TOEIC
NEW

新制多益閱讀全真模擬試題
金色證書╳一擊必殺

1

經驗分享談；
制定讀書計畫

2

新舊制閱讀題型
分析與比較

3

考試時間分配、技巧
不藏私大公開

學習有捷徑
夢想最接近

使用說明之 *1*
多益的閱讀部分有哪些題型？

多益的閱讀部分分為三個大題，分別為第五大題「句子填空」、第六大題「段落填空」，第七大題可再細分為「單篇閱讀」及「多篇閱讀」，各大題的詳細內容介紹及做答方式請看以下：

▶ Part 5：「句子填空」

在 Part 5 的題目中，每一題各會有一個句子，考生必須從下列的四個選項中選出一個最適合的答案填入句子中。

例題：

101 _____ you get to the final stage of the interview, I will email you all the necessary documents.

(A) By

(B) Even

(C) Once

(D) Though

解題小撇步：

· 考生在選擇答案時務必要依據上下文來判斷需填入單字的詞性及時態，若不符合條件的選項請立即刪去。

· 若為有上、下句關係的兩個句子之間的關聯要先確認清楚，例如句子間的時序關係或因果關係。

▶ Part 6：「段落填空」

　　Part 6 的題目均是以一篇篇的文章呈現，於文章中會出現填空題，考生必須從四個選項中選出最適合的答案填入。

例題：

Questions 130～133 refer to the following email.

Dear Mr. Cheng,

Maxton Law Office is hiring for the position of law administrator and I am ___130___ information about this opportunity.

The law office administrator will be ___131___ for providing administrative support in our law office. The duties ___132___ overseeing budgeting and payroll operations, managing office space arrangements and gathering supplies.

___133___ in Business, legal administration or a related field. Please contact me if there are any adequate candidates that meet our qualifications for this position.

Sincerely,
Ariana

130 (A) disseminating
(B) recommending
(C) expressing
(D) acknowledging

131 (A) irrational
(B) informative
(C) responsible
(D) chargeable

132 (A) inclusive
(B) including
(C) include
(D) included

133 (A) All candidates show great interests
(B) That's the reason why I chose this major
(C) The focus was put on the thorough investigation
(D) A candidate should have a Bachelor's degree

解題小撇步：

・此部分考題其實與第五部分題型有異曲同工之妙，只是這部分各題目內容再稍長一點，但基本的解題方法與第五部分差異不大，且關鍵解題線索通常就在填空空格附近。

・在本次多益改制後此部分增加了「句子填空」題型，因此考生要更加注意上、下句之間的關係及文章內容的理解。

▶ Part 7：「單篇閱讀」、「多篇閱讀」

Part 7 為閱讀題，此部分又分為「單篇閱讀」和「多篇閱讀」，考生在閱讀完文章後需針對文章下方的各項題目，從四個答案選項中選出最正確的其中一項回答。

「單篇閱讀」例題：

Questions 154-156 refer to the following advertisement.

Holiday House for Rent

This newly built, light and airy 2-bedroom holiday cottage is perfect for a city break in one of England's most vibrant cities. The house is centrally located in the beautiful neighborhood of Clifton with shops, cafes and restaurants nearby.

- The interior is furnished and equipped to a high standard, with high quality linen and towels provided.

- The open plan sitting room and the kitchen with separate utility room on the first floor provide all the amenities for a comfortable stay.

- On the second floor you will find two double bedrooms - a king-size bed in the master and two singles in the second room. The second floor also has its own tiled shower room.

- Guests will have access to the entire premises, as well as a private courtyard at the rear.

154 What can be found near the cottage mentioned in the advertisement?
(A) A hospital
(B) An elementary school
(C) A supermarket
(D) Dining places

155 Which of following is not provided in this holiday house?
(A) Linens and towels
(B) Kitchenware
(C) A private courtyard
(D) Rain gear

156 Where is the courtyard?
(A) Near the cottage
(B) In front of the cottage
(C) At the back of the house
(D) Next to the house

「多篇閱讀」例題：

Questions 173~177 refer to the following advertisement, reservation and e-mail.

Sky Tower Restaurant

Champ de Mars, 101 Avenue Anatole France, 75007 Paris, France
dineandwine@skytower.paris
+33-1-4573-8666

Sky Tower Restaurant is a food experience not to be missed - the menu is best described as French contemporary with a delicious selection of exceptional dishes beautifully presented. Sky Tower offers splendid views of city Paris and sumptuous interiors, including the deluxe private dining room, Adèle, which is suitable for up to 16 guests. To reserve this space please contact our events team groups@skytower.paris.

Dining at our rooftop bar is also a delightfully classy experience where guests can enjoy an impressive list of wine and cocktails as well as the full a la carte menu. Bookings for tables at the bar can also be made through our reservations system.

We welcome and encourage style, but please note that we do not permit shorts, sportswear, sports trainers or flip flops. Our management reserves the right to refuse admission to anyone we feel is inappropriately dressed. Guests aged 16-17 are welcome in our bar and lounge areas accompanied by an adult (aged 21+).

Lunch: Mon-Sun: 11:45am-2:45pm / Dinner: Mon-Sun: 5:45pm-10:15pm

We accept bookings 60 days in advance.

From: Josephine Cochran
To: <groups@skytower.paris>
Subject: Adèle Reservation

Hi,

I read an article about your restaurant in Top Paris magazine Issue March 2018 and found it a nice place for my family gathering. Therefore I am writing this letter to reserve the private dining room on April 24, Tuesday. There are 15 of us, and we'll be needing the room from 6 pm to 9 pm for a family dinner in celebration of my grandparents' 60th anniversary. Please let me know whether Adèle is available at the time mentioned above.

Also, I'd like to know if we could bring our own wine to the restaurant. I understand that your rooftop bar provides the guests with a wide range of wines and cocktails, but we'd like to bring our own special wine from my grandpa's vineyard.

Looking forward to your prompt response.

Regards,
Josephine

From: Adèle Room
To: Josephine Cochran
Subject: Re: Adèle Reservation

Dear Ms. Cochran,
Thanks for your making a reservation with us. Adèle Room is reserved for you for your designated date and time. We will be very glad to receive you in our establishment. We warmly welcome you and your family to spend the meaningful and memorable night of celebration with us.

In regard to your request to bring your own wine, please

note that according to the restaurant's policy, we will charge a €30 corkage fee for wine (€60 for a magnum) and €75 for Champagne (€150 for a magnum). Thanks for your understanding.

We look forward to receiving you on April 24.

Best wishes

_____

173 What does "Adèle" refer to in the advertisement?
   (A) The restaurant manager
   (B) The private dining rooms
   (C) The rooftop bar
   (D) The chef's signature dish

174 Which of the following is most likely the restaurant's dress code?
   (A) Cocktail attire
   (B) Business attire
   (C) Beach attire
   (D) Smart casual

175 Where does Josephine hear about the restaurant?
   (A) From a journal
   (B) From the social media
   (C) From TV
   (D) From a friend

176 According to the first e-mail, what is the purpose of the dinner gathering?

(A) To celebrate a colleague's promotion

(B) To celebrate a couple's anniversary

(C) To celebrate a friend's birthday

(D) To welcome new employees

177 According to the second e-mail, when will the restaurant charge a "corkage fee"?

(A) When the guests bring their own food

(B) When the guests don't reserve in advance

(B) When the guests don't show up on time

(D) When the guests bring their own wine

解題小撇步：

· 建議考生在正式閱讀文章之前能先大略看過題目及選項，以便在閱讀文章的同時快速地找到相關資訊，並且能夠清楚知道需多加注意的內容。

· 信件及報章雜誌常將主旨設為標題或放在前幾句出現，考生可以由此快速得知文章通篇重點。另外，文章中的「日期」、「時間」等細節也有可能做為題目考出，請考生別輕忽。

新制多益改了哪些部分？

　　接下來就是大家最關心的：「新制多益到底是什麼？到底改了什麼？」最新多益改制除了改變題型之外，各大題題目量的分配也有調整，以下為各位考生簡單整理出了新制多益閱讀部分所做的更改！

▶ Part 5：「句子填空」

	舊制題型	新制題型
題數	40 題	30 題
題目類型	從選項中選出最正確的選項填入句子中	題目類型不變

▶ Part 6：「段落填空」

	舊制題型	新制題型
題數	12 題（3*4）	16 題（4*4）
題目類型	● 3 篇文章，每篇 4 個問題	● 4 篇文章，每篇 4 個問題 ● 選項中新增完整句子的選項

▶ Part 7：「單篇閱讀」、「多篇閱讀」

「單篇閱讀」

	舊制題型	新制題型
題數	28 題	29 題
題目類型	● 9 篇文章，每篇約 2～5 個問題	● 10 篇文章，每篇約 2～4 個問題 ● 加入測驗篇章結構能力，並在選項裡新增句子填空題型 ● 新增引述文章部分內容題型

「多篇閱讀」

	舊制題型	新制題型
題數	20 題	25 題
題目類型	● 4 組雙篇閱讀文章，每個 5 個問題	● 新增多篇閱讀題型，題目比例改為 2 組雙篇閱讀、3 組多篇閱讀，每組 5 個問題 ● 新增簡訊、線上聊天內容題型 ● 新增引述文章部分內容題型

使用說明之 *3*

新增 3 支多益閱讀高分攻略影片

　　在影音修訂版中，我們邀請到國立成功大學外文系畢業，擁有多益金色證書的 Laura 老師來和大家分享她的多益實戰經驗。

　　在影片中，首先 Laura 老師會分享自己考多益的經驗，並教大家如何根據自己的目標下訂適合自己的讀書計畫，再根據準備時間立出階段性目標。

　　接下來，老師會替讀者們不藏私分析新舊制多益閱讀題型的差別，更會針對每個類型的常見考題做分析。

　　最後則是考試當天，閱讀測驗不會寫不完的「考試時間分配」以及「考試技巧大公開」！實力需要長時間養成，但考試技巧一定可以迅速建立，為了能夠迅速抓到考試當天所需要注意到的眉眉角角，快點開這三支影片吧！

1

經驗分享談；
制定讀書計畫

2

新舊制閱讀題型
分析與比較

3

考試時間分配、技巧
不藏私大公開

主編的話

各位讀者好，我是這本書的主編 Laura。

近年來，因為國內大學及企業採用多益成績作為門檻，很多人為了在多益考試中拿到高分而苦思不已，花了大把鈔票買書、補習、刷題，分數卻還是止步不前。

為了幫助廣大讀者在多益考試中可以少花一點力氣、多拿一點分數，在這次的影音增修版中，我錄了三支影片，在影片中現身說法，和讀者們不藏私分享自己從小到大不補習英文成績一路頂尖的秘密，同時也會聊到，為了攻克多益閱讀，平時可以怎麼做準備，讓自己在考試當天發揮最大實力。

學習雖然沒有捷徑，但一定有「相對來說更適合自己的方法」以及「最有效率的方法」，多益考試只要找對方法，一定能夠拿高分。在影片中，我們也會分析比較新舊制多益的差別、題型的差異，讓你不用花錢請英文家教，就可以一掃 QR code，把多益高手精心準備的應試小祕訣通通免費送給你，就不用額外花錢請名師或補習囉。

最後，祝福大家都能夠在準備考試的過程中紮紮實實的學習透徹、考試當天穩定的把實力發揮出來，一舉拿到金色證書！

Preface 作者序－李宇凡

「什麼！多益又要改制了！」、「天啊！
改制多益要怎麼應考啊！」這兩個問題大概是
從 ETS 官方宣布將於台灣正式實施新制多益
考試的新聞稿出來之後，學生最常跟我說的
話。可以看出這次多益大動作改制，已經有許
多考生開始尋求對應措施，我想這時候正是我
該出馬的時候了！

　　新制多益，新的考試不只對學生，對我們這些老師來說也是一種考
驗，要怎麼去幫助學生應考、要從什麼角度去剖析考試，一個個都在測
試老師們的專業度，以我來說，我最建議的就是從模擬試題做起了。充
分的練習除了讓自己訓練在指定時間內完成試題，培養在閱讀部分的理
解力及學習分配解題時間，同時也是認識新式題型的好機會。

　　為什麼必須要先透過模擬題來認識新題型呢？那是因為，考生必須
要先借由自己實際的操作、練習才可以得知自己不擅長新制題型的部
分，從而才能進一步想辦法去解決它、克服它。

另外，在練習模擬試題後的參閱解析動作也極其重要，解析中包含了詳細的題目內容、題型分析、單字補充以及解題說明，反覆的琢磨其中內容，一定能夠有效地獲取優良學習成果。特別是閱讀部分這次除了增加不少符合現在世代的即時通訊內容，考生所要閱讀的文章內容更是大幅增加，除了在做答時要更加注意時間調配及細心程度之外，經由解析反覆確認快速答題技巧更是極其重要。

　　模擬試題看起來普通，卻是對付新制多益考試的第一道防線，希望考生們務必在正式上場之前先小試身手一番，並期盼能藉由這些試題給予各位應考新制多益的信心，進而獲取理想佳績。

Preface 作者序－蔡文宜

TOEIC 多益考試是現今主流的英語能力測驗之一，不只時常被用來測試自我英語能力，甚至是許多的學校機關畢業門檻以及求職的利器。其主要針對的是在英語社會求職的需要，因此出題方向也著重於商業實用性質，有著如此信效度的多益考試據上次於 2006 年改制以來，時隔 10 年以上再度改制，臺灣也開始實施，許多考生開始侷促不安，到底多益改制要怎麼因應才好？

多益的閱讀考試一直以來都會讓眾多考生大喊「寫不完題目啊！！」，尤其是測驗中第七部份的文章內容可以說是一篇比一篇還要長，且題型越發與時俱進，這次改制，不只段落填空出現句子選項，考生最害怕的「大魔王」第七大題除了增加多篇閱讀題型，內容更是有多樣化的趨勢，新增了線上聊天訊息等可以反映出現今日常生活之中社交及職場英語使用習慣，這對學習實用英文絕對是有效的，但也就意味著考生不能再讀死書了，而是要靈活著用，這無疑對某些考生來說是一大考驗。

考生除了能在自己的日常生活中運用報章雜誌增進「讀」的能力之外，更可藉由以我們多年教學經驗出題的本書，搭配精心設計的閱讀新題型來做練習，詳解更是除了中譯、單字之外更添加了出題類型說明及分析，讓考生能「懂」，有「看」有「懂」，考生才能百「考」百勝。

　　這次多益官方瞬違已久的改制，相信許多人已經很有感了，尤其是望一眼市面上的多益參考書籍無一不與考生心情「神同步」，紛紛推出了本次改制多益的解題方法、新題目解析等書籍，要我們來說，這當然也是對應改制的一種方式，但練習模擬題也不枉是另一種有效備考的好招式。

　　透過系列模擬題的考驗並進行解題練習，相信考生定能獲得不小的學習成效，更重要的是能加以理解改制新題目的內容，即使明年將迎來新考驗也可以輕鬆面對，將新改制的多益迎刃而解、一擊必殺。

Wenny Tsai

Preface 作者序－徐培恩

　　很榮幸有這次機會參與本書的製作，身為一名針對多益考試的英語講師，這次的多益改制想當然爾是不可輕忽的，考生緊張，我們這些講師也同樣緊張啊！但是緊張歸緊張，還是要盡到身為老師的責任，於是這本全真模擬試題就這樣誕生了。

　　以本書作者的角度來看，要配合此次改制的題型出題並不容易，除了閱讀題組增加為多篇閱讀，內容整體要有所增加之外，題型要更加地貼近現實日常運用，譬如說兩人以上的互動式訊息便是其中一種，不過要說最難出題的還是這次加入的篇章結構題型，這類題型必須綜觀整個文章結構，出起來沒有這麼容易。

　　拼了命寫出題目後，我轉念一想：「我在出題時感到困難的部分，不就跟要去參加新制多益的考生會遇到的一樣嗎？」因此，我覺得在對新制多益題型還尚未熟悉的情況下，對各位考生們來說要

在有限時間內準確解題是有難度的，尤其是閱讀題組的部分，除了過往的時間掌控之外，對新題型的熟悉度也攸關了考試的關鍵，考生還必須保持清楚的思緒才有辦法理出整體篇章結構以及作者於文章中想表達的意思，模擬試題於熟悉改制多益題型的重要度由此可見一斑。

　　做為一名老師，最期望的不外乎是學生們能夠獲得自己所期望的佳績，希望各位能藉由本全真模擬試題熟悉新題型，並帶著胸有成竹的自信走向考場，大家加油！

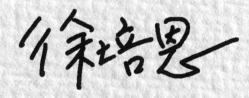

Contents目錄

002 | 使用說明
015 | 主編的話
016 | 作者序——李宇凡
018 | 作者序——蔡文宜
020 | 作者序——徐培恩

PART 1
金色證書一擊必殺
閱讀全真**模擬試題**

024 | 新多益閱讀全真模擬**試題** — **第 1 回**
066 | 新多益閱讀全真模擬**試題** — **第 2 回**
108 | 新多益閱讀全真模擬**試題** — **第 3 回**
150 | 新多益閱讀全真模擬**試題** — **第 4 回**
188 | 新多益閱讀全真模擬**試題** — **第 5 回**
230 | 新多益閱讀全真模擬**試題** — **第 6 回**

PART 2
金色證書一擊必殺
閱讀關鍵**解題分析**

274 | 新多益閱讀全真模擬**試題解析** — **第 1 回**
336 | 新多益閱讀全真模擬**試題解析** — **第 2 回**
398 | 新多益閱讀全真模擬**試題解析** — **第 3 回**
462 | 新多益閱讀全真模擬**試題解析** — **第 4 回**
528 | 新多益閱讀全真模擬**試題解析** — **第 5 回**
592 | 新多益閱讀全真模擬**試題解析** — **第 6 回**

閱讀全真模擬試題

新多益閱讀全真模擬試題 — 第1~6回

金色證書一擊必殺 Part 1

New TOEIC Reading Test 1

新多益**閱讀**全真模擬**試題第1回**

> ### ▶ READING TEST
>
> In the Reading Test, you will read a variety of texts and answer several different types of reading comprehension questions. The entire Reading Test will last 75 minutes. There are three parts, and directions are given for each part. You are encouraged to answer as many questions as possible within the time allowed.
>
> You must mark your answers on the separate answer sheet. Do not write your answers in the test book.
>
> ### ▶ PART 5
>
> **Directions:** A word or phrase is missing in each of the sentences below. Four answer choices are given below each sentence. Select the best answer to complete the sentence. Then mark the letter (A), (B), (C), or (D) on your answer sheet.

101 The _____ problem with our software will be investigated by the developers.

(A) rewarding
(B) awarding
(C) recurring
(D) occurring

102 Please keep this ticket until the specified date, _____ you may be charged a fine of NT 5,000.

(A) otherwise
(B) although
(C) moreover
(D) despite

103 Mr. Fisher _____ to the branch in San Francisco in a couple of weeks.

(A) transfer
(B) is transferred
(C) will transfer
(D) will be transferred

104 This email is for the attention of the employees on probation _____ those who have completed all the assessments and are awaiting the results.

(A) in addition
(B) unless
(C) due to
(D) except

105 Remember to _____ inventory before you get off work today.

(A) take
(B) get
(C) draw
(D) meet

106 Despite the _____ of social media, face-to-face conversations are still a crucial way to build up business relationships.

(A) authenticity
(B) decrease
(C) emergency
(D) prevalence

107 It is important for us to equip _____ with all the knowledge and skills needed in the training program.

(A) we
(B) us
(C) ours
(D) ourselves

108 Our department has _____ a refund to your account for the cancelled ticket. Please allow three days for this to be processed.

(A) booked
(B) issued
(C) launched
(D) withdrew

109 We will be grateful if you could spare up to ten minutes to complete this survey _____ looks into how you are satisfied with our product.

(A) who
(B) it
(C) which
(D) whose

110 We are sorry to tell you that this service is not _____ in Asia; however, we do provide similar service that suits your needs.

(A) responsible
(B) available
(C) reversible
(D) susceptible

111 The film was made in _____ with Dreamland Studio featuring its state-of-the art animation and visual effects.

(A) collection
(B) celebration
(C) calibration
(D) collaboration

112 Customers _____ on an early morning flight are allowed to check in their baggage at the airport the evening before their departure day.

(A) traveling
(B) travel
(C) to travel
(D) traveled

113 International students who are _____ for the scholarship should submit the application form to the admissions office by March 1st.

(A) accessible
(B) eligible
(C) capable
(D) renewable

114 Mrs. White has been unemployed since she _____ her job in the economic recession a decade ago.

(A) loses
(B) lost
(C) has lost
(D) was lost

115 We offer _____ corporate and school catering services in Cardiff.

(A) neither
(B) either
(C) not only
(D) both

116 A _____ salesperson always speaks eloquently.

(A) success
(B) succeed
(C) successful
(D) successive

117 Sara _____ a note on your desk when she left the office yesterday.

(A) leaves
(B) left
(C) has left
(D) has been left

118 They bought a new projector _____ the old one is beyond repair.

(A) but
(B) so
(C) since
(D) thus

119 We must not give up _____ tough the situation is.

(A) however
(B) whenever
(C) whatever
(D) wherever

120 This email is a reminder of the _____ of the proposal. No late submission is accepted.

(A) obsession
(B) deadline
(C) procedure
(D) procurement

121 Despite his high reputation, many people voted _____ Jason as the president.

(A) to
(B) from
(C) for
(D) against

122 The attendance rate of the seminar is higher _____ expected.

(A) than
(B) to
(C) then
(D) since

123 _____ is the price of the office space in this area?

(A) How much
(B) How many
(C) What
(D) Where

124 If you have any queries about renting your property, please contact our _____ via 01908871024 or the email listed.

(A) agent
(B) broker
(C) spokesperson
(D) engineer

125 _____ the bad weather condition, we have to postpone the event.

(A) Since
(B) Because of
(C) In spite of
(D) As of

126 Simply type in your location and find our most cost-effective car _____ deals.

(A) letting
(B) lending
(C) exchange
(D) rental

127 _____ in the heart of London, Berjaya Hotel is your perfect choice of accommodation when you travel to this amazing city.

(A) To locate
(B) Locating
(C) Located
(D) Locate

128 The receptionist will call you _____ she receives your package.

(A) not only
(B) as soon as
(C) other than
(D) as far as

129 _____ my vacation, I traveled to Shanghai, Taipei and Hong Kong.

(A) Between
(B) On
(C) During
(D) From

130 We recommend _____ this app to keep yourself updated and connected.

(A) to use
(B) use
(C) using
(D) used

▶ PART 6

Directions: Read the texts on the following pages. A word or phrase is missing in some of the sentences. Answer choices are given below each of these articles. Select the best answer to complete the text. Then mark the letter (A), (B), (C) or (D) on your answer sheet.

Questions 131-134 refer to the following email.

Date: 31 July, 2017
To: Ben Lim
From: Tally Tours
Subject: Refund Issue

Dear Ben Lim,

Thank you for letting us know about the issue of your Tally Tours ticket. The tickets you ___131___ for the one-day tour in Galway are refundable until as late as three days prior to the date of travel. In order to make a claim for the refund, you will need to complete the online refund application form and send it to us in an attachment no later ___132___ three days before departure. As soon as the application form is received, we will start to process your refund immediately. Please allow five working days for ___133___ to be processed. It may take another three days for any credit to appear in your account. ___134___. We are looking forward to having you on board next time.

Kind Regards,

Ellen

131 (A) developed
    (B) progressed
    (C) purchased
    (D) utilized

132 (A) than
    (B) as
    (C) to
    (D) in

133 (A) me
    (B) it
    (C) them
    (D) either

★ 134 (A) We sincerely welcome you to join this journey
    (B) We are confident that we have the best price among other companies
    (C) Please note that our accountant will be on leave for the next couple of days
    (D) We do apologize if this causes any inconvenience to you

Questions 135-138 refer to the following letter.

Dear employee,

Public Health England has been notified that a Spring Airline employee who ___135___ to the hospital has been confirmed to have a Meningococcal Meningitis Group B infection. I am happy to inform you that he is recovering well and will be discharged soon.

___136___ this, we are working closely with the staff at the company's health service in an attempt to reduce the chances of bacteria spreading. We have conducted a risk assessment and concluded that there is currently no need to take any specific action or change the routine for our staff. However, we still strongly recommend that you ___137___ vaccinated as soon as possible if you have not been offered an antibiotic.

Spring Airline's health service has recently been running vaccination sessions for new employees who had not been vaccinated prior to entering our company. For the other staff, you can still have this vaccination if you are eligible. ___138___, you can either contact your doctor or visit our website at www.springairline.co.uk/meningitis for further information.

Yours sincerely,

Mike Wilson
Deputy Director of Health Protection

135 (A) admitted
(B) has admitted
(C) was admitting
(D) was admitted

136 (A) In light of
(B) In spite of
(C) Because
(D) Since

137 (A) get
(B) got
(C) have got
(D) are getting

★ **138** (A) If you have difficulties accessing our website
(B) If you are uncertain about your eligibility
(C) If you are skeptical about the diagnosis
(D) If you are not contacted by our practice nurse

Questions 139-142 refer to the following post.

Happy New Year! We trust you had a restful Christmas vacation and are raring to get back to your classroom. If not, here are some wonderful activities to make your transition a little more palatable. Why not ___139___ this brand new semester with some exciting and motivational basketball from Craig Wade and Ryan Anderson? Not that into sports? Well, we also have plans for moviegoers. Come on Sunday and sink into a chair in our school theater and enjoy a movie! If you ___140___ to do some preparations for your studies, Paul Newman and Sue Chen have a tutorial session on Monday for those who wish to hone their essay writing skills. Plus, on the same day, there will be a peer feedback task which helps to increase the ___141___ of your presentations. No matter which you choose, ___142___.

139 (A) start
  (B) starting
  (C) to start
  (D) to starting

140 (A) suggest
  (B) compromise
  (C) prefer
  (D) register

141 (A) intelligent
  (B) intelligence
  (C) intelligible
  (D) intelligibility

★ **142** (A) we hope that these activities will make your school return a little more enjoyable
  (B) we only accept sign-ups prior to the aforementioned date
  (C) make sure you verify whether you meet the requirements of each position
  (D) we wish you a pleasant new year holiday and look forward to having you back soon

Questions 143-146 refer to the following review.

REVIEWS OF LOTTIE'S APARTMENT

Laura
11 October, 2017

Lottie's home was a wonderful place to ___143___ a weekend in Paris. The apartment was in a fantastic location from where you can walk to the metro station in just six minutes. It was also within walking distance to plenty of good restaurants and well-known tourist ___144___, such as the Louvre Palace and Champs-Élysées. The apartment looked exactly the same as shown on the website and was everything we needed for our little adventure in Paris. Although our flight arrived a little late that night, Lottie was still extremely friendly and helpful in accommodating our late ___145___. She even made some delicious cookies for us! We also had a chance to meet her husband, who was also very kind to us throughout our stay. However, ___146___. Overall, it was a nice stay and we will definitely come back again.

143 (A) take
(B) spend
(C) cost
(D) pay

144 (A) accommodations
(B) appreciations
(C) transportations
(D) attractions

145 (A) arrive
(B) arriving
(C) arrived
(D) arrival

★ **146** (A) the Wi-Fi network in my room was a little unstable
(B) the price of the room is very reasonable
(C) the living room was pretty spacious and cozy
(D) the room was so immaculate

▶ PART 7

Directions: In this part, you will read a selection of texts, such as magazine and newspaper articles, letters, and advertisements. Each text is followed by several questions. Select the best answer for each question and mark the letter (A), (B), (C), or (D) on your answer sheet.

Questions 147-148 refer to the following notice.

The Deadline for The Second Tuition Fee Installment Is 5th June 2017

Please ensure the payment is made before this date.

The amount payable is $4,253

If you encounter any problems paying, you must contact the income office.

Late payment will incur a $50 late payment charge.

Failure to pay your tuition fee will lead to legal action.

To discuss anything related to tuition fee payment, please contact
Mary Conn – Income Officer

Tel. 141-6172-8930

---

147 What is the main purpose of this notice?

(A) To announce payment extension procedures

(B) To call for rent payment

(C) To introduce a new officer

(D) To ask for tuition fee payment

148 What might happen if the payment is made one day after the due date?

(A) The payer might face legal consequences.

(B) The payer will have to file for an extension.

(C) The payer will need to pay an extra $50.

(D) The payer will be removed from the university.

Looking for someone to help (PAID)

From: Sami Wright   Aug, 10
To: me

Hi everyone,

I am currently looking for somebody to help me with transcribing video clips. You SHOULD be very good at English listening. I have a total of 48 video clips and each lasts from approximately five to twenty minutes. All you need to do is to transcribe the lines (word by word) spoken in the clips. Usually, the transcription of each video takes around twenty minutes to an hour. You will be paid $50 for the videos under five minutes, $80 for the ones between five to ten minutes, and $120 for the ones between ten to twenty minutes. You can choose to do as many clips as you can. I expect to receive all the completed transcript files no later than August 31.

Please let me know asap if you are interested in doing this job.

Best,

Sami

149 Why is this email written?

(A) To introduce a newly launched movie

(B) To offer assistance in translation

(C) To look for transcribers with excellent listening skills

(D) To search for video editing experts

150 How much can one earn if he/she completes a transcription of a fifteen-minute video?

(A) $50

(B) $80

(C) $120

(D) $200

151 When is the deadline for this task?

(A) August 5

(B) August 10

(C) August 20

(D) August 31

Questions 152-155 refer to the following advertisement.

EASYGO.COM

BOOK YOUR TRIP NOW!

Low Fare/ High Quality

Your amazing trip is just a click away.

Travelling on luxurious coaches across the country does not have to hurt your wallet. You can either book online in advance or buy on the day at a coach station. You can enjoy the low fare ticket with great value.

We take you to thousands of destinations in the UK where amazing stories are waiting.

Check out the lowest fares from where you are:

LONDON to BIRMINGHAM *one-way* *Journey time: 02h30m*	**£10 BOOK NOW**
LONDON to BATH *one-way* *Journey time: 02h05m*	**£5 BOOK NOW**
LONDON to CARDIFF *one-way* *Journey time: 02h40m*	**£8 BOOK NOW**
LONDON to YORK *one-way* *Journey time: 03h30m*	**£25 BOOK NOW**
LONDON to EDINBURGH *one-way* *Journey time: 05h25m*	**£40 BOOK NOW**

All the prices are subject to change. Be quick and book your ticket as early as you can. Click _HERE_ to download our app which keeps you updated on our low price tickets. For more information, go on our website at www.easygo.co.uk.

152 What most likely is EASYGO?

(A) An airline

(B) A ferry operator

(C) An automobile manufacturer

(D) A coach company

153 According to the ad, which journey is the longest?

(A) London to Bath

(B) London to York

(C) London to Edinburgh

(D) London to Birmingham

154 Which of the following statements is true?

(A) The tickets can only be purchased online.

(B) A journey from London to York takes no longer than four hours.

(C) A one-way ticket from London to Bath costs £10.

(D) The ticket prices are fixed all year round.

155 What can be inferred from the advertisement?

(A) The company is based in the US.

(B) Customers can get a discount only when booking online.

(C) Customers can check ticket prices in the company's app.

(D) Customers can only buy one-way tickets at coach stations.

Questions 156-160 refer to the following information.

Job Hunter

Are you looking for a job?

Go on Job Hunter and find out the tips to help you stand out from thousands of candidates.

Human Resources Advisor/ Phoenix Personnel Ltd/ Manila/ the Philippines

About the job:

Title: Human Resources Advisor

No.: H2827400010

Location: Manila, the Philippines

Job Type: 1 Year Fixed Term Contract

Salary: $28,000-$30,000 **per annum**

Closing Date: 15 Nov, 2017

Phoenix Personnel is recruiting for an experienced HR advisor who can provide effective and efficient support to join our well-versed team on a fixed term contract until the end of October 2018.

Your tasks are to…

- Serve as a link between management and employees by providing advice, guidance and support on all kinds of matters regarding employee relations
- Examine and modify compensation and benefits policies and ensure compliance with legal requirements
- Assist recruitment campaigns twice a year and take part in new employee selection
- Conduct seasonal job evaluations and provide advice on job reviews
- Support the HR manager with staffing duties, such as understaffing, hearings and disciplinary procedures

What's on offer:

- $28,000-$30,000 **per annum**
- Hours: 09:00-5:00
- Free lunch meal at the cafeteria

If you find this position a good match with your personality and professional background, please send your resume to us at pprecruitment@phoenix.co.ph. Please specify you are applying for HR advisor in the subject box. Our staff will contact you very soon. All good wishes with your search for employment.

156 Where most likely can this information be seen?

(A) At an electronics show

(B) At a book fair

(C) On a job searching website

(D) In a resort

157 What is suggested about the position being advertised?

(A) It is a half-year contract position.

(B) Its contract will end in November 2017.

(C) It is restricted to Filipino applicants.

(D) It is based in the capital of the Philippines.

158 According to the information, what is NOT a stated duty of this position?

(A) Handling hiring matters

(B) Communicating with employees and managers

(C) Analyzing the company's salary policies

(D) Delivering speeches on university campus

159 What should applicants do when applying for this position?

(A) Bring an application form to the HR department

(B) Phone the HR director

(C) Email a CV to the company

(D) Identify their college major in the email

160 What does the phrase "per annum" mean?

(A) daily

(B) weekly

(C) monthly

(D) annual

Questions 161-165 refer to the following article.

Rice and Sea—Traditional Paella

Once you try it, you will get addicted. Hurry and try this fabulous dish yourself!

Ingredients

- 180 grams of medium grain rice
- 5 boneless chicken thighs
- 225 grams of sliced squid (rings)
- 100 grams of well-scrubbed mussels with beards removed
- 0.5 tablespoon of ground sea salt
- 0.5 tablespoon of ground black pepper
- 1 tablespoon of olive oil
- 2 chopped onions

Steps

1. Heat the olive oil in a non-stick medium size pan with medium heat.

2. Put the chicken thighs in a bowl and season them with sea salt and black pepper. Leave it for 10 minutes. —[1]—

3. Fry the chicken over medium heat for 5 minutes until both sides turn lightly colored. Transfer the chicken to a large plate. —[2]—

4. Add the onions to the pan and fry for 3 minutes over a gentle fire until softened and lightly brown.

5. —[3]—Mix the chicken with the fried onions, stir in the rice and cook for another 3 to 4 minutes until the rice is evenly mixed with the other ingredients.

6. Scatter the sliced squid over the partly cooked rice mixture. Continue cooking for 5 minutes until the squid is perfectly cooked.

7. Place the lid over the pan and keep simmering for 10 minutes until the rice is softened and a bit sticky. Be careful not to burn the rice. —[4]—

8. Add a few drops of lemon onto the rice and get ready to dig in!

161 Where most likely can this article be found?

(A) In a cookbook
(B) In a financial newspaper
(C) In a sports car magazine
(D) In a church leaflet

162 What is NOT a required ingredient?

(A) black pepper
(B) chicken breast
(C) paella rice
(D) squid

163 What is indicated about preparing the onions?

(A) They should be red onions.
(B) They should be cooked in boiled water first.
(C) They should be cut into pieces.
(D) They should be marinated with soy sauce.

164 How should the rice be cooked eventually?

(A) It should be slightly burned,
(B) It should be soggy.
(C) It should be soft and sticky.
(D) It should be half-cooked.

★ 165 In which of the positions marked [1], [2], [3] and [4] does the following sentence best belong? "Return the fried chicken thighs to the pan."

(A) [1]
(B) [2]
(C) [3]
(D) [4]

Questions 166-170 refer to the following information.

Introducing Landmark: The Best Educational Institute for the Elderly

For whom

The course is aimed at people who are over 50 years old and are still active and keen on lifelong learning.

Facilitators

Peter Tan, specialist in National Senior Education Center, Head Teacher in Westlake Community College

Description

Landmark is an institute that provides specially-designed courses and activities for elders. In response to the "**silver tsunami**", which has posed an impact on all respects of human society, including political, economic and cultural domains, Landmark pioneers in contributing to older adults' educational development, which in turn is beneficial to maintaining mental, social and physical health. Our program is full of rich learning and development activities that are very popular with elders.

Date: 14 January 2016
Time: 8:00-15:00
Venue: St Stephen's Building
Cost: £ 20
Contact <u>kimsu1912@pioneer.co.uk</u> to book a place.

If booked in a group of three, the cost will be £15 per person.

166 Who most likely would participate in this event?

(A) An active duty soldier

(B) A retired teacher

(C) A preschool child

(D) A university student

167 What is probably the cause of "silver tsunami"?

(A) aging population

(B) an earthquake

(C) global warming

(D) financial crisis

168 According to this information, what is NOT a benefit of providing old adults with educational opportunities?

(A) Political stability can be ensured.

(B) Psychological wellness can be attended to.

(C) Social relationship can be maintained.

(D) The elderly can be physically well.

169 What can we infer from this information?

(A) The course will last a month.

(B) The event will take place at St. Stephen's Building.

(C) Group registration is not permitted.

(D) People over 60 years old can get 20% off the price.

170 If three people sign up as a group, how much will they have to pay in total?

(A) £15

(B) £20

(C) £45

(D) £60

Questions 171-175 refer to the following email.

Materials for Friday's Seminar   20 Oct 2016

From: Thomas Summers   To: you

Dear All,

I am including some of the materials in the attachment we will be talking about on Friday during our seminar. This time we will be looking into how to best prepare for the upcoming FET annual project. In preparation for the seminar, I would like you to do the following in advance:

1. Read through the sample project proposal. You will notice there will be some sections missing. This is done on purpose in order to avoid revealing personal information.

2. Highlight the keywords related to this year's subject and try to think about the relevance between the two years' focuses.

3. Try to assess the old project proposal based on the criteria attached as a Word document.

4. Next, see the department directors' detailed evaluation and see what they liked and what they thought could be improved.

5. Finally, think about some ideas that are applicable to this year's year-end project and bring them to this Friday's seminar. There will be a brainstorming session for your ideas to be shared.

Please note that due to the length of the documents necessary for the seminar, I will not print them out for you. It would be good therefore if all of you could bring either e-copies or hard copies of the documents to the seminar to be able to access the information.

You will also find it useful to read through some parts of the online documents in the resources portal which you can log into with your employee ID and password. I am also attaching the copies of some of them just in case you can't find them.

Finally, it has been brought up to me that some of you will have to attend the weekly meeting at the same time. This is rather unfortunate. Although I would normally not encourage you to skip weekly meetings, on this occasion I would hope that you treat this seminar as a priority.

Best wishes,

Thomas Summers

171 What is the purpose of this email?

(A) To inquire the prices of Christmas decoration materials

(B) To remind parents of the dates of the final exams

(C) To inform preparation of a seminar discussion

(D) To request an employee leave application form

172 Why is part of the content of the sample project proposal concealed?

(A) To avoid plagiarism

(B) To protect personal information

(C) To save space

(D) To elicit inspiration

173 What are the seminar attendees asked to do on Friday?

(A) Highlighting the key words in the old proposal

(B) Logging into the resources portal

(C) Asking the supervisors about their comments on the proposals

(D) Bringing the printed documents to the discussion

174 What can be inferred about the seminar?

(A) It is considered more important than weekly meetings at the moment.

(B) It will be held in December.

(C) It is only for department directors.

(D) It is a monthly event.

175 Who most likely is Thomas?

(A) The organizer of the weekly meeting

(B) The IT supplier

(C) The website designer

(D) The host of the seminar

★Questions 176-180 refer to the following conversation, table and email.

Super Sales Group

Nov 3

2017 Sports Club List
Click here to download this file

Jennifer H 17:01

Good afternoon everyone! As most of you may know, the registration for this year's sports clubs has already begun. Your physical wellbeing, healthy living awareness and teamwork spirit are something our company holds in high regard. In order to maintain productivity and promote an active lifestyle, we have the responsibility to ensure that every one of you participate in at least one sports club organized and funded by our company. We provide professional tutorial and training sessions each week. Attendance will be taken on a regular basis and will be counted towards your reward package at the end of the year. We are also excited to tell you that this year we have two new clubs which you can find in the above file. According to the record, most of our clubs are very popular, so early registration is advisable. Please do not hesitate to seek counsel if you are confused about anything regarding this matter. Good luck with your club picking and as always enjoy your fantastic weekend!

Jennifer H 17:04

Thank you!
Jennifer!
Elisa W. 17:04

Have a great
weekend!
Stefanie 17:10

2017 Sport Club List			
Monday	**Tuesday**	**Thursday**	**Friday**
18:00-20:30	18:00-20:30	18:00-20:30	18:00-21:00
Table Tennis	Jogging	Indoor Climbing NEW	Aerobic Dance
Yoga NEW	Swimming	Belly Dance	Badminton
Aerobic Dance	Badminton	Table Tennis	Jogging

From: Ivy Wang   **Nov 6, 2017**

To: Jennifer Hendryx

Subject: Inquiry about sports club registration

Dear Jennifer,

Thank you for your information. I am really interested in the clubs you run this year. They all look very attractive to me. Here I have a few points I am not clear about. First, how many clubs can we enroll in at most? Second, is there any possibility that you can open another belly dance session on Tuesday? As far as I know, many people in my department are super interested in joining the new indoor climbing club and the belly dance club. However, the two are unfortunately on the same day. Plus, as an old member of the belly dance club which was extremely full last year, I am sure this year it will still be in great demand.

On behalf of the department, I would very much appreciate if you could rearrange the timetable to **accommodate** this condition. I am looking forward to your reply.

Best regards,

Ivy Wang
Sales Department

176 Who most likely is Jennifer?

(A) A yoga therapist

(B) A new employee

(C) An old member of the climbing club

(D) A department director

177 What are employees advised to do?

(A) To sign up as early as possible

(B) To rearrange their own schedule

(C) To spend weekend time exercising

(D) To research each sport before joining

178 What is TRUE about the sports club policy?

(A) Everyone only get to apply for one club at a time.

(B) Each member can skip classes up to three times a year.

(C) Club attendance is closely related to employees' salary.

(D) Membership fee should be paid to the accounting department.

179 What is NOT the reason why Ivy was concerned about the club arrangement?

(A) The coach of the indoor climbing club is frequently absent.

(B) Two popular sessions are scheduled on the same day.

(C) Too many people want to join the belly dance club.

(D) A large number of people may want to continue their membership in the belly dance club.

180 In the email, the word "accommodate" in paragraph 2, line 2, is closest in meaning to

(A) purchase

(B) lodge

(C) fit

(D) return

★Questions 181-185 refer to the following itinerary, timetable and notice.

Western Airline
Your amazing journey starts here.

<u>Manage My Trip</u>

Your booking is successfully confirmed. Thank you for choosing Western Airline.
Now it's time to check in to get a boarding pass.

CHECK IN ONLINE NOW

BOOKING REFERENCE: WA13100394
STATUS: Checked-in/ Seat 15A reserved

To Dublin
Flight No. TR301

Departure: Prague	Arrival: Dublin
Date: 4 February 2016	Date: 4 February 2016
Time: 13:55	Time: 16:20
Passenger 1	Passenger 2
Chris Walker	Emma Chase
Flight No. TR301	Flight No. TR301

Click **HERE** to reserve your seat for free if you haven't yet.
Click **HERE** to protect your trip with travel insurance.
Click **HERE** to rent a car with exclusive deals.

Receipt
Total paid: 108 EUR with no insurance
via Visa ending in 1939
Card holder's name: Chris Walker
Paid on 31 January 2016

WESTERN AIRLINE

International Departures

Flight No	Destination	Time	Gate	Remarks
CF8977	Berlin	12:07	A-19	Gate Closing
BA386	London	12:40	A-38	Boarding
QF9281	Barcelona	13:25	B-20	Delayed
TR301	Dublin	13:55	C-32	Check-in at R19
PR9011	Milan	14:22	B-12	Check-in at C10

Gate C-32

NOTICE

For passengers boarding Flight number TR301 leaving for Dublin, the boarding gate has been changed to C-02 due to temporary renovation. We apologize for the inconvenience.

181 According to the information, what is indicated about Chris Walker's flight?

(A) The seat has been reserved.

(B) The payment is due in a week.

(C) It flies from Dublin to Prague.

(D) The payment was made in cash.

182 What is TRUE about Western Airline?

(A) It does not allow online check-in.

(B) Car rental service is available.

(C) It costs 8 euros to reserve a seat.

(D) Travel insurance fee is included in the ticket price.

183 What does the departure timetable tell us?

(A) The departure gate of the flight leaving for Berlin is under construction.

(B) Passengers going to London are allowed to board now.

(C) Flight QF9281 will arrive in Barcelona at 13:25.

(D) The check-in counter for Flight PR9011 is open at B12.

184 What change was made to Flight No. TR301?

(A) It was cancelled.

(B) It was delayed for over an hour.

(C) Its departure gate was moved to another one.

(D) Its check-in counter was changed to C10.

185 What can be inferred from the information?

(A) Chris was traveling alone to Dublin.

(B) Chris booked the flight one month ahead of the departure time.

(C) It was around noon when Chris saw the departure timetable.

(D) Several flights were delayed or cancelled due to bad weather condition.

★Questions 186-190 refer to the following ticket, signboard and email.

Welcome to St. Thomas Church

---General Admission Ticket---

The entrance fee will go towards the renovation of the St. Thomas Church. Your patronage makes a huge contribution to this great work.

Date: September 21, 2017	Ticket No.: 32038238214
Entrance Time: 14:00	Reservation No.: 1000500234
Ticket Type: Student	Date Booked: August 21, 2017
Price: 10 EUR (VAT included)	Date Printed: August 21, 2017

Please retain this ticket until the end of the visit and the ticket must be presented at the venue upon request. The church reserves the right to deny admission when any behavior is found suspicious and detrimental to other visitors or our properties. Please note that smoking, eating and drinking are strictly prohibited on the premises. No pets or dangerous items are allowed on the premises. Children under 12 must be accompanied by an adult. The church reserves the right to change the routes or visiting time due to adverse weather conditions, safety issues or emergent events. This ticket is non-refundable. If you have any questions, please go on our website at www.sthomaschurch.com, call 076-302-1364 or email admission@sthomaschurch.org.uk for information.

Renovation Project of St. Thomas Church

Temporary Closure of St. Thomas Church

Please be advised that St. Thomas Church will be officially closed for renovations in the east wing of the property from 15 September 2017 to 15 October 2017. The renovation project will include the damaged pavement repair at the porch, foyer floor leveling, installment of new clocks on the south exterior, fallen steeple resurrection and drainage additions at the chapel building. For visitors, do not enter the construction area unless authorized. We apologize for any inconvenience caused. We look forward to seeing you again soon.

Request for refund of the ticket
From- David (davidtan310050@my.uba.ac.uk)
To- admission@sthomaschurch.org.uk
22 September 2017

To whom it may concern,

I purchased a single admission ticket to the church for September 21 on your official website on August 21. Not until I arrived at the church that day did I realize the site had been closed for refurbishment. Between the time when I booked the ticket and when I traveled to the church, I did not receive notification of any kind regarding the church closure. Since this is a rather special condition, I suppose your refund policy does not apply. I tried to contact your customer service department on September 21 but the phone wasn't answered and so far I haven't got any reply from you. Therefore, I am writing this email to request a full refund of the ticket. Please handle this as soon as possible. If you received this email, please answer me as fast as you can.

David Tan

186 Which of the following cannot be brought into the church?

(A) tickets
(B) 12-year-old children
(C) digital camera
(D) hamburgers

187 Which of the following is NOT TRUE about St. Thomas Church?

(A) It is free of entry fee.
(B) Some parts of it are currently being refurbished.
(C) It might be closed on a stormy day.
(D) The funding of its renovation is based on its proceeds from admission.

188 What is indicated about the renovation of the church?

(A) It will take one week to complete.
(B) The broken gate of the east wing will be fixed.
(C) New clocks will be installed on the north interior surface.
(D) Some drainages will be added to the chapel.

189 What is David asking for from the church official?

(A) He is asking for the specific date of its reopening.
(B) He would like to know the details of its remodeling.
(C) He is requesting his money be returned.
(D) He is complaining about the customer service.

190 What is TRUE about David's ticket?

(A) It is purchased over a month before the first day of the church being closed.
(B) It is a student ticket booked on the website.
(C) The price has been refunded to David's account.
(D) The church official had notified David about the renovation before the ticket was booked.

------*Sandwich Theory*------

We want you!!!

We are looking for several clerks who can…

- Operate the cash register, receive money, issue receipts, and register the money received with efficiency and accuracy
- Serve customers courteously and ensure all customers have a wonderful dining experience in our store
- Monitor stock and order ingredients on a daily basis, contact food supplier and distributor
- Carry out cleaning of store area before and after our opening hours

Required Working Hours…

- A minimum of 24 hours per week
- Availability to work on Saturday is preferable.

Salary

- Full-time: $800 / month
- Part-time: $12 / hour

How to apply…

- Download the application form from www.sandwichtheory.com, fill it out and email to recruitment2017@swtr.com before 7 Nov 2017.

If you have any queries, you can…

- Email us at recruitment2017@swtr.com

or

- Add us on Let's TALK and ask our most friendly staff directly.

Let's TALK

<u>Nov 9</u>

> Hello, my name is Celia. I am interested in the job advertised on the bulletin board on our campus. I was wondering if this is still available to apply for.
>
> **Celia Chen**

The clerk one?

Stefanie Feng

> Yes. Is it too late?
>
> **Celia Chen**

Well, technically, it's well past the application deadline. But you are welcome to apply if you'd like. You can complete the application form, print it out and bring it to our store. Our manager will usually be in store from Monday thru Thursday in the afternoon.

Stefanie Feng

> That's fantastic! Thank you so much! I will come to your store on Thursday afternoon. Is that OK for you?
>
> **Celia Chen**

Great! See you then!

Stefanie Feng

Sandwich Theory

<u>Employment Application</u>

Personal Information

NAME _____ CELIA CHEN _____ DATE OF BIRTH _____ 24 MARCH 1996 _____

NATIONALITY _____ CHINA _____ PLACE OF BIRTH _____ CHINA _____

ADDRESS _JINXIN ROAD HUAXIN CITY JIANGSU PROVINCE_ POST CODE _____ 002001 _____

TELEPHONE (86) _____ 15400758894 _____ GENDER _____ FEMALE _____

EMERGENCY CONTACT:

NAME _____ TELEPHONE ( )_____

ADDRESS _____ POST CODE _____

EDUCATION MOST RECENTLY ATTAINEED _____ BU Economy BA _____

RECENT EMPLOYMENT RECORD

○NONE

COMPANY _____ POSITION _____ PERIOD _____

PAYMENT _____ REASON FOR LEAVING _____

I USED TO WORK IN SANDWICH THEORY BEFORE. ○Y ●N

I AM LOOKING FOR A ○ full time ● part time job

I AM ABLE TO WORK ___3___ DAYS AFTER BEING NOTIFIED I AM HIRED.

I AM ABLE TO WORK IN THE FOLLOWING HOURS

	MON	TUE	WED	THU	FRI	SAT
08:00-12:00	V	V		V	V	V
12:00-16:00	V	V		V	V	
16:00-20:00	V	V				
20:00-23:30	V	V				

I hereby certify that the information given above is accurate and complete.

Sign _____ CELIA CHEN _____

Date _____ 10 Nov 2017 _____

191 Which of the following is NOT the duty of the job?

(A) Keeping sanitation of the workplace

(B) Serving diners at the store

(C) Delivering food to customers

(D) Carrying out stock replenishment

192 What most likely is Celia's current job?

(A) A student

(B) A store owner

(C) A factory worker

(D) A plumber

193 When is the deadline of the job application?

(A) March 24

(B) November 7

(C) November 9

(D) November 10

194 According to the information, what would be Celia's advantage as the job applicant?

(A) Her previous working experience

(B) Her education

(C) Her application time

(D) Her being able to work on weekends

195 What can be inferred from the information above?

(A) Celia met the deadline of the application.

(B) If hired, Celia will be paid at an hourly rate.

(C) Celia is not able to meet the requirement of the minimum working hours.

(D) The store manager is usually out of the store on Wednesdays.

Dear Residents of Paris Garden Condominium,

Time flies unbelievably fast. It is always sad to say good-bye. Your time at Paris Garden Condominium is almost over and your tenancy will soon end on 5th September 2017. I am sure you'd found your check-out envelopes by the time you saw this letter. Please read the following information carefully. It tells you what to do when moving out.

- Your last check-out time is 16:00 5th September 2017. You are suggested to allow four days to a week to pack your belongings. Last minute packing is always exhausting.
- Please notify the office your departure time one day ahead of time and arrange an appointment with our housing assistant for the checkout inspection of your room.
- Before you leave, you should clean up your room and bathroom. Anything unwanted should be properly disposed of. You may lose your money from the deposit if you fail to complete a thorough cleaning.
- Please make sure you don't owe any rent or damage any properties of the condominium. Natural wear-out should be reported to us in advance. If we find any unreported damage, you may be charged the cost of the repair work needed. In the worst case, you may face legal action.
- To claim your $1,000 deposit, you need to fill out the deposit refund form which can be found in the envelope along with this letter, and return a signed copy along with your room key to the office. Your deposit will be returned to you within a month.
- Our office is open 8:00-17:00 from Monday to Saturday during this period. Please don't hesitate to contact us if you have any questions. Our extension number is 6500.

We hope you enjoyed your stay in Paris Garden Condominium. Thank you and wish you all the best in the future.

Kind Regards,

Mary Keith

Deposit Return Form

Full Name: Kimberley Conn Resident Number: 105766 Room Number: 9010	Building: North Floor: 9th Room Type: Studio

Bank Details (Please make sure you provide accurate and complete information)

Name of Bank: Eastern Bank

Name of the Account Holder: Kimberley Conn

Account Number: 009887194730921

Zip Code: 005479

Your Signature: *Kimberley Conn*
Date: 4 September 2017

---

25 September 2017
Subject: Deposit Return Notice
Sender: Paris Garden Condo
Receiver: Kimberley

Dear Kimberley,

We hope this email finds you well. We have returned the deposit to your bank account. The amount returned is $798. The following list shows the details of the charge from the original deposit.

- Utility bill: $127 (August 2 – September 1)
- Cleaning work of the <u>limescale</u> in the bathroom and kitchen: $25
- Removal of the adhesive mark on the wall and door: $25
- Repair work of the vacuum: $25

If you have any questions about your refund, please reply to us.
Hope all is well on your side.

Jack Mill
Paris Garden Condo

196 What is the topic of the information above?

(A) Bidding for janitorial work
(B) Office square letting
(C) Moving out of a property
(D) Application for bank clerks

197 Which of the following is NOT the thing the tenants were asked to do?

(A) Filling in an application form
(B) Returning the key
(C) Cleaning up the room
(D) Filing for rent payment extension

198 What is TRUE about Kimberley?

(A) She is an officer at Paris Garden Condominium.
(B) She lived in the ninth floor of the north building.
(C) She failed to provide the correct bank information.
(D) She failed to turn in the application form in time.

199 How much did Kimberley owe for the electricity and water bill?

(A) $25
(B) $50
(C) $127
(D) $798

200 What is the word "limescale" in line 10 closest in meaning to?

(A) watermark
(B) bathtub
(C) toiletry
(D) cutlery

New TOEIC Reading Test 2
新多益閱讀全真模擬試題第2回

▶ **READING TEST**

In the Reading Test, you will read a variety of texts and answer several different types of reading comprehension questions. The entire Reading Test will last 75 minutes. There are three parts, and directions are given for each part. You are encouraged to answer as many questions as possible within the time allowed.

You must mark your answers on the separate answer sheet. Do not write your answers in the test book.

▶ **PART 5**

Directions: A word or phrase is missing in each of the sentences below. Four answer choices are given below each sentence. Select the best answer to complete the sentence. Then mark the letter (A), (B), (C), or (D) on your answer sheet.

101 The shipping delay was caused by an unexpected problem that _____ in our delivery system.
(A) occurred
(B) occurring
(C) occurs
(D) has occurred

102 Mr. Jefferson proved himself an outstanding salesperson as his sales performance _____ exceeded our expectation.
(A) periodically
(B) coincidentally
(C) accidently
(D) consistently

103 This is an urgent project that we need to get _____ within three working days.
(A) done
(B) all
(C) well
(D) over

104 Ms. Leech has been _____ to the position of the Manager of the Research and Development Department.
(A) raised
(B) promoted
(C) increased
(D) enhanced

105 Since you are not satisfied with the product, we respect your decision if you wish to get a full _____ of your purchase.
(A) refund
(B) return
(C) payment
(D) attendance

106 We have just been _____ that our supplier is unable to provide us the computer components we need.
(A) expected
(B) talked
(C) informed
(D) involved

107 To schedule an appointment with Mr. Nelson, please contact his secretary _____ the hours of 10 a.m. and 6 p.m.
(A) between
(B) from
(C) within
(D) besides

108 All employees are _____ to attend the year-end banquet at Grand Hyatt Hotel on December 23rd.
(A) achieved
(B) benefited
(C) invited
(D) revised

109 Ms. Woodfield will be _____ her annual leave for two weeks, starting January 12th.
(A) on
(B) in
(C) for
(D) at

110 Normally, our employees are _____ to their first annual leave after working for one year.
(A) given
(B) entitled
(C) taken
(D) allocated

111 Helen Spencer was _____ as the General Manager because of her strong educational background and her considerable work experience.
(A) employed
(B) pointed
(C) assigned
(D) offered

112 There is a long queue of customers _____ to be served at the checkout.
(A) awaited
(B) waited
(C) waiting
(D) are waiting

113 This proposal requires some _____ as we have made a change in our plan.
(A) declaration
(B) encouragement
(C) modification
(D) communication

114 All _____ please bring your highest diplomas and English proficiency certificates with you to the interview.
(A) applicants
(B) contestants
(C) consultants
(D) investigators

115 The _____ salary for a mechanical engineer in our company will be NT$45,000 per month.
(A) initial
(B) intimate
(C) initiate
(D) early

116 The designated operators must _____ inspect all the elevators and escalators to ensure they are in satisfactory working order.
(A) perfunctorily
(B) thoroughly
(C) reluctantly
(D) dilatorily

117 We have to _____ this proposal, as it does not meet our current need.
(A) promote
(B) adopt
(C) encourage
(D) decline

118 Even though our office will be relocated, both our office phone number and fax number remain _____.
(A) usual
(B) same
(C) similar
(D) unchanged

119 Once you receive your renewal notice, you should renew your registration online as soon as possible _____ it expires.
(A) until
(B) before
(C) after
(D) when

120 According to our contract, our order _____ arrived two days ago. However, we haven't received our commodities up to now.
(A) should have
(B) will have
(C) had
(D) have

121 _____ some personal factors, Mr. Crooks will not be able to attend the new branch office's opening ceremony.
(A) In case
(B) Due to
(C) Because
(D) So that

122 The central air-conditioning system of the office building is currently out of service _____ annual maintenance.
(A) plus
(B) with
(C) for
(D) around

123 The department dinner has been postponed because it has a time _____ with an employee-training course.
(A) conflict
(B) difference
(C) break
(D) fight

124 To make up for our mistake, we would like to offer you a coupon for two _____ dinners in our restaurant.
(A) complimentary
(B) complicated
(C) compulsory
(D) complementary

125 From now on, besides large event planning and arrangement, we also provide activity consultation services _____ production promotion services.
(A) as well as
(B) as long as
(C) as soon as
(D) as far as

126 Your request for a seven-day leave of absence will not be approved _____ you can't find anyone to cover your position.
(A) whether
(B) if
(C) although
(D) unless

127 The budget for this project is
_____; therefore we must get
this contract within the budget.
(A) limited
(B) sufficient
(C) ineffective
(D) precise

128 We should _____ a meeting
this week to discuss the details
of the development project.
(A) experience
(B) schedule
(C) gather
(D) invite

129 Whether you would _____ this
job offer or not, please get back
to us with your decision no later
than this Friday.
(A) admit
(B) return
(C) accept
(D) declare

130 Our HR secretary will answer any
questions _____ employment
policies and procedures.
(A) connecting
(B) regarding
(C) considering
(D) according

▶ PART 6

Directions: Read the texts on the following pages. A word or phrase is missing in some of the sentences. Answer choices are given below each of these articles. Select the best answer to complete the text. Then mark the letter (A), (B), (C) or (D) on your answer sheet.

Questions 131-134 refer to the following e-mail.

To: Last-year students
From: Career Service
Subject: Career Event for International Students

Dear Students,
The Careers Service is happy to bring you an event that may be of interest to you.
— A pre-employment workshop run by PBA Company on December 2nd, Saturday.

PBA Company, is the largest recruitment platform ___131___ in supporting International students. They deliver a ___132___ pre-employment workshop to help you find jobs in Asia.

In this workshop you will learn
• Latest information about Asia's job market
• When you should start seeking job opportunities
• Application strategy and skills ___133___
• Introductions to write a CV/resume that will bring you through the screening
• How to prepare for different types of interviews

____134____

Kind regards,
Emily
Career Service

---

131 (A) specialize
    (B) specializes
    (C) specializing
    (D) specialized

132 (A) professional
    (B) skillful
    (C) proficient
    (D) manageable

133 (A) day by day
    (B) one by one
    (C) page by page
    (D) step by step

★ **134** (A) Sign up immediately to secure place - places are limited.
    (B) Contact our staff if you wish to cancel your appointment.
    (C) Thanks again for your warmest hospitality.
    (D) Please send us the signed contract without delay.

Questions 135-138 refer to the following announcement.

Announcement-Office Closing

Please be ___135___ that MBP Shanghai Office has declared a business closure for the Annual Company Trip from 30 November (Thursday) to 3 December (Sunday). As such, all MBP delivery services will be ___136___ put on hold during the time. Our office will resume its operation as usual on 4 December (Monday) and will respond to all queries thereafter.

For any ___137___, please contact us at 2412-1234 or send an email to customerservice99@mbp.com.

___138___

From the Management & Staff of **MBP Shanghai Office**

135 (A) inform
(B) informs
(C) informing
(D) informed

136 (A) permanently
(B) temporarily
(C) surprisingly
(D) constantly

137 (A) comprehension
(B) congregation
(C) modification
(D) clarification

★ 138 (A) We are grateful for your speedy reply.
(B) We look forward to hearing from you soon.
(C) We apologize for any inconvenience it may cause.
(D) Please let me know if you are unable to come.

Questions 139-142 refer to the following e-mail.

From: Ellen Hathaway <Ellen.Hathaway@westengland.ac.uk>

To: cliftonhouse-studio-residents@westengland.ac.uk

Date: Tue, Feb 27, 2018 at 1:46 PM

Subject: Disposing of unwanted or broken small electrical items

Hello

Our Accommodation Manager has asked me to contact you on her __139__ . Hall staff have noticed a number of broken small items of electrical equipment __140__ in the waste and recycling area near Clifton House recently. Please __141__ that the contractors who pick up our waste and recycling from there are not able to take away any electrical equipment.

If you have any items of electrical equipment you want to dispose of, __142__ and a member of staff will come and collect the item from you and dispose of it appropriately.

Thank you.

Ellen Hathaway

Student Support Adviser, Clifton House

139 (A) own
(B) behalf
(C) back
(D) conscience

140 (A) are appearing
(B) to have appeared
(C) appearing
(D) to appear

141 (A) note
(B) remind
(C) find
(D) notify

★ 142 (A) please take a minute to review the attached list of items
(B) please complete the on-line waste collection request form
(C) please fill out the leave request form at the reception counter
(D) please arrive at the conference venue two hours ahead

Questions 143-146 refer to the following invitation.

To: Prof. Helen Hutchinson

From: William Marsh

Subject: Invitation Letter for Alumni Reunion Party

Dear Prof. Hutchinson

I hope this letter find you in the best ___143___ of your health. The purpose of writing is to inform you regarding the Annual Alumni Reunion Party of Department of Business Administration in the University of Clifton. Many of our distinguished alumni including Joseph Martinez and Ryder Hernandez will attend the event. We want to earnestly invite you as chief guest in this reunion party, as you have always been a ___144___ of achievement and inspiration for students in the Department of BA. It would be a pleasant surprise for them to see you as Chief Guest in between them.

If you could kindly spare some precious time and come to this alumni reunion party we shall be ___145___. The decided date is 8th March, 2018 on Thursday. Time is from 6 pm to 9 pm and venue is the UOC Business School Building.

We understand your busy schedule, but the management and Preparatory Team are extremely eager to receive a positive response from your side. ___146___

We shall wait for your reply.

With Warm Regards,

William

Prof. William Marsh

Dean of Department of Business Administration

University of Clifton

143 (A) condition
   (B) term
   (C) period
   (D) circumstance

144 (A) feature
   (B) characteristic
   (C) idol
   (D) symbol

145 (A) fortunate
   (B) privileged
   (C) confidential
   (D) satisfied

★ 146 (A) We hope that you will not turn us down in this regard.
   (B) We hope to receive the samples within this week.
   (C) We hope there are other opportunities to do business with you.
   (D) We hope you commence the production immediately.

▶ PART 7

Directions: In this part, you will read a selection of texts, such as magazine and newspaper articles, letters, and advertisements. Each text is followed by several questions. Select the best answer for each question and mark the letter (A), (B), (C), or (D) on your answer sheet.

Questions 147-148 refer to the following invitation.

The Charity League of Leicester
invites you to a
Harvest Banquet

Sunday, December 17, 12:30 PM

Caesar Hotel Leicester
185 West Minister Road
44 (0) 116 255 0000

Generously Sponsored by
Angel Garden Foundation
St. George Children's Safety Culture and Education Foundation

RSVP
to Rachel Brown by November 30th

147 What is the invitation for?
(A) A job fair
(B) A charity event
(C) A housewarming party
(D) A home party

148 When should the invitees reply to this invitation?
(A) The sooner the better
(B) A week before the banquet
(C) By the end of November
(D) Within seven days

Questions 149-151 refer to the following poster.

Arirang Korean Restaurant

Open: Tuesday to Sunday at 12 PM

❧ Authentic Korean cuisine in the heart of New York ❦

Everything on our menu is made from scratch.

Check out our new expansion & Stay tuned for our Patio Grand Opening!

66 New Garden Road, New York City

www.arirang-newyork.com

149 What is this poster advertising for?
(A) Business lunch sets
(B) Special meal deals
(C) All-you-can-eat buffet lunch
(D) Authentic Korean dishes

150 On Which day of the week is the restaurant closed?
(A) Sunday
(B) Monday
(C) Tuesday
(D) Saturday

151 According to the poster, which statement is correct?
(A) The restaurant will close for a month.
(B) The chef of the restaurant is from South Korea.
(C) The owner of the restaurant is a Korean.
(D) The restaurant is scaling up its business.

Questions 152-153 refer to the following message.

Telephone Message

For: <u>Ashley</u>

From: <u>Mr. Walsh</u>

Message: Due to poor visibility caused by dense fog, all flights from Penghu to Taipei today have been cancelled. Thus, I don't think I will be able to make it to the office for the meeting scheduled tomorrow morning. Please let the meeting attendees know the meeting is cancelled. I will reschedule it sometime next week.

Action required: ☐ Please call back

☐ Caller will call back later

☑ No action required

Date: November 29   Time: 14:33   Message taken by: ___*Linda*___

---

152 According to this message, what will be changed?
(A) The meeting location
(B) The meeting time
(C) The meeting agenda
(D) The meeting moderator

153 What should Ashley do when she gets the message?
(A) Send the meeting cancellation notice
(B) Meet Mr. Walsh at the airport
(C) Return Mr. Walsh's call immediately
(D) Cancel her flight to Penghu

Questions 154-156 refer to the following memorandum.

Date: May 23
To: Daniel Murray
From: Lisa Louis

Daniel,

Below is the first draft of the timeline for our new product launch. Please take a look at it and let me know if you can have everything ready by the indicated dates:

① First week of June – Marketing team will visit the venue where the launch press conference will take place and meet several times with event planning team to discuss their specific concerns and needs.

② Second week of June – Miranda Fletcher will prepare an official announcement to issue to the news media as well as the list of guests we will invite to celebrate the product launch with us.

③ Third week of June – Jessica Ruther will present the guidelines and programs for the advertising and promotional campaign to Mr. Morgan and Mr. Morris.

154 What is the main purpose of the memo?

(A) To provide a rough schedule

(B) To reserve a venue for launch event

(C) To publish a press release

(D) To identify problems with a speech draft

155 Who most likely are Mr. Morgan and Mr. Morris?

(A) Security guards

(B) Senior executives

(C) New employees

(D) The interviewers

156 What will happen in the second week of June?

(A) The guidelines for the advertising will be proposed.

(B) The press release will be ready.

(C) The venue of the press conference will be decided.

(D) The invitation will be sent.

★Questions 157-159 refer to the following text message chain.

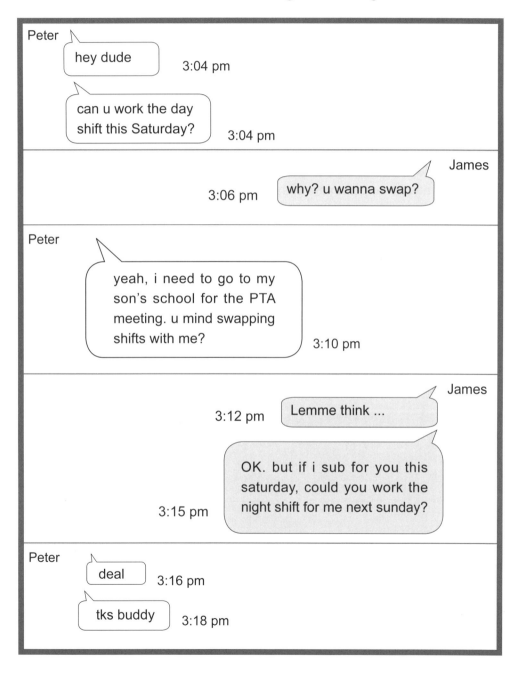

Peter

hey dude   3:04 pm

can u work the day shift this Saturday?   3:04 pm

James

3:06 pm   why? u wanna swap?

Peter

yeah, i need to go to my son's school for the PTA meeting. u mind swapping shifts with me?   3:10 pm

James

3:12 pm   Lemme think ...

OK. but if i sub for you this saturday, could you work the night shift for me next sunday?   3:15 pm

Peter

deal   3:16 pm

tks buddy   3:18 pm

157 Why is this text message chain mainly about?

(A) Swapping shifts with colleagues
(B) Calling an emergency meeting
(C) Developing a meeting agenda
(D) Negotiating for a lower price

158 Why is Peter unable to work the day shift this Saturday?

(A) He has to go on a blind date.
(B) He has an appointment with his dentist.
(C) He has to go to his son's school.
(D) He needs to pick up his client at the airport.

159 According to the message chain, which is true?

(A) James will work Peter's shift on Saturday.
(B) Peter has a day off next Sunday.
(C) James will go to the PTA meeting with Peter.
(D) James helps Peter out unconditionally.

Questions 160-161 refer to the following information.

Christmas Delivery Information

Christmas is a busy and important time of year. To support you in your shopping plans over this period, we offer different options to have your purchase delivered to your home. Whether you choose truck delivery or picking with delivery, please check the estimated delivery date by entering your postcode as you start the checkout process. Same/next day delivery is subject to availability at our local transport partner. Please understand that conditions beyond our control such as adverse weather could delay your order.

If you need your order quicker, you can visit your local store and take your purchases home yourself, or have the order delivered the same day or next day within the store delivery area*. The last day before Christmas to receive a delivery from the store will be 23rd December.

*An additional £10 charge will be incurred for truck deliveries outside of the store delivery area.

---

160 What do customers need to estimate the delivery date of their purchase?
(A) Postcode
(B) Membership number
(C) Order number
(D) ID number

161 Which statement is true about truck deliveries outside the store delivery area?
(A) It takes two days longer.
(B) It costs an extra £10.
(C) It needs earlier reservation.
(D) It's cheaper than picking with delivery.

Questions 162-165 refer to the following e-mail.

From: Rebecca Turner <r_turner@cosmail.com>
To: <customerservice@langalino.com>
Date/Time: March 19/ 12:01:45
Subject: Appreciation from a customer

Dear Langalino Customer Service,
I am writing this letter in regard to my experience at your location on Rainbow Blvd. earlier today. I arrived with my young girl as well as my girlfriends and their children at 11:30 a.m. —[1]— We were greeted by an attendant named Vincent, who held the door for us and helped us fold the strollers. He quickly led us to our table and fetched high chairs for all the little ones.

Although Langalino is a self-service establishment, and customers are supposed to order at the counter and get stuff by themselves, Vincent not only took our orders at our table so we didn't have to leave our little ones, but also refilled our drinks and brought us items that we required.—[2]— When we were about to leave, he was thoughtful enough to escort us out, holding the door for all of us and our children. While the restaurant was bustling with patrons, we still felt as if we were dining with our own private wait staff. —[3]—

My girlfriends and I are all frequent visitors to your establishment. Service like this is definitely the very reason for our return visits. Please pass along our appreciation to Vincent and the rest of the staff at your Rainbow branch. —[4]—

Your loyal customer,
Connie Chessman

162 What is the purpose of this letter?
(A) To make a complaint
(B) To express regrets
(C) To express gratitude
(D) To postpone a payment

163 According to this letter, what is Langalino?
(A) A child-friendly restaurant
(B) A pet-friendly restaurant
(C) A staff cafeteria
(D) A school dining hall

164 Which word can replace the word "escort" in this letter?
(A) escape
(B) accompany
(C) educate
(D) control

★ **165** In which of the positions marked [1], [2], [3], and [4] does the sentence "They are a credit to your organization." best belong?
(A) [1]
(B) [2]
(C) [3]
(D) [4]

Questions 166-168 refer to the following advertisement.

Holiday House for Rent

This newly built, light and airy 2-bedroom holiday cottage is perfect for a city break in one of England's most vibrant cities. The house is centrally located in the beautiful neighborhood of Clifton with shops, cafes and restaurants nearby.

- The interior is furnished and equipped to a high standard, with high quality linen and towels provided.
- The open plan sitting room and the kitchen with separate utility room on the first floor provide all the amenities for a comfortable stay.
- On the second floor you will find two double bedrooms - a king-size bed in the master and two singles in the second room. The second floor also has its own tiled shower room.
- Guests will have access to the entire premises, as well as a private courtyard at the rear.

---

166 What can be found near the cottage mentioned in the advertisement?
(A) A hospital
(B) An elementary school
(C) A supermarket
(D) Dining places

167 Which of following is not provided in this holiday house?
(A) Linens and towels
(B) Kitchenware
(C) A private courtyard
(D) Rain gear

168 Where is the courtyard?
(A) Near the cottage
(B) In front of the cottage
(C) At the back of the house
(D) Next to the house

Questions 169-171 refer to the following advertisement.

Interview Events for Formosa Aircraft Catering Company

We are searching for talented individuals to fill the vacancies at Formosa Aircraft Catering Company in our base in Taoyuan, Taiwan.

☞Organization: Formosa Aircraft Catering Company

☞Job Function: Catering, Food & Beverage

☞Employment Type: Full Time - Permanent

☞Last date of application: 31-January-2018

Formosa Aircraft Catering Company (FACC) provides exclusive catering services to Formosa Airways. You will be responsible for the execution of work assigned by the supervisor to provide and accommodate all daily food products as airline requirements and menu cycle. Furthermore, you will also facilitate at all times proper cleanliness in all work, storage space and refrigeration areas.

You should have basic English communication skills and up to 2 years of experience. High school or above education level is preferred. Moreover, it is essential that you have basic knowledge in food hygiene, and basic food cooking techniques.

To apply for the job you will be required to attach the following:

1. Resume / CV

2. Copy of Passport

3. Copy of Highest Educational Certificate

169 What is this company recruiting?
(A) Flight attendants
(B) Catering staff
(C) Kitchen apprentices
(D) Senior executives

170 What is NOT mentioned in the advertisement?
(A) Applicants must be available to work immediately.
(B) Applicants must be able to speak simple English.
(C) Applicants must have at least 2 years of experience.
(D) Applicants should have basic cooking skills.

171 What should one provide in order to apply for the job?
(A) Copy of highest educational certificate
(B) English proficiency certificate
(C) Bank statement
(D) Copy of statement of academic records

Questions 172-175 refer to the following information.

Trial Period Policy

✦Policy Statement

A 90-calendar day trial period applies to all current staff that transfer into or are promoted to a new position. The staff member's trial period starts on the first day of the job change and lasts until the staff member has completed 90 consecutive calendar days of regular employment status. During this time, the staff member determines whether or not the position meets his or her expectations, and the supervisor determines whether or not the staff member has the knowledge and skills to perform the job expectations.

✦Completion of the Trial Period

Supervisors must evaluate the staff member during the trial period. A performance review should be initiated within the first 15 days of hire. The supervisor should obtain and complete a Trial Period Review Form. Upon obtaining the form, the supervisor and staff member should meet to discuss performance and determine whether the staff member is performing at his or her expected level of performance during the trial period.

The review form should be completed as well as signed and dated by both the supervisor and staff member before the 90th calendar day of the trial period.
A decision should be made by the supervisor to recommend:
successful completion of the review period,
extension of the review period for 30 days, or
discharge because of unsuccessful completion of the review period.

Any extension or discharge must be reviewed with the HR leader and a representative of Staff and Labor Relations at least 14 calendar days before the end of the 90-calendar day period.

172 How long does this company run trial periods?
(A) 30 working days
(B) Two months
(C) 90 calendar days
(D) 30 – 90 days

173 When should supervisors start evaluating the staff member's performance?
(A) From the 90th calendar day
(B) Within the first 15 days of hire
(C) Two weeks before the end of the trial period
(D) From the first day of hire

174 Which statement is incorrect about the Trial Period Review Form?
(A) It needs both the supervisor's and the staff member's signatures.
(B) It should be completed by the end of the trial period.
(C) The supervisor must fill it out secretly.
(D) It's to review the staff member's performance.

175 Who is irrelevant to a decision of extension or discharge?
(A) Director of the HR Department
(B) The representative of Staff and Labor Relations
(C) The supervisor of the staff member
(D) The fellow colleagues of the staff member

★**Questions 176-180 refer to the following advertisement, form, and letter.**

ABOUT Gala CLUB

Say goodbye to plastic membership cards. It's all happening in your smartphone! The Gala app is your portal to great fashion rewards, special offers, discounts, and invitations to exclusive events. Every time you buy something from Gala you earn points - in Gala stores and online. These points can be used towards fabulous rewards and perks. Visit the club pages often to keep up to date with the latest club offers.

✳**Offers**

As a Club member you have access to customized offers. Everything from special discounts, reduced sale prices, to 3 for 2 deals. The possibilities are endless.

✳**Events**

Welcome to the guest list! We love throwing parties. As a Gala Club member you can join us at fashion shows, exclusive shopping events, music events, etc.

You find all available events in your club pages. To attend simply click on the event and book your seat, or place on the list.

Wait no more! Download the app and create an account to sign up right now!

Email: michael_pa28@cosmail.com

Title: ◉ Mr.   ○ Mrs.   ○ Miss

First name: Michael   Last name: Parsons

Date of birth: 28/11/1998

Phone number: +44   7784756886

Address: Manor Hall, Lower Clifton Rd   Postcode: BS8 1BU

Country: United Kingdom

Subscription:

☑ I am interested in receiving printed marketing material from Gala.

By clicking "Save details" I accept the Privacy Policy.

Cancel   Save Details

Hi, **Michael**! Welcome to the club!

You have successfully become a member of Gala! Congratulations!

You can now enjoy your Gala Club benefits: collect points on everything you buy, redeem offers in store and access exclusive content. Just show your phone to the cashier every time you shop to collect points, and use them to unlock great offers, fashionable rewards and access to exclusive events. When you shop online, your points are registered automatically.

Gala is giving all new individual members 20% off for the first online purchase. Before April 29, 2018, 24:00 AM, you can make extra savings on your online order with the voucher code NEWMEMBER-281198 .

Enjoy your shopping!

176 What is the purpose of the advertisement?
- (A) To recruit new members
- (B) To update club offers
- (C) To announce year-end sale
- (D) To recruit franchisees.

177 What type of industry most likely is Gala?
- (A) Apparel Accessories
- (B) Finance and insurance
- (C) Culture and education
- (D) Catering service

178 Which of the following will not be provided to the member?
- (A) Special discounts
- (B) A physical membership card
- (C) Fashion rewards
- (D) Fashion event invitations

179 Why did Michael submit the form?
- (A) To sign up for the club
- (B) To update his contact information
- (C) To renew his membership
- (D) To activate his bank account

180 What does the voucher code entitle Michael to?
- (A) A free standard delivery
- (B) A free same-day delivery
- (C) A discount of 20%
- (D) A free cup of coffee in store

From: Tiffany Taylor <ttiffany@ttevents.com>
To: Mr. Davies <jabst@autotradecenter.com.tw>
Date/Time: January 23/14:02:56
Subject: Business Introduction

Dear Mr. Davies,

I am Tiffany Taylor from Tiffany Events. Please allow me to take this opportunity to introduce our company and our services. We are a company that specializes in event organizing business. We have more than 10 years of experience in organizing private parties, charitable events, and weddings. With a wide range of resources we are able to help you find the perfect venue, plan the event, connect you with the best vendors and produce any aspect of the event. We will do the design, set-up the location, invite the guests, and even find the talent wanted in the event. To put it briefly, you can be a guest of your own event and celebrate while we take care of everything.

If you are interested in learning any further information regarding our services, please contact me at (02)2929-6868.
Looking forward to working with you in the near future.

Best wishes,
Tiffany Taylor, Owner

From: Johnny Davies <jabst@qmpmotorcorp. com.tw>

To: Tiffany Taylor <ttiffany@ttevents.com>

Date/Time: February 10/11:32:45

Subject: Re: Business Introduction

Dear Tiffany,

Thanks for your letter dated January 23. The services you provide are exactly what we need for our company anniversary on April 18. The company anniversary is usually the QMP Motor Corporation's most important event of the year. This year we're planning to have an even bigger celebration party because it's our 20th anniversary. As usual, the party should be held on the basement floor of our office building.

We would like to invite you or your sales representative to our company for a meeting next Tuesday morning around ten to negotiate a tie-up with you. Please let me know if it is a convenient time for you.

Look forward to your reply.

Sincerely,

Johnny Davies, Office Assistant

From: Tiffany Taylor <ttiffany@ttevents.com>

To: Johnny Davies <jabst@qmpmotorcorp. com.tw>

Date/Time: February 10/14:02:10

Subject: Re: Re: Business Introduction

Dear Johnny,

Thank you for considering our firm to assist you with your annual event. I will arrive at your office at the designated time together with our Event Specialists, Ivy and Yolanda, to present the services we provide in detail.

Looking forward to our meeting.

Sincerely,

Tiffany

181 Why is the first letter written?
- (A) To poach talent from a competitor
- (B) To find new customers and increase sales
- (C) To introduce a new sales representative
- (D) To announce temporary closure

182 What kind of service does Tiffany Events provide?
- (A) Location catering service
- (B) Airport pickup service
- (C) Event planning service
- (D) Lift repairs and maintenance service

183 According to the second e-mail, which event is taking place in the coming April?
(A) The Company Sports Day
(B) The annual company trip
(C) The company founder's birthday
(D) The company 20th anniversary party

184 Which of the following has the most similar meaning to the word "tie-up" in the second e-mail?
(A) Postponement
(B) Relationship
(C) Deal-making
(D) Compensation

185 What's the purpose of the third e-mail?
(A) To accept the meeting invitation
(B) To make an appointment
(C) To offer a special discount
(D) To ask for a rain check

SUBJECT: INVITATION TO QUOTE PRICE OF GOODS

Dear. Mr. Wright,

We are interested in purchasing 120 exhaust mufflers and 200 fuel filters from you.

Please quote your ordinary unit price for supplying the goods together with your discount for volume purchases. Please indicate whether your quotes are inclusive or exclusive of sales taxes and delivery costs. Please state these clearly, otherwise we will assume they are both included.

Sincerely,

Allen Brunner

Subject: Re: INVITATION TO QUOTE PRICE OF GOODS

Attachment: Quotation.doc 📄

Dear Mr. Brunner,

With reference to your letter dated June 29, inquiring about our auto parts - exhaust mufflers and fuel filters, we are grateful for your interest in our products and are pleased to provide the quotation as attached for your consideration.

Both sales taxes and delivery costs are covered in the price. Please note that the prices listed are only valid for this quarter.

Should there be any questions regarding the quotation or you need further details to meet your requirement, please feel free to contact me anytime during 9 am to 5 pm.
Looking forward to receiving your order.

Yours faithfully,
Jeffery

Quotation

Prepared for			Sales Representative		
Allen Brunner			Jeffery Wright		
KOHEN Mobile Manufaturer 3566 Rainbow Blvd- Suite 440 2305-468-343			Product Specialist 4464-569-304/ wjeffery@autoparts. com		
Date: 28/01/2018			Valid Until: 31/03/2018		
No.	Item	Qty	Unit Price	Discount	Amount
1	Exhaust Muffler EM3-28	120	NT$12,000	5%	1,368,000.00
2	Fuel Filter FF5-16DL	200	NT$500	5%	95,000.00
Total					1,463,000.00

On orders for 100 pieces we allow a discount of 5%.

On orders for 500 pieces we allow a discount of 20%.

Prices are inclusive of VAT and delivery charges.

Payment is due seven days after the invoice.

186 What is the purpose of the first e-mail?

(A) To request an invoice

(B) To request a quote

(C) To change an order

(D) To request a product sample

187 According to the second e-mail, when should Mr. Brunner contact Jeffery for further details regarding the quotation?

(A) During the working hours

(B) No earlier than 5 pm

(C) Anytime before 9 am

(D) Anytime during the day

188 According to the two e-mails, which statement is correct about the quote?

(A) It is exclusive of delivery charge.

(B) It is inclusive of service charge.

(C) It is valid until the end of February.

(D) It is inclusive of taxes.

189 What percentage discount is offered on the quote?

(A) A discount of 5%

(B) A discount of 10%

(C) A discount of 15%

(D) A discount of 20%

190 Which of the following is not given in the quotation?

(A) Discount for volume purchases

(B) Estimated delivery date

(C) The customer's contact info

(D) The supplier's contact info

14 Days Work (20 positions!)

☛ 2 shifts— ① **10 am ~ 6 pm** ② **1 pm ~ 9 pm**
☛ Work Location— **GoGo Shopping Mall Food Court**
☛ Job Description— **Selling Dairy Products**
☛ Pay range from **£10~£12/per hour** based on experience

- Training will be provided by the company
- Able to speak simple English
- Please call 928-405-766 (10 am-6 pm) or
 email your resume to stevenchuang@gogomall.com

To: Albert Hsiang <albert_hsiang66@qmail.com>
From: Rebecca Lin <linrebecca@dcmedairysupplies.com>
Date/Time: April 26/16:12:48
Subject: Interview Invitation

Dear Mr. Hsiang,

Thank you for your resume and application letter. DCME Company would like to invite you to interview for the position of counter crew. Please click on the link below and sign in to select your preferred interview time.
http://www.dcmedairyproducts.interviewassistant.menu=candidate&even tToken=d8r838r8t880085324144dhug7
Your interview will take place at: 307 Royal Building, Christopher Road. When you arrive for your interview, please report to the receptionist on the 10th Floor.
Thank you.

Candidate ⊙ Mr. ○Mrs. ○ Ms.	**Albert Hsiang**
Position Applied for :	○Supervisor ⊙ Counter crew
Preferred Interview Date:	○May 3 ⊙ May 4 ○ May 5
Preferred Interview Time:	○10:30 ○11:00 ○11:30 ○13:30 ○14:00 ○14:30 ○15:00 ○15:30 ⊙16:00 ○16:30
SUBMIT	

191 What is the purpose of the advertisement?
(A) To recruit helpers
(B) To promote a new product
(C) To advertise a movie
(D) To announce a flash sale

192 Which information is not given in the advertisement?
(A) The salary
(B) The working time
(C) The work location
(D) The starting time

193 Why was the email written?
(A) To request a meeting
(B) To submit an assignment
(C) To send an interview invitation
(D) To introduce the company

194 What position is Albert applying for?
(A) The supervisor
(B) The counter crew
(C) The delivery driver
(D) The express courier

195 When will Albert's interview take place?
(A) 2 pm on May 3
(B) 4 pm on May 4
(C) 10 am on May 4
(D) 3:30 pm on May 5

RETURNS

The Eastern Lake® stands behind the quality of everything we sell and hope you're happy with your gear. Our products are fully warranted against defects in materials and workmanship with a lifetime guarantee. Footwear holds a limited one-year guarantee.

If you're unsatisfied with products you purchased from The Eastern Lake, you can return your item(s) as follows:

- Items purchased online can be returned online or at our retail stores within 60 days of purchase.
- Items purchased in a retail store must be returned in-store within 60 days of purchase.
- You must have an original receipt or packing slip to complete your return.
- Items must be unused and unwashed.
- Custom products are final and are not eligible for returns, exchanges, changes or alterations.

Dear Sir,

The Men's Thermoball Lifty 400 Winter Boots that I ordered from you have arrived this morning. Thank you very much.

Nevertheless, I regret to tell you that I need to return the item because they are too small for me. They are the size that I usually wear but I just can't fit in.

Attached to this letter and the parcel is the goods return note. Please let me know when I will get a refund of my purchase. Thanks.

Look forward to hearing from you soon.

Regards,
Derrick Long

Goods Return Note

Purchase Order No. ___439908124___

Date Goods Received: _26 January, 2018___

Reasons for Returning:

☐ Defective product
☐ Product no longer needed
☐ Product did not match description on website or in catalog
☑ Product did not meet customer's expectations
☐ Incorrect product or size ordered
☐ Incorrect product or size delivered

Signed: _Derrick Long_   Dated: _February 27, 2018___

196 What kind of product does The Eastern Lake sell?

(A) Household appliances
(B) Outdoor products
(C) Electronic components
(D) Books and magazines

197 How long is footwear guaranteed for?

(A) Lifetime
(B) 60 days
(C) One year
(D) Two years

198 What is the purpose of Derrick's letter?

(A) To place a purchase order
(B) To request a proof of purchase

(C) To return an item he ordered
(D) To change the delivery address

199 What is Derrick's reason for returning the product?

(A) He doesn't like the color.
(B) He ordered the wrong size.
(C) It doesn't meet his needs.
(D) The product arrived damaged.

200 When does Derrick return the product?

(A) Seven days after purchase
(B) One month after receipt of goods
(C) Two months before guarantee expires
(D) After guarantee expired

New TOEIC Reading Test 3

新多益閱讀全真模擬試題第3回

► **READING TEST**

In the Reading Test, you will read a variety of texts and answer several different types of reading comprehension questions. The entire Reading Test will last 75 minutes. There are three parts, and directions are given for each part. You are encouraged to answer as many questions as possible within the time allowed.

You must mark your answers on the separate answer sheet. Do not write your answers in the test book.

► **PART 5**

Directions: A word or phrase is missing in each of the sentences below. Four answer choices are given below each sentence. Select the best answer to complete the sentence. Then mark the letter (A), (B), (C), or (D) on your answer sheet.

---

101 Before submitting your request, please_____ you specify the amount you need.
(A) assure
(B) ensure
(C) insure
(D) reassure

102 Office staff who need to use the paper shredder are required to get_____ from director David first.
(A) prove
(B) approve
(C) approving
(D) approval

103 Some critics are skeptical about the _____ of the industry.
(A) sustain
(B) sustaining
(C) sustainable
(D) sustainability

104 The unemployment rate this year rose _____ due to the country's withdrawal from the union.
(A) dramatically
(B) periodically
(C) consistently
(D) anxiously

105 Congratulations to you for _____ to manager.
(A) promote
(B) promoting
(C) promoted
(D) being promoted

106 Please turn off the machine when it is not _____ use.
(A) to
(B) with
(C) in
(D) on

107 She had her luggage _____ to her home address.
(A) shipping
(B) shipped
(C) to ship
(D) for shipping

108 _____ a broader perspective, some gaping holes in the system need to be addressed with priority.
(A) From
(B) On
(C) With
(D) Along

109 Most airlines would _____ overbook knowing that a percentage of passengers will not show up.
(A) unexpectedly
(B) considerably
(C) intentionally
(D) arguably

110 _____ you get to the final stage of the interview, I will email you all the necessary documents.
(A) By
(B) Even
(C) Once
(D) Though

111 When you need to stay in the office for a/an _____ period of time, you can ask your company to cover the meal for you.
(A) extended
(B) predicted
(C) delayed
(D) intended

112 A potential crisis has been _____ after he appealed for help.
(A) converted
(B) averted
(C) perverted
(D) reverted

113 A decade has _____ since she last left her hometown.
(A) intervened
(B) fantasized
(C) enunciated
(D) retrieved

114 Please remind the seminar attendees to bring _____ IDs to the venue.
(A) his
(B) her
(C) their
(D) your

115 _____ anonymity is concerned, it is your responsibility to inform the participants that their identities will be safely protected.
(A) As far as
(B) As soon as
(C) As tardy as
(D) As well as

116 Congratulations to an alumnus of our university, Kris Cape, _____ has won the best mobile app award this year.
(A) that
(B) who
(C) whose
(D) which

117 A coach will be booked to _____ you to and from the event.
(A) transcribe
(B) transport
(C) translate
(D) traverse

118 How much does the collection of lipsticks _____ ?
(A) take
(B) spend
(C) pay
(D) cost

119 After trying to contact her _____ times, I finally got hold of her.
(A) occasional
(B) multiple
(C) valueless
(D) binary

120 If anybody has issues _____ accessing the signup list, please do let me know.
(A) with
(B) in
(C) among
(D) for

121 We regret that we have to cancel the event due to the _____ circumstances.
(A) indirect
(B) acute
(C) unforeseen
(D) diverse

122 Mr. Lee will be on his annual leave _____ December 22 to January 1.
(A) from
(B) on
(C) during
(D) between

123 _____ the difficulties faced, we need to be brave and tough it out.
(A) On account of
(B) Resulting from
(C) Regardless of
(D) With regard to

124 _____ all the competitors, Sherman is the most articulate speaker.
(A) Of
(B) In
(C) Along
(D) For

125 Please carefully read through the contract _____ the obligations.
(A) detail
(B) details
(C) detailing
(D) detailed

126 Do you understand the requirements expected to be _____ ?
(A) met
(B) composed
(C) purchased
(D) breached

127 It is important that the standard operating procedures _____ when you apply for reimbursement.
(A) follow
(B) be followed
(C) following
(D) be following

128 Sophie brought up the issue to her direct supervisor _____ the risk of losing her job.
(A) at
(B) in
(C) with
(D) as

129 Both parties have to sign the document _____ they understand the terms.
(A) indicate
(B) which indicate
(C) indicates
(D) to indicate

130 _____ is the average length of each video clip?
(A) How
(B) What
(C) How long
(D) When

▶ PART 6

Directions: Read the texts on the following pages. A word or phrase is missing in some of the sentences. Answer choices are given below each of these articles. Select the best answer to complete the text. Then mark the letter (A), (B), (C) or (D) on your answer sheet.

Questions 131-134 refer to the following information.

Dental Assistant Job in London

Adriana Dental Office- London SE7
Part-time

Our office, conveniently ___131___ near a Piccadilly line metro station, is seeking an experienced and reliable dental surgery assistant who is certified by General Dental Council for weekday work. The role of a dental assistant which we highly ___132___ is key to creating for patients the best experience of dental treatment.

Your duties are

• assisting dental operation by preparing the surgery instruments, sterilizing the instruments after use, passing and holding the surgery devices during the procedure

• arranging ___133___ with customers and ensuring the dentists' schedules run smoothly

• offering friendly help to customers and easing their anxiety

Please send your CV, and ___134___ .

131 (A) locates
(B) locating
(C) is located
(D) located

132 (A) consider
(B) recognize
(C) perceive
(D) conceive

133 (A) appointments
(B) conferences
(C) summits
(D) meetings

★ 134 (A) you should have at least
1 year of clinic experience
(B) we will be in touch to arrange
a telephone interview
(C) we can officially welcome
you on board
(D) qualifications are essential
to the job requirements

Questions 135-138 refer to the following email.

Dear New Ocean Bell Resident,

As you may know, the heater in your room stops working from time to time recently. ___135___ our contractor, an operative will be coming and carrying out some remedial works to the heating system at New Ocean Bell on 17th and 18th September 2017.

We are writing this email to formally notify you that for these essential works to be completed, access to your room may be required at some point during the days. These works will be carried out with minimum ___136___. You do not have to be present while the heater check-up which will only last no more than five minutes is carried out but ___137___.

If for any reason these dates need to be changed, please notify us ___138___. Please, if you have any queries, do not hesitate to let us know.

Kind regards,

Ray

135 (A) Ring
(B) Rang
(C) Being rung
(D) Having rung

136 (A) disruption
(B) distortion
(C) fragility
(D) agility

★ 137 (A) no-show will lead to serious penalty
(B) your presence may disrupt the procedures of the works
(C) are more than welcome to do so should you wish
(D) I understand how busy your schedule is

138 (A) with patience
(B) in advance
(C) for instance
(D) on a short notice

Questions 139-142 refer to the following post.

The 2nd Music Wave Award is Open NOW!

The 2nd Music Wave Award offers amateur music composers the chance to win 12 thousand dollars and a work placement in Beta Music. The award,   139   by Beta Music and My-Line, gives the country's brightest music composers and producers a head start in the highly competitive music industry. Participants should first become a member of My-Line by   140   on www.myline.com. Next, submit your work which should be saved in an mp3 file to the MyMusic portal. Finally, fill out the personal information chart and click "submit". You will receive an email   141   that your file is successfully received.   142 . No late submission would be acceptable. Your work will go through three rating phases reviewed by the country's prestigious music producers and songwriters. The results will be released on the official website of MyMusic on the first day of December.

139 (A) sponsored
(B) rewarded
(C) compensated
(D) expanded

140 (A) register
(B) registering
(C) registered
(D) registration

141 (A) confirm
(B) confirms
(C) to confirm
(D) confirming

★ 142 (A) Please be constantly updated about the latest results.
(B) The deadline for submitting your work is November 5th.
(C) Your willingness to share your work with us is appreciated.
(D) Further details will be circulated near the time of early December.

★Questions 143-146 refer to the following conversation.

Southwest Branch Office 2017 (65)

09:00

Stefanie

Hey, Eve. Good morning. I have been told to speak to you about ___143___ a request for my office door to be fixed.

Eve

Can you be specific about the problem? What is the room number?

10:00

Stefanie

My room is 1414. My door knob keeps locking and takes a long to unlock ___144___ any key. Sometimes the door will not even stay latched closed.

Eve

Okay! I got it. I will put through your request to the ___145___ department when I am back in the office this afternoon. They will send an operative over by 5 pm today.

16:09

Stefanie

___146___ .

Eve

Alright. If you've got any problem next time, just let me know.

143 (A) giving in
   (B) gearing up
   (C) putting in
   (D) holding up

144 (A) in
   (B) by
   (C) with
   (D) to

145 (A) logistics
   (B) financial
   (C) administrative
   (D) human resources

★ 146 (A) I am locked out of my room again.
   (B) The technician went late this afternoon.
   (C) My door is good to use now. You are my hero!
   (D) Can I ask for the extension number of the department?

▶ PART 7

Directions: In this part, you will read a selection of texts, such as magazine and newspaper articles, letters, and advertisements. Each text is followed by several questions. Select the best answer for each question and mark the letter (A), (B), (C), or (D) on your answer sheet.

Questions 147-148 refer to the following notice.

Notice

We're appealing for the public help locating a missing women Cecily
McCarthy. Ms. McCarthy comes from little Timber, Bristol. She was last
seen in Bath on July 20th.

Cecily is described as white, approximately five feet 2 inches tall and
a slim build. She has dark brown hair and is about 48 years old in
appearance. Please contact Mary

Wilson on 131-6274-2618. You will get a £800 reward.

---

147 What is the purpose of the notice?
(A) To call for public donation
(B) To search for a missing woman
(C) To notify an area of danger
(D) To describe a public figure

148 Which of the following feature is not specified in the notice?
(A) The woman's figure
(B) The woman's color of hair
(C) The woman's color of skin
(D) The woman's date of birth

March 3

09:32

George

Hello, Amanda, I have reserved the stay in your place from March 16 to March 18. My friend, Wen and I will arrive at Vienna airport at 8:10 PM on March 16. We were wondering if you are available to check us in around that time. We think it is going to take us a while to get to the city center from the airport. Could you please let us know the easiest way to get to your place? Train or coach? Or is there an express link from the airport? Looking forward to your reply. Have a nice day!

Amanda

The easiest way to get to my place is to catch the OBB train to Vienna main station. From there you switch to a train going to Wiener Meidling and from there take the U6 line to Alserstraße and finally tram 43 to Elterleinplatz. It is only three minute walk up to St. Kalvarine. If you got any questions, just call me.

149 What is the conversation about?
(A) An upcoming trip
(B) The history of a city
(C) Pros and cons of the city's transportation service
(D) The development of a city's metro system

150 How long will George stay in Vienna?
(A) one day
(B) two days
(C) three days
(D) twelve hours

151 According to the information, which of the following is CORRECT?
(A) George will go to Vienna alone.
(B) Amanda is going to host George for a week.
(C) George will arrive in Vienna in the early morning.
(D) George is suggested to transfer more than two times.

Questions 152-156 refer to the following message.

Hello All,

On Saturday, November 25, we are planning on hosting a Thanksgiving feast at Da'Tony's! Tony will provide us with a turkey and pumpkin pie, and those of us that attend will cook side dishes to bring potluck style.

The celebration will begin at 2pm at Tony's, and dinner will be served at 3pm. We would like for everyone to bring a dish to share. We will need the following: Stuffing, Candied Yams, Green Bean Casserole, Apple pie, one or two soups, corn bread, roasted vegetables, dinner rolls, miscellaneous desserts, cranberry sauce, or any traditional dishes that you cook for your own family's Thanksgiving celebration. When you know what you want to make please send a direct message to Brian Lehrwyn, and I will make sure to let the whole group know what is still needed so that we don't double up on anything!

Also, please feel free to add others to this group, including Chinese staff so we can share this wonderful bit of our culture. Please let me know by November 14 so I can give the specific number to Tony. Please copy and repost this message when you invite someone new. If you respond after November 14, sorry, but you won't be able to join as the cost of the event and amount of food prepared depends on the number of people. Once I have a definite number I will let Tony know, and he will make sure to have a bird large enough for all of us. Additionally, Tony is willing to offer a deal in which you can order 3 drinks (beer, wine, or a simple mixed drink) for 100 RMB. Gobble! Gobble! Everyone!

Courtney

152 Why is this message sent?
(A) To advertise a sport event
(B) To announce the duty arrangement
(C) To call for volunteers for an activity
(D) To invite people to a festive event

153 What are participants asked to bring to the event?
(A) a pumpkin pie
(B) a half turkey
(C) Chinese tea
(D) a small side dish

154 What is Brian most likely in charge of?
(A) putting up the decorations
(B) building the list of food
(C) publicizing the celebration event
(D) contacting the Chinese staff

155 What should one do if he/she invites someone new?
(A) post this message again in the group
(B) pay 100 RMB to Tony
(C) report to Brian in advance
(D) bring an extra dish

156 Which of the following is NOT true?
(A) The event will begin in the afternoon.
(B) The event is restricted to Chinese staff.
(C) Tony will offer some free drinks for people.
(D) The event is held on November 25.

Questions 157-161 refer to the following notice.

Association of Social Workers in Scotland

Meeting Notice

Meeting: Children Social Care Department Meeting

Time: Tuesday, 21 November 2017, 16:00

Venue: Conference Room 201

Participants: Director Irene, Maya, Noah, Sharon, Ryan, Eve, Faye, David

Minute taker: Eve Sawyer

Agenda:

Agenda	Speaker
• Evening sport sessions stay in Building A • Fire Drills on Friday, November 24, 2017 • Thanksgiving Dinner on Friday, November 24, 2017 • Report of Interviews with families of school non-attenders on Monday, November 27,2017	Director Irene
• What will be in the Package of Support of 2019 version? • Social workers' participation in training, supervision and team meetings • Weekend safeguarding duties	Maya
• The protocol of office staff late for post	Sharon

157 What day is the meeting scheduled on?
(A) Monday
(B) Tuesday
(C) Friday
(D) Saturday

158 Who will record the proceedings of the meeting?
(A) Irene
(B) Maya
(C) Sharon
(D) Eve

159 How many people will speak at the meeting?
(A) 1
(B) 3
(C) 8
(D) 9

160 According to the agenda, what will take place the next week of the meeting?
(A) fire drill
(B) report of previous interviews
(C) Thanksgiving dinner
(D) social workers' training

161 What most likely is Sharon responsible for?
(A) attendance management
(B) employee professional training
(C) office procurement
(D) course organization

Employees' Health Service

Update your details

It is important to keep your contact details up to date. Hospitals will typically send appointments by post. If you miss your appointment due to a wrong address, then you will need to be referred again and this can often lead to long delays. —[1]—

If the health service needs to contact you, they will do this by phone or mail, so please update your information and let us know if you have changed your phone number or address. You can either update your details online or by using a change-of-contact-details form that is available from reception at the Employees' Health Service at General Hospital. —[2]—

If you are not yet registered with the online service, you will need to visit the reception in person and register for online access, with which you can do the followings. —[3]—

• Book appointments or cancel booked appointments
• Order repeat prescriptions
• Update your address details

Please kindly note that we process over 150 new registrations as new employees arrive at Dong-Tai in the middle of September. —[4]— Therefore, if you are a newly registered employee in the third quarter of the year, you may not be able to get online access until after Christmas. We appreciate your understanding.

162 What is the main idea of the first half of the notice?

(A) update of personal details

(B) procedures of resignation

(C) how to make medical appointments

(D) how to refill prescriptions

163 How can online registration be done?

(A) By visiting the Employee Health Service

(B) By mailing to Dong-Tai

(C) By calling the clinician

(D) By phoning the receptionist

164 What can be inferred from the information?

(A) Online registration is often busy in spring.

(B) Dong-Tai provides employee health services in cooperation with General Hospital.

(C) Those who are already registered online must still go to the reception to change details.

(D) Over a hundred and fifty new staff are recruited every month.

★ 165 In which of the positions marked [1], [2], [3] and [4] does the following sentence best belong? "We employ extra staff to help us with this, but it often takes a long time to fully register everyone."

(A) [1]

(B) [2]

(C) [3]

(D) [4]

Green Spirit Brand

Thank you for using this Green Spirit Brand product which is designed and manufactured to the highest quality standards. Please read these instructions carefully and retain for future reference in order to gain **optimal** use from your product.

USE

• Please note that this product contains a glass liner and should be treated with care at all times.

• Prior to initial use of the product, please clean your flask with warm water and glass protection washing-up liquid.

• DO NOT put the flask into a microwave or conventional oven. —[1]—

• Always leave sufficient space in the neck and do not overfill.

• After filling, ensure both the outside cup and stopper are always tightly closed. —[2]—

CLEANING

• If your flask has not been used for some time, rinse it with warm water and dish washing liquid in the interest of hygiene.

• After cleaning, leave it to drain and with the stopper off. —[3]—

• DO NOT use a dishwasher to clean your flask.

• DO NOT use abrasive sponge pads to remove difficult stains. —[4]—

• Avoid storing any carbonated drink or milk as it may cause breakage to the glass liner.

• Always clean it after use to avoid the possibility of bacteria growth.

166 What is the Green Spirit Brand product?
(A) a dishwashing soap
(B) a cupboard
(C) a vacuum flask
(D) a washing machine

167 What is advised after the product has been cleaned?
(A) It should be filled with hot water.
(B) It should be stored on a dish dryer rack.
(C) It should be left without the stopper.
(D) It should be soaked with soap.

168 Which of the following is CORRECT?
(A) This product is microwave-safe.
(B) This product is not good for fizzy drink.
(C) This product should be rinsed with cold water before use.
(D) This product would be damaged by dishwashing liquid.

★ **169** In which of the positions marked [1], [2], [3] and [4] does the following sentence best belong? "Adding a teaspoon of bicarbonate of soda produces excellent results."
(A) [1]
(B) [2]
(C) [3]
(D) [4]

170 The word "optimal" in paragraph 1, line 4, is closest in meaning to
(A) best
(B) optimistic
(C) exterior
(D) complete

Office Closure during Christmas

From- Paul Newman

To: all

13 December 2016

Dear Residents of Burberry Apartment,

Please note that the Burberry Apartment office will be closed from 22 December to 1 January due to Christmas and New Year's holidays. We will reopen on 3 January, 2017.

Emergency contact

If there is an emergency, you can still contact a duty warden during this period. The phone numbers of the duty wardens will be posted on the office door.

Cleaning and recycling collections

As all cleaners will not be onsite during the vacation, the regular weekly cleaning will not take place until 2 January. Therefore, you must keep clean and tidy your own kitchens and hallways.

Security

As you are celebrating the holidays, please also be vigilant by making sure all your flat doors and windows are kept locked at all times. Call 999 if there is an emergency.

Post collections

The office will be open for an hour between 12 and 1pm for post collection on the following days:

- 24 December 2016
- 27 December 2016
- 29 December 2016
- 30 December 2016
- 31 December 2016

Finally, we sincerely wish you a happy Christmas and new year.

Paul Newman

171 Who was the email sent to?
   (A) the officers of the apartment building
   (B) the tenants of the apartment building
   (C) the contractor of the apartment building
   (D) the cleaning staff of the apartment building

172 Who most likely is Paul Newman?
   (A) the executive officer of the apartment
   (B) the cleaner of the apartment
   (C) the tenant of the apartment
   (D) the designer of the apartment

173 When will the office open again?
   (A) 29 December
   (B) 30 December
   (C) 1 January
   (D) 3 January

174 Which of the following services is still available during the vacation?
   (A) repairs
   (B) post collections
   (C) security
   (D) cleaning

175 Which of the following is WRONG?
   (A) There won't be anyone on duty during the vacation.
   (B) Cleaning staff usually come on a weekly basis.
   (C) Residents are advised to stay alert during Christmas.
   (D) Residents can receive packages on December 31.

Hop-On-Go Takes Taxi-riding Experience to the Next Level

Hop-On-Go is the first brand in the country to transform the conventional taxi hailing. With the latest transportation technology, you can get to where you want to go anywhere, anytime and with just a click.

Passengers just need to download the Hop-On-Go mobile app and get registered with their phone number and bank account. Whenever you need a ride, send a request, select the driver and the driver will come pick you up in no time. As soon as you get to the destination, the bill will be sent to your phone and can be automatically paid off from the bank. More importantly, it saves your money as the fare is nearly half as expensive as the regular taxi fare. So far, we have already had 1.5 million Hop-On-Go riders with us!

Your Friday morning trip with Hop-On-Go
RECEIPT

Thank you for choosing Hop-On-Go.
$ 9/ paid via device/ September 15 2017/ Hop-On-Go Express

Please note that the fare does not include the fees that may be charged
by your bank.
• Pick-up @ 20 Albert Street/ 07:32
• Drop-off @ 57 Tank Road/ 07: 45

You rode with Stephen Wong.
Distance: 5.52 miles
Trip time: 13 minutes

Hop-On-Go
Get a $10 coupon for Hop-On-Go Express if you invite a new friend to try
Hop-On-Go.
Share Code: RD77O

Contact us.
Left personal belongings behind? Track it down by emailing at
lostproperties@hopongo.com

From: Sherry

To: lostproperties@hopongo.com

Subject: Lost laptop bag

Hello,

Last Friday morning, I rode your taxi with Stephen Wong. As soon as I got out of the car, I noticed my laptop bag was not with me. I must have left it in the car. But I did not have the driver's number which should normally show in the app. So I am writing to request that you help track down the driver and have him contact me as soon as possible. It is a 13-inch black laptop bag in which there are my wallet, glasses and some medications. The bag is my birthday gift from my husband and therefore means a lot to me, so I would appreciate if you could find it for me. Thank you very much.

Sherry

176 What is Hop-On-Go?
  (A) a taxi hailing platform
  (B) a newly launched car brand
  (C) a mobile company
  (D) a telecom company

177 According to the advertisement, which of the following is true?
  (A) Passengers must carry with them their laptops when getting a ride.
  (B) Passengers do not need to carry cash with them when getting a ride.
  (C) The Hop-On-Go services are usually more expensive than regular taxis.
  (D) There are around 150,000 members on Hop-On-Go.

178 What can be inferred from the receipt?
(A) The fare had not yet been paid.
(B) The fare including the bank charge may be more than $9.
(C) The passenger's last name is Wong.
(D) The passenger had used the coupon.

179 According to the email, what information should have appeared in the app?
(A) The driver's birthday
(B) The driver's bank account
(C) The driver's license number
(D) The driver's phone number

180 What is indicated about Sherry's bag?
(A) It is purple.
(B) It is 15 inches of size.
(C) It is a birthday gift.
(D) It has been found.

La Siene Apartment

La Siene Apartment is located opposite the contemporary art museum and within only a five-minute walk from National Botanic Garden. The self-catering studio apartment also features an on-site restaurant, a lounge and a standard swimming pool. Other amenities are such as a rooftop terrace, a gaming area and a common room with table tennis and table football facilities. Free Wi-Fi is provided in all public areas. There are computers at every corner of each floor for your use.

Each studio has a flat-screen TV and a multi-function work desk specially designed for business people. The luxury bathroom is equipped with a whirlpool bathtub. Hairdryers and irons are available upon request and La Siene also has a guest laundry room for you. Kitchenettes are fully equipped with an induction hotplate, an oven, a microwave and a fridge. A 24-hour supermarket is just at the Harbor Street which is 30 seconds away from the apartment by walking.

We speak your languages.

La Siene Apartment
Room Tariff

Room Class	Regular Rate	Promotion Rate
Tourist Class	€ 150 per day	€ 110 per day
Ambassador Class	€ 180 per day	€ 150 per day
Corporate Class	€ 220 per day	€ 180 per day
Annex Room	€ 50 per person	

Anna
March 2017

We spent our time in La Siene tourist-class studio for three nights in early March. The room was gorgeous, clean and warm as described on the website. I like the tastefully furnished interior and the wonderfully bright room which gets ample sunlight. The receptionists are open, easygoing and friendly. They passionately told us where we could go sightseeing and experience the amazing local street food. However, as we booked the room for the weekend time where there was no promotion deal, the room rate was a little high for us, but overall we enjoyed our time there and I will definitely come back next time. Couldn't have thought of a better place to stay in Paris. This is absolutely my best highlight on Resort.com so far.

181 In which city is La Siene Apartment?
(A) London
(B) Dublin
(C) Prague
(D) Paris

182 What is indicated about the apartment?
(A) It is close to a museum.
(B) Wi-Fi data are €10 per day.
(C) It takes 30 minutes to walk to the nearest superstore.
(D) The bathrooms are equipped with hairdryers.

183 Which of the following is not included in the studio amenities?
(A) whirlpool bathtub
(B) work desk
(C) fridge
(D) tennis court

184 What was Anna slightly dissatisfied with?
(A) the receptionists
(B) the room rate
(C) the furnishings
(D) the sport facilities

185 How much did Anna spend on her room in total?
(A) € 330
(B) € 450
(C) € 150
(D) € 540

★**Questions 186-190 refer to the following letter, information and email.**

Letter of Intent

Survey of Administrative Specialists

To:

From:Lydia Liao

Date:December 7th, 2017

In an effort to determine our staff for the 2017-2018 year, Da-Deng Ltd. would like to know if you intend to sign a new contract for the next year. Please be reminded that if you check the box 'I do not intend to return to Da-Deng Ltd. next year.' Your position will be advertised and a new candidate will be replacing your post.

[ ] I intend to return to Da-Deng Ltd. next year.

[ ] I do not intend to return to Da-Deng Ltd. next year.

Your signature:_____   Date: _____

Please return this survey to Lydia by 12:00 on Friday 5 January 2018. If we do not receive your response by this date, your position may be advertised. Confirmation of contract renewal will be issued in the beginning of March. Thank you.

Administrative Specialist

Job Description

Your responsibility is to assist office duties in a variety of areas including scheduling office meetings, managing incoming and outgoing mail, responding to, redirecting incoming calls, completing special projects, applying for project resources and managing all sorts of reimbursements.

Job Type

Full-time

Job Number

8506

Department

Information Technology

Salary

$ 400,000 Annually

Subject: Queries about contract renewal

From: Jessie

To: Lydia

Dear Lydia,

Please accept this letter as notification of my plan to commence maternity leave in two months' time. As my baby is due in May 2018, my doctor advised me to cease working three months ahead of time. I have enclosed my medical certificate that confirms my pregnancy.

Because of my pregnancy, I was wondering if I need to sign the contract renewal letter you sent to us. Since I understand I am entitled to 52 weeks of maternity leave which is specified in the employment handbook, I am confused about if there is necessity for me to sign the letter of intent for the next year's employment.

Looking forward to hearing from you.

Jessie

186 Who most likely was this letter sent to?
(A) current staff
(B) expectant mothers
(C) job candidates
(D) board of directors

187 Who most likely is Lydia?
(A) an accountant
(B) a human resources officer
(C) an engineer
(D) a salesperson

188 What is not likely to be a specialist's duty?
(A) reminding the director of the weekly meeting
(B) putting through a customer to the director
(C) going on a business trip with the president
(D) contacting the financial department for reimbursement

189 When most likely did Jessie send the email?
(A) In December
(B) In January
(C) In February
(D) In March

190 What was Jessie's major inquiry?
(A) whether to take a leave
(B) whether to stay in the company
(C) whether to go to the doctor
(D) whether to sign the letter of intent

★**Questions 191-195 refer to the following reminder, information and calendar.**

Dear Sales Department Employees,

Thank you so much for sparing some time to go through this weekly reminder. First of all, it is Friday again! I would like to wish you all a happy, safe weekend. Besides, as Chinese New Year is fast approaching, celebrations are being held in various parts of the city, including Timmy's café just beside our office building. Check this website for more details: http://www.juniormerry/chinesenewyear.

I would also like to take this opportunity to thank you for your individual and collective contributions to our sale effort as of last year. Your sales record is impressive and has even exceeded our goal. Keep up the good work. In the meantime, there are a few things I would like to remind you.

- You are required to respond to customers' messages before 21:00. Even if you are not able to sort out their issues immediately, please at least leave a message saying with courtesy that you will attend to them the next day.

- With regard to mileage reimbursement, you must be able to substantiate the mileage with the original documentation or receipts. According to the policy of the Internal Revenue Service, please be aware that only the mileage costs incurred while conducting business can qualify for reimbursement.

- All sales staff have a Chinese New Year vacation which this year will start on the 10th of February all the way to 21st of February. Everyone should return to work on the 22nd of February. However, due to the fact that this year we have a longer holiday than usual, we all need to work for extra hours to make up for the holiday. Please refer to the attachment detailing the specific work time.

Finally, it is getting cold. Please bundle up and take care! Let's keep fighting till the end of this year.

Danielle Wu

Timmy's Café

Friday Night Live- 9 Feb

Free live music from local and student bands, cheap beer and tasty traditional Chinese food. Pretty much the perfect Friday night. See you there.
Venue: Timmy's Café
Start Time: 19:00

Karaoke

It's karaoke night - The Timmy's wildest night, guaranteed. Belt out a classic, or force a mate to do it for you.
Venue: Timmy's Café
Start Time: 20:00

The Big Fat Pub Quiz at Timmy's

We expect hilarious fun facts about Chinese New Year. Beat your colleagues to be the best team in town. By far the best thing to do in Timmy's. Free fizzy drinks and pizza are provided.
Venue: Timmy's Café
Start Time: 18:00

Sun	Mon	Tue	Wed	Thu	Fri	Sat
				1	2	3
4	5	6	7	8	9	10 Vacation Starts
11	12	13	14	15 Chinese New Year	16 Chinese New Year	17 Chinese New Year
18 Chinese New Year	19 Chinese New Year	20 Chinese New Year	21 Last Day of Vacation	22 Working Day All Day	23 Working Day All Day	24 Working Day All Day
25 Working Day Half Day	26	27	28			

191 What information does the first paragraph of the reminder give?
(A) the date of Chinese New Year's Eve
(B) some festive celebration events
(C) a newly open restaurant
(D) the latest office regulations

192 What is indicated about mileage reimbursement application?
(A) The original proof should be presented.
(B) There is an amount limit.
(C) Mileage costs incurred during Chinese New Year do not qualify.
(D) The policy has been changed recently.

193 According to Timmy's Café, which event provides free food?
(A) Friday Night Live
(B) Karaoke
(C) The Big Fat Pub Quiz
(D) All of the above

194 Why should the employees have to work for extra hours?
(A) To reach the annual goal of the department
(B) To make up for the holiday
(C) To prepare for the next year
(D) To pay off the penalty

195 On which day should the employees work for a half day?
(A) 10 February
(B) 22 February
(C) 24 February
(D) 25 February

★**Questions 196-200 refer to the following CV, invitation and certificate.**

Romina Champion

Phone: 44-9408-2260/ Email: romina_2003@mail2008.com/
Address: 10 Chong Jiang Road, HGTF, Singapore

Academic Background

MSc. Computer Science Information Engineering, School of Technology, University of Ming-Hua
BA. English culture and literature, College of Arts, University of National Education

Professional Background

2012-2014 Information Technology Engineer, Deli Communication, Singapore
2014-2016 Field Engineer, New Vision Technology, Singapore

Internship

2011-2012 Intern, Deli Communication, Singapore

Languages

English, Mandarin, Japanese, Thai

Thank you for your consideration.

Dear Ms. Romina Champion,

Congratulations to you on being selected by our human resource officers as one of the candidates for the position of Field Engineer at Sun Power Ltd. We would like to invite you to attend an interview on 29 December, 2016, at 2 PM, at our office in Clark.

You will have an interview with our department manager, Frank Oliver. The interview will last about 30 minutes. Please bring one employment reference and your resume to the interview.

If you cannot make it to the interview, please contact the office by phone (555-8148). We can rearrange the appointment with you.

We look forward to seeing you.

Best regards,

Faye Edy

Certificate of Employment

39 Vanilla Road, MTXC, Singapore
6 December 2016

To whom it may concern,

This letter is to certify that **Ms. Romina Champion** has been employed by New Vision Technology from 1 November 2014 to 30 November 2016 in the position of field engineer. During the period, her duty were :

- Dealing with 2nd Line support
- Face-to-Face Support
- Networking Maintenance

This letter also recognizes her outstanding performance and massive contribution to our Company over the past two years and one month.

Respectfully Yours,
New Vision Technology

Bella Fang
Human Resource Management Officer

---

196 Which of the following is NOT included in the CV?
(A) address
(B) phone number
(C) date of birth
(D) educational background

197 What job is Romina seeking?
(A) human resource officer
(B) director of management
(C) field engineer
(D) account analyst

198 According to the information above, which of the following is True of Romina?

(A) She can speak five languages.

(B) She has over ten years of work experience.

(C) She studied English literature in college.

(D) She has worked for three different companies so far.

199 Who is Frank Oliver?

(A) a manager at New Vision Technology

(B) a manager at Sun Power Ltd.

(C) a field engineer at Deli Communication

(D) a human resource officer at New Vision

200 When was the employment certificate issued?

(A) On 6 December 2016

(B) On 1 November 2014

(C) On 30 November 2016

(D) On 29 December 2016

New TOEIC Reading Test 4
新多益閱讀全真模擬試題第4回

▶ **READING TEST**

In the Reading Test, you will read a variety of texts and answer several different types of reading comprehension questions. The entire Reading Test will last 75 minutes. There are three parts, and directions are given for each part. You are encouraged to answer as many questions as possible within the time allowed.

You must mark your answers on the separate answer sheet. Do not write your answers in the test book.

▶ **PART 5**

Directions: A word or phrase is missing in each of the sentences below. Four answer choices are given below each sentence. Select the best answer to complete the sentence. Then mark the letter (A), (B), (C), or (D) on your answer sheet.

101 If you are between the ages of 16 and 21, you are _____ to the support we offer.
(A) prone
(B) inclined
(C) entitled
(D) susceptible

102 Emma is the person _____ opinion I respect.
(A) that
(B) which
(C) who
(D) whose

103 He is ill and _____ needs to take a sick leave today.
(A) therefore
(B) however
(C) hereby
(D) moreover

104 As managers, it is _____ on us to be accepting to different opinions.
(A) derogatory
(B) incumbent
(C) superfluous
(D) facetious

105 All of you should make punctuality your priority, _____ for those of you working as salespersons.
(A) hardly
(B) deliberately
(C) especially
(D) scarcely

106 _____ in 2002, the band rapidly rose to fame with their debut album.
(A) Forms
(B) Forming
(C) Formed
(D) Formation

107 Hangzhou is the _____ point of trade and commerce in Zhejiang province.
(A) suburban
(B) modern
(C) rebellious
(D) focal

108 Over the past decade, they have turned _____ into a globally well-known team.
(A) theirs
(B) they
(C) their
(D) themselves

109 The evaluation process _____ of three main stages.
(A) consists
(B) revolves
(C) composes
(D) resists

110 The presentation demonstrated the major _____ of the project.
(A) achievement
(B) distance
(C) revenge
(D) personality

111 The report made a few _____ references to the sensitive issue.

(A) sublime
(B) inductive
(C) oblique
(D) authentic

112 Every teacher should _____ their recess duties and report back to supervisors.

(A) succeed
(B) fulfill
(C) pursue
(D) behold

113 The director asked the attendants to share their reflections _____ this issue.

(A) in
(B) with
(C) over
(D) on

114 During the week to come, participants _____ a development plan in collaboration with one another.

(A) complete
(B) completed
(C) will complete
(D) have completed

115 Read through the instructions and get the gist of _____ to create your own website.

(A) what
(B) how
(C) whether
(D) whom

116 We hope you find our workshop _____ .

(A) help
(B) helping
(C) helpful
(D) to help

117 The analysis approach will be described _____ more details in the following section.

(A) in
(B) upon
(C) with
(D) by

118 _____ I want to achieve by this proposal is to sketch an outline for the seasonal project.

(A) Which
(B) What
(C) How
(D) That

119 Initially, we did not plan _____ so many evaluators.
(A) recruitment
(B) recruiting
(C) to recruit
(D) for recruiting

120 We are in a predicament _____ a single mistake can lead to an enormous chain reaction.
(A) that
(B) where
(C) which
(D) when

121 We based our reasoning on the assumption _____ everyone has at least one year of professional experience.
(A) that
(B) which
(C) whose
(D) why

122 This session _____ you to voice your concern about your working conditions.
(A) provides
(B) forewarns
(C) admits
(D) allows

123 _____ the handbook, every teacher at the university has the right to take a sabbatical leave after working for seven years.
(A) In addition to
(B) According to
(C) Applicable to
(D) In light of

124 We are proud to be able to _____ aesthetic design with innovative technology in our home appliances.
(A) reply
(B) involve
(C) compare
(D) combine

125 Hotel Amanda is easily _____ by metros, buses or taxis.
(A) available
(B) acceptable
(C) accessible
(D) amendable

126 The seaside shopping malls are _____ in winter.
(A) deserted
(B) instructed
(C) rescheduled
(D) conserved

127 Justin just started a project you may be interested _____ .
(A) of
(B) with
(C) about
(D) in

128 _____ migration is an important global phenomenon that needs to be tackled seriously.
(A) Forcing
(B) Forced
(C) Force
(D) Forces

129 _____ of you who participated in the event can apply for reimbursement by the end of this month.
(A) Those
(B) These
(C) Whom
(D) Ones

130 Make sure the size and color of the signboard are in _____ with the state laws.
(A) agree
(B) agreed
(C) agreeing
(D) agreement

▶ **PART 6**

Directions: Read the texts on the following pages. A word or phrase is missing in some of the sentences. Answer choices are given below each of these articles. Select the best answer to complete the text. Then mark the letter (A), (B), (C) or (D) on your answer sheet.

Questions 131-134 refer to the following letter.

Dear all,

We are delighted to invite you to attend the STC year-end party ___131___ will take place on 27 December 2017 at 4 pm. Please access the year-end party website at www.stc.com/yearendparty. This will provide all ___132___ information regarding the party including timetable, ticket information, costume hire and photography and much more. It is vital that you read this information carefully. If your query is not covered on the website, please contact the HR department at 9876-0534.

The deadline to register for the year-end party is 11 December 2017 and registration only ___133___ a few minutes. You should complete your form even if you do not wish to attend the party by selecting the "in absentia" option. If you are still not sure about whether you will be able to come, you must still register. ___134___ if you register after the deadline.

With best wishes,

HR office

131 (A) what
(B) which
(C) who
(D) it

132 (A) state-of-the-art
(B) down-to-earth
(C) up-to-date
(D) last-minute

133 (A) spends
(B) takes
(C) costs
(D) pays

★ 134 (A) We would be unable to guarantee you a place at the party
(B) We are pleased to have you with us
(C) You can even choose to invite your family
(D) You will be offered an extra ticket

Questions 135-138 refer to the following letter.

Dear Mr. Peters

I am writing to express my dissatisfaction with my stay at Belarus Studio, Minsk Belarus, on July 10th- 13th, which I booked on iHotel.com for my company colleagues.

My central complaint is that the hotel amenities provided fell ___135___ short of the description on the website. I booked five studio-type rooms in room 0401 to 0405. The actual rooms were hardly like the pictures shown on the website. As soon as we entered the rooms, we were extremely terrified by the scattered wall mold. The bathtubs have gathered limescale and looked terribly rusty. The overall furnishings, ___136___ on the website as "modern and charming", were in fact old and worn.

We tried to speak to your ___137___ who promised to arrange a room change for us but it took one day to happen. We were asked to fill out a complaint form detailing the issues we encountered and I enclose a copy for your information.

We feel that ___138___ as it completely ruined our vacation and we consider the description on the website false advertising. We look forward to hearing from you within the next three days.

Sincerely yours,

Cindy Johnson

135 (A) very
(B) far
(C) many
(D) too

136 (A) describing
(B) described
(C) descriptive
(D) description

137 (A) clerk
(B) broker
(C) spokesperson
(D) representative

★ 138 (A) we deserve a free upgrade to the presidential suite
(B) you should handle this issue with more discretion next time
(C) we are due a full refund for the hotel stay
(D) it is worth the stay considering the low room rate

Questions 139-142 refer to the following advertisement.

English Villagers

Current Job Opening

Software quality assurance engineer

Our team is fully committed to ___139___ software quality, and takes user experience seriously. We are currently seeking a highly skilled software engineer who is willing to join us in taking our quality to the next level and building the next generation online English learning tools.

REQUIREMENTS

- You must possess the latest technology and programming techniques to bring out the full ___140___ of the interactive website.
- You must have a minimum of 1 year of experience in C/C++ or debugging skills.
- You must be strong in system level programming including Python/ Ruby scripting.
- You must have good system level understanding of Linux.

Detail-oriented perfectionists are welcome. ___141___ , we will support your further professional training to hone your expertise. Most importantly, you must have passion for ___142___ .

139 (A) insuring
　　(B) ensuring
　　(C) assuring
　　(D) reassuring

140 (A) capacity
　　(B) requirement
　　(C) standard
　　(D) protocol

★ 141 (A) If you prefer flexible working hours
　　(B) If you consider yourself communicative
　　(C) For those who have an unquenchable thirst for knowledge
　　(D) For those who love dealing with customer affairs

★ 142 (A) how you do
　　(B) how do you do
　　(C) what you do
　　(D) what do you do

Questions 143-146 refer to the following newsletter.

Welcome to Leicester Bank Newsletter. We aim to give you an insight in the latest trends in finance and trade ___143___ covering various subjects relevant for your business.

If you are a regular reader of Leicester Bank Newsletter, you probably know at least something about the current market instability in Europe. ___144___, you may still occasionally come across some pervasive myths about the status of the European market. For instance, some, such as the belief that how the governments will manage the new political landscape would bring about uncertainty, actually require more context to ___145___ true. Others, such as the idea that the drastic slide in global stock markets in the first weeks of this year means that the major market will be covered in the unremitting gloom, are just wrong.

Also, this week our technology sector has a go at digitization in business. ___146___.

Finally, our "hear from you" section presents the opinions and questions you had for us in the previous two months. Thank you for your feedback. Every reader is an inextricable element of us.

Have a great weekend.

Newsletter Team

143 (A) in
(B) by
(C) with
(D) along

144 (A) For example
(B) Therefore
(C) However
(D) Consequently

145 (A) hold
(B) make
(C) tell
(D) determine

★ **146** (A) Why bank rankings really matter for investment is well explained
(B) It demonstrates the steps to get a personal loan
(C) Tips to improve your credit rating are provided
(D) Those who are tech-savvy must not miss out.

▶ **PPART 7**

Directions: In this part, you will read a selection of texts, such as magazine and newspaper articles, letters, and advertisements. Each text is followed by several questions. Select the best answer for each question and mark the letter (A), (B), (C), or (D) on your answer sheet.

Questions 147-148 refer to the following warning sign.

ACTION IN CASE OF EMERGENCY

Do not use the lift in event of a fire alarm

If you become trapped in this lift, you should take the following action:

• Press the alarm button on the switch panel (bell symbol) and wait for a reply.
• If there is no reply, press the alarm button again.
• When your call is answered, speak into the grill on the switch panel and say that you are trapped in lift HDS 41 in the Heather Road branch Goldenmill road.

147 What is the main purpose of the sign?
(A) To demonstrate the maintenance standards of the lift
(B) To advertise the lift brand
(C) To illustrate the lift installment procedure
(D) To showcase the safety guidelines of the lift

148 What should be indicated to the security personnel in case of emergency?
(A) the location of the lift
(B) the time of the emergency
(C) the names of the people trapped
(D) the floor at which the lift is

Questions 149-151 refer to the following email.

To: Luke Glover
From: Industrial Bank Survey
May 14, 2017

We welcome your feedback

Dear Luke Glover,

Thank you for visiting Industrial Bank Hoping Road.

We're committed to making our customer experience the best it can be. In order to strengthen the already good customer relationship, we would appreciate your feedback on your recent experience with us by responding to the survey which takes only 3 minutes to complete. We always take your opinions seriously to better understand how to improve the service we provide. Please be assured that we will never use your feedback to sell or market anything to you.

Please begin by answering the question below.

Based on your recent in-branch experience, how likely are you to recommend Industrial Bank Hoping Road to a friend?

Please give your answer on a scale where '1' means 'not at all likely' and '5' means 'extremely likely'.

1 not at all likely	2	3	4	5 extremely likely

149 What is Luke Glover asked to do in the email?
(A) To open a bank account
(B) To contact the branch manager
(C) To check in with the online banking account
(D) To complete a customer survey

150 When did Luke Glover most likely visit the bank recently?
(A) January 30
(B) May 13
(C) July 1
(D) December 22

151 What does answer 4 mean on the scale given?
(A) Mr. Glover is not happy with the service.
(B) Mr. Glover would never visit the branch again.
(C) Mr. Glover is willing to get a loan from the bank.
(D) Mr. Glover is happy to recommend the bank to his friends.

Questions 152-156 refer to the following announcement.

David Morrison, a security officer in the Atlantic International School, will be retiring effective 19 November 2017. David has been an excellent employee. He was a keen and dedicated security officer who appreciated the student population and was always on hand to assist and advise with their problems. His calming, friendly presence resolved many difficult situations.

David joined the school security services team in 2002 after a period of working in the private security sector. As a door supervisor at the school, he quickly adapted to school life and was swiftly appointed as the campus society workforce representative. His energy and drive, combined with excellent knowledge of his role, soon made him a much-respected person both within his own department and in the wider school community, where he received many requests for advice and assistance.

David's retirement is our loss but a well-deserved **respite** for him. A retirement party will be held in his honor at Marina Restaurant on the evening of 19 November 2017, at 6:00 pm. All are invited to share in this celebration. We all extend our best wishes to David and express our appreciation to his dedication. In the meantime, we wish David a wonderful retirement.

152 Who is David Morrison?
(A) a university teacher
(B) a mechanical engineer
(C) a school officer
(D) a children's nurse

153 What was David's first position at the school?
(A) security supervisor
(B) recruitment director
(C) campus society workforce representative
(D) door supervisor

154 How long has David worked in the school?
(A) 10 years
(B) 15 years
(C) 19 years
(D) 20 years

155 What is the main idea of the last paragraph?
(A) an invitation to the retirement party
(B) a job description of the position
(C) an overview of David's career
(D) David's contribution to the school

156 The word "respite" in paragraph 3, line 1, is closest in meaning to
(A) respect
(B) employment
(C) entertainment
(D) rest

Questions 157-161 refer to the following letter.

Queen Square Accommodation Offer

Dear Monica Tsai,

Origin Amaze Co. is delighted to offer, on behalf of Florabridge Housing, the following accommodation at Rainbow Court. —[1]—

Room Type: double-bed studio
Rent: $160 per week

All rooms are offered and accepted on the basis of single occupation as of the start date of the tenancy on September 3, 2017. If you wish to accept this offer, you must pay the reservation fee by July 3, 2017, otherwise this offer will be withdrawn. —[2]— Your room is not reserved until you have made your payment.

—[3]— Once you accept this offer of the room, the rent payment will be due as on the 5th of each month as set out in the tenancy contract. If you wish to move in later than September 3, 2017 or leave earlier than September 2, 2018, you will still have to pay the rent on a monthly basis unless you find a replacement tenant.

—[4]— Once you accept this offer, an email confirming your reservation will be sent to you and you will be required to complete the online induction before moving into your room. The room key will be ready for you to collect on arrival at the accommodation.

If you need more information, please go on our accommodation website at www.originamaze.com/benefits.

Origin Amaze Co.

157 How much is the rent for the double-bed studio per month?
(A) $160
(B) $320
(C) $480
(D) $640

158 What should Monica do to accept the offer?
(A) pay the reservation fee
(B) pay the monthly rent
(C) complete the online induction
(D) register on the company website

159 What should be done if one wishes to leave before the tenancy ends?
(A) pay an extra amount of rent
(B) find a replacement
(C) complete an online application
(D) contact the landlord

160 Which of the following statements is WRONG?
(A) The property is let on a one-year tenancy.
(B) The rent payment should be made in the beginning of each month.
(C) The room key will be sent to the tenant's current address.
(D) Monica is likely an employee in Origin Amaze Co.

★ **161** In which of the positions marked [1], [2], [3] and [4] does the following sentence best belong? "The tenancy is for a fixed length"
(A) [1]
(B) [2]
(C) [3]
(D) [4]

Questions 162-166 refer to the following information.

Room Bookings Information

The information below relates to room bookings in Northwest Technology Park in Shanghai during the term of 2016-2017. The regulations may be subject to change due to the availability of particular rooms, national holidays and inclement weather.

• Regular weekly bookings

For evening sports sessions, we have given a set of usernames and passwords for weekly bookings to the session leaders. All your need to do is to log into our online system where you can amend, add notes to, or cancel your bookings. Most in-door activities will be usually held in the Richmond Rooms. All the other outdoor sports events will be held at the court east off the Richmond Rooms.

Please be aware that the Richmond Rooms will be used for the ID office bimonthly meeting every other month. Exact dates to be confirmed.

• Special events

Special events can be held at Woodland Room on the nights of Tuesday, Thursday, Friday and Saturday. When you place your bookings, you will be asked for some basic information regarding the purpose, duration and special requirements of your event. With the information, we will check the technical requirements, let you know the costs, any additional information we require and provided all is in order approve your booking.

If we think the technical requirement is of too much complexity, you may be required to meet with the Tech and Logistics Team. If we think your requirement is inappropriate, we will be in contact to discuss details and further advice.

More information about charges for technical equipment and support can be obtained from the events team.

162 Which of the following information is NOT provided?
(A) The names of the rooms
(B) The available time of the rooms
(C) The directions for booking the rooms
(D) The cancellation policies

163 Which may NOT be the cause of the regulations being altered?
(A) storms
(B) departmental meetings
(C) the complexity of the event
(D) bank holidays

164 What is indicated about Richmond Rooms?
(A) They would be used for meetings.
(B) They are for special events.
(C) Most outdoor events are held in them.
(D) Registration forms are to be filled out at the venue.

165 Why would some information be required when booking for special events?
(A) To check the identity of the event organizer
(B) To ensure the prepayment is made in time
(C) To check for the technical requirements of the rooms
(D) To update the organizers on the latest room hire policy

166 What would happen if the requirement of the event is too complicated?
(A) The event will need to be cancelled.
(B) The organizer will face a financial penalty.
(C) The organizer will have to discuss with the logistics team.
(D) Additional paperwork will need to be completed.

Questions 167-171 refer to the following information.

Happy Holidays Everyone!

It's that time of year to start spreading holiday cheer! One of the fun ways to do this is through our departmental Secret Santa gift exchange. Last year those of us who participated had a blast (just ask any of us), and this year I have a feeling we'll have even more fun (we certainly deserve it)!!! To sign up, please follow the instructions below:

• Find the special box in Office 303 and take a form beside it. On this form write your name and 3 things that you would like to receive from your Secret Santa (ex. socks, mugs, wine, chocolate, Star Wars stuff, face masks, whatever you fancy). There is no guarantee that you will get all of these things—it's just to give your special someone some ideas. —[1]—

• The budget is $60, so keep that in mind when listing your items. Fold the form and put it into the box by Wednesday, December 6th. —[2]—

• Write your name on the sign-up sheet.

• Secret Santas will be randomly chosen on Thursday, December 7th.

So what are you signing up for exactly? Let me give it to you straight: For those who choose to participate, the Secret Santa festivities will commence on Monday, December 18th. From Monday (Dec 18) to Wednesday (Dec 20), you will give your Secret Santa small gifts (candy, socks, etc.) each day, along with **quirky** clues so they can slowly try to guess who you are. —[3]— Be creative!

On Thursday, December 21st during 3rd and 4th periods, we will have our Secret Santa revealing party. This is where we will guess our sneaky co-workers and receive the 'biggest' gift from them. To remain anonymous, there will be a location where you can stealthily drop your gift off sometime during the week before Thursday's party. —[4]—

This is especially merry the more people that participate, so hopefully there's a great turn out (no pressure)!

Happy Holidays and Happy E-bay Hunting!
Danielle

167 What holiday is the event most likely for?
(A) Chinese New Year
(B) Summer Bank Holiday
(C) Easter Monday
(D) Christmas Day

168 Who will be the Secret Santas?
(A) The department officers
(B) Danielle
(C) Everyone who doesn't sign up
(D) Yet to be confirmed

169 When will the Secret Santa activity begin?
(A) On December 6
(B) On December 7
(C) On December 18
(D) On December 21

★ 170 In which of the positions marked [1], [2], [3] and [4] does the following sentence best belong? "This can be done via scavenger hunt or secret placements around school."
(A) [1]
(B) [2]
(C) [3]
(D) [4]

171 The word "quirky" in paragraph 2, line 5, is closest in meaning to
(A) peculiar
(B) rapid
(C) furious
(D) straightforward

Questions 172-175 refer to the following message.

Dear employees,

This is a reminder that the common room located on the 2nd floor of the Senate Hall is an area restricted for the income house and health center staff use only and therefore should not be being used as a break facility by Beacon House administrators.

Please be advised that Beacon House administrators have access to the ground floor foyer within the Beacon House to use as a break/ recreational area, and are welcome to use other locations within the office building including, and not restricted to, the Hawthorns and Broomhill House café. There is also a café and group meeting facilities available for all staff within the Staff Union (Tyndall Building).

Many thanks in advance.
With best wishes,

Tara Thorne

172 Why is this message sent?
(A) To make clear the rest area for certain staff
(B) To remind staff of the weekly activities
(C) To notice the construction to be carried out
(D) To advertise the newly built café

173 Which area can income house staff use?
(A) 2nd floor of Senate Hall
(B) ground floor foyer at Beacon House
(C) Hawthorns House
(D) Broomhill House café

174 Which area can be accessed by all staff?

(A) Hawthorns House

(B) Broomhill House café

(C) Tyndall Building café

(D) Beacon House common room

175 Which can be inferred from this message?

(A) Some Beacon House administrators have used the Senate House the common room.

(B) Some health center staff have used the break facility on the ground floor foyer at Beacon House.

(C) The Tyndall Building café has been refurbished recently.

(D) The Senate House common room will soon be closed for renovation.

★**Questions 176-180 refer to the following advertisement, coupon and reviews.**

Motorway Car

Motorway Car Rental offers you 25,000 cars and various types of quality vehicles. We will help you dig out the best deals from the leading rental agents and find the car you need from various corners of the world such as Tokyo, Shanghai, Taipei, Amsterdam, London, Paris, Berlin and Milan. Become a member of Motorway Car Rental and win a 50% off discount off your first car hire. Book your rental car through Motorway Car Rental Today.

50%

off your car hire

- Copy this code: TR82016 and use it at checkout.
- Valid within one month after registration.
- Valid for all destinations worldwide. Search, compare and Save!

We had to wait about an hour when we arrived to get the car we wanted. We were tired after the flight arrived after midnight. We would have appreciated it to be a little bit faster.

From Ryan

I don't think the website is user-friendly enough. As I canceled my booking, I didn't get the confirmation email right away. Because of that, my credit card had to be re-credited in three to five days, so I had to wait for that before putting a new booking.

From Danielle

I was traveling in Paris, but my location was directed to London's site, costing valuable time, and my plans were delayed afterwards.

From Austin

176 What is Motorway Car?
(A) an automobile manufacturer
(B) a travel agency
(C) a car dealing company
(D) an online car rental platform

177 In which of the following cities can't customers enjoy Motorway Car's service?
(A) Taipei
(B) Berlin
(C) Melbourne
(D) Milan

178 Which of the following is TRUE of the coupon?
(A) It can only be retained by an old member.
(B) Customers will need a code to use the coupon.
(C) It is only valid in Asian countries.
(D) It offers one free car hire to new members.

179 Who most likely are Ryan, Danielle and Austin?
(A) Motorway Car customers
(B) Motorway Car agents
(C) Motorway Car co-founders
(D) Motorway Car officers

180 What is Danielle's major complaint?
(A) The car arrived late.
(B) The car's quality was poor.
(C) The booking system was slow.
(D) The information provided was not accurate.

Airport Link Opens for Operations Today

By Irene Kramer
11 September 2015

After 10 years of planning, construction and testing, Bath Mead's airport link officially opened for business today. According to the official news released just earlier, Bath Mead's Airport Link Corporation offers customers a discount of 40% off for all types of tickets during the first two months of the operation.

The airport line connects the major points in central business district of Bath Mead, such as Denmark Shopping Mall, City Hall and Monumental Square with each terminal of International Bath Mead Airport. Compared to having to spend ninety minutes on the Airport coach, passengers can now travel between Bath Mead and the airport for merely twenty-five minutes.

Luggage check-in services for a variety of airlines are also available at Mt. Jade station, Lavender Road station and Airport Park station. The check-in has to be carried out three hours before the flight leaves. Information about the regulations for all airlines can be found at the check-in counters at the aforementioned stations.

Standard Seat		
Children	Adult	Group
$14	$20	$15
Premium Seat		
Children	Adult	Group
$18	$30	$22

Notice of Correction

The recent news release dated 11 September 2015 misidentified the ticket fares of Bath Mead Airport Link premium seat. According to the official information obtained from Bath Mead's Airport Link Corporation, the correct fares for premium seats are $20 for children, $34 for adults and $25 for groups. We are deeply sorry for the inconvenience.

181 Who is Irene Kramer?
- (A) a government officer
- (B) a delegate from the airport link corporation
- (C) a journalist
- (D) a passenger

182 Since when has the airport link construction been planned?
- (A) 1995
- (B) 2005
- (C) 2010
- (D) 2015

183 What is TRUE of the airport link?
- (A) It majorly connects the rural areas to the airport.
- (B) It takes an hour and a half to get to the airport from the city center.
- (C) Passengers can check in their luggage at certain stations.
- (D) Passengers can check in their luggage three days prior to flight departure.

184 During the first month of its operation, what is the fare for an adult's standard seat ticket?
- (A) $8
- (B) $12
- (C) $14
- (D) $20

185 What is the notice mainly about?
- (A) the recent fare adjustment
- (B) the errors in the previous news
- (C) the operation of the airport link
- (D) the end date of the discount offer

Project Material Request

Please be aware that the application of project materials for the winter term will be open from 15 November to 8 December. As usual, the budget limit for each department is $500. If your request is over the limit, we cannot accept it. To save time, I would like each department to control their budget within the limit before submitting your request since it would take extra time to handle the rejection and resubmitting process. Plus, according to our record, it usually takes a long time before our supplier, Mr. Morris, quotes to us. Therefore, in order to be able to distribute the resources to everyone by the end of this year, I would like you to send your request list to me no later than the deadline, 8 December. Please note that no late submission is accepted.

With regard to the form of the request list, please specify the number of each item you need, the specific name of the item and most importantly, the department for which you are requesting. You still need to put the item in the list even if we already have it in storage. As soon as the materials arrive, we will contact the department individually. If you have any questions, feel free to contact me by marydublin@mail.2010.us.

Mary Dublin

Item	Number	Price per unit	Total
Twin adhesive tape	30	$1.1	$33
Craft paper	200	$0.6	$120
Crepe paper	50	$1	$50
Pipe cleaner	50	$0.3	$15
Wild flower seed	2	$12.5	$25
Color paint	10	$50	$500

Requested by Jeremy Zhong
Date: 7 December 2016

Project Material Request
From: Jeremy Zhong
To: Mary Dublin
Cc: Kathryn Culhane
Date: 7 December 2016

Dear Mary,

I have sent you the request form just earlier this afternoon. Please check. The total price is a little bit over the limit. However, I understand that you have the color paints in stock as you told me last time I dropped by your office, so I assume that will not go into our estimated budget. As for the craft paper, can we get it in different colors?

Thank you.

Jeremy

186 Who is Mr. Morris?
(A) an office assistant
(B) a department officer
(C) a stationery supplier
(D) a delivery driver

187 When can the requested materials be given to the departments?
(A) by 8 December, 2016
(B) by 15 November, 2016
(C) by 22 December, 2016
(D) by 31 December, 2016

188 Which of the following is CORRECT?
(A) The submission should be made by the end of December.
(B) The name of the department supervisor should be written down.
(C) The budget cannot be over $100.
(D) Mr. Morris is often slow to handle the quotation.

189 What did Jeremy fail to do in meeting the submission requirements?
(A) identify his department
(B) specify the number of the item
(C) put down the items' names
(D) hand in the list in time

190 What did Jeremy mention in his email?
(A) That the craft paper is out of stock
(B) That the color paints are in storage
(C) That the twin adhesive tapes are too expensive
(D) That if the deadline can be extended

★**Questions 191-195 refer to the following emails and ticket.**

To: oxford-booking

From: Stefanie Wang

Subject: Refund Issue

To whom it may concern,

I purchased on your website five tickets for

① London to Cambridge 6:45AM (via National Link)

② Cambridge day tour

③ Cambridge to London Evening Service

But unfortunately three of us are not able to go. Therefore, I was wondering if we could get a full refund for three of the tickets. I have attached the tickets I bought as proof of purchase. Hope to hear from you soon. Thank you.

Stefanie

To: Stefanie Wang
From: oxford-booking
Subject: Re: Refund Issue

Hi Stefanie,

I have issued a refund to your account for three tickets. Please allow 5-6 working days for this to be processed.

Only two of these tickets will now be valid for your London transfers, Cambridge transfer and the Cambridge day tour.

Looking forward to welcoming you on board the tour.

Kind Regards,

Molly Yang

---

oxford-booking

TICKET
London to Cambridge 6:45AM (via National Link)
8/23/17 06:45
5 x Student / Return Rate

Ticket Information
G01K7785S3 V16401K763000HBE3KQT

Date of Purchase
8/7/17 20:01 GMT

£ 56.30

TICKET

Cambridge to London 18:15PM (via National Link)

8/27/17 06:45

5 x Student / Return Rate

Ticket Information

G01K7BF5S4 V16401K763000HBE3KQT

Date of Purchase

8/7/17 20:03 GMT

£ 56.30

TICKET

Cambridge Day Tour Tour Only

8/24/17 10:00

5 x Student / Standard / Tour Only

Ticket Information

G01K7BF5S4 V16401K76390HBE3KQT

Date of Purchase

8/7/17 20:04 GMT

£ 60.00

191 Why was the first email sent?

(A) To ask for travel information

(B) To request a refund

(C) To book a tour

(D) To reserve a coach seat

192 How many tickets were refunded?

(A) one

(B) two

(C) three

(D) five

193 What most likely is Oxford-booking?

(A) a department store

(B) a travel agency

(C) a metro company

(D) a hotel

194 What is indicated about the tickets?

(A) They were bought at a railway station.

(B) They all became invalid.

(C) They were bought with a student discount.

(D) They were all train tickets.

195 Which of the following is INCORRECT?

(A) The train bound for Cambridge leaves in the morning.

(B) The tickets were purchased on the same day.

(C) The total cost of the tickets is £172.6

(D) One of the tickets is for London tour.

★**Questions 196-200 refer to the following emails and information.**

Inquiry of print credit refund

To: libraryadmin@york.ac.uk

From: joanna09013@york.ac.uk

To anyone it may concern,

I am a master student in the school of education. Considering the fact that I will be leaving the university in early September, the validity of my library card will soon expire. However, there are still plenty of print credits left in the card, and I doubt there will be a chance for me to use up the remaining credits by the time I leave. Therefore, I would like to request a refund of the unused credits. If this is doable, I would like to know how long it will take for the refund to be processed, and if the money will be wired back to my bank account. Thank you.

Joanna Chang

Re: Inquiry of print credit refund
To: joanna09013@york.ac.uk
From: libraryadmin@york.ac.uk

Dear Joanna,

Unfortunately, we cannot refund unused print credits. Like book tokens, print credit can only be used for the purpose it was bought for. It is not a refundable deposit.

We will however transfer your credit to another user's account if you reply with their username and confirm this is what you would like.

You might be interested to know how the University uses the income from printing. It is used to keep our student printers and photocopiers working and stocked with sufficient paper and toner; to purchase new or replacement equipment; and to fund new and improved service.

Best wishes,

Amy Peterson
Librarian
University of York

University of York
Student Card Information

Card Holder: Ms. Joanna Chang
Student No.: 1607660
Program: International Education (Full-Time) School of Education
Course Start Date: 20 September 2016
Course End Date: 3 September 2017
Print Credit: £53.05
Recent **Top-up**: £20

196 What were the emails about?

(A) graduation procedures

(B) print credit refund

(C) tuition payment

(D) assignment deadline

197 How much are Joanna requesting for refund?

(A) £20

(B) £33.05

(C) £43.05

(D) £53.05

198 What is indicated in the second email?

(A) It will take over a week for the money to be transferred back.

(B) The unused credits can be transferred to another student with permission.

(C) Students would be charged extra for the printers to be upgraded.

(D) The printers and photocopiers in the university are all brand new.

199 How long is the course Joanna is enrolled in?

(A) about six months

(B) about a year

(C) about two years

(D) about three years

200 The phrase "top-up" in the last line in the card information, is closest in meaning to

(A) fine

(B) withdrawal

(C) deposit

(D) transfer

New TOEIC Reading Test 5
新多益**閱讀**全真模擬**試題第5回**

▶ **READING TEST**

In the Reading Test, you will read a variety of texts and answer several different types of reading comprehension questions. The entire Reading Test will last 75 minutes. There are three parts, and directions are given for each part. You are encouraged to answer as many questions as possible within the time allowed.

You must mark your answers on the separate answer sheet. Do not write your answers in the test book.

▶ **PART 5**

Directions: A word or phrase is missing in each of the sentences below. Four answer choices are given below each sentence. Select the best answer to complete the sentence. Then mark the letter (A), (B), (C), or (D) on your answer sheet.

101 We cannot put your order into production without a _____ contract.

(A) sign
(B) signs
(C) signed
(D) signing

102 Both parties have agreed _____ all the terms and conditions after negotiation.

(A) at
(B) with
(C) by
(D) in

103 Thank you for giving me the privilege of having an _____ with you yesterday.

(A) interview
(B) interpretation
(C) induction
(D) instruction

104 Gillian has replaced Mr. Garcia, who is no longer in our _____.

(A) regulation
(B) consideration
(C) employment
(D) reinforcement

105 Raymond is not a good boss to work with as he changes his mind _____ and asks you your opinion more than once.

(A) constantly
(B) generously
(C) perceivably
(D) preferably

106 I would like to set up a meeting to discuss the details of _____ of the proposal.

(A) compensation
(B) recreation
(C) aggregation
(D) implementation

107 The date and time of the meeting has been changed but the location _____ the same.

(A) contains
(B) expects
(C) remains
(D) maintains

108 The menu of the staff canteen _____ change according to the availability of ingredients.

(A) is eligible for
(B) is subject to
(C) is aware of
(D) is used to

109 Bellavita Coffee is offering a 20% discount on all its beverages this month _____ their grand opening.

(A) in celebration of
(B) in accordance with
(C) with respect to
(D) for the sake of

110 In _____ to expanding its presence in the Europe market, Max Auto is also planning to explore opportunities in Asia.

(A) order
(B) relation
(C) addition
(D) regard

111 _____ employees who want to participate in the company trip must sign up by the end of this week.

(A) Both
(B) All
(C) Each
(D) None

112 The processing time for the Taiwan compatriot permit is _____ a week.

(A) normally
(B) considerably
(C) permanently
(D) surprisingly

113 For _____ reasons, swimwear and underwear may not be returned or exchanged.

(A) personal
(B) operational
(C) confidential
(D) hygienic

114 Curtis didn't have much success in the workplace _____ he was fired repeatedly from his jobs for not being productive.

(A) while
(B) although
(C) even
(D) as

115 All dishes in this restaurant are cooked for immediate _____.

(A) activation
(B) consumption
(C) assumption
(D) constituent

116 Audio guides are free with your _____ entry tickets at the main entrance.

(A) ultimate
(B) intentional
(C) individual
(D) successful

117 If you don't go to the restroom right now, you'll have to wait _____ intermission.

(A) since
(B) until
(C) when
(D) after

118 It's not _____ to tip the drivers, but $1-$5 would be appropriate if you want to.

(A) obligatory
(B) complimentary
(C) comprehensive
(D) expensive

119 An in-car navigation system _____ $15 per day or $70 per week.

(A) spends
(B) costs
(C) takes
(D) consumes

120 This coupon is only valid on weekdays and cannot be combined with _____ offer.

(A) else
(B) one another
(C) each other
(D) any other

121 All items in our store _____ a one-year limited warranty.

(A) render up
(B) stand for
(C) come with
(D) set up

122 The term paper needs _____ to Prof. Adams by September 8th.

(A) to submit
(B) submitting
(C) to be submitted
(D) being submitted

123 The mayor was arrested for taking bribes _____ the use of his official position.

(A) in support of
(B) in memory of
(C) in charge of
(D) in exchange for

124 The coroner _____ that the woman's death was an accident and not murder.

(A) promised
(B) concluded
(C) integrated
(D) appended

125 The premiere will begin with a tea party _____ guests can mingle and relax before the start of the film.

(A) which
(B) what
(C) where
(D) those

126 _____ the fire last month, the opening of the branch office was postponed.

(A) Due to
(B) Because
(C) Owing
(D) Resulted in

127 The gym offers a free session to help their new members _____ the machines.

(A) get acquainted with
(B) be informed of
(C) stay clear of
(D) get familiar with

128 The price does not include breakfast _____ you can add it for £7.50 per person.

(A) but
(B) although
(C) or
(D) nor

129 If you feel airsick, _____ is a bag in the seat pocket in front of you.

(A) which
(B) there
(C) that
(D) what

130 All elevators within the building are _____ a preventative maintenance.

(A) taking
(B) undergoing
(C) experimenting
(D) practicing

▶ PART 6

Directions: Read the texts on the following pages. A word or phrase is missing in some of the sentences. Answer choices are given below each of these articles. Select the best answer to complete the text. Then mark the letter (A), (B), (C) or (D) on your answer sheet.

Questions 131-134 refer to the following letter.

Dear Ms. Tucker,

This is in response to your letter concerning the issues you experienced while staying at our hotel.

As you wrote, your troubles began when you heard ___131___ noise from the walls. Our apologies. This hotel is a 70-year-old structure, and the walls are thin, so the noises made by other guests can be heard easily. We're currently in the process of soundproofing the building to solve this problem.

Then, you found that the air conditioner in your room didn't work. You mentioned that you wanted to change a room but your request was ___132___ by our front desk representative, Samantha. I would like to beg for your understanding that we were unable to move you to another room, as our hotel was fully booked on that day.

In this letter you will find an enclosed voucher for a free night's stay and a complimentary breakfast at the hotel. We hope the voucher can ___133___ the unpleasant experience you had at our hotel this time, and ___134___ .

All best,
Daniel Knight
General Manager, Truncheon Hotel

131 (A) incessant
    (B) attractive
    (C) prestigious
    (D) imperative

132 (A) welcomed
    (B) declined
    (C) invented
    (D) processed

133 (A) put up with
    (B) stay away from
    (C) drop in on
    (D) make up for

★ **134** (A) we thank you for your cooperation
    (B) we hope to receive your order soon
    (C) we look forward to serving you again soon
    (D) we hope you make the payment without delay

Questions 135-138 refer to the following advertisement.

Are you ready for the ultimate Chinese New Year at the Tutu Malaysia Resort?

Join us this February and discover a CNY land with over 30 rides, shows and attractions to create most ___135___ family memories! If you are lucky enough, you will spot Tutu Rabbit, our mascot, ___136___ red envelopes in Dream Park!

You and your family can even extend the celebratory fun by staying in our amazing Tutu Malaysia Resort Hotel for a whole night of Chinese New Year's entertainment and jolly fun that ___137___ kids and adults will enjoy.

Please note that ___138___ for entry into the park.

135 (A) festive
(B) cautious
(C) persuasive
(D) holistic

136 (A) deliver
(B) delivering
(C) delivered
(D) being delivering

137 (A) only
(B) none
(C) both
(D) every

★ 138 (A) tickets can only be purchased online in advance
(B) you may be asked to overwork on the weekend
(C) we will not open for business for the next week
(D) you must bring your original purchase receipt

Questions 139-142 refer to the following email.

From: Joseph Thomas
To: crownhouse-residents@clifton.ac.uk
Date: Tue, Mar 20, 2018 at 5:13 PM
Subject: Notice of Routine Boiler Inspection

Hi,

This is to give notice to residents in Crown House that personnel from the University's Estates staff are due to carry out routine inspection and maintenance of the boilers (providing hot water and central heating) in the flats ___139___ today, Tuesday 20th March. It is ___140___ that this work will take 2 to 3 days.

Work will take place from 9am to not later than 5pm daily.

They will require ___141___ the kitchens and various boiler rooms in the flats but will not require access to bedrooms. The hall will give them access if you are not in your flat when they call. All Estates personnel carry University identification.

___142___

Thank you.

Joseph

139 (A) commence
(B) commenced
(C) commencing
(D) will commence

140 (A) estimate
(B) estimated
(C) estimating
(D) estimation

141 (A) access to
(B) charge for
(C) recess of
(D) appeal to

★ 142 (A) Please respond ASAP.
(B) Looking forward to seeing you.
(C) Please fill out the form below.
(D) Apologies for the short notice.

Questions 143-146 refer to the following email.

Dear Mr. Cheng,

Maxton Law Office is hiring for the position of law administrator and I am ___143___ information about this opportunity.

The law office administrator will be ___144___ for providing administrative support in our law office. The duties ___145___ overseeing budgeting and payroll operations, managing office space arrangements and gathering supplies.

___146___ in Business, legal administration or a related field. Please contact me if there are any adequate candidates that meet our qualifications for this position.

Sincerely,
Selena

143 (A) disseminating
    (B) recommending
    (C) expressing
    (D) acknowledging

144 (A) irrational
    (B) informative
    (C) responsible
    (D) chargeable

145 (A) inclusive
    (B) including
    (C) include
    (D) included

★ 146 (A) All candidates show great interests
    (B) That's the reason why I chose this major
    (C) The focus was put on the thorough investigation
    (D) A candidate should have a Bachelor's degree

▶ PART 7

Directions: In this part, you will read a selection of texts, such as magazine and newspaper articles, letters, and advertisements. Each text is followed by several questions. Select the best answer for each question and mark the letter (A), (B), (C), or (D) on your answer sheet.

Questions 147-149 refer to the following post.

Event: Alumni Dinner Gathering Set For December 30th
Come join us on Dec 30th at 5:30pm (sharp!) til 7:30 pm for our annual Alumni dinner for UCS at Tapatili downtown!
The evening promises to be a fun time full of fellowship and catching up with friends. In addition, if you haven't received your UCS alumni pin we will be handing them out at the dinner! Bring $30 for dinner and drinks!

DEC 30 UCS Alumni Dinner
Public · Hosted by UCS Alumni Association

🕐 Saturday, December 30 at 5:30 PM - 7:30 PM CST
Next Week

Border Cafe Tapatili
89 N Queens Rd, Tapatili, Oklahoma 74103

27 Going • 15 Interested

147 What's the purpose of this post?

(A) To call an emergency meeting

(B) To promote an event

(C) To invite sponsors to an event

(D) To advertise for a restaurant

148 What will the attendees receive at the dinner?

(A) The UCS alumni pin

(B) The Alumni brochure

(C) The Membership application form

(D) The degree certificate

149 Who's going to pay for the dinner?

(A) The event organizer

(B) The attendees

(C) The Alumni Association

(D) The event sponsors

Questions 150-152 refer to the following notice.

Closure of Car Park 1

To facilitate the construction of developing the airport into a Three-runway System, Car Park 1 is closed from 14 January 2018. Hourly parking spaces are available at Car Park 2, 3 and Takashima Outlet Car Park while daily and long-term parking spaces are also available at Car Park 3 and Takashima Outlet Car Park. These car parks provide a total of over 3,000 parking spaces. For any further enquiries, please contact airport car park customer service hotline at 3300-3300.

150 What is this notice about?

(A) Temporary closing of an auto company

(B) Permanent closing of a parking area

(C) Change of business hours

(D) Business closing for Thanksgiving

151 What is the purpose of closing Car Park 1?

(A) For airport renovation

(B) For runway expansion

(C) To reduce personnel expenses

(D) To build a gourmet court

152 Which car park only provides hourly parking spaces?

(A) Car Park 1

(B) Car Park 2

(C) Car Park 3

(D) Takashima Outlet Car Park

Questions 153-155 refer to the following information.

Transport for Special Needs

In addition to public transport, we have a variety of options available for passengers with mobility difficulties, offering more flexible and personalized transport services through advance booking.

★Coach

① Rehabus	Telephone +852 2827 0023
② Easy-Access Bus	Telephone +852 2770 0023
★ Limousine	Telephone +852 8103 0023
★ Taxi	Telephone +852 2766 0023

Please request a quote before booking. Thanks!

153 Who is the information for?

(A) People carrying large luggage
(B) People with limited mobility
(C) People who are short of cash
(D) Women who travel alone

154 Which statement is correct about the transport services?

(A) It needs booking in advance.
(B) It's a popular public transport.
(C) It's an airport pickup service.
(D) It's unaffordable for most people.

155 What is one encouraged to do before reserving the transport service?

(A) Visit the tourist center
(B) Inquire about prices
(C) Rent an audio guide
(D) Take a number

Questions 156-158 refer to the following letter.

December 2017

Dear Michelle,

We received the deposit Rotary Club of Youth made.

We would like to thank you and all your Rotarians for this huge effort. We are definitely sure that this will be of great help for those in need of housing.

We plan to build, at least, twenty houses in March, and there will probably be a second construction in May. We will be sending pictures and whatever news we have concerning the project.

Thank you for becoming a blessing for Mexico.

You set an example of the real essence of Christmas.

We wish you all a very merry Christmas.

Norma Robles,
Rural Reconstruction, Mexico

156 Why is this letter written?

(A) To inquire about a house

(B) To discuss a house renovation

(C) To express thankfulness

(D) To renew the contract

157 According to the letter, what did Rotary Club of Youth do?

(A) The provided medical assistance.

(B) They established a school.

(C) They volunteered for community service.

(D) They made a donation.

158 What will the donated money probably be used for?

(A) Building temporary accommodation

(B) Buying Christmas decorations

(C) Renovating an office

(D) Establishing a general hospital

Questions 159-161 refer to the following email.

Dear Mr. Adams,

With regard to your application and the subsequent interview you had with us, we are pleased to offer you the position of Purchasing Assistant in WALTS Company.

As we discussed, this is a full-time position of 40 working hours a week, and your initial salary will be £14,000 per year. Your first day in this position will be March 19th, 2018.

Please confirm your acceptance of this offer by replying to this letter no later than Feb. 28, 2018.

We are looking forward to your joining our staff.

Best wishes,
Diana Watkins, HR Manager

159 What is the purpose of this e-mail?

(A) To confirm the time of a meeting
(B) To invite an applicant to an interview
(C) To negotiate salary
(D) To offer a position

160 Which statement about the position offered to Mr. Adams is true?

(A) It's a contract position.
(B) It's an executive position.
(C) It's a full-time position.
(D) It involves a lot of business travel.

161 What is Mr. Adams supposed to do next?

(A) Prepare for the second-round interview
(B) Reply to this e-mail with his decision
(C) Call Diana to reschedule the appointment
(D) Send his resume and application letter

★Questions 162-164 refer to the following text message chain.

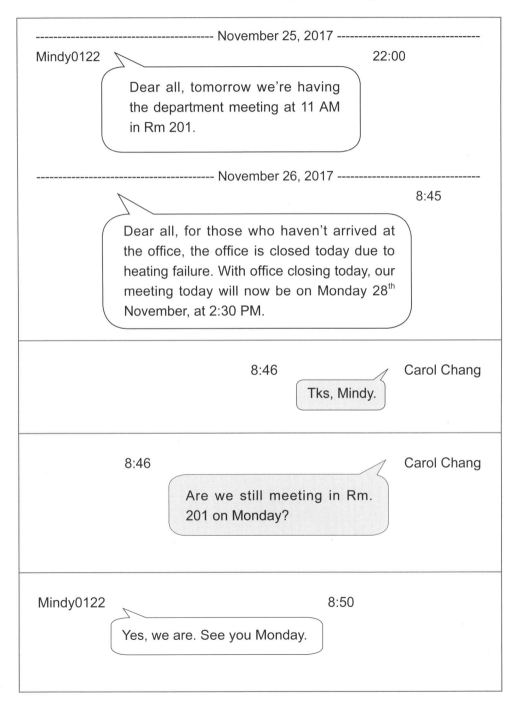

------------------------- November 25, 2017 -------------------------

Mindy0122   22:00

> Dear all, tomorrow we're having the department meeting at 11 AM in Rm 201.

------------------------- November 26, 2017 -------------------------

                                                   8:45

> Dear all, for those who haven't arrived at the office, the office is closed today due to heating failure. With office closing today, our meeting today will now be on Monday 28th November, at 2:30 PM.

8:46   Carol Chang

> Tks, Mindy.

8:46   Carol Chang

> Are we still meeting in Rm. 201 on Monday?

Mindy0122   8:50

> Yes, we are. See you Monday.

162 What is the purpose of the first text message?

(A) It's a reminder.
(B) It's a reservation.
(C) It's an offer.
(D) It's a purchase order.

163 Why is the office closed today?

(A) The heating is not working.
(B) There is a typhoon.
(C) There is a power failure.
(D) It's a national holiday.

164 What has been changed due to office closing?

(A) The minute taker
(B) The meeting location
(C) The meeting time
(D) The meeting moderator

Questions 165-167 refer to the following information.

👍 *A Tour of Central Library*

🗓 Thu, Feb 8 2018   🕐 2:30 pm – 4:00 pm   🚌 Central Library

This tour will explore the architectural significance and history of Kingsland Public Library's (KPL) landmark Central Library at Grand Crown Plaza. The tour will introduce attendees to the history of the library's spaces and its services. The tour will also give attendees a behind-the-scenes glimpse at the library's underground storage "Cellars" and the Kingsland Collection's "Morgue" of archival materials.

This tour can accommodate up to 20 people on a first-come, first-served basis.

The tour involves climbing and descending stairs. Tours meet in the Grand Lobby next to the Reception Desk and depart 5 minutes after the start time.

---

165 How long will this library tour take?

(A) One and a half hours
(B) Two hours
(C) Two and a half hours
(D) Three hours

166 Where is the assembly point for the tour?

(A) At the entrance
(B) In the lobby
(C) By the fountain
(D) At the escalator

167 Which of the following is incorrect about the tour?

(A) To join you need to book in advance.
(B) It can accommodate up to 20 people.
(C) The tour involves stair climbing.
(D) The attendees will visit places not open to the public.

Questions 168-171 refer to the following post.

 Charlotte Cunningham ▶ Air Rosa
21 hours • Le Mesnil-Amelot, France • 🌐

Yesterday we had a flight with Air Rosa from Maldives to Amsterdam Netherland with a connection at CDG, Paris. The flight from Maldives was delayed and we missed our connecting flight, which we fully understand can happen. However, instead of helping us, your "customer service" would rather treat us as if we were a problem to your company. Your staff sent us in different directions and no one took responsibility or was even nice to us. On top of this you lost our baggage.

We understand mistakes happen and flights get delayed. But our advice is that you shape up your customer experience and start taking care of the people that pays for traveling with you. We are disappointed and will actively advise our friends and family not to travel with you if your don't start showing consideration for your customers.

👍Like　　💬 comment　　➡share

Air Rosa　　Good morning Charlotte,

Thank you for contacting us here. We are very sorry to hear about the unsatisfying service you have received at our airport in Paris. This concerns us deeply and does not conform with our usual high standard of customer care. Feedback like yours is invaluable to us and will always be forwarded to the departments concerned. We would like to follow up on it further and therefore kindly ask you to send us your booking reference and/or ticket number in a private message.

We're further sorry to hear about your baggage delay. We will gladly look into it for you, if you could provide your baggage reference, tag number or the full name as it appears on the booking. We are happy to help in any way we can and once again apologize for the troubles you've endured.

Like 1 • Reply　18h

168 What is the post mainly about?

(A) A customer complaint

(B) A promotional campaign

(C) A hotel renovation

(D) A wonderful travel experience

169 How did Charlotte Cunningham feel when she wrote the post?

(A) Excited

(B) Miserable

(C) Furious

(D) Calm

170 According to the post, which of the following didn't happened to Charlotte?

(A) Her flight was delayed.

(B) Her baggage was lost.

(C) She missed her connecting flight.

(D) She was forced to give up her seat.

171 According to the reply from Air Rosa, what did they offer to do for Charlotte?

(A) To compensate for her loss

(B) To inquire into her missing baggage

(C) To help her book another flight

(D) To provide free pickup service

Questions 172-173 refer to the following advertisement.

Here at Flying Fur, we groom and board dogs of all shapes and sizes. We have been serving the community since 2003. Our experienced pet groomers attend grooming seminars annually to learn the latest techniques as well as important information regarding pet grooming. We were voted Belfast's Best Pet Groomers 2011-2017, and won three successive British Dog Grooming Championships from 2015-2017.

We treat your pets as our own. Our certified groomers and stylists are here at Flying Fur to give your dogs the special attention they deserve.

We are by appointment only, so please call us at 0113-4408-9935 for all your grooming and boarding needs.

172 What kind of service does Flying Fur provide?

(A) Elderly care service
(B) Dog grooming service
(C) Child care service
(D) Hairdressing services

173 How does Flying Fur do business?

(A) By appointment only
(B) On a first-come, first served basis
(C) By online reservations
(D) By affiliate programs

Questions 174-175 refer to the following message.

Message for: Louisa Greene
Date/Time: June 18/2:30 p.m.
Caller: Julia Elliot

Message: Ms. Elliot would like to meet one hour earlier tomorrow morning at the headquarters. Please be there by 9:30 instead of 10:30. She requests the change of meeting time because heads of other departments want to join the meeting as well. She wants to make sure there's enough time to get everything ready before they arrive. Please check your schedule to make sure the time works for you and call Ms. Elliot on her cellphone.

Message taken: Angela Bradley

174 What time was tomorrow's meeting originally scheduled?

(A) 10:30 a.m.
(B) 11:30 a.m.
(C) 9:30 a.m.
(D) 8:30 a.m.

175 What is Louisa Greene supposed to do when receiving the message?

(A) Send an e-mail message to Angela
(B) Take a cab to the headquarters
(C) Look at her schedule for June 19
(D) Meet Ms. Elliot at her office

★**Questions 176-180 refer to the following e-mails and form.**

From: Jerry Moore
To: Steven Harris
Subject: Party Invitation

Attached: Ticket Order Form.doc ,📄

Dear Mr. Harris,

The Campbell Foundation invites you to attend a special benefit performance featuring Purple Ladybug, one of the most famous and popular theatre troupes in Barcelona. All <u>proceeds</u> will go towards the Animal Protection Association Barcelona.

You may already know that the Campbell Foundation has saved over 1,000 dogs from the streets in the Summerfield area since 2009. But perhaps you didn't know that we created programs that focus on sterilization and vaccination, and donate thousands of euros every year to public and private dog shelters to help local organizations implement spay and neuter programs all throughout Spain to humanely address the overpopulation of street dogs.

You can also make a contribution to these efforts by purchasing a ticket to the benefit performance, which will be held on March 15 at 7:00 p.m. in the Summerfield University auditorium. The cost of the ticket is only €20.00 per person.

Please click here to order your tickets. If you cannot attend but would still like to make a donation, we will receive it appreciatively.

We await your response with anticipation.

Best wishes,
Jerry Moore

Ticket Order Form

To reserve tickets please complete and submit the booking form

Full name: | Steven Harris |

E-mail: S_Harris0918@fmail.com

Phone number: | 077-8475-6884 |

Number of tickets: ◉ | 5 |

Total amount of payment: | €100 |

Donation options:

◉ Custom; Enter your own amount: | €300 |

○ Predefined: ☐ €10 ☐ €20 ☐ €50 ☐ €100

Credit card information:

◉ Visa   ○ Master   ○ JCB   ○ American Express

Credit card number: 5433-XXXX-XXXX-0059

Please mail the tickets to: | Avenida Diagonal 731, **Barcelona**, 08014 |

| **Submit** |

From: Steven Harris

To: Jerry Moore

Subject: RE: Party Invitation

Dear Jerry,

Thank you for your invitation. You know that I have always concerned myself with the welfare of the street dogs. Cruel means such as poisoning, electrocution and shooting are never appropriate solutions to stray dog overpopulation. I deeply appreciate your efforts in leading the way to a better future for stray dogs.

This is a very meaningful event and I am very glad to help support your efforts. I just submitted the online ticket order form. My wife and children are all going with me. Hopefully together with everyone's efforts we can rescue as many dogs as possible from a variety of bad situations.

See you on March 15.

Best wishes,
Steven

176 Why is the first email written?

(A) To evaluate a new employee's performance
(B) To request financial support
(C) To introduce a company
(D) To sell tickets to a benefit performance

177 Which of the following is most similar to a "benefit performance"?

(A) Charitable entertainment
(B) Earning power
(C) Profit-making program
(D) sales volume

178 What does the word "proceeds" in the invitation letter refer to?

(A) Original receipts
(B) Annual income
(C) Discount provided
(D) Money donated

179 According to the ticket order form, what else did Steven do in addition to purchasing tickets?

(A) He signed up to be a volunteer at the foundation.
(B) He made a donation of €300.
(C) He introduced some potential clients.
(D) He recommended a few animal welfare groups.

180 What is the purpose of the second letter?

(A) To decline the invitation
(B) To accept the invitation
(C) To invite proposals
(D) To confirm an agreement

★**Questions 181-185 refer to the following advertisement, information and letter.**

MD Towel Industrial Tourism & Explore Factory

Situated by Sunny Lake in Somerset County, MD Towel Industrial Tourism & Explore Factory is one of the biggest domestic and international towel producers in the U.S. Established in the 1970s, MD Towel Manufacturer remodeled its business, setting up its first tourism factory by Sunny Lake in 2012 and became a popular tourist attraction in the southwest Oklahoma. MD Towel Manufacturer's award-winning tourist factory opens its plants to tourists, introducing visitors how towels that we use on a daily basis are made.

The factory offers a variety of DIY sessions for both adults and children to learn to fold towels into different shapes such as cupcakes, lollipops, ice cream, animals, flowers and other designs and have fun. In addition, group tours of the factory are available to students of primary school, middle school and community-based organizations.

To book a group tour please click **_here_** for more details.

Choose a group tour and save big with MD Towel Industrial Tourism & Explore Factory!

➤ **Group Tour Times/** Monday through Friday at 9:30 a.m. and 2:30 p.m.
➤ **Group Tour options (for groups of less than 20 people)**

	Length of time	Rates (per person)
Tour A	2 hours— 1 hour for the factory tour and 1 hour for DIY session: cupcake towel + lollipop towel	$10
Tour B	1 1/2 hours – 1 hour for the factory tour and 1/2 hour for DIY session: cupcake towel or lollipop towel	$8
Tour C	1 hour – 1/2 hour for the factory tour and 1/2 hour for DIY session: cupcake towel or lollipop towel	$5
Tour D	1 hour— factory tour	$4
Tour E	1 hour – DIY session: cupcake towel + lollipop towel	$6

Please contact +1 405-525-7788 or e-mail to jasonbradman@mdtowel.com to make an appointment for a tour. Tours are available by appointment only.

From: Katrina Blacks

To: jasonbradman@mdtowel.com

Subject: Factory Tour Reservation

Hi,

My name is Katrina Blacks and I'm a teacher at St. George Primary School. After reading the article about your Towel Industrial Tourism & Explore Factory on your website, I believe taking a tour of your factory would be a nice field trip for my Year 6 class. I'd like to reserve a 2-hour tour on October 25th at 2:30 p.m. for my 20 students.

Please let me know if the factory can take my reservation on the above-mentioned date and time.

Regards,

Katrina Blacks

181 Which statement is true about the towel factory?

(A) It is a newly built modern factory.
(B) It specializes in manufacturing towels.
(C) It is not open to the public.
(D) Their DIY sessions are designed for children.

182 How many sessions of group tours does the factory provide a day?

(A) Five
(B) Four
(C) Three
(D) Two

183 Where did Katrina learn obtain the information about the Towel Factory?

(A) From the factory's website
(B) From a monthly magazine
(C) From classified ads in newspaper
(D) From a TV interview

184 How much will the factory charge Katrina's class for their visit on October 25th?

(A) $80
(B) $100
(C) $160
(D) $200

185 Why is Katrina taking her class to the factory?

(A) To go on a picnic
(B) To listen to a speech
(C) For a field trip
(D) To give a singing performance

★**Questions 186-190 refer to the following information.**

Welcome to the California Country House in Palm Springs!

Situated in the Southern California desert of Palm Springs, the California Country House is all about relaxing, putting your feet up and enjoying a vacation escape. Our classic Italian farm hotel provides just the right amount of rustic charm and fascination. Eighteen comfortable guest rooms surround a swimming pool amid a lush courtyard where palm trees and birds of paradise sway in the breeze complimenting spectacular mountains views!

Vacation Advisor Travelers' Choice Awards

California Country House is voted Number One in service on Vacation Advisor in Palm Springs among 180 properties competing for the spot. We look forward to having you stay with us, by the pool, at California Country House in Palm Springs. Book the room for your stay right now and see why our guests rate us so well time and time again, and year after year. Believe it or not, you'll never want to check out!

Vacation. com

Dear Miranda H, your booking is guaranteed and all paid for. There's no need to call us – it's all booked!

California Country House	$89
	nightly price per room

335 E Palm Canyon, Palm Springs, CA 92264-5523
+1 831-228-1234
☑ Free breakfast   ☑ Free WiFi   ☑ Free parking

Vacation.com confirmation no.	10934694756
Check in date	Tuesday, May 30, 2017 (2PM)
Check out date	Friday, June 2, 2017 (noon)
Your stay	3 nights, 1 room
Amount paid	$267.00
Cancellation policy	Free cancellation before May 27, 2017 (0AM)
Required at check in	• Credit card or cash deposit required • Government-issued photo ID required • Minimum check-in age is 18

Great stay at California Country House- highly recommended

Miranda H from Chatham, Canada ★★★★☆

California Country House was a great home away from home. A very clean, friendly atmosphere provided a great vacation. We were picked up at the airport and dropped off too at the end of our stay. The limo service is a great addition to the many offerings here. It is available to arrive in style at the down town restaurant of your choosing. Bicycles on the property are also another convenient way of getting around.

The House is located in a great spot with easy walking distance to downtown as well as grocery stores and pharmacies. Ralphs, a supermarket just a few blocks east, has all the fixings for self-catering travellers. We really liked having the kitchen to use to cook meals so we didn't have to go out and eat.

The service and the hotel facility is OUTSTANDING. The staff at California Country House cannot do enough for you during your stay, from offering fresh fruit, a glass of wine, a towel for the pool to a suggestion for an outing such as a hike. Nina and Jake, and the rest of the crew there, made me feel so welcome.

I highly recommend staying here—with the great amenities, service, friendly faces and reasonable rates, you can't go wrong! I will definitely go back and stay here again and look forward to going back! This family-owned business offers it all!

186 According to the first piece of information, what is California Country House?

(A) A leisure farm
(B) A ski resort
(C) A resort hotel
(D) A local hospital

187 According to the second piece of information, what is not included in the price?

(A) Parking fee
(B) Breakfast
(C) Internet connection
(D) Extra beds

188 According to the booking confirmation, what is required at check in?

(A) The confirmation letter
(B) Proof of identity
(C) Copy of flight ticket
(D) Original purchase receipt

189 What does "Ralphs" in Miranda's comment refer to?

(A) A Mexican restaurant
(B) A fitness center
(C) A supermarket
(D) A beauty salon

190 According to Miranda's comment, who most likely can Nina and Jake be?

(A) The owners of California Country House
(B) Regular customers of Ralphs
(C) Guests at California Country House.
(D) Companions of Miranda.

★**Questions 191-195 refer to the following information and e-mails.**

Floyds Books Order Confirmation

Order Number: GB035346   Date: August 29

This notice is to inform you that your order for the following items has been received and is currently being processed. Please check the following details to confirm that they are accurate:

Customer Name: Stacy Perry
Contact Phone: 012-2485-8888
Shipping Address: 45 Smith House, Lakeside Valley, Manchester M12

Requested items:	Qty	Unit price
#59247346 *The Pearl Thief* (by Elizabeth Wein -published 2017)	1	$7.99
#23042309 Moonstone: *The Boy Who Never Was* (by Sjon -published 2013)	1	$8.59
#12083466 *One Year in Provence* (by Peter Mayle -published 1989)	1	$7.99
Subtotal		$24.57
New Member Discount		-2.45
Shipping		$3.00
Total		$25.12

Payment Details:

Debit/Credit Card Number: 22XX-XXXX-XXXX-6609

Card Owner: Stacy Perry

Billing Address: 45 Smith House, Lakeside Valley, Manchester M12

★All orders from Floyds Books ship within 12 hours of this confirmation notice and should be received within 3 business days.

Thank you for purchasing with Floyds.

From: Stacy Perry

To: Floyds Books <customerservice@floydsbooks.com.uk>

Date: Sep 5, 2018

Subject: My Book Order

Dear Floyds Customer Service,

I am writing this letter to inquire about my book order, GB035346, with you for three books on August 29. I received a confirmation letter, which informed me that my order would be delivered within three business days. In other words, I should have received my order no later than September 1st; however, it's already been a week and I'm still waiting for my books.

The delay of the delivery has caused considerable inconvenience as the books are supposed to be a birthday present for my daughter. I must receive them by tomorrow, otherwise I won't be needing them anymore, and I'll definitely cancel my order and ask for a full refund.

Please could you check the status of my order immediately and let me know what is going on.

Please respond as soon as possible.

Regards,
Stacy Perry

From: Floyds Books
To: Stacy Perry <stacy0318_sperry@netmail.com.uk>
Date: Sep 5, 2018
Subject: RE: My Book Order

Dear Ms. Perry

In reply to your letter concerning your book order, GB035346, I on behalf of Floyds Books sincerely apologize for the inconvenience that you faced because of the delivery delay. We checked the status of your order as soon as we received your letter. Your order was dispatched on the day the confirmation letter was sent to you, but unfortunately, it was delivered to the wrong address. The books have been retrieved and will be delivered to your designated address by our express courier by today.

To make up for the inconvenience we have caused, with your books we are sending a coupon for a discount of 30% on your next purchase.

Again, our apologies.

Best wishes,
Fiona Schmidt
Manager of Floyds Books Customer Service

191 According to the first e-mail, how did Stacy Perry make the payment?

(A) By credit card
(B) By cash
(C) By installments
(D) By phone

192 Which statement about Tracy's order is true?

(A) She was provided a free delivery.
(B) She was offered a discount of 10%.
(C) She will collect her order at the store.
(D) She is a regular customer of Floyds Books.

193 Why did Stacy write the e-mail?

(A) She received a damaged book.
(B) She wanted to change the delivery address.
(C) Her order didn't arrive on schedule.
(D) She received incorrect items.

194 What is the purpose of the third e-mail?

(A) To confirm a purchase order
(B) To verify membership information
(C) To deal with a complaint
(D) To apologize for being absent

195 According to the third e-mail, what will Stacy get along with her books?

(A) A discount coupon
(B) A free book
(C) A discount code
(D) A purchase receipt

★**Questions 196-200 refer to the following information, advertisement and e-mail.**

◇Working Holiday Visa Information◇

If you're between 18 and 30 (or 35 for certain countries), you could be eligible for a Working Holiday Scheme visa, which enables you to earn a bit of cash as well as acquire some overseas work experience while traveling in New Zealand.

At present, New Zealand has a Working Holiday Scheme agreement with 42 countries around the world. Please note that some countries have quotas, so make sure you get your application in quickly once the quota opens.

The agreements we have with the 42 countries vary, but there are a few rules that apply for everyone. All applicants from all countries must—

➢ Have a passport valid for at least three months after your planned departure from New Zealand.

➢ Be at least 18 years old and not older than 30 (or 35 depending on your nationality).

➢ Meet our health and character requirements.

➢ Not bring dependents with you.

➢ Hold a return air ticket, or sufficient funds to purchase such a ticket.

➢ Have not previously visited New Zealand using the Working Holiday Scheme visa (or been approved for one).

➢ Be coming to New Zealand for a holiday, with working being the secondary reason for your visit.

About Us

Founded in 2010, W&T is a company specializes in providing personal assistance to backpackers arriving in New Zealand. We offer groups no bigger than 5 people professional assistance and personalized support throughout the whole process of a working holiday in New Zealand. Over the seven years we have obtained an excellent reputation for high job placement rate and high referral rate. Our Beginner Kit that covers all the services you need at a reasonable price of NZ$600 will help you make the most of your working holiday.

Contact us for more information.
www.workntravel.com
information@workntravel.com
+64 9 363 1833
or visit us at our office: 25 Gorge Road Queenstown 9300

To: information@workntravel.com
From: DAISUKE MATSUSHIMA
Subject: Questions Regarding Working Holiday Visa

Hi,
I am Daisuke Matsushima from Japan. I am currently traveling in New Zealand and planning to stay here longer. According to the regulations, I'm only allowed to stay in your country up to three months. Therefore I'm thinking maybe applying for a working holiday visa is an option for me. Your Beginner Kit helped a friend of mine get hired in NZ fast and thus she recommended me to seek your advice and assistance. I'm wondering if your Beginner Kit also includes working holiday visa application. As I'm already in New Zealand, is it possible for me to apply for such a visa, and how long does it take to get the visa? It is very important that I get my working holiday visa before the expected departure date and get employed as soon as possible; otherwise I'll have to leave on November 19, 2018, and then come back.
I would like to stop by your Queenstown office to inquire about further membership details tomorrow morning. If you wish to contact me, I am only reachable via e-mail as I do not have a phone and contact number in NZ.
See you soon.

Warm wishes
Daisuke Matsushima

196 What is the first piece of information about?

(A) How to apply for an immigrant visa

(B) How to extend the visitor visa

(C) The working holiday visa scheme

(D) How to transfer from student visa to work visa

197 What kind of company is W&T?

(A) A working holiday service provider

(B) A travel agency

(C) An international human resources agency

(D) An immigration agency

198 Where did Daisuke hear about W&T?

(A) From a TV commercial

(B) From the radio

(C) From the Internet

(D) From a friend

199 Which word has the closest meaning to the word "quota" in the first piece of information?

(A) situation

(B) allocation

(C) application

(D) segregation

200 What's the best way to reach Daisuke in New Zealand at present?

(A) By cellphone

(B) By fax

(C) By e-mail

(D) By Skype

New TOEIC Reading Test 6
新多益**閱讀**全真模擬**試題第6回**

▶ **READING TEST**

In the Reading Test, you will read a variety of texts and answer several different types of reading comprehension questions. The entire Reading Test will last 75 minutes. There are three parts, and directions are given for each part. You are encouraged to answer as many questions as possible within the time allowed.

You must mark your answers on the separate answer sheet. Do not write your answers in the test book.

▶ **PART 5**

Directions: A word or phrase is missing in each of the sentences below. Four answer choices are given below each sentence. Select the best answer to complete the sentence. Then mark the letter (A), (B), (C), or (D) on your answer sheet.

---

101 The training program will run from October 12th to 20th,_____ which you will work in a team with other attendants.
(A) for
(B) during
(C) by
(D) at

102 Protecting our customers _____ fraud and financial crime is of utmost importance to our company.
(A) against
(B) upon
(C) with
(D) among

103 Homeowners have raced to prepay property taxes before the new tax law _____ .
(A) takes place
(B) takes exception
(C) takes effect
(D) takes sides

104 The price of bitcoins has _____ more than 25 percent from an all-time high of nearly $20,000 reached last month.
(A) discriminated
(B) duplicated
(C) deliberated
(D) depreciated

105 The theme park is _____ closed and is expected to reopen on November 1st.
(A) personally
(B) temporarily
(C) successively
(D) constantly

106 Passengers without electronic tickets need to pay the traffic fees _____ .
(A) in cash
(B) in turn
(C) in addition
(D) in common

107 Consumption of alcoholic beverages _____ your ability to drive a car or operate machinery.
(A) prejudices
(B) advances
(C) captures
(D) transpires

108 All questions concerning personnel salary should be _____ to Emily Waltz at extension 1181.
(A) introduced
(B) contributed
(C) directed
(D) attributed

109 I'll have to discuss this matter with my supervisor _____ I can give you an answer.
(A) as long as
(B) before
(C) while
(D) besides

110 Owing to the dense fog, the airport will be closed for at least a _____ 6 hours, until 8 p.m.
(A) more
(B) other
(C) further
(D) past

111 Let's look over the numbers to see _____ workable this plan is.
(A) where
(B) how
(C) whether
(D) however

112 To everyone's surprise, the new restaurant is _____ the competition.
(A) edging out
(B) digging out
(C) reaching out
(D) letting out

113 Unfortunately, I won't be able to join you for the celebration because of a _____ arrangement.
(A) prior
(B) inferior
(C) better
(D) former

114 Our salespeople are _____ on a commission-based pay system.
(A) assigned
(B) employed
(C) dispatched
(D) underscored

115 Employees _____ to take their seven-day annual leave at once must submit application two months in advance.
(A) planning
(B) to plan
(C) plans
(D) planned

116 Instead of _____ their hours on paper, part-time employees are required to do that on the company website, starting from July 1st.
(A) recorded
(B) recording
(C) being recorded
(D) been recorded

117 The exact date of the Company Sports Day has not been _____ , but it will definitely be sometime in April.
(A) integrated
(B) preserved
(C) modified
(D) determined

118 _____ creating a TV commercial, Zinova will launch its new smart phone with an Internet advertising campaign.
(A) Even though
(B) So as to
(C) Rather than
(D) With regard to

119 Production at the factory was temporarily _____ yesterday afternoon when the main machine broke down.
(A) closed
(B) halted
(C) arrested
(D) ended

120 VeMo Auto will soon _____ a new CEO to succeed Allen Freeman who is retiring at the end of the month after 40 years of dedicated service.
(A) nominate
(B) assign
(C) allocate
(D) indicate

121 East Asia Plastics, one of the country's largest plastic goods _____ , failed to meet this year's revenue target of $5 billion.
(A) provide
(B) provisions
(C) provider
(D) providers

122 The main advantage this new multi-function printer has _____ previous models is its photocopy function.
(A) over
(B) on
(C) from
(D) with

123 The couple would like _____ Angela Deli or Veronica's Restaurant to take charge of catering for the reception after their wedding ceremony.
(A) both
(B) neither
(C) either
(D) whether

124 It is _____ that no information concerning our business contract should be disclosed to third parties.
(A) publishable
(B) imperative
(C) confidential
(D) apparent

125 Under the terms of your warranty for this air conditioner, you can receive free maintenance for twelve months _____ the date of purchase.
(A) undergoing
(B) following
(C) passing
(D) preceding

126 During the last year, U.S. exports to China expanded by 18%, _____ U.S. imports from China increased by 12%.
(A) as
(B) while
(C) because
(D) since

127 After recent negotiations with government officials, Manila Spinning & Weaving Corp. has announced the _____ of a brand new textile mill in Quezon City, the Philippines.
(A) open
(B) opens
(C) opening
(D) opened

128 Unemployment is estimated to be at a gigantic 28% in the North Yorkshire, _____ many residents to seek employment in nearby cities.
(A) leave
(B) to leave
(C) left
(D) leaving

129 To maintain its position as a leading contributor to regional development, M&Mars Inc. will _____ work with local suppliers as far as possible.
(A) seldom
(B) never
(C) once again
(D) briefly

130 By offering same day delivery services in major 25 markets, we _____ increasing our revenue by 20% over the next quarter.
(A) anticipate
(B) believe
(C) consent
(D) participate

▶ PART 6

Directions: Read the texts on the following pages. A word or phrase is missing in some of the sentences. Aanswer choices are given below each of these articles. Select the best answer to complete the text. Then mark the letter (A), (B), (C) or (D) on your answer sheet.

Questions 131-134 refer to the following e-mail.

Dear Ms. Wilson,

I am Julia Robinson, the Purchasing Specialist of A&D Garment Company. We learn that your company is a leading manufacturer that produces high ___131___ fabrics; therefore we are very interested in purchasing products from you.

We would greatly appreciate it ___132___ you could send us your latest product catalogue, ___133___ .

As we wish to discuss what products to purchase in our department meeting held this Friday afternoon, we will need the catalogue by Tuesday ___134___ have enough time to review it before the meeting.

Looking forward to hearing from you as promptly as possible.

Best wishes,

Julia

131 (A) quality
(B) qualitative
(C) qualification
(D) qualify

132 (A) whether
(B) although
(C) if
(D) because

★ **133** (A) as we've already made our decision
(B) around two hours ahead of the meeting
(C) either a soft copy or a hard copy is fine
(D) while the salary is not as good as expected

134 (A) so as to
(B) according to
(C) in relation to
(D) with reference to

Questions 135-138 refer to the following information.

We believe in investing in the future and ___135___ young talent. That's why, as far back as 1975, Zap Inc. started its undergraduate scholarship scheme to help individuals realize their full potential.

As a Zap scholar, you will not only have the opportunity to work on projects that are ___136___ to your field of studies, but will also be able to experience the Zap work culture through our internship scheme. ___137___ completion of studies, Zap scholars will be deployed on various career tracks.

The application cycle will open following the release of JUPAS results and close two weeks later. Please apply via the ZapScholarship website. We thank all applicants for their interest in Zap Inc. and ___138___ .

135 (A) prepare
    (B) to prepare
    (C) preparation
    (D) preparing

136 (A) relevant
    (B) relate
    (C) reliable
    (D) relative

137 (A) For
    (B) With
    (C) On
    (D) At

★ 138 (A) believe that all applicants deserve a second chance
    (B) regret that only shortlisted applicants will be notified
    (C) welcome any comments you may wish to make
    (D) apologize for all inconvenience we may have caused

Questions 139-142 refer to the following advertisement.

All-inclusive Tour Package

We are well aware that handling the small details before a big trip is anything but relaxing. So, we're more than happy to ___139___ it for you.

By train or by plane, we organize the appropriate transportation. You receive all the necessary information before departure. ___140___ .

Your rooms and suites are waiting for you in the very comfortable Village. Lazy sleep in mornings, ___141___ naps, beauty moments, ... you'll love every minute you spend in the room.

Your meals and refreshments are also ___142___ in your package. From breakfast to the evening meal without forgetting breaks for snacks, each Village offers a generous selection of varied dishes and snacks, at practically all hours.

---

139 (A) look after
(B) take care of
(C) get on with
(D) put up with

★ **140** (A) All you need to do is to pack your bag
(B) Our room services are available 7/24
(C) As long as you make a reservation in advance.
(D) Your taxi will arrive in five minutes.

141 (A) prospective
(B) restorative
(C) innovative
(D) concentrative

142 (A) includable
(B) included
(C) including
(D) inclusive

Questions 143-146 refer to the following notice.

=== Home Investment Loans ===

If you are considering __143__ an income property, or finally buying that home-away-from-home, a First Bank Home investment loan which allows you to finance the purchase of a second property using the equity in your primary home is definitely ideal for you.

Compared __144__ a personal loan, the First Bank Home investment loan provides a better interest rate and a longer term. Generally, you'll need a down payment of 25% of the purchase price. First Bank will work with you to arrange a smaller down payment by leveraging your own assets depending on your personal circumstances.

Our mortgage specialists can quickly __145__ a mortgage amount that is comfortable for you based on your personal income and expenses. In many cases, we can even pre-approve to a specified fair market value. Once we receive your application, your First Bank mortgage specialist will contact you within 48 hours, and following the consultation, __146__ .

143 (A) purchase
(B) to purchase
(C) purchasing
(D) purchases

144 (A) to
(B) against
(C) over
(D) with

145 (A) eliminate
(B) plan
(C) calculate
(D) subtract

★ 146 (A) your order will arrive at your designated address
(B) we are looking forward to seeing you again
(C) you will receive a decision within another 72 hours
(D) the exact meeting date and time will be announced

▶ PART 7

Directions: In this part, you will read a selection of texts, such as magazine and newspaper articles, letters, and advertisements. Each text is followed by several questions. Select the best answer for each question and mark the letter (A), (B), (C), or (D) on your answer sheet.

Questions 147-149 refer to the following poster.

Christmas Bazaar

December 14-24, 2017   11 AM – 9 PM DAILY

£5 for a single day pass   £20 for a season pass

Kids 12 and under free

Kids Activities

Food • Beverages • Vendors & Crafters

Raffles • Silent Auction • Home Baked Goods

Lower Hill Park

1200 Lower Hill Road, Clifton, BS2

www.lowerhillchristmasbazaar.com

Parking is available in the Lower Hill Public Car Park £4/per day.

147 What is this poster for?
(A) To invite vendors
(B) To advertise for a car park
(C) To promote an event
(D) To recruit event planners

148 What do we know about the bazaar according to the poster?
(A) It's an 11-day event.
(B) It's an annual event.
(C) It's a campus event.
(D) It's a company event.

149 What can't people do at the bazaar?
(A) Bid for the items they like
(B) Draw lots
(C) Watch animals doing tricks
(D) Enjoy handmade cookies

Questions 150-152 refer to the following advertisement.

Unlike many news organizations, we haven't put up a pay wall so as to keep our journalism as open as we can. Investigative journalism takes a lot of time, money and hard work to produce. With the proceeds we get from advertising coming down, we increasingly need our readers to fund us. If you read our reporting and you like it and you're willing to help fund it, our future would be much more secure. Support us for £4.99 a month.

Click here to become a supporter

150 Where most likely can we see this advertisement?
(A) On a news website
(B) In a storybook
(C) In a medical journal
(D) On a class bulletin board

151 What's the purpose of this advertisement?
(A) To give a warning
(B) To announce an event
(C) To raise money
(D) To recruit volunteers

152 Who is most likely to become a supporter?
(A) A party goer
(B) A workaholic
(C) A loyal reader
(D) A shopping queen

Questions 153-155 refer to the following notice.

Introduction to Funding Further Study

Thu 19 Jan 2018, 3:15 PM to 4:00 PM
Careers Service, 6 Christopher Avenue - Training Room 2

This 45-minute short talk will help you come to grips with funding Masters and PhDs, including scholarships, grants, government loans and other funding opportunities.

This session covers:

• Useful resources you can use when applying for funding

• Some examples of funders, including research councils and charities

• Where to find PG student case studies

• Experience sharing: Two examples of students who have been granted funding

The seminar is free but places are limited, so registration is required. To register, please email Catherine Rubens (C.Rubens630@clifton.ac.uk).

153 What is the purpose of this seminar?
(A) To provide funding information
(B) To recruit higher education students
(C) To train a group of new employees
(D) To present a business proposal

154 Who is this seminar for?
(A) Those who needs funding for business
(B) Those who needs support for higher education
(C) Those who are seeking employment
(D) Those who are getting married

155 What should one do before attending the seminar?
(A) Fill out the request form
(B) Pay a registration fee
(C) Contact Catherine Rubens
(D) Purchase a ticket

Questions 156-159 refer to the following news.

Daily London

Charlie Harvey for dailylondon.co.uk   Monday 23 Jan 2017 5:25 pm

For the first time, London Mayor Sadiq Khan issued the highest air pollution alert today, indicating that the capital's air is a 'health crisis'. Figures showed that at 3pm today, the air in the capital city was even worse than that in smoggy Beijing. Public Health England suggests that people who live in the capital, or anywhere else subject to an alert, should reduce exercise outside.

Experts from King's College believe the recent spell of air pollution in London was the worst since 2011, and was resulted from the combination of traffic pollution and air pollution from wood burning, which was to keep households warm during the winter.

Cancer research proved that air pollution is carcinogenic to humans and can lead to lung cancer. According to the statistics, outdoor air pollution contributes to 9,500 premature deaths in London every year. It not only worsens existing lung conditions but also increases the risk of getting lung cancer.

Some schools have banned children from playing outdoors over the past few days, as the air pollution is excess of tolerable levels. "It is a shameful fact that more than 360 of our primary schools are in areas breaching legal pollution limits," said Mr. Khan.

156 Which is the best title for the news?

(A) Air Pollution Crisis in London

(B) Top Attractions in London

(C) The Worst Victims of Air Pollution

(D) How Air Pollution Measured

157 What do authorities discourage Londoners from doing?

(A) Smoking in public places

(B) Using a wood-burning stove

(C) Doing outdoor physical exercise

(D) Taking children to the parks

158 Which of the following does not contribute to London's air pollution?

(A) Vehicle exhaust

(B) Wood-burning emissions

(C) Kitchen waste

(D) Household CO2 emissions

159 Who is Sadiq Khan?

(A) The spokesman of PHE

(B) The Mayor of London

(C) An expert from King's College

(D) A cancer researcher

Questions 160-162 refer to the following post.

---

used_auto_supervisor Want to own a Mercedes-Benz E Class E350? We have a beautiful used 2015 Mercedes-Benz E Class E350 for sale and you can have it for only $18,999 now! BlueTEC AMG Night Edition 4dr 9G-Tronic available. Heated leather seats – 18" alloy wheels - Cruise Control. Bluetooth-Electric Folding Mirrors - Paddle Shift.

We are here Mon-Fri 9AM-6PM and Sat 9AM-4PM and ready to get you approved. Give us a call at (313) 635-7600, stop in, or visit our website www.usedautosupervisor.com for more info.

#usedcarforsale #benz_e350

 252 ▪ 3

---

diva_magicgirl   Nice. Wish I could afford it.

....

jonathan_1227   @samwang check this out

....

serena2001   @jackwu88 this might be the one you're looking for!

---

160 What is the purpose of this post?
(A) To promote a tour package
(B) To sell a used car
(C) To rent an apartment
(D) To find a roommate

161 Who of the following was most likely to write this post?
(A) A used car dealer
(B) A bookstore owner
(C) A fire fighter
(D) A middle school student

162 Which is NOT a means to get further details about the used car?
(A) Visit the website
(B) Inquire via e-mail
(C) Inquire via phone
(D) Visit the dealership

Questions 163-164 refer to the following advertisement.

2018 Rosa Airlines
Rock 'n' Roll Buckingham
Marathon & 1/2 Marathon

Saturday, March 10, 2018
Rock 'n' Roll Buckingham Square
3218 West Regent Street, Buckingham, BC10903

The Rosa Airlines Rock 'n' Roll Buckingham Marathon & 1/2 Marathon returns March 10, 2018 and you're invited to ROCK the biggest running festival to hit the city!

More than just a financial city, Buckingham is a cultural city with an endless list of things to do and experience during race weekend. Meet us at the Starting Line and experience it for yourself!

| Register Now for ~~$109.99~~ $99 | Price Increase In: 5 days 13 hours 21 min |

163 Who is the event organizer?
(A) The Buckingham city government
(B) The Rosa Airlines
(C) The International Marathon Association
(D) None of the above

164 According to this advertisement, which statement is true?
(A) Reduced registration fee is available for the time being.
(B) Participants must be at least 18 years old.
(C) The event is for the staff of Rosa Airlines only.
(D) Buckingham is a political city rather than a cultural city.

★Questions 165-166 refer to the following text message.

< **FE Telecom** ⠀⠀⠀⠀⠀⠀⠀⠀⠀⠀⠀⠀⠀⠀⠀⠀⠀⠀⠀⠀⠀⠀⠀⠀⠀⠀⠀⠀⠀⠀⠀⠀⠀ Delete

--------------------------- February 24, 2018 ----------------------------------

Dear Ms. Thomason, you have missed your last month's mobile phone payment of $139.59.

Please settle the overdue amount immediately to avoid extra charges. If the payment has already been settled, please accept our apologies and disregard this message.

Thank you very much.

⠀⠀ 11:02

---

165 What is the purpose of this text message?
(A) It's a payment reminder.
(B) It's a reservation confirmation.
(C) It's an apology for a late payment.
(D) It's an appointment reminder.

166 Which of the following can replace the word "disregard" in this message?
(A) dismiss
(B) eliminate
(C) ignore
(D) disvalue

Questions 167-169 refer to the following e-mail.

Dear Mr. Jackson,

I on behalf of G&P Inc. would like to thank you for your time and effort that you have put into offering us this proposal. We have reviewed your proposal in detail. Overall we're quite happy with it, except your proposed price was too high. We hope you understand that our team has been given a specific budget for this project and therefore we must get this contract within the budget.

Your price needs to be lower than what you have quoted in your initial proposal; otherwise we'll have to look for other suppliers. Please consider our offer and look forward to your positive reply.

Best regards,
Jennifer Booth

---

167 What is the purpose of this e-mail?
(A) To request for compensation
(B) To negotiate for a lower price
(C) To request a deadline extension
(D) To propose a business plan

168 Who most likely is Mr. Jackson?
(A) Jennifer Booth's supervisor
(B) Marketing Manager of G&P Inc.
(C) A major shareholder of G&P Inc.
(D) A contracted supplier of G&P Inc.

169 What will G&P Inc. do if Mr. Jackson won't change his quote?
(A) Increase their budget
(B) Seek other suppliers
(C) Accelerate their production
(D) Reduce their office expenses

RECYCLE YOUR CLOTHES— New Life to Old Clothes
Bring It to CAP Stores!

If you have any clothes or textiles that are no longer wanted or needed, no matter what brand or what condition, bring them to CAP to give them a new purpose through our garment collecting scheme and receive a $5 voucher for your next purchase in return!

It is now as easy as possible for you to give your unwanted garments a new life.
Once the old garments have been dropped off in a store, our partner W-Pigeon collects and sort them into three categories of :

• To be reworn – wearable clothing will be sold as second-hand clothes.
• To be reused – old clothes and textiles that are no longer wearable will be turned into other products, such as cleaning cloths.
• To be recycled – everything else is turned into textile fibres.

For each kilogram of textiles that CAP collects, 0.05 US Dollars will be donated to a local charity organization. Please read more at www.cap. charity.com.

170 What is the purpose of the garment-collecting scheme?
(A) To give unwanted clothes a new purpose
(B) To recruit talented fashion designers
(C) To increase the sales volume
(D) To improve the store's reputation

171 What most likely is "W-Pigeon"?
(A) A clothes recycling provider
(B) A fabric supplier
(C) A cleaner
(D) A hypermarket

172 What will the store offer in exchange for the unwanted garments?
(A) A free membership
(B) A $5 voucher for the next purchase
(C) A thank you card
(D) A donation certificate

Questions 173-175 refer to the following webpage.

Visit Ada Müller's Family Homes
A unique opportunity to explore Ada Müller's world

Discover the life and times of Ada Müller across five unique properties in and around Cologne-upon-Rhine and let your imagination run wild. Find out where this great writer of all time was born and where she and her family lived, the places she visited, and gained a new perspective on life in the sixteenth and seventeenth centuries. You'll be amazed just how much of Ada Müller's world remains.

All properties are open daily throughout the year unless otherwise specified below –

– Ada Müller's Birthplace opens daily from 10am- 4pm except:
24 Dec: 10am - 2pm (Last entry 1pm)
25 Dec: Closed
26 Dec: 11am - 4pm (Last entry 3pm)
1 Jan: 11am- 4pm
– Ada Müller's Studio opens daily from 10am- 4pm except:
24 Dec: 10am - 1.30pm (Last entry 1pm)
25 Dec: Closed
26 Dec: 11am - 4pm (Last entry 3pm)
1 Jan: 11am- 4pm
– Ada Müller's House opens daily from 10am- 4pm except:
24 Dec: 10am - 1.30pm (Last entry 1pm)
25 & 26 Dec: Closed
1 Jan: 11am- 4pm
– Eva Müller's Cottage opens daily from 10am- 4pm except:
24 Dec: 10am - 2pm (Last entry 1pm)
25 & 26 Dec: Closed
1 Jan: 11am- 4pm
– Evans Müller's Farm is now closed for the winter.
It will be open 10 March - 4 November 2018

Click here to book now and save 10%!

173 About Ada Müller, which statement is correct?

(A) She was a famous actress in sixteenth century.

(B) She was the wife of a great writer.

(C) Her homes have become tourist attractions.

(D) She lived alone by herself in a cottage.

174 On which day are all Ada Müller's properties closed?

(A) The first day of the year

(B) The last day of the year

(C) Christmas

(D) Ada Müller's birthday

175 Which property is open throughout the year except the winter?

(A) Evans Müller's Farm

(B) Ada Müller's Birthplace

(C) Ada Müller's Studio

(D) Eva Müller's Cottage

Isabella Clothing Inc. Order Confirmation

Order Number: AH23986BL235
Order Date: February 12, 2018
Customer Name: Joanna Press
Contact Phone: 033-1288-8821

Dear Ms. Press,

Thank you for ordering products from our company. Your order for the following items has been received and has been processed:

Requested items:	Size	Qty	Price
#35346093 *Ribbed jumper --grey*	L	1	£11.99
#73012948 *Denim super-stretch trousers*	28"	1	£25.99
#88239424 *Hooded fleece top --pink*	14	1	£14.99
Subtotal			£52.97
First online purchase discount -20%			-£10.59
Delivery			£0.00
Total			£42.38

Your order has been shipped to the designated convenience store as below:

LORRY's **Hartcliff Store:** 128 Hartcliff Road, Leicester LC2

★We will send you a text message on the day your item has arrived at your designated convenience store for you to collect.

Thank you for shopping with Isabella Clothing Inc.

< **QB Logistics** | Delete |

---------------------------- February 14, 2018 ----------------------------------

Dear Ms. Joanna Press, your order # AH-23986BL235 has been successfully delivered and is available for pickup at LORRY's Hartcliff Store. Please collect your item before 5:00 PM, February 21, 2018; otherwise your order will be returned to sender. The total amount of your order is £42.38. Thank you very much.

09:12

From: Joanna Press
To: Isabella Clothing <customerservice@isabellaclothing.co.uk>
Date: Feb 14, 2018
Subject: Item Arrived Defective

Hi,

I am writing this letter regarding my order, AH23986BL235, with you for three items on Feb 12. I hate to cause trouble but an item I purchased arrived defective. The zipper of the denim trousers is broken. The zipper cannot work at all because the teeth don't line up. I have taken some pictures of the defect and would like to return this item for a full refund. Please contact me as soon as possible.

Looking forward to your prompt reply.

Regards,
Joanna Press

176 About the order, which of the following is true?

(A) The payment was settled by installments.

(B) The order will be delivered to the buyer's place.

(C) The buyer was charged a delivery fee of £3.00.

(D) The order will be collected at a convenience store.

177 What is the purpose of the text message?

(A) It's a pickup notice.

(B) It's a meeting notice.

(C) It's an invitation.

(D) It's an order cancellation.

178 According to the text message, how long will the convenience store keep the item for the buyer?

(A) Two days

(B) Five days

(C) Seven days

(D) Two weeks

179 Why is Joanna writing this e-mail?

(A) She is pleased with the items.

(B) One of her items arrived defective.

(C) She wants to change the order.

(D) Her order has not arrived yet.

180 What will Joanna do with the trousers?

(A) Return it for a refund

(B) Exchange it at the store

(C) Give it to her sister

(D) Take it to the store for alteration

★Questions 181-185 refer to the following message and e-mails.

Telephone Message

For: <u>Prof. Wellington</u>   From: <u>Ms. Davenport</u>
Date: <u>December 12</u>   Time: <u>16:02</u>

Message: Brighten City University of Science & Technology wants to invite you to be the Chief Guest as well as deliver a speech on their commencement on June 16, 2018. The school sent you a formal invitation on December 1st, but hasn't received a reply from you. Please could you confirm your attendance by sending an e-mail at your earliest convenience. The management and the Graduation Preparation Team are expecting your positive response. Thank you.

Action required: ☐ Please call back Tel No. _____
                 ☐ Caller will call back later
                 ☐ No action required
                 ☑ Other: <u>Please confirm by e-mail</u>

Message taken by: <u>Brenda</u>

From: David Wellington   December 13, 8:25AM
To: Linda Davenport
Subject: Invitation Acceptance

Dear Ms. Davenport,

I got a message from you yesterday regarding the commencement speech invitation. Please accept my sincere apology for not replying earlier. I was attending an academic conference in Beijing when I received your invitation and just returned to UK two days ago. I had been considering whether to accept the invitation before my assistant handed me the message note yesterday.

It's an honor for me to be invited to give a speech as the Chief Guest. I am pleased to accept your invitation to address the graduates at the Commencement on June 16th, 2018. As you requested, I am sending you this letter to confirm my attendance.

Best wishes,
David Wellington

From: Linda Davenport   December 13 at 10:11AM
To: David Wellington
Subject: Re: Invitation Acceptance

Dear Prof. Wellington,

We would like to extend our sincere gratitude and appreciation to you
for kindly accepting our invitation to be our Chief Guest and speak
to our graduates at their commencement on June 16th 2018. Your
presence will grace this memorable occasion. The ceremony begins
at 9:45 AM at Brighten Hall and is estimated to end by 11:00 AM. The
preparation team is planning on giving a lunch party following the
commencement, and we would like to invite you to join us.

I will contact you the first week in June to finalize the arrangements.
Once again, thank you for taking part in our commencement.

Warm wishes,
Linda Davenport
Director of Graduation Preparation Team

181 What is the purpose of the telephone message?
(A) To request an interview
(B) To request a meeting
(C) To ask for a reply to an invitation
(D) To ask for payment

182 What is Prof. Wellington invited to do at the commencement?
(A) To award prizes
(B) To address the graduates
(C) To give a presentation
(D) To interview the job candidates

183 How long is the commencement estimated to last?

(A) One hour

(B) One and a half hours

(C) One hour and a quarter

(D) Two hours

184 According to the second e-mail, what will be held following the ceremony?

(A) A lunch party

(B) A tea party

(C) An academic conference

(D) A impromptu meeting

185 When will Prof. Wellington be informed of the final arrangement?

(A) Before Christmas

(B) A week before the graduation

(C) At the beginning of June

(D) By the end of June

★Questions 186-190 refer to the following advertisement, reservation and e-mail.

Sky Tower Restaurant

Champ de Mars, 101 Avenue Anatole France, 75007 Paris, France
dineandwine@skytower.paris
+33-1-4573-8666

Sky Tower Restaurant is a food experience not to be missed - the menu is best described as French contemporary with a delicious selection of exceptional dishes beautifully presented. Sky Tower offers splendid views of city Paris and sumptuous interiors, including the deluxe private dining room, Adèle, which is suitable for up to 16 guests. To reserve this space please contact our events team
groups@skytower.paris.

Dining at our rooftop bar is also a delightfully classy experience where guests can enjoy an impressive list of wine and cocktails as well as the full a la carte menu. Bookings for tables at the bar can also be made through our reservations system.

We welcome and encourage style, but please note that we do not permit shorts, sportswear, sports trainers or flip flops. Our management reserves the right to refuse admission to anyone we feel is inappropriately dressed. Guests aged 16-17 are welcome in our bar and lounge areas accompanied by an adult (aged 21+).

Lunch: Mon-Sun: 11:45am-2:45pm / Dinner: Mon-Sun: 5:45pm-10:15pm
We accept bookings 60 days in advance.

From: Josephine Cochran

To: <groups@skytower.paris>

Subject: Adèle Reservation

Hi,

I read an article about your restaurant in Top Paris magazine Issue March 2018 and found it a nice place for my family gathering. Therefore I am writing this letter to reserve the private dining room on April 24, Tuesday. There are 15 of us, and we'll be needing the room from 6 pm to 9 pm for a family dinner in celebration of my grandparents' 60th anniversary. Please let me know whether Adèle is available at the time mentioned above.

Also, I'd like to know if we could bring our own wine to the restaurant. I understand that your rooftop bar provides the guests with a wide range of wines and cocktails, but we'd like to bring our own special wine from my grandpa's vineyard.

Looking forward to your prompt response.

Regards,

Josephine

From: Adèle Room

To: Josephine Cochran

Subject: Re: Adèle Reservation

Dear Ms. Cochran,

Thanks for your making a reservation with us. Adèle Room is reserved for you for your designated date and time. We will be very glad to receive you in our establishment. We warmly welcome you and your family to spend the meaningful and memorable night of celebration with us.

In regard to your request to bring your own wine, please note that according to the restaurant's policy, we will charge a €30 corkage fee for wine (€60 for a magnum) and €75 for Champagne (€150 for a magnum). Thanks for your understanding.

We look forward to receiving you on April 24.

Best wishes

186 What does "Adèle" refer to in the advertisement?
(A) The restaurant manager
(B) The private dining rooms
(C) The rooftop bar
(D) The chef's signature dish

187 Which of the following is most likely the restaurant's dress code?
(A) Cocktail attire
(B) Business attire
(C) Beach attire
(D) Smart casual

188 Where does Josephine hear about the restaurant?
(A) From a journal
(B) From the social media
(C) From TV
(D) From a friend

189 According to the first e-mail, what is the purpose of the dinner gathering?
(A) To celebrate a colleague's promotion
(B) To celebrate a couple's anniversary
(C) To celebrate a friend's birthday
(D) To welcome new employees

190 According to the second e-mail, when will the restaurant charge a "corkage fee"?
(A) When the guests bring their own food
(B) When the guests don't reserve in advance
(C) When the guests don't show up on time
(D) When the guests bring their own wine

★Questions 191-195 refer to the following e-mails and agenda.

From: Abby Gilmore
To: R&D Department
Subject: Monthly Meeting Notice
Attachment: 📄 Meeting Agenda for March 2018. doc

Dear all,

We have scheduled our monthly Research & Development meeting in the conference room at 10:00 a.m. on Friday, March 16.

Each of us should be prepared to give an update on our current projects, following Brian and Lillian's report on the meeting with their Japanese counterparts. We will also discuss the upcoming projects for the next six months in the meeting. Attached please find a draft agenda for our meeting.

Should there be any questions with regard to information contained in this meeting notice, or if the scheduled date, time or location of the meeting is not convenient for you, please do not hesitate to contact me on extension #331.

We look forward to your participation in this important meeting.

Sincerely,
Abby Gilmore
R&D Department Assistant

Agenda for March Meeting, 2018

10:00 -	-Meeting begins-
10:00 – 10:15	-Brian and Lillian's report-
10:15 – 10:45	-Updates on current projects-
10:45 – 12:20	-New product development- 1. New product ideas 2. Possible applications of new product 3. Cost of product development 4. Workable development plan 5. Realistic schedule
12:30	-Meeting adjourns-

From: Helena Sunders

To: R&D Department

Subject: Monthly Meeting Minutes

_____

Dear all,

Thank you all for another worthwhile meeting yesterday. I am excited about all the accomplishments we have made in the meeting.

The meeting minutes have been compiled, transcribed and proofread and are now attached to this mail for your review. Please take a few minutes to review the meeting minutes and feel free to contact me if you notice any discrepancies between the minutes and the actual meeting content.

The R&D Monthly Meeting will reconvene in the main conference room at 10:00am on April 13th. Look forward to seeing you again and brainstorming with you all.

Best wishes,

Helena Sunders

---

191 What are all attendants of the meeting asked to do?
(A) Have a short talk with the moderator
(B) Register for the meeting
(C) Give an update on the current projects
(D) Add an agenda item

192 What will Brian and Lillian report on?
(A) The meeting with their Japanese counterparts
(B) New product development schedule
(C) New production launch plan
(D) The on-the-job training program

193 According to the agenda, what will the meeting focus on?
(A) New product development
(B) New marketing strategies
(C) Staff requirement
(D) Budget revision

194 Who is most likely in charge of the minutes in the meeting?
(A) Brian
(B) Helena Sunders
(C) Abby Gilmore
(D) Lillian

195 Which of the following is closest to the word "reconvene" in meaning?
(A) Reunite
(B) Redeem
(C) Rewind
(D) Revert

Position: Senior Office Manager
Employer: Halvard Financial Edinburg

Halvard Financial Planning Inc. is opening a branch office in Edinburg in May 2018. Renovation on the location is expected to be concluded by the end of April. Thus, Halvard Financial Planning is interested in hiring a Senior Office Manager for our new location.

Candidates must have at least five years experience as an Office Manger in a related field. A Bachelor's Degree or higher is required. Preference will be given to those who hold degrees in business administration and finance. Experience in financial planning is a considerable asset.

Key responsibilities of this position include hiring new staff members, payroll managements, accounts management, responding to customer service issues in a timely manner and all other duties related to the smooth operation of an office environment.

We welcome anyone that can creatively perform in this demanding environment to apply for this position. Please send an application letter including your resume to hr_hiring@hvfinancialplanning.com no later than Mach 20th.

Dear Sir/Ma'am,

I saw, with interest, your advertisement looking for a Senior Office Manager on your website and would like to recommend myself for this position at Halvard Financial Planning Inc.

I am currently employed as the Financial Controller for NHP Corp, where I have been working for 6 years since I earned my Master's degree in Business Administration from the University of Washington. I believe the skills and experiences I have obtained make me an ideal candidate for the position.

My experience in NHP Corp as a financial controller has afforded me the opportunity to develop considerable skills in payroll management and accounts management. In addition, through my work with NHP Corp., I have become heavily involved in handling customer complaints and related issues. I am confident that my experience in NHP and my academic background in business administration qualify me for consideration.

I am enclosing my latest resume for your review in hopes of meeting with you to discuss my qualifications in more detail.

Sincerely,
Danny Peterson

Dear Mr. Peterson,

Thank you for submitting an application for the position of Senior Office Manager with Halvard Financial Planning Inc. in Edinburg.

We have looked over your resume and would like to invite you to have an interview with us. Your interview has been scheduled for April 2, 2018, 10 am in our head office, located at 212 N Business Highway 181, Edinburg TX15845-6264

Please bring along the following documentation with you to the interview: two passport-size photos, proof of ID, and your highest degree diploma.

Please call Becky at 877-222-3333 to confirm your attendance by 5pm on March 30th or email me if you have any questions or need to reschedule.

Regards,
Patty Johnson
HR Manager
Halvard Financial Planning Inc.

196 What's the purpose of the notice?

(A) To announce a job fair

(B) To announce a renovation

(C) To announce a holiday closing

(D) To announce a vacancy

197 Which is excluded from the qualifications for the Senior Office Manager?

(A) A Bachelor's degree

(B) Management experience

(C) Excellent English proficiency

(D) Work experience in related field

198 What's the purpose of the first e-mail?

(A) To request for a meeting

(B) To inquire about the status of application

(C) To apply for a job vacancy

(D) To reply to a request

199 According to the Danny's e-mail, which statement is correct?

(A) Danny doesn't meet the academic qualifications.

(B) Danny is planning to change jobs.

(C) Danny lacks experience in management.

(D) Danny is now between jobs.

200 What is Danny supposed to do by March 30th?

(A) Pay Patty Johnson a visit

(B) Register for a place online

(C) Resign his position at NHP

(D) Confirm his attendance

閱讀關鍵解題分析

新多益閱讀全真模擬試題解析 — 第1~6回

New TOEIC Reading Analysis 1
新多益閱讀全真模擬試題解析第1回

我們在軟體上經常性出現的問題將會交給開發人員檢驗。

【類型】形容詞詞彙題型

【詞彙】
software 軟體／
investigate 調查／
developer 開發者／
rewarding 有回報的／
award 獎項／
recurring 一再發生的／
occur 發生

【正解】(C)

101 The _____ problem with our software will be investigated by the developers.
(A) rewarding
(B) awarding
(C) recurring
(D) occurring

【解析】本題空格出現在名詞problem之前,因此必須選填一個形容詞。根據語義最符合的選項為(C)。(B)(D)選項的動詞並無用現在分詞當形容詞的用法。

請在指定日期之前妥善保留此張票,否則您可能被收取五千元新台幣的罰款。

【類型】連接詞題型

【詞彙】
retain保留／specify明確說明／
charge收費／otherwise否則／
moreover再者／despite即使

【正解】(A)

102 Please keep this ticket until the specified date, _____ you may be charged a fine of NT 5,000.
(A) otherwise
(B) although
(C) moreover
(D) despite

【解析】本題空格於兩個句子之間,因此需選填一個連接詞。根據語義應選(A)否則。(C)選項為副詞。(D)選項為介系詞。

費雪先生再過幾週將會被調派至舊金山的分行。

【類型】動詞時態題型

【詞彙】
branch 分行;分公司／
transfer 調派;轉學;轉帳;換乘交通工具

【正解】(D)

103 Mr. Fisher _____ to the branch in San Francisco in a couple of weeks.
(A) transfer
(B) is transferred
(C) will transfer
(D) will be transferred

【解析】題幹的時間為in+一段時間表示「再過……時間」,為未來式。而費雪先生是「被」調派,因此應選未來式被動態的(D)選項。

104 This email is for the attention of the employees on probation _____ those who have completed all the assessments and are awaiting the results.

(A) in addition
(B) unless
(C) due to
(D) except

【解析】空格後方接的those為代名詞,可知此空格為一介系詞。In addition為副詞片語;unless為連接詞;due to雖為介系詞片語但其語義為「由於」。因此,綜合詞性及語義判斷,正解為(D)。

此封電子郵件敬呈於試用期期間之員工,已完成全數考核並等待結果通知的員工可不加以理會。

【類型】介系詞題型

【詞彙】
probation 試用／
assessment 考核;評量／
await 等待／
announcement 宣布／
unless 除非／except 除了

【正解】(D)

---

105 Remember to _____ inventory before you get off work today.

(A) take
(B) get
(C) draw
(D) meet

【解析】take inventory意思為「檢查庫存」。take是固定動詞搭配語。

今天下班前記得要清點庫存。

【類型】動詞搭配語題型

【詞彙】
inventory 庫存／
get off work 下班

【正解】(A)

---

106 Despite the _____ of social media, face-to-face conversations are still a crucial way to build up business relationships.

(A) authenticity
(B) decrease
(C) emergency
(D) prevalence

【解析】despite是「即使」的意思。表示承認社交媒體的「盛行」或「普及」,但是也不能否認面對面交談的重要性。根據語義判斷,正解為(D)。

即使社交媒體十分盛行,面對面的交談仍然是建立貿易關係的一個重要方式。

【類型】名詞詞彙題型

【詞彙】
despite 即使／crucial 重要的／
business relationship 貿易關係／
authenticity 真實性／
decrease 減少／
emergency 緊急狀況／
prevalence 盛行

【正解】(D)

對我們而言，在這個培訓課程中讓自己獲得所需的知識和技能是相當重要的。

【類型】代名詞題型

【詞彙】
equip 裝備／program 課程

【正解】(D)

107 It is important for us to equip _____ with all the knowledge and skills needed in the training program.

(A) we
(B) us
(C) ours
(D) ourselves

【解析】題意為「為我們自己獲取知識和技能」，需用「反身代名詞」ourselves。

本部門已將您取消門票的退款匯回您的帳戶。退款日程需三天。

【類型】動詞詞彙題型

【詞彙】
refund 退款／account 帳戶／process 處理／book 預訂／issue 派發／launch 發起；上映／withdraw 取回

【正解】(B)

108 Our department has _____ a refund to your account for the cancelled ticket. Please allow three days for this to be processed.

(A) booked
(B) issued
(C) launched
(D) withdrew

【解析】issue的意思為官方「核發」某筆款項或「發行」某物。launch的意思是「發起」或「發動」某項運動。

如果您能撥空十分鐘完成此份產品滿意度的調查問卷，我們將非常感激。

【類型】關係代名詞題型

【詞彙】
grateful 感激／spare 空出／survey 調查／satisfied 感到滿意的／product 產品

【正解】(C)

109 We will be grateful if you could spare up to ten minutes to complete this survey _____ looks into how you are satisfied with our product.

(A) who
(B) it
(C) which
(D) whose

【解析】當先行詞為survey事物時，關係代名詞需用which或that引導關係子句。

110 We are sorry to tell you that this service is not _____ in Asia; however, we do provide similar service that suits your needs.

(A) responsible
(B) available
(C) reversible
(D) susceptible

【解析】題幹語義為「此服務在亞洲地區不可獲得」，根據語義，答案為available。

我們很遺憾必須告知您我們在亞洲地區並無提供此項服務。然而，我們有提供類似的服務同樣能滿足您的需求。

【類型】形容詞詞彙題型

【詞彙】
provide 提供／suit 符合／
responsible 負責任的／
available 可得到的／
reversible 可恢復的／
susceptible 易受到……影響的

【正解】(B)

---

111 The film was made in _____ with Dreamland Studio featuring its state-of-the art animation and visual effects.

(A) collection
(B) celebration
(C) calibration
(D) collaboration

【解析】in collaboration with表示「與……合作」。

這部片子特與Dreamland工作室合作，置入了該工作室最先進的動畫及視覺特效技術。

【類型】名詞詞彙題型

【詞彙】
feature 以……為特色／
state-of-the-art 最先進的／
animation 動畫／visual effect
視覺特效／collection 收集組／
celebration 慶祝／calibration
校準／collaboration 合作

【正解】(D)

---

112 Customers _____ on an early morning flight are allowed to check in their baggage at the airport the evening before their departure day.

(A) traveling
(B) travel
(C) to travel
(D) traveled

【解析】原句Customers who travel on an early morning flight are...經過分詞構句簡化，將who省略並將動詞改為現在分詞traveling。

搭乘早班班機的旅客可在出發日前一晚於機場辦理行李托運。

【類型】動詞型態題型

【詞彙】
customer 顧客／flight 班機／
allow 允許／baggage 行李／
departure 離開

【正解】(A)

符合獎學金申請資格的國際學生應於三月一日前將申請表提交給註冊組。

【類型】形容詞詞彙題型

【詞彙】
scholarship 獎學金／
submit 呈交／application form
申請表／admission 錄用／
accessible 可獲得的／eligible
有資格的／capable 有能力的／
renewable 可更新的

【正解】(B)

---

113 International students who are _____ for the scholarship should submit the application form to the admissions office by March 1st.

(A) accessible
(B) eligible
(C) capable
(D) renewable

【解析】be eligible for：在……方面有資格，根據語義，答案選(B)。

自從懷特女士在十年前的經濟大蕭條中失業後一直未能找到工作。

【類型】動詞時態題型

【詞彙】
unemployed 失業的／
economic recession 經濟衰退／
decade 十年

【正解】(B)

---

114 Mrs. White has been unemployed since she _____ her job in the economic recession a decade ago.

(A) loses
(B) lost
(C) has lost
(D) was lost

【解析】since引導的子句的時態為a decade ago十年前，為一過去的時間點，因此動詞用lose的過去式lost。

我們提供卡迪夫地區的公司以及學校餐飲服務。

【類型】連接詞題型

【詞彙】
corporate 公司的／
catering service 餐飲提供服務／
both...and... 兩者都……

【正解】(D)

---

115 We offer _____ corporate and school catering services in Cardiff.

(A) neither
(B) either
(C) not only
(D) both

【解析】neither...nor...不是……也不是……／either...or...不是……就是……／not only...but also...不僅……還……／both...and...兩者都

116 A _____ salesperson always speaks eloquently.

(A) success
(B) succeed
(C) successful
(D) successive

【解析】success成功（名）／succeed成功（動）／
successful成功的（形）／successive連續的（形）

一位成功的銷售員說話總能滔滔雄辯。

【類型】詞類變化題型

【詞彙】
salesperson 銷售員／
eloquently 滔滔雄辯地

【正解】(C)

---

117 Sara _____ a note on your desk when she left the office yesterday.

(A) leaves
(B) left
(C) has left
(D) has been left

【解析】本題時間提示when she left the office yesterday為過去一個時間點，因此動詞選leave的過去式left。

當Sara昨天離開辦公室時，她在你的桌上留了一張便條紙。

【類型】動詞時態題型

【詞彙】
note 便條紙／leave 留下

【正解】(B)

---

118 They bought a new projector _____ the old one is beyond repair.

(A) but
(B) so
(C) since
(D) thus

【解析】since在本題的語義為「因為」，表因果關係。另外考生須注意so跟thus雖然語意相近，但so為連接詞，用於連接兩個句子；而thus為副詞，不能充當連接詞用。

他們買了一台新投影機，因為舊的那台已經無法修理了。

【類型】連接詞題型

【詞彙】
projector 投影機／repair 修理／
thus 於是

【正解】(C)

無論處境多艱困，我們都不能放棄。

【類型】副詞題型

【詞彙】
give up 放棄／tough 艱困／
however 無論如何

【正解】(A)

119 We must not give up _____ tough the situation is.
(A) however
(B) whenever
(C) whatever
(D) wherever

【解析】however在本題為「無論如何……」的意思，可理解為no matter how...,而非表示轉折的「然而」。另外，whenever可理解為no matter when；whatever可理解為no matter what；wherever可理解為no matter where。

這封電子郵件提醒您這份提案的截止日期。逾期不收。

【類型】名詞詞彙題型

【詞彙】
reminder 提醒／proposal 提案／
submission 提交／
obsession 執迷／deadline
截止日期／procedure 流程／
procurement 採購

【正解】(B)

120 This email is a reminder of the _____ of the proposal. No late submission is accepted.
(A) obsession
(B) deadline
(C) procedure
(D) procurement

【解析】A of B翻譯成「B的A」。the deadline of the proposal翻譯成「提案的截止日期」。

儘管Jason的聲望頗高，許多人還是不選他為會長。

【類型】片語動詞題型

【詞彙】
reputation 聲望；名譽／
president 會長

【正解】(D)

121 Despite his high reputation, many people voted _____ Jason as the president.
(A) to
(B) from
(C) for
(D) against

【解析】vote for意思為「投票給……」；vote against意思為「投反對票給……」。本題需注意despite「即使」有條件與結果互相牴觸的語義。因此根據語義邏輯，應選vote against。

122 The attendance rate of the seminar is higher _____ expected.

(A) than
(B) to
(C) then
(D) since

【解析】比較級句型：S1+V+比較級+than+S2。then是副詞，不能當作連接詞用。

本次研討會的出席率比預期的高。

【類型】比較級題型

【詞彙】
attendance rate 出席率／
seminar 研討會

【正解】(A)

---

123 _____ is the price of the office space in this area?

(A) How much
(B) How many
(C) What
(D) Where

【解析】跟price連用的疑問詞為what。What is the price of...? 相當於How much is...?考生容易犯的錯誤為How much is the price...?。

這個區域的辦公室價格多少？

【類型】疑問詞題型

【詞彙】
office space 辦公室空間

【正解】(C)

---

124 If you have any queries about renting your property, please contact our _____ via 01908871024 or the email listed.

(A) agent
(B) broker
(C) spokesperson
(D) engineer

【解析】agent的意思為經紀人，代理人。broker則是比agent職等更高的經紀人。

如果您有任何關於房產出租的疑問，請撥打01908871024或發信到以上郵箱與我們的仲介員聯繫。

【類型】名詞詞彙題型

【詞彙】
query 疑問／property 房地產／
agent 仲介；代理人／
broker 仲介；經紀人／
spokesperson 代言人

【正解】(A)

由於天氣狀況惡劣，我們必須延遲活動。

【類型】介系詞片語題型

【詞彙】
postpone 延遲／
in spite of 即使／as of 自從

【正解】(B)

125 _____ the bad weather condition, we have to postpone the event.
(A) Since
(B) Because of
(C) In spite of
(D) As of

【解析】the bad weather condition為一名詞片語，因此前面必須接介系詞片語。since為連接詞。(B), (C), (D)皆為介系詞片語，根據語義判斷，答案應選because of「由於」。

只要輸入您的位置，您就可以找到我們最實惠的租車服務。

【類型】名詞片語題型

【詞彙】
location 位置／cost-effective 經濟實惠／deal 交易／
letting 租（房）／lend 出借／
exchange 交換／rental 出租

【正解】(D)

126 Simply type in your location and find our most cost-effective car _____ deals.
(A) letting
(B) lending
(C) exchange
(D) rental

【解析】letting與rental意思皆為「出租」，但let為英式英語裡專指「房屋出租」，而rent泛指廣義的租賃或租費。另外，let是指房東將房子出租給租屋人，而rent是指租屋（物）人向房東（所有人）租用。

位於倫敦中心，Berjaya飯店是你探索這座奇幻城市的最佳住宿選擇。

【類型】動詞型態題型

【詞彙】
locate 位於

【正解】(C)

127 _____ in the heart of London, Berjaya Hotel is your perfect choice of accommodation when you travel to this amazing city.
(A) To locate
(B) Locating
(C) Located
(D) Locate

【解析】locate something in somewhere是指將某物安置於某處。因此改為被動的表示法為: something is located in somewhere。本題運用分詞構句將主詞和動詞省略，變成Located in the heart of London...。

128 The receptionist will call you _____ she receives your package.

(A) not only
(B) as soon as
(C) other than
(D) as far as

【解析】as soon as表示「一……就……」，用於連接兩個句子。not only...but also表示「不僅……還……」。other than表示「除了」。as far as表示「達到……的程度」。

前台接待人員一收到您的包裹會立即打電話給您。

【類型】連接詞題型

【詞彙】
receptionist 接待人員／
package 包裹／
as soon as 一……就……／
other than 除了／
as far as 達到……的程度

【正解】(B)

---

129 _____ my vacation, I traveled to Shanghai, Taipei and Hong Kong.

(A) Between
(B) On
(C) During
(D) From

【解析】vacation為一段時間，與during或in連用。between指「在兩個時間點之間」，如between 6:00 a.m. and 8:00 a.m.。on用於「某一天有關的任何時間」，如on Saturday；on Monday morning。from是指「從某點時間起」，如from the end of September。

在我的假期中，我去了上海，台北和香港。

【類型】介系詞題型

【詞彙】
vacation 假期

【正解】(C)

---

130 We recommend _____ this app to keep yourself updated and connected.

(A) to use
(B) use
(C) using
(D) used

【解析】recommend+ V-ing為固定用法。另外recommend可用於虛擬語氣句型：S+ recommend+(that)+ S+ Vr....，如Don recommends that the office stay open until 6 p.m.

我們推薦您使用這個應用程式獲得最新資訊。

【類型】動詞型態題型

【詞彙】
recommend 推薦／app 應用程式 (application)／update 更新

【正解】(C)

Directions: Read the texts on the following pages. A word or phrase is missing in some of the sentences. Answer choices are given below each of these articles. Select the best answer to complete the text. Then mark the letter (A), (B), (C) or (D) on your answer sheet.

Questions 131-134 refer to the following email.

日期：2017年7月31日
收件人：Ben Lim
寄件人：泰利旅行社
主旨：退款問題

親愛的Ben Lim,

感謝您告知我們關於您先前在泰利旅行的購票事宜。您之前購買的高威一日遊券在出發日期前三天都能退票。若您欲退票，您需要在出發日三天前填妥線上退票申請表並發送到我們的郵箱。一旦我們收到您的申請表，我們會立即處理您的退票事宜。退票手續需五個工作日。該筆款項可能會在手續完成後三天之後才能匯到您的帳戶。造成您的不便，我們深感抱歉。希望您下次有機會再來體驗我們為您安排的行程。

敬祝順心

Ellen

Date: 31 July, 2017
To: Ben Lim
From: Tally Tours
Subject: Refund Issue

Dear Ben Lim,

Thank you for letting us know about the issue of your Tally Tours ticket. The tickets you ___131___ for the one-day tour in Galway are refundable until as late as three days prior to the date of travel. In order to make a claim for the refund, you will need to complete the online refund application form and send it to us in an attachment no later ___132___ three days before departure. As soon as the application form is received, we will start to process your refund immediately. Please allow five working days for ___133___ to be processed. It may take another three days for any credit to appear in your account. ___134___. We are looking forward to having you on board next time.

Kind Regards,

Ellen

131 (A) developed
(B) progressed
(C) purchased
(D) utilized

【解析】題幹的主詞根據上下文語義推敲可知為「您購買的高威一日遊券」。加上根據關鍵字refundable「可退費的」，可推理出前方的動詞應為purchase「購買」。因此答案應選(C)。

【類型】動詞詞彙題型

【詞彙】
develop 研發／progress 進步／
purchase 購買／utilize利用

【正解】(C)

---

132 (A) than
(B) as
(C) to
(D) in

【解析】題幹的意思為「在出發日期三天前將申請表寄送給我們」。其中no later than意思為「不晚於」某個時間點。為一個片語連接詞，意思與before, by相近。另外，我們也可以從later推敲出後方應該接一個比較級連接詞than，因此答案應選(A)。

【類型】連接詞題型

【詞彙】
make a claim for 申請／
application form 申請表／
attachment 附件／
departure 出發

【正解】(A)

---

133 (A) me
(B) it
(C) them
(D) either

【解析】根據前一句語義「我們會立即處理您的退款事宜」。本句的代名詞明顯是代指前一句的「退款事宜」，性質為單數的事物，因此應用代名詞it。(D)選項either用在兩個選項之間的其中一個，但上下文並沒有兩者擇一的線索，因此答案應選(B)。

【類型】代名詞題型

【詞彙】
working day 工作日／
process 處理

【正解】(B)

【類型】句子插入題型

【詞彙】

credit 帳面餘額／appear 出現／
sincerely 誠心地／
accountant 會計師／
inconvenience 不便

【正解】(D)

★ 134 (A) We sincerely welcome you to join this journey
(B) We are confident that we have the best price among other companies
(C) Please note that our accountant will be on leave for the next couple of days
(D) We do apologize if this causes any inconvenience to you

【解析】根據前一句語義「款項須等到額外的三天之後才會匯入您的帳戶」。加上先前退款手續的五天，加起來一共八天。因此根據文義，應選「造成對方不便」的選項。(D)選項「如果造成您的不便，我們誠心感到抱歉」文義最為符合。

敬愛的員工：

英國公衛中心收到消息，一名春日航空的員工在住院期間確診罹患B型流行性腦脊髓膜炎。慶幸的是，該名病患已逐漸康復並很快就能出院。

有鑑於此，我們目前正與公司的健康中心同仁密切合作，努力阻止細菌的傳播。經過我們的風險評估，我們總結出目前尚無必要採取特別措施或更改任何工作行程。然而，我們依然強烈建議若您尚未接受抗體注射，請盡快施打疫苗。

Questions 135-138 refer to the following letter.

Dear employee,

Public Health England has been notified that a Spring Airline employee who ___135___ to the hospital has been confirmed to have a Meningococcal Meningitis Group B infection. I am happy to inform you that he is recovering well and will be discharged soon.

___136___ this, we are working closely with the staff at the company's health service in an attempt to reduce the chances of bacteria spreading. We have conducted a risk assessment and concluded that there is currently no need to take any specific action or change the routine for our staff. However, we still strongly recommend that you ___137___ vaccinated as soon as possible if you have not been offered an antibiotic.

Spring Airline's health service has recently been running vaccination sessions for new employees who had not been vaccinated prior to entering our company. For the other staff, you can still have this vaccination if you are eligible. ___138___, you can either contact your doctor or visit our website at www.springairline.co.uk/meningitis for further information.

Yours sincerely,

Mike Wilson
Deputy Director of Health Protection

春日航空目前正在提供就職前還未接受過疫苗的新員工疫苗施打的服務。其他員工若符合資格，您同樣也能享受疫苗施打的服務。若您對於是否符合資格有任何疑問，可以聯繫您的醫師或到我們的官網www.springairline.co.uk/meningitis瀏覽進一步的資訊。

敬祝 健康

Mike Wilson
健康中心主任

---

135 (A) admitted

(B) has admitted

(C) was admitting

(D) was admitted

【解析】本句文義表達的是「住院的員工」。由於admit為「使⋯⋯住院」，因此欲表達「某人住院」在英文中應轉換為被動語態someone is/was admitted to...。另外discharge為「使⋯⋯出院」，因此「某人出院」同樣使用被動語態someone is/was discharged from...。

【類型】動詞型態題型

【詞彙】
notify 通知／
admit 使⋯⋯住院／
confirm 確認／
meningitis 腦膜炎／
infection 感染

【正解】(D)

【類型】介系詞題型

【詞彙】
in light of 有鑒於／
in spite of 即使／
with an attempt to V. 為了／
bacteria 細菌／spread 傳播

【正解】(A)

136 (A) In light of
(B) In spite of
(C) Because
(D) Since

【解析】本題須考慮上一段的文義。在上文中提到一名春日航空的員工確診出流行性腦膜炎。因此此句應是承接此因果關係，後面接著表示公司同仁正積極與健康中心緊密合作。in light of或in the light of表示「鑑於」或「根據」，意思和because of, due to, in view of意思相近。because和since皆為連接詞，後面須接完整句子。本題空格後方為一名詞，因此選項僅須考慮介系詞。

【類型】動詞型態題型

【詞彙】
recommend 建議；推薦／
vaccinate 施打疫苗／
as soon as possible 盡快／
offer 提供／antibiotic 抗體

【正解】(A)

137 (A) get
(B) got
(C) have got
(D) are getting

【解析】vaccinate表示讓某人施打疫苗，因此某人接受疫苗在英文中比須轉換為被動語態。be/get vaccinated。recommend為與虛擬語氣連用的動詞。其句型為S+ recommend+(that)+ S+ Vr....。recommend之後接的名詞子句中的動詞應為原形動詞。因此答案選(A)。

【類型】句子插入題型

【詞彙】
eligible 有資格的／
access 取得／
uncertain 不確定／
eligibility 資格／
skeptical 懷疑／
diagnosis 診斷／contact 聯絡

【正解】(B)

★ **138** (A) If you have difficulties accessing our website
(B) If you are uncertain about your eligibility
(C) If you are skeptical about the diagnosis
(D) If you are not contacted by our practice nurse

【解析】根據前句語義「其他員工如果符合資格也可以接受疫苗施打」，後句應承接此語意，也是關於「接受疫苗施打的資格」。選項(A)關於是否能進入網站，與後句visit our website at www.springairline.co.uk/meningitis for further information矛盾。選項(C)關於對於診斷的真實性感到懷疑，與後句文義不相干。選項(D)關於與護士聯繫，但前文中沒有任何關於護士會與任何員工聯繫的資訊，因此跟文義不相干。因此，答案選(B)。

288

Questions 139-142 refer to the following post.

Happy New Year! We trust you had a restful Christmas vacation and are raring to get back to your classroom. If not, here are some wonderful activities to make your transition a little more palatable. Why not ___139___ this brand new semester with some exciting and motivational basketball from Craig Wade and Ryan Anderson? Not that into sports? Well, we also have plans for moviegoers. Come on Sunday and sink into a chair in our school theater and enjoy a movie! If you ___140___ to do some preparation, for your studies, Paul Newman and Sue Chen have a tutorial session on Monday for those who wish to hone their essay writing skills. Plus, on the same day, there will be a peer feedback task which helps to increase the ___141___ of your presentations. No matter which you choose, ___142___.

新年快樂！相信你過了一個相當放鬆的聖誕假期，而你也迫不及待想要返回校園了吧！如果還沒準備好的話，這裡有一些精彩的活動，能夠讓您一邊收心同時不會有假日症候群喔！讓有趣又充滿活力的籃球課帶領你開啟全新的學期吧！課程由Craig Wade和Ryan Anderson指導。如果你不那麼熱愛運動，我們也有專為電影愛好者量身打造的計畫！星期天在我們的校園電影院有電影欣賞的活動！如果您想要為下學期的課程做一些準備，Paul Newman和Sue Chen在星期一會開設論文寫作指導的教學課程。另外，在同一天也有一場學生討論會，幫助你讓你的簡報更加清晰易懂。無論你選擇了哪個活動，我們希望這些活動能讓各位的開學準備更加愉快喔！

---

139 (A) start
(B) starting
(C) to start
(D) to starting

【解析】why not後面加原形動詞。另外，why後面同樣加原形動詞。

【類型】動詞型態題型

【詞彙】
brand new 嶄新的／
semester 學期／
motivational 激勵人心的

【正解】(A)

---

140 (A) suggest
(B) compromise
(C) prefer
(D) register

【解析】根據語義判斷，前文提過了籃球課和電影欣賞，而此處話題轉向論文寫作，顯示了一個語意的轉折，兩方的比較。因此我們可判斷該句應是要表達「如果你比較喜歡……」。因此答案選(C)。選項(A)suggest後面須接V-ing。

【類型】動詞詞彙題型

【詞彙】
suggest 建議／
compromise 妥協／prefer 偏愛／
register 註冊／
preparation 準備／
tutorial 家教／session 課程／
hone 鑽研／essay 論文

【正解】(C)

【類型】詞類變化題型

【詞彙】

plus 另外／peer 同儕／
task 任務／increase 提升／
intelligence 智商／
intelligent 聰明的／
intelligible 可讀的；清晰的／
intelligibility 可讀性／
presentation 簡報

【正解】(D)

141 (A) intelligent
(B) intelligence
(C) intelligible
(D) intelligibility

【解析】根據語義判斷，該課程是幫助學生提高「簡報製作的清晰度」，因此答案應選(D)。

【類型】句子插入題型

【詞彙】

no matter which 無論哪個／
enjoyable 令人愉悅／
sign-up 登記／
prior to 在……之前／
aforementioned 前面提過的／
verify 查證／
requirement 需求／
position 職位／
look forward to 期待

【正解】(A)

★ **142** (A) we hope that these activities will make your school return a little more enjoyable
(B) we only accept sign-ups prior to the aforementioned date
(C) make sure you verify whether you meet the requirements of each position
(D) we wish you a pleasant new year holiday and look forward to having you back soon

【解析】根據全文語意，此處結尾應表達「所有的活動旨在幫助學生過渡收假期」的意思。選項(B)關於活動登記，但前文中並無提到任何需要登記的信息。選項(C)關於職位的要求，有關申請工作，與本文無關。選項(D)應用在放假前的祝福語，與本文的語境恰巧相反。

Questions 143-146 refer to the following review.

REVIEWS OF LOTTIE'S APARTMENT

Laura
11 October, 2017

Lottie's home was a wonderful place to ___143___ a weekend in Paris. The apartment was in a fantastic location from where you can walk to the metro station in just six minutes. It was also within walking distance to plenty of good restaurants and well-known tourist ___144___ , such as the Louvre Palace and Champs-Élysées. The apartment looked exactly the same as shown on the website and was everything we needed for our little adventure in Paris. Although our flight arrived a little late that night, Lottie was still extremely friendly and helpful in accommodating our late ___145___ . She even made some delicious cookies for us! We also had a chance to meet her husband, who was also very kind to us throughout our stay. However, ___146___ . Overall, it was a nice stay and we will definitely come back again.

Lottie公寓的評論

Laura
2017年10月11日

Lottie的公寓非常適合週末來巴黎旅行時來入住。公寓的地理位置極佳,距離地鐵站走路僅需六分鐘。許多餐廳和知名景點如:羅浮宮、香榭大道也都在步行範圍內。公寓看起來和網站照片上完全一樣,非常適合我們在巴黎的小旅行。雖然我們的班機稍有延遲,Lottie依然非常友善熱情地接待我們入住。她甚至還做了些手工餅乾給我們!我們也有機會見到她的先生,同樣也非常友善。但是,我房間的無線網路是有點不穩定。但總體來說,這次的經驗非常棒,我們下次一定會再回來。

---

143 (A) take
　　(B) spend
　　(C) cost
　　(D) pay

【解析】本題考點為四個易混淆的動詞。take為「某事物花了多少時間」。spend為「某人花了多少時間或金錢」。cost為「某事物花了多少金錢」。pay為「某人付了多少錢」。本題題幹意思為「在巴黎花了一個週末的時間」,因此答案選(B)。

【類型】動詞詞彙題型

【詞彙】
take 事物花時間／
spend 人花時間或金錢／
cost 事物花錢／pay 人付錢

【正解】(B)

【類型】名詞詞彙題型

【詞彙】
within 在……之內／
walking distance 步行距離／
well-known 知名的／
tourist attraction 觀光景點／
accommodation 住宿／
appreciation 欣賞／
transportation 交通

【正解】(D)

144 (A) accommodations
(B) appreciations
(C) transportations
(D) attractions

【解析】tourist attraction為「觀光景點」，如羅浮宮和香榭大道。因此答案選(D)。

【類型】詞類變化題型

【詞彙】
flight 班機／extremely 極度／
accommodate 使……適應；幫
忙／arrival 到達

【正解】(D)

145 (A) arrive
(B) arriving
(C) arrived
(D) arrival

【解析】accommodate our late arrival迎接遲來的我們。空格處應填一名詞，arrive的名詞為arrival，因此答案應選(D)。

【類型】句子插入題型

【詞彙】
unstable 不穩定的／
reasonable 合理的／
spacious 空間大的／
cozy 舒適的／
immaculate 完美的

【正解】(A)

★ **146** (A) the wi-fi network in my room was a little unstable
(B) the price of the room is very reasonable
(C) the living room was pretty spacious and cozy
(D) the room was so immaculate

【解析】本題關鍵詞為However「然而」轉折語。因此應選一個語意與前文相反的選項。由於前文都是對於住所的讚美，此處是稍微表達一點不完美之處。因此選項(A)無線網路稍微不穩定最符合語意。

▶ PART 7

Directions: In this part, you will read a selection of texts, such as magazine and newspaper articles, letters, and advertisements. Each text is followed by several questions. Select the best answer for each question and mark the letter (A), (B), (C), or (D) on your answer sheet.

Questions 147-148 refer to the following notice.

The Deadline for The Second Tuition Fee Installment Is 5th June 2017

Please ensure the payment is made before this date.

The amount payable is $4,253

If you encounter any problems paying, you must contact the income office.

Late payment will incur a $50 late payment charge.

Failure to pay your tuition fee will lead to legal action.

To discuss anything related to tuition fee payment, please contact
Mary Conn – Income Officer

Tel. 141-6172-8930

第二期的學費繳費截止日期為
2017年6月5日

請在截止日期前完成繳費。
金額：4,253元

若您遇到任何繳費困難，
務必與財務部連絡。
逾期繳費需額外負擔
50元的逾期費用。
若您不繳費，
您將面臨法律責任。
若您有任何問題，請連絡財務
Mary Conn。

電話：141-6172-8930

【詞彙】
deadline 截止日期／
tuition fee 學費／
payable 可支付的／
encounter 遭遇／
income office 財務部／
charge 收費／lead to 導致／
legal 法律／discuss 討論

這則通知的目的是什麼？

(A) 宣布申請延期繳費的步驟

(B) 催繳租房費用

(C) 介紹新進長官

(D) 催繳學費

【類型】尋找主旨題型

【詞彙】

announce 宣佈／

extension 延期／

procedure 手續／

call for 徵求／tuition 學費

【正解】(D)

如果學費延遲一天交會發生什麼事？

(A) 付費者可能會面臨法律責任。

(B) 付費者必須申請延期。

(C) 付費者必須額外支付50元。

(D) 付費者會被大學開除。

【類型】尋找細節題型

【詞彙】

due date 截止日／

legal 法律的／

consequence 後果／

file for 申請／remove 移除

【正解】(C)

---

147 What is the main purpose of this notice?

(A) To announce payment extension procedures

(B) To call for rent payment

(C) To introduce a new officer

(D) To ask for tuition fee payment

【解析】此篇文章的主旨貫串文章各處。只要抓住關鍵字 tuition即可知道文章的主旨是關於學費繳交。另外，通常文章主旨會顯示在標題部份，此篇標題The Deadline for The Second Tuition Fee Installment Is 5th June 2017即告訴讀者，這篇是關於學費繳交的截止時間。

---

148 What might happen if the payment is made one day after the due date?

(A) The payer might face legal consequences.

(B) The payer will have to file for an extension.

(C) The payer will need to pay an extra $50.

(D) The payer will be removed from the university.

【解析】本題問「若遲一天付款會發生什麼事？」線索藏在文中的中段Late payment will incur a $50 late payment charge. 延期付款需額外支付50元。因此答案選(C)。

Questions 149-151 refer to the following email.

Looking for someone to help (PAID)

From: Sami Wright   Aug, 10
To: me

Hi everyone,

I am currently looking for somebody to help me with transcribing video clips. You SHOULD be very good at English listening. I have a total of 48 video clips and each lasts from approximately five to twenty minutes. All you need to do is to transcribe the lines (word by word) spoken in the clips. Usually, the transcription of each video takes around twenty minutes to an hour. You will be paid $50 for the videos under five minutes, $80 for the ones between five to ten minutes, and $120 for the ones between ten to twenty minutes. You can choose to do as many clips as you can. I expect to receive all the completed transcript files no later than August 31.

Please let me know asap if you are interested in doing this job.

Best,
Sami

徵求協助（有報酬）

寄件人：Sami Wright　八月十日
收件人：我

大家好，

我目前在徵求人幫忙打影片逐字稿。您的英語聽力必須非常好。我共有48段影片，每段長約五到二十分鐘。您需要將影片中的台詞一字一句打出來。一般而言，每段影片會花上大約二十分鐘到一小時不等。每完成一個五分鐘以內的影片，您可獲得50元。完成一個五到十分鐘的影片，您可獲得80元。完成一個十到二十分鐘的影片，您可獲得120元。您接的影片數量由您決定。所有完成的逐字稿須在8月31日前回傳給我。

若您對這份工作有興趣，請盡快與我連絡。

平安

Sami

【詞彙】
currently 目前／
transcribe 抄寫／
approximately 大約／
line 台詞／
file 檔案／
asap 盡快

為何Sami要寫這封電郵？
(A) 介紹一部新上映的電影
(B) 提供翻譯協助
(C) 徵求聽力極佳的逐字稿聽打者
(D) 尋找影片編輯專家

【類型】尋找主旨題型

【詞彙】
introduce 介紹／launch 上映／
assistance 協助／
translation 翻譯／
search for 尋找／expert 專家

【正解】(C)

如果完成了一個十五分鐘的影片
聽打，他／她可以賺到多少錢？
(A) 50元
(B) 80元
(C) 120元
(D) 200元

【類型】尋找細節題型

【詞彙】
earn 賺

【正解】(C)

這個任務的截止日期是？
(A) 八月五日
(B) 八月十日
(C) 八月二十日
(D) 八月三十一日

【類型】尋找細節題型

【詞彙】
deadline 截止日期／task 任務

【正解】(D)

---

149 Why is this email written?

(A) To introduce a newly launched movie
(B) To offer assistance in translation
(C) To look for transcribers with excellent listening skills
(D) To search for video editing experts

【解析】主旨題的線索通常都藏在文章的前段。這封電郵的主旨就在內容的第一句I am currently looking for somebody to help me with transcribing video clips. You SHOULD be very good at English listening. 因此答案應選(C)。

150 How much can one earn if he/she completes a transcription of a fifteen-minute video?
(A) $50
(B) $80
(C) $120
(D) $200

【解析】此細節題包含了數字，因此在文章中需特別留意數字。從此句and $120 for the ones between ten to twenty minutes可得知十到二十分鐘的影片一則是120元。因此本題應選(C)。

151 When is the deadline for this task?

(A) August 5
(B) August 10
(C) August 20
(D) August 31

【解析】此細節題包含了日期，因此在文中需特別留意日期的線索。從此句I expect to receive all the completed transcript files no later than August 31.可得知截止日期為八月三十一日。no later than表示不能晚於，等同於截止日期的意思。因此答案應選(D)。

Questions 152-155 refer to the following advertisement.

EASYGO.COM
BOOK YOUR TRIP NOW!
Low Fare/ High Quality

Your amazing trip is just a click away.
Travelling on luxurious coaches across the country does not have to hurt your wallet. You can either book online in advance or buy on the day at a coach station. You can enjoy the low fare ticket with great value.
We take you to thousands of destinations in the UK where amazing stories are waiting.

Check out the lowest fares from where you are:

LONDON to BIRMINGHAM *one-way* *Journey time: 02h30m*	£10 BOOK NOW
LONDON to BATH *one-way* *Journey time: 02h05m*	£5 BOOK NOW
LONDON to CARDIFF *one-way* *Journey time: 02h40m*	£8 BOOK NOW
LONDON to YORK *one-way* *Journey time: 03h30m*	£25 BOOK NOW
LONDON to EDINBURGH *one-way* *Journey time: 05h25m*	£40 BOOK NOW

All the prices are subject to change. Be quick and book your ticket as early as you can. Click HERE to download our app which keeps you updated on our low price tickets. For more information, go on our website at www.easygo.co.uk.

EASYGO.COM
現在就預訂您的行程
低價／高品質

您的精彩旅程在一次點擊之後展開。
搭乘豪華的旅行巴士環遊全國再也不用讓您的荷包大失血了。您可以在事先在網上購票或在任一巴士站購票,即可享受物超所值的票價。我們帶您到英國境內數千個景點,在那裡有精彩的故事等著您!

從您的出發地發現低價車票:

倫敦到伯明罕 *單程* *旅程時間:兩小時三十分*	10鎊 立即預訂
倫敦到巴斯 *單程* *旅程時間:兩小時五分*	5鎊 立即預訂
倫敦到卡蒂夫 *單程* *旅程時間:兩小時四十分*	8鎊 立即預訂
倫敦到約克 *單程* *旅程時間:三小時三十分*	25鎊 立即預訂
倫敦到愛丁堡 *單程* *旅程時間:五小時二十五分*	40鎊 立即預訂

所有票價可能變動。請即早預訂。點擊這裡下載我們的應用程式通知您最新的低價車票。也可上www.easygo.co.uk搜索更多資訊。

【詞彙】
book 預訂／fare 票價／
quality 品質／luxurious 豪華的／
coach 長途巴士／
in advance 事先／
destination 目的地／
journey 旅程／
subject to 受制於／update 更新

EASYGO最有可能是什麼？
(A) 一間航空公司
(B) 一間郵輪公司
(C) 一間汽車製造商
(D) 一間巴士公司

【類型】尋找主旨題型

【詞彙】
likely 可能

【正解】(D)

152 What most likely is EASYGO?

(A) An airline
(B) A ferry operator
(C) An automobile manufacturer
(D) A coach company

【解析】本題問EASYGO最有可能是何種公司，也是在考驗考生抓主旨的能力。透過標題和全篇內容，我們可以發現這篇廣告是有關於英國的一間巴士公司宣傳的低價車票。內文的第二行Travelling on luxurious coaches across the country does not have to hurt your wallet.即透露是長途巴士的車票廣告。另外從book your trip和fare等字眼也可以推敲出這篇廣告是跟巴士票有關的。因此答案選(D)。

根據廣告，哪一段旅程最長？
(A) 倫敦到巴斯
(B) 倫敦到約克
(C) 倫敦到愛丁堡
(D) 倫敦到伯明罕

【類型】尋找細節題型

【詞彙】
ad 廣告／journey 旅程

【正解】(C)

153 According to the ad, which journey is the longest?

(A) London to Bath
(B) London to York
(C) London to Edinburgh
(D) London to Birmingham

【解析】本題考驗考生抓時間細節的能力。時間及數字等資訊比較容易在英文字中凸顯，因此只要在文章中特別留意數字，並仔細核對信息，便可輕鬆找到答案。在五段路線中，倫敦到愛丁堡的車程為五小時二十五分，是所有路線中最久的，因此答案選(C)。

154 Which of the following statements is true?

(A) The tickets can only be purchased online.

(B) A journey from London to York takes no longer than four hours.

(C) A one-way ticket from London to Bath costs £10.

(D) The ticket prices are fixed all year round.

【解析】本題為是非敘述題，考生須對文章細節通篇理解後方能判斷。根據You can either book online in advance or buy on the day at a coach station.選項(A)票只能線上購買為非。根據票價表內倫敦到巴斯的單程票價5鎊，選項(C)一張倫敦到巴斯的單程票需10鎊為非。根據文末All the prices are subject to change.選項(D)車票票價全年一致為非。根據倫敦到約克的車程Journey time: 03h30m，選項(B)為正確答案。

下列敘述何者正確？

(A) 票只能線上購買。

(B) 倫敦到約克的車程少於四小時。

(C) 一張倫敦到巴斯的單程票需10鎊。

(D) 車票票價全年一致。

【類型】是非題型

【詞彙】
purchase 購買／
no longer than 不長於／
fixed 固定的

【正解】(B)

---

155 What can be inferred from the advertisement?

(A) The company is based in the US.

(B) Customers can get a discount only when booking online.

(C) Customers can check ticket prices in the company's app.

(D) Customers can cnly buy one-way tickets at coach stations.

【解析】本題為推論題。考生須從文中的資訊，進一步推理出答案。根據We take you to thousands of destinations in the UK where amazing stories are waiting.我們得知這間公司是在英國，因此選項(A)為非。根據You can enjoy the low fare ticket with great value.我們僅能得知我們能享受到低價車票，但文中並無指明只有透過線上購票才能享有優惠。因此選項(B)為非。根據You can either book online in advance or buy on the day at a coach station.我們能得知票可以在線上或任一巴士站購買。因此選項(D)為非。根據Click *HERE* to download our app which keeps you updated on our low price tickets.我們能得知下載應用程式即能隨時掌握最新的低價資訊，因此答案應選(C)。

從廣告中我們能推斷？

(A) 這間公司根據在美國。

(B) 旅客線上購票能享有折扣。

(C) 旅客能透過公司的應用程式查詢票價。

(D) 旅客只能在巴士站購買到單程車票。

【類型】推理題型

【詞彙】
infer 推理／advertisement 廣告

【正解】(C)

工作獵手

你在找工作嗎？

上找工作獵手發掘讓你脫穎而出的訣竅

人資顧問／鳳凰人事有限公司／馬尼拉／菲律賓

關於這份工作：
職稱：人資顧問
編號：H2827400010
地點：菲律賓馬尼拉
工作種類：一年期合約
薪資：每年$28,000—$30,000
申請截止日期：2017年11月15日

鳳凰人事正招聘有經驗的人資顧問加入我們的資深團隊，提供我們有效的協助。定期合約直到2018年10月底。

工作任務：
* 作為主管和員工間的橋樑，在一切員工關係的議題上提供建議，指導和協助。
* 檢視並修改薪資福利政策，確保其與法律規範相符。
* 每年兩次支援招聘活動，並參與新員工揀選過程。
* 辦理每季的職員評估並提供意見。
* 支援人資經理各項業務，如：人手短缺應變，公聽會以及紀律懲戒等。

Job Hunter

Are you looking for a job?

Go on Job Hunter and find out the tips to help you stand out from thousands of candidates.

Human Resources Advisor / Phoenix Personnel Ltd / Manila / the Philippines

About the job:
Title: Human Resources Advisor
No.: H2827400010
Location: Manila, the Philippines
Job Type: 1 Year Fixed Term Contract
Salary: $28,000-$30,000 **per annum**
Closing Date: 15 Nov, 2017

Phoenix Personnel is recruiting for an experienced HR advisor who can provide effective and efficient support to join our well-versed team on a fixed term contract until the end of October 2018.

Your tasks are to...
* Serve as a link between management and employees by providing advice, guidance and support on all kinds of matters regarding employee relations
* Examine and modify compensation and benefits policies and ensure compliance with legal requirements
* Assist in recruitment campaigns twice a year and take part in new employee selections
* Conduct seasonal job evaluations and provide advice on job reviews
* Support the HR manager with staffing duties, such as understaffing, hearings and disciplinary procedures

What's on offer:

- $28,000-$30,000 **per annum**
- Hours: 09:00-5:00
- Free lunch meal at the cafeteria

If you find this position a good match with your personality and professional background, please send your resume to us at pprecruitment@phoenix.co.ph. Please specify you are applying for HR advisor in the subject box. Our staff will contact you very soon. All good wishes with your search for employment.

我們提供您：

- 年薪$28,000-$30,000
- 上班時間：09:00-05:00
- 在員工餐廳免費供餐

如果您認為您的個性和專業背景相當符合本職缺，請將您的履歷寄到pprecruitment@phoenix.co.ph。請在標題欄標明您是申請人資顧問一職。相關人員很快會跟您聯繫。祝您求職順利！

【詞彙】

candidate 候選人／human resources 人資／advisor 顧問／
contract 合約／per annum 每年／personnel 人事／
recruit 招聘／experienced 有經驗的／effective 有效的／
efficient 有效率的／well-versed 成熟的／
management 管理／guidance 指導／modify 修改／
compensation 薪資／compliance 符合／campaign 活動／
seasonal 季的／evaluation 評估／understaffing 人手短缺／
hearing 公聽會／disciplinary 紀律的／personality 個性／
professional 專業的

---

156 Where most likely can this information be seen?

(A) At an electronics show
(B) At a book fair
(C) On a job searching website
(D) In a resort

【解析】本題問這則訊息最有可能在哪裡被看見，實際上是考驗考生把握主旨的能力。從標題Job Hunter和文中各處皆可發現本文跟求職相關。因此最有可能的地方是選項(C)。

這則訊息最有可能在哪裡被看見？

(A) 在電子展上
(B) 在書展上
(C) 在求職網上
(D) 在度假村中

【類型】尋找主旨題型

【詞彙】
electronics 電子／
book fair 書展／resort 度假村

【正解】(C)

關於本職缺的敘述文中提及了？
(A) 本工作為半年一期的合約。
(B) 合約在2017年11月到期。
(C) 僅限於菲律賓的申請者。
(D) 本職缺在菲律賓的首都。

【類型】尋找細節題型

【詞彙】
position 職缺／
advertise 廣告／restrict 限制／
capital 首都

【正解】(D)

157 What is suggested about the position being advertised?

(A) It is a half-year contract position.
(B) Its contract will end in November 2017.
(C) It is restricted to Filipino applicants.
(D) It is based in the capital of the Philippines.

【解析】本題問關於這個職缺的資訊。考生須詳讀相關信息後方能作答。根據Job Type: 1 Year Fixed Term Contract我們能得知合約是一年。因此選項(A)為非。根據on a fixed term contract until the end of October 2018我們得知合約將於2018年十月底結束。因此選項(B)為非。我們從文中得知這份工作在菲律賓馬尼拉，但文中並無提及只限於菲律賓的求職者，因此選項(C)為非。根據Location: Manila, the Philippines我們得知該職缺位於菲律賓的首都馬尼拉。因此答案應選(D)。

根據文中資訊，下列何者不是本職缺的職務？
(A) 處理招聘事宜
(B) 與員工和主管溝通
(C) 分析公司的薪資政策
(D) 於大學演講

【類型】是非題型

【詞彙】
duty 職務／handle 處理／
matter 事宜／analyze 分析／
deliver 發表（演說）／
speech 演講

【正解】(D)

158 According to the information, what is NOT a stated duty of this position?

(A) Handling hiring matters
(B) Communicating with employees and managers
(C) Analyzing the company's salary policies
(D) Delivering speeches on university campus

【解析】本題為是非題，考生須仔細閱讀並過濾資訊才能正確作答。在Your tasks are to...的下方，我們可以找到本工作要求的內容，其中我們無法找到「於大學演講」的項目。因此答案應選(D)。

159 What should applicants do when applying for this position?

(A) Bring an application form to the HR department

(B) Phone the HR director

(C) Email a CV to the company

(D) Identify their college major in the email

求職者申請時須做什麼？
(A) 將申請表帶到人資部
(B) 打電話給人資主管
(C) 將履歷寄到公司
(D) 在電郵中標明大學專業

【類型】尋找細節題型

【詞彙】
applicant 申請者／
phone 打電話／CV 履歷／
identify 標明／major 主修

【解析】根據If you find this position a good match with your personality and professional background, please send your resume to us at pprecruitment@phoenix.co.ph.我們能得知求職者需把履歷寄到公司電郵信箱。其中resume和CV同義，因此答案應選(C)。

【正解】(C)

---

160 What does the phrase "per annum" mean?

(A) daily

(B) weekly

(C) monthly

(D) annual

"per annum" 在文中代表什麼意思？
(A) 每天的
(B) 每週的
(C) 每月的
(D) 每年的

【類型】同義字題型

【詞彙】
per annum 每年／
annual 每年的

【正解】(D)

【解析】我們可以發現annum和annual的字首十分相近，因此考生能在不認識該字的情況透過這個線索推斷答案應選(D)。per為「每……」的意思。

米與海之歌—傳統海鮮飯

一旦你試了，你就會上癮！趕快試試這道美味的料理吧！

原料
- 180克的中米
- 5個去骨雞腿
- 225克的魷魚片（圈）
- 100克的去鱗去鬚貽貝
- 0.5茶匙的粗海鹽
- 0.5茶匙的粗黑胡椒
- 1茶匙的橄欖油
- 2顆切丁洋蔥

步驟

1. 在中等大小的不沾鍋上用中火加熱橄欖油。

2. 在雞腿置入碗中加入海鹽和黑胡椒調味。放置十分鐘。—[1]—

3. 以中火煎雞腿肉直到顏色微微變色。將雞腿肉裝到大盤上。—[2]—

4. 在鍋中加入洋蔥以文火煎三分鐘直到洋蔥變軟變微微金黃。

5. —[3]—將雞肉與洋蔥拌勻，加入米飯攪拌並烹煮三至四分鐘直到米飯均勻地與其他食材混合。

6. 在半熟的米飯堆上撒上魷魚片。繼續煮五分鐘直到魷魚煮熟。

7. 蓋上鍋蓋燜煮十分鐘直到米飯軟化且稍微黏糊。小心不要燒焦。—[4]—

8. 於飯上加入幾滴檸檬汁便可以享用了！

【詞彙】
paella 海鮮燉飯／
addict 使上癮／
boneless 去骨的／slice 切片／
scrub 刮除／mussel 貽貝／
non-stick pan 不沾鍋／
season 調味／scatter 散布／
lid 蓋子／simmer 燉

Questions 161-165 refer to the following article.

Rice and Sea—Traditional Paella

Once you try it, you will get addicted. Hurry and try this fabulous dish yourself!

Ingredients

- 180 grams of medium grain rice
- 5 boneless chicken thighs
- 225 grams of sliced squid (rings)
- 100 grams of well-scrubbed mussels with beards removed
- 0.5 tablespoon of ground sea salt
- 0.5 tablespoon of ground black pepper
- 1 tablespoon of olive oil
- 2 chopped onions

Steps

1. Heat the olive oil in a non-stick medium size pan with medium heat.

2. Put the chicken thighs in a bowl and season them with sea salt and black pepper. Leave it for 10 minutes. —[1]—

3. Fry the chicken over medium heat for 5 minutes until both sides turn lightly colored. Transfer the chicken to a large plate. —[2]—

4. Add the onions to the pan and fry for 3 minutes over a gentle fire until softened and lightly brown.

5. —[3]—Mix the chicken with the fried onions, stir in the rice and cook for another 3 to 4 minutes until the rice is evenly mixed with the other ingredients.

6. Scatter the sliced squid over the partly cooked rice mixture. Continue cooking for 5 minutes until the squid is perfectly cooked.

7. Place the lid over the pan and keep simmering for 10 minutes until the rice is softened and a bit sticky. Be careful not to burn the rice. —[4]—

8. Add a few drops of lemon onto the rice and get ready to dig in!

161 Where most likely can this article be found?

    (A) In a cookbook
    (B) In a financial newspaper
    (C) In a sports car magazine
    (D) In a church leaflet

【解析】根據標題及內文，我們能輕易發現本文跟食物烹飪有關。因此最有可能找到本文的地方為選項(A)食譜裡。

這篇文章最有可能在哪裡被發現？
(A) 在食譜裡
(B) 在金融報刊裡
(C) 在跑車雜誌裡
(D) 在教堂手冊裡

【類型】尋找主題題型

【詞彙】
article 文章／cookbook 食譜／
financial 金融的／
leaflet 摺頁手冊

【正解】(A)

---

162 What is NOT a required ingredient?

    (A) black pepper
    (B) chicken breast
    (C) paella rice
    (D) squid

【解析】根據指示，考生須在所需原料的下方細讀之後方可找出答案。所有選項中，唯有選項(B)雞胸肉沒有在所需原料清單裡。所需的應為chicken thighs雞腿肉。因此答案應選(B)。

下列何者不是所需的材料？
(A) 黑胡椒
(B) 雞胸肉
(C) 海鮮米飯
(D) 魷魚

【類型】尋找細節題型

【詞彙】
required 需要的／
ingredient 原料／breast 胸部

【正解】(B)

---

163 What is indicated about preparing the onions?

    (A) They should be red onions.
    (B) They should be cooked in boiled water first.
    (C) They should be cut into pieces.
    (D) They should be marinated with soy sauce.

【解析】根據原料清單中的chopped onions，我們能得知洋蔥須被切成小塊，因此答案應選(C)。

準備洋蔥時須注意什麼？
(A) 須準備紅洋蔥。
(B) 須在沸水裡煮過。
(C) 須切成小片。
(D) 須用醬油醃漬過。

【類型】尋找細節題型

【詞彙】
indicate 指出／
boiled water 滾水／
marinate 醃漬／soy sauce 醬油

【正解】(C)

米飯最後應被煮成怎樣？
(A) 稍微燒焦
(B) 溼糊狀
(C) 軟軟黏黏
(D) 半熟

【類型】尋找細節題型

【詞彙】
eventually 最後／soggy 溼糊

【正解】(C)

164 How should the rice be cooked eventually?

(A) It should be slightly burned,
(B) It should be soggy.
(C) It should be soft and sticky.
(D) It should be half-cooked.

【解析】根據Place the lid over the pan and keep simmering for 10 minutes until the rice is softened and a bit sticky. Be careful not to burn the rice.我們能得知最終米飯應該呈現 softened and a bit sticky「軟軟黏黏」的樣子。因此答案應選(C)。

"Return the fried chicken thighs to the pan." 這個句子最適合放在 [1], [2], [3], [4]哪個位置？
(A) [1]
(B) [2]
(C) [3]
(D) [4]

【類型】句子插入題型

【詞彙】
pan 平底鍋

【正解】(C)

★ 165 In which of the positions marked [1], [2], [3] and [4] does the following sentence best belong? "Return the fried chicken thighs to the pan."

(A) [1]
(B) [2]
(C) [3]
(D) [4]

【解析】Return the fried chicken thighs to the pan.「將煎過的雞腿放回鍋中」。根據此句我們可以推斷本句一定是放在步驟Transfer the chicken to a large plate. 之後。根據文中的插入位置判斷，[3]是最合理的位置。因其後接了Mix the chicken with the fried onions... ，與該句的語意最為連貫。「將煎過的雞腿放回鍋中之後，將雞肉與洋蔥混合均勻……」。因此答案應選(C)。

Questions 166-170 refer to the following information.

Introducing Landmark: The Best Educational Institute for the Elderly

For whom
The course is aimed at people who are over 50 years old and are still active and keen on lifelong learning.

Facilitators
Peter Tan, specialist in National Senior Education Center, Head Teacher in Westlake Community College

Description
Landmark is an institute that provides specially-designed courses and activities for elders. In response to the "**silver tsunami**", which has posed an impact on all respects of human society, including political, economic and cultural domains, Landmark pioneers in contributing to older adults' educational development, which in turn is beneficial to maintaining mental, social and physical health. Our program is full of rich learning and development activities that are very popular with elders.

Date: 14 January 2016
Time: 8:00-15:00
Venue: St Stephen's Building
Cost: £ 20
Contact kimsu1912@pioneer.co.uk to book a place.

If booked in a group of three, the cost will be £ 15 per person.

Landmark簡介：銀髮族的最佳教育中心

對象
本課程特別為五十歲以上積極好學的人士設計。

推動者
Peter Tan，國立終身教育中心專員，西湖社區大學教學組長

介紹
Landmark機構為老年人提供特殊設計的課程及活動。因應近年來對社會造成鉅大影響的銀髮海嘯，包含政治、經濟及教育層面，Landmark為致力老年人終身學習的先鋒，進而對老年人心理、社會及身體健康等方面啟到正面的影響。我們的課程有豐富的學習內容及有趣的活動，非常受到銀髮族的歡迎。

日期：2016年1月14日
時間：8:00-15:00
地點：St Stephen's大樓
費用：20鎊
聯繫 kimsu1912@pioneer.co.uk 報名。

三人團報，每人優惠價15鎊。

【詞彙】
institute 機構／elderly 長輩／course 課程／be aimed at 針對／keen 熱衷／lifelong learning 終身學習／facilitator 促成者／specialist 專員／in response to 為回應／tsunami 海嘯／respect 方面／domain 領域／contribute to 貢獻／beneficial 有助益的／maintain 維持／mental 心智的

誰最有可能參加這個活動？
(A) 現役軍人　　(B) 退休教師
(C) 學齡前兒童　(D) 大學生

【類型】推理題型

【詞彙】

participate 參加／
active duty 現役的／
retired 退休／
preschool 學齡前的

【正解】(B)

166 Who most likely would participate in this event?

  (A) An active duty soldier

  (B) A retired teacher

  (C) A preschool child

  (D) A university student

【解析】我們從本文標題及內文各處能發現本文是關於老年人的教育課程的推廣。因此選項(B)退休教師最有可能去參加。

銀髮海嘯的原因最有可能是什麼？
(A) 人口老化　　(B) 地震
(C) 全球暖化　　(D) 金融危機

【類型】推理題型

【詞彙】

probably 可能／cause 成因／
silver 銀色的／tsunami 海嘯／
aging 老化的／
population 人口／crisis 危機

【正解】(A)

167 What is probably the cause of "silver tsunami"?

  (A) aging population

  (B) an earthquake

  (C) global warming

  (D) financial crisis

【解析】因本題在文中並無明確的答案。因此我們須從silver tsunami字面意思上推理。銀髮海嘯最有可能的成因是人口老化，因此答案應選(A)。

根據信息，下列何者不是提供老年人教育機會的優點？
(A) 政治局面得以穩定
(B) 心理健康能被照護到
(C) 社會關係可以被維持
(D) 老年人能保持身體健康

【類型】是非題型

【詞彙】

stability 穩定性／
ensure 保證／
psychological 心理的／
wellness 健康／attend to 關切／
well 健康的

【正解】(A)

168 According to this information, what is NOT a benefit of providing old adults with educational opportunities?

  (A) Political stability can be ensured.

  (B) Psychological wellness can be attended to.

  (C) Social relationship can be maintained.

  (D) The elderly can be physically well.

【解析】根據which in turn is beneficial to maintaining mental, social and physical health.老年人教育的好處有維持心理上、社會上和身體上的健康。並無穩定政治局面的效果。因此答案應選(A)。

169 What can we infer from this information?

(A) The course will last a month.

(B) The event will take place at St. Stephen's Building.

(C) Group registration is not permitted.

(D) People over 60 years old can get 20% off the price.

【解析】根據Venue: St Stephen's Building，我們能得知地點是在St Stephen's大樓。選項(A)的資訊我們無法從文中找到。根據If booked in a group of three, the cost will be £15 per person.我們知道選項(C)是錯誤的。選項(D)的資訊我們也無法從文中找到。

我們能從此信息裡推理出？
(A) 本課程為時一個月。
(B) 本課程在 St. Stephen's大樓舉辦。
(C) 本課程不接受團報。
(D) 六十歲以上的人能打八折。

【類型】細節題型

【詞彙】
infer 推理／last 持續／
permit 允許

【正解】(B)

---

170 If three people sign up as a group, how much will they have to pay in total?

(A) £15

(B) £20

(C) £45

(D) £60

【解析】根據If booked in a group of three, the cost will be £15 per person.三人團報，每人的特價為15鎊，因此三人為45鎊。因此答案應選(C)。

如果三人一起報名，他們總共需繳多少錢？
(A) 15鎊
(B) 20鎊
(C) 45鎊
(D) 60鎊

【類型】推理題型

【詞彙】
sign up 報名／in total 總共

【正解】(C)

週五研討會資料

2016年10月20日
寄件人: Thomas Summers
收件人: 你

大家好：

我在附件中夾帶了一些週五研討會我們會討論到的資料。這次我們將探討如何準備即將到來的FET年度專案。為了更好的準備這次的研討會，我希望你們事先做到以下：

1. 瀏覽過專案的提案樣本。您會發現某些部分缺失。這是故意為了防止個人資訊外流。

2. 將關於今年專案的關鍵詞標記出來，並想想想關於這兩年專案重點的相關性。

3. 嘗試根據附檔的標準表評估去年的舊專案。

4. 接著，瀏覽部門主任的詳細評估，並找出他們發現的優缺點。

5. 最後，想出一些能運用到今年的年終專案的點子，並在週五的研討會中提出。會中會有腦力激盪的環節讓您分享您的想法。

請知悉由於本次研討會需要的文件數量過多，我不會一一為你們列印。請自行攜帶電子檔或紙本版到研討會上。

您也可以使用您的員工編號和密碼登入資源專區，預先瀏覽過部分的線上文件，將會對您的思考有幫助。若您找不到，我也將它們夾帶在附檔中了。

Materials for Friday's Seminar   20 Oct 2016

From: Thomas Summers   To: you

Dear All,

I am including some of the materials in the attachment we will be talking about on Friday during our seminar. This time we will be looking into how to best prepare for the upcoming FET annual project. In preparation for the seminar, I would like you to do the following in advance:

1. Read through the sample project proposal. You will notice there will be some sections missing. This is done on purpose in order to avoid revealing personal information.

2. Highlight the keywords related to this year's subject and try to think about the relevance between the two years' focuses.

3. Try to assess the old project proposal based on the criteria attached as a Word document.

4. Next, see the department directors' detailed evaluation and see what they liked and what they thought could be improved.

5. Finally, think about some ideas that are applicable to this year's year-end project and bring them to this Friday's seminar. There will be a brainstorming session for your ideas to be shared.

Please note that due to the length of the documents necessary for the seminar, I will not print them out for you. It would be good therefore if all of you could bring either e-copies or hard copies of the documents to the seminar to be able to access the information.

You will also find it useful to read through some parts of the online documents in the resources portal which you can log into with your employee ID and password. I am also attaching the copies of some of them just in case you can't find them.

Finally, it has been brought up to me that some of you will have to attend the weekly meeting at the same time. This is rather unfortunate. Although I would normally not encourage you to skip weekly meetings, on this occasion I would hope that you treat this seminar as a priority.

Best wishes,

Thomas Summers

最後，我得知有些人必須在同一時間參加週會。這是比較不巧的。雖然我不鼓勵大家翹掉週會，但在這種情況下我還是希望各位以這次的研討會為優先。

祝 順心

Thomas Summers

【詞彙】
seminar 研討會／
attachment 附件／
upcoming 即將來臨的／
project 專案／
in preparation for 為準備／
in advance 事先／
sample 樣本／revelation 曝光／
relevance 相關性／
assess 評估／criteria 標準／
applicable 可應用的／
brainstorm 腦力激盪／
length 長度／e-copy 電子檔／
hard copy 紙質檔／portal 專區／
bring up to 向某人提起／
unfortunate 不幸／priority 優先

---

171 What is the purpose of this email?

(A) To inquire the prices of Christmas decoration materials

(B) To remind parents of the dates of the final exams

(C) To inform preparation of a seminar discussion

(D) To request an employee leave application form

【解析】根據文中標題及第一段，我們能得知本文旨在提醒員工星期五研討會的準備事項。因此答案選(C)。

本電郵的主旨為何？
(A) 詢問聖誕裝飾品的材料價格
(B) 提醒家長期末考的日期
(C) 提醒研討會的準備事項
(D) 申請員工請假單

【類型】尋找主旨題型

【詞彙】
inquire 詢問／inform 通知／
request 申請／leave 請假

【正解】(C)

為何專案提案樣本的部分內容被隱藏？
(A) 避免抄襲
(B) 保護個人資訊
(C) 省空間
(D) 激發靈感

【類型】尋找細節題型

【詞彙】
plagiarism 抄襲／elicit 引導／
inspiration 靈感

【正解】(B)

172 Why is part of the content of the sample project proposal concealed?
(A) To avoid plagiarism
(B) To protect personal information
(C) To save space
(D) To elicit inspiration

【解析】根據You will notice there will be some sections missing. This is done on purpose in order to avoid revealing personal information.我們能得知部分內容被隱藏是為了保護個資。因此答案選(B)。

研討會參與者星期五時需要做什麼？
(A) 在去年的專案中標出關鍵詞
(B) 登入資源專區
(C) 詢問主管對於專案的評價
(D) 將紙本文件帶到研討會討論中

【類型】尋找細節題型

【詞彙】
attendee 參加者／
highlight 標出重點

【正解】(D)

173 What are the seminar attendees asked to do on Friday?
(A) Highlighting the key words in the old proposal
(B) Logging into the resources portal
(C) Asking the supervisors about their comments on the proposals
(D) Bringing the printed documents to the discussion

【解析】根據It would be good therefore if all of you could bring either e-copies or hard copies of the documents to the seminar to be able to access the information.我們能得知在星期五的研討會中，參與者必須自行攜帶文件。選項(A)(B)都是在研討會之前需要做的事。選項(C)並無在文中提及。因此答案應選(D)。

174 What can be inferred about the seminar?

    (A) It is considered more important than weekly meetings at the moment.

    (B) It will be held in December.

    (C) It is only for department directors.

    (D) It is a monthly event.

【解析】根據文末...on this occasion I would hope that you treat this seminar as a priority.我們能得知Thomas Summers 認為研討會目前是比週會更重要的。根據電郵中的日期，我們可以推測研討會是在十月舉辦。因此選項(B)為非。文中並無提及研討會只有部門主管可以參加，以及研討會一個月舉行一次，因此選項(C)(D)皆為非。答案應選(A)。

關於研討會，我們可以推論出？

(A) 研討會目前被認為比週會更重要

(B) 研討會將會在十二月舉行。

(C) 研討會只有部門主管可以參加。

(D) 研討會一個月舉行一次。

【類型】推理題型

【詞彙】

monthly 每月的

【正解】(A)

---

175 Who most likely is Thomas?

    (A) The organizer of the weekly meeting

    (B) The IT supplier

    (C) The website designer

    (D) The host of the seminar

【解析】根據本文推理，Thomas為電郵的寄件人，並提醒員工關於研討會的準備事項，因此他很有可能是研討會的主持人。因此答案應選(D)。

Thomas最有可能是誰？

(A) 週會的主辦者

(B) 資訊供應商

(C) 網站設計者

(D) 研討會主持人

【類型】推理題型

【詞彙】

organizer 主辦者／

supplier 供應商／

designer 設計者／host 主持人

【正解】(D)

超級銷售員群組

十一月三日

2017 運動社團清單
點此下載檔案

Jennifer H 17:01

大家早！相信多數人都知道，今年的體育社團已經開始報名了。我們公司非常重視您的身體健康，健康意識以及團隊精神。為了維持生產力並提倡運動精神，我們有責任確保每個人至少參加一門體育社團，所有的社團都由我們公司組織並提供資金。我們提供專業的指導以及每週的訓練課程。我們會經常性點名，而出席率會計算在你的年終績效內。我們很開心告知您今年我們加入了兩個新社團。您可以在以上的檔案中找到。根據以往經驗，多數的社團都很受歡迎，因此我們呼籲您儘早報名。如果您有任何疑問，請不要猶豫來聯絡我們。祝您選擇社團順利，週末大快樂！

Jennifer H 17:04

謝謝Jennifer！
Elisa W. 17:04

週末愉快！
Stefanie 17:10

Super Sales Group

Nov 3

2017 Sports Club List
Click here to download this file

Jennifer H 17:01

Good afternoon everyone! As most of you may know, the registration for this year's sports club has already begun. Since your physical wellbeing, healthy living awareness and teamwork spirit are something our company holds in high regard. In order to maintain productivity and promote an active lifestyle, we have the responsibility to ensure that every one of you participate in at least one sports club organized and funded by our company. We provide professional tutorial and training sessions each week. Attendance will be taken on a regular basis and will be counted towards your reward package at the end of the year. We are also excited to tell you that this year we have two new clubs which you can find in the above file. According to the record, most of our clubs are very popular, so early registration is advisable. Please do not hesitate to seek counsel if you are confused about anything regarding this matter. Good luck with your club picking and as always enjoy your fantastic weekend!

Jennifer H 17:04

Thank you! Jennifer!
Elisa W.
17:04

Have a great weekend!
Stefanie
17:10

2017 Sport Club List			
Monday	**Tuesday**	**Thursday**	**Friday**
18:00-20:30	18:00-20:30	18:00-20:30	18:00-21:00
Table Tennis	Jogging	Indoor Climbing NEW	Aerobic Dance
Yoga NEW	Swimming	Belly Dance	Badminton
Aerobic Dance	Badminton	Table Tennis	Jogging

2017 運動社團清單			
週一	週二	週四	週五
18:00-20:30	18:00-20:30	18:00-20:30	18:00-21:00
乒乓球	慢跑	室內攀岩（新）	有氧舞蹈
瑜珈（新）	游泳	肚皮舞	羽球
有氧舞蹈	羽球	乒乓球	慢跑

From: Ivy Wang　　　　　　　　　　　Nov 6, 2017
To: Jennifer Hendryx
Subject: Inquiry about sports club registration

Dear Jennifer,

Thank you for your information. I am really interested in the clubs you run this year. They all look very attractive to me. Here I have a few points I am not clear about. First, how many clubs can we enroll in at most? Second, is there any possibility that you can open another belly dance session on Tuesday? As far as I know, many people in my department are super interested in joining the new indoor climbing club and the belly dance club. However, the two are unfortunately on the same day. Plus, as an old member of the belly dance club which was extremely full last year, I am sure this year it will still be in great demand.

On behalf of the department, I would very much appreciate if you could rearrange the timetable to **accommodate** this condition. I am looking forward to your reply.

Best regards,

Ivy Wang
Sales Department

寄件人：Ivy Wang
　　　　2017年11月6日
收件人：Jennifer Hendryx
主旨：運動社團報名相關疑問

親愛的Jennifer：

感謝您的告知。我對於今年的社團非常感興趣。每個社團都非常吸引我。我有幾點問題想釐清。首先，我們最多能加入幾個社團？第二，有沒有可能在星期二增開一堂肚皮舞課呢？據我所知，我部門很多人對新開設的室內攀岩和肚皮舞社團非常感興趣，但是這兩堂課在同一天。另外，因為我去年也在肚皮舞社，人數爆滿，我相信今年也會供不應求。

如果您能夠重新調整時間表以因應我們的需求，我代表我的部門向您道謝。期待您的回覆。

祝 安好

Ivy Wang
銷售部門

【詞彙】

awareness 意識／hold in high regard 重視／
productivity 生產力／responsibility 責任／participate 參加／
fund 資助／on a regular basis 經常／reward package
獎勵辦法／advisable 可取的／counsel 諮詢／
aerobic dance 有氧舞蹈／attractive 吸引人的／
As far as I know 就我所知／in great demand 需求量高／
on behalf of 代表／accommodate 使適應

Jennifer最有可能是誰？
(A) 瑜珈師
(B) 新進員工
(C) 攀岩社的舊社員
(D) 部門主管

【類型】推理題型

【詞彙】
therapist 治療師／
director 主管

【正解】(D)

176 Who most likely is Jennifer?

　　(A) A yoga therapist
　　(B) A new employee
　　(C) An old member of the climbing club
　　(D) A department director

【解析】在群組對話中，Jennifer是發送社團開放報名消息的人。也是員工寫電郵詢問相關信息的對象，因此我們能推論Jennifer非常有可能是某個部門的主管。因此答案選(D)。

員工被建議做什麼？
(A) 儘早報名
(B) 重新安排他們的行程表
(C) 利用週末時間運動
(D) 加入前研究過每項運動

【類型】尋找細節題型

【詞彙】
advise 建議／
rearrange 重新安排／
research 研究

【正解】(A)

177 What are employees advised to do?

　　(A) To sign up as early as possible
　　(B) To rearrange their own schedule
　　(C) To spend weekend time exercising
　　(D) To research each sport before joining

【解析】根據According to the record, most of our clubs are very popular, so early registration is advisable.我們能得知員工最好儘早報名，因此答案應選(A)。

關於運動社團規定何者正確？
(A) 每個人一次只能報名一個社團。
(B) 社員每年可以不出席三次。
(C) 社團出席率與員工薪水緊密相關。
(D) 社費須繳交到會計部門。

【類型】是非題型

【詞彙】
at a time 一次／skip 跳過／
attendance 出席／membership
fee 會員費／accounting 會計

【正解】(C)

178 What is TRUE about the sports club policy?

　　(A) Everyone only get to apply for one club at a time.
　　(B) Each member can skip classes up to three times a year.
　　(C) Club attendance is closely related to employees' salary.
　　(D) Membership fee should be paid to the accounting department.

【解析】根據Attendance will be taken on a regular basis and will be counted towards your reward package at the end of the year.出席率會被計算到年終的獎勵辦法，表示與薪水有密切關係，因此答案應選(C)。

179 What is NOT the reason why Ivy was concerned about the club arrangement?

(A) The coach of the indoor climbing club is frequently absent.
(B) Two popular sessions are scheduled on the same day.
(C) Too many people want to join the belly dance club.
(D) A large number of people may want to continue their membership in the belly dance club.

【解析】根據電郵中的內容，Ivy提到了肚皮舞社和室內攀岩社都非常受歡迎。而兩者被安排在同一天。也提到了去年的肚皮舞社很搶手，今年應該也會是。因此除了選項(A)沒有被提及，其餘皆是Ivy提到的問題。因此答案應選(A)。

下列何者不是Ivy對於社團安排的疑慮？
(A) 室內攀岩的教練常常缺席。
(B) 兩個受歡迎的社團被安排在同一天。
(C) 太多人想加入肚皮舞社。
(D) 很多人想要繼續待在肚皮舞社。

【類型】是非題型

【詞彙】
concern 憂心／
arrangement 安排／
coach 教練／
frequently 經常／
absent 缺席

【正解】(A)

---

180 In the email, the word "accommodate" in paragraph 2, line 2, is closest in meaning to

(A) purchase
(B) lodge
(C) fit
(D) return

【解析】accommodate和fit皆有使某物符合或適應某種情況的意思。因此答案應選(C)。

在電郵中，第二段第二行的 "accommodate" 最接近？
(A) 購買
(B) 住宿
(C) 符合
(D) 返回

【類型】同義字題型

【詞彙】
accommodate 處理／
lodge 住宿／
fit 使符合

【正解】(C)

西方航空

精彩旅程始於此

管理我的行程

您的預定已成功確認。
感謝您選擇西方航空。
現在您可以登記並取得登機證。

線上登記

預訂代號: WA13100394
狀態: 已登記／座位15A已預訂

往都柏林
班機號 TR301

出發: 布拉格 日期: 2016年2月4日 時間: 13:55	到達: 都柏林 日期: 2016年2月4日 時間: 16:20
乘客1 Chris Walker 班機號TR301	乘客2 Emma Chase 班機號TR301

點擊這裡免費預訂您的座位
點擊這裡購買旅行保險
點擊這裡划算租車

收據
總共支付：108歐元無保險費
透過Visa尾號：1939
卡片擁有人姓名：Chris Walker
於2016年1月31日付款

西方航空

★**Questions 181-185 refer to the following itinerary, timetable and notice.**

Western Airline

Your amazing journey starts here.

Manage My Trip

Your booking is successfully confirmed. Thank you for choosing Western Airline.
Now it's time to check in to get a boarding pass.

CHECK IN ONLINE NOW

BOOKING REFERENCE: WA13100394
STATUS: Checked-in/ Seat 15A reserved

To Dublin
Flight No. TR301

Departure: Prague Date: 4 February 2016 Time: 13:55	Arrival: Dublin Date: 4 February 2016 Time: 16:20
Passenger 1 Chris Walker Flight No. TR301	Passenger 2 Emma Chase Flight No. TR301

Click **HERE** to reserve your seat for free if you haven't yet.
Click **HERE** to protect your trip with travel insurance.
Click **HERE** to rent a car with exclusive deals.

Receipt
Total paid: 108 EUR with no insurance
via Visa ending in 1939
Card holder's name: Chris Walker
Paid on 31 January 2016

WESTERN AIRLINE

International Departures				
Flight No	Destination	Time	Gate	Remarks
CF8977	Berlin	12:07	A-19	Gate Closing
BA386	London	12:40	A-38	Boarding
QF9281	Barcelona	13:25	B-20	Delayed
TR301	Dublin	13:55	C-32	Check-in at R19
PR9011	Milan	14:22	B-12	Check-in at C10

Gate C-32

NOTICE

For passengers boarding Flight number TR301 leaving for Dublin, the boarding gate has been changed to C-02 due to temporary renovation. We apologize for the inconvenience.

國際出發航班				
班機號	目的地	時間	登機門	備註
CF8977	柏林	12:07	A-19	登機門即將關閉
BA386	倫敦	12:40	A-38	正在登機
QF9281	巴賽隆納	13:25	B-20	班機延遲
TR301	都柏林	13:55	C-32	於R19辦理登機
PR9011	米蘭	14:22	B-12	於C10辦理登機

登機門 C-32

通知
搭乘班機號TR301前往都柏林的旅客，因暫時維修緣故，登機門改為C-02。抱歉造成您的不便。

【詞彙】
boarding pass 登機證／
exclusive 獨家的／
insurance 保險／
inconvenience 不方便

---

181 According to the information, what is indicated about Chris Walker's flight?

(A) The seat has been reserved.
(B) The payment is due in a week.
(C) It flies from Dublin to Prague.
(D) The payment was made in cash.

【解析】根據電子機票中STATUS: Checked-in/ Seat 15A reserved表示座位已預訂。款項已用信用卡付清，而班機是由布拉格飛往都柏林。因此答案應選(A)。

根據信息，關於Chris Walker的航班何者正確？
(A) 座位已預訂。
(B) 款項在一週後到期付款。
(C) 班機從都柏林飛往布拉格。
(D) 款項已現金付清。

【類型】尋找細節題型

【詞彙】
reserve 預定／due 到期／
payment 付款

【正解】(A)

關於西方航空何者正確？
(A) 無法線上登記。
(B) 提供租車服務。
(C) 預約座位需要8歐元。
(D) 機票內包含旅行保險。

【類型】是非題型

【詞彙】
allow 允許／car rental 出車／
insurance 保險

【正解】(B)

182 What is TRUE about Western Airline?

(A) It does not allow online check-in.
(B) Car rental service is available.
(C) It costs 8 euros to reserve a seat.
(D) Travel insurance fee is included in the ticket price.

【解析】根據電子機票中的資訊我們能得知乘客可以辦理線上登記。根據Click HERE to reserve your seat for free if you haven't yet.我們得知預訂座位是免費的。而文中並無提到旅行保險是免費的。而由Click HERE to rent a car with exclusive deals.我們得知租車服務是有提供的。因此答案應選(B)。

班機出發時間表透露何資訊？
(A) 飛往柏林班機的登機門正維修中。
(B) 前往倫敦的乘客現在可以登機。
(C) QF9281班機會在13:25抵達巴賽隆納。
(D) 班機PR9011的登機櫃檯在B12開放。

【類型】尋找細節題型

【詞彙】
departure 出發／
construction 建造／
board 登機／counter 櫃檯

【正解】(B)

183 What does the departure timetable tell us?

(A) The departure gate of the flight leaving for Berlin is under construction.
(B) Passengers going to London are allowed to board now.
(C) Flight QF9281 will arrive in Barcelona at 13:25.
(D) The check-in counter for Flight PR9011 is open at B12.

【解析】根據信息，前往都柏林的班機登機門正在維修，並非柏林。QF9281會在13:25分起飛前往巴賽隆納，並非抵達。PR9011的登記櫃檯在C-10並非B12。因此答案應選(B)。

184 What change was made to Flight No. TR301?

   (A) It was cancelled.
   (B) It was delayed for over an hour.
   (C) Its departure gate was moved to another one.
   (D) Its check-in counter was changed to C10.

【解析】根據通知，the boarding gate has been changed to C-02 due to temporary renovation.我們能得知登機門改到 C-02，因此答案應選(C)。

班機TR301有什麼改變？
(A) 被取消了。
(B) 延遲超過一小時。
(C) 登機門改變。
(D) 登記櫃檯改到C10.

【類型】尋找細節題型

【詞彙】
　cancel 取消

【正解】(C)

---

185 What can be inferred from the information?

   (A) Chris was traveling alone to Dublin.
   (B) Chris booked the flight one month ahead of the departure time.
   (C) It was around noon when Chris saw the departure timetable.
   (D) Several flights were delayed or cancelled due to bad weather condition.

【解析】根據電子機票，共有兩位旅客，因此Chris並非獨自前往都柏林。Chris機票付款的時間為1月31日，而班機出發時間為2月4日，因此是四天前預訂的。在班機表和通知中，並無提及天候不佳的因素。而在班機表中，飛往柏林和倫敦的班機一個登機門即將關閉，另一個正在登機。因此我們能推斷Chris在現場看到登機表的時間也差不多是中午十二點多。因此答案應選(C)。

從以上信息我們可以得知？
(A) Chris獨自前往都柏林。
(B) Chris在出發時間的一個月前訂了本班機。
(C) 當Chris看到班機出發時間表時時間約是中午。
(D) 天候不佳，許多班機取消或延誤了。

【類型】推理題型

【詞彙】
　ahead of 提前／condition 狀況

【正解】(C)

歡迎來到聖湯瑪士教堂

---一般入場票---

入場費將會用於教堂翻修。
感謝您的貢獻。

日期：2017年9月21日	票號：32038238214
入場時間：14:00	預訂號：1000500234
門票種類：學生票	預訂日：2017年8月21日
價格：10歐元（含稅）	列印日期：2017年8月21日

請保留本票券直到參觀結束，請在參觀地點應要求出示此門票。當發現任何可疑行為可能傷及遊客或本場地，本教堂保留拒絕旅客進入的權利。在場內嚴禁吸菸、飲食。場內嚴禁危險物品。十二歲以下孩童需有成人陪伴。若因天候因素、安全因素或緊急事件，本教堂保留更動參觀路線或時間的權利。本票不能退費。如果有任何疑問，請上www.sthomaschurch.com。或撥076-302-1364，或發信到admission@sthomaschurch.org.uk獲取更多資訊。

聖湯瑪士教堂翻修計畫

暫時關閉

聖湯瑪士教堂的東側將於2017年9月15日到2017年10月15日正式關閉進行維修。本次維修工程包含門廊的走道維修、大廳的地面重整、南面的新鐘安裝、

Welcome to St. Thomas Church

---General Admission Ticket---
The entrance fee will go towards the renovation of the St. Thomas Church. Your patronage makes a huge contribution to this great work.

Date: September 21, 2017	Ticket No.: 32038238214
Entrance Time: 14:00	Reservation No.: 1000500234
Ticket Type: Student	Date Booked: August 21, 2017
Price: 10 EUR (VAT included)	Date Printed: August 21, 2017

Please retain this ticket until the end of the visit and the ticket must be presented at the venue upon request. The church reserves the right to deny admission when any behavior is found suspicious and detrimental to other visitors or our properties. Please note that smoking, eating and drinking are strictly prohibited on the premises. No pets or dangerous items are allowed on the premises. Children under 12 must be accompanied by an adult. The church reserves the right to change the routes or visiting time due to adverse weather conditions, safety issues or emergent events. This ticket is non-refundable. If you have any questions, please go on our website at www.sthomaschurch.com, call 076-302-1364 or email admission@sthomaschurch.org.uk for information.

Renovation Project of St. Thomas Church

Temporary Closure of St. Thomas Church

Please be advised that St. Thomas Church will be officially closed for renovations in the east wing of the property from 15 September 2017 to 15 October 2017. The renovation project will include the damaged pavement repair at the porch, foyer floor leveling, installment of new clocks on the south exterior, fallen steeple resurrection and drainage additions at the chapel building. For visitors, do not enter the construction area unless authorized. We apologize for any inconvenience caused. We look forward to seeing you again soon.

塔尖重建，以及小教堂的排水系統增設等。旅客未經允許請勿擅闖建地。造成不便敬請見諒。期待再見。

Request for refund of the ticket
From- David (davidtan310050@my.uba.ac.uk)
To- admission@sthomaschurch.org.uk
22 September 2017

To whom it may concern,

I purchased a single admission ticket to the church for September 21 on your official website on August 21. Not until I arrived at the church that day did I realize the site had been closed for refurbishment. Between the time when I booked the ticket and when I traveled to the church, I did not receive notification of any kind regarding the church closure. Since this is a rather special condition, I suppose your refund policy does not apply. I tried to contact your customer service department on September 21 but the phone wasn't answered and so far I haven't got any reply from you. Therefore, I am writing this email to request a full refund of the ticket. Please handle this as soon as possible. If you received this email, please answer me as fast as you can.

David Tan

要求退費
寄件人- David
(davidtan310050@my.uba.ac.uk)
收件人-
admission@sthomaschurch.org.uk
2017年9月22日

給相關人員：

我在八月二十一日於你們的官網上買了一張九月二十一日的教堂單次票。直到當天到達教堂我才知道教堂已關閉維修了。在我訂票到到達現場這段時間裡，我沒有收到任何關於教堂關閉的消息。由於情況特殊，我想你們的退款規定應該不適用。在九月二十一日時我嘗試與你們的客服聯絡，但電話無人接聽。到現在我仍然沒有得到任何回覆。因此我寫這封信來要求你們給我全額退票。請儘速處理。如果你收到這封信，請儘速回信。

David Tan

【詞彙】

admission 入場／entrance fee 入場費／renovation 翻修／patronage 施捨／pavement 人行道／retain 保留／venue 地點／suspicious 可疑的／detrimental 有害的／prohibit 禁止／premise 房屋場地／accompany 陪伴／adverse 惡劣的／emergent 緊急的／wing 房屋側／porch 門廊／foyer 大廳／installment 安裝／exterior 外部的／steeple 尖塔／resurrection 重新樹立／drainage 排水口／addition 添加／chapel 小教堂／refurbishment 翻修／notification 通知

下列何者不能被帶到教堂裡？
(A) 門票
(B) 12歲小孩
(C) 數位相機
(D) 漢堡

【類型】尋找細節題型

【詞彙】
digital camera 數位相機

【正解】(D)

186 Which of the following cannot be brought into the church?

(A) tickets
(B) 12-year-old children
(C) digital camera
(D) hamburgers

【解析】根據Please note that smoking, eating and drinking are strictly prohibited on the premises.教堂內嚴禁飲食，因此漢堡不能帶入內。

關於聖湯瑪士教堂的敘述何者不正確？
(A) 入場免費。
(B) 某些區域正在翻修。
(C) 颱風天可能會關閉。
(D) 翻修的經費源自於門票收入。

【類型】是非題型

【詞彙】
entry 入場／refurbish 翻修／
stormy 風雨交加的／
proceeds 收入

【正解】(A)

187 Which of the following is NOT TRUE about St. Thomas Church?

(A) It is free of entry fee.
(B) Some parts of it are currently being refurbished.
(C) It might be closed on a stormy day.
(D) The funding of its renovation is based on its proceeds from admission.

【解析】根據門票上的資訊Price: 10 EUR (VAT included)我們能得知票不是免費的，因此選項(A)為非。根據公告，我們能得知教堂的某些區域正在翻修。根據門票上的說明The church reserves the right to change the routes or visiting time due to adverse weather conditions, safety issues or emergent events. 我們能得知天氣狀況不佳時，教堂可能會關閉。根據門票上的資訊The entrance fee will go towards the renovation of the St. Thomas Church. 我們能得知門票收入將運用於教堂的翻修計畫。因此，選項(B) (C) (D)皆正確，答案應選(A)。

關於教堂翻修的敘述何者正確？
(A) 要花一個禮拜。
(B) 東側壞掉的大門會進行維修。
(C) 北面內側會安裝新的時鐘。
(D) 小教堂會增加排水設施。

【類型】是非題型

【詞彙】
indicate 提及／install 安裝／
interior 內部的／surface 表面

【正解】(D)

188 What is indicated about the renovation of the church?

(A) It will take one week to complete.
(B) The broken gate of the east wing will be fixed.
(C) New clocks will be installed on the north interior surface.
(D) Some drainages will be added to the chapel.

【解析】根據公告，翻修時間為九月十五到十月十五，因此為期一個月，而非一周。因此選項(A)為非。文中並無提及教堂東側的大門壞掉的事情。因此選項(B)為非。新的時鐘是安裝在南面的外側，而非北面的內側。根據drainage additions at the chapel building，選項(D)是正確的。

---

189 What is David asking for from the church official?

(A) He is asking for the specific date of its reopening.
(B) He would like to know the details of its remodeling.
(C) He is requesting his money be returned.
(D) He is complaining about the customer service.

【解析】根據電郵中內容Therefore, I am writing this email to request a full refund of the ticket.我們能得知David要求教堂官方全額退費。因此答案應選(C)。

David要求教堂人員做什麼？
(A) 他想知道重新開張的具體時間。
(B) 他想知道裝修的細節。
(C) 要求退費。
(D) 抱怨客服。

【類型】尋找細節題型

【詞彙】
official 官方人員／
remodel 重新裝潢／
request 要求／
customer service 客戶服務

【正解】(C)

---

190 What is TRUE about David's ticket?

(A) It is purchased over a month before the first day of the church being closed.
(B) It is a student ticket booked on the website.
(C) The price has been refunded to David's account.
(D) The church official had notified David about the renovation before the ticket was booked.

【解析】根據電郵中內容，David的票是在八月二十一日買的，而教堂從九月十五日起進行翻修。因此買票日期到開始翻修日期並未超過一個月，因此選項(A)為非。從電郵中我們未能得知款項是否已退回給David，因此選項(C)為非。根據電郵中內容Between the time when I booked the ticket and when I traveled to the church, I did not receive notification of any kind regarding the church closure.表示David在買票之前或之後都沒有接受到關於教堂關閉的任何訊息。因此選項(D)為非。根據門票上的資訊Ticket Type: Student我們能得知David買的是學生票。因此答案應選(B)。

關於David的入場卷何者為真？
(A) 在教堂關閉的一個月前就買了。
(B) 是在網站上訂的學生票。
(C) 已經退款到David的帳戶裡了。
(D) 訂票之前，教堂人員就已經告知David整修的消息。

【類型】是非題型

【詞彙】
notify 通知

【正解】(B)

-------三明治理論-------

我們在找你！！！

我們在徵求店員！幫我們……

- 操作收銀機、收錢、發收據、有效並準確地登錄帳目。
- 親切地服務顧客並確保顧客在我們店裡用餐愉快。
- 管理存貨並每天訂原料，聯絡供應商和送貨員。
- 於營業時間前後打掃店裡環境。

工作時間……
- 每週至少24小時
- 能在週六上班更好

薪水……
- 全職：每月800元
- 兼職：每小時12元

如何應徵……
- 於www.sandwichtheory.com下載申請表，填妥之後於2017年11月7日之前寄到recruitment2017@swtr.com

如果您有任何疑問，請……
- 電郵聯絡我們 recruitment2017@swtr.com
或者
- 加我們Let's TALK直接詢問我們友善的員工

---------*Sandwich Theory*---------

We want you!!!

We are looking for several clerks who can...

- Operate the cash register, receive money, issue receipts, and register the money received with efficiency and accuracy
- Serve customers courteously and ensure all customers have a wonderful dining experience in our store
- Monitor stock and order ingredients on a daily basis, contact food supplier and distributor
- Carry out cleaning of store area before and after our opening hours

Required Working Hours...
- A minimum of 24 hours per week
- Availability to work on Saturday is preferable.

Salary...
- Full-time: $800 / month
- Part-time: $12 / hour

How to apply...
- Download the application form from www.sandwichtheory.com, fill it out and email to recruitment2017@swtr.com before 7 Nov 2017.

If you have any queries, you can...
- Email us at recruitment2017@swtr.com
or
- Add us on Let's TALK and ask our most friendly staff directly.

Let's TALK
Nov 9

Hello, my name is Celia. I am interested in the job advertised on the bulletin board on our campus. I was wondering if this is still available to apply for.

Celia Chen

The clerk one?

Stefanie Feng

Yes. Is it too late?

Celia Chen

Well, technically, it's well past the application deadline. But you are welcome to apply if you'd like. You can complete the application form, print it out and bring it to our store. Our manager will usually be in store from Monday thru Thursday in the afternoon.

Stefanie Feng

That's fantastic! Thank you so much! I will come to your store on Thursday afternoon. Is that OK for you?

Celia Chen

Great! See you then!

Stefanie Feng

Let's TALK
十一月九日

您好我叫Celia。我在我們校園的布告欄看到您的徵才信息。不曉得現在是否還能應徵?

Celia Chen

店員嗎?

Stefanie Feng

是!還來得及嗎?

Celia Chen

原則上現在已經超過截止日期一段時間了。但如果您要應徵還是歡迎的。你可以填好申請表,印出來帶到店裡。我們經理通常週一到週四下午都會在店裡。

Stefanie Feng

太棒了!非常感謝你!我週四下午去,可以嗎?

Celia Chen

好的!到時候見。

Stefanie Feng

三明治理論　　　求職申請表

Sandwich Theory　　　Employment Application

個人資料
姓名　CELIA CHEN
出生日期　1996年3月24日
國籍　中國　出生地　中國
地址　江蘇省花新市金鑫路
郵遞區號　002001
電話 (86) 15400758894　性別　女
緊急聯絡人
姓名　　　電話（　）　　　
地址　　　　　　　　　　
郵遞區號　　　　　
最高學歷　波士頓大學經濟學學士
近期工作經驗

◉ 無

公司　　職位　　在職期間　　
薪酬　　　　　　離職原因　　　
我曾在三明治理論工作過
○ 是　◉ 否
我在找　○ 全職　◉ 兼職工作
我在被通知錄取後　3　天能到
崗位
可工作時間

	一	二	三	四	五	六
08:00-12:00	V	V		V	V	V
12:00-16:00	V	V		V	V	
16:00-20:00	V	V				
20:00-23:30	V	V				

我在此確認以上資料正確無誤。

簽名　CELIA CHEN

日期　2017年11月10日

Personal Information
NAME　CELIA CHEN　DATE OF BIRTH　24 MARCH 1996
NATIONALITY　CHINA　PLACE OF BIRTH　CHINA
ADDRESS　JINXIN ROAD HUAXIN CITY JIANGSU PROVINCE
POST CODE　002001
TELEPHONE (86)　15400758894　GENDER　FEMALE
EMERGENCY CONTACT:
NAME　　　　　　TELEPHONE (　)　　　　
ADDRESS　　　　　POST CODE　　　　
EDUCATION MOST RECENTLY ATTAINEED　BU Economy BA
RECENT EMPLOYMENT RECORD

◉ NONE

COMPANY　　　POSITION　　　PERIOD　　　
PAYMENT　　　　　　REASON FOR LEAVING　　　　
I USED TO WORK IN SANDWICH THEORY BEFORE.　○ Y　◉ N
I AM LOOKING FOR A　○ full time　◉ part time job
I AM ABLE TO WORK　3　DAYS AFTER BEING NOTIFIED I AM HIRED.
I AM ABLE TO WORK IN THE FOLLOWING HOURS

	MON	TUE	WED	THU	FRI	SAT
08:00-12:00	V	V		V	V	V
12:00-16:00	V	V		V	V	
16:00-20:00	V	V				
20:00-23:30	V	V				

I hereby certify that the information given above is accurate and complete.

Sign　CELIA CHEN

Date　10 Nov 2017

【詞彙】
operate 操作／cash register 收銀機／issue 發送／
efficiency 效率／accuracy 準確／courteously 有禮地／
monitor 監控／stock 存貨／on a daily basis 每天／
distributor 配送員／minimum 最低／availability 可行性／
preferable 更可取的／recruitment 招聘／query 疑問／
bulletin board 布告欄／technically 技術上／nationality 國籍／
hereby 特此／certify 證明／accurate 準確的

191 Which of the following is NOT the duty of the job?

(A) Keeping sanitation of the workplace
(B) Serving diners at the store
(C) Delivering food to customers
(D) Carrying out stock replenishment

【解析】在徵才文中，根據Monitor stock and order ingredients on a daily basis我們可得知其中一項工作需要清點庫存並訂貨、補貨。根據Serve customers courteously我們可得知需要服務客人。根據Carry out cleaning of store area before and after our opening hours我們可得知需要保持店內衛生清潔。因此沒有被提及的選項是(C)外送食物。

下列何者不是這份工作的任務?
(A) 保持工作環境的衛生
(B) 服務店裡的顧客
(C) 外送食物給顧客
(D) 補貨

【類型】是非題型

【詞彙】
duty 責任／sanitation 衛生／workplace 工作場所／diner 用餐的人／deliver 遞送／replenishment 補充

【正解】(C)

---

192 What most likely is Celia's current job?

(A) A student
(B) A store owner
(C) A factory worker
(D) A plumber

【解析】根據第二則對話中Hello, my name is Celia. I am interested in the job advertised on the bulletin board on our campus.我們可推斷Celia仍然在校園中活動，因此可能是位學生。因此答案應選(A)。

Celia目前的工作最有可能是?
(A) 學生
(B) 店主
(C) 工廠工人
(D) 水管工

【類型】推論題型

【詞彙】
store owner 店主／plumber 水管工

【正解】(A)

---

193 When is the deadline of the job application?

(A) March 24
(B) November 7
(C) November 9
(D) November 10

【解析】根據徵才文章中Download the application form from www.sandwichtheory.com, fill it out and email to recruitment2017@swtr.com before 7 Nov 2017.可以知道截止日期是十一月七日。這類時間的題型相對較好把握，考生只需留心文章中日期的資訊。

工作應徵的截止日是甚麼時候?
(A) 3月24日
(B) 11月7日
(C) 11月9日
(D) 11月10日

【類型】尋找細節題型

【詞彙】
deadline 截止日期

【正解】(B)

根據信息，Celia應徵該工作的優勢為何？
(A) 她之前的工作經驗
(B) 她的教育背景
(C) 她的申請時間
(D) 她能在週末上班

【類型】推理題型

【詞彙】
advantage 優勢／
previous 先前的／
education 學歷

【正解】(D)

194 According to the information, what would be Celia's advantage as the job applicant?

(A) Her previous working experience
(B) Her education
(C) Her application time
(D) Her being able to work on weekends

【解析】本題須綜合第一篇及第三篇文章的細節資訊方能推理得出答案。在第一篇徵才文章中指出Availability to work on Saturday is preferable.而第三篇的申請表中Celia在週末的時間是勾選可以上班的，因此我們可推論這會是她的申請優勢。因此答案應選(D)。

從上述資訊我們能推論出？
(A) Celia在截止日前提出申請。
(B) 錄用之後Celia將領時薪。
(C) Celia無法符合最低工作時數的要求。
(D) 店經理每逢週三經常不在店裡。

【類型】推理題型

【詞彙】
meet 符合／
hourly 每小時的

【正解】(B)

195 What can be inferred from the information above?

(A) Celia met the deadline of the application.
(B) If hired, Celia will be paid at an hourly rate.
(C) Celia is not able to meet the requirement of the minimum working hours.
(D) The store manager is usually out of the store on Wednesdays.

【解析】本題須綜合三篇閱讀的細節資訊仔細過濾篩選。第二篇的對話透露了Celia申請的時間遠晚於截止日期了。因此選項(A)為非。根據第一篇Part-time: $12 / hour兼職員工薪資每小時12元計。而在第三篇的申請表中Celia勾選的是兼職人員，因此我們可推斷她錄用後將會領時薪。因此選項(B)正確。根據第一篇的說明最低工作時數為24小時，而Celia在申請表中勾選了52個小時的工作時數，因此選項(C)為非。根據第二篇對話，Stefanie說店經理通常週一到週四的下午都在店裡，因此選項(D)為非。

★**Questions 196-200 refer to the following letter, form and email.**

Dear Residents of Paris Garden Condominium,

Time flies unbelievably fast. It is always sad to say good-bye. Your time at Paris Garden Condominium is almost over and your tenancy will soon end on 5th September 2017. I am sure you'd found your check-out envelopes by the time you saw this letter. Please read the following information carefully. It tells you what to do when moving out.

- Your last check-out time is 16:00 5th September 2017. You are suggested to allow four days to a week to pack your belongings. Last minute packing is always exhausting.
- Please notify the office your departure time one day ahead of time and arrange an appointment with our housing assistant for the checkout inspection of your room.
- Before you leave, you should clean up your room and bathroom. Anything unwanted should be properly disposed of. You may lose your money from the deposit if you fail to complete a thorough cleaning.
- Please make sure you don't owe any rent or damage any properties of the condominium. Natural wear-out should be reported to us in advance. If we find any unreported damage, you may be charged the cost of the repair work needed. In the worst case, you may face legal action.
- To claim your $1,000 deposit, you need to fill out the deposit refund form which can be found in the envelope along with this letter, and return a signed copy along with your room key to the office. Your deposit will be returned to you within a month.

各位巴黎花園公寓的居民好：

時光飛逝。再見總難說出口。您在巴黎公寓的租約即將在2017年9月5日到期。相信您看到這封信的時候也應該拿到退宿信封了。請詳閱下列資訊，關於您離宿的手續。

- 您最晚離宿的時間為2017年9月5日下午四點。您最好提前四天開始整理行李，不然會很累人的。
- 請提前一天告知辦公室同仁您的離宿時間並和我們的房仲助理約時間檢查您的房間。
- 離宿之前請清潔您的房間及浴室。請丟棄廢棄物。如果您沒有確實清潔，我們將會從您的押金中扣取款項。
- 請不要積欠房租或破壞房屋設施。自然損壞應提前報備辦公室。如果我們發現任何沒有通報的損壞，您需要負擔修理費。情節嚴重者須面臨法律責任。
- 您需填妥押金退還表來領取您的1,000元押金。表格在此信的附件。填妥後簽名，連同房間鑰匙交還到辦公室。押金會在一個月之內退還給您。

- 此段期間辦公室開放時間為週一到週六8:00-17:00。如有任何問題請不吝與我們聯繫。我們的分機為6500。

希望您這段時間在巴黎花園公寓居住愉快。非常感謝您，祝您未來一切順利。

祝　安好

Mary Keith

押金退還表	
全名： Kimberley Conn	大樓：北棟 樓層：9樓
居住號：105766	房型：
房間號：9010	公寓型臥室

銀行資料　（請提供正確完整的資料）
銀行名稱：東方銀行
戶名：Kimberley Conn
帳號：009887194730921
郵遞區號：005479

簽名：*Kimberley Conn*
日期：2017年9月4日

2017年9月25日
主旨：押金返還通知
寄件人：巴黎花園公寓
收件人：Kimberley

親愛的Kimberley：

願您安好。我們已將押金退到您的銀行帳戶。金額為798元。下列表格為收費信息。

- Our office is open 8:00-17:00 from Monday to Saturday during this period. Please don't hesitate to contact us if you have any questions. Our extension number is 6500.

We hope you enjoyed your stay in Paris Garden Condominium. Thank you and wish you all the best in the future.

Kind Regards,

Mary Keith

Deposit Return Form	
Full Name: Kimberley Conn	Building: North
Resident Number: 105766	Floor: 9th
Room Number: 9010	Room Type: Studio

Bank Details (Please make sure you provide accurate and complete information)
Name of Bank: Eastern Bank
Name of the Account Holder: Kimberley Conn
Account Number: 009887194730921
Zip Code: 005479

Your Signature: *Kimberley Conn*
Date: 4 September 2017

---

25 September 2017
Subject: Deposit Return Notice
Sender: Paris Garden Condo
Receiver: Kimberley

Dear Kimberley,

We hope this email finds you well. We have returned the deposit to your bank account. The amount returned is **$798**. The following list shows the details of the charge from the original deposit.

- Utility bill: $127 (August 2 – September 1)
- Cleaning work of the <u>limescale</u> in the bathroom and kitchen: $25
- Removal of the adhesive mark on the wall and door: $25
- Repair work of the vacuum: $25

If you have any questions about your refund, please reply to us.
Hope all is well on your side.

Jack Mill
Paris Garden Condo

- 電費：127元（八月二日到九月一日）
- 浴室及廚房的水垢清理費25元
- 牆上及門上的膠帶痕清除費：25元
- 吸塵器修理費：25元

如您對退款有任何疑問，請立即聯絡我們。
願您一切順利。

Jack Mill
巴黎花園公寓

【詞彙】

resident 居民／condominium 公寓／tenancy 租約／
belonging 所有物／exhausting 累人的／inspection 檢查／
unwanted 廢棄的／dispose of 丟棄／deposit 押金／
thorough 完整的／property 不動產／claim 領取／
utility bill 電費單／limescale 水垢／adhesive 黏著的／
vacuum 吸塵器

196 What is the topic of the information above?
(A) Bidding for janitorial work
(B) Office square letting
(C) Moving out of a property
(D) Application for bank clerks

【解析】根據第一封信的內容第一段，我們可得知這是有關一間公寓正辦理的離宿手續。因此答案應選(C)。

以上資訊的主題是什麼？
(A) 衛生工程的招標
(B) 辦公室出租
(C) 離宿手續
(D) 應徵銀行行員

【類型】尋找主題題型

【詞彙】
bid 招標／janitorial 衛生的／
let 出租

【正解】(C)

下列何者不是租屋人需做的事？
(A) 填妥申請表
(B) 歸還鑰匙
(C) 打掃房間
(D) 申請租金延期繳費

【類型】是非題型

【詞彙】
tenant 租屋人／fill in 填寫／
extension 延期

【正解】(D)

197 Which of the following is NOT the thing the tenants were asked to do?

(A) Filling in an application form
(B) Returning the key
(C) Cleaning up the room
(D) Filing for rent payment extension

【解析】根據第一封信的資訊you should clean up your room and bathroom、you need to fill out the deposit refund form、return a signed copy along with your room key to the office 等，選項(A)(B)(C)皆是租屋人需要做的事。選項(D)在文中找不到任何資訊。因此答案應選(D)。

關於Kimberley何者正確？
(A) 她是巴黎花園公寓的職員。
(B) 她住在北棟9樓。
(C) 她沒有提供正確的銀行資訊。
(D) 她沒有準時交申請表。

【類型】是非題型

【詞彙】
officer 官員／fail to 未能／
in time 即時

【正解】(B)

198 What is TRUE about Kimberley?

(A) She is an officer at Paris Garden Condominium.
(B) She lived in the ninth floor of the north building.
(C) She failed to provide the correct bank information.
(D) She failed to turn in the application form in time.

【解析】根據第二篇的押金退還表中，我們能得知Kimberley 住在巴黎花園公寓的北棟9樓。因此答案應選(B)。

Kimberley欠了多少水電費？
(A) 25元
(B) 50元
(C) 127元
(D) 798元

【類型】尋找細節題型

【詞彙】
owe 欠／electricity 電

【正解】(C)

199 How much did Kimberley owe for the electricity and water bill?

(A) $25
(B) $50
(C) $127
(D) $798

【解析】根據第三篇的電郵中Utility bill: $127 (August 2 – September 1)，積欠的水電費為127元，因此答案應選(C)。

200 What is the word "limescale" in line 10 closest in meaning to?

(A) watermark
(B) bathtub
(C) toiletry
(D) cutlery

【解析】limescale為「水垢」的意思，與watermark「水漬」意思最相近。

第十行的limescale最接近下列何者？
(A) 水漬
(B) 浴缸
(C) 廁所設備
(D) 刀具

【類型】同義字題型

【詞彙】
watermark 水漬／
bathtub 浴缸／
toiletry 浴室設備／cutlery 刀具

【正解】(A)

交貨延遲為本公司配送系統所發生的意外問題所導致。

【類型】動詞時態題型

【詞彙】
shipping delay交貨延遲／
unexpected 預期外的／
occur 發生／
delivery system配送系統／
trick 詭計／request 請求

【正解】(A)

101 The shipping delay was caused by an unexpected problem that _____ in our delivery system.

(A) occurred (B) occurring

(C) occurs (D) has occurred

【解析】本題的空格接在that之後，因此判斷從空格處開始，是一個形容詞子句，用來形容先行詞unexpected problem（意料之外的問題）是出在配送系統上。這個形容詞子句，動詞必須跟前面句子的時態一致，同為過去簡單式，故選(A)。

傑佛遜先生證明了自己是個優異的銷售人員，因為他的業績表現不斷超越我們的期待。

【類型】副詞詞彙題型

【詞彙】
outstanding出色的／
salesperson 銷售人員／
expectation 期待／periodically
定期地；偶爾／coincidentally
碰巧地／accidently 偶然地／
consistently一貫地

【正解】(D)

102 Mr. Jefferson proved himself an outstanding salesperson as his sales performance _____ exceeded our expectation.

(A) periodically (B) coincidentally

(C) accidently (D) consistently

【解析】要選出適合本題空格的副詞，必須考量整個句子的脈絡關係。要證明自己是個出色的銷售人員，業績表現以 (A)所表示的「偶爾」、(B)所表示的「碰巧」以及(C)所表示的「偶然」的頻率超越期待，並不足以顯現一個銷售人員的優異，而(D)所表示的「持續不斷地」超越期待，恰能呼應這個句子所想呈現的讚揚之意，故為最適當的選項。

這是一個緊急的案子，我們必須在三個工作日內將它完成。

【類型】形容詞詞彙題型

【詞彙】
urgent 緊急的／
working day工作日

【正解】(A)

103 This is an urgent project that we need to get _____ within three working days.

(A) done (B) all

(C) well (D) over

【解析】【解析】get sth. done 為「將某事完成」的用法，get sth. +adj.這個用法中所用的形容詞為「動狀詞」，即以過去分詞做形容詞用，表示「某件事」以「被動的形式」呈現某種狀態，如get the project finished即「將案子做完」。本題選項中只有(A)是分詞形容詞，其他都是一般形容詞，故選(A)。

104 Ms. Leech has been ＿＿＿ to the position of the Manager of the Research and Development Department.

(A) raised

(B) promoted

(C) increased

(D) enhanced

【解析】本題是要根據句子前後文的意思，選出適合放在空格中的動詞。題目的意思要表達的「李琪小姐被晉升至研發部經理一職」，因此空格中必須是可以表達「晉升」的動詞。(A)的raise有「提升、提高」之意，但是多用來表示「薪資的提升」；(C)的increase多用在表示「數量的增加」；(D)的enhance則用在表示「價值或品質的提升」，只有(B)的promote是用來表示「職務或地位」的提升，故正解為(B)。

李琪小姐已經被晉升至研發部門的經理一職。

【類型】動詞詞彙題型

【詞彙】
position職位／
the Research and Development Department 研發部門／
raise提高／
promote晉升／
increase增加／
enhance提升

【正解】(B)

---

105 Since you are not satisfied with the product, we respect your decision if you wish to get a full ＿＿＿ of your purchase.

(A) refund

(B) return

(C) payment

(D) attendance

【解析】由句子前半句提到not satisfied with the product「對產品不滿意」，可知句子後半句所提到的decision「決定」，應該是與「退回商品」有關。(A)的refund與(B)的return都有「退還」的意思，但是看到空格前出現get a full，便可知這裡要用get a full refund of sth.「將某物全額退費」的片語用法，故(A)為正解。其他選項中的名詞並沒有與get a full合在一起使用的相關用法。(C)的payment是指購買者支付給供貨者的費用；(D)的attendance與full放在一起指full attendance「全勤」，與本題句意無關。

既然您對產品不滿意，如果您希望能全額退回您購買的商品，我們將尊重您的決定。

【類型】名詞選擇題型

【詞彙】
be satisfied with sth. 對某事滿意／refund退費／purchase購買的商品

【正解】(A)

我們剛剛收到通知，說我們的供應商無法提供我們所需要的電腦零件。

【類型】動詞詞彙題型

【詞彙】
supplier 供應商／
computer component 電腦零件／
expect 期待／inform通知／
involve包含；涉及

【正解】(C)

106 We have just been _____ that our supplier is unable to provide us the computer components we need.

(A) expected   (B) talked

(C) informed   (D) involved

【解析】根據空格前面的現在完成式助動詞可知空格中應選出適當的現在完成式動詞。這裡要表達的是「被告知」某訊息，因此選項中只有(C)的inform「通知、告知」是能確實傳達此意的動詞。(B)的talk為「說話」的意思，不能用來表示「告知」；(A)的expect與(D)的involve放入空格中都無法表達出正確的句意，故不選。

要安排與尼爾森先生會面的時間，請於上午十時至下午六時這段時間跟他的秘書聯絡。

【類型】介系詞題型

【詞彙】
schedule 安排／
appointment 會面

【正解】(A)

107 To schedule an appointment with Mr. Nelson, please contact his secretary _____ the hours of 10 a.m. and 6 p.m.

(A) between   (B) from

(C) within   (D) besides

【解析】此題示要選出適合放在空格中的介系詞。要判斷出適當的介系詞，句子中10 a.m.與6 p.m.中間的連接詞and是重要關鍵字。between A and B為表示「在A與B之間」的用法，而from A to B為表示「從A到B」的用法。within表示「在……範圍內」，後面通常接「一段時間」，如three hours等；besides則表示「除……之外」，後面通常接名詞。故(A)為正確答案。

所有的員工都受邀出席十二月廿三日在君悅酒店舉行的尾牙餐會。

【類型】動詞詞彙題型

【詞彙】
employee 員工／year-end banquet 年終、尾牙餐會／
achieve達到/benefit 得益／
invite邀請／revise修改

【正解】(C)

108 All employees are _____ to attend the year-end banquet at Grand Hyatt Hotel on December 23rd.

(A) achieved   (B) benefited

(C) invited   (D) revised

【解析】本題為被動語態的題型，空格中的動詞要根據句意選出適當的過去分詞。本題的句子主要是要表達「受邀出席餐會」之意，選項中的動詞中只有(C)能適當表達出句意，其他動詞放入空格中都無法讓句子有意義，故選(C)。

109 Ms. Woodfield will be _____ her annual leave for two weeks, starting January 12th.

(A) on

(B) in

(C) for

(D) at

伍菲德小姐從一月12日開始將會休兩個星期的年假。

【類型】介系詞題型

【詞彙】
on leave休假／
annual leave年假

【正解】(A)

【解析】本題的空格要依前後文選出能與名詞leave「休假」合用的介系詞。be on leave為表示「休假」的片語用法，on在這個片語中是「處於……狀態中」的用法。其他選項的介系詞都無此用法，故(A)為正解。

---

110 Normally, our employees are _____ to their first annual leave after working for one year.

(A) given   (B) entitled

(C) taken   (D) allocated

一般而言，我們的員工在工作一年後才能享有第一次年假。

【類型】動詞詞彙題型

【詞彙】
be entitled to 給予權利；使有資格／annual leave 年休

【正解】(B)

【解析】本題是要考應試者是否會使用be entitled to「給予權利」這個片語動詞的用法。根據空格的前後文，可知本句意在表示「工作一年後使能享有年假」，故選(B)。(A)的動詞原形give為授與動詞，介系詞to必須放在employee前；(C)之take所表示的「拿、取」與(D)之allocate所表示的「分派、分配」，放在本句空格中均無法使本句具有意義，因此不選。

---

111 Helen Spencer was _____ as the General Manager because of her strong educational background and her considerable work experience.

(A) employed   (B) pointed

(C) assigned   (D) offered

海倫史賓塞因其優秀的教育背景及重要的工作經歷而被任命為總經理。

【類型】動詞詞彙題型

【詞彙】
employ 聘雇／general manager 總經理／educational background學歷背景／work experience工作經歷

【正解】(A)

【解析】本題的空格，是要根據句意及前後文選出正確的動詞過去分詞。要選出正確的動詞，空格後面的介系詞as是個不能忽略的關鍵。(C)的assign雖有「指派、任命」之意，但是不與as連用；(B)的point為「指」，容易與appoint「指派」這個動詞混淆，要小心不要上當；(D)的offer指「提供」，用來表示「提供工作機會或優惠等」，亦不宜放在這裡使用。(A)的employ指「聘雇」，employ sb. as+職稱，為用來表示「聘雇某人做某職」的片語用法，故為正解。

結帳區有一長排顧客等著被服務。

【類型】動詞時態題型

【詞彙】
queue 隊伍／customer 顧客／
checkout 結帳區

【正解】(C)

---

112 There is a long queue of customers _____ to be served at the checkout.

(A) awaited   (B) waited

(C) waiting   (D) are waiting

【解析】此題主要是要考以there+be+名詞+V-ing來表示「有……在做某事」的句型用法。空格中的動詞為表示there be句型中的真主詞customer所正在進行的動作，因此這個動詞必須是現在分詞，故選(C)。

由於我們的計劃做了異動，這份提案需要做點修改。

【類型】動詞詞彙題型

【詞彙】
modification 修改／
declaration 聲明／
encouragement 鼓勵／
communication溝通

【正解】(C)

---

113 This proposal requires some _____ as we have made a change in our plan.

(A) declaration

(B) encouragement

(C) modification

(D) communication

【解析】 句子中的連接詞as在此為「因為」之意，可知句子前後彼此有因果關係。句子中提到的「因」為「計劃做了異動」，由於計劃有所改變，使得提案需要做些(C)修改，才合乎常理。若是空格中放入(A)聲明、(B)鼓勵或(D)溝通，都會讓整個句子變得令人難以理解。故選(C)。

所有應徵者請帶著您最高學歷證明及英語能力證明來參加面試。

【類型】主詞選擇題型

【詞彙】
applicant 申請人／
diploma 學位證書；文憑／
English proficiency certificate
英文能力證明／
interview 面試

【正解】(A)

---

114 All _____ please bring your highest diplomas and English proficiency certificates with you to the interview.

(A) applicants   (B) contestants

(C) consultants   (D) investigators

【解析】本題空格為能符合句子情境的人物主詞。本句的最關鍵字為最後一個字：interview「面試」。依據句子中的其他詞彙如diploma學歷文憑及English proficiency certificate英語能力證明，便可依常理推斷出需要攜帶這兩樣東西參加「面試」的人應該是某職務的「應徵者」，故選項中以(A)為最適合的答案。

115 The _____ salary for a mechanical engineer in our company will be NT$45,000 per month.

(A) initial   (B) intimate

(C) initiate   (D) early

【解析】本題要選出放在名詞salary「薪資」前的形容詞。將選項中的形容詞分別放在名詞salary前，便可選出正確的答案。initial salary表示「起始薪資」，即「起薪」，是為正解。(B)的intimate表「親密的」及(C)的initiate表「新加入的」，都不是適合用來形容salary的形容詞。要注意的是(D)的early有「提早的」之含意，early salary在英文中有「提前預支薪水」之意，與本題句意並不相符，故非適當的選擇。

本公司技術工程師的起薪為每個月新台幣45,000元。

【類型】形容詞選擇題型

【詞彙】
initial salary 起薪／
mechanical engineer 技術工程師／
intimate親密的／
initiate新加入的／
early 早期的、提早的

【正解】(A)

---

116 The designated operators must _____ inspect all the elevators and escalators to ensure they are in satisfactory working order.

(A) perfunctorily   (B) thoroughly

(C) reluctantly   (D) dilatorily

【解析】此題空格中應填入能適當形容句子中的動詞inspect的副詞。根據本句前後文意，(B)的thoroughly表「徹底仔細地」，放在空格中能表達「為了確保電梯及電扶梯能維持良好運作，操作員應對其做徹底檢查」的完整句意，是為正解。若用(A)的perfunctorily來形容動詞，則表示「敷衍地檢查」；用(C)的reluctantly來形容，則表示「勉為其難地檢查」；用(D)的dilatorily來形容則為「慢吞吞地檢查」，依常理判斷，以上三種檢查方式都無法確實讓機器設備維持良好運作，故皆非適當副詞選項。

指定操作員必須徹底檢查所有電梯及電扶梯，以確保良好運作。

【類型】副詞詞彙題型

【詞彙】
designated operator 操作員／
inspect檢查／elevator電梯／
escalator 手扶梯／satisfactory
令人滿意的／perfunctorily敷衍地／thoroughly徹底仔細地／
reluctantly 勉強地／
dilatorily慢吞吞地

【正解】(B)

---

117 We have to _____ this proposal, as it does not meet our current need.

(A) promote   (B) adopt

(C) encourage   (D) decline

【解析】由句子中的連接詞as「因為」，可之本句前後互為因果關係。連接詞as之後已說明了「不符目前所需」，可知這項提案是「不可用的」，因此(A)放入空格後表示「促進此提案」、(B)放入空格後表示「採用此提案」及(C)放入空格後表示「鼓勵此提案」，都與句意不合。只有(D)的decline，放入空格後意指「回絕此提案」，是能夠與「不符合目前所需」相呼應的結果。

由於此項提案不符合我們目前的需要，我們必須予以回絕。

【類型】動詞詞彙題型

【詞彙】
proposal 提案／meet符合／
need 需求／decline 拒絕／
adopt 採用／encourage 鼓勵

【正解】(D)

雖然我們的辦公室將遷移，電話和傳真號碼還是維持不變。

【類型】形容詞題型

【詞彙】
relocate 遷移

【正解】(D)

118 Even though our office will be relocated, both our office phone number and fax number remain _____ .

(A) usual   (B) same

(C) similar   (D) unchanged

【解析】本句的重點是要表示公司電話維持不變，空格中要填入適當的形容詞。本題的困難處在於選項中的形容詞皆有類似的含義，因此要確實認識每個形容詞的用法，才能作出正確選擇。(A)的usual指「平常的、慣常的、一如以往的」，通常與as連用，如remain as usual，即可表示「維持與以往一樣」；(B)的same指「相同的」，通常與the連用，如remain the same 即表示「維持相同」；(C)的similar則指「相似的」，並不表示「相同」或「不變」，因此以上三個形容詞都不適用於本句的空格。(D)的unchanged指「未改變的、無變化的」，放在空格中恰能表示公司電話「維持不變」。

您一旦收到更新通知，就應該儘快在到期之前上網更新您的註冊資訊。

【類型】連接詞選擇題型

【詞彙】
renewal notice更新通知／
renew更新／
registration註冊；登記／
as soon as possible儘快／
expire到期

【正解】(B)

119 Once you receive your renewal notice, you should renew your registration online as soon as possible _____ it expires.

(A) until   (B) before

(C) after   (D) when

【解析】本題要依空格前面句子所描述的內容來選擇一個適當的連接詞。依句意可知註冊資訊要儘快更新，句子最後又提到expire「到期」，可知時間上有其急迫性，因此填入(A)until表「直到到期」、(C)after表「到期之後」或(D) when表「到期之時」，這些在時間上都不符合「儘快更新」的概念，只有填入(B)before表「到期之前」，才符合常理，故選(B)。

根據合約內容，我們的訂單兩天前就該到了。但是我們卻至今都尚未收到商品。

【類型】動詞時態題型

【詞彙】
contract合約／order訂購的東西／receive收到／commodity商品

【正解】(A)

120 According to our contract, our order _____ arrived two days ago. However, we haven't received our commodities up to now.

(A) should have   (B) will have

(C) had   (D) have

【解析】描述「應發生而未發生之事」時，時態上會用「should＋現在完成式」來表示。由本題後句描述之內容可知「還未收到商品」，而前句要表達的內容即「兩天前就應該收到訂單了」，因此時態上要選(A)should have，以表示商品「應該早已經要寄到卻還未寄到」。

121 _____ some personal factors, Mr. Crooks will not be able to attend the new branch office's opening ceremony.

(A) In case　　　　　(B) Due to

(C) Because　　　　　(D) So that

由於某些個人因素，克魯克斯先生將無法出席新分公司的開幕會。

【類型】連接詞選擇題型

【詞彙】
personal factor 個人因素／
branch office 分公司／opening ceremony 開幕典禮

【正解】(B)

【解析】【解析】本句空格處是要填入一個可以呼應前後句因果關係的連接詞。後面的句子內容「無法出席開幕會」乃結果，故前面的空格必須是能陳述「原因」的連接詞。由於空格後為名詞，表示原因的連接詞如果要用(C) because，必須與of連用，故不選(C)；(A) in case為表示「假如；萬一」，並無表達因果關係的用法，故不選(A)；(D) so that表「結果」，並不是用來陳述原因的連接詞，故(D)亦不可選。(B) due to後面接名詞，表示「由於……之故」，是為正解。

122 The central air-conditioning system of the office building is currently out of service _____ annual maintenance.

(A) plus　　　　　(B) with

(C) for　　　　　(D) around

此辦公大樓的中央空調系統目前因為年度保養而暫停使用。

【類型】介系詞選擇題型

【詞彙】
central air-conditioning system 中央空調系統／office building 辦公大樓／out of service 暫停服務／annual maintenance 年度保養

【正解】(C)

【解析】以句子的整體脈絡來看，「做年度保養」是「中央空調系統暫停使用」的原因，四個選項的介系詞中，只有(C) for有「為了……」的含義，可用來表示「為了某種目的或原因」，故正解為(C)。

123 The department dinner has been postponed because it has a time _____ with an employee-training course.

(A) conflict　　　　　(B) difference

(C) break　　　　　(D) fight

因為時間跟一場員工訓練課程衝突，部門聚餐時間已經被延後了。

【類型】名詞選擇題型

【詞彙】
department dinner 部門聚餐／time conflict 時間衝突／employee-training course 員工訓練課程

【正解】(A)

【解析】空格中要填入的名詞與空格前的time一起使用，為一個複合名詞。英文中並沒有time break或time fight這兩個複合名詞，故(C)與(D)可先刪除不選；time difference指的是不同地域之間的「時差」，亦與本句文意不符，故(B)也非適當答案。time conflict指「時間衝突」，表示兩件事將發生在同一時間，故正解為(A)。

為了彌補我方失誤，我們想提供您一張本餐廳兩客免費晚餐的優惠券。

【類型】形容詞選擇題型

【詞彙】
make up 彌補／
coupon 優惠券／
complimentary 贈送的／
complicated 複雜的／
compulsory 強制的／
complementary 互補的

【正解】(A)

124 To make up for our mistake, we would like to offer you a coupon for two _____ dinners in our restaurant.
(A) complimentary
(B) complicated
(C) compulsory
(D) complementary

【解析】本題空格處要填入修飾名詞dinners的形容詞。由句子中的coupon「優惠券」這個字可知這份晚餐內容在消費上是對顧客有利的。用(B) complicated形容dinner將表示「複雜的晚餐」，而用(C) compulsory形容將表示「強迫的晚餐」，都不符合常理。值得特別留意的是(A) complimentary所表示的「贈送的、免費的」與(D) complementary所表示的「互補的」，這兩個形容詞的拼字只有一字之差，一不小心很容易選錯。complimentary dinners意指「免費晚餐」，符合句意，故(A)為正解。

從現在起，除了大型活動策劃及佈置之外，我們也將提供活動咨詢服務以及產品促銷服務。

【類型】連接詞選擇題型

【詞彙】
from now on 從現在起／
planning 策劃／
arrangement 佈置安排／
activity consultation service 活動諮詢服務／
production promotion service 產品促銷服務

【正解】(A)

125 From now on, besides large event planning and arrangement, we also provide activity consultation services _____ production promotion services.
(A) as well as
(B) as long as
(C) as soon as
(D) as far as

【解析】觀察本題空格前後，為兩個詞性相同的名詞詞組，而選項中只有(A) as well as「不但……而且……；和」，為可以用來連接兩個相同詞性的詞組的連接詞，故正確答案為(A)。(B)的as long as「只要」及(C)的as soon as「一……就……」，都是後面要連接完整句子的連接詞；至於(D)的as far as則是用來表示「遠至……」的連接詞，皆不適合放在本句空格中。

126 Your request for a seven-day leave of absence will not be approved _____ you can't find anyone to cover your position.

(A) whether   (B) if

(C) although   (D) unless

如果你無法找到代理職務的人，你的七天休假申請將不會被批准。

【類型】連接詞選擇題型

【詞彙】
request申請／leave of absence 休假／approve批准／cover sb.'s position 負責某人職務

【正解】(B)

【解析】本句空格處要填入一個能表示前後句彼此的條件關係之連接詞，也就是某事只有在條件成立時，才有可能發生。(A)的whether為「是否」之意，(C)的although表「雖然」，都不能放在條件句中表示條件。(B)的if指「如果」，表示「若無法找到代理人」，休假申請就無法獲准，是為正解。(D)的unless表「除非」，雖然也可以放在條件句中表示條件，但是必須是在「排除某種狀況」時使用，因此若要放在本句空格中，後面的句子要改成you can find someone to cover your position才能成立。

---

127 The budget for this project is _____ ; therefore we must get this contract within the budget.

(A) limited   (B) sufficient

(C) ineffective   (D) precise

這項提案的預算有限，因此我們必須在預算內拿到這份合約。

【類型】形容詞選擇題型

【詞彙】
budget 預算／limited 有限的／sufficient 充足的／ineffective無效的／precise 精確的

【正解】(A)

【解析】本句空格中的形容詞是要修飾名詞budget「預算」。由後面的句子表示「要在預算內拿到合約」，可知這份預算是有所限制的，因此選項中以(A)limited 所表示的「有限的」最適當，故為正解。

---

128 We should _____ a meeting this week to discuss the details of the development project.

(A) experience   (B) schedule

(C) gather   (D) invite

我們應該在本週找個時間開會，以討論這份開發案的細節。

【類型】動詞詞彙題型

【詞彙】
detail細節／development project 開發案／experience 體驗／schedule安排時間／gather 集合／invite 邀請

【正解】(B)

【解析】本句空格處應填入一個可以與名詞meeting搭配使用的動詞。(A)的experience通常用來表示「體驗或經歷」某個事件或過程」；(C)的gather通常用來表示「集合」某事物，後面不為單數名詞；(D)的invite通常用來「邀請」某人參加某活動，後面要接人物，因此這三個動詞皆不適合放在本句空格。(B)的schedule意指「安排……的時間」，schedule a meeting即表示「安排會議時間」，故為正解。

無論您是否接受這份工作,請在本週五之前回覆我們您的決定。

【類型】動詞詞彙題型

【詞彙】
job offer工作機會／
get back to sb. 回覆某人／
no later than不遲於……／
admit承認／
return返還／
accept 接受／
declare 宣布

【正解】(C)

---

129 Whether you would _____ this job offer or not, please get back to us with your decision no later than this Friday.
(A) admit
(B) return
(C) accept
(D) declare

【解析】本句空格要填入一個與名詞job offer「工作機會」搭配使用之動詞。一般而言,面對工作機會不外兩個選擇,一是「接受」,二是「回絕」,選項中只有(C) accept為適當動詞,其他選項內皆非適合job offer的動詞選擇,故正解為(C)。

我們的人資部秘書將會回答有關聘雇政策及程序的任何問題。

【類型】介系詞選擇題型

【詞彙】
HR secretary 人資部秘書／
employment policy 聘雇政策／
procedure程序

【正解】(B)

---

130 Our HR secretary will answer any questions _____ employment policies and procedures.
(A) connecting
(B) regarding
(C) considering
(D) according

【解析】本句空格要填入能表示「有關」聘雇政策及程序之問題的介系詞。選項中只有(B)的regarding有「關於」的含義,是為正解。(A)的connecting為動詞connect的現在分詞,並非介系詞;(C)的considering為「考慮到……」之意,considering加上後面的名詞並無法形成一個可以用來形容前面的名詞questions的介系詞片語,故不適用;(D)的according通常要與to連用,以表示「根據」,而且語意上亦與本句不符,亦非適當選擇。

▶ PART 6

Directions: Read the texts on the following pages. A word or phrase is missing in some of the sentences. Answer choices are given below each of these articles. Select the best answer to complete the text. Then mark the letter (A), (B), (C) or (D) on your answer sheet.

Questions 131-134 refer to the following email.

To: Last-year students
From: Career Service
Subject: Career Event for International Students

Dear Students,
The Careers Service is happy to bring you an event that may be of interest to you.
── A pre-employment workshop run by PBA Company on December 2nd, Saturday.

PBA Company, is the largest recruitment platform ___131___ in supporting International students. They deliver a ___132___ pre-employment workshop to help you find jobs in Asia.

In this workshop you will learn
• Latest information about Asia's job market
• When you should start seeking job opportunities
• Application strategy and skills ___133___
• Introductions to write a CV/resume that will bring you through the screening
• How to prepare for different types of interviews

___134___

Kind regards,
Emily
Career Service

收件人：畢業生
寄件人：求職服務
主旨：針對國際學生的求職服務

親愛的學生們，
求職服務中心很高興致上一場您可能會有興趣的活動──一場由PBA公司所辦的職前座談會將於十二月二日星期六舉行。

PBA公司是專門支持國際學生最大的求職平台。他們提供專業的職前座談會，幫助您找到亞洲的工作。

在這場座談會您將學習
• 有關亞洲職場的最新資訊
• 何時應開始尋找工作機會
• 按部就班的應徵策略與技巧
• 一份助您通過篩選的履歷之撰寫入門
• 如何準備不同類型的面試

名額有限，請立刻報名以確保名額。

謹致問候，
艾蜜莉
求職服務處

131 (A) specialize

(B) specializes

(C) specializing

(D) specialized

【解析】這裡要考的是be specialized in sth. 這個表示「專門從事；專攻」的片語用法。本處空格前省略了關係代名詞及be動詞，空格處應填入specialize（專門從事）的過去分詞specialized，故正解 (D)。

【類型】形容詞選擇題型

【正解】(A)

132 (A) professional

(B) skillful

(C) proficient

(D) manageable

【解析】根據前文「PBA公司唯一專門支持國際學生的最大招募平台」，因此在協助學生求職上應俱有一定的專業度，故此公司所提供給學生的職前座談會，以(A)「專業的」來形容最為適當，故選(A)。選項(B)的skillful通常用來形容「技術純熟的」職能專家；選項(C)的proficient通常用來表示「精通」某事，並與介系詞in或at搭配使用；選項(D)的manageable則為「可控制的；可管理的」之意，將這個字放在此處形容pre-employment似乎並無法收「吸引學生參與」之效。因此以上三個選項皆不是適當的答案。

【類型】副詞選擇題型

【正解】(D)

133 (A) day by day

(B) one by one

(C) page by page

(D) step by step

【解析】這一句要表示座談會中能提供與會者「以什麼方式」習得求職策略與技巧，把選項(A)的day by day（日復一日地）、選項(B)的one by one（一個接一個地）或選項(C)的page by page（一頁一頁地）放進空格，在句意上都顯得詞不達意而通暢不足；只有選項(D)的「一步步地循序漸進」，能表示「讓參與者按部就班地學到求職技巧」的意思，故以(D)為最適當的答案。

★ **134** (A) Sign up immediately to secure place - places are limited.
(B) Contact our staff if you wish to cancel your appointment.
(C) Thanks again for your warmest hospitality.
(D) Please send us the signed contract without delay.

【類型】句子插入題型

【詞彙】
sign up 報名、簽到／
secure確保／
place名額／
hospitality招待／
without delay即刻

【正解】(A)

【解析】新制多益閱讀測驗增加了與托福測驗一樣的「句子插入題型」，應試者根據前後文，將一個最適當的句子插入文章適當的位置中。因此應試者必須確實理解前後文意，對整篇文章脈絡有更好地掌握，才能夠選出正確的答案。根據前文，本篇郵件內容主要是在「宣傳一個職前座談會活動」，因此此處應該是一個給「有興趣參與活動的人」的提醒。選項(B)提到「取消預約」；選項(C)提到「溫暖款待」以及選項(D)提到「簽好的合約」，以上均跟前面內容的「職前座談會活動宣傳」無關，因此皆非適當選項。選項(A)提醒此活動「名額有限」，因此有興趣的人應「立刻報名」，是最適當的答案，故為正解。

Questions 135-138 refer to the following announcement.

Announcement-Office Closing

Please be ___135___ that MBP Shanghai Office has declared a business closure for the Annual Company Trip from 30 November (Thursday) to 3 December (Sunday). As such, all MBP delivery services will be ___136___ put on hold during the time. Our office will resume its operation as usual on 4 December (Monday) and will respond to all queries thereafter.

For any ___137___, please contact us at 2412-1234 or send an email to customerservice99@mbp.com.
___138___

From the Management & Staff of **MBP Shanghai Office**

公司停業公告

在此通知您MBP上海分公司已經宣布11月30日（星期四）至12月3日（星期日）因為年度公司旅遊將暫時停業。因此，所有MBP配送服務在這段時間將會暫時擱置。我們公司將會在12月4日（星期一）恢復往常運作，並在之後回覆所有詢問。需要任何說明，請來電2412-1234與我們聯絡，或將郵件寄至customerservice99@mbp.com . 我們為所可能造成的不便致歉。

MBP上海公司管理部及員工敬上

【詞彙】
put on hold擱置／
resume重新開始

135 (A) inform
(B) informs
(C) informing
(D) informed

【解析】空格前有be動詞，可知空格中的動詞一定是「現在分詞」或「過去分詞」。使用現在分詞表示「主動的正在進行某動作」，而使用過去分詞則表示「被動的接受某動作」。inform表「通知」，這一句是要通知對方that引導出來的公告內容，因此對方是處於「被通知」的狀態，因此空格內的動詞應為過去分詞informed。please be informed that... 即「在此通知您……」。正解為(D)。

【類型】副詞選擇題型

【詞彙】
permanently 永久地；長期地／
temporarily暫時地／
constantly 持續發生地

【正解】(B)

136 (A) permanently
(B) temporarily
(C) surprisingly
(D) constantly

【解析】本處空格要填入能形容put on hold這個動詞片語的副詞。根據本句前後語意，MBP公司要從星期四公休至星期日，並在星期一恢復營業，因此配送服務的擱置只是暫時，而非永久，故這個空格應填入temporarily，正解為(B)。

【類型】名詞選擇題型

【詞彙】
comprehension 理解／
congregation集會／
modification修改／
clarification説明

【正解】(D)

137 (A) comprehension
(B) congregation
(C) modification
(D) clarification

【解析】根據本句語意，逗號前的句子表目的，意指「若您需要任何……」，請來電聯絡……。因此空格中可以是「資訊」、「細節」或「説明」等需要詳細解釋的名詞，選項中以(D)最適合這句的語意，其他選項的名詞放在空格裡，都無法使句意完整，故正解為(D)。

★ **138** (A) We are grateful for your speedy reply.
(B) We look forward to hearing from you soon.
(C) We apologize for any inconvenience it may cause.
(D) Please let me know if you are unable to come.

【類型】句子插入題型

【詞彙】
speedy快速的／
inconvenience 不便

【正解】(C)

【解析】由於前文是在發出「暫時休業」通知，並且無法在休業期間提供任何配送服務，按常理推測，暫時休業無法提供顧客平常的服務，可能會對顧客造成些許不便，因此最適合放在此處的句子應為(C)，對休業造成的不便向顧客致歉。

Questions 139-142 refer to the following e-mail.

From: Ellen Hathaway <Ellen.Hathaway@westengland.ac.uk>

To: cliftonhouse-studio-residents@westengland.ac.uk

Date: Tue, Feb 27, 2018 at 1:46 PM

Subject: Disposing of unwanted or broken small electrical items

Hello,

Our Accommodation Manager has asked me to contact you on her ___139___. Hall staff have noticed a number of broken small items of electrical equipment ___140___ in the waste and recycling area near Clifton House recently. Please ___141___ that the contractors who pick up our waste and recycling from there are not able to take away any electrical equipment.

If you have any items of electrical equipment you want to dispose of, ___142___ and a member of staff will come and collect the item from you and dispose of it appropriately.

Thank you.

Ellen Hathaway
Student Support Adviser, Clifton House

寄件人：Ellen Hathaway<Ellen.Hathaway@westengland.ac.uk>
收件人：cliftonhouse-studio-residents@westengland.ac.uk
日期：2018年二月27日星期二 下午1:46
主旨：處理不要或壞掉的小件電器

哈囉！

我們的宿舍經理要我代表她聯絡各位。大樓員工在Clifton宿舍附近的垃圾回收區發現一些壞掉的小件電器。請你們注意，到那裡收我們的垃圾及回收物的契約人員並無法取走任何電器。

如果你們有任何想要處理掉的電器，請填寫線上廢棄物回收申請表，我們的人員會來跟你收走並做適當處理。
謝謝你們。

Ellen Hathaway
Clifton宿舍學生支援輔導員

【詞彙】
dispose處理／
contractor 契約人員／
waste 垃圾

139 (A) own
(B) behalf
(C) back
(D) conscience

【解析】這句空格是要完成一個副詞片語。本句的主詞為our Accommodation Manager（我們的宿舍經理），並非寫信者本人，因此這裡的副詞片語是要表示這封信是「代表」宿舍經理而寫的。將選項中的名詞放入空格中，由on one's own 為「獨立」之意、on one's behalf 為「代表某人」之意、on one's back 表示「某人臥病在床」，而on one's conscience 則為「耿耿於懷」之意，可知適合本句句意的片語應為on her behalf，正解為(B)。

---

140 (A) are appearing
(B) to have appeared
(C) appearing
(D) to appear

【解析】這個句子的動詞為notice（注意），這個動詞的用法有兩種，一種是notice後面接that所引導的名詞子句，表示注意到某件事；另一種則為notice sb./sth. V-ing，notice接受詞，受詞後的動詞以「現在分詞」呈現，表示「注意到某人正在做某動作」或「注意到某事的發生」。本句notice後並非that名詞子句，而是直接接受詞a number of broken small items of electrical equipment（一些壞掉的小型電器），因此空格中的動詞應為現在分詞appearing，正解為(C)。

141 (A) note

(B) remind

(C) find

(D) notify

【解析】本句that後面引導的名詞子句是要向對方提出説明，please note that ...為用來提示對方注意即將説明的事項的句型用法，故此空格應填入(A)。

【類型】動詞選擇題行

【詞彙】
note注意／
notify通知

【正解】(A)

★ **142** (A) please take a minute to review the attached list of items

(B) please complete the on-line waste collection request form

(C) please fill out the leave request form at the reception counter

(D) please arrive at the conference venue two hours ahead

【解析】本處空格前的句子意指「如果你有任何想處理掉的電器」，空格後的句子表示「會有人來收走並作適當處理」，可知空格處要插入的句子應與「處理電器」有關。選項(A)(C)(D)句子所述均與「處理電器」無關，因此可以逐一刪除；選項(B)表示「請填寫線上廢棄物回收申請表」是最合乎文意的句子，故應選(B)。

【類型】句子插入題型

【詞彙】
reception counter接待櫃檯

【正解】(B)

収件人：Helen Hutchinson教授
寄件人：William Marsh
主旨：校友會邀請函

親愛的Hutchinson教授，
希望這封信得知您身體健康。寫信的目的是要通知您有關Clifton大學企業管理學系年度校友聯歡會一事。我們許多傑出校友包括Joseph Martinez及Ryder Hernandez都會出席這次盛會。我們想誠摯地邀請您當我們的首席貴賓，因為一直以來，您對企管系的學生來說象徵著成就與靈感啟發。他們若看到您是他們的首席貴賓，一定會感到非常驚喜。
如果您能撥出一些寶貴的時間參加這次校友聯歡會，我們將感到無比榮幸。時間已經決定是在2018年的三月八日星期四。時間是下午六點至九點，而地點是Clifton大學的商學院大樓。
我們知道您每天行程都很忙碌，但是管理部及籌備小組都殷切地希望能收到您正面的回覆。我們希望您不會在這件事上拒絕我們。我們等著您的回音。

溫暖祝福
William

William Marsh教授
企業管理學系主任
University of Clifton

【詞彙】
alumni 校友／reunion 再團聚；聯歡／Business Administration 企業管理／
distinguished傑出的／achievement成就／inspiration靈感；鼓舞人心

354

Questions 143-146 refer to the following invitation.

To: Prof. Helen Hutchinson
From: William Marsh
Subject: Invitation Letter for Alumni Reunion Party

Dear Prof. Hutchinson,
I hope this letter find you in the best ___143___ of your health. The purpose of writing is to inform you regarding the Annual Alumni Reunion Party of Department of Business Administration in the University of Clifton. Many of our distinguished alumni including Joseph Martinez and Ryder Hernandez will attend the event. We want to earnestly invite you as chief guest in this reunion party, as you have always been a ___144___ of achievement and inspiration for students in the Department of BA. It would be a pleasant surprise for them to see you as Chief Guest in between them.

If you could kindly spare some precious time and come to this alumni reunion party we shall be ___145___. The decided date is 8th March, 2018 on Thursday. Time is from 6 pm to 9 pm and venue is the UOC Business School Building.
We understand your busy schedule, but the management and Preparatory Team are extremely eager to receive a positive response from your side. ___146___
We shall wait for your reply.

With Warm Regards,
William

Prof. William Marsh
Dean of Department of Business Administration
University of Clifton

143 (A) condition
(B) term
(C) period
(D) circumstance

【解析】這個句子要表達的是「希望您收到這封信時，是非常健康的狀態」，這是英語信件中常見的開頭問候句。空格前後要表達的意思是「您的健康處在最佳狀態」，用來形容健康情況時，通常用condition這個字，因此正解為(A)。選項(D)的circumstance也可做「情況」解，但通常指的是「周圍環境」或「情勢」，不是適合放在此處的名詞，故不選。

【類型】名詞選擇題型

【詞彙】
circumstance 環境；情況；情勢

【正解】(A)

---

144 (A) feature
(B) characteristic
(C) idol
(D) symbol

【解析】這個空格是要用來表示主詞you的，選項(A)(B)指「特色」，不適合用來表示「人」，故不考慮。根據空格後面的語意，這句是在表示對方對企管系的學生來說代表著成就與靈感啟發，因此填入表示「象徵、代表」的symbol，會比表示「偶像」的idol來的適切，故正解為(D)。

【類型】名詞選擇題型

【詞彙】
feature特色／
characteristic特色、特性

【正解】(D)

---

145 (A) fortunate
(B) privileged
(C) confidential
(D) satisfied

【解析】這句要表達的意思是「您的蒞臨將使我們感到很榮幸」，因此選項(B)應是選項中最適當的形容詞，正解為(B)。fortunate指「幸運的」，通常是與自己無法操控的「運氣」有關，因此不適合放在這個句子中；其他兩個形容詞更是不符句意，故不選。

【類型】形容詞選擇題型

【詞彙】
fortunate幸運的／
privileged榮幸的／
confidential機密的

【正解】(B)

【詞彙】
turn down 拒絕／
commence 開始進行

【正解】(A)

★ 146 (A) We hope that you will not turn us down in this regard.
(B) We hope to receive the samples within this week.
(C) We hope there are other opportunities to do business with you.
(D) We hope you commence the production immediately.

【解析】這裡要插入一個適合前後文語意的句子。空格前的句子意在向收信人表達「希望收到對方肯定的回覆」的殷切之意，選項中的四個句子中，以選項(A)表示「希望您不會拒絕我們」最適合接在後面，加強「希望對方能答應邀約」的語氣，故(A)為正解。其他句子語意都與本信內容無甚相關，故不選。

▶ **PART 7**

Directions: In this part, you will read a selection of texts, such as magazine and newspaper articles, letters, and advertisements. Each text is followed by several questions. Select the best answer for each question and mark the letter (A), (B), (C), or (D) on your answer sheet.

Questions 147-148 refer to the following invitation.

The Charity League of Leicester
invites you to a
Harvest Banquet

Sunday, December 17, 12:30 PM

Caesar Hotel Leicester
185 West Minister Road
44 (0) 116 255 0000

Generously Sponsored by
Angel Garden Foundation
St. George Children's Safety Culture and Education Foundation

RSVP
to Rachel Brown by November 30th

Leicester慈善聯盟團體
邀請您參加
收成餐會

12月17日星期日中午12點30分

Leicester凱薩飯店
西部長路185 號
44 (0) 116 255 0000

慷慨贊助
天使園基金會
聖喬治兒童文教基金會

敬請回覆
11月30前與Rachel Brown 聯繫

【詞彙】
charity慈善／league聯盟／sponsor 贊助／
Children's Safety Culture and Education Foundation兒童安全文教基金會／RSVP 敬請回覆

這是為了什麼活動而發的邀請函？
(A) 就業博覽會
(B) 慈善活動
(C) 新居喬遷派對
(D) 家庭派對

【類型】內容主題題型

【詞彙】
retirement退休

【正解】(B)

---

147 What is the invitation for?
(A) A job fair
(B) A charity event
(C) A housewarming party
(D) A home party

【解析】由本邀請函上的餐會地點是在飯店舉辦，可知在家舉辦的新居喬遷派對即家庭派對皆不是可能的活動，故選項(C)(D)可刪除不考慮。邀請函上未提到任何有關求職或就業的訊息，因此選項(A)亦非適當選項。由邀請函上的主辦單位為The Charity League of Leicester（Leicester 慈善聯盟團體），可推測這最有可能是一場慈善活動的邀請函，正解為(B)。

受邀者何時應該回覆這張邀請函？
(A) 越快越好
(B) 餐會前一星期
(C) 十一月底前
(D) 七天之內

【類型】提問細節題型

【正解】(C)

---

148 When should the invitees reply to this invitation?
(A) The sooner the better
(B) A week before the banquet
(C) By the end of November
(D) Within seven days

【解析】由邀請函最後表示RSVP to Rachel Brown by November 30th（敬請在十一月30日之前回覆Rachel Brown），可知受邀者應在十一月底前回覆邀請函，正解為(C)。

Questions 149-151 refer to the following poster.

Arirang Korean Restaurant

Open: Tuesday to Sunday at 12 PM

☙ Authentic Korean cuisine
in the heart of New York ❧

Everything on our menu is made
from scratch.

Check out our new expansion & Stay tuned
for our Patio Grand Opening!

66 New Garden Road, New York City

··

www.arirang-newyork.com

阿里郎韓式餐廳

開門營業：
週二至週日中午十二點

☙ 紐約市中心的
道地韓式料理 ❧

菜單上所有菜色皆
從頭開始製作

請來看看我們的新擴充的
餐廳並敬請期待我們的露
台盛大開幕會！

紐約市新公園路66號

www.arirang-newyork.com

【詞彙】
authentic道地的／cuisine料理／
from scratch從頭開始／patio露台

---

149 What is this poster advertising for?

(A) Business lunch sets

(B) Special meal deals

(C) All-you-can-eat buffet lunch

(D) Authentic Korean dishes

【解析】由海報上內容提到authentic Korean cuisine（道地韓
式料理），可知這是在為「道地的韓式菜餚」做宣傳，正解為
(D)。

這則海報是在為什麼做宣傳？
(A) 商業午餐
(B) 特別套餐
(C) 吃到飽自助午餐
(D) 道地韓式菜餚

【類型】內容主題題型

【詞彙】
business lunch set商業午餐

【正解】(D)

每星期哪一天餐廳休息？
(A) 星期天
(B) 星期一
(C) 星期二
(D) 星期六

【類型】提問細節題型

【正解】(B)

根據海報內容，哪項敘述正確？
(A) 餐廳將會關閉一個月。
(B) 餐廳主廚來自南韓。
(C) 餐廳老闆是韓國人。
(D) 餐廳正要擴大營業。

【類型】提問細節題型

【詞彙】
scale up 提高規模

【正解】(D)

150 On Which day of the week is the restaurant closed?

(A) Sunday

(B) Monday

(C) Tuesday

(D) Saturday

【解析】由海報上表示開門營業的時間為週二至週日的中午十二點，營業時間不包含星期一，可推測星期一應為餐廳公休日，正解為(B)。

151 According to the poster, which statement is correct?

(A) The restaurant will close for a month.

(B) The chef of the restaurant is from South Korea.

(C) The owner of the restaurant is a Korean.

(D) The restaurant is scaling up its business.

【解析】由海報上提到check out our new expansion（請來看看我們新擴充的餐廳），關鍵字expansion（擴充）透露這家餐廳增加了營業空間，選項(D)所述符合海報內容，故為正解。

Questions 152-153 refer to the following message.

Telephone Message

For: <u>Ashley</u>

From: <u>Mr. Walsh</u>

Message: Due to poor visibility caused by dense fog, all flights from Penghu to Taipei today have been cancelled. Thus, I don't think I will be able to make it to the office for the meeting scheduled tomorrow morning. Please let the meeting attendees know the meeting is cancelled. I will reschedule it sometime next week.

Action required: ☐ Please call back
　　　　　　　　 ☐ Caller will call back later
　　　　　　　　 ☑ No action required

Date: November 29　　Time: 14:33

Message taken by: 　<u>Linda</u>　

電話留言

致： <u>Ashley</u>

留言者： <u>Mr. Walsh</u>

留言內容：由於濃霧造成的能見度不佳，今天所有從澎湖飛往台北的班機都已經被取消。因此，我不認為我能趕得上預定在明天早上舉行的會議。請讓會議與會者知道會議被取消了。我會在下週找個時間重新安排會議。

行動要求：☐ 請回電
　　　　　 ☐ 來電者會稍後再打來
　　　　　 ☑ 不需要行動

日期：11月29日　時間：14:33

記錄留言者： <u>Linda</u>

【詞彙】

visibility 能見度／dense fog 濃霧／attendee 出席者

---

152 According to this message, what will be changed?

(A) The meeting location

(B) The meeting time

(C) The meeting agenda

(D) The meeting moderator

【解析】由留言內容表示meeting is canceled（會議已被取消），留言者會reschedule it sometime next week（下週找個時間重新安排會議），可知會議時間將被重新安排，故正解為(B)。

根據留言內容，什麼將有所變更？

(A) 會議地點

(B) 會議時間

(C) 會議議程

(D) 會議主席

【類型】提問細節題型

【詞彙】

moderator 主席

【正解】(B)

Ashley 看到留言後應該要做什麼？
(A) 發出會議取消通知
(B) 到機場接Walsh先生
(C) 立刻回Walsh先生電話
(D) 取消到澎湖的班機

【類型】提問細節題型

【正解】(A)

日期：五月23日
致：Daniel Murray
自：Lisa Louis

Daniel，
以下為我們新品上市的時間表初稿。請你看一下，並讓我知道你是否能在指定日期之前將一切準備好：

①六月第一週—行銷團隊將會勘察舉行上市記者會的場地，並會與活動籌備團隊開幾次會，討論他們具體關心的事項與需要。

②六月第二週—Miranda Fletcher 會將要發給新聞媒體的新聞稿以及我們將邀請來跟我們一起慶祝新品上市的貴賓名單準備好。

③六月第三週—Jessica Ruther 會將宣傳及促銷活動的指導方針及活動計劃向Morgan先生及Morris先生報告。

【詞彙】
official announcement正式發佈稿／
advertising and promotional campaign宣傳促銷活動

153 What should Ashley do when she gets the message?
(A) Send the meeting cancellation notice
(B) Meet Mr. Walsh at the airport
(C) Return Mr. Walsh's call immediately
(D) Cancel her flight to Penghu

【解析】由留言中指示Please let the meeting attendees know the meeting is cancelled.（請讓與會者知道會議取消），可知Ashley在看到留言後應該要「發出會議取消通知」，讓與會者知道會議取消的消息，正解為(A)。

Questions 154-156 refer to the following memorandum.

Date: May 23
To: Daniel Murray
From: Lisa Louis

Daniel,
Below is the first draft of the timeline for our new product launch. Please take a look at it and let me know if you can have everything ready by the indicated dates:

① First week of June – Marketing team will visit the venue where the launch press conference will take place and meet several times with event planning team to discuss their specific concerns and needs.

② Second week of June – Miranda Fletcher will prepare an official announcement to issue to the news media as well as the list of guests we will invite to celebrate the product launch with us.

③ Third week of June – Jessica Ruther will present the guidelines and programs for the advertising and promotional campaign to Mr. Morgan and Mr. Morris.

154 What is the main purpose of the memo?
(A) To provide a rough schedule
(B) To reserve a venue for launch event
(C) To publish a press release
(D) To identify problems with a speech draft

這則備忘錄的主要目的為何？
(A) 提供初步的時間表
(B) 預訂發表會的場地
(C) 發出一篇新聞稿
(D) 指出演講草稿的問題

【解析】由備忘錄一開始便表示Below is the first draft of the timeline for...（這是……的時間表初稿），draft指「草稿」，first draft則為「第一次草稿」，可知這個timeline（時間表）只是初步草擬的時間表，正解為(A)。

【類型】內容主題題型

【詞彙】
press release新聞稿

【正解】(A)

155 Who most likely are Mr. Morgan and Mr. Morris?
(A) Security guards
(B) Senior executives
(C) New employees
(D) The interviewers

Morgan先生及Morris先生最有可能是什麼身份？
(A) 安全警衛
(B) 高階主管
(C) 新進員工
(D) 面試官

【解析】由備忘錄上的內容，Morgan先生及Morris先生是呈報宣傳活動的對象，按常理推斷，接受呈報的人經常具備公司主管等級的身份，選項中以(B)的「高階主管」為最有可能的答案，故為正解。

【類型】提問細節題型

【詞彙】
security guard 安全警衛／
senior executive高階主管

【正解】(B)

156 What will happen in the second week of June?
(A) The guidelines for the advertising will be proposed.
(B) The press release will be ready.
(C) The venue of the press conference will be decided.
(D) The invitation will be sent.

六月的第二週將會發生什麼事？
(A) 會報告宣傳方針。
(B) 新聞稿會準備好。
(C) 決定記者會地點。
(D) 寄出邀請函。

【解析】由備忘錄上表示六月第二週預定完成事項為Miranda Fletcher會將an official announcement to issue to the news media（要發給新聞媒體的正式通知）準備好，可知選項(B)所述為正確答案，故為正解。

【類型】提問細節題型

【正解】(B)

Peter：
嘿，老兄
你這星期六可以上早班嗎？
James：
問這幹嘛？你想換班嗎？
Peter：
對啊，我得去我兒子學校參加家長座談會。你介意跟我換班嗎？
James：
我想想……
好，但如果我這星期六幫你代班，你下星期天可以幫我值晚班嗎？
Peter：
就這麼說定了。
謝啦，兄弟。

【詞彙】
dude 男子間的互相稱呼；老兄／
swap 交換／
PTA（=Parent-Teacher Association）家長座談會／
lemme（=let me）讓我……
let尾音與me連續發音而出現的口語字彙／
sub 替代／
buddy 夥伴

Peter
hey dude 3:04 pm

can u work the day shift this Saturday? 3:04 pm

James
3:06 pm why? u wanna swap?

Peter
yeah, i need to go to my son's school for the PTA meeting. u mind swapping shifts with me? 3:10 pm

James
3:12 pm Lemme think ...

OK. but if i sub for you this saturday, could you work the night shift for me next sunday?
3:15 pm

Peter
deal 3:16 pm

tks buddy 3:18 pm

157 Why is this text message chain mainly about?
(A) Swapping shifts with colleagues
(B) Calling an emergency meeting
(C) Developing a meeting agenda
(D) Negotiating for a lower price

這則文字訊息串主要是關於什麼內容？
(A) 與同事換班
(B) 召開緊急會議
(C) 建立會議議程
(D) 商議一個較低的價格

【類型】內容主題題型

【正解】(A)

【解析】由此文字訊息串中Peter詢問James可否幫他上星期六早班，而James最後以Peter幫他上下週日的晚班作為交換條件，答應幫忙，可知這則文字訊息串主要跟同事討論換班事宜，正解為(A)。

---

158 Why is Peter unable to work the day shift this Saturday?
(A) He has to go on a blind date.
(B) He has an appointment with his dentist.
(C) He has to go to his son's school.
(D) He needs to pick up his client at the airport.

Peter這星期六為何不能上日班？
(A) 他必須去相親。
(B) 他跟牙醫有約。
(C) 他必須去兒子的學校。
(D) 他要去機場接客戶。

【類型】提問細節題型

【正解】(C)

【解析】由Peter在文字訊息串上表示I need to go to my son's school...（我必須去我兒子的學校），可知選項(C)所述符合對話內容，故為正解。

---

159 According to the message chain, which is true?
(A) James will work Peter's shift on Saturday.
(B) Peter has a day off next Sunday.
(C) James will go to the PTA meeting with Peter.
(D) James helps Peter out unconditionally.

根據訊息串，何者正確？
(A) James星期六會值Peter的班。
(B) Peter下星期天將放一天假。
(C) James會跟Peter一起去家長座談會。
(D) James無條件地幫Peter的忙。

【類型】提問細節題型

【詞彙】
help sb. out 幫某人擺脫困難／
unconditionally 無條件地

【正解】(A)

【解析】由訊息內容中James答應幫Peter上星期六的早班，可知選項(A)為正解

聖誕節寄貨資訊

聖誕節是一年中的一個忙碌及重要時刻。為了支持您在這段時間的購物計劃，我們提供您不同選擇，幫您將購買的東西寄送到家。無論您選擇貨運或是提貨＋寄貨服務，請在您開始結帳過程時輸入郵遞區號以查詢預定寄達日期。當日／隔日到貨將依我們合作的當地貨運公司工作時間而有所不同。請您理解若發生超出我們所能控制的情況，如不利的天氣，可能會延遲您收到訂購商品的時間。

如果您需要快一點拿到訂購商品，您可以到您當地的分店自己取回購買的商品，或是在分店配送區域內*讓您訂購的商品當天或隔日送達。聖誕節前收到店內寄出貨物的最後一天將會是十二月二十三日。

*分店配送區域外的貨運服務將額外收取十鎊的費用。

【詞彙】
picking with delivery 提貨＋運送服務／
availability 可利用性／
adverse不利的

Christmas Delivery Information

Christmas is a busy and important time of year. To support you in your shopping plans over this period, we offer different options to have your purchase delivered to your home. Whether you choose truck delivery or picking with delivery, please check the estimated delivery date by entering your postcode as you start the checkout process. Same/next day delivery is subject to availability at our local transport partner. Please understand that conditions beyond our control such as adverse weather could delay your order.

If you need your order quicker, you can visit your local store and take your purchases home yourself, or have the order delivered the same day or next day within the store delivery area*. The last day before Christmas to receive a delivery from the store will be 23rd December.

*An additional £10 charge will be incurred for truck deliveries outside of the store delivery area.

160 What do customers need to estimate the delivery date of their purchase?
(A) Postcode
(B) Membership number
(C) Order number
(D) ID number

【解析】由第一段的please check the estimated delivery date by entering your postcode...（請輸入您的郵遞區號，以查詢預定到貨日期），故可知要預估何時可以到貨，需要postcode（郵遞區號），正解為(A)。delivery date指「到貨日期」。

顧客需要什麼以預估他們所購物品的到貨時間？
(A) 郵遞區號
(B) 會員號碼
(C) 訂單編號
(D) 身分證字號

【類型】提問細節題型

【正解】(A)

---

161 Which statement is true about truck deliveries outside the store delivery area?
(A) It takes two days longer.
(B) It costs an extra £10.
(C) It needs earlier reservation.
(D) It's cheaper than picking with delivery.

【解析】由最後附註的這句An additional £10 charge will be incurred for truck deliveries outside of the store delivery area.（分店配送區外的貨運將額外收取十鎊費用），可知選項(B)為正確描述。至於配送時間多長、是否需要提前預約、比起picking with delivery（提貨＋運送服務）費用如何，在文中並未提及，故(A)(C)(D)皆可不需考慮。

關於分店配送區外的貨運哪一項敘述正確？
(A) 它需要再多兩天的時間。
(B) 它要多花十鎊費用。
(C) 它需要提前預約。
(D) 它比提貨運送服務便宜。

【類型】提問細節題型

【正解】(B)

寄件人：Rebecca Turner
<r_turner@cosmail.com>
收件人：
<customerservice@langalino.com>
日期／時間：三月19日／12:01:45
主旨：一位顧客的感謝

親愛的安格里諾客服部，
我是為了今天稍早在貴公司彩虹大道的分店得到的經歷而寫這封信的。我帶著我的小女兒與我的女朋友及他們的孩子在上午十一點三十分到達。—[1]— 接待我們的是一位名叫Vincent的服務員，他幫我們開門，並且幫我們折好嬰兒車。他很快地領我們到座位，並為所有的小孩拿高腳椅來。

雖然安格里諾是一家自助式場所，顧客應該要到櫃檯點餐，並且自己拿東西，但是Vincent不僅到桌邊幫我們點菜，好讓我們不用離開我們的小孩，而且還幫我們重新加滿飲料，還有幫我們拿我們需要的東西。—[2]— 我們要離開的時候，他非常貼心地護送我們出去，為我們和我們的孩子拉著門。雖然餐廳因為顧客很多正忙，我們仍然感覺自己彷彿有私人服務員隨侍在側。—[3]—

我和我的女朋友們都是你們餐廳的常客。像這樣的服務絕對是我們一再回訪的原因。請將我們的感謝轉達給Vincent以及彩虹分店的其他員工。—[4]—

你們的忠實顧客
Connie Chessman

Questions 162-165 refer to the following e-mail.

From: Rebecca Turner <r_turner@cosmail.com>
To: <customerservice@langalino.com>
Date/Time: March 19/12:01:45
Subject: Appreciation from a customer

Dear Langalino Customer Service,
I am writing this letter in regard to my experience at your location on Rainbow Blvd. earlier today. I arrived with my young girl as well as my girlfriends and their children at 11:30 a.m. —[1]— We were greeted by an attendant named Vincent, who held the door for us and helped us fold the strollers. He quickly led us to our table and fetched high chairs for all the little ones.

Although Langalino is a self-service establishment, and customers are supposed to order at the counter and get stuff by themselves, Vincent not only took our orders at our table so we didn't have to leave our little ones, but also refilled our drinks and brought us items that we required.—[2]— When we were about to leave, he was thoughtful enough to escort us out, holding the door for all of us and our children. While the restaurant was bustling with patrons, we still felt as if we were dining with our own private wait staff. —[3]—

My girlfriends and I are all frequent visitors to your establishment. Service like this is definitely the very reason for our return visits. Please pass along our appreciation to Vincent and the rest of the staff at your Rainbow branch. —[4]—

Your loyal customer,
Connie Chessman

162 What is the purpose of this letter?
(A) To make a complaint
(B) To express regrets
(C) To express gratitude
(D) To postpone a payment

這封信的目的為何？
(A) 提出抱怨
(B) 表達遺憾
(C) 表達感謝
(D) 延後支付款項

【解析】由信件主旨為Appreciation from a customer（來自一位顧客的感謝），可知這封信的目的是要表達感謝，appreciation與gratitude都是「感謝、感激」之意，故(C)為正解。

【類型】內容主題題型

【詞彙】gratitude 感激

【正解】(C)

---

163 According to this letter, what is Langalino?
(A) A child-friendly restaurant
(B) A pet-friendly restaurant
(C) A staff cafeteria
(D) A school dining hall

根據信件內容，Langalino是什麼地方？
(A) 親子餐廳
(B) 寵物餐廳
(C) 員工餐廳
(D) 學校食堂

【解析】由信件內容提到自己與其他朋友都是帶著孩子前往，而且服務生為小孩都準備了孩童使用的high chair（高腳椅），可推測這家餐廳是一家適合帶小孩前往用餐的餐廳，選項中以(A)的child-friendly restaurant（親子餐廳）為最有可能的答案，故正解為(A)。

【類型】提問細節題型

【正解】(A)

(A) 逃開
(B) 陪伴
(C) 教育
(D) 控制

【類型】相似字義題型

【正解】(B)

164 Which word can replace the word "escort" in this letter?
(A) escape
(B) accompany
(C) educate
(D) control

【解析】文章出現escort的句子為：he was thoughtful enough to escort us out, holding the door for all of us and our children.（他非常體貼地送我們離開，為我們及孩子所有人拉著門），escort 有「護送」的意思。若將四個選項的動詞都取代escort，放入句中，(A)(C)(D)的動詞放入句中都讓句義變得難以理解，只有選項(B)的accompany（陪同、伴隨）放入句中，表示「陪我們出去」，與原句escort us out（護送我們出去）意義相去不遠，故(B)為正解。

「他們真的能為貴公司增光」這個句子最適合放在標示[1][2][3][4]的哪一個位置？

【類型】句子插入題

【正解】(D)

★ 165 In which of the positions marked [1], [2], [3], and [4] does the sentence "They are a credit to your organization." best belong?
(A) [1]
(B) [2]
(C) [3]
(D) [4]

【解析】要插入的句子主詞為they，因此這個句子前面必須出現可以用複數代名詞they取代的人。[1][2][3][4]的位置，只有[4]的前文提到Please pass along our appreciation to Vincent and the rest of the staff...（請將我們的感謝傳達給Vincent及其他員工……），插入句的主詞they指得就是「Vincent和其他員工」，故(D)為正解。

Questions 166-168 refer to the following advertisement.

Holiday House for Rent

This newly built, light and airy 2-bedroom holiday cottage is perfect for a city break in one of England's most vibrant cities. The house is centrally located in the beautiful neighborhood of Clifton with shops, cafes and restaurants nearby.

- The interior is furnished and equipped to a high standard, with high quality linen and towels provided.
- The open plan sitting room and the kitchen with separate utility room on the first floor provide all the amenities for a comfortable stay.
- On the second floor you will find two double bedrooms - a king-size bed in the master and two singles in the second room. The second floor also has its own tiled shower room.
- Guests will have access to the entire premises, as well as a private courtyard at the rear.

度假小屋出租

這幢新建成、明亮通風的兩房度假別墅非常適合在英國最活躍的城市之一中偷閒。房子座落於近美麗的克利夫頓區的中心,附近有商店、咖啡館及餐廳。

- 屋內配有高規格的裝潢設施,且提供高品質的床單與毛巾。
- 一樓的開放式起居室及與洗衣間分開的廚房提供舒適住宿之所有備品。
- 二樓有兩間雙人房:主臥室有一個特大號床,第二個房間則為兩張單人床。二樓也有自己的鋪磚浴室。
- 房客能夠使用整棟房屋,還有後面的私人庭院。

【詞彙】
cottage別墅／linen床單／utility room洗衣房;雜物間／
amenity 便利設施／premises 房宅／courtyard庭院

---

166 What can be found near the cottage mentioned in the advertisement?

(A) A hospital

(B) An elementary school

(C) A supermarket

(D) Dining places

廣告中提到的別墅附近可以找到什麼?

(A) 一間醫院

(B) 一間小學

(C) 一間超市

(D) 用餐的地方

【類型】提問細節題型

【正解】(D)

【解析】廣告中提到The house is... with shops, cafes and restaurants nearby(這房子……附近有商店、咖啡店及餐廳),除了選項(D)的「餐廳」之外,其他選項所述在廣告中均未提及,故(D)為正解。

以下何者在這間度假屋中沒有提供？
(A) 床單與毛巾
(B) 廚具
(C) 私人庭院
(D) 雨具

【類型】提問細節題型

【詞彙】
kitchenware廚具／
rain gear雨具（包含雨衣、雨傘、雨鞋等）

【正解】(D)

---

167 Which of following is not provided in this holiday house?
(A) Linens and towels
(B) Kitchenware
(C) A private courtyard
(D) Rain gear

【解析】有廣告介紹中提到kitchen及utility room配有各種amenities（便利設施），以提供舒適住宿，因此推測廚房中應配有基本廚具，唯一沒有在文中提到的為選項(D)的rain gear（雨具），故正解為(D)。

庭院在哪裡？
(A) 別墅附近
(B) 別墅前面
(C) 房子後面
(D) 房子隔壁

【類型】提問細節題型

【正解】(C)

---

168 Where is the courtyard?
(A) Near the cottage
(B) in front of the cottage
(C) At the back of the house
(D) Next to the house

【解析】廣告最後提到courtyard的位置是at the rear（在後方），rear即「後部」，因此可知庭院位在房屋後方，正解為(C)。

Questions 169-171 refer to the following advertisement.

Interview Events for
Formosa Aircraft Catering Company

We are searching for talented individuals to fill the vacancies at Formosa Aircraft Catering Company in our base in Taoyuan, Taiwan.
☞Organization: Formosa Aircraft Catering Company
☞Job Function: Catering, Food & Beverage
☞Employment Type: Full Time - Permanent
☞Last date of application: 31-January-2018

Formosa Aircraft Catering Company (FACC) provides exclusive catering services to Formosa Airways. You will be responsible for the execution of work assigned by the supervisor to provide and accommodate all daily food products as airline requirements and menu cycle. Furthermore, you will also facilitate at all times proper cleanliness in all work, storage space and refrigeration areas.

You should have basic English communications skills and up to 2 years of experience. High school or above education level is preferred. Moreover, it is essential that you have basic knowledge in food hygiene, and basic food cooking techniques.

To apply for the job you will be required to attach the following:
1. Resume / CV
2. Copy of Passport
3. Copy of Highest Educational Certificate

【詞彙】

vacancy 職缺／permanent 長期的／execution 執行／
facilitate 促進；幫助／hygiene衛生／
CV (=curriculum vitae)簡歷

福爾摩沙航空餐飲公司
面試活動

我們正在為福爾摩沙航空餐飲公司在台灣桃園總部的職務空缺尋找優異人才。
☞公司：福爾摩沙航空餐飲公司
☞工作內容：餐飲服務、餐點及飲品準備
☞聘雇形式：全職──長期
☞應徵截止日：2018年1月31日

福爾摩沙航空餐飲公司（FACC）為福爾摩沙航空公司提供獨一無二的餐飲服務。你將負責執行主管指派的工作，依照航空要求標準以及菜單提供每日食物。而且你也將協助讓所有工作台、儲藏空間及冷藏區域隨時保持適當的清潔。

你必須具備基本的英語溝通技能，並且有兩年以上的經驗。有高中以上學歷較佳。此外，你必須要有基本的食物衛生知識，以及基本的食物烹調技巧。

應徵此工作你將需要附上以下文件：
1. 履歷表／簡歷
2. 護照影本
3. 最高學歷影本

這家公司在招募什麼？
(A) 空服員
(B) 餐飲服務人員
(C) 廚房學徒
(D) 高階主管

【類型】內容主題題型

【詞彙】
apprentice 學徒／executive 主管

【正解】(B)

169 What is this company recruiting?
(A) Flight attendants
(B) Catering staff
(C) Kitchen apprentices
(D) Senior executives

【解析】由標題可知這是一個附屬在航空公司下，以提供航空餐點為主的catering company（餐飲公司）的徵才廣告，職務內容的說明表示要找的人才與提供catering, food and beverage（餐飲服務）有關，因此正解為(B)。

何者未在廣告中提及？
(A) 應徵者必須能立刻開始上班。
(B) 應徵者必須能夠說簡單的英文。
(C) 應徵者必須要有至少兩年的經驗。
(D) 應徵者應該要有基本的烹飪技術。

【類型】提問細節題型

【正解】(A)

170 What is NOT mentioned in the advertisement?
(A) Applicants must be available to work immediately.
(B) Applicants must be able to speak simple English.
(C) Applicants must have at least 2 years of experience.
(D) Applicants should have basic cooking skills.

【解析】這則徵才廣告中對應徵者的要求條件中，提到需要有basic English communications skills（基本英語溝通能力）、up to 2 years of experience（至少兩年經驗）以及basic food cooking techniques（基本食物烹調技巧），因此選項(B)(C)(D) 所述都符合要求條件。廣告中並未提到選項(A)所述之「必須能立刻開始上班」，故選項(A)為正解。

為了應徵此工作，需要提供什麼？
(A) 最高學歷影本
(B) 英語能力證明
(C) 銀行財力證明
(D) 成績單影本

【類型】提問細節題型

【詞彙】
proficiency 精通／
bank statement 財力證明

【正解】(A)

171 What should one provide in order to apply for the job?
(A) Copy of highest educational certificate
(B) English proficiency certificate
(C) Bank statement
(D) Copy of statement of academic record

【解析】廣告最後說明應徵者所應附文件，包含resume / CV（履歷）、copy of passport （護照影本）及copy of highest educational certificate（最高學歷證明影本），選項中只有(A)在應附文件之列，故正解為(A)。

Questions 172-175 refer to the following information.

Trial Period Policy

✦ Policy Statement
A 90-calendar day trial period applies to all current staff that transfer into or are promoted to a new position. The staff member's trial period starts on the first day of the job change and lasts until the staff member has completed 90 consecutive calendar days of regular employment status. During this time, the staff member determines whether or not the position meets his or her expectations, and the supervisor determines whether or not the staff member has the knowledge and skills to perform the job expectations.

✦ Completion of the Trial Period
Supervisors must evaluate the staff member during the trial period. A performance review should be initiated within the first 15 days of hire. The supervisor should obtain and complete a Trial Period Review Form. Upon obtaining the form, the supervisor and staff member should meet to discuss performance and determine whether the staff member is performing at his or her expected level of performance during the trial period.

The review form should be completed as well as signed and dated by both the supervisor and staff member before the 90th calendar day of the trial period.
A decision should be made by the supervisor to recommend:
successful completion of the review period,
extension of the review period for 30 days, or
discharge because of unsuccessful completion of the review period.

試用期政策

✦ 政策聲明
九十天的試用期適用於所有轉調或晉升至新職位的現任員工。員工的適用期從職務變更起第一天開始至員工完成一般任用情況的連續九十天止。在這段時間，員工可以決定這個職務是否符合其期待，且主管也決定該員工是否具備符合職務需要的知識或技能。

✦ 完成試用期
主管必須在試用期間評估員工。員工表現評估應該在聘雇日起前十五天開始。主管必須取得並填寫試用期評估表。拿到評估表後，主管及員工應該要開會討論其表現，並決定該員工在試用期間的表現是否達到期望程度。

評估表應於試用期的第九十天之前，由主管及員工雙方共同填寫、簽名及押日期。
主管應做出建議決定：
順利完成觀察期，
延長觀察期30天，或
因為無法順利完成觀察期而予以解僱。

延長或解僱，必須在九十天的試用期之前的十四天，經人資部主管及勞資關係代表審核決定。

Any extension or discharge must be reviewed with the HR leader and a representative of Staff and Labor Relations at least 14 calendar days before the end of the 90-calendar day period.

【詞彙】

trial period 試用期／consecutive連續的／evaluate評估／extension延長／discharge解僱

這家公司的試用期多長？
(A) 三十個工作天
(B) 兩個月
(C) 九十天
(D) 三十至九十天

【類型】提問細節題型

【詞彙】

working day（不含週六日的）工作天／calendar day（包含週六日的）曆日

【正解】(C)

172 How long does this company run trial periods?
   (A) 30 working days
   (B) Two months
   (C) 90 calendar days
   (D) 30 – 90 days

【解析】由政策聲明中一開始便表示A 90-calendar day trial period applies to all current staff...（九十天的試用期適用所有現任員工……），可知這家公司的試用期為90天，正解為(C)。

直屬主管何時應該開始評估員工的表現？
(A) 從第九十天起
(B) 在受僱日起前十五天內
(C) 試用期結束兩週前
(D) 從受僱的第一天開始

【類型】提問細節題型

【正解】(B)

173 When should supervisors start evaluating the staff member's performance?
   (A) From the 90th calendar day
   (B) Within the first 15 days of hire
   (C) Two weeks before the end of the trial period
   (D) From the first day of hire

【解析】由聲明中表示A performance review should be initiated within the first 15 days of hire.（表現評估應於受僱日起十五天內開始），可知正解為(B)。

174 Which statement is incorrect about the Trial Period Review Form?
(A) It needs both the supervisor's and the staff member's signatures.
(B) It should be completed by the end of the trial period.
(C) The supervisor must fill it out secretly.
(D) It's to review the staff member's performance.

關於試用期評估表的敘述，何者不正確？
(A) 它需要主管及員工的簽名。
(B) 它要在試用期結束前完成。
(C) 主管必須秘密地填寫此表。
(D) 它是用來評估員工的表現。

【類型】提問細節題型

【詞彙】
signature 簽名

【正解】(C)

【解析】聲明中表示試用期評估should be completed as well as signed and dated by both the supervisor and staff member before the 90th calendar day of the trial period（應於試用期的第九十天之前，由主管及員工雙方共同完成、簽名及押日期），因此選項(A)(B)(D)皆為符合聲明內容之敘述，選項(C)不符所述，故此題應選(C)。

---

175 Who is irrelevant to a decision of extension or discharge?
(A) Director of the HR Department
(B) The representative of Staff and Labor Relations
(C) The supervisor of the staff member
(D) The fellow colleagues of the staff member

誰與延長試用期或解僱的決定無關？
(A) 人資部主管
(B) 勞資關係代表
(C) 員工的直屬主管
(D) 員工的同事

【類型】提問細節題型

【詞彙】
fellow colleague 同事

【正解】(D)

【解析】聲明最後表示supervisor將做出「完成試用期」、「延長試用期」或「解僱」的決定，而此決定必須由the HR leader（人事部主管）以及a representative of Staff and Labor Relations（勞資關係代表）做審核，可知(A))B)(C)皆與此決定有關聯，因此這三個選項皆可確定刪除不選。正解為(D)。

ABOUT Gala CLUB

Say goodbye to plastic membership cards. It's all happening in your smartphone! The Gala app is your portal to great fashion rewards, special offers, discounts, and invitations to exclusive events. Every time you buy something from Gala you earn points - in Gala stores and online. These points can be used towards fabulous rewards and perks. Visit the club pages often to keep up to date with the latest club offers.

★Offers

As a Club member you have access to customized offers. Everything from special discounts, reduced sale prices, to 3 for 2 deals. The possibilities are endless.

★Events

Welcome to the guest list! We love throwing parties. As a Gala Club member you can join us at fashion shows, exclusive shopping events, music events, etc.

You find all available events in your club pages. To attend simply click on the event and book your seat, or place on the list.

Wait no more! Download the app and create an account to sign up right now!

關於Gala俱樂部

跟塑膠會員卡說再見吧。一切都在您的智慧型手機裡了！Gala 應用程式軟體就是您拿到超棒時尚獎品、特別優惠、折扣以及獨家活動邀請函的入口網站。每次在Gala購物──店內或線上──都能賺取點數。這些點數能夠用來獲得超棒的獎品及購物金。常常上俱樂部網頁就能得到最新的會員優惠。

★優惠

身為俱樂部會員，您將取得為您量身訂做的優惠。從特別折扣、商品減價到買二送一優惠，優惠的可能性永無止盡。

★活動

歡迎進入嘉賓名單！我們超愛舉辦派對。身為Gala俱樂部會員，您將能參加我們的時裝秀、獨家購物活動、音樂活動等等。在您的會員網頁上您就能找到所有開放參加的活動。只要點選活動並訂位就能參加了。

別再等了！現在就下載應用程式軟體並開戶註冊吧！

Email: michael_pa28@cosmail.com

Title: ⦿ Mr.　○ Mrs.　○ Miss

First name: Michael　Last name: Parsons

Date of birth: 28/11/1998

Phone number: +44　7784756886

Address: Manor Hall, Lower Clifton Rd

Postcode: BS8 1BU

Country: United Kingdom

Subscription:

☑ I am interested in receiving printed marketing material from Gala.

By clicking "Save details" I accept the Privacy Policy.

Cancel　Save Details

Hi, *Michael*! Welcome to the club!

You have successfully become a member of Gala! Congratulations!

You can now enjoy your Gala Club benefits: collect points on everything you buy, redeem offers in store and access exclusive content. Just show your phone to the cashier every time you shop to collect points, and use them to unlock great offers, fashionable rewards and access to exclusive events. When you shop online, your points are registered automatically.

Gala is giving all new individual members 20% off for the first online purchase. Before April 29, 2018, 24:00 AM, you can make extra savings on your online order with the voucher code NEWMEMBER-281198 .

Enjoy your shopping!

電子郵件信箱：
michael_pa28@cosmail.com
稱謂：⦿Mr.○ Mrs.○ Miss

名：Michael　姓：Parsons
出生日期：28/11/1998
電話號碼：+44 7784756886
地址：Manor Hall, Lower Clifton Rd
郵遞區號：BS8 1BU
國家：United Kingdom
訂閱：
☑ 我有興趣收到Gala的廣告信件。

點選「存取資料」表示接受隱私政策。

取消　存取資料

嗨，*Michael*！歡迎加入俱樂部！您已經成功成為Gala的會員了！恭喜！
你現在可以享有Gala俱樂部的權益：收集每次購物的點數、兌換店內優惠以及取得獨家內容。每次購物時只要讓收銀員看你的手機，就能收集點數並取得超棒的優惠、流行獎品以及參加獨家活動的資格。當您在線上購物時，會自動為您記錄點數。

Gala目前提供所有新會員首次線上購物八折優惠。在2018年4月29日零點零分之前，您都可以用 NEWMEMBER-281198 這組優惠碼，為您的線上訂購省下更多錢。
請您盡情購物吧！

【詞彙】
perk額外補貼；購物金／
3 for 2 deal 買二送一優惠（三樣商品以價高的兩樣商品計價）／subscription 訂閱

廣告的目的為何？
(A) 招募新會員
(B) 更新會員優惠
(C) 宣布年終特賣
(D) 招募加盟業者

【類型】內容主題題型

【詞彙】
franchisee 加盟業者

【正解】(A)

176 What is the purpose of the advertisement?
　　(A) To recruit new members
　　(B) To update club offers
　　(C) To announce year-end sale
　　(D) To recruit franchisees.

【解析】由廣告內容說明會員可以得到的各種優惠，以及最後建議download the app（下載應用程式軟體），create an account to sign up（設立帳號並註冊），可知這是這家公司用來招募會員的廣告，正解為(A)。

Gala最有可能是哪一種產業的公司？
(A) 服飾業
(B) 金融保險業
(C) 文教業
(D) 餐飲服務業

【類型】提問細節題型

【正解】(A)

177 What type of industry most likely is Gala?
　　(A) Apparel Accessories
　　(B) Finance and insurance
　　(C) Culture and education
　　(D) Catering service

【解析】廣告中雖未明白表示Gala是販售何種商品的商店，但是在給Michael的會員歡迎信上表示會員可以參加他們舉辦的fashion shows（時裝秀），可推測Gala應該是與fashion（時裝）有關的產業，選項中以(A)的服飾業與fashion最有關，故答案應為(A)。

以下何者不會提供給會員？
(A) 特別折扣
(B) 實體會員卡
(C) 時尚獎品
(D) 時尚活動邀請卡

【類型】提問細節題型

【正解】(B)

178 Which of the following will not be provided to the member?
　　(A) Special discounts
　　(B) A physical membership card
　　(C) Fashion rewards
　　(D) Fashion event invitations

【解析】由廣告一開始就表示say goodbye to plastic membership card（跟塑膠會員卡道別），且接著表示會員的一切相關事物都在手機裡，可知這家公司不會發給會員一張實質的會員卡，而是以手機軟體取代，正解為(B)。

179 Why did Michael submit the form?
(A) To sign up for the club
(B) To update his contact information
(C) To renew his membership
(D) To activate his bank account

【解析】本題問的是Michael提交表格的目的。根據本題所提供此表格前後兩份資料內容，可知Michael是照第一份廣告資料推薦，下載應用軟體並設立帳號以註冊會員，並成功加入會員，因此這份表格的目的即「註冊成為會員」，正解為(A)。

Michael為何要提交這份表格？
(A) 註冊參加俱樂部
(B) 更新他的聯絡資訊
(C) 辦理續會
(D) 啟用他的銀行帳號

【類型】提問目的題型

【詞彙】
renew 重新開始、繼續／
activate啟用

【正解】(A)

180 What does the voucher code entitle Michael to?
(A) A free standard delivery
(B) A free same-day delivery
(C) A discount of 20%
(D) A free cup of coffee in store

【解析】由第三份資料上提供新會員一個voucher code（優惠碼），提供新會員20% off for the first online purchase（第一次線上購物八折），可知答案為(C)。

優惠碼可以讓Michael享有什麼？
(A) 一次免費一般寄貨服務
(B) 一次免費當日到貨服務
(C) 八折的優惠
(D) 店內一杯免費咖啡

【類型】提問細節題型

【詞彙】
standard delivery 一般寄送

【正解】(C)

寄件人：Tiffany Taylor
<ttiffany@ttevents.com>
收件人：Mr. Davies
<jabst@autotradecenter.com.tw>
日期／時間: 1月23日/ 14:02:56
主旨：業務介紹

親愛的Davies先生，

我是Tiffany活動策劃公司的Tiffany Taylor。請容我藉這個機會向您介紹本公司以及我們的服務項目。我們是一家專門做活動策劃的公司。我們有超過十年策劃私人派對、慈善活動及婚禮的經驗。我們有很多的資源能夠幫您找到適合的場地、規劃活動、聯絡最棒的攤位，並針對活動各方面做各種策劃。我們會負責設計、佈置場地、邀請來賓，甚至幫您找活動中需要的藝人。簡單來說，我們負責搞定一切，您只要可以當自己活動的賓客並慶祝就可以了。

如果您有興趣知道有關我們服務項目的進一步資訊，請打(02)2929-6868這支電話與我聯絡。

期待能在不久的將來與您合作。

獻上最佳祝福，

負責人 Tiffany Taylor

寄件人：Johnny Davies
<jabst@qmpmotorcorp. com.tw>
收件人：Tiffany Taylor
<ttiffany@ttevents.com>
日期／時間：
2月10日／11:32:45
主旨：回覆：業務介紹

From: Tiffany Taylor <ttiffany@ttevents.com>
To: Mr. Davies <jabst@autotradecenter.com.tw>
Date/Time: January 23/ 14:02:56
Subject: Business Introduction

Dear Mr. Davies,

I am Tiffany Taylor from Tiffany Events. Please allow me to take this opportunity to introduce our company and our services. We are a company that specializes in event organizing business. We have more than 10 years of experience in organizing private parties, charitable events, and weddings. With a wide range of resources we are able to help you find the perfect venue, plan the event, connect you with the best vendors and produce any aspect of the event. We will do the design, set-up the location, invite the guests, and even find the talent wanted in the event. To put it briefly, you can be a guest of your own event and celebrate while we take care of everything.

If you are interested in learning any further information regarding our services, please contact me at (02)2929-6868.
Looking forward to working with you in the near future.

Best wishes,
Tiffany Taylor, Owner

From: Johnny Davies <jabst@qmpmotorcorp. com. tw>
To: Tiffany Taylor <ttiffany@ttevents.com>
Date/Time: February 10/ 11:32:45
Subject: Re: Business Introduction

Dear Tiffany,

Thanks for your letter dated January 23. The services you provide are exactly what we need for our company anniversary on April 18. The company anniversary is usually the QMP Motor Corporation's most important event of the year. This year we're planning to have an even bigger celebration party because it's our 20th anniversary. As usual, the party should be held on the basement floor of our office building.

We would like to invite you or your sales representative to our company for a meeting next Tuesday morning around ten to negotiate a <u>tie-up</u> with you. Please let me know if it is a convenient time for you.

Look forward to your reply.

Sincerely,

Johnny Davies, Office Assistant

親愛的Tiffany，
謝謝您一月二十三日的來信。貴公司所提供的服務正是我們四月十八日的公司週年紀念日所需要的。公司創立紀念日一向是QMP汽車公司每年最重要的活動。今年我們計劃舉辦更大的慶祝活動，因為這是我們的二十週年紀念。跟往常一樣，派對將會在本公司辦公大樓的地下樓層舉行。

我們希望能邀請您及您的業務代表下週二早上大約十點到我們公司來開會，討論與貴公司的合作事宜。請告訴我這是不是您方便的時間。

期待您的回覆。

誠摯地，
Johnny Davies 辦公室助理

From: Tiffany Taylor <ttiffany@ttevents.com>
To: Johnny Davies <jabst@qmpmotorcorp. com.tw>
Date/Time: February 10/14:02:10
Subject: Re: Re: Business Introduction

Dear Johnny,

Thank you for considering our firm to assist you with your annual event. I will arrive at your office at the designated time together with our Event Specialists, Ivy and Yolanda, to present the services we provide in detail.

Looking forward to our meeting.

Sincerely,
Tiffany

寄件人：Tiffany Taylor <ttiffany@ttevents.com>
收件人：Johnny Davies <jabst@qmpmotorcorp. com.tw>
日期／時間：
February 10／14:02:10
主旨：回覆：回覆：業務介紹

親愛的Johnny，
謝謝您考慮讓我們公司來協助您的年度大事。我會跟我們的活動策劃專員Ivy及Yolanda一起在您指定的時間到貴公司，向您提出我們所提供的服務各項細節。
期待我們的會面。

誠摯地
Tiffany

【詞彙】
specialize 專攻／negotiate 協商／
tie-up 合作／designated 指定的

第一封信的撰寫目的為何？
(A) 從對手挖角人才
(B) 找新客戶以增加業務
(C) 介紹新的業務代表
(D) 宣布暫時歇業

【類型】提問原因題型

【詞彙】
poach挖角／talent 有天份的人

【正解】(B)

181 Why is the first letter written?
(A) To poach talent from a competitor
(B) To find new customers and increase sales
(C) To introduce a new sales representative
(D) To announce temporary closure

【解析】第一封信的主旨為business introduction（業務介紹），內容主要在介紹公司業務內容及強項，並希望對方如果有興趣可以進一步聯繫，可知這封信的目的應該是要開發潛在的客戶以增加業務，選項(B)為最適當的答案，故選(B)。

Tiffany活動策劃公司提供什麼樣的服務？
(A) 定點外燴服務
(B) 接機服務
(C) 活動籌劃服務
(D) 電梯維修服務

【類型】提問細節題型

【詞彙】
lift 電梯／repairs and maintenance 維修／airport pickup接機

【正解】(C)

182 What kind of service does Tiffany Events provide?
(A) Location catering service
(B) Airport pickup service
(C) Event planning service
(D) Lift repairs and maintenance service

【解析】由信中表示We are a company that specializes in event organizing business.（我們是一間專門從事活動策劃的公司），可知這間公司提供event organizing（活動規劃）的服務，正解為(C)。

根據第二封郵件，哪個活動將在四月進行？
(A) 公司運動會
(B) 年度公司旅遊
(C) 公司創辦人生日
(D) 公司廿年紀念派對

【類型】提問細節題型

【詞彙】
founder創辦人

【正解】(D)

183 According to the second e-mail, which event is taking place in the coming April?
(A) The Company Sports Day
(B) The annual company trip
(C) The company founder's birthday
(D) The company 20th anniversary party

【解析】由第二封信件中提到 ...our company anniversary on April 18（……我們公司在四月十八日的週年紀念日），可知四月份將舉行公司廿年紀念派對活動，正解為(D)。

184 Which of the following has the most similar meaning to the word "tie-up" in the second e-mail?
(A) Postponement
(B) Relationship
(C) Deal-making
(D) Compensation

下列哪個字與第二封郵件中的「tie up」這個字意義最相近？
(A) 延緩
(B) 關係
(C) 交易
(D) 賠償

【類型】相似字義題型

【詞彙】
postponement延後／
compensation賠償

【正解】(C)

【解析】tie-up意指「聯合」，在此有「合作」的含義，選項中以(C)的deal-making（交易）字義上與tie-up最接近，其他選項的字義皆與tie-up毫無相關性可言，故正解為(C)。

---

185 What's the purpose of the third e-mail?
(A) To accept the meeting invitation
(B) To make an appointment
(C) To offer a special discount
(D) To ask for a rain check

第三封郵件的目的為何？
(A) 接受會議邀請
(B) 確定約會時間
(C) 提供特別折扣
(D) 請求改期

【類型】內容主題題型

【詞彙】
rain check 延期、改期

【正解】(A)

【解析】由第三封信件中表示I will arrive at your office at the designated time...（我會在指定時間到達貴公司……），可知此信目的為「接受會議邀請」，正解為(A)。

主旨：請求產品報價

親愛的Wright先生，
我們有意向貴公司購買120個排氣消音器及200個燃油濾清器。
請您為提供以上產品的一般單價以及大量採購折扣做報價。請註明您的報價是否包含營業稅以及運費。請您說明清楚，否則我們將認定兩者皆含在報價內。

誠摯地
Allen Brunner

SUBJECT: INVITATION TO QUOTE PRICE OF GOODS

Dear. Mr. Wright,
We are interested in purchasing 120 exhaust mufflers and 200 fuel filters from you.
Please quote your ordinary unit price for supplying the goods together with your discount for volume purchases. Please indicate whether your quotes are inclusive or exclusive of sales taxes and delivery costs. Please state these clearly, otherwise we will assume they are both included.

Sincerely,
Allen Brunner

主旨：回覆：請求產品報價
附件：報價單.doc
親愛的Brunner先生，

有關您六月二十九日詢問有關本公司汽車零件一排氣消音器及燃油濾清器的來信，我們很感謝您對我們的產品有興趣，並很樂意提供您報價單，茲附件在此供您參考。
營業稅及運費都已經包含在報價裡。請注意所列價格都只在當季有效。
若您有任何有關報價的問題，或是您需要滿足您要求的進一步細節，請儘管在上午九點至下午五點這段時間與我聯絡。
期待能收到您的訂單。

您忠實的，
Jeffery

Subject: Re: INVITATION TO QUOTE PRICE OF GOODS
Attachment: Quotation.doc 🖹

Dear Mr. Brunner,
With reference to your letter dated June 29, inquiring about our auto parts - exhaust mufflers and fuel filters, we are grateful for your interest in our products and are pleased to provide the quotation as attached for your consideration.
Both sales taxes and delivery costs are covered in the price. Please note that the prices listed are only valid for this quarter.
Should there be any questions regarding the quotation or you need further details to meet your requirement, please feel free to contact me anytime during 9 am to 5 pm.
Looking forward to receiving your order.

Yours faithfully,
Jeffery

Quotation

Prepared for	Sales Representative
Allen Brunner	Jeffery Wright
KOHEN Mobile Manufaturer 3566 Rainbow Blvd- Suite 440 2305-468-343	Product Specialist 4464-569-304/ wjeffery@autoparts. com
Date: 28/01/2018	Valid Until: 31/03/2018

No.	Item	Qty	Unit Price	Discount	Amount
1	Exhaust Muffler EM3-28	120	NT$12,000	5%	1,368,000.00
2	Fuel Filter FF5-16DL	200	NT$500	5%	95,000.00
Total					1,463,000.00

On orders for 100 pieces we allow a discount of 5%.
On orders for 500 pieces we allow a discount of 20%.
Prices are inclusive of VAT and delivery charges.
Payment is due seven days after the invoice.

報價單

報價對象	業務代表
Allen Brunner 可汗汽車製造廠 3566 彩虹大道 440室 2305-468-343	Jeffery Wright 產品專員 4464-569-304/ wjeffery@autoparts. com
日期: 28/01/2018	有效日至: 31/03/2018

No	品項	數量	單價	折扣	金額
1	排氣消音器 EM3-28	120	12,000 元	5%	1,368,000.00
2	燃油濾清器 FF5-16DL	200	500元	5%	95,000.00
總價					1,463,000.00

一次訂100個可獲95折。
一次訂500個可獲8折。
價格包含增值稅與運費。
請款單收到後7天內需付款。

【詞彙】

exhaust muffler 排氣消音器／fuel filter 燃油濾清器／unit price 單價／volume purchase大宗採購／inclusive 包含的／exclusive 不包含的/with reference to有關／quotation報價單／VAT =value added tax 增值稅／invoice 請款單

第一封郵件的目的為何？

(A) 要求請款單

(B) 要求報價

(C) 更改訂單

(D) 要求樣品

【類型】內容主題題型

【正解】(B)

186 What is the purpose of the first e-mail?

    (A) To request an invoice

    (B) To request a quote

    (C) To change an order

    (D) To request a product sample

【解析】由第一封信主旨為INVITATION TO QUOTE PRICE OF GOODS（邀請產品報價），可知這封信是要請對方為特定產品報價，正解為(B)。

根據第二封郵件，Brunner先生應該何時與Jeffery聯絡，以詢問有關報價單的進一步細節？

(A) 上班時間

(B) 下午五點以後

(C) 上午九點前任何時間

(D) 一天內任何時間

【類型】提問細節題型

【詞彙】
working hour上班時間

【正解】(A)

187 According to the second e-mail, when should Mr. Brunner contact Jeffery for further details regarding the quotation?

    (A) During the working hours

    (B) No earlier than 5 pm

    (C) Anytime before 9 am

    (D) Anytime during the day

【解析】第二封郵件中提到若有任何問題請在during 9 am-5 pm這段時間聯絡，可知選項(B)(C)(D)所述皆不正確。一般日間上班公司的工作時間通常為朝九晚五，故可推測9 am-5 pm這段時間為Jeffery的上班時間，故(A)為最有可能的答案。

根據兩封郵件內容，關於此報價哪項敘述正確？

(A) 報價不含運費。

(B) 報價含服務費。

(C) 報價有效至二月底。

(D) 報價含稅。

【類型】提問細節題型

【詞彙】
service charge服務費

【正解】(D)

188 According to the two e-mails, which statement is correct about the quote?

    (A) It is exclusive of delivery charge.

    (B) It is inclusive of service charge.

    (C) It is valid until the end of February.

    (D) It is inclusive of taxes.

【解析】由第二封郵件內容可知報價含稅及運費，可知選項(A)所述錯誤，而選項(D)所述正確，正解為(D)。由附件的報價單上顯示報價有效至三月31日，因此選項(C)亦非正解。本題提供的信件及資訊中均未提到service charge（服務費），因此選項(B)所述可不考慮。

189 What percentage discount is offered on the quote?

(A) A discount of 5%

(B) A discount of 10%

(C) A discount of 15%

(D) A discount of 20%

【解析】由報價單上的discount（折扣）欄顯示報價提供5%優惠，可知(A)為正解。

這份報價提供多少折扣？

(A) 九五折

(B) 九折

(C) 八五折

(D) 八折

【類型】提問細節題型

【正解】(A)

190 Which of the following is not given in the quotation?

(A) Discount for volume purchases

(B) Estimated delivery date

(C) The customer's contact info

(D) The supplier's contact info

【解析】由報價單上顯示內容，可以得到(A)(C)(D)等資訊，唯獨選項(B)的交貨日期並未在報價單上出現，故正解為(B)。

報價單尚未提供下列哪一項資訊？

(A) 大量採購的折扣

(B) 預計交貨日期

(C) 顧客聯絡資訊

(D) 供應商的聯絡資訊

【類型】提問細節題型

【詞彙】

estimated 預估的／

info=information 資料

【正解】(B)

14日短期工作（20個職缺！）
☛ 輪班制— ①上午10點至下午6點②下午一點至下午九點
☛ 工作地點— GoGo 購物城美食廣場
☛ 工作內容— 販售乳製品
☛ 薪資範圍— 依經驗每小時10英鎊～12英鎊

- 公司將提供訓練
- 需會說簡單英語
- 請來電928-405-766（上午十點至下午六點）或
  將您的履歷寄至
  stevenchuang@gogomall.com

14 Days Work (20 positions!)
☛ 2 shifts— ① 10 am ~ 6 pm ② 1 pm ~ 9 pm
☛ Work Location— GoGo Shopping Mall Food Court
☛ Job Description— Selling Dairy Products
☛ Pay range from £10~£12/per hour based on experience

- Training will be provided by the company
- Able to speak simple English
- Please call 928-405-766 (10 am-6 pm) or
  email your resume to stevenchuang@gogomall.com

收件人：Albert Hsiang <albert_hsiang66@qmail.com>
寄件人：Rebecca Lin <linrebecca@dcmedairysupplies.com>
日期／時間：四月26日／16:12:48
主旨：面試邀請

親愛的向先生，
謝謝您的履歷表及應徵信。
DCME公司希望能邀請您來面試櫃檯人員一職。請點選以下連結，登入後選擇您希望的面試時間。
http://www.dcmedairyproducts.interviewassistant.menu=candidate&eventToken=d8r838r8t880085324144dhug7
您的面試將會在Christopher路上的307皇家大樓舉行。
當您抵達面試地點時，請至十樓向櫃檯人員報到。
謝謝您。

To: Albert Hsiang <albert_hsiang66@qmail.com>
From: Rebecca Lin <linrebecca@dcmedairysupplies.com>
Date/Time: April 26/16:12:48
Subject: Interview Invitation

Dear Mr. Hsiang,
Thank you for your resume and application letter. DCME Company would like to invite you to interview for the position of counter crew. Please click on the link below and sign in to select your preferred interview time.
http://www.dcmedairyproducts.interviewassistant.menu=candidate&eventToken=d8r838r8t880085324144dhug7
Your interview will take place at: 307 Royal Building, Christopher Road.
When you arrive for your interview, please report to the receptionist on the 10th Floor.
Thank you.

Candidate ⊙ Mr. ○Mrs. ○ Ms.	Albert Hsiang
Position Applied for :	○Supervisor ⊙ Counter crew
Preferred Interview Date:	○May 3 ⊙ May 4 ○ May 5
Preferred Interview Time:	○10:30 ○11:00 ○11:30 ○13:30 ○14:00 ○14:30 ○15:00 ○15:30 ⊙16:00 ○16:30
	SUBMIT

應徵者 ⊙Mr. ○Mrs. ○ Ms.	Albert Hsiang
應徵職務	○主管 ⊙櫃檯人員
希望面試日期	○五月三日 ⊙五月四日 ○五月五日
希望面試時間	○10:30 ○11:00 ○11:30 ○13:30 ○14:00 ○14:30 ○15:00 ○15:30 ⊙16:00 ○16:30
送出	

【詞彙】
receptionist 櫃檯人員／submit 送出；提交

191 What is the purpose of the advertisement?
(A) To recruit helpers
(B) To promote a new product
(C) To advertise a movie
(D) To announce a flash sale

【解析】由廣告標題為14天的短期工作，內容為徵求在購物城美食廣場的乳製品販售員，可知這則廣告目的應該是在招募短期工作人員，選項中以(A)為最適當的答案，故(A)為正解。

這篇廣告的目的為何？
(A) 招募幫手
(B) 促銷新品
(C) 幫一部電影打廣告
(D) 公佈一場限時搶購

【類型】內容主題題型

【詞彙】
advertise 廣告宣傳／flash sale 限時特賣

【正解】(A)

這篇廣告沒有提供哪一項訊息？
(A) 報酬
(B) 工作時間
(C) 工作地點
(D) 開始時間

【類型】提問細節題型

【正解】(D)

192 Which information is not given in the advertisement?
(A) The salary
(B) The working time
(C) The work location
(D) The starting time

【解析】這則徵人廣告上提到了工作時間為兩班輪班制，工作時間、地點及薪資報酬都清楚列出，唯獨沒有提到這份短期工作從何時開始，故答案要選(D)。

這封電子郵件為何而寫？
(A) 請求會面
(B) 提交作業
(C) 邀請面試
(D) 介紹公司

【類型】提問原因題型

【詞彙】
submit 提交／assignment 作業

【正解】(C)

193 Why was the email written?
(A) To request a meeting
(B) To submit an assignment
(C) To send an interview invitation
(D) To introduce the company

【解析】由郵件主旨為interview invitation（面試邀請），可知寫這封郵件的原因是為了邀請對方來面試，故正解為(C)。

194 What position is Albert applying for?
(A) The supervisor
(B) The counter crew
(C) The delivery driver
(D) The express courier

【解析】由面試邀請信件及Albert在應徵時間選擇表上的應徵職務欄圈選counter crew（櫃檯人員），可知他應徵的是櫃檯人員，正解為(B)。

Albert應徵的是哪一個職務？
(A) 主管
(B) 櫃檯人員
(C) 送貨司機
(D) 快遞員

【類型】提問細節題型

【詞彙】
delivery driver送貨司機／
express courier快遞員

【正解】(B)

195 When will Albert's interview take place?
(A) 2 pm on May 3
(B) 4 pm on May 4
(C) 10 am on May 4
(D) 3:30 pm on May 5

【解析】由Albert在應徵時間選擇表上圈選May 4的16:00，可知他的面試將在五月四日下午四點舉行，正解為(B)。

Albert的面試何時進行？
(A) 五月三日下午兩點
(B) 五月四日下午四點
(C) 五月四日上午十點
(D) 五月五日下午三點半

【類型】圖表閱讀題型

【正解】(B)

退貨

Eastern Lake® 為所有我們販售的商品品質做後盾，希望您能對您的服飾用品感到滿意。我們的產品在材質方面都有完整的保固，手工製品則有終身保固。鞋類商品則為有限制的一年保固。

如果您對您在Eastern Lake購買的產品不滿意，您可以用以下方式退貨：

• 線上購買的商品可以在六十天內在線上或是至我們零售商店辦理退貨。

• 在零售商店購買的商品一定要在六十天內到店內辦理退貨。

• 您必須要有原購物發票或裝箱單才能完成退貨手續。

• 商品必須未經使用或未過水。

• 訂製產品都是完成品，不適用於退貨、換貨、變更或修改。

RETURNS

The Eastern Lake® stands behind the quality of everything we sell and hope you're happy with your gear. Our products are fully warranted against defects in materials and workmanship with a lifetime guarantee. Footwear holds a limited one-year guarantee.

If you're unsatisfied with products you purchased from The Eastern Lake, you can return your item(s) as follows:

• Items purchased online can be returned online or at our retail stores within 60 days of purchase.

• Items purchased in a retail store must be returned in-store within 60 days of purchase.

• You must have an original receipt or packing slip to complete your return.

• Items must be unused and unwashed.

• Custom products are final and are not eligible for returns, exchanges, changes or alterations.

先生您好，

我跟你們訂購的男子保暖提升400冬靴已經在今天早上送來了。非常謝謝。

但是，很遺憾必須告訴你們我必須退掉這件商品，因為它們對我來說太小了。它們是我平常穿的尺寸，但我就是穿不下。

Dear Sir,

The Men's Thermoball Lifty 400 Winter Boots that I ordered from you have arrived this morning. Thank you very much.

Nevertheless, I regret to tell you that I need to return the item because they are too small for me. They are the size that I usually wear but I just can't fit in.

Attached to this letter and the parcel is the goods return note. Please let me know when I will get a refund of my purchase. Thanks.
Look forward to hearing from you soon.

Regards,
Derrick Long

隨信及包裹附上的是商品退貨單。請讓我知道何時能拿到退款。謝謝。
期待很快有您的消息。

Derrick Long 謹上

Goods Return Note

Purchase Order No. ___439908124___

Date Goods Received: ___26 January, 2018___

Reasons for Returning:

☐ Defective product

☐ Product no longer needed

☐ Product did not match description on website or in catalog

☑ Product did not meet customer's expectations

☐ Incorrect product or size ordered

☐ Incorrect product or size delivered

Signed: _Derrick Long_

Dated: ___February 27, 2018___

商品退貨單

購物訂單編號 ___439908124___

商品到貨日期 __2018年一月26日__

退貨原因：

☐ 商品瑕疵

☐ 不需要了

☐ 商品與網站或型錄上描述不符

☑ 商品不符合顧客期待

☐ 訂購錯誤商品或尺寸

☐ 寄送錯誤商品或尺寸

簽名：Derrick Long

日期：___2018年二月27日2018___

【詞彙】

stand behind 做後盾／workmanship 手工製品／
lifetime 終身的／packing list 裝箱單／
custom product 訂製產品／eligible 適合／alteration 修改

The Eastern Lake是賣什麼商品的？

(A) 家用電器

(B) 戶外用品

(C) 電子零件

(D) 書與雜誌

【類型】提問細節題型

【詞彙】

household appliance家用電器／
electronic component電子零件

【正解】(B)

鞋類的保固時間是多久？

(A) 終身

(B) 六十天

(C) 一年

(D) 兩年

【類型】提問細節題型

【正解】(C)

Derrick的信件目的為何？

(A) 下購買訂單

(B) 請求購買憑證

(C) 退訂購物品

(D) 更改寄貨地址

【類型】內容主題題型

【詞彙】

proof 證明／delivery address
寄貨地址

【正解】(C)

---

196 What kind of product does The Eastern Lake sell?

(A) Household appliances

(B) Outdoor products

(C) Electronic components

(D) Books and magazines

【解析】雖然本題提供的資訊中並未明白說明The Eastern Lake是什麼商店，但由「商品退貨須知」提到他們的其中一項商品有footwear（鞋類），而且退貨信上也提到要將訂購的winter boots（冬季靴子）退貨，footwear與選項(A)(C)(D)等商品都毫無關係，刪除不可能的選項後，只有(B)的戶外用品是最有可能的答案，故正解為(B)。

---

197 How long is footwear guaranteed for?

(A) Lifetime

(B) 60 days

(C) One year

(D) Two years

【解析】由「退貨須知」上提到Footwear holds a limited one-year guarantee.（鞋類商品提供有限的一年保固），可知答案為(C)。

---

198 What is the purpose of Derrick's letter?

(A) To place a purchase order

(B) To request a proof of purchase

(C) To return an item he ordered

(D) To change the delivery address

【解析】由Derrick的信件提到... I need to return the item（……我需要退貨），可知這封信的目的是要「退貨」，正解為(C)。

199 What is Derrick's reason for returning the product?
(A) He doesn't like the color.
(B) He ordered the wrong size.
(C) It doesn't meet his needs.
(D) The product arrived damaged.

Derrick退貨的理由是什麼？
(A) 他不喜歡顏色。
(B) 他訂購錯誤的尺碼。
(C) 不符合他的需要。
(D) 產品到貨時已損毀。

【類型】提問細節題型

【正解】(C)

【解析】Derrick在信中強調自己訂購的尺寸是他平常穿的尺寸，可知他不認為自己訂到錯誤的尺碼，故選項(B)並非正確答案。根據Derrick的商品退貨單上勾選的退貨原因為Product did not meet customer's expectations（商品不符合期待），可知選項(C)為最適當的描述，故為正解。

---

200 When does Derrick return the product?
(A) Seven days after purchase
(B) One month after receipt of goods
(C) Two months before guarantee expires
(D) After guarantee expired

Derrick是何時退的貨？
(A) 購買後七天
(B) 收到貨後一個月
(C) 保固到期前兩個月
(D) 保固到期之後

【類型】圖表閱讀題型

【詞彙】
expire 到期

【正解】(B)

【解析】由Derrick填寫的商品退貨單上的到貨日期為2018年1月26日，根據「退貨須知」，鞋類商品保固期為一年，因此保固到期為2019年1月25日。Derrick的退貨日期為2018年2月27日，離保固到期還很久。可知他是在到貨後一個月左右退貨的，正解為(B)。

New TOEIC Reading Analysis 3
新多益閱讀全真模擬試題解析第3回

提出申請之前請確認你已標明所需數量。

【類型】動詞相似詞彙題型

【詞彙】

submit繳交／assure使某人放心／ensure確認某事物／insure保險／reassure再三使某人放心／specify詳細標明／amount數量

【正解】(B)

101 Before submitting your request, please _____ you specify the amount you need.

(A) assure　　　　(B) ensure

(C) insure　　　　(D) reassure

【解析】assure表示「使某人放心」，如：I can assure you that this is 100% safe. ensure表示「確認某事物」，如：He ensured that the doors were all locked. insure表示「將某物保險」，如：insure my car for $100,000。reassure表示「使某人放心」，如：She tried to reassure her mother.

需要使用碎紙機的辦公室職員需要先得到David主任的同意。

【類型】詞類變化題型

【詞彙】

staff員工／paper shredder 碎紙機／require需要／prove證明／approve允許／approval允許（名）／director主管

【正解】(D)

102 Office staff who need to use the paper shredder are required to get _____ from director David first.

(A) prove　　　　(B) approve

(C) approving　　　(D) approval

【解析】prove為動詞，表示「證明」。用法為：prove something/ someone+ (to be)+adj. approve為同意的動詞，名詞變化為approval。根據題幹，動詞get後方應接名詞，因此答案應選(D)。

某些評論家對於這個產業的續航力感到懷疑。

【類型】詞類變化題型

【詞彙】

critics評論家／skeptical懷疑／sustain維持／sustainable能夠持久的／sustainability持久力／industry產業

【正解】(D)

103 Some critics are skeptical about the _____ of the industry.

(A) sustain　　　　(B) sustaining

(C) sustainable　　(D) sustainability

【解析】空格為一名詞片語的部分。因此應填入名詞。sustain為動詞，表示「持久」，sustaining為動詞詞形式，意思同為「持久」。根據本題的語意，空格處的意思應為「持久力；續航力」，因此應選(D)表示「續航力」。

104 The unemployment rate this year rose _____ due to the country's withdrawal from the union.

(A) dramatically

(B) periodically

(C) consistently

(D) anxiously

【解析】根據題幹的語意「國家退出聯盟」，我們可推斷失業率應該是急劇攀升。因此只有選項(A)符合語意。

由於國家退出聯盟，今年的失業率急劇攀升。

【類型】副詞詞彙題型

【詞彙】
unemployment rate失業率／
rise提升／
dramatically戲劇性地／
periodically定期地／
consistently連貫地／
anxiously焦慮地／
due to因為／
withdrawal退出／
union聯盟

【正解】(A)

---

105 Congratulations to you for _____ to manager.

(A) promote   (B) promoting

(C) promoted   (D) being promoted

【解析】promote表示「使某人升遷」。因此某人升遷到某職位應該用被動語態來表示，如：be promoted to。而空格前方有介系詞for，因此be應變化為being動名詞形式。因此答案應選(D)。

恭喜你晉升經理。

【類型】動詞型態題型

【詞彙】
congratulations恭喜／
promote升遷／
manager經理

【正解】(D)

---

106 Please turn off the machine when it is not _____ use.

(A) to   (B) with

(C) in   (D) on

【解析】in use表示「東西使用中」。out of use表示「東西不使用」。如：This platform is not in use.

機器不使用時請將它關掉。

【類型】介系詞題型

【詞彙】
machine機器／
in use使用中

【正解】(C)

她將她的行李托運回家。

【類型】動詞型態題型

【詞彙】
luggage行李／
ship托運

【正解】(B)

107 She had her luggage _____ to her home address.

(A) shipping   (B) shipped

(C) to ship   (D) for shipping

【解析】此處的have為使役動詞。have something V-pp表示「將某物做某種處置」，如I had my hair cut.表示「我剪了頭髮」。另外have someone Vr. 表示「讓某人做某事」，如：She had him collect the tickets for her.表示「她讓他幫她收集門票」。

從宏觀的角度看，這個系統內部存在的某些大問題需要優先被解決。

【類型】介系詞題型

【詞彙】
broad寬廣的／
perspective觀點／
gaping hole明顯的大問題／
address處理／priority優先

【正解】(A)

108 _____ a broader perspective, some gaping holes in the system need to be addressed with priority.

(A) From   (B) On

(C) With   (D) Along

【解析】與perspective這個字連用的介系詞為from，表示「從……角度來看」。因此答案應選(A)。

大部分的航空公司都知道某些旅客不會出現，因此都會刻意超賣機位。

【類型】副詞詞彙題型

【詞彙】
airline航空公司／unexpectedly出乎預期地／considerably可觀地／intentionally故意地／arguably可論證地／overbook使過量預定／percentage百分比／passenger乘客／show up出現

【正解】(C)

109 Most airlines would _____ overbook knowing that a percentage of passengers will not show up.

(A) unexpectedly   (B) considerably

(C) intentionally   (D) arguably

【解析】題幹後方的knowing that a percentage of passengers will not show up表示航空公司已知特定的乘客不會出現，因此會「故意」超賣機票。因此答案應選(C)。

110 _____ you get to the final stage of the interview, I will email you all the necessary documents.

(A) By   (B) Even
(C) Once   (D) Though

【解析】本題有兩個句子，缺少連接詞。因此我們可確定空格處必填從屬連接詞。by為介系詞。even為副詞。though為連接詞，表示「雖然」。綜合文法和語意，答案應選(C)。

一旦你到達面試的最後一關，我會把需要的文件都電郵給你。

【類型】連接詞題型

【詞彙】
by到某個時間點之前／
once一旦／though雖然／
stage階段／necessary需要的／
document文件

【正解】(C)

---

111 When you need to stay in the office for a/an _____ period of time, you can ask your company to cover the meal for you.

(A) extended
(B) predicted
(C) delayed
(D) intended

【解析】extend有延長的意思，過去分詞extended表示「延長的」。題幹意思為「在辦公室待的更久一點」，因此答案應選(A)。

當你需要在辦公室待晚一點的時候，你可以要求公司幫你支付你的餐點。

【類型】形容詞詞彙題型

【詞彙】
extended延長的／
predicted預料中的／
delayed延期的／
intended刻意地／
cover付

【正解】(A)

---

112 A potential crisis has been _____ after he appealed for help.

(A) converted
(B) averted
(C) perverted
(D) reverted

【解析】此題的選項能跟crisis危機語意符合的選項為(B)避開。選項(D)revert為不及物動詞。

在他求助之後，潛在的危機已經避免了。

【類型】動詞型態題型

【詞彙】
potential潛在的／
crisis危機／convert轉換／
avert避開／pervert使腐壞／
revert回復／appeal for訴諸

【正解】(B)

自從她上次離開家鄉已經過了十年。

【類型】動詞詞彙題型

【詞彙】
decade十年／intervene介入／
fantasize幻想／
enunciate讀出發音／
retrieve拿回

【正解】(A)

113 A decade has _____ since she last left her hometown.

(A) intervened　　　(B) fantasized

(C) enunciated　　　(D) retrieved

【解析】題幹的意思為「自從她上次離開家鄉已經過了十年」，換句話説自從上次她離家之後，十年已經介入了這段時間內。因此，選項(A)最符合本句語意。

請提醒參加研討會的人將他們的身分證帶到會場。

【類型】所有格題型

【詞彙】
remind提醒／seminar研討會／
attendee參與者／venue會場

【正解】(C)

114 Please remind the seminar attendees to bring _____ IDs to the venue.

(A) his　　　　　　(B) her

(C) their　　　　　(D) your

【解析】本題的所有格是代指前面提過的seminar attendees 因此為第三人稱複數所有格their，因此答案應選(C)。

有關匿名性的問題，你有責任告知參與者他們的身份信息都會受到保護。

【類型】連接詞片語題型

【詞彙】
as far as...concerned有關／
as soon as一……就……／
tardy緩慢／as well as和／
anonymity匿名／
responsibility責任／
participant參加者／
identity身份／protect保護

【正解】(A)

115 _____ anonymity is concerned, it is your responsibility to inform the participants that their identities will be safely protected.

(A) As far as　　　(B) As soon as

(C) As tardy as　　(D) As well as

【解析】as far as something is/are concerned表示「關於某事情」，為連接詞片語。因此答案應選(A)。

116 Congratulations to an alumnus of our university, Kris Cape, _____ has won the best mobile app award this year.

(A) that   (B) who

(C) whose   (D) which

【解析】本題的先行詞為Kris Cape是一個人。並且空格前方有逗點，表示非限定用法。因此不能用that，符合的選項為(B)。whose則是代表先行詞和關係代名詞後方的名詞有所有格關係。

恭喜本校校友Kris Cape榮獲今年度最佳手機軟體獎。

【類型】關係代名詞題型

【詞彙】
alumnus校友／
university大學／award獎項

【正解】(B)

---

117 A coach will be booked to _____ you to and from the event.

(A) transcribe   (B) transport

(C) translate   (D) traverse

【解析】coach意思為「長途巴士」，因此巴士是用來「運輸」人的。根據語義，選項(B)最為符合。

我們會預訂一輛巴士接送你來回活動現場。

【類型】動詞詞彙題型

【詞彙】
coach長途巴士／book預定／
transcribe抄寫／transport運輸／
translate翻譯／traverse橫渡

【正解】(B)

---

118 How much does the collection of lipsticks _____ ?

(A) take   (B) spend

(C) pay   (D) cost

【解析】本題考點為四個易混淆的動詞。take為「某事物花了多少時間」。spend為「某人花了多少時間或金錢」。cost為「某事物花了多少金錢」。pay為「某人付了多少錢」。本題題幹意思為「這組口紅多少錢」，因此答案選(D)。

這組口紅多少錢？

【類型】動詞相近詞彙題型

【詞彙】
collection組合／lipstick口紅

【正解】(D)

試著與她聯絡好幾次之後，我終於聯繫上她了。

【類型】形容詞詞彙題型

【詞彙】
occasional偶然的／
multiple多次的／
valuable有價值的／
binary二元的／get hold of聯繫

【正解】(B)

---

119 After trying to contact her _____ times, I finally got hold of her.

(A) occasional   (B) multiple

(C) valueless   (D) binary

【解析】time在本題中為「次數」的意思。本題表示「聯絡她很多次」，因此選項(B)multiple語義最符合。

如果任何人有關於取得報名名單的問題，請務必通知我。

【類型】介系詞題型

【詞彙】
issue議題／
access取得／
signup報名

【正解】(A)

---

120 If anybody has issues _____ accessing the signup list, please do let me know.

(A) with   (B) in

(C) among   (D) for

【解析】have issues/problems with表示「在某方面有問題」，為固定搭配的介系詞。因此答案應選(A)。

我們感到抱歉由於未預期因素，我們必須取消本次活動。

【類型】形容詞詞彙題型

【詞彙】
regret遺憾／indirect間接的／
acute急性的／
unforeseen未預期的／
diverse多樣的／
circumstance情形

【正解】(C)

---

121 We regret that we have to cancel the event due to the _____ circumstances.

(A) indirect   (B) acute

(C) unforeseen   (D) diverse

【解析】本題語意為「因為未預料的情況，我們必須取消活動」，根據語意，選項(C)最符合題意。

122 Mr. Lee will be on his annual leave _____ December 22 to January 1.

(A) from　　　　　　(B) on

(C) during　　　　　(D) between

【解析】from A to B表示「從A點到B點」；on後面加「跟一天有關」的時間點，如：on Monday, on December 12th。during後面加一段時間，如：during the vacation。between A and B表示「在A和B之間」。題幹中有to，並且有兩個時間點，因此答案應選(A)。

李先生從十二月二十二日到一月一日休年假。

【類型】介系詞題型

【詞彙】
annual年度的／
leave假

【正解】(A)

---

123 _____ the difficulties faced, we need to be brave and tough it out.

(A) On account of　　(B) Resulting from

(C) Regardless of　　(D) With regard to

【解析】regardless of表示「無論」，同義的單字片語還有despite, in spite of, no matter what, irrespective of等。

無論遇到什麼困難，我們都必須勇敢撐過去。

【類型】介系詞片語題型

【詞彙】
on account of因為／
result from由……導致／
regardless of無論／
with regard to關於／
difficulty困難／brave勇敢／
tough out艱難渡過

【正解】(C)

---

124 _____ all the competitors, Sherman is the most articulate speaker.

(A) Of　　　　　　(B) In

(C) Along　　　　(D) For

【解析】最高級句型：S+V+最高級+of群體／in範圍。本題把後面的介系詞片語移到句首。因此答案應選(A)。

在所有的競爭者中，Sherman是口齒最清晰的演說者。

【類型】介系詞題型

【詞彙】
competitor競爭者／
articulate口齒清晰的

【正解】(A)

請仔細閱讀這份合約，裡面詳細
說明有哪些義務。

【類型】動詞型態題型

【詞彙】
contract合約／
detail詳細說明／
obligation義務

【正解】(C)

125 Please carefully read through the contract _____ the obligations.

(A) detail
(B) details
(C) detailing
(D) detailed

【解析】本題考的是形容詞子句簡化的形容詞片語。本句的先行詞為contract。原本的修飾語為which/that details the obligations。經過分詞構句簡化之後將which/that刪除，並將動詞改為現在分詞detailing。因此答案應選(C)。

你了解必須達到的要求嗎？

【類型】動詞詞彙題型

【詞彙】
requirement要求／meet達到／
compose組成／purchase購買／
breach裂開

【正解】(A)

126 Do you understand the requirements expected to be _____ ?

(A) met
(B) composed
(C) purchased
(D) breached

【解析】meet the requirement表示「達到要求」。為固定用法。meet表示「達到」或「符合」的意思。其他用法還有meet the expectation符合期望、make ends meet讓收支平衡。

當你們申請報銷時，按照標準程
序走是很重要的。

【類型】動詞型態題型

【詞彙】
standard operating procedures
標準作業程序／
apply for申請／
reimbursement報銷

【正解】(B)

127 It is important that the standard operating procedures _____ when you apply for reimbursement.

(A) follow
(B) be followed
(C) following
(D) be following

【解析】It is important/ crucial/ recommended that S Vr.為虛擬語氣的句型，其中子句中的動詞須為原型動詞。而標準作業程序是「被遵循的」，因此使用被動語態be+ V-pp.。因此答案應選(B)。

128 Sophie brought up the issue to her direct supervisor _____ the risk of losing her job.

(A) at   (B) in

(C) with   (D) as

【解析】at the risk of表示「冒著⋯⋯風險」做某事。通常放在動詞片語之後。為固定用法，因此答案應選(A)。

Sophie冒著被辭退的風險向她的直屬主管提起這個問題。

【類型】介系詞題型

【詞彙】
bring up something to someone向某人提起某事／
direct supervisor直屬主管／
at the risk of冒著⋯⋯風險

【正解】(A)

---

129 Both parties have to sign the document _____ they understand the terms.

(A) indicate   (B) which indicate

(C) indicates   (D) to indicate

【解析】本題語意為「雙方簽署條款，目的是為了表示雙方都明白其中的條款」。表示目的性需用不定詞to Vr.。因此答案應選(D)。

雙方必須簽署這份文件以表示他們都了解了這些條款。

【類型】動詞型態題型

【詞彙】
sign簽署／
document文件／
indicate標示／
term條款

【正解】(D)

---

130 _____ is the average length of each video clip?

(A) How   (B) What

(C) How long   (D) When

【解析】本題的主詞為the average length of each video clip，關鍵詞為length，搭配的疑問詞為what，非how long。換句話說，what is the length of something也可以用how long is something來表示。How long is the length of something是錯誤用法。另外，what is the size of something也可以說how large is something。what is the age of someone也可以說how old is someone。

每個影片長度平均多長？

【類型】疑問詞題型

【詞彙】
average平均的／
length長度／
video clip短片

【正解】(B)

▶ **PART 6**

Directions: Read the texts on the following pages. A word or phrase is missing in some of the sentences. Answer choices are given below each of these articles. Select the best answer to complete the text. Then mark the letter (A), (B), (C) or (D) on your answer sheet.

Questions 131-134 refer to the following information.

倫敦地區牙醫助理職缺

Adriana牙醫診所-倫敦SE7區 兼職

我們的診所位於地鐵Piccadilly 線附近，目前正在徵求一位有經 驗、能力強並通過牙醫協會認證 的牙醫助理，上班時間為週間時 段。牙醫助理的任務是幫助病人 擁有一個很棒的就診經驗，我們 十分看重這點。

你的任務是

• 協助手術進行，準備器具，消 毒使用過的器具，在手術過程中 遞送器具。
• 安排病人預約看診，確保手術 日程進行順利
• 幫助病患，減輕病患焦慮情緒

請將履歷寄來，我們會與您聯絡 安排電話面試。

Dental Assistant Job in London

Adriana Dental Office- London SE7
Part-time

Our office, conveniently ___131___ near a Piccadilly line metro station, is seeking an experienced and reliable dental surgery assistant who is certified by General Dental Council for weekday work. The role of a dental assistant which we highly ___132___ is key to creating for patients the best experience of dental treatment.

Your duties are

• assisting dental operation by preparing the surgery instruments, sterilizing the instruments after use, passing and holding the surgery devices during the procedure

• arranging ___133___ with customers and ensuring the dentists' schedules run smoothly

• offering friendly help to customers and easing their anxiety

Please send your CV, and ___134___.

---

131 (A) locates
(B) locating
(C) is located
(D) located

【解析】locate表示「定位」或「使……座落於」，因此某人事物位於何處應用被動語態表達（be located...）。而此題為經分詞構句省略後的分詞片語，原本是which is conveniently located near a Piccadilly line metro station，簡化後變成conveniently located near a Piccadilly line metro station。因此答案應選(D)。

【類型】動詞型態題型

【詞彙】
conveniently方便地／
locate位於／
metro地鐵／seek尋找／
experienced有經驗的／
reliable靠得住的／
dental牙齒的／
surgery手術／
assistant助理／
certify認證／
weekday週間

【正解】(D)

【詞彙】
highly高度／consider考慮／
recognize認可／
perceive認為／
conceive認為／
treatment治療

【正解】(B)

132 (A) consider
(B) recognize
(C) perceive
(D) conceive

【解析】根據題幹語意，空格處應填入「認可」。選項中(B)最符合。consider為「考慮」的意思。perceive表示「感官上的知道」，而conceive表示「經過思考後的知道」。

【類型】名詞詞彙題型

【詞彙】
arrange安排／
appointment約會／
conference會議／
summit高峰會／
meeting會議／
ensure確保／dentist牙醫／
schedule行程／
smoothly順暢地

【正解】(A)

133 (A) appointments
(B) conferences
(C) summits
(D) meetings

【解析】appointment為人與人之間約定的見面。conference為大型的主題會議。summit為政府或國家元首聚集的高峰會。meeting是公司內部例行的小型會議。本題語境為牙醫與病患間的約診，因此答案應選(A)。

【類型】句子插入題型

【詞彙】
CV履歷／clinic診所的／
in touch可聯繫／telephone
interview電話面試／officially
正式地／qualification資格／
essential重要的

【正解】(B)

★ **134** (A) you should have at least 1 year of clinic experience
(B) we will be in touch to arrange a telephone interview
(C) we can officially welcome you on board
(D) qualifications are essential to the job requirements

【解析】根據題幹語意，在寄履歷之後，接選項(B)會使語意最為通順。選項(C)是正式歡迎入職，不適用本題語境。選項(A)(D)應出現在工作資格要求的區域。

Questions 135-138 refer to the following email.

Dear New Ocean Bell Resident,
As you may know, the heater in your room stops working from time to time recently. ___135___ our contractor, an operative will be coming and carrying out some remedial works to the heating system at New Ocean Bell on 17th and 18th September 2017.

We are writing this email to formally notify you that for these essential works to be completed, access to your room may be required at some point during the days. These works will be carried out with minimum ___136___. You do not have to be present while the heater check-up which will only last no more than five minutes is carried out but ___137___.

If for any reason these dates need to be changed, please notify us ___138___. Please, if you have any queries, do not hesitate to let us know.

Kind regards,
Ray

親愛的New Ocean Bell住戶
你們好：

誠如你們所知，最近房間內的暖氣常常故障。在我們與承包商聯繫後，技師會在2017年9月17、18日到New Ocean Bell公寓修理暖氣系統。

我們正式告知您為了讓修繕工程順利完成，技師可能需要在該時段進入你們的房間。我們會盡量把干擾降到最低。在暖氣檢修的過程中，通常只需要不到五分鐘，你不需要在場，但如果你需要在場當然也歡迎。

如果因為任何原因，維修日期需要更動，請提前通知我們。若有疑問，歡迎聯繫我們。

祝 順利
Ray

---

135 (A) Ring
(B) Rang
(C) Being rung
(D) Having rung

【解析】本題空格到逗點處為分詞構句後的分詞片語。原本是 We have rung our contractor and...。經過主詞和連接詞省略，動詞改為現在分詞後，變成Having rung our contractor, ...。因此答案應選(D)。

【類型】動詞型態題型

【詞彙】
ring打電話／
contractor承包商／
operative技術工人／
carry out進行／
remedial修繕的

【正解】(D)

【類型】名詞詞彙題型

【詞彙】
minimum最低的／
disruption干擾／
distortion變形／
fragility脆弱／
agility敏捷

【正解】(A)

136 (A) disruption
(B) distortion
(C) fragility
(D) agility

【解析】根據本題語意，修繕工程應盡量避免干擾住戶。因此根據語義，答案應選(A)。

【類型】句子插入題型

【詞彙】
present在場的／
penalty懲罰／
procedure流程

【正解】(C)

★ 137 (A) no-show will lead to serious penalty
(B) your presence may disrupt the procedures of the works
(C) are more than welcome to do so should you wish
(D) I understand how busy your schedule is

【解析】題幹表示「修理期間不需在場」，因此選項(A)變矛盾。而空格之前的連接詞為but，代表後方語意轉折。接選項(B)會呈現因果關係。因此選項(C)最合適。

【類型】副詞片語題型

【詞彙】
notify通知／
patience耐心／
in advance事先／
for instance例如／
on a short notice很晚通知

【正解】(B)

138 (A) with patience
(B) in advance
(C) for instance
(D) on a short notice

【解析】題幹語意為「若有任何問題請提前通知」，因此選項(B)語意最通順。

Questions 139-142 refer to the following post.

The 2nd Music
Wave Award is Open NOW!

第二屆音浪獎現在開跑

The 2nd Music Wave Award offers amateur music composers the chance to win 12 thousand dollars and a work placement in Beta Music. The award, ___139___ by Beta Music and My-Line, gives the country's brightest music composers and producers a head start in the highly competitive music industry. Participants should first become a member of My-Line by ___140___ on www.myline.com. Next, submit your work which should be saved in an mp3 file to the MyMusic portal. Finally, fill out the personal information chart and click "submit". You will receive an email ___141___ that your file is successfully received. ___142___ . No late submission would be acceptable. Your work will go through three rating phases reviewed by the country's prestigious music producers and songwriters. The results will be released on the official website of MyMusic on the first day of December.

第二屆的音浪獎為業餘音樂創作者提供一個贏得一萬兩千元和在Beta音樂公司工作的機會。本獎項由Beta音樂與My-Line贊助提供。提供給國內最傑出的作曲家和製作人在競爭激烈的音樂產業中一個拔得頭籌的機會。參加者須先上www.myline.com註冊My-Line會員。接著將您的作品存成mp3檔上傳到MyMusic空間。最後填妥個人資料表並點擊上傳。您將會收到一封確認作品上傳成功的電郵。繳交截止日為十一月五日。逾期不受理。您的作品將會經過三輪評審，評審為享譽國內的音樂製作人及詞曲創作人。評選結果會在十二月一日在MyMusic的官方網站上公布。

【類型】動詞詞匯題型

【詞彙】
award獎項／
sponsor贊助／reward回饋／
compensate補償／
expand擴張／bright傑出／
composer作曲者／
producer製作人／
head start先機／
competitive競爭的／
industry產業

【正解】(A)

139 (A) sponsored
　　(B) rewarded
　　(C) compensated
　　(D) expanded

【解析】本句主詞「獎項」與「贊助」一詞最為搭配。根據語意，答案應選(A)。

【類型】動詞型態題型

【詞彙】
participant參加者／
register註冊

【正解】(B)

140 (A) register
　　(B) registering
　　(C) registered
　　(D) registration

【解析】空格前方有介系詞by。因此應填動名詞registering。動名詞有名詞的詞性，但仍保留動詞的特徵，如：後方能接受詞。選項(D)registration雖為名詞，可放在介系詞後方，但後面不能在接受詞。因此不能說by registration on...。因此答案應選動名詞的選項(B)。

141 (A) confirm

(B) confirms

(C) to confirm

(D) confirming

【解析】本題原句應為You will receive an email that confirms that your file is successfully received.經過分詞構句，省略 that並把動詞改為現在分詞後變為You will receive an email confirming that your file is successfully received.。因此答案 應選(D)。

【類型】動詞型態題型

【詞彙】
confirm確認／
file檔案／
successfully成功地

【正解】(D)

★ **142** (A) Please be constantly updated about the latest results.

(B) The deadline for submitting your work is November 5th.

(C) Your willingness to share your work with us is appreciated.

(D) Further details will be circulated near the time of early December.

【解析】句子插入題須考慮上下文語意的連貫。根據空格後方 No late submission would be acceptable.我們能推斷前一句 必定跟截止日期相關。因此選項(B)的語意最符合。

【類型】句子插入題型

【詞彙】
submission呈交／
acceptable可接受的／
constantly經常／
deadline截止日期／
willingness意願／
appreciate感激／
further進一步的／
circulate散布

【正解】(B)

西南區營業處 2017 (65)

09:53

Stefanie

Eve早安。 我被告知要跟你講關於申請修理我的辦公室門的事情。

Eve

能具體說明問題嗎？第幾號房間？

10:00

Stefanie

房間號碼是1414。門把一直鎖上，用什麼鑰匙都要很久才能打開。有時候門鏈也鎖不上。

Eve

好的，我知道了。我今天下午回辦公室後會將您的申請提出到後勤部門。他們會在今天下午五點前派專人去修理。

16:09

Stefanie

門修好了！感謝您！你是我的英雄！

Eve

好的，有什麼問題再跟我說。

Southwest Branch Office 2017 (65)

Stefanie　　　09:53

Hey, Eve. Good morning. I have been told to speak to you about ___143___ a request for my office door to be fixed.

Eve

Can you be specific about the problem? What is the room number?

10:00

Stefanie

My room is 1414. My door knob keeps locking and takes a long to unlock ___144___ any key. Sometimes the door will not even stay latched closed.

Eve

Okay! I got it. I will put through your request to the ___145___ department when I am back in the office this afternoon. They will send an operative over by 5 pm today.

16:09

Stefanie

___146___ .

Eve

Alright. If you've got any problem next time, just let me know.

416

143 (A) giving in

(B) gearing up

(C) putting in

(D) holding up

【解析】本題語意為「提出修門的申請」。與提出申請連用的
片語動詞為put in或put through。因此答案應選(C)。

【詞彙】
give in屈服／
gear up整裝準備／
put in呈交／
hold up阻礙

【正解】(C)

---

144 (A) in

(B) by

(C) with

(D) to

【解析】with+工具；by+手段。空格後方接的是key，因此空
格應填入with。

【類型】介系詞題型

【詞彙】
door knob門把／
unlock解鎖

【正解】(C)

---

145 (A) logistics

(B) financial

(C) administrative

(D) human resources

【解析】根據本文，主題為門的修繕。因此根據通篇語意判
斷，負責修繕的相關部門應為後勤部logistics department。因
此答案應選(A)。

【類型】名詞片語題型

【詞彙】
put through提交／
request申請／
logistics後勤／
financial財務的／
administrative行政的／
human resources人力資源／
department部門

【正解】(A)

【類型】句子插入題型

【詞彙】
technician技術人員／
extension number分機號碼

【正解】(C)

★ 146 (A) I am locked out of my room again.
(B) The technician went late this afternoon.
(C) My door is good to use now. You are my hero!
(D) Can I ask for the extension number of the department?

【解析】本篇為通訊軟體的對話。因此句子插入題必須根據對話的上下文來判斷答案。在Stefanie說完之後，Eve接著說 Alright. If you've got any problem next time, just let me know. 我們能判斷修門的問題很可能已經解決了。因此根據語意判斷，答案應為(C)。

▶ **PART 7**

Directions: In this part, you will read a selection of texts, such as magazine and newspaper articles, letters, and advertisements. Each text is followed by several questions. Select the best answer for each question and mark the letter (A), (B), (C), or (D) on your answer sheet.

Questions 147-148 refer to the following notice.

Notice

We're appealing for the public help locating a missing women Cecily McCarthy. Ms. McCarthy comes from little Timber, Bristol. She was last seen in Bath on July 20th.

Cecily is described as white, approximately five feet 2 inches tall and a slim build. She has dark brown hair and is about 48 years old in appearance. Please contact Mary Wilson on 131-6274-2618. You will get a £800 reward.

公告

我們正徵求大家的幫忙找一位走失的女士Cecily McCarthy。McCarthy女士來自布里斯托小木鎮。上次有人見到她是七月二十日在巴斯。Cecily是白皮膚，身高大約五尺二吋，身材纖細。頭髮深棕色，看上去大約四十八歲。請撥打131-6274-2618聯繫Mary Wilson。您可以得到800鎊作為獎勵。

【詞彙】
appeal for尋求／locate定位／describe描述／approximately大約／feet英尺／inch英吋／slim纖細的／build身型

這則公告的目的是什麼？
(A) 呼籲大眾捐款
(B) 尋找一名走失的女人
(C) 告知危險區域
(D) 描述一位公眾人物

【類型】尋找主旨題型

【詞彙】
call for呼籲／
donation捐款／
notify通知／
figure人物

【正解】(B)

147 What is the purpose of the notice?
(A) To call for public donation
(B) To search for a missing woman
(C) To notify an area of danger
(D) To describe a public figure

【解析】尋找主旨題型須留意文章的前段或標題。根據文中第一句We're appealing for the public help locating a missing women Cecily McCarthy.我們便能判斷本文是有關尋找一位失蹤人士。因此答案應選(B)。

下列哪項特徵沒有出現在這則公告中？
(A) 這位女人的身材
(B) 這位女人的髮色
(C) 這位女人的膚色
(D) 這位女人的生日

【類型】是非題型

【詞彙】
feature特徵

【正解】(D)

148 Which of the following feature is not specified in the notice?
(A) The woman's figure
(B) The woman's color of hair
(C) The woman's color of skin
(D) The woman's date of birth

【解析】根據文中細節Cecily is described as white, approximately five feet 2 inches tall and a slim build. She has dark brown hair and is about 48 years old from her look.裡面包含了膚色、身高、身材以及髮色，並無提到生日。因此答案應選(D)。

★**Questions 149-151** **refer to the following conversation.**

March 3

09:32

George

Hello, Amanda, I have reserved the stay in your place from March 16 to March 18. My friend, Wen and I will arrive at Vienna airport at 8:10 PM on March 16. We were wondering if you are available to check us in around that time. We think it is going to take us a while to get to the city center from the airport. Could you please let us know the easiest way to get to your place? Train or coach? Or is there an express link from the airport? Looking forward to your reply. Have a nice day!

Amanda

The easiest way to get to my place is to catch the OBB train to Vienna main station. From there you switch to a train going to Wiener Meidling and from there take the U6 line to Alserstraße and finally tram 43 to Elterleinplatz. It is only three minute walk up to St. Kalvarine. If you got any questions, just call me.

三月三日

09:32

George

你好Amanda，我已經預訂了三月十六日到十八日在您的住所待兩晚。我跟我朋友Wen會在三月十六日晚上八點十分到達維也納機場。不曉得那時候您可否幫我們辦理入住。我們想從機場到市區應該會耽誤一陣子。您可以告訴我們到您住所最簡單的方式嗎？搭火車還是巴士？或是有沒有機場快捷呢？等待您的回答。祝您愉快。

Amanda

到我住所最簡單的方法就是搭火車OBB到維也納中央車站。從車站轉乘前往Wiener Meidling的火車。再從那裡搭乘U6線到Alserstraße。最後再搭有軌電車43號到Kalvarine街。有任何問題再打給我。

【詞彙】
reserve預定／wonder想知道／a while一會兒／coach長途巴士／express link快捷運輸／switch轉換／tram有軌電車

這段對話是有關什麼？
(A) 即將到來的旅程
(B) 一座城市的歷史
(C) 這座城市交通的利與弊
(D) 這座城市地鐵系統的發展

【類型】尋找主題題型

【詞彙】
upcoming即將來臨的／
pros and cons好處與壞處／
transportation交通／
development發展／metro地鐵

【正解】(A)

---

149 What is the conversation about?

(A) An upcoming trip

(B) The history of a city

(C) Pros and cons of the city's transportation service

(D) The development of a city's metro system

【解析】根據對話的前段，我們能發現George提到預定房間和到達機場等信息。並詢問是否能幫忙辦理入住，以及如何從機場到達住宿地點等問題。我們可推斷本文是有關一段即將到來的旅行。因此答案應選(A)。

George會待在維也納多久？
(A) 一天
(B) 兩天
(C) 三天
(D) 十二小時

【類型】尋找細節題型

【詞彙】
Vienna維也納

【正解】(C)

---

150 How long will George stay in Vienna?

(A) one day

(B) two days

(C) three days

(D) twelve hours

【解析】根據George的對話的前半部分。他提到他預訂了十六日到十八日的房間。因此至少有三天是待在維也納的。因此最佳的答案為(C)。

根據信息，下列何者正確？
(A) George回獨自去維也納。
(B) Amanda會招待George一週。
(C) George會在清晨到達維也納。
(D) George被建議要轉車超過兩次。

【類型】是非題型

【詞彙】
host招待／transfer轉乘

【正解】(D)

---

151 According to the information, which of the following is CORRECT?

(A) George will go to Vienna alone.

(B) Amanda is going to host George for a week.

(C) George will arrive in Vienna in the early morning.

(D) George is suggested to transfer more than two times.

【解析】根據對話，George會跟朋友Wen一起前往維也納，因此選項(A)為非。Amanda只會招待George三天，因此選項(B)為非。而George到達維也納機場的時間是晚上八點十分。因此選項(C)為非。整段旅行中，根據Amanda的建議，必須轉乘三次。因此選項(D)正確。

Questions 152-156 refer to the following message.

Hello All,

On Saturday, November 25, we are planning on hosting a Thanksgiving feast at Da'Tony's! Tony will provide us with a turkey and pumpkin pie, and those of us that attend will cook side dishes to bring potluck style.

The celebration will begin at 2pm at Tony's, and dinner will be served at 3pm. We would like for everyone to bring a dish to share. We will need the following: Stuffing, Candied Yams, Green Bean Casserole, Apple pie, one or two soups, corn bread, roasted vegetables, dinner rolls, miscellaneous desserts, cranberry sauce, or any traditional dishes that you cook for your own family's Thanksgiving celebration. When you know what you want to make please send a direct message to Brian Lehrwyn, and I will make sure to let the whole group know what is still needed so that we don't double up on anything!

Also, please feel free to add others to this group, including Chinese staff so we can share this wonderful bit of our culture. Please let me know by November 14 so I can give the specific number to Tony. Please copy and repost this message when you invite someone new. If you respond after November 14, sorry, but you won't be able to join as the cost of the event and amount of food prepared depends on the number of people. Once I have a definite number I will let Tony know, and he will make sure to have a bird large enough for all of us. Additionally, Tony is willing to offer a deal in which you can order 3 drinks (beer, wine, or a simple mixed drink) for 100 RMB. Gobble! Gobble! Everyone!

Courtney

各位好：

星期六，十一月二十五日，我們預定在Da'Tony餐廳舉辦感恩節大餐。Tony會提供一隻火雞和南瓜派。參加的人會準備配菜。

活動下午裡點在Tony餐廳開始，晚餐三點上桌。我們希望大家都帶一道菜來。我們需要：餡料、冰糖地瓜、焗烤綠豆派、蘋果派、一到兩道湯、玉米麵包、烤蔬菜、餐包、各種甜點、蔓越梅醬或任何其他你感恩節大餐會煮給家人吃的傳統菜。如果你決定好要準備什麼，請直接發訊息給Brian Lehrwyn，我會讓群組的人知道還缺什麼，才不會重複準備。

然後，歡迎把其他人拉近這個群組，包括中國員工，我們才能分享這個那麼棒的文化。請在十一月十四日讓我知道，我才能把確切的人數交給Tony。如果你邀請人進群組，請複製貼上這個消息。如果你在十一月十四日之後才回覆，非常抱歉，你將無法參加，因為活動的經費和食物的數量都是根據人數決定的。一旦我有了確切的人數之後，我會告訴Tony。他會幫我們準備一隻夠大的火雞。另外，Tony可以請我們點三種飲料（啤酒，酒類或混合的飲料），上限100人民幣。吃吧！大家！

Courtney上

【詞彙】

feast大餐／attend參加／side dish配菜／potluck主人準備
餐具，客人準備菜餚的聚餐文化／stuffing餡料／casserole
砂鍋菜／roast烤／dinner roll餐包／miscellaneous各式各
樣的／double up重複／specific明確的／definite確定的／
additionally另外／gobble狼吞虎嚥

這則消息是有關什麼？
(A) 宣傳一個運動賽事
(B) 公布職務分配
(C) 徵求活動自願者
(D) 邀請人參加一個節慶活動

【類型】尋找主旨題型

【詞彙】
advertise廣告／
announce公佈／
volunteer志願者／
festive節慶的

【正解】(D)

152 Why is this message sent?

    (A) To advertise a sport event

    (B) To announce the duty arrangement

    (C) To call for volunteers for an activity

    (D) To invite people to a festive event

【解析】根據開頭we are planning on hosting a Thanksgiving
feast at Da'Tony's，我們能得知本文是有關感恩節的慶祝活
動。因此答案應選(D)。

參加者被要求帶什麼到現場？
(A) 南瓜派
(B) 半隻火雞
(C) 中國茶
(D) 小配菜

【類型】尋找細節題型

【詞彙】
participant參加者／
pumpkin南瓜

【正解】(D)

153 What are participants asked to bring to the
    event?

    (A) a pumpkin pie

    (B) a half turkey

    (C) Chinese tea

    (D) a small side dish

【解析】根據文內信息those of us that attend will cook side
dishes to bring potluck style以及We would like for everyone
to bring a dish to share，參加的人必須帶一道配菜跟大家分
享，因此答案應選(D)。

154 What is Brian most likely in charge of?

(A) putting up the decorations

(B) building the list of food

(C) publicizing the celebration event

(D) contacting the Chinese staff

Brian最有可能負責什麼？

(A) 安裝裝飾品

(B) 列食物清單

(C) 宣傳慶祝活動

(D) 聯絡中國員工

【類型】尋找細節題型

【詞彙】

in charge of負責／

publicize宣傳

【解析】根據文內信息When you know what you want to make please send a direct message to Brian Lehrwyn，因此Brian很有可能是負責統計參加者帶的食物。因此答案應選(B)。

【正解】(B)

155 What should one do if he/she invites someone new?

(A) post this message again in the group

(B) pay 100 RMB to Tony

(C) report to Brian in advance

(D) bring an extra dish

如果某人邀請了新的人加入，他／她需要做什麼？

(A) 把這則消息再次貼在群組裡

(B) 交100人民幣給Tony

(C) 事先回報給Brian

(D) 多帶一道菜

【類型】尋找細節題型

【詞彙】

post張貼／in advance事先

【解析】根據文內信息Please copy and repost this message when you invite someone new.其中repost代表「再次張貼」，因此答案應選(A)。

【正解】(A)

156 Which of the following is NOT true?

(A) The event will begin in the afternoon.

(B) The event is restricted to Chinese staff.

(C) Tony will offer some free drinks for people.

(D) The event is held on November 25.

下列何者不正確？

(A) 活動會在下午開始。

(B) 活動只有中國員工才能參加。

(C) Tony會請大家免費喝飲料。

(D) 活動在十一月二十五日舉行。

【類型】是非題型

【詞彙】

restrict限制／hold舉辦

【解析】根據文內信息The celebration will begin at 2pm at Tony's活動下午兩點開始，因此選項(A)正確。Tony is willing to offer a deal in which you can order 3 drinks (beer, wine, or a simple mixed drink) for 100 RMB，Tony會免費請大家喝飲料，上限100人民幣，因此選項(C)正確。文章第一句On Saturday, November 25，活動是在十一月二十五日，因此選項(D)正確。文中並無提到活動只有中國員工才能參加，因此答案應選(B)。

【正解】(B)

蘇格蘭社工協會 會議通知	
會議：兒童社會關懷部門會議 時間：2017年11月21日星期二，下午四點 地點：會議室201 參加者：Irene主任, Maya, Noah, Sharon, Ryan, Eve, Faye, David 會議記錄：Eve Sawyer 議程：	

議程	主講人
• 晚間運動課程仍在A棟進行 • 2017年11月24日星期五防火演習 • 2017年11月24日星期五感恩節晚餐 • 2017年11月27日星期一回報輟學生家庭訪談報告	Irene 主任
• 2019年助學專案內容 • 社工參加訓練，督導以及團隊會議事宜 • 週末巡邏職務	Maya
• 員工遲到規章	Sharon

Association of Social Workers in Scotland
Meeting Notice

Meeting: Children Social Care Department
Meeting Time: Tuesday, 21 November 2017, 16:00
Venue: Conference Room 201
Participants: Director Irene, Maya, Noah, Sharon, Ryan, Eve, Faye, David
Minute taker: Eve Sawyer
Agenda:

Agenda	Speaker
• Evening sport sessions stay in Building A • Fire Drills on Friday, November 24, 2017 • Thanksgiving Dinner on Friday, November 24, 2017 • Report of Interviews with families of school non-attenders on Monday, November 27,2017	Director Irene
• What will be in the Package of Support of 2019 version? • Social workers' participation in training, supervision and team meetings • Weekend safeguarding duties	Maya
• The protocol of office staff late for post	Sharon

【詞彙】

association協會／social worker社會工作者／Scotland蘇格蘭／meeting notice會議通知／department meeting部門會議／venue地點／conference會議／director主管／minute taker會議記錄／agenda議程／session課程／drill演練／supervision監督／safeguarding巡邏／protocol規定

157 What day is the meeting scheduled on?

(A) Monday

(B) Tuesday

(C) Friday

(D) Saturday

本次會議訂於星期幾？

(A) 星期一

(B) 星期二

(C) 星期五

(D) 星期六

【類型】尋找細節題型

【詞彙】

schedule計畫行程

【正解】(B)

【解析】根據文中資訊Time: Tuesday, 21 November 2017, 16:00。答案應選(B)。關於時間的資訊，需要特別留意數字或日期。在文中通常數字的訊息相對比較容易找到。

---

158 Who will record the proceedings of the meeting?

(A) Irene

(B) Maya

(C) Sharon

(D) Eve

誰會記錄會議內容？

(A) Irene

(B) Maya

(C) Sharon

(D) Eve

【類型】尋找細節題型

【詞彙】

proceedings流程

【正解】(D)

【解析】根據文中資訊Minute taker: Eve Sawyer答案應選(D)。其中minute taker代表「會議記錄者」，而meeting minutes表示「會議記錄」。

---

159 How many people will speak at the meeting?

(A) 1

(B) 3

(C) 8

(D) 9

在會議上會有幾個人發表？

(A) 1人

(B) 3人

(C) 8人

(D) 9人

【類型】尋找細節題型

【詞彙】

meeting會議

【正解】(B)

【解析】根據議程，只有Irene，Maya跟Sharon會發表。因此答案應選(B)。

根據議程，會議的下一週有什麼事？
(A) 防火演練
(B) 報告先前的訪談內容
(C) 感恩節晚餐
(D) 社工訓練

【類型】尋找細節題型

【詞彙】
take place發生

【正解】(B)

160 According to the agenda, what will take place the next week of the meeting?
(A) fire drill
(B) report of previous interviews
(C) Thanksgiving dinner
(D) social workers' training

【解析】根據議程，表定於下週一的事項是Report of Interviews with families of school non-attenders on Monday, November 27, 2017。選項(D)社工訓練只在討論項目中，並沒有說到具體時間。而選項(A)和(C)都在當週週五。因此答案應選(B)。

Sharon最有可能是負責什麼？
(A) 出勤管理
(B) 員工職訓
(C) 辦公室採購
(D) 課程安排

【類型】推理題型

【詞彙】
responsible負責的／
attendance出席／
management管理／
professional training職業訓練／
procurement採購／
organization安排

【正解】(A)

161 What most likely is Sharon responsible for?
(A) attendance management
(B) employee professional training
(C) office procurement
(D) course organization

【解析】根據議程，Sharon發表的項目是有關員工遲到規章，跟員工的出勤管理比較有關係，因此我們可以推斷Sharon應是負責出勤管理的業務，因此答案應選(A)。

Questions 162-165 refer to the following notice.

Employees' Health Service

Update your details

It is important to keep your contact details up to date. Hospitals will typically send appointments by post. If you miss your appointment due to a wrong address, then you will need to be referred again and this can often lead to long delays. —[1]—

If the health service needs to contact you, they will do this by phone or mail, so please update your information and let us know if you have changed your phone number or address. You can either update your details online or by using a change-of-contact-details form that is available from reception at the Employees' Health Service at General Hospital. —[2]—

If you are not yet registered with the online service, you will need to visit the reception in person and register for online access, with which you can do the followings. —[3]—

- Book appointments or cancel booked appointments
- Order repeat prescriptions
- Update your address details

Please kindly note that we process over 150 new registrations as new employees arrive at Dong-Tai in the middle of September. —[4]— Therefore, if you are a newly registered employee in the third quarter of the year, you may not be able to get online access until after Christmas. We appreciate your understanding.

員工保健服務

更新個人資料
隨時更新個人資料非常重要。醫院通常都會將掛號通知透過郵件寄給你。如果因為地址填錯而未能接收到掛號通知，醫院會需要再一次將你轉診，這樣通常會導致看診延遲。—[1]—

如果健康中心需要通知你，他們會打電話或發郵件，因此請更新你的個人資料，如果你更換電話號碼或地址，請告知我們。你可以選擇在線上更新個人資料或在總醫院的員工保健服務前台領取更改聯繫資料的表格直接更改。—[2]—

如果你還沒線上註冊，你需要親自到前台申請線上註冊。線上註冊後，你可以：—[3]—

- 預約掛號或取消掛號
- 續訂處方
- 更新地址

請知悉九月中將會有新員工入職東泰，屆時我們會需要處理超過一百五十名員工的註冊。—[4]—因此，如果你是在今年的第三個季度剛註冊的員工，可能直到聖誕節之後你才能登入線上平台。感謝你的理解。

【詞彙】

update更新／up to date最新的／typically一般地／appointment預約／post郵件／refer轉診／lead to導致／reception前台／appointment預約／repeat重複的／prescription處方／process處理／quarter季；四分之一／appreciate感謝／understanding理解

本通知前半部的主旨為何？
(A) 更新個人資料
(B) 離職手續
(C) 如何預約掛號
(D) 如何續處方

【類型】尋找主旨題型

【詞彙】
personal個人的／
procedure手續／
resignation辭職／
refill重新裝滿／
prescription處方

【正解】(A)

162 What is the main idea of the first half of the notice?

(A) update of personal details

(B) procedures of resignation

(C) how to make medical appointments

(D) how to refill prescriptions

【解析】根據文章開頭第一句It is important to keep your contact details up to date.我們能知道本文的前半部是有關更新個人資料的重要性和方法。因此答案應選(A)。

如何申請線上註冊？
(A) 前往員工保健服務
(B) 寫信給東泰
(C) 打電話給診所醫師
(D) 打電話給前台人員

【類型】尋找細節題型

【詞彙】
online線上的／
clinician診所醫師／
phone打電話／
receptionist前台人員

【正解】(A)

163 How can online registration be done?

(A) By visiting the Employee Health Service

(B) By mailing to Dong-Tai

(C) By calling the clinician

(D) By phoning the receptionist

【解析】根據if you are not yet registered with the online service, you will need to visit the reception in person and register for online access說到如果要申請線上註冊，必須本人親自到前台辦理。因此答案應選(A)。

164 What can be inferred from the information?

(A) Online registration is often busy in spring.

(B) Dong-Tai provides employee health services in cooperation with General Hospital.

(C) Those who are already registered online must still go to the reception to change details.

(D) Over a hundred and fifty new staff are recruited every month.

【解析】根據文中資訊Therefore, if you are a newly registered employee in the third quarter of the year, you may not be able to get online access until after Christmas.表示在第三季時，系統會很繁忙。而第三季通常是七月到九月，為夏天到秋天，因此選項(A)為非。You can either update your details online or by using a change-of-contact-details form that is available from reception at the Employees' Health Service at General Hospital.説明已經線上註冊的員工可以直接在網上更改個人資料，不需要到前台更改。因此選項(C)為非。Please kindly note that we process over 150 new registrations as new employees arrive at Dong-Tai in the middle of September.表示今年九月會有超過150名新員工入職，不代表每個月都有那麼多人入職，因此選項(D)為非。根據本文訊息，我們可以推斷東泰公司和總醫院合作提供員工的保健服務，因此答案應選(B)。

從文中我們能推斷？

(A) 春季的線上註冊通常很繁忙。

(B) 東泰與總醫院合作提供員工保健的服務。

(C) 已經線上註冊的員工仍需要到前台更改個人資料。

(D) 每個月有超過一百五十名新員工招聘入職。

【類型】推理題型

【詞彙】
in cooperation with與……合作／recruit招聘

【正解】(B)

★ **165** In which of the positions marked [1], [2], [3] and [4] does the following sentence best belong? "We employ extra staff to help us with this, but it often takes a long time to fully register everyone."

(A) [1]　　　　(B) [2]

(C) [3]　　　　(D) [4]

【解析】本句表示「我們額外請了員工來幫忙處理，但通常將每個人都完成註冊仍須很長一段時間。」在[4]的位置最合適，與Therefore, if you are a newly registered employee in the third quarter of the year, you may not be able to get online access until after Christmas.產生合理的因果關係，因此答案應選(D)。

"We employ extra staff to help us with this, but it often takes a long time to fully register everyone." 這個句子最適合放在[1], [2], [3], [4]哪個位置？

(A) [1]

(B) [2]

(C) [3]

(D) [4]

【類型】句子插入題型

【詞彙】
employ雇用

【正解】(D)

Questions 166-170 refer to the following manual.

綠能牌

感謝您使用綠能牌產品。綠能牌產品有最高規格的設計與製造流程。請仔細閱讀以下說明,並妥善保存以便維持產品的最大使用效能。

使用說明

- 請注意本產品含有玻璃夾層,使用時請務必小心。
- 使用前務必用溫水和保護玻璃的洗潔精清洗此保溫杯。
- 請勿將保溫杯放入微波爐或傳統烤箱中。—[1]—
- 請預留杯頸空間,請勿過度裝填。
- 裝滿之後,確保外杯和杯蓋保持緊蓋狀態。—[2]—

清洗說明

- 如果保溫杯一段時間未使用,請用溫水和洗潔精沖洗,確保衛生。
- 清洗後,打開杯蓋晾乾。—[3]—
- 請勿使用洗碗機來清洗保溫杯。
- 請勿使用粗糙的洗碗海綿來除去頑固髒污。—[4]—
- 請勿裝碳酸飲料或牛奶,以免造成玻璃夾層破裂。
- 使用後請務必清洗以免細菌滋生。

Green Spirit Brand

Thank you for using this Green Spirit Brand product which is designed and manufactured to the highest quality standards. Please read these instructions carefully and retain for future reference in order to gain **optimal** use from your product.

USE

- Please note that this product contains a glass liner and should be treated with care at all times.
- Prior to initial use of the product, please clean your flask with warm water and glass protection washing-up liquid.
- DO NOT put the flask into a microwave or conventional oven. —[1]—
- Always leave sufficient space in the neck and do not overfill.
- After filling, ensure both the outside cup and stopper are always tightly closed. —[2]—

CLEANING

- If your flask has not been used for some time, rinse it with warm water and dish washing liquid in the interest of hygiene.
- After cleaning, leave it to drain and with the stopper off. —[3]—
- DO NOT use a dishwasher to clean your flask.
- DO NOT use abrasive sponge pads to remove difficult stains. —[4]—
- Avoid storing any carbonated drink or milk as it may cause breakage to the glass liner.
- Always clean it after use to avoid the possibility of bacteria growth.

【詞彙】

product產品／design設計／manufacture生產／standard標準／instruction指示／retain保留／reference參考／gain獲得／optimal最佳的／contain包含／liner夾層／treat對待／prior to 在……之前／initial最初的／flask保溫杯／washing-up liquid 洗潔液／microwave微波爐／conventional傳統的／oven烤箱／sufficient足夠的／neck杯頸／overfill過度裝填／stopper杯蓋／rinse沖洗／in the interest為……著想／hygiene衛生／drain瀝乾／dishwasher洗碗機／abrasive粗糙的／sponge pad洗碗海綿／stain髒污／store裝／carbonated drink碳酸飲料／breakage裂開／possibility可能性／bacteria細菌／growth生長

---

166 What is the Green Spirit Brand product?

(A) a dishwashing soap

(B) a cupboard

(C) a vacuum flask

(D) a washing machine

【解析】根據文中訊息Prior to initial use of the product, please clean your flask with warm water and glass protection washing-up liquid.其中的單字flask我們可得知本產品為「真空保溫杯」。再加上其他關鍵字眼fill, overfill, stopper, outside cup等，也能幫助考生判斷主旨。

此綠能牌產品是什麼？

(A) 洗碗皂

(B) 櫃子

(C) 真空保溫杯

(D) 洗衣機

【類型】尋找主旨題型

【詞彙】
dishwashing洗碗的／
cupboard櫥櫃／
vacuum真空的／
flask保溫杯

【正解】(C)

---

167 What is advised after the product has been cleaned?

(A) It should be filled with hot water.

(B) It should be stored on a dish dryer rack.

(C) It should be left without the stopper.

(D) It should be soaked with soap.

【解析】根據文中資訊After cleaning, leave it to drain and with the stopper off.表示清洗之後必須打開杯蓋靜置。因此答案應選(C)。

本產品在清潔之後需要如何處理？

(A) 需裝滿熱水。

(B) 需要放在碗架上瀝乾

(C) 需要打開杯蓋放置

(D) 需要浸在肥皂水裡

【類型】尋找細節題型

【詞彙】
advise建議／store存放／
rack架子／soak浸泡

【正解】(C)

下列何者正確？
(A) 本產品可放到微波爐裡。
(B) 本產品不宜裝氣泡飲料。
(C) 本產品使用前要用冷水清洗。
(D) 本產品會被洗碗精損傷。

【類型】是非題型

【詞彙】
microwave-safe可放進微波爐的／
fizzy drink氣泡飲料／
rinse清洗／
damage損壞

【正解】(B)

168 Which of the following is CORRECT?

(A) This product is microwave-safe.

(B) This product is not good for fizzy drinks.

(C) This product should be rinsed with cold water before use.

(D) This product would be damaged by dishwashing liquid.

【解析】根據文中資訊DO NOT put the flask into a microwave or conventional oven.請勿放入微波爐，因此選項(A)為非。Avoid storing any carbonated drink or milk as it may cause breakage to the glass liner.請勿裝碳酸飲料carbonated drink，也就是氣泡飲料fizzy drink，因此選項(B)正確。Prior to initial use of the product, please clean your flask with warm water and glass protection washing-up liquid.表示本產品需要用溫水清洗，並且可以使用洗碗精。因此選項(C)(D)為非。

"Adding a teaspoon of bicarbonate of soda produces excellent results." 這個句子最適合放在[1], [2], [3], [4]哪個位置？
(A) [1]   (B) [2]
(C) [3]   (D) [4]

【類型】句子插入題型

【詞彙】teaspoon茶匙／
bicarbonate碳酸氫鈉

【正解】(D)

★ 169 In which of the positions marked [1], [2], [3] and [4] does the following sentence best belong? "Adding a teaspoon of bicarbonate of soda produces excellent results."
(A) [1]   (B) [2]
(C) [3]   (D) [4]

【解析】根據本句判斷，加入一茶匙的碳酸氫鈉蘇打粉能產生絕佳的效果，因此套入[1]到[4]的位置中，[4]的位置最合理，都與清潔難去除的污漬相關。因此答案應選(D)。

第一段第四行的 "optimal" 意思最接近？
(A) 最佳的   (B) 樂觀的
(C) 外部的   (D) 完整的

【類型】同義字題型

【詞彙】
optimistic樂觀的／
exteriors外部的／complete完整的

【正解】(A)

170 The word "optimal" in paragraph 1, line 4, is closest in meaning to

(A) best

(B) optimistic

(C) exterior

(D) complete

【解析】optimal表示「最佳的」，與best語意最接近，因此答案應選(A)。

Questions 171-175 refer to the following email.

Office Closure during Christmas

From- Paul Newman
To: all
13 December 2016

Dear Residents of Burberry Apartment,
Please note that the Burberry Apartment office will be closed from 22 December to 1 January due to Christmas and New Year's holidays. We will reopen on 3 January, 2017.

Emergency contact

If there is an emergency, you can still contact a duty warden during this period. The phone numbers of the duty wardens will be posted on the office door.

Cleaning and recycling collections

As all cleaners will not be onsite during the vacation, the regular weekly cleaning will not take place until 2 January. Therefore, you must keep clean and tidy your own kitchens and hallways.

Security

As you are celebrating the holidays, please also be vigilant by making sure all your flat doors and windows are kept locked at all times. Call 999 if there is an emergency.

Post collections

The office will be open for an hour between 12 and 1pm for post collection on the following days:

- 24 December 2016
- 27 December 2016
- 29 December 2016
- 30 December 2016
- 31 December 2016

Finally, we sincerely wish you a happy Christmas and new year.
Paul Newman

聖誕期間辦公室休息

寄件人- Paul Newman
收件人: 全體
2016年12月13日

親愛的Burberry公寓居民：
請知悉Burberry公寓從十二月二十二日到一月一日由於聖誕假期及新年假期即將關閉。我們在2017年一月三日會重新開啟。

緊急聯絡
如果有緊急事件，你可以在這期間內聯絡留守的守衛。守衛的電話號碼會公告在辦公室門上。

清潔及回收
假期期間清潔工不會到場清潔。每週的定期清潔直到一月二日之前都不會有人來處理。因此你必須自行保持廚房及走道的整潔。

安全注意事項
在慶祝假期的同時，請時刻留意公寓門窗是否關閉。如有緊急事件，請撥打999。

郵件包裹接收
辦公室在下列日期內會於12點到1點開放一小時接受郵件或包裹。
• 2016年12月24日
• 2016年12月27日
• 2016年12月29日
• 2016年12月30日
• 2016年12月31日

最後，我們衷心祝福你聖誕及新年快樂。
Paul Newman

這封電子郵件是寄給誰？
(A) 公寓大樓的官員
(B) 公寓大樓的住戶
(C) 公寓大樓的承包商
(D) 公寓大樓的清潔人員

【類型】尋找細節題型

【詞彙】
tenant租屋人／
contractor承包商

【正解】(B)

171 Who was the email sent to?

(A) the officers of the apartment building

(B) the tenants of the apartment building

(C) the contractor of the apartment building

(D) the cleaning staff of the apartment building

【解析】根據郵件一開始的信息Dear Residents of Burberry Apartment明白告訴我們此信是寄給公寓的住戶，因此答案應選(B)。

Paul Newman最有可能是誰？
(A) 公寓的行政負責人
(B) 公寓的清潔工
(C) 公寓的住戶
(D) 公寓的設計師

【類型】推理題型

【詞彙】
executive行政的／
designer設計師

【正解】(A)

172 Who most likely is Paul Newman?

(A) the executive officer of the apartment

(B) the cleaner of the apartment

(C) the tenant of the apartment

(D) the designer of the apartment

【解析】在文章一開始跟結束，我們可以發現Paul Newman是這封信的寄件人，而內文是有關聖誕新年假期期間的各項宣導，因此我們可以推斷Paul Newman可能是負責這幢公寓的行政負責人。因此答案應選(A)。

辦公室什麼時候會再開？
(A) 十二月二十九日
(B) 十二月三十日
(C) 一月一日
(D) 一月三日

【類型】尋找細節題型

【詞彙】
office辦公室

【正解】(D)

173 When will the office open again?

(A) 29 December

(B) 30 December

(C) 1 January

(D) 3 January

【解析】根據文中信息We will reopen on 3 January, 2017.明白說明一月三日辦公室恢復辦公。因此答案應選(D)。

174 Which of the following services is still available during the vacation?

(A) repairs

(B) post collections

(C) security

(D) cleaning

【解析】根據文中post collection的部分，假期期間仍有五天是開放收取郵遞包裹的。因此答案應選(B)。

下列哪項服務在假期期間仍有提供？

(A) 修繕

(B) 郵件包裹接收

(C) 安全管理

(D) 清潔

【類型】尋找細節題型

【詞彙】

repair修繕／

security安全

【正解】(B)

---

175 Which of the following is WRONG?

(A) There won't be anyone on duty during the vacation.

(B) Cleaning staff usually come on a weekly basis.

(C) Residents are advised to stay alert during Christmas.

(D) Residents can receive packages on December 31.

【解析】根據文中資訊If there is an emergency, you can still contact a duty warden during this period.，表示假期期間仍有守衛留守，因此選項(A)錯誤。the regular weekly cleaning will not take place until 2 January透露平時的清潔都是每週一次的，其中weekly表示「每週的」。As you are celebrating the festival, please also be vigilant by making sure all your flat doors and window are kept locked at all times.表示住宿在聖誕假期間仍需提高警覺。其中vigilant與alert意思相近，皆為「警覺的」的意思。根據包裹接收日期資訊，十二月三十一日是有接收包裹的。因此選項(B)(C)(D)皆正確。因此答案應選(A)。

下列何者錯誤？

(A) 假期期間沒有人執勤。

(B) 清潔人員通常是一週來一次。

(C) 住戶在聖誕期間被建議要提高警覺。

(D) 住戶在十二月三十一日可以接收包裹。

【類型】是非題型

【詞彙】

on duty執勤／

alert警覺的

【正解】(A)

Hop-On-Go讓你的
搭車體驗更上一層樓

Hop-On-Go是國內第一個改造傳統計程車搭乘模式的品牌。擁有最新的交通運輸科技，只要點擊一下，無論何時何地你都能去到你想去的地方。乘客只需要下載Hop-On-Go手機應用程式並使用電話號碼及銀行帳號註冊即可使用。想搭車時，發送要求，選取司機，司機會立即前往接送。一到達目的地，帳單會寄到你的手機並自動從銀行扣款。更重要的，它幫你省錢，因為車費比一般的計程車便宜將近一半。到目前為止，我們已經擁有一百五十萬個會員了！

Hop-On-Go Takes Taxi-riding Experience to the Next Level

Hop-On-Go is the first brand in the country to transform the conventional taxi hailing. With the latest transportation technology, you can get to where you want to go anywhere, anytime and with just a click.

Passengers just need to download the Hop-On-Go mobile app and get registered with their phone number and bank account. Whenever you need a ride, send a request, select the driver and the driver will come pick you up in no time. As soon as you get to the destination, the bill will be sent to your phone and can be automatically paid off from the bank. More importantly, it saves your money as the fare is nearly half as expensive as the regular taxi fare. So far, we have already had 1.5 million Hop-On-Go riders with us!

您星期五早上的
Hop-On-Go搭車記錄
收據

謝謝你選擇Hop-On-Go。
9元／由手機付款／2017年9月15日／Hop-On-Go快車

請知悉車費不包含銀行手續費。
• 上車@ Albert街20號／07:32
• 下車@ Tank路57號／07:45

司機Stephen Wong
距離：5.52英里
時間：13分鐘

Your Friday morning trip with Hop-On-Go RECEIPT

Thank you for choosing Hop-On-Go.
$ 9/ paid via device/ September 15 2017/ Hop-On-Go Express

Please note that the fare does not include the fees that may be charged by your bank.
• Pick-up @ 20 Albert Street/ 07:32
• Drop-off @ 57 Tank Road/ 07: 45

You rode with Stephen Wong.
Distance: 5.52 miles
Trip time: 13 minutes

Hop-On-Go

Get a $10 coupon for Hop-On-Go Express if you invite a new friend to try Hop-On-Go.

Share Code: RD77O

Contact us.

Left personal belongings behind? Track it down by emailing at lostproperties@hopongo.com

Hop-On-Go

邀請新朋友加入Hop-On-Go即可得到10元快車優惠券。

分享碼：RD77O

聯絡我們

東西忘在車上了嗎？發電郵到lostproperties@hopongo.com找回遺失物。

From: Sherry
To: lostproperties@hopongo.com
Subject: Lost laptop bag

Hello,

Last Friday morning, I rode your taxi with Stephen Wong. As soon as I got out of the car, I noticed my laptop bag was not with me. I must have left it in the car. But I did not have the driver's number which should normally show in the app. So I am writing to request that you help track down the driver and have him contact me as soon as possible. It is a 13-inch black laptop bag in which there are my wallet, glasses and some medications. The bag is my birthday gift from my husband and therefore means a lot to me, so I would appreciate if you could find it for me. Thank you very much.

Sherry

收件人：
lostproperties@hopongo.com
主旨：遺失筆電包

您好，

上週五早上，我搭乘Stephen Wong司機的車。下車時，我發現筆電包不在身上了。我一定是掉在車上了。但我並沒有司機的電話，通常應用程式裡都會顯示司機電話的。所以我想請你們幫我找到那位司機讓他盡快跟我聯絡。是一個十三寸的筆電包，裡面有我的皮夾、眼鏡和一些藥。這個電腦包是我先生送我的生日禮物，因此對我意義重大。如果你們能幫我找回來我會非常感激。感謝！

Sherry

【詞彙】

brand品牌／transform改造／conventional傳統的／hail招呼／transportation運輸／technology科技／passenger乘客／mobile手機／app應用程式／register註冊／account帳戶／in no time立刻／destination目的地／automatically自動地／fare車費／regular一般的／via透過／charge收費／

distance距離／express快車／code密碼／coupon優惠券／belonging所有物／track down找到／as soon as一……就……／laptop筆電／normally一般地／medication藥物／appreciate感恩

Hop-On-Go是什麼？
(A) 計程車呼叫平台
(B) 新發表的汽車品牌
(C) 手機公司
(D) 電信公司

【類型】尋找主旨題型

【詞彙】
hail呼叫／
launch發表／
telecom電信

【正解】(A)

176 What is Hop-On-Go?

(A) a taxi hailing platform

(B) a newly launched car brand

(C) a mobile company

(D) a telecom company

【解析】根據廣告的第一句台詞Hop-On-Go is the first brand in the country to transform the conventional taxi hailing.其中的taxi hailing表示呼叫計程車，我們能得知Hop-On-Go是一個呼叫計程車的平台，因此答案應選(A)。

根據廣告，下列何者正確？
(A) 乘客搭車時要攜帶他們的筆電。
(B) 乘客搭車時不需要攜帶現金。
(C) Hop-On-Go搭車通常比一般計程車貴。
(D) Hop-On-Go目前大約有15萬會員。

【類型】是非題型

【詞彙】
advertisement廣告／
laptop筆電／
get a ride搭乘／
cash現金／
service服務

【正解】(B)

177 According to the advertisement, which of the following is true?

(A) Passengers must carry with them their laptops when getting a ride.

(B) Passengers do not need to carry cash with them when getting a ride.

(C) The Hop-On-Go services are usually more expensive than regular taxis.

(D) There are around 150,000 members on Hop-On-Go.

【解析】根據廣告內文，As soon as you get to the destination, the bill will be sent to your phone and can be automatically paid off from the bank.我們能得知車費會自動從銀行扣款，因此不需要帶現金是正確的。而文中並沒有提到乘客搭車時需要攜帶筆電，因此選項(A)為非。More importantly, it saves your money as the fare is nearly half as expensive as the regular taxi fare.表示Hop-On-Go通常是計程車的半價，因此選項(C)為非。So far, we have already had 1.5 million Hop-On-Go riders with us! 表示目前該平台已有一百五十萬人，而非十五萬人使用，因此選項(D)為非。

178 What can be inferred from the receipt?

    (A) The fare had not yet been paid.

    (B) The fare including the bank charge may be more than $9.

    (C) The passenger's last name is Wong.

    (D) The passenger had used the coupon.

【解析】根據收據內容的細節，車費是九元。再加上Please note that the fare does not include the fees that may be charged by your bank.因此銀行手續費加上去後一定是多於九元的。因此答案應選(B)。而根據paid via device表示車費已付清。You rode with Stephen Wong.表示姓Wong的是司機。而優惠券信息是顯示在收據上，表示乘客搭車之後才可得知優惠券信息，因此我們無從判斷優惠券是否已被使用。

從這張收據我們能推論？
(A) 車費還沒付清。
(B) 包含銀行手續費的車資可能會貴於九元。
(C) 乘客姓Wong。
(D) 乘客已使用優惠券。

【類型】推理題型

【詞彙】
receipt收據／
last name姓

【正解】(B)

---

179 According to the email, what information should have appeared in the app?

    (A) The driver's birthday

    (B) The driver's bank account

    (C) The driver's license number

    (D) The driver's phone number

【解析】根據電子郵件內容But I did not have the driver's number which should normally show in the app.表示司機的電話一般情況會顯示在應用程式中。因此答案應選(D)。

根據電子郵件，在應用程式中應該顯示什麼資訊？
(A) 司機的生日
(B) 司機的銀行帳號
(C) 司機的駕照號碼
(D) 司機的電話號碼

【類型】尋找細節題型

【詞彙】
appear出現／license執照

【正解】(D)

---

180 What is indicated about Sherry's bag?

    (A) It is purple.

    (B) It is 15 inches of size.

    (C) It is a birthday gift.

    (D) It has been found.

【解析】根據電子郵件內容It is a 13-inch black laptop bag in which there are my wallet, glasses and some medications. The bag is my birthday gift from my husband and therefore means a lot to me, so I would appreciate if you could find it back for me.其中提到了是一個十三吋的黑色電腦包。並且是一個生日禮物。而郵件發出的時候，電腦包還沒找到，因此答案應選(C)。

關於Sherry的筆電包何者正確？
(A) 是紫色的。
(B) 是15吋大。
(C) 是一個生日禮物。
(D) 已經找到了。

【類型】尋找細節題型

【詞彙】
indicate標明／
inch英寸

【正解】(C)

La Siene公寓

La Siene公寓位於當代藝術博物館對面，從國立植物園走路只要五分鐘內即可到達。本自助式公寓還附有餐廳、起居室和一座標準游泳池。其他設施還有頂樓陽台、遊戲間和公共設施空間，其中有乒乓球和桌上足球。所有公共空間都提供免費無線網路。

每間公寓房都有一台平面電視和一張多功能工作桌，特別為商業人士設計。豪華浴室配有按摩浴缸。吹風機和電熨斗可要求提供。La Siene還為您提供客人專用的洗衣間。小型廚房設配齊全，附有導熱爐盤，烤箱，微波爐和冰箱。二十四小時的超市就在距離公寓走路三十秒的Harbor街上。

我們會說您的語言。

La Siene Apartment

La Siene Apartment is located opposite the contemporary art museum and within only a five-minute walk from National Botanic Garden. The self-catering studio apartment also features an on-site restaurant, a lounge and a standard swimming pool. Other amenities are such as a rooftop terrace, a gaming area and a common room with table tennis and table football facilities. Free Wi-Fi is provided in all public areas. There are computers at every corner of each floor for your use.

Each studio has a flat-screen TV and a multi-function work desk specially designed for business people. The luxury bathroom is equipped with a whirlpool bathtub. Hairdryers and irons are available upon request and La Siene also has a guest laundry room for you. Kitchenettes are fully equipped with an induction hotplate, an oven, a microwave and a fridge. A 24-hour supermarket is just at the Harbor Street which is 30 seconds away from the apartment by walking.

We speak your languages.

La Siene公寓 房價		
房間等級	一般價	促銷價
旅遊房	一天150歐	一天110歐
大使房	一天180歐	一天150歐
企業房	一天220歐	一天180歐
附屬房	每人50歐	

La Siene Apartment Room Tariff		
Room Class	Regular Rate	Promotion Rate
Tourist Class	€ 150 per day	€ 110 per day
Ambassador Class	€ 180 per day	€ 150 per day
Corporate Class	€ 220 per day	€ 180 per day
Annex Room	€ 50 per person	

Anna
March 2017

We spent our time in La Siene tourist-class studio for three nights in early March. The room was gorgeous, clean and warm as described on the website. I like the tastefully furnished interior and the wonderfully bright room which gets ample sunlight. The receptionists are open, easygoing and friendly. They passionately told us where we could go sightseeing and experience the amazing local street food. However, as we booked the room for the weekend time where there was no promotion deal, the room rate was a little high for us, but overall we enjoyed our time there and I will definitely come back next time. Couldn't have thought of a better place to stay in Paris. This is absolutely my best highlight on Resort.com so far.

Anna
2017年3月

我們三月初在La Siene的旅遊房待了三個晚上。房間如同網站上描述的一樣美麗，乾淨溫暖。我喜歡品味獨到的室內裝潢和日照採光充足的房間。前台服務人員非常大方、隨和、友善。他們還很熱情地跟我們推薦可以去哪裡觀光和吃好吃的小吃。但是由於是週末的時間，我們訂的房型沒有優惠價，因此房價對我們來說有點高。但整體來講我們非常滿意，下次一定會再來。在巴黎找不到更好的地方住了。這絕對是目前為止我在Resort.com上最棒的經驗。

【詞彙】

opposite相反／contemporary當代的／botanic植物的／self-catering自行開伙的／studio家庭式公寓／feature以……為特色／on-site在現場的／lounge起居室／amenity設施／terrace陽台／facility設施／multi-function多功能／specially特別地／design設計／luxury豪華／equip配有／whirlpool bathtub按摩浴缸／iron熨斗／upon一經……／laundry洗衣間／kitchenette小廚房／induction導熱／hotplate導熱盤／oven烤箱

La Siene公寓在哪個城市？

(A) 倫敦

(B) 都柏林

(C) 布拉格

(D) 巴黎

【類型】尋找細節題型

【詞彙】

apartment公寓／

London倫敦／

Dublin都柏林／

Prague布拉格／

Paris巴黎

【正解】(D)

---

181 In which city is La Siene Apartment?

(A) London

(B) Dublin

(C) Prague

(D) Paris

【解析】根據最後一篇評價內容Couldn't have thought of a better place to stay in Paris., 我們能得知這間公寓是在巴黎。因此答案應選(D)。

關於公寓的描述何者正確？

(A) 距離博物館很近。

(B) 無線網路一天10歐元。

(C) 到最近的超市走路要三十分鐘。

(D) 浴室附有吹風機。

【類型】尋找細節題型

【詞彙】

data數據流量／

superstore超市

【正解】(A)

---

182 What is indicated about the apartment?

(A) It is close to a museum.

(B) Wi-Fi data are €10 per day.

(C) It takes 30 minutes to walk to the nearest superstore.

(D) The bathrooms are equipped with hairdryers.

【解析】根據廣告內文La Siene Apartment is located opposite the contemporary art museum，這間公寓離當代藝術博物館非常近。Free Wi-Fi is provided in all public areas. 表示無線網路是免費的。24-hour supermarket is just at the Harbor Street which is 30 seconds away from the apartment walking.表示超市離公寓只要三十秒路程。Hairdryers and irons are available upon request表示吹風機和熨斗要跟服務人員索取，並不是配備在浴室裡的。因此答案應選(A)。

183 Which of the following is not included in the studio amenities?

(A) whirlpool bathtub

(B) work desk

(C) fridge

(D) tennis court

【解析】本題信息散佈在廣告內文各處。根據內文在交誼廳有乒乓球和桌上足球檯。並沒有網球場，因此答案應選(D)。

下列何者不包含在公寓設施裡？

(A) 按摩浴缸

(B) 工作桌

(C) 冰箱

(D) 網球場

【類型】是非題型

【詞彙】

amenity設施／

whirlpool bathtub按摩浴缸／

court球場

【正解】(D)

---

184 What was Anna slightly dissatisfied with?

(A) the receptionists

(B) the room rate

(C) the furnishings

(D) the sport facilities

【解析】根據Anna的評價the room rate was a little high for us，我們能得知她認為房價有一點高，因此答案應選(B)。

Anna對於什麼稍微有點不滿意？

(A) 前台人員

(B) 房價

(C) 裝潢

(D) 運動設施

【類型】尋找細節題型

【詞彙】

slightly稍微地／

dissatisfied感到不滿意的／

receptionist前台人員／

rate房價／furnishing裝潢／

facility設施

【正解】(B)

---

185 How much did Anna spend on her room in total?

(A) € 330

(B) € 450

(C) € 150

(D) € 540

【解析】本題須綜合後兩篇閱讀線索方能找出答案。根據房價表和Anna的評價，Anna在週末時段入住，因此沒有享受到促銷價，而Anna住了三個晚上的旅遊房。因此以一晚150歐元來計算，三個晚上共450歐元。因此答案應選(B)。

Anna總共付了多少房費？

(A) 330歐元

(B) 450歐元

(C) 150歐元

(D) 540歐元

【類型】推理題型

【詞彙】

in total總共

【正解】(B)

續聘意向書

行政專員調查
收件人：
寄件人：Lydia Liao
日期：2017年12月7日

為了確定我們2017-2018年度的職員，大登有限公司想知道您是否明年還願意跟我們簽合約。請知悉如果您勾選「我明年不再與大登有限公司續約」的選項，我們會開始廣告您的職缺，並會有新進人員取代您的崗位。

[ ] 我明年與大登有限公司續約

[ ] 我明年不再與大登有限公司續約

簽名：＿＿＿＿＿＿＿＿＿＿

日期：＿＿＿＿＿＿＿＿＿＿

請在2018年1月5日星期五12:00之前回傳這份調查。如果在該日期前我們還未收到你的回覆，你的職位可能就會被刊登。續約確認信會在三月初發送。謝謝。

Letter of Intent

Survey of Administrative Specialists
To:
From: Lydia Liao
Date: December 7th, 2017

In an effort to determine our staff for the 2017-2018 year, Da-Deng Ltd. would like to know if you intend to sign a new contract for the next year. Please be reminded that if you check the box 'I do not intend to return to Da-Deng Ltd. next year.' Your position will be advertised and a new candidate will be replacing your post.

[ ] I intend to return to Da-Deng Ltd. next year.

[ ] I do not intend to return to Da-Deng Ltd. next year.

Your signature: ＿＿＿＿＿＿ Date: ＿＿＿＿＿＿

Please return this survey to Lydia by 12:00 on Friday 5 January 2018. If we do not receive your response by this date, your position may be advertised. Confirmation of contract renewal will be issued in the beginning of March. Thank you.

Administrative Specialist
Job Description

Your responsibility is to assist office duties in a variety of areas including scheduling office meetings, managing incoming and outgoing mail, responding to, redirecting incoming calls, completing special projects, applying for project resources and managing all sorts of reimbursements.

Job Type
Full-time

Job Number
8506

Department
Information Technology

Salary
$ 400,000 Annually

行政專員
工作說明

你的職責為協助辦公室項目，包含各類領域，如安排辦公室會議、管理郵件進出、接聽或轉接電話、完成特殊專案、申請專案材料並管理各類報銷。

工作類別
全職

工作編號
8506

部門
資訊部

薪資
年薪400,000元

Subject: Queries about contract renewal
From: Jessie
To: Lydia

Dear Lydia,

Please accept this letter as notification of my plan to commence maternity leave in two months' time. As my baby is due in May 2018, my doctor advised me to cease working three months ahead of time. I have enclosed my medical certificate that confirms my pregnancy.

Because of my pregnancy, I was wondering if I need to sign the contract renewal letter you sent to us. Since I understand I am entitled to 52 weeks of maternity leave which is specified in the employment handbook, I am confused about if there is necessity for me to sign the letter of intent for the next year's employment.
Looking forward to hearing from you.

Jessie

主旨：續約問題
寄件人：Jessie
收件人：Lydia

親愛的Lydia,

我想寫這封郵件告知您我兩個月後會開始請產假。我的寶寶會在2018年五月出生。因此我的醫師建議我生產前三個月不要工作。我已附上醫生證明。

由於我懷孕，我不知道我還需不需要簽您先前寄給我們的續聘意向書。我從員工手冊中了解到我有52週的育嬰假。我不清楚是否還有必要簽明年的續聘意向書。

希望盡快得到您的答覆。
Jessie

intent意圖／survey調查／administrative行政的／specialist專員／in an effort to為了／determine決定／staff員工／intend意圖要／contract合約／position職位／advertise廣告／candidate候選人／replace取代／post崗位／signature簽名／response回覆／confirmation確認／renewal更新／issue發送／description描述／responsibility責任／assist協助／a variety of各類的／incoming進來的／outgoing出去的／redirect轉接／project專案／apply for申請／resource資源／reimbursement報銷／full-time全職／information technology資訊科技／annually每年地／query疑問／notification通知／commence開始／maternity leave產假／due預產的／advise建議／cease停止／ahead of time提前／enclose附帶／medical醫學的／certificate證明／confirm確認／pregnancy懷孕／wonder想知道／be entitled to有……的資格／specify標明／handbook手冊／necessity必要性

這封信最有可能是寄給誰？
(A) 現職員工
(B) 未來的媽媽
(C) 工作應徵者
(D) 董事會

【類型】推理題型

【詞彙】
current目前的／staff員工／
expectant即將成為的／
candidate候選人／
board of director董事會

【正解】(A)

186 Who most likely was this letter sent to?

　　(A) current staff

　　(B) expectant mothers

　　(C) job candidates

　　(D) board of directors

【解析】根據信中的內容判斷，這封信是問大家明年是否願意續留在公司。因此我們能判斷這封信是寄給目前公司的員工。因此答案應選(A)。

187 Who most likely is Lydia?

(A) an accountant

(B) a human resources officer

(C) an engineer

(D) a salesperson

Lydia最有可能是誰？
(A) 會計
(B) 人資職員
(C) 工程師
(D) 銷售員

【類型】推理題型

【詞彙】

accountant會計／

human resource人力資源／

salesperson銷售員

【正解】(B)

【解析】根據信中的內容判斷，這封信是有關員工續聘問題，因此應該是由與人資相關的部門發送的，因此答案應選(B)。

---

188 What is not likely to be a specialist's duty?

(A) reminding the director of the weekly meeting

(B) putting through a customer to the director

(C) going on a business trip with the president

(D) contacting the financial department for reimbursement

下列何者最不可能是專員的職責？
(A) 提醒主管開週會
(B) 將客戶電話轉接給主管
(C) 陪總裁出差
(D) 聯絡財務部門報銷事宜

【類型】推理題型

【詞彙】

duty職責／

remind提醒／

director主任／

weekly每週的／

put through呈交／

business trip出差／

president總裁／

financial財務的／

reimbursement報銷

【正解】(C)

【解析】根據第二篇文章的細節Your responsibility is to assist office duties in a variety of areas including scheduling office meetings, managing incoming and outgoing mail, responding to, redirecting incoming calls, completing special projects, applying for project resources and managing all sorts of reimbursements.選項(A)(B)(D)都有被提及，除了選項(C)陪總裁出差，因此答案應選(C)。

Jessie最有可能在什麼時候寄這
封電郵？
(A) 十二月
(B) 一月
(C) 二月
(D) 三月

【類型】推理題型

【詞彙】
likely可能地

【正解】(A)

189 When most likely did Jessie send the email?

(A) In December

(B) In January

(C) In February

(D) In March

【解析】根據第三篇文章信息Please accept this letter as notification of my plan to commence maternity leave in two months' time.首先我們知道Jessie在兩個月後要請產假。As my baby is due in May 2018, my doctor advised me to cease working three months ahead of time.小孩是在五月出生，而醫生建議小孩出生前三個月停止工作。因此我們可判斷Jessie會在二月停止工作。如果二月對於Jessie寄信的時間來說是兩個月後，表示Jessie是在十二月寄這封信的。因此根據推理，答案應選(A)。

Jessie主要的疑問是什麼？
(A) 是否要請假
(B) 是否要續留公司
(C) 是否要去看醫生
(D) 是否要簽續聘意向書

【類型】尋找主旨題型

【詞彙】
major主要的／
inquiry疑問／
take a leave請假／
sign簽署

【正解】(D)

190 What was Jessie's major inquiry?

(A) whether to take a leave

(B) whether to stay in the company

(C) whether to go to the doctor

(D) whether to sign the letter of intent

【解析】根據電子郵件中的第二段信息Because of my pregnancy, I was wondering if I need to sign the contract renewal letter you sent to us.此處Jessie提出了疑問，是有關是否需要簽署續聘意向書。因此答案應選(D)。

★**Questions 191-195 refer to the following reminder, information and calendar.**

Dear Sales Department Employees,

Thank you so much for sparing some time to go through this weekly reminder. First of all, it is Friday again! I would like to wish you all a happy, safe weekend. Besides, as Chinese New Year is fast approaching, celebrations are being held in various parts of the city, including Timmy's café just beside our office building. Check this website for more details: http://www.juniormerry/chinesenewyear.

I would also like to take this opportunity to thank you for your individual and collective contributions to our sale effort as of last year. Your sales record is impressive and has even exceeded our goal. Keep up the good work. In the meantime, there are a few things I would like to remind you.

- You are required to respond to customers' messages before 21:00. Even if you are not able to sort out their issues immediately, please at least leave a message saying with courtesy that you will attend to them the next day.

- With regard to mileage reimbursement, you must be able to substantiate the mileage with the original documentation or receipts. According to the policy of the Internal Revenue Service, please be aware that only the mileage costs incurred while conducting business can qualify for reimbursement.

- All sales staff have a Chinese New Year vacation which this year will start on the 10th of February all the way to 21st of February. Everyone should return to work on the 22nd of February. However, due to the fact that this year we have a longer holiday than usual, we all need to work for extra hours to make up for the holiday. Please refer to the attachment detailing the specific work time.

Finally, it is getting cold. Please bundle up and take care! Let's keep fighting till the end of this year.

Danielle Wu

親愛的銷售部員工，

非常感謝您撥空閱讀這封週報。首先，又到了星期五。祝你們有個開心又安全的週末。由於中國新年快到了，城市各地都在舉辦慶祝活動，包括公司旁邊的提米咖啡廳。更多資訊都在這個網站http://www.juniormerry/chinesenewyear。

我也想藉此感謝全體自從去年來對我們業務的貢獻。你們的業績非常驚人，甚至早已超過我們的目標。繼續努力。同時，我想告知各位幾件事。

- 晚上九點前必須回覆客戶訊息。即使你無法立即解決，請至少留個訊息禮貌的跟他們說你明天會處理。

- 至於路費報銷的問題，你必須提供證明路費的原始單據或收據。根據內部利潤中心政策，只有在跑業務的過程中產生的交通里程才能申請報銷。

- 所有業務員的中國新年將會在二月十日開始，一直到二月二十一日。所有人在二月二十二日都必須返回工作崗位。但是，因為今年我們的假期比較長，大家都必須加班來補回上班時數。請參考附件說明。

最後，天冷了。請多穿點衣服多保重！年底前大家加油！

Danielle Wu

提米咖啡廳

星期五夜晚現場演出-二月九日

本地樂團和學生樂團的免費現場表演秀，有廉價啤酒、美味的傳統中國料理，陪你度過一個完美週五。到時候見！

地點：提米咖啡廳
開始時間：19:00

卡拉OK

又到了K歌的晚上。提米的最瘋狂之夜。高歌一曲經典，或讓你的好朋友上台獻醜吧！

地點：提米咖啡廳
開始時間：20:00

瘋狂猜燈謎

來説説關於新年的趣事。打敗你的同事成為冠軍吧！提米咖啡最棒的活動！提供免費氣泡飲料和披薩。

地點：提米咖啡廳
開始時間：18:00

Timmy's Café

Friday Night Live- 9 Feb

Free live music from local and student bands, cheap beer and tasty traditional Chinese food. Pretty much the perfect Friday night. See you there.
Venue: Timmy's Café
Start Time: 19:00

Karaoke

It's karaoke night - The Timmy's wildest night, guaranteed. Belt out a classic, or force a mate to do it for you.
Venue: Timmy's Café
Start Time: 20:00

The Big Fat Pub Quiz at Timmy's

We expect hilarious fun facts about Chinese New Year. Beat your colleagues to be the best team in town. By far the best thing to do in Timmy's. Free fizzy drinks and pizza are provided.
Venue: Timmy's Café
Start Time: 18:00

日	一	二	三	四	五	六
				1	2	3
4	5	6	7	8	9	10 假期開始
11	12	13	14	15 中國新年	16 中國新年	17 中國新年
18 中國新年	19 中國新年	20 中國新年	21 假期最後一天	22 全天工作天	23 全天工作天	24 全天工作天
25 半天工作天	26	27	28			

Sun	Mon	Tue	Wed	Thu	Fri	Sat
				1	2	3
4	5	6	7	8	9	10 Vacation Starts
11	12	13	14	15 Chinese New Year	16 Chinese New Year	17 Chinese New Year
18 Chinese New Year	19 Chinese New Year	20 Chinese New Year	21 Last Day of Vacation	22 Working Day All Day	23 Working Day All Day	24 Working Day All Day
25 Working Day Half Day	26	27	28			

【詞彙】

spare空出／go through瀏覽／reminder提醒／approach接近／various各式各樣的／individual個別的／collective集體的／contribution貢獻／exceed超過／meantime同時／sort out解決／immediately立即／courtesy禮貌／attend to照顧／with regard to關於／mileage里程／reimbursement報銷／substantiate使具體／original原始的／documentation文件／revenue收入／make up補足／refer to參考／make up補足／bundle up多穿衣服／tasty美味的／guarantee保證／belt out撕扯嗓音／force強迫／hilarious好笑的／beat打敗／colleague同事／by far目前為止／fizzy含氣泡的

---

191 What information does the first paragraph of the reminder give?

(A) the date of Chinese New Year's Eve

(B) some festive celebration events

(C) a newly open restaurant

(D) the latest office regulations

【解析】第一篇文章中的第一段是在談論即將到來的中國新年，並介紹了一個慶祝活動資訊的網站。因此答案應選(B)。

這封提醒的第一段告訴我們什麼？

(A) 除夕的日期

(B) 一些節慶慶祝活動

(C) 一間新開的餐廳

(D) 最新的辦公室規章

【類型】尋找主旨題型

【詞彙】

paragraph段落／reminder提醒／festive節慶的／regulation規定

【正解】(B)

關於路程費用報銷何者正確？

(A) 必須出示原始證明單據。

(B) 有報銷上限。

(C) 中國新年期間的路程費不予以報銷。

(D) 最近的政策有所改變。

【類型】是非題型

【詞彙】

mileage里程／

reimbursement報銷／

application申請／

proof證明／

present呈獻／

amount數量／

limit限制／

incur招致／

qualify符合資格／

policy政策

【正解】(A)

192 What is indicated about mileage reimbursement application?

(A) The original proof should be presented.

(B) There is an amount limit.

(C) Mileage costs incurred during Chinese New Year do not qualify.

(D) The policy has been changed recently.

【解析】根據第一篇文中的第二點you must be able to substantiate the mileage with the original documentation or receipts我們能得知報銷申請需要提出原始的文件或收據，因此答案應選(A)。

根據提米咖啡廳的資訊，哪一個活動有提供免費的食物？

(A) 星期五夜晚現場演出

(B) 卡拉OK

(C) 瘋狂猜燈謎

(D) 以上皆是

【類型】尋找細節題型

【詞彙】

above以上的

【正解】(C)

193 According to Timmy's Café, which event provides free food?

(A) Friday Night Live

(B) Karaoke

(C) The Big Fat Pub Quiz

(D) All of the above

【解析】根據第二篇文中Free fizzy drinks and pizza are provided.表示第三個活動瘋狂猜燈謎有提供免費食物及飲料。因此答案應選(C)。

194 Why should the employees have to work for extra hours?

(A) To reach the annual goal of the department

(B) To make up for the holiday

(C) To prepare for the next year

(D) To pay off the penalty

【解析】根據第一篇文中However, due to the fact that this year we have a longer holiday than usual, we all need to work for extra hours to make up for the holiday.表示由於今年假期較長,員工必須加班補足工時。因此答案應選(B)。

為何員工需要加班?
(A) 為了達到部門的年度目標
(B) 為了補足假期期間的工時
(C) 為了明年準備
(D) 為了償還罰金

【類型】尋找細節題型

【詞彙】
annual年度的／
department部門／
make up補足／
pay off付清／
penalty罰金

【正解】(B)

---

195 On which day should the employees work for a half day?

(A) 10 February

(B) 22 February

(C) 24 February

(D) 25 February

【解析】根據第三篇月曆,二月二十五日是working day half day。因此答案應選(D)。

哪一天所有的員工上半天班?
(A) 二月十日
(B) 二月二十二日
(C) 二月二十四日
(D) 二月二十五日

【類型】尋找細節題型

【詞彙】
employee員工／
half一半的

【正解】(D)

Romina Champion

電話： 44-9408-2260／
電子信箱：
romina_2003@mail2008.
com／地址：新加坡HGTF重
江路10號

學術背景
明華大學科技學院資訊工程
科學碩士
國立教育大學人文學院英語
系學士

專業背景
2012-2014新加坡德里通訊
資訊工程師
2014-2016新加坡新象科技
駐場工程師

實習
2011-2012新加坡德里通訊
實習生

語言
英語，華語，日語，泰語

感謝您的考慮。

Romina Champion

Phone: 44-9408-2260/ Email:
romina_2003@mail2008.com/ Address: 10
Chong Jiang Road, HGTF, Singapore

Academic Background
MSc. Computer Science Information
Engineering, School of Technology, University
of Ming-Hua
BA. English culture and literature, College of
Arts, University of National Education

Professional Background
2012-2014 Information Technology Engineer,
Deli Communication, Singapore
2014-2016 Field Engineer, New Vision
Technology, Singapore

Internship
2011-2012 Intern, Deli Communication,
Singapore

Languages
English, Mandarin, Japanese, Thai

Thank you for your consideration.

Dear Ms. Romina Champion,

Congratulations to you on being selected by our human resource officers as one of the candidates for the position of Field Engineer at Sun Power Ltd. We would like to invite you to attend an interview on 29 December, 2016, at 2 PM, at our office in Clark.

You will have an interview with our department manager, Frank Oliver. The interview will last about 30 minutes. Please bring one employment reference and your resume to the interview.

If you cannot make it to the interview, please contact the office by phone (555-8148). We can rearrange the appointment with you.

We look forward to seeing you.

Best regards,
Faye Edy

親愛的Romina Champion小姐,

恭喜您通過我們太陽能有限公司人資專員的篩選成為駐場工程師的應徵候選人之一。特邀請您來參加面試。日期：2016年12月29日下午兩點。地點：克拉克處辦公室。

您將會與我們的部門經理Frank Oliver面談。面談時間大約三十分鐘。請攜帶一份在職證明和簡歷到面試現場。

如果您不克前來面試,請聯絡辦公室。撥打555-8148。我們將重新為您安排面試。

期待與您相見。

祝　平安
Faye Edy

在職證明

新加坡MTXC香草路39號
2016年12月6日

給相關人員
我特此證實Romina Champion
小姐從2014年11月1日到2016
年11月30日在新象科技公司擔
任職駐場工程師一職。

在職期間，她負責：

• 處理第二號線的支援
• 面對面支援
• 網路維修
我們公司高度肯定她兩年一
個月來的傑出表現，以及對
公司作出的突出貢獻。

衷心祝福
新象科技公司

Bella Fang
人資部門專員

Certificate of Employment

39 Vanilla Road, MTXC, Singapore
6 December 2016

To whom it may concern,
This letter is to certify that **Ms. Romina Champion** has been employed by New Vision Technology from 1 November 2014 to 30 November 2016 in the position of field engineer. During the period, her duty were：

• Dealing with 2nd Line support
• Face-to-Face Support
• Networking Maintenance
This letter also recognizes her outstanding performance and massive contribution to our Company over the past two years and one month.

Respectfully Yours,
New Vision Technology

Bella Fang
Human Resource Management Officer

【詞彙】
academic學術的／background背景／information engineering資訊工程／literature文學／intern實習生／internship實習／consideration考慮／attend參加／reference參考資料／rearrange重新安排／appointment約會／certificate證明／certify證明／employ僱用／field engineer駐場工程師／deal with處理／maintenance維修／recognize認可／outstanding傑出的／massive巨大的／contribution貢獻／respectfully尊敬地

196 Which of the following is NOT included in the CV?

(A) address

(B) phone number

(C) date of birth

(D) educational background

【解析】根據履歷表資訊Phone: 44-9408-2260/ Email: romina_2003@mail2008.com/ Address: 10 Chong Jiang Road, HGTF, Singapore提供了電話號碼，電子郵箱和地址。Academic Background MSc. Computer Science Information Engineering, School of Technology, University of Ming-Hua BA. English culture and literature, College of Arts, University of National Education提供了教育背景。因此文中沒有提及出生日期，因此答案應選(C)。

下列何者沒有包含在履歷表裡？

(A) 地址

(B) 電話號碼

(C) 出生日期

(D) 教育背景

【類型】尋找細節題型

【詞彙】

CV履歷表

【正解】(C)

---

197 What job is Romina seeking?

(A) human resource officer

(B) director of management

(C) field engineer

(D) account analyst

【解析】根據第二封邀請函中的資訊Congratulations to you on being selected by our human resource officers as one of the candidates for the position of Field Engineer at Sun Power Ltd.我們能得知Romina應徵的是field engineer駐場工程師。因此答案應選(C)。

Romina在找什麼工作？

(A) 人資專員

(B) 管理主管

(C) 駐場工程師

(D) 財會分析師

【類型】尋找細節題型

【詞彙】

seek尋找／

human resource人力資源／

director主管／

management管理／

field engineer駐場工程師／

analyst分析師

【正解】(C)

根據以上關於Romina的資訊，下列何者正確？

(A) 她能說五種語言。

(B) 她有十年以上工作經驗。

(C) 她在大學期間主修英國文學。

(D) 到目前為止她在三間公司上班過。

【類型】是非題型

【詞彙】
literature文學

【正解】(C)

198 According to the information above, which of the following is True of Romina?

(A) She can speak five languages.

(B) She has over ten years of work experience.

(C) She studied English literature in college.

(D) She has worked for three different companies so far.

【解析】根據履歷表中資訊BA. English culture and literature, College of Arts, University of National Education，其中BA表示Bachelor of Arts「學士」，而主修為英國文化與文學。因此選項(C)正確。根據Languages English, Mandarin, Japanese, Thai我們能得知她能說四種語言，而非五種，因此選項(A)為非。而她的工作經驗是從2012年到2016年，共有四年的時間，並沒有超過十年，因此選項(B)為非。而她待過的公司是德里通訊和新象科技，共兩間不同的公司，因此選項(D)為非。因此答案應選(C)。

199 Who is Frank Oliver?

(A) a manager at New Vision Technology

(B) a manager at Sun Power Ltd.

(C) a field engineer at Deli Communication

(D) a human resource officer at New Vision

【解析】根據第二封邀請函內容You will have an interview with our department manager, Frank Oliver.我們能得知Frank Oliver 是Romina正應徵的公司Sun Power Ltd的部門經理。因此答案 應選(B)。

Frank Oliver是誰？

(A) 新象科技的經理

(B) 太陽能有限公司的經理

(C) 德里通訊科技的駐場工程師

(D) 新象科技的人資專員

【類型】尋找細節題型

【詞彙】

manager經理

【正解】(B)

---

200 When was the employment certificate issued?

(A) On 6 December 2016

(B) On 1 November 2014

(C) On 30 November 2016

(D) On 29 December 2016

【解析】根據第三篇文章的日期，我們能得知這份在職證明是 在2016年12月6日頒發的。因此答案應選(A)。此類尋找數字或 日期的題目要確實把握，閱讀時多留意數字類信息。

這封在職證明是何時頒發的？

(A) 2016年12月6日

(B) 2014年11月1日

(C) 2016年11月30日

(D) 2016年12月29日

【類型】尋找細節題型

【詞彙】

issue頒發

【正解】(A)

New TOEIC Reading Analysis 4
新多益閱讀全真模擬試題解析第4回

如果你介於16到21歲之間，你就有資格申請我們提供的協助。

【類型】形容詞詞彙題型

【詞彙】
prone易於……的／incline傾向／be entitled to有資格／susceptible易受……的／support支持／offer提供

【正解】(C)

101 If you are between the ages of 16 and 21, you are _____ to the support we offer.
(A) prone
(B) inclined
(C) entitled
(D) susceptible

【解析】根據題意，我們能根據the support we offer來判斷，前方的形容詞應該是填「有資格申請」相關的詞彙。因此答案應選(C)。

Emma是那位我非常尊重她想法的人。

【類型】關係代名詞題型

【詞彙】
opinion意見／respect尊重

【正解】(D)

102 Emma is the person _____ opinion I respect.
(A) that
(B) which
(C) who
(D) whose

【解析】本題題幹的主詞補語意思為「那位我非常尊重她想法的人」，因此先行詞the person與空格之後的名詞opinion之間有所有格關係。因此關係代名詞須填whose。因此答案應選(D)。

他生病了因此今天需要請病假。

【類型】副詞題型

【詞彙】
ill生病的／therefore因此／however然而／hereby藉此／moreover而且／take a sick leave請病假

【正解】(A)

103 He is ill and _____ needs to take a sick leave today.
(A) therefore
(B) however
(C) hereby
(D) moreover

【解析】本題須考慮連接詞and之前的語意「他生病了」，與後半句有因果關係，而表示因果關係的副詞為therefore「因此」。however表示轉折語氣。hereby表示「藉此」，通常用在正式的公務場合，表達「藉由這些話語或行動，進行某種決定或行動」，如I hereby pronounce you man and wife.而moreover表示「而且」，有添加信息的功能。因此答案應選(A)。

104 As managers, it is _____ on us to be accepting to different opinions.

(A) derogatory

(B) incumbent

(C) superfluous

(D) facetious

【解析】be incumbent on somebody表示「某人有某責任……」，因此根據語意，答案應選(B)。

身為經理，我們就應該要對不同的意見保持開放的態度。

【類型】形容詞詞彙題型

【詞彙】
manager經理／
derogatory貶義的／
incumbent負有義務的／
superfluous過多的／
facetious詼諧的／
accepting樂於接納的

【正解】(B)

---

105 All of you should make punctuality your priority, _____ for those of you working as salespersons.

(A) hardly

(B) deliberately

(C) especially

(D) scarcely

【解析】本題後段必須承接前句語意，並特別強調特定族群。因此especially用來強調或確切說明。因此答案應選(C)。

你們大家應該要把準時當作首要條件，特別是業務員。

【類型】副詞題型

【詞彙】
take something as the priority
將某事視為優先／
punctuality準時／
hardly幾乎不／
deliberately故意／
especially特別／scarcely鮮少／
salesperson業務員

【正解】(C)

---

106 _____ in 2002, the band rapidly rose to fame with their debut album.

(A) Forms   (B) Forming

(C) Formed   (D) Formation

【解析】本題原句為The band was formed in 2002, and the band rapidly rose to fame with their debut album.經過分詞構句省略相同主詞the band和BeV.，並省略連接詞and之後，即變成題幹的句子。因此答案應選(C)。

於2002年成軍，這個樂團迅速以他們的第一張專輯成名。

【類型】動詞型態題型

【詞彙】
form形成／rapidly迅速地／
rise to fame成名／
debut album首張專輯

【正解】(C)

杭州是浙江省貿易與商業的樞紐。

【類型】形容詞詞彙題型

【詞彙】
suburban郊區的／
modern現代的／
rebellious反叛的／
focal中心的／trade貿易／
commerce商業／
province省

【正解】(D)

過去十年來，他們已經蛻變為一個全球知名的團隊。

【類型】代名詞題型

【詞彙】
decade十年／turn into轉變為／
globally全球地／
well-known知名的／
team團隊

【正解】(D)

評選的過程共有三個主要階段。

【類型】動詞詞彙題型

【詞彙】
evaluation評估／
process過程／
consist of由……組成／
revolve圍繞／compose組成／
resist抗拒／main主要的／
stage階段

【正解】(A)

---

107 Hangzhou is the ＿＿＿＿＿ point of trade and commerce in Zhejiang province.
(A) suburban
(B) modern
(C) rebellious
(D) focal

【解析】根據語意，本句表達「貿易與商業的中心」，因此答案應選(D)。其名詞為focus。

---

108 Over the past decade, they have turned ＿＿＿＿＿ into a globally well-known team.
(A) theirs
(B) they
(C) their
(D) themselves

【解析】themselves反身代名詞代替前面提過的相同指稱的名詞。根據語意「他們將他們自己轉變成全球知名的團隊」。因此答案應選(D)。

---

109 The evaluation process ＿＿＿＿＿ of three main stages.
(A) consists
(B) revolves
(C) composes
(D) resists

【解析】consist of表示「由……組成」，需用主動語態。因此答案應選(A)。

110 The presentation demonstrated the major _____ of the project.

(A) achievement

(B) distance

(C) revenge

(D) personality

【解析】「本次專案的成就」，能與project一字搭配並語意通順的選項為(A)。

這個簡報呈現了本次專案的重要成績。

【類型】名詞詞彙題型

【詞彙】
presentation呈現／
demonstrate展現／
major主要的／
achievement成就／
distance距離／revenge復仇／
personality個性／
project專案

【正解】(A)

---

111 The report made a few _____ references to the sensitive issue.

(A) sublime

(B) inductive

(C) oblique

(D) authentic

【解析】oblique reference表示「旁敲側擊；隱晦地提到」。根據語意，答案應選(C)。

這則報告旁敲側擊了這個敏感議題。

【類型】形容詞詞彙題型

【詞彙】
sublime卓越的／
inductive歸納式的／
oblique隱晦的／
authentic真實的／
reference提及／
sensitive敏感的／issue議題

【正解】(C)

---

112 Every teacher should _____ their recess duties and report back to supervisors.

(A) succeed

(B) fulfill

(C) pursue

(D) behold

【解析】本題能與duty搭配的動詞為fulfill。fulfill duties表示「盡到職責」。表示「盡到職責」的動詞還有meet, carry out, perform等。因此答案應選(B)。

每位老師都應該完成課間值勤並且回報給主管。

【類型】動詞詞彙題型

【詞彙】
succeed成功／fulfill達成／
pursue追求／behold看／
recess中場休息／duty職責／
supervisor主管

【正解】(B)

這位主管要求與會者分享他們對這個議題的感想。

【類型】介系詞題型

【詞彙】
director主管／
attendant參加者／
reflection感想／
issue議題

【正解】(D)

113 The director asked the attendants to share their reflections _____ this issue.
(A) in
(B) with
(C) over
(D) on

【解析】與reflection連用等介系詞為on。因此答案應選(D)。

下週，參加者會彼此合作完成一份發展計畫。

【類型】動詞型態題型

【詞彙】
participant參加者／
complete完成／
development發展／
in collaboration with與……合作

【正解】(C)

114 During the week to come, participants _____ a development plan in collaboration with one another.
(A) complete
(B) completed
(C) will complete
(D) have completed

【解析】根據時間the week to come表示「下一週」，為未來式。因此應選未來式動詞，選項(C)。

讀過這些指南並抓到如何架設自己的網站的精髓。

【類型】疑問詞題型

【詞彙】
instruction說明／
gist主旨／
create創造

【正解】(B)

115 Read through the instructions and get the gist of _____ to create your own website.
(A) what
(B) how
(C) whether
(D) whom

【解析】how表示「如何」，問方法。根據語意「如何打造自己的網站」，答案應選(B)。另外，what問東西；whether問「是否」；whom問「人」。

116 We hope you find our workshop _____ .

(A) help

(B) helping

(C) helpful

(D) to help

【解析】find something adj.表示「覺得某物……」。因此空格應選一個形容詞,因此答案應選(C)。

我們希望你能覺得我們的說明會有幫助。

【類型】動詞型態題型

【詞彙】
find認為／
workshop說明會／
helpful有幫助的

【正解】(C)

---

117 The analysis approach will be described _____ more details in the following section.

(A) in

(B) upon

(C) with

(D) by

【解析】in details為介系詞片語當副詞的功能,表示「詳細地」。本題表達「詳細地說明」,因此答案應選(A)。

這個分析方法會在下個部分有更詳細的描述。

【類型】介系詞題型

【詞彙】
analysis分析／
approach方法／
describe描述／
in details詳細地／
following接續的／
section區;部分

【正解】(A)

---

118 _____ I want to achieve by this proposal is to sketch an outline for the seasonal project.

(A) Which

(B) What

(C) How

(D) That

【解析】本題的主詞為空格到proposal,需用間接問句充當主詞。而間接問句缺失的部分為achieve的受詞,因此疑問詞應用what。因此答案應選(B)。

我希望這個提案的目的是為這個季度專案構思一個大綱。

【類型】疑問詞題型

【詞彙】
achieve達成／
proposal提案／
sketch勾勒／
outline大綱／
seasonal季節性的／
project計劃

【正解】(B)

起初，我們並沒有計劃招聘那麼多評估人員。

【類型】詞類變化題型

【詞彙】
initially起初／plan計劃／recruitment招聘／recruit招聘／evaluator評估人員

【正解】(C)

---

119 Initially, we did not plan _____ so many evaluators.

(A) recruitment

(B) recruiting

(C) to recruit

(D) for recruiting

【解析】plan後面須接不定詞to Vr.表示「計劃做某事」。因此答案應選(C)。

我們正處於一個一犯小錯誤就會導致巨大的連鎖效應的困境。

【類型】關係副詞題型

【詞彙】
predicament困境／lead to導致／enormous巨大的／chain reaction連鎖反應

【正解】(B)

---

120 We are in a predicament _____ a single mistake can lead to an enormous chain reaction.

(A) that

(B) where

(C) which

(D) when

【解析】本題考點為關係副詞。我們必須根據空格前方的先行詞屬性判斷。predicament表示「艱難的處境」，我們可理解為「處所」。因此與「處所」搭配的關係副詞為where，因此答案應選(B)。

我們這個推理的假設前提是每個人至少都有一年的專業經驗。

【類型】連接詞題型

【詞彙】
base something on something 把某事建立在某事上／assumption假設／at least至少／professional專業的／experience經驗

【正解】(A)

---

121 We based our reasoning on the assumption _____ everyone has at least one year of professional experience.

(A) that

(B) which

(C) whose

(D) why

【解析】本題的受詞補語從空格開始到experience，受詞補語用於補充說明受詞。連接詞需用that。因此答案應選(A)。本題容易與關係代名詞that混淆。考生須注意受詞補語連接詞that後方應接「完整名詞子句」，而關係代名詞that後方應接「不完整形容詞子句」。

122 This session ＿＿＿＿ you to voice your concern about your working conditions.

(A) provides

(B) forewarns

(C) admits

(D) allows

【解析】provide的用法為provide somebody with something/provide something for somebody，並沒有provide somebody to Vr.的用法。allow的用法為allow somebody to Vr.表示「允許某人做某事」。因此答案應選(D)。

這個環節讓你有機會發表你對工作情況的疑慮。

【類型】動詞詞彙題型

【詞彙】
session環節；課程／
provide提供／
forewarn提前警告／
admit承認／allow允許／
voice發表／concern擔憂／
condition狀況

【正解】(D)

---

123 ＿＿＿＿ the handbook, every teacher at the university has the right to take a sabbatical leave after working for seven years.

(A) In addition to

(B) According to

(C) Applicable to

(D) In light of

【解析】根據本文語意「根據手冊」，因此表示「根據」的選項為(B)。另外還有based on也可以表示「根據」。

根據手冊，這所大學裡的每位老師在工作七年之後都有一次請公假的權利。

【類型】介系詞片語題型

【詞彙】
in addition to除了／
according to根據／
applicable to能適用於……／
in light of有鑒於／
handbook手冊／right權利／
sabbatical leave大學職員的公假

【正解】(B)

---

124 We are proud to be able to ＿＿＿＿ aesthetic design with innovative technology in our home appliances.

(A) reply

(B) involve

(C) compare

(D) combine

【解析】combine A with B表示「將AB兩事物結合」。而compare A with B表示「將AB兩事物相比較」。根據語意，選項(D)比較符合語意。

我們非常自豪能夠在家電用品上結合美學設計與創新的科技。

【類型】動詞詞彙題型

【詞彙】
proud驕傲的／reply回覆／
involve包含／compare比較／
combine結合／aesthetic美學的／design設計／innovative創新的／technology科技／
appliance家電用品

【正解】(D)

搭地鐵，巴士或計程車都能很容易到達Amanda旅館。

【類型】形容詞詞彙題型

【詞彙】
available可得到的／
acceptable可接受的／
accessible可得到的；可接觸到的／amendable可修改的／
metro地鐵

【正解】(C)

---

125 Hotel Amanda is easily _____ by metros, buses or taxis.

(A) available

(B) acceptable

(C) accessible

(D) amendable

【解析】available表示某事物是「可取得的」；而accessible則表示某事物是「可被接觸到的」或「可進入的」。

這些濱海的購物中心冬天時完全鬧空城。

【類型】動詞詞彙題型

【詞彙】
seaside濱海的／
desert廢棄／
instruct指導／
reschedule更改行程／
conserve保存

【正解】(A)

---

126 The seaside shopping malls are _____ in winter.

(A) deserted

(B) instructed

(C) rescheduled

(D) conserved

【解析】本題語意能與主詞seaside shopping mall搭配的動詞只有選項(A)表示「廢棄」。

Justin剛開始一個你可能會感興趣的計劃。

【類型】介系詞題型

【詞彙】
project計劃／
be interested in感到有興趣的

【正解】(D)

---

127 Justin just started a project you may be interested _____ .

(A) of

(B) with

(C) about

(D) in

【解析】be interested in表示「感到興趣」；be interesting to表示「對某人來說是有趣的」。因此答案應選(D)。

128 _____ migration is an important global phenomenon that needs to be tackled seriously.

(A) Forcing

(B) Forced

(C) Force

(D) Forces

被迫移民是一個需要被嚴肅處理的重要的全球現象。

【類型】動詞型態題型

【詞彙】
force強迫／
migration移民／
global全球的／
phenomenon現象／
tackle處理／seriously嚴肅地

【解析】根據題幹語意，forced migration表示「受迫的移民現象」。因過去分詞表達「被動」的語意。現在分詞表達「主動」的語意。因此答案應選(B)。

【正解】(B)

---

129 _____ of you who participated in the event can apply for reimbursement by the end of this month.

(A) Those

(B) These

(C) Whom

(D) Ones

那些參加這個活動的人在這個月底之前都可以申請報銷。

【類型】代名詞題型

【詞彙】
participate參加／
event活動／
apply for申請／
reimbursement報銷

【解析】those of you表示「那些……的人」。為固定用法。those通常用來指代「某些人」。因此答案應選(A)。

【正解】(A)

---

130 Make sure the size and color of the signboard are in _____ with the state laws.

(A) agree

(B) agreed

(C) agreeing

(D) agreement

確認招牌的大小跟顏色都是符合州法的。

【類型】詞類變化題型

【詞彙】
make sure確認／
signboard招牌／
in agreement with與……符合／
state州

【解析】in agreement with表示「與……符合」，為固定用法。in後面通常加名詞形式，再加上介系詞可充當介系詞片語使用。如：in search for「尋找」；in conjunction with「連接」；in remembrance of「懷念」等。

【正解】(D)

大家好，

非常高興邀請大家在2017年12月27日下午四點來參加STC的年終派對。請上www.stc.com/yearendparty網站詳讀年終派對資訊。網站提供所有有關年終派對的最新資訊，包含：時程表，門票資訊，服裝租借和照相等更多資訊。請確實詳讀這些資訊。如果在網站上找不到關於你的問題的資訊，請撥打9876-0534聯絡人力資源部。

報名參加年終派對在2017年12月11日截止，報名只需花你幾分鐘的時間。如果你不參加，你也需要填妥表格，勾選「缺席」的選項。如果你不確定能否到場，你也必須申請。如果你超過截止日期才報名，我們無法保證你的名額。

祝大家順心愉快

人資辦公室

Directions: Read the texts on the following pages. A word or phrase is missing in some of the sentences. Answer choices are given below each of these articles. Select the best answer to complete the text. Then mark the letter (A), (B), (C) or (D) on your answer sheet.

Questions 131-134 refer to the following letter.

Dear all,

We are delighted to invite you to attend the STC year-end party ___131___ will take place on 27 December 2017 at 4 pm. Please access the year-end party website at www.stc.com/yearendparty. This will provide all ___132___ information regarding the party including timetable, ticket information, costume hire and photography and much more. It is vital that you read this information carefully. If your query is not covered on the website, please contact the HR department at 9876-0534.

The deadline to register for the year-end party is 11 December 2017 and registration only ___133___ a few minutes. You should complete your form even if you do not wish to attend the party by selecting the "in absentia" option. If you are still not sure about whether you will be able to come, you must still register. ___134___ if you register after the deadline.

With best wishes,

HR office

131 (A) what

(B) which

(C) who

(D) it

【解析】本句的先行詞year-end party為事物，因此關係代名詞需用which或that。因此答案應選(B)。

【類型】關係代名詞題型

【詞彙】

delighted高興的／

invite邀請／

attend參加／

year-end年終的／

take place發生

【正解】(B)

---

132 (A) state-of-the-art

(B) down-to-earth

(C) up-to-date

(D) last-minute

【解析】根據本文語意，網站上公布的是「最新的」資訊。因此符合語意的為選項(C)。state-of-the-art表示「運用最新科技的」；last-minute表示「最後一分鐘倉促決定或完成的」。語意上有所區分。

【類型】形容詞詞彙題型

【詞彙】

provide提供／

state-of-the-art高科技的／

down-to-earth樸實的／

up-to-date最新的／

last-minute倉促完成；決定的／

regarding關於／

timetable時間表／

costume道具服／hire租用／

photography拍照

【正解】(C)

---

133 (A) spends

(B) takes

(C) costs

(D) pays

【解析】本題考點為四個易混淆的動詞。take為「某事物花了多少時間」。spend為「某人花了多少時間或金錢」。cost為「某事物花了多少金錢」。pay為「某人付了多少錢」。本題主詞為registration「註冊」，因此需選選項(B)。

【類型】相似動詞詞彙題型

【詞彙】

deadline截止日期／

register註冊報名／

registration註冊報名

【正解】(B)

【類型】句子插入題型

【詞彙】
unable無法／
guarantee保證／
pleased開心的／
extra額外的

【正解】(A)

★ **134** (A) We would be unable to guarantee you a place at the party
(B) We are pleased to have you with us
(C) You can even choose to invite your family
(D) You will be offered an extra ticket

【解析】根據後半句「如果你在截止日期後報名」，最適合的句子為選項(A)，「我們無法保證你能來參加」。

Questions 135-138　refer to the following letter.

Peters先生您好，

我來信告知我從七月十號到十三號在白俄羅斯明斯克的Belarus公寓房入住時不滿意的經驗。我是在愛旅館網站上幫我同事預訂的房間。

我主要要反映的是旅館所提供的設施遠遠不如網站上所描述的樣子。我預訂了五間公寓式套房，房號0401到0405。但實際的房間完全不是網站上那一回事。我們一進房就被牆上散佈的霉嚇到。浴缸積滿了水垢而且看上去都生鏽了。大致上的裝潢，在網站上標榜是「現代且迷人」，但實際上卻又舊又爛。

我們試著跟你們的旅館代表反應過，他當時答應我們幫我們換房，但花了一天才換好。我們當時被要求填寫一張客訴單，詳細說明我們遇到的問題。我也夾帶於附件供您參考。

Dear Mr. Peters

I am writing to express my dissatisfaction with my stay at Belarus Studio, Minsk Belarus, on July 10th- 13th, which I booked on iHotel.com for my company colleagues.

My central complaint is that the hotel amenities provided fell ____135____ short of the description on the website. I booked five studio-type rooms in room 0401 to 0405. The actual rooms were hardly like the pictures shown on the website. As soon as we entered the rooms, we were extremely terrified by the scattered wall mold. The bathtubs have gathered limescale and looked terribly rusty. The overall furnishings, ____136____ on the website as "modern and charming", were in fact old and worn.

We tried to speak to your ____137____ who promised to arrange a room change for us but it took one day to happen. We were asked to fill out a complaint form detailing the issues we encountered and I enclose a copy for your information.

We feel that ___138___ as it completely ruined our vacation and we consider the description on the website false advertising. We look forward to hearing from you within the next three days.
Sincerely yours,
Cindy Johnson

我們認為我們應該得到所有的房價退還，因為這次經驗已經完全破壞了我們的假期，而且我們認為網站上的廣告不實。希望我們能在三天之內得到您的回覆。

Cindy Johnson敬上

---

135 (A) very
    (B) far
    (C) many
    (D) too

【解析】fall short of表示「不比……」。而加上副詞far表示「遠遠不比……」。有加強語氣的作用。因此答案應選(B)。

【類型】副詞詞彙題型

【詞彙】
central中心的／
complaint抱怨／
amenity設施／
provide提供／
fall short of不比／
description描述／
far遠遠地

【正解】(B)

---

136 (A) describing
    (B) described
    (C) descriptive
    (D) description

【解析】本題原句應為The overall furnishings, which were described on the website as...經過分詞構句省略關係代名詞與BeV.之後，變成本題的句子。因此，答案應選(B)。考生也可以直接從主被動語態判斷。主動語態會用現在分詞，被動語態會用過去分詞。而此處的裝潢是在網站上「被描述」，因此會使用被動語態。

【類型】詞類變化題型

【詞彙】
overall大致上的／
furnishing裝潢／
describe描述／
descriptive描述的／
description描述／
modern現代的／
charming迷人的／
worn磨損的

【正解】(B)

【詞彙】

clerk店員／
broker經紀人／
spokesperson代言人／
representative代表／
arrange安排

【正解】(D)

137 (A) clerk
(B) broker
(C) spokesperson
(D) representative

【解析】根據本題語意，顧客應是找到旅館的「代表人」。clerk為「商店或銀行的店員」。broker為「仲介」。spokesperson為「代言人」。因此最合適的選項為(D)。

【類型】句子插入題型

【詞彙】

deserve應得／
upgrade升級／
presidential suite總統套房／
handle處理／
discretion謹慎／
due應付帳的／
worth值得／
rate房價／
ruin毀壞／
false假的

【正解】(C)

★ **138** (A) we deserve a free upgrade to the presidential suite
(B) you should handle this issue with more discretion next time
(C) we are due a full refund for the hotel stay
(D) it is worth the stay considering the low room rate

【解析】根據文意，顧客應是要求退費，因不滿旅館的設施與廣告不實。因此答案應選(C)。

Questions 139-142 refer to the following advertisement.

English Villagers

Current Job Opening

Software quality assurance engineer

Our team is fully committed to ___139___ software quality, and takes user experience seriously. We are currently seeking a highly skilled software engineer who is willing to join us in taking our quality to the next level and building the next generation online English learning tools.

REQUIREMENTS

- You must possess the latest technology and programming techniques to bring out the full ___140___ of the interactive website.
- You must have a minimum of 1 year of experience in C/C++ or debugging skills.
- You must be strong in system level programming including Python/Ruby scripting.
- You must have good system level understanding of Linux.

Detail-oriented perfectionists are welcome. ___141___, we will support your further professional training to hone your expertise. Most importantly, you must have passion for ___142___.

英語村村民

目前工作職缺
軟體品質維護工程師
我們的團隊致力於確保軟體的品質並且非常看重顧客使用經驗。我們目前正徵求一位能力好的軟體工程師，願意加入我們的團隊精進我們公司產品的品質並打造新世代的線上英語學習工具。

條件：

- 你必須擁有最新的科技及編程技術，將互動式網站的功能達到最高效能。

- 你至少要有一年的C或C++或軟體除錯的技能

- 你必須擅長系統規格的程式編寫，包括Python和Ruby程式編寫

- 你必須有完備的Linux系統的知識

我們非常歡迎注重細節的完美主義者。如果你是精益求精的好學人士，我們會提供你專業訓練以完善你的專業能力。最重要的，你必須對你的工作充滿熱情。

【詞彙】
commit致力／
insure保險／ensure確保／
assure向某人確定／
reassure使某人安心／
software軟體／
quality品質／
seriously認真地

【正解】(B)

139 (A) insuring
(B) ensuring
(C) assuring
(D) reassuring

【解析】ensure表示「確認某事物」，如：He ensured that the doors were all locked. insure表示「將某物保險」，如：insure my car for $100,000。assure表示「使某人放心」，如：I can assure you that this is 100% safe. reassure表示「使某人放心」，如：She tried to reassure her mother. 本題語意為「確保軟體的品質」，因此答案應選(B)。

【類型】名詞詞彙題型

【詞彙】
possess擁有／
program編程／
technique技術／
bring out發揮／
capacity能力／
requirement要求／
standard標準／
protocol規定／
interactive互動的

【正解】(A)

140 (A) capacity
(B) requirement
(C) standard
(D) protocol

【解析】根據語意「將互動式網站的功能發揮到極致」。因此應選選項(A)。

★ **141** (A) If you prefer flexible working hours
(B) If you consider yourself communicative
(C) For those who have an unquenchable thirst for knowledge
(D) For those who love dealing with customer affairs

【解析】根據後半句「我們會幫助你專業進修」，我們能推測前半句是有關「專業訓練」的條件子句。因此答案應選(C)。

【類型】動詞詞彙題型

【詞彙】
prefer比較喜歡／
flexible彈性的／
consider認為／
communicative善於溝通的／
unquenchable不滅的／
thirst渴／
deal with處理／
customer顧客／
affair事務／
further進一步的／
professional專業的／
training培訓／
hone磨礪／
expertise專業技能／

【正解】(C)

★ **142** (A) how you do
(B) how do you do
(C) what you do
(D) what do you do

【解析】空格處應填間接問句當作名詞子句當for的受詞。間接問句結構：wh+S+V。根據語意「對於你做的事情有熱情」，因此答案應選(C)。

【類型】名詞子句題型

【詞彙】
passion熱情

【正解】(C)

歡迎觀閱Leicester銀行新聞報。我們致力於報導與您理財相關的各類主題，提供你財經界最新的潮流見解。

如果你是我們新聞報的忠實讀者，你可能已經知道一些關於目前歐洲市場的不穩定。然而，你可能還是會偶爾聽到一些關於歐洲市場狀態的某些廣為流傳的迷思。例如，有些消息，像是政府如何處理新的政治局面會帶來不穩定性，其實是需要更多背景資訊才能斷定的。其他消息，像是今年最開始的幾個星期的全球股市戲劇性地大跌意味著主要市場會籠罩著不散的陰霾，根本就是錯誤的。

更多的是，我們的科技專欄對於商業數位化的議題有深入報導。科技迷一定不能錯過喔！

最後，我們的「聽見你的聲音」專欄公布了過去兩個月來你們給予我們的意見與問題。感謝你的意見。你們每位讀者都是我們不可分割的一部份。

祝 週末愉快

新聞報團隊敬上

Welcome to Leicester Bank Newsletter. We aim to give you an insight in the latest trends in finance and trade ___143___ covering various subjects relevant for your business.

If you are a regular reader of Leicester Bank Newsletter, you probably know at least something about the current market instability in Europe. ___144___, you may still occasionally come across some pervasive myths about the status of the European market. For instance, some, such as the belief that how the governments will manage the new political landscape would bring about uncertainty, actually require more context to ___145___ true. Others, such as the idea that the drastic slide in global stock markets in the first weeks of this year means that the major market will be covered in the unremitting gloom, are just wrong.

Also, this week our technology sector has a go at digitization in business. ___146___.

Finally, our "hear from you" section presents the opinions and questions you had for us in the previous two months. Thank you for your feedback. Every reader is an inextricable element of us.

Have a great weekend.

Newsletter Team

143 (A) in
　　(B) by
　　(C) with
　　(D) along

【解析】空格處應填表示手段的介系詞by，表示「藉由某種方法」。with後面通常接名詞。因此答案應選(B)。

【類型】介系詞題型

【詞彙】
aim目標／
insight見解／trend趨勢／
finance財經／trade貿易／
cover報導／
various各類的／
subject主題／
relevant有關的

【正解】(B)

---

144 (A) For example
　　(B) Therefore
　　(C) However
　　(D) Consequently

【解析】本題需要考慮前一句If you are a regular reader of Leicester Bank Newsletter, you probably know at least something about the current market instability in Europe.「如果你是我們報紙的忠實讀者，你可能已經知道一點歐洲市場目前不穩定的狀況」與本句有轉折的關係。因此答案應選(C)。therefore與consequently都表示因果關係。

【類型】副詞題型

【詞彙】
therefore因此／
however然而／
consequently因此／
occasionally偶爾地／
come across遇到／
pervasive廣為流傳的／
myth迷思／
status狀態／
European歐洲的

【正解】(C)

【詞彙】

for instance例如／
manage處理／
political政治的／
landscape局面／
bring about帶來／
uncertainty不確定／
require需要／
context背景資訊／
hold true為真實／
determine決定

【正解】(A)

【類型】句子插入題型

【詞彙】

sector領域；部門；行業／
have a go at試一試／
digitization數位化／
ranking排名／
matter重要／
investment投資／
explain解釋／
demonstrate展示／
step步驟／
loan貸款／
credit信用／
provide提供／
tech-savvy對科技痴迷的／
miss out錯過

【正解】(D)

---

145 (A) hold
　　(B) make
　　(C) tell
　　(D) determine

【解析】hold true表示「某事為真」。為固定搭配語，因此答案應選(A)。

★ 146 (A) Why bank rankings really matter for investment is well explained
　　(B) It demonstrates the steps to get a personal loan
　　(C) Tips to improve your credit rating are provided
　　(D) Those who are tech-savvy must not miss out.

【解析】本題空格應填與前半句「商業數位化」相關的句子，因此選項(D)關於「科技迷」為最適合的答案。

▶ PART 7

Directions: In this part, you will read a selection of texts, such as magazine and newspaper articles, letters, and advertisements. Each text is followed by several questions. Select the best answer for each question and mark the letter (A), (B), (C), or (D) on your answer sheet.

Questions 147-148 refer to the following warning sign.

ACTION IN CASE OF EMERGENCY

Do not use the lift in event of a fire alarm

If you become trapped in this lift, you should take the following action:

- Press the alarm button on the switch panel (bell symbol) and wait for a reply.
- If there is no reply, press the alarm button again.
- When your call is answered, speak into the grill on the switch panel and say that you are trapped in lift HDS 41 in the Heather Road branch Goldenmill road.

緊急狀況應變措施

遇到火災請勿搭乘電梯。

如果你被困在電梯裡，你應該依照下列指示行動。

- 按壓在控制板上有鐘形狀的緊急按鈕，等待回應。
- 如果沒有回應，再次按壓按鈕。
- 如果有人回應，請對著控制板上的對講口講話。說明你被困在Goldenmill路上Heather路分部的HDS 41電梯。

【詞彙】
in case of萬一／emergency緊急狀況／lift電梯／alarm警報／trap困住／take action採取行動／switch轉換／panel平板／symbol符號／grill對講口／branch分部

這個標誌的主要目的是什麼？
(A) 展示電梯維修標準
(B) 廣告電梯品牌
(C) 說明電梯安裝程序
(D) 展示電梯安全說明

【類型】尋找主旨題型

【詞彙】

demonstrate展示／
maintenance維修／
standard標準／lift電梯／
advertise廣告／brand品牌／
illustrate說明／
installment安裝／
procedure程序／
showcase展示／
guideline大綱

【正解】(D)

---

147 What is the main purpose of the sign?

(A) To demonstrate the maintenance standards of the lift

(B) To advertise the lift brand

(C) To illustrate the lift installment procedure

(D) To showcase the safety guidelines of the lift

【解析】根據本文標題及內容，我們能得知本文說明了搭乘電梯遇到緊急狀況時應採取的步驟。因此答案應選(D)。

緊急狀況中，需向安全人員提供何種訊息？
(A) 電梯的位置
(B) 意外的時間點
(C) 受困人的姓名
(D) 電梯所在樓層

【類型】尋找細節題型

【詞彙】
indicate標明／
security安全／
personnel人員／
location位置／
emergency緊急況狀／
trap困住

【正解】(A)

---

148 What should be indicated to the security personnel in case of emergency?

(A) the location of the lift

(B) the time of the emergency

(C) the names of the people trapped

(D) the floor at which the lift is

【解析】根據文末When your call is answered, speak into the grill on the switch panel and say that you are trapped in lift HDS 41 in the Heather Road branch Goldenmill road.告訴人們必須說出電梯的位置。因此答案應選(A)。

Questions 149-151 refer to the following email.

To: Luke Glover
From: Industrial Bank Survey
May 14, 2017
We welcome your feedback
Dear Luke Glover,

Thank you for visiting Industrial Bank Hoping Road.

We're committed to making our customer experience the best it can be. In order to strengthen the already good customer relationship, we would appreciate your feedback on your recent experience with us by responding to the survey which takes only 3 minutes to complete. We always take your opinions seriously to better understand how to improve the service we provide. Please be assured that we will never use your feedback to sell or market anything to you.

Please begin by answering the question below. Based on your recent in-branch experience, how likely are you to recommend Industrial Bank Hoping Road to a friend?

Please give your answer on a scale where '1' means 'not at all likely' and '5' means 'extremely likely'.

1 not at all likely	2	3	4	5 extremely likely

收件人：Luke Glover
寄件人：工業銀行調查部門
2017年5月14日
歡迎您的意見
親愛的Luke Glover，
感謝您蒞臨工業銀行和平路分行。

我們致力於提供最棒的客戶服務。為了加強已經很優的客戶關係，我們希望您能花個三分鐘完成這份調查，告訴我們您最近的對我們客服的寶貴意見。我們一直以來都非常珍惜您寶貴的意見，以優化我們提供的服務品質。請知悉我們從來不會利用您的意見來推銷任何產品。

請回答以下問題。
根據您最近到和平分行的經驗，您有多大的可能性會將我們的服務推薦給您的朋友？
請在量表上圈選，數字1代表完全不可能，數字5代表非常有可能。

1 完全 不 可能	2	3	4	5 非常 有 可能

【詞彙】
industrial產業的／survey調查／commit投入／strengthen強化／relationship關係／respond to回應／assure向某人確認／market行銷／recommend推薦／scale量表

Luke Glover在電郵中被要求做什麼？
(A) 開戶
(B) 聯絡分行經理
(C) 以線上帳戶登錄
(D) 完成客服調查

【類型】尋找細節題型

【詞彙】
branch分行

【正解】(D)

149 What is Luke Glover asked to do in the email?

(A) To open a bank account

(B) To contact the branch manager

(C) To check in with the online banking account

(D) To complete a customer survey

【解析】根據文中信息In order to strengthen the already good customer relationship, we would appreciate your feedback on your recent experience with us by responding to the survey which takes only 3 minutes to complete.我們能得知Glover先生被要求完成一份顧客滿意度調查。因此答案應選(D)。

Luke Glover最有可能什麼時候造訪這間銀行的？
(A) 1月30日
(B) 5月13日
(C) 7月1日
(D) 12月22日

【類型】尋找細節題型

【詞彙】
visit造訪

【正解】(B)

150 When did Luke Glover most likely visit the bank recently?

(A) January 30

(B) May 13

(C) July 1

(D) December 22

【解析】根據電郵中的時間May 14, 2017與文中提到Thank you for visiting Industrial Bank Hoping Road.我們能推測Glover先生可能在收到這封電郵不久之前去過這間銀行分行。因此最接近的時間為選項(B)。

數字4在取向表上代表什麼？
(A) Glover先生對於服務不滿意。
(B) Glover先生不會再拜訪這間分行了。
(C) Glover先生願意從這間銀行申請貸款。
(D) Glover先生願意把這間銀行推薦給朋友。

【類型】推理題型

【詞彙】
service服務／loan貸款／
recommend推薦

【正解】(D)

151 What does answer 4 mean on the scale given?

(A) Mr. Glover is not happy with the service.

(B) Mr. Glover would never visit the branch again.

(C) Mr. Glover is willing to get a loan from the bank.

(D) Mr. Glover is happy to recommend the bank to his friends.

【解析】根據量表上的說明，5代表「非常有可能推薦給朋友」。1代表「完全不可能推薦給朋友」因此我們能推測4代表「滿有可能推薦給朋友」。因此答案應選(D)。

Questions 152-156 refer to the following announcement.

David Morrison, a security officer in the Atlantic International School, will be retiring effective 19 November 2017. David has been an excellent employee. He was a keen and dedicated security officer who appreciated the student population and was always on hand to assist and advise with their problems. His calming, friendly presence resolved many difficult situations.

David joined the school security services team in 2002 after a period of working in the private security sector. As a door supervisor at the school, he quickly adapted to school life and was swiftly appointed as the campus society workforce representative. His energy and drive, combined with excellent knowledge of his role, soon made him a much-respected person both within his own department and in the wider school community, where he received many requests for advice and assistance.

David's retirement is our loss but a well-deserved **respite** for him. A retirement party will be held in his honor at Marina Restaurant on the evening of 19 November 2017, at 6:00 pm. All are invited to share in this celebration. We all extend our best wishes to David and express our appreciation to his dedication. In the meantime, we wish David a wonderful retirement.

David Morrison一位在亞特蘭大國際學校服務的安全人員,將在2017年11月19日退休。David一直是位非常優異的員工。他非常熱心勤懇,對於全校學生瞭如指掌,對於學生事務都親力親為地協助,給予建議。他那令人心安、友善的存在解決了校園中許多堅難的問題。

David在私人保安部門工作了一段時間後於2002年加入了本校的維安團隊。身為本校的門衛主管,他很快地適應了學校的運作,也很快被指派為校園人力代表。他的活力與精力,加上他豐富的專業職務知識,很快地就讓他不管在部門內或整個校園內都成為了一位備受尊敬的人,許多人有困難都會去找他解決或詢問意見。

David的退休是我們的損失,但他也值得好好地休息一段時間了。2017年11月19日晚上六點,我們會在Marina餐廳為他舉辦一場退休派對。大家一起來共襄盛舉。我們會在派對上對David表達我們的祝福與感謝。同時,我們也祝他退休快樂。

【詞彙】
security安全／officer官員／retire退休／effective有效的／keen熱衷的／dedicated致力的／appreciate理解／population人口／on hand委身從事／assist協助／advise建議／calming另人安心的／presence存在／resolve解決／situation處境／private私人的／sector部門／supervisor主管／adapt to適應／swiftly迅速地／appoint指派／workforce人力／representative代表／drive精力／combine結合／community社區／request要求／assistance協助／loss損失／well-deserved應得的／respite休息／retirement退休／in one's honor以某人名義／celebration慶祝／extend延伸／express表達／appreciation感謝／dedication付出／in the meantime同時

David Morrison是誰？
(A) 一位大學教師
(B) 一位機械工程師
(C) 一位學校的職員
(D) 一位兒童護士

【類型】尋找細節題型

【詞彙】
university大學／
mechanical機械的

【正解】(C)

152 Who is David Morrison?

    (A) a university teacher

    (B) a mechanical engineer

    (C) a school officer

    (D) a children's nurse

【解析】根據第一段David Morrison, a security officer in the Atlantic International School告訴我們David是亞特蘭大國際學校的維安職員。因此答案應選(C)。

153 What was David's first position at the school?

(A) security supervisor

(B) recruitment director

(C) campus society workforce representative

(D) door supervisor

【解析】根據第二段第二行信息As a door supervisor at the school，我們能得知David是位門衛主管，因此答案應選(D)。

David在這間學校的第一個職位是什麼？

(A) 維安主管

(B) 召聘部主任

(C) 校園人力代表

(D) 門衛主管

【類型】尋找細節題型

【詞彙】

position職位／

security安全／

supervisor主管／

recruitment招聘／

director主管／

campus校園／workforce人力／

representative代表

【正解】(D)

---

154 How long has David worked in the school?

(A) 10 years

(B) 15 years

(C) 19 years

(D) 20 years

【解析】根據文中資訊，David是在2002年入職於這所學校，並在2017年退休，前後共15年的時間在學校服務。因此答案應選(B)。

David在這間學校服務多久了？

(A) 10 年

(B) 15 年

(C) 19 年

(D) 20 年

【類型】尋找細節題型

【詞彙】

work工作

【正解】(B)

本文最後一段的主旨為何？
(A) 退休派對的邀請
(B) 職位說明
(C) David職涯概要
(D) David在學校的貢獻

【類型】尋找主旨題型

【詞彙】
main主要的／
paragraph段落／
invitation邀請／
description描述／
overview概要／
contribution貢獻

【正解】(A)

155 What is the main idea of the last paragraph?

(A) an invitation to the retirement party

(B) a job description of the position

(C) an overview of David's career

(D) David's contribution to the school

【解析】根據最後一段A retirement party will be held in his honor at Marina Restaurant on the evening of 19 November 2017, at 6:00 pm.告訴我們學校即將為David辦一場退休派對，並邀請大家參加，因此答案應選(A)。

第三段第一行的respite與下列何者意思最接近？
(A) 尊敬
(B) 僱用
(C) 娛樂
(D) 休息

【類型】同義字題型

【詞彙】
respite休息／
respect尊敬／
employment雇用／
entertainment娛樂／
rest休息

【正解】(D)

156 The word "respite" in paragraph 3, line 1, is closest in meaning to

(A) respect

(B) employment

(C) entertainment

(D) rest

【解析】respite表示「長期工作後的休息」，因此與rest「休息」意思最相近。因此答案應選(D)。

Questions 157-161 refer to the following letter.

Queen Square Accommodation Offer

Dear Monica Tsai,

Origin Amaze Co. is delighted to offer, on behalf of Florabridge Housing, the following accommodation at Rainbow Court. —[1] —

Room Type: double-bed studio
Rent: $160 per week

All rooms are offered and accepted on the basis of single occupation as of the start date of the tenancy on September 3, 2017. If you wish to accept this offer, you must pay the reservation fee by July 3, 2017, otherwise this offer will be withdrawn. —[2]— Your room is not reserved until you have made your payment.

—[3]— Once you accept this offer of the room, the rent payment will be due as on the 5th of each month as set out in the tenancy contract. If you wish to move in later than September 3, 2017 or leave earlier than September 2, 2018, you will still have to pay the rent on a monthly basis unless you find a replacement tenant.

—[4]— Once you accept this offer, an email confirming your reservation will be sent to you and you will be required to complete the online induction before moving into your room. The room key will be ready for you to collect on arrival at the accommodation.

If you need more information, please go on our accommodation website at www.originamaze.com/benefits.

Origin Amaze Co.

皇后城公寓住宿錄取通知

親愛的Monica Tsai：

Origin Amaze公司非常高興代表Florabridge房屋公司通知您錄取了以下在Rainbow Court的住宿。

房型：雙人床公寓式套房
租金：每週160元

所有的房間都是從2017年9月3日起以單人間的形式出租的。如果您欲接受這個條件，您必須在2017年7月3日前將訂金繳清，否則我們將取消您的資格。在您付清款項之前您的房間都不會被預約。

一旦您接受了這個入住資格，房租如同租約記載的需在每個月的5號繳交。如果您要在2017年9月3日之後入住或在2018年9月2日之前搬離，您仍需要每個月繳清房租，除非您找到頂替您的人。

一旦您接受了這個入住資格，您會接收到一封確認預約的電子郵件，而您必須在入住之前辦妥線上入住手續。房間鑰匙會在您到達宿舍當天供您領取。

如果您需要更多資訊，請上我們的宿舍官網www.originamaze.com/benefits。

Origin Amaze公司 敬上

雙人套房的房租每個月多少錢？
(A) 160元
(B) 320元
(C) 480元
(D) 640元

【類型】尋找細節題型

【詞彙】
double-bed雙人床／
studio公寓式套房

【正解】(D)

157 How much is the rent for the double-bed studio per month?
(A) $160
(B) $320
(C) $480
(D) $640

【解析】根據文中細節Rent: $160 per week，表示「每週160元」，因此每月應該約為640元。因此答案應選(D)。

Monica如果要接受住宿資格的話必須做什麼？
(A) 付清訂金
(B) 付清月租
(C) 完成線上入住手續
(D) 在公司官網上登錄

【類型】尋找細節題型

【詞彙】
reservation預約／
fee費用／
monthly每月的／
induction入住；就任／
register註冊

【正解】(A)

158 What should Monica do to accept the offer?
(A) pay the reservation fee
(B) pay the monthly rent
(C) complete the online induction
(D) register on the company website

【解析】根據文中資訊If you wish to accept this offer, you must pay the reservation fee by July 3, 2017 otherwise this offer will be withdrawn.如果要接受入住資格，必須先繳清訂金。因此答案應選(A)。完成線上入住手續則是在入住之前必須完成的。

159 What should be done if one wishes to leave before the tenancy ends?

(A) pay an extra amount of rent

(B) find a replacement

(C) complete an online application

(D) contact the landlord

【解析】根據文中資訊If you wish to move in later than September 3, 2017 or leave earlier than September 2, 2018, you will still have to pay the rent on a monthly basis unless you find a replacement tenant.表示即使提前離宿，仍然需要交房租，除非找到替代人選。因此答案應選(B)。

如果有人想在租約到期之前離宿必須做什麼？

(A) 付額外的租金

(B) 找到替代的人

(C) 完成線上申請

(D) 聯繫房東

【類型】尋找細節題型

【詞彙】
amount數量／replacement取代／landlord房東

【正解】(B)

---

160 Which of the following statements is WRONG?

(A) The property is let on a one-year tenancy.

(B) The rent payment should be made in the beginning of each month.

(C) The room key will be sent to the tenant's current address.

(D) Monica is likely an employee in Origin Amaze Co.

【解析】根據文中資訊If you wish to move in later than September 3, 2017 or leave earlier than September 2, 2018, you will still have to pay the rent on a monthly basis unless you find a replacement tenant.我們能推測租約可能是從2017年9月3日起到2018年9月2日止。因此選項(A)正確。the rent payment will be due as on the 5th of each month as set out in the tenancy contract表示房租需在每個月5號繳清。因此選項(B)正確。Origin Amaze Co. is delighted to offer, on behalf of Florabridge Housing, the following accommodation at Rainbow Court.由此句我們能推測Monica很可能是Origin Amaze公司的員工，而公司與Florabridge房屋公司合作提供員工的宿舍。因此選項(D)正確。The room key will be ready for you to collect on arrival at the accommodation. 則透露房間鑰匙在房客到達當天才能領取，並不會寄到房客當前的住址。因此選項(C)為非。

下列敘述何者錯誤？

(A) 房屋是以一年期出租的。

(B) 房租需在月初繳清。

(C) 房間鑰匙會寄到租屋人目前的地址。

(D) Monica可能是Origin Amaze公司的員工。

【類型】是非題型

【詞彙】
statement敘述／
property不動產／
current目前的

【正解】(C)

"The tenancy is for a fixed length"這個句子最適合放在[1], [2], [3], [4]哪個位置？

(A) [1]

(B) [2]

(C) [3]

(D) [4]

【類型】句子插入題型

【詞彙】

fixed固定的／

length長度

【正解】(C)

★ 161 In which of the positions marked [1], [2], [3] and [4] does the following sentence best belong? "The tenancy is for a fixed length"

(A) [1]

(B) [2]

(C) [3]

(D) [4]

【解析】本句意思為「租約為固定時程的」。因此我們必須尋找與本句信息相關的段落插入。[1]所在的段落表達恭賀錄取住宿資格。[2]所在的段落是有關預約費的繳交。[3]所在的段落是有關租約的固定時程。[4]所在的段落是有關線上辦理入住。因此答案應選(C)。

Questions 162-166 refer to the following information.

Room Bookings Information

The information below relates to room bookings in Northwest Technology Park in Shanghai during the term of 2016-2017. The regulations may be subject to change due to the availability of particular rooms, national holidays and inclement weather.

• Regular weekly bookings
For evening sports sessions, we have given a set of usernames and passwords for weekly bookings to the session leaders. All your need to do is to log into our online system where you can amend, add notes to, or cancel your bookings. Most in-door activities will be usually held in the Richmond Rooms. All the other outdoor sports events will be held at the court east off the Richmond Rooms.

Please be aware that the Richmond Rooms will be used for the ID office bimonthly meeting every other month. Exact dates to be confirmed.

• Special events
Special events can be held at Woodland Room on the nights of Tuesday, Thursday, Friday and Saturday. When you place your bookings, you will be asked for some basic information regarding the purpose, duration and special requirements of your event. With the information, we will check the technical requirements, let you know the costs, any additional information we require and provided all is in order approve your booking.

場地預訂資訊

以下的資訊關於上海西北科技園區2016-2017年度的場地預定。所有的規定可能受到場地使用、國定假日和天氣因素的影響而改變。

• 每週一般預定
晚間運動課程的場地，我們已經將一組帳號密碼交給每星期預定場地的課程組長。你只要登入線上系統修改，增添或取消您的預定。大多數的室內活動通常都會在Richmond的房間舉行。其他的室外活動都會在Richmond大樓東邊的球場舉行。

請知悉每兩週Richmond大樓的房間都會被ID辦公室用作雙月會的場地。確切的日期還未定。

• 特殊活動
特殊活動可以在星期二、星期四、星期五及星期六的晚上在Woodland樓舉辦。預定時，我們會詢問一些基本資訊，包括活動目的，時長和特殊需求。根據這些資訊，我們會確認一些技術上的要求，通知你所需費用，詢問任何必要的資訊，如果一切就緒，我們便可批准你的預定。

如果我們認為技術需求過於複雜，你可能需要親自與科技後勤部門面談。如果我們認為你的要求不恰當，我們會與你聯繫討論更深入的作法。

更多關於技術設備的收費和援助可以從活動組詢問到。

If we think the technical requirement is of too much complexity, you may be required to meet with the Tech and Logistics Team. If we think your requirement is inappropriate, we will be in contact to discuss details and further advice.

More information about charges for technical equipment and support can be obtained from the events team.

【詞彙】
book預訂／relate有關／term期／regulation規定／subject to受制於／due to由於／availability可取得性／particular特定的／inclement惡劣的／regular普通的／session課程／username使用名稱／password密碼／amend更改／activity活動／outdoor戶外的／court球場／aware知道的／bimonthly每兩個月的／exact準確的／confirm確認／duration長度／requirement需求／provided假設／in order整理好的／approve同意／technical技術上的／complexity複雜度／logistics後勤／inappropriate不合適的／charge收費／equipment設備／obtain獲得

下列何種資訊沒有提供？
(A) 房間名稱
(B) 房間可預約的時間
(C) 房間預訂步驟
(D) 取消預訂政策

【類型】是非題型

【詞彙】
directions步驟／
cancellation取消

【正解】(D)

162 Which of the following information is NOT provided?

(A) The names of the rooms

(B) The available time of the rooms

(C) The directions for booking the rooms

(D) The cancellation policies

【解析】根據文中資訊、房間名稱，可預約時間以及預訂步驟都在細項裡有提及。而取消政策並沒有被提到，因此答案應選 (D)。

163 Which may NOT be the cause of the regulations being altered?

(A) storms

(B) departmental meetings

(C) the complexity of the event

(D) bank holidays

【解析】根據文中資訊The regulations may be subject to change due to the availability of particular rooms, national holidays and inclement weather.會影響規定的因素有空間的使用、例假日與天氣因素,與活動複雜度無關,因此答案應選(C)。

下列何者不是預訂規定更改的原因?

(A) 暴雨

(B) 部門會議

(C) 活動複雜度

(D) 銀行例假日

【類型】是非題型

【詞彙】

cause原因／

regulation規定／

alter更改／

storm暴雨／

departmental部門的／

complexity複雜度

【正解】(C)

---

164 What is indicated about Richmond Rooms?

(A) They would be used for meetings.

(B) They are for special events.

(C) Most outdoor events are held in them.

(D) Registration forms are to be filled out at the venue.

【解析】根據文中資訊Please be aware that the Richmond Rooms will be used for the ID office bimonthly meeting every other month. Exact dates to be confirmed.表示該場地會被用作會議室。而特殊活動是在Woodland Room舉行。戶外活動是在Richmond的東側戶外舉辦。而文中提到場地申請是在線上完成。因此答案應選(A)。

關於Richmond樓房間的敘述何者正確?

(A) 會議會在裡面舉行。

(B) 用來舉辦特殊活動。

(C) 大部分的戶外活動在裡面舉辦。

(D) 申請表必須當場填妥。

【類型】尋找細節題型

【詞彙】

outdoor戶外的／

registration申請／

fill out填寫／

venue場地

【正解】(A)

為什麼預訂特殊活動場地時需要提供某些資訊？
(A) 為了確認活動主辦人的身份
(B) 為了確認費用準時交齊
(C) 為了確認場地的技術需求
(D) 為了通知活動主辦人最新的場地出租政策

【類型】尋找細節題型

【詞彙】
identity身份／
organizer主辦者／
ensure確保／
prepayment預付款／
in time即時／
technical技術的／
update更新／
hire租用／policy政策

【正解】(C)

如果活動需求過於複雜會發生什麼事？
(A) 活動會被取消。
(B) 活動主辦者需要繳交罰金。
(C) 活動主辦人需要與後勤組討論。
(D) 需要填寫額外的申請文件。

【類型】尋找細節題型

【詞彙】
requirement需求／
complicated複雜的／
financial財務的／
penalty處罰／
additional額外的／
paperwork文件

【正解】(C)

---

165 Why would some information be required when booking for special events?

(A) To check the identity of the event organizer

(B) To ensure the prepayment is made in time

(C) To check for the technical requirements of the rooms

(D) To update the organizers on the latest room hire policy

【解析】根據文中資訊When you place your bookings, you will be asked for some basic information regarding the purpose, duration and special requirements of your event. With the information, we will check the technical requirements...。表示場地方需要進一步的資訊來確定場地的技術需求。因此答案應選(C)。

166 What would happen if the requirement of the event is too complicated?

(A) The event will need to be cancelled.

(B) The organizer will face a financial penalty.

(C) The organizer will have to discuss with the logistics team.

(D) Additional paperwork will need to be completed.

【解析】根據文中資訊If we think the technical requirement is of too much complexity, you may be required to meet with the Tech and Logistics Team.表示活動主辦者必須與科技後勤組討論協商。因此答案應選(C)。

Questions 167-171 refer to the following information.

Happy Holidays Everyone!

It's that time of year to start spreading holiday cheer! One of the fun ways to do this is through our departmental Secret Santa gift exchange. Last year those of us who participated had a blast (just ask any of us), and this year I have a feeling we'll have even more fun (we certainly deserve it)!!! To sign up, please follow the instructions below:

• Find the special box in Office 303 and take a form beside it. On this form write your name and 3 things that you would like to receive from your Secret Santa (ex. socks, mugs, wine, chocolate, Star Wars stuff, face masks, whatever you fancy). There is no guarantee that you will get all of these things—it's just to give your special someone some ideas. —[1]—

• The budget is $60, so keep that in mind when listing your items. Fold the form and put it into the box by Wednesday, December 6th. —[2]—

• Write your name on the sign-up sheet.

• Secret Santas will be randomly chosen on Thursday, December 7th.

假期愉快！

又到了散播歡樂散播愛的佳節時期。過節的最佳選擇就是參加本部門的小天使小主人交換禮物遊戲。去年參加的人玩得可開心了，不信可以去問他們。今年我感覺會更好玩喔！我們應得的！報名説明如下：

• 在303辦公室找到那只特別的箱子，在箱子旁邊拿一張表格。填入你的名字和三樣你想要小天使送你的禮物，例如：襪子、馬克杯、酒、巧克力、星際大戰的東西、面膜或任何想要的東西。你不一定能拿到你想要的東西，只是給你的小天使一些想法罷了。

• 預算為60元。在想禮物的時候稍微考慮一下金額。把表格折起來放到箱子裡。截止日期為12月6日星期三。

• 在報名表上填上姓名。

• 小天使會在12月7日星期四隨機決定。

那麼你們究竟是報名什麼樣的活動呢？讓我直接告訴你：

小天使小主人的遊戲會在12月18日星期一開始。從星期一（12/18）到星期三（12/20），你每天要給你的小天使一些小禮物，像是糖果，襪子等等，還要給一些奇怪的線索，讓他們猜猜你是誰。你可以透過尋寶遊戲或是公司內的神祕角落來達到這點，發揮你們的創意！

12月21日星期四時，在第三和第四節時段，我們會舉辦小天使揭露派對。這時候我們就會猜出我們狡猾的同事是誰了，並且能從他們手上得到最大禮。為維持匿名性，我們會安排一個地方讓你們偷偷地在星期四的派對之前放禮物。

越多人參加越好玩！希望會有大驚喜喔。但不要有壓力。祝大家假期愉快，E-bay採購愉快！

So what are you signing up for exactly? Let me give it to you straight:

For those who choose to participate, the Secret Santa festivities will commence on Monday, December 18th. From Monday (Dec 18) to Wednesday (Dec 20), you will give your Secret Santa small gifts (candy, socks, etc.) each day, along with **quirky** clues so they can slowly try to guess who you are. —[3]— Be creative!

On Thursday, December 21st during 3rd and 4th periods, we will have our Secret Santa revealing party. This is where we will guess our sneaky co-workers and receive the 'biggest' gift from them. To remain anonymous, there will be a location where you can stealthily drop your gift off sometime during the week before Thursday's party. —[4]—

This is especially merry the more people that participate, so hopefully there's a great turn out (no pressure)!

Happy Holidays and Happy E-bay Hunting!
Danielle

【詞彙】

spread散步／departmental部門的／exchange交換／participate參加／have a blast玩得愉快／certainly一定／deserve應得／sign up報名／instruction說明／form表格／mug馬克杯／fancy想要／guarantee保證／budget預算／list列出／randomly隨機地／straight直接地／festivity節慶活動／commence開始／quirky奇怪的／creative有創意的／reveal顯露／sneaky狡猾的／remain保持／anonymous匿名的／stealthily偷偷地／especially特別地／merry快樂的／pressure壓力

167 What holiday is the event most likely for?

(A) Chinese New Year

(B) Summer Bank Holiday

(C) Easter Monday

(D) Christmas Day

【解析】根據文中關鍵字眼Santa，我們可以判斷這個活動最有可能是聖誕節的活動，因此答案應選(D)。

這個活動最有可能是為了什麼節日？

(A) 中國新年

(B) 夏季的銀行例假日

(C) 復活節星期一

(D) 聖誕節

【類型】尋找主旨題型

【詞彙】
Easter復活節

【正解】(D)

168 Who will be the Secret Santas?

(A) The department officers

(B) Danielle

(C) Everyone who doesn't sign up

(D) Yet to be confirmed

【解析】根據文中資訊On Thursday, December 21st during 3rd and 4th periods, we will have our Secret Santa revealing party. This is where we will guess our sneaky co-workers and receive the 'biggest' gift from them.告訴我們神秘的小天使在12月21日才會公佈，因此答案應選(D)。

小天使是誰？

(A) 部門職員

(B) Danielle

(C) 每個沒報名的人

(D) 還未決定

【類型】尋找細節題型

【詞彙】
yet還未／
confirm確認

【正解】(D)

169 When will the Secret Santa activity begin?

(A) On December 6

(B) On December 7

(C) On December 18

(D) On December 21

【解析】根據文中資訊For those who choose to participate, the Secret Santa festivities will commence on Monday, December 18th.因此答案應選(C)。

小天使小主人活動何時開始？

(A) 12月6日

(B) 12月7日

(C) 12月18日

(D) 12月21日

【類型】尋找細節題型

【詞彙】
activity活動

【正解】(C)

"This can be done via scavenger hunt or secret placements around the company."這個句子最適合放在[1], [2], [3], [4]哪個位置？
(A) [1]
(B) [2]
(C) [3]
(D) [4]

【類型】句子插入題型

【詞彙】
position位置／
scavenger清道夫／
hunt狩獵／
placement位置

【正解】(C)

★ 170 In which of the positions marked [1], [2], [3] and [4] does the following sentence best belong? "This can be done via scavenger hunt or secret placements around the company."
(A) [1]
(B) [2]
(C) [3]
(D) [4]

【解析】本句表示「你可以透過尋寶遊戲或是公司內的神秘角落來達到這點。」與前句you will give your Secret Santa small gifts (candy, socks, etc.) each day, along with quirky clues so they can slowly try to guess who you are.表示「給你的小天使一些暗示」有關。而本句提供了一些意見和辦法，提到舉例子的效果。因此答案應選(C)。

第二段第五行的quirky與下列何者意思最接近？
(A) 奇怪的
(B) 快速的
(C) 暴怒的
(D) 直接的

【類型】同義字題型

【詞彙】
quirky奇怪的／
peculiar奇怪的／
rapid快速的／
furious憤怒的／
straightforward直接的

【正解】(A)

171 The word "quirky" in paragraph 2, line 5, is closest in meaning to
(A) peculiar
(B) rapid
(C) furious
(D) straightforward

【解析】quirky與peculiar都表示「奇怪的」的意思，因此答案應選(A)。

Questions 172-175 refer to the following message.

Dear employees,

This is a reminder that the common room located on the 2nd floor of the Senate Hall is an area restricted for the income house and health center staff use only and therefore should not be being used as a break facility by Beacon House administrators.

Please be advised that Beacon House administrators have access to the ground floor foyer within the Beacon House to use as a break/recreational area, and are welcome to use other locations within the office building including, and not restricted to, the Hawthorns and Broomhill House café. There is also a café and group meeting facilities available for all staff within the Staff Union (Tyndall Building).

Many thanks in advance.
With best wishes,

Tara Thorne

【詞彙】
reminder提醒／common room交誼廳／locate位於／restrict限制／income收入／staff員工／therefore因此／break休息／facility設施／administrator行政人員／advise建議／access管道／foyer大廳／recreational休閒的／in advance事先

親愛的員工，

在此提醒大家Senate大樓二樓的交誼廳只限於財務部以及健康中心的職員使用，因此Beacon House的行政人員沒有權限使用該場地作為休息場所。

Beacon House的行政職員可以使用Beacon House的一樓大廳作為休息區，並歡迎使用辦公樓內的其他區域，如：Hawthorns樓和Broomhill樓的咖啡廳，可使用區域不限於以上區域。在員工協會（Tyndall樓）也有供全體員工使用的咖啡廳和群組會議室。

感謝大家
祝 萬事順心

Tara Thorne

這則訊息的主旨為何？
(A) 說明特定員工的休息區
(B) 提醒員工每週活動
(C) 提醒即將進行的施工
(D) 宣傳新開的咖啡廳

【類型】尋找主旨題型

【詞彙】
make clear釐清／
rest area休息區／
certain特定的／remind提醒／
weekly每週的／activity活動／
notice通知／
construction施工／
carry out進行／
advertise廣告／
newly新

【正解】(A)

172 Why is this message sent?
    (A) To make clear the rest area for certain staff
    (B) To remind staff of the weekly activities
    (C) To notice the construction to be carried out
    (D) To advertise the newly built café

【解析】根據本文的首句及各段強調的重點，內容都是圍繞員工休息區域的劃分說明。因此答案應選(A)。

財務部的員工可以使用哪一個區域？
(A) Senate Hall二樓
(B) Beacon House的一樓大廳
(C) Hawthorns樓
(D) Broomhill House咖啡廳

【類型】尋找細節題型

【詞彙】
foyer大廳

【正解】(A)

173 Which area can income house staff use?
    (A) 2nd floor of Senate Hall
    (B) ground floor foyer at Beacon House
    (C) Hawthorns House
    (D) Broomhill House café

【解析】根據本文的首句This is a reminder that the common room located on the 2nd floor of the Senate Hall is an area restricted for the income house and health center staff use only表示財務部的員工和健康中心的員工可以使用的是Senate Hall的二樓區。因此答案應選(A)。

174 Which area can be accessed by all staff?

(A) Hawthorns House

(B) Broomhill House café

(C) Tyndall Building café

(D) Beacon House common room

【解析】根據There is also a café and group meeting facilities available for all staff within the Staff Union (Tyndall Building). 因此答案應選(C)。

哪一個區域供全體員工使用？

(A) Hawthorns樓

(B) Broomhill樓咖啡廳

(C) Tyndall樓咖啡廳

(D) Beacon House交誼廳

【類型】尋找細節題型

【詞彙】

access使用／

common room交誼廳

【正解】(C)

175 Which can be inferred from this message?

(A) Some Beacon House administrators have used the Senate House the common room.

(B) Some health center staff have used the break facility on the ground floor foyer at Beacon House.

(C) The Tyndall Building café has been refurbished recently.

(D) The Senate House common room will soon be closed for renovation.

【解析】根據This is a reminder that the common room located on the 2nd floor of the Senate Hall is an area restricted for the income house and health center staff use only and therefore should not be being used as a break facility by Beacon House administrators.我們可以推斷某些Beacon House的行政職員可能最近使用了Senate Hall二樓的員工休息設施，因此官方才寄出了此信通知大家。因此答案應選(A)。

從本訊息我們可以推斷？

(A) 某些Beacon House的行政職員使用了Senate House的交誼廳。

(B) 某些健康中心的員工使用了Beacon House一樓大廳的休息設施。

(C) Tyndall樓的咖啡廳最近在翻修。

(D) Senate House的交誼廳很快會關閉翻新。

【類型】推理題型

【詞彙】

facility設施／

refurbish翻修／

renovation翻新

【正解】(A)

Motorway租車

Motorway租車給你兩萬五千台租車選擇與各式各樣的高品質車種。我們幫助你從各大租車平台找到最佳價格，並幫助你在世界各個角落，包括東京、上海、台北、阿姆斯特丹、倫敦、巴黎、柏林和米蘭，找到你需要的車子。加入Motorway租車會員，享有首次租車五折優惠。今天就在Motorway租車吧！

| **50%
租車
五折** | 複製此碼：
TR82016於租車時使用
註冊後一個月內有效。
全世界各點有效。
找車！比價！
省荷包！ |

我們等了一個小時才等到我們想要的車。飛機半夜之後才到達，我們都很累了。如果服務能再快一點會更好。

Ryan留言

我覺得這個網站對使用者還不夠便利。當我取消預訂的時候，我沒有立即收到確認信。因此，我的信用卡要過三到五天後才能重設完成，所以我在下新訂單之前都必須浪費這段時間。

Danielle留言

Motorway Car

Motorway Car Rental offers you 25,000 cars and various types of quality vehicles. We will help you dig out the best deals from the leading rental agents and find the car you need from various corners of the world such as Tokyo, Shanghai, Taipei, Amsterdam, London, Paris, Berlin and Milan. Become a member of Motorway Car Rental and win a 50% off discount off your first car hire. Book your rental car through Motorway Car Rental Today.

| **50%
off your car
hire** | Copy this code: TR82016 and use it at checkout.
Valid within one month after registration.
Valid for all destinations worldwide.
Search, compare and Save! |

We had to wait about an hour when we arrived to get the car we wanted. We were tired after the flight arrived after midnight. We would have appreciated it to be a little bit faster.

From Ryan

I don't think the website is user-friendly enough. As I canceled my booking, I didn't get the confirmation email right away. Because of that, my credit card had to be re-credited in three to five days, so I had to wait for that before putting a new booking.

From Danielle

I was traveling in Paris, but my location was directed to London's site, costing valuable time, and my plans were delayed afterwards.

From Austin

我當時在巴黎,但定位卻定到了倫敦的位置。浪費了寶貴的時間,我之後的計劃也因此延誤了。

Austin留言

【詞彙】

rental租用／offer提供／various各類的／quality高品質的／vehicle車／dig挖／deal交易／agent仲介／discount折扣／hire租用／through透過／code碼／valid有效的／registration註冊／destination目的／worldwide世界各地／flight班機／appreciate感激／user friendly方便使用這的／confirmation確認／direct指引／site地址／valuable寶貴的／afterwards後來

---

176 What is Motorway Car?

(A) an automobile manufacturer

(B) a travel agency

(C) a car dealing company

(D) an online car rental platform

【解析】根據廣告中的資訊We will help you dig out the best deals from the leading rental agents我們能得知Motorway是幫助消費者從各大租車平台中選出最佳的租車價格,因此是一個租車的平台。因此答案應選(D)。

Motorway租車是什麼?

(A) 一間汽車製造商

(B) 一間旅行社

(C) 一間售車行

(D) 一個線上租車平台

【類型】尋找主旨題型

【詞彙】

automobile汽車／

manufacturer製造商／

deal販售／

platform平台

【正解】(D)

消費者在下列哪一個城市使用不到Motorway租車的服務？

(A) 台北

(B) 柏林

(C) 墨爾本

(D) 米蘭

【類型】尋找細節題型

【詞彙】

customer消費者

【正解】(C)

下列對於優惠券的描述何者正確？

(A) 只有舊會員才能得到。

(B) 消費者需要密碼才能使用該優惠券。

(C) 只有在亞洲國家有效。

(D) 它提供新會員一次免費租車的服務。

【類型】是非題型

【詞彙】

coupon優惠券／

retain獲得／

valid有效的／

hire租用

【正解】(B)

177 In which of the following cities can't customers enjoy Motorway Car's service?

(A) Taipei

(B) Berlin

(C) Melbourne

(D) Milan

【解析】根據廣告中的資訊find the car you need from various corners of the world such as Tokyo, Shanghai, Taipei, Amsterdam, London, Paris, Berlin and Milan.其中並沒有墨爾本，因此答案應選(C)。

178 Which of the following is TRUE of the coupon?

(A) It can only be retained by an old member.

(B) Customers will need a code to use the coupon.

(C) It is only valid in Asian countries.

(D) It offers one free car hire to new members.

【解析】根據廣告以及優惠券中的資訊，Become a member of Motorway Car Rental and win a 50% off discount off your first car hire.我們能得知，新註冊的會員才享有此優惠折扣。因此選項(A)為非。Copy this code: TR82016 and use it at checkout.表示需要代碼才能使用。因此選項(B)正確。Valid for all destinations worldwide.表示世界各地的服務點都有效，因此選項(C)為非。而新會員註冊是享有五折優惠，而非免費租車。因此選項(D)為非。

179 Who most likely are Ryan, Danielle and Austin?

(A) Motorway Car customers

(B) Motorway Car agents

(C) Motorway Car co-founders

(D) Motorway Car officers

【解析】根據最後一篇文中資訊，我們能發現這三位發表的都是對Motorway租車服務的評價，因此我們合理推測他們都是使用過該平台服務的消費者。因此答案應選(A)。

Ryan, Danielle and Austin最有可能是誰？

(A) Motorway租車的消費者

(B) Motorway租車的仲介

(C) Motorway租車的共同創辦人

(D) Motorway租車的職員

【類型】推理題型

【詞彙】
agent仲介／
co-founder共同創辦人

【正解】(A)

---

180 What is Danielle's major complaint?

(A) The car arrived late.

(B) The car's quality was poor.

(C) The booking system was slow.

(D) The information provided was not accurate.

【解析】根據最後一篇文中資訊As I canceled my booking, I didn't get the confirmation email right away. Because of that, my credit card had to be re-credited in three to five days, so I had to wait for that before putting a new booking.表示系統運作緩慢，導致時間的浪費。因此答案應選(C)。

Danielle主要的不滿是什麼？

(A) 車子晚到了。

(B) 車子品質低劣。

(C) 預訂系統緩慢。

(D) 系統提供的資訊不準確。

【類型】尋找細節題型

【詞彙】
major主要的／
complaint抱怨／
quality品質／
accurate準確的

【正解】(C)

機場捷運
今天開始營運

Irene Kramer撰寫
2015年9月11日

經過了十年的規劃,建造與測試,Bath Mead的機場捷運今天正式開啟營運。根據稍早的官方新聞稿,Bath Mead機場捷運公司於營運後兩個月內提供乘客所有票種六折優惠。

機場捷運連結了Bath Mead中心商業區的幾個主要節點,如:丹麥購物中心,市政廳,紀念碑廣場,與Bath Mead國際機場的每個航站樓。與過去必須搭乘九十分鐘的機場巴士相比,現在乘客可以只花二十五分鐘就能往返Bath Mead與機場。

在玉山站、香草路站與機場公園站提供各家航空的行李托運登記服務。行李托運必須於飛機起飛前三個小時完成辦理。各家航空的資訊都可在上述車站的登記櫃檯詢問得到。

Airport Link Opens for Operations Today

By Irene Kramer
11 September 2015

After 10 years of planning, construction and testing, Bath Mead's airport link officially opened for business today. According to the official news released just earlier, Bath Mead's Airport Link Corporation offers customers a discount of 40% off for all types of tickets during the first two months of the operation.

The airport line connects the major points in central business district of Bath Mead, such as Denmark Shopping Mall, City Hall and Monumental Square with each terminal of International Bath Mead Airport. Compared to having to spend ninety minutes on the Airport coach, passengers can now travel between Bath Mead and the airport for merely twenty-five minutes.

Luggage check-in services for a variety of airlines are also available at Mt. Jade station, Lavender Road station and Airport Park station. The check-in has to be carried out three hours before the flight leaves. Information about the regulations for all airlines can be found at the check-in counters at the aforementioned stations.

Standard Seat		
Children	Adult	Group
$14	$20	$15
Premium Seat		
Children	Adult	Group
$18	$30	$22

標準座		
兒童	成人	團體
14元	20元	15元
頭等座		
兒童	成人	團體
18元	30元	22元

Notice of Correction

The recent news release dated 11 September 2015 misidentified the ticket fares of Bath Mead Airport Link premium seat. According to the official information obtained from Bath Mead's Airport Link Corporation, the correct fares for premium seats are $20 for children, $34 for adults and $25 for groups. We are deeply sorry for the inconvenience.

更正通知

2015年9月11日發表的新聞稿對於Bath Mead機場捷運的頭等座票價資訊的報導出現錯誤。根據Bath Mead機場捷運公司的官方資訊，頭等座的正確票價為：兒童20元，成人34元，團體25元。造成任何不便我們深感抱歉。

【詞彙】
operation運行／construction建造／test測試／officially正式地／release發表／corporation公司／discount折扣／connect連結／central business district中心商業區／monumental紀念碑／terminal航站樓／coach長途巴士／merely只有／luggage行李／a variety of各式各樣的／regulation規定／counter櫃台／aforementioned前面提過的／premium頭等的／correction改正／misidentify誤報／obtain獲得／inconvenience不便之處

Irene Kramer是誰？
(A) 一位政府官員
(B) 一位機場捷運公司的代表
(C) 一名記者
(D) 一名乘客

【類型】推理題型

【詞彙】
delegate代表／
journalist記者

【正解】(C)

181 Who is Irene Kramer?

    (A) a government officer

    (B) a delegate from the airport link corporation

    (C) a journalist

    (D) a passenger

【解析】由於第一篇文章是一篇新聞稿，因此我們能推斷Irene Kramer是一位記者，因此答案應選(C)。

機場捷運的建造是從何時開始計畫的？
(A) 1995
(B) 2005
(C) 2010
(D) 2015

【類型】尋找細節題型

【詞彙】
construction建造／
plan規劃

【正解】(B)

182 Since when has the airport link construction been planned?

    (A) 1995

    (B) 2005

    (C) 2010

    (D) 2015

【解析】根據新聞稿中的時間與第一句話After 10 years of planning, construction and testing, Bath Mead's airport link officially opened for business today.我們可推斷機場捷運是在這篇報導發出的時間2015年往前推的十年前的時候開始規劃的，因此為2005年。

183 What is TRUE of the airport link?

(A) It majorly connects the rural areas to the airport.

(B) It takes an hour and a half to get to the airport from the city center.

(C) Passengers can check in their luggage at certain stations.

(D) Passengers can check in their luggage three days prior to flight departure.

【解析】根據新聞中的資訊The airport line connects the major points in central business district of Bath Mead表示捷運是連結了機場與中心商業區的地點，而非鄉下地區。因此選項(A)為非。passengers now can travel between Bath Mead and the airport for merely twenty-five minutes.表示往返Bath Mead與機場只需25分鐘，因此選項(B)為非。Luggage check-in services for a variety of airlines are also available at Mt. Jade station, Lavender Road station and Airport Park station. 表示行李托運服務可在以上三個車站辦理，因此選項(C)正確。The check-in has to be carried out three hours before the flight leaves.表示行李托運必須在飛機起飛前三小時辦理，因此選項(D)為非。

關於機場捷運何者正確？
(A) 它連結了機場與鄉下地區。
(B) 從市區到機場需要一個半小時。
(C) 乘客可在指定車站辦理行李托運。
(D) 乘客可在班機起飛三天前辦理行李托運。

【類型】是非題型

【詞彙】
connect連結／
rural鄉下的／
luggage行李／
certain特定的／
prior to之前／
departure離開

【正解】(C)

---

184 During the first month of its operation, what is the fare for an adult's standard seat ticket?

(A) $8
(B) $12
(C) $14
(D) $20

【解析】根據新聞中的資訊與票價資訊，營運後的首兩個月內票價為原價的60%。因此原價20元的票價打折後為12元。因此答案應選(B)。

在機場捷運營運的第一個月內，一張成人標準座的票價為何？
(A) 8元
(B) 12元
(C) 14元
(D) 20元

【類型】推理題型

【詞彙】
fare車費／
standard標準的

【正解】(B)

本通知主要是關於什麼？

(A) 最近的票價更動

(B) 先前新聞中的錯誤資訊

(C) 機場捷運的營運

(D) 優惠的截止日期

【類型】尋找主旨題型

【詞彙】

adjustment調整／error錯誤／

previous先前的／discount折扣

【正解】(B)

185 What is the notice mainly about?

(A) the recent fare adjustment

(B) the errors in the previous news

(C) the operation of the airport link

(D) the end date of the discount offer

【解析】根據最後一篇公告的內容表示，先前的新聞稿將頭等座的票價誤寫了。因此答案應選(B)。

★**Questions 186-190 refer to the following information, chart, email.**

Project Material Request

Please be aware that the application of project materials for the winter term will be open from 15 November to 8 December. As usual, the budget limit for each department is $500. If your request is over the limit, we cannot accept it. To save time, I would like each department to control their budget within the limit before submitting your request since it would take extra time to handle the rejection and resubmitting process. Plus, according to our record, it usually takes a long time before our supplier, Mr. Morris, quotes to us. Therefore, in order to be able to distribute the resources to everyone by the end of this year, I would like you to send your request list to me no later than the deadline, 8 December. Please note that no late submission is accepted.

With regard to the form of the request list, please specify the number of each item you need, the specific name of the item and most importantly, the department for which you are requesting. You still need to put the item in the list even if we already have it in storage. As soon as the materials arrive, we will contact the department individually. If you have any questions, feel free to contact me by marydublin@mail.2010.us.

Mary Dublin

專案材料申請

通知大家本次冬季專案材料從11月15日到12月8日期間開放申請。與先前一樣，每個部門的預算限制為500元。如果你的申請超過預算，我們無法接受。為了節省時間，請每個部門在呈交申請之前先控制好預算，因為處理駁回和重交的流程又會耗掉很長時間。再者，為了在年底前將材料分發給各位，希望各位在截止日期12月8日前將需求單傳給我。請注意逾期不受理。

關於需求單的格式，請標明你需要的每項物品的數量，確切的名稱，最重要的，申請使用的部門名稱。即使你申請的物品在我們的庫存已經有了，你也要列入表中。一旦材料到了，我會個別通知每個部門。如果你有任何問題，請不吝透過marydublin@mail.2010.us與我聯繫。

Mary Dublin

Item	Number	Price per unit	Total
Twin adhesive tape	30	$1.1	$33
Craft paper	200	$0.6	$120
Crepe paper	50	$1	$50
Pipe cleaner	50	$0.3	$15
Wild flower seed	2	$12.5	$25
Color paint	10	$50	$500

Requested by Jeremy Zhong
Date: 7 December 2016

品項	數量	單價	總價
雙面膠	30	$1.1	$33
硬卡紙	200	$0.6	$120
皺紙	50	$1	$50
毛根	50	$0.3	$15
野花種子	2	$12.5	$25
水彩	10	$50	$500

Jeremy Zhong申請
日期: 2016年12月7日

Project Material Request
From: Jeremy Zhong
To: Mary Dublin
Cc: Kathryn Culhane
Date: 7 December 2016

Dear Mary,

I have sent you the request form just earlier this afternoon. Please check. The total price is a little bit over the limit. However, I understand that you have the color paints in stock as you told me last time I dropped by your office, so I assume that will not go into our estimated budget. As for the craft paper, can we get it in different colors?

Thank you.
Jeremy

專案材料申請
寄件人: Jeremy Zhong
收件人: Mary Dublin
副本: Kathryn Culhane
日期: 2016年12月7日

Mary您好,

我今天下午剛把需求表寄給你了。請查收。總價稍微超出了預算。我記得我上次到你辦公室時你上次告訴我庫存還有水彩,所以我想這應該不會算到預算額內。至於卡紙,我們可以要不同顏色的嗎?

感謝你

Jeremy

project專案／material材料／request申請／aware知道的／application申請／term期／as usual如同往常／budget預算／limit限制／department部門／submit呈交／handle處理／rejection駁回／resubmit重新呈交／process流程／supplier供應商／quote報價／distribute分發／resource資源／submission呈交／with regard to有關／specify標明／storage倉庫／individually個別地／twin adhesive tape雙面膠／craft paper卡紙／crepe paper皺紙／pipe cleaner毛根／wild野生的／seed種子／unit單位／drop by路過／assume假設／estimate預估

Morris先生是誰？
(A) 一位辦公室助理
(B) 一位部門職員
(C) 一位文具供應商
(D) 一位貨車司機

【類型】推理題型

【詞彙】
assistant助理／
stationery文具／
supplier供應商／
delivery配送

【正解】(C)

186 Who is Mr. Morris?

(A) an office assistant

(B) a department officer

(C) a stationery supplier

(D) a delivery driver

【解析】根據第一篇文中Plus, according to our record, it usually takes a long time before our supplier, Mr. Morris, quotes to us. Morris先生負責報價，我們能判斷Morris先生很有可能是一位文具供應商。

187 When can the requested materials be given to the departments?

(A) by 8 December, 2016

(B) by 15 November, 2016

(C) by 22 December, 2016

(D) by 31 December, 2016

【解析】根據第一篇文中in order to be able to distribute the resources to everyone by the end of this year我們能得知在年底之前材料能交給各個部門。因此答案應選(D)。

申請的材料何時能交給個部門？
(A) 2016年12月8日前
(B) 2016年12月15日前
(C) 2016年12月22日前
(D) 2016年12月31日前

【類型】尋找細節題型

【詞彙】
request申請

【正解】(D)

---

188 Which of the following is CORRECT?

(A) The submission should be made by the end of December.

(B) The name of the department supervisor should be written down.

(C) The budget cannot be over $100.

(D) Mr. Morris is often slow to handle the quotation.

【解析】根據第一篇文中資訊Please be aware that the application of project materials for the winter term will be open from 15 November to 8 December.表示料申請的截止日期應是12月8日，而非十二月底，因此選項(A)為非。the department for which you are requesting表示申請人需要寫下申請的部門名稱，而非部門主管名稱，因此選項(B)為非。the budget limit for each department is $500表示每個部門的預算是500元，而非100元，因此選項(C)為非。根據according to our record, it usually takes a long time before our supplier, Mr. Morris, quotes to us表示Morris先生通常報價都給得很慢。因此選項(D)正確。

下列何者正確？
(A) 材料申請需在十二月底之前完成。
(B) 部門主管的名字需要寫下來。
(C) 預算不能超過100元。
(D) Morris先生通常報價都很慢。

【類型】是非題型

【詞彙】
submission呈交／
supervisor主管／
budget預算／
quotation報價

【正解】(D)

Jeremy沒有做到哪一項申請規定？
(A) 標明他的部門名稱
(B) 標明所需的物品數量
(C) 標明物品名稱
(D) 準時呈交申請

【類型】尋找細節題型

【詞彙】
fail to未能做到／
meet符合／
requirement需求／
identify標明／
specify標明／
hand in繳交／
in time即時

【正解】(A)

Jeremy在信中提到了什麼？
(A) 卡紙庫存沒有貨了。
(B) 水彩庫存有貨。
(C) 雙面膠太貴了。
(D) 截止日期能否延遲。

【類型】尋找細節題型

【詞彙】
out of stock沒有存貨／
extend延期

【正解】(B)

---

189 What did Jeremy fail to do in meeting the submission requirements?

(A) identify his department

(B) specify the number of the item

(C) put down the items' names

(D) hand in the list in time

【解析】根據第二篇及第三篇文章，Jeremy都有標明申請的品項數量和名稱，並在12月7日就完成了申請，但並沒有標明部門的名稱。因此答案應選(A)。

190 What did Jeremy mention in his email?

(A) That the craft paper is out of stock

(B) That the color paints are in storage

(C) That the twin adhesive tapes are too expensive

(D) That if the deadline can be extended

【解析】根據第三篇電子郵件中信息I understand that you have the color paints in stock as you told me last time I dropped by your office表示水彩是有庫存的，因此答案應選(B)。

★**Questions 191-195 refer to the following emails and ticket.**

To: oxford-booking

From: Stefanie Wang

Subject: Refund Issue

To whom it may concern,

I purchased on your website five tickets for

① London to Cambridge 6:45AM (via National Link)

② Cambridge day tour

③ Cambridge to London Evening Service

But unfortunately three of us are not able to go. Therefore, I was wondering if we could get a full refund for three of the tickets. I have attached the tickets I bought as proof of purchase. Hope to hear from you soon. Thank you.

Stefanie

收件人：oxford-booking

寄件人：Stefanie Wang

主旨：退費問題

給相關人員

我在你們網站上買了五張票券：

① 倫敦到劍橋 早上6:45 搭乘全國連通

② 劍橋一日遊券

③ 劍橋到倫敦 晚間班車

但很不幸的是我們有三個人沒有辦法去了。因此，我想請問我們能否要回三張票券的全額退費呢？我在附檔夾帶了我購買的票券作為證明。希望盡快得到您的回覆。感謝。

Stefanie

收件人: Stefanie Wang
寄件人: oxford-booking
主旨: 回覆：退費問題

Stefanie您好：
我已經將三張票券的費用退到您的帳戶。需要5到6天才能匯到您的戶頭。
因此目前只有兩張票券是有效的，包括倫敦班車，劍橋班車以及劍橋一日遊券。
期待您下次搭乘。

祝 愉快
Molly Yang

To: Stefanie Wang
From: oxford-booking
Subject: Re: Refund Issue

Hi Stefanie,

I have issued a refund to your account for three tickets. Please allow 5-6 working days for this to be processed.

Only two of these tickets will now be valid for your London transfers, Cambridge transfer and the Cambridge day tour.
Looking forward to welcoming you on board the tour.

Kind Regards,

Molly Yang

牛津訂票
票券
倫敦到劍橋 早上6:45 搭乘全國連通
8/23/17 06:45
學生票5張/ 來回

票券資訊
G01K7785S3
V16401K763000HBE3KQT

購買日期
8/7/17 20:01格林威治標準時間

56.30鎊

oxford-booking

TICKET
London to Cambridge 6:45AM (via National Link)
8/23/17 06:45
5 x Student / Return Rate

Ticket Information
G01K7785S3 V16401K763000HBE3KQT

Date of Purchase
8/7/17 20:01 GMT

£ 56.30

TICKET

Cambridge to London 18:15PM (via National Link)

8/27/17 06:45

5 x Student / Return Rate

Ticket Information

G01K7BF5S4 V16401K763000HBE3KQT

Date of Purchase

8/7/17 20:03 GMT

£ 56.30

- -

TICKET

Cambridge Day Tour Tour Only

8/24/17 10:00

5 x Student / Standard / Tour Only

Ticket Information

G01K7BF5S4 V16401K76390HBE3KQT

Date of Purchase

8/7/17 20:04 GMT

£ 60.00

票券

劍橋到倫敦 晚上18:15 搭乘全國連通

8/27/17 06:45

學生票5張／來回

票券資訊

G01K7BF5S4

V16401K763000HBE3KQT

購買日期

8/7/17 20:03格林威治標準時間

56.30鎊

- -

票券

劍橋一日遊 8/24/17

10:00 學生票5張／標準／旅遊券

票券資訊

G01K7BF5S4

V16401K76390HBE3KQT

購買日期

8/7/17 20:04格林威治標準時間

60.00鎊

【詞彙】

refund退費／concern有關／purchase購買／unfortunately不幸地／attach附帶／proof證明／issue核發／account帳戶／process處理／valid有效的／on board上車

第一封電子郵件的主旨是什麼？
(A) 詢問旅遊資訊
(B) 要求退費
(C) 預訂行程
(D) 預訂巴士座位

【類型】尋找主旨題型

【詞彙】
tour旅遊／
reserve預訂／
coach長途巴士

【正解】(B)

幾張票申請了退費？
(A) 一張
(B) 兩張
(C) 三張
(D) 五張

【類型】尋找細節題型

【詞彙】
refund退費

【正解】(C)

牛津訂票最有可能是什麼？
(A) 百貨公司
(B) 旅行社
(C) 地鐵公司
(D) 旅館

【類型】推理題型

【詞彙】
metro地鐵

【正解】(B)

---

191 Why was the first email sent?

(A) To ask for travel information

(B) To request a refund

(C) To book a tour

(D) To reserve a coach seat

【解析】根據第一封電郵內容Therefore, I was wondering if we could get a full refund for three of the tickets. 我們能得知此電郵是有關票券退費事宜。因此答案應選(B)。

---

192 How many tickets were refunded?

(A) one

(B) two

(C) three

(D) five

【解析】根據第一封電郵內容Therefore, I was wondering if we could get a full refund for three of the tickets.以及第二封電郵內容I have issued a refund to your account for three tickets. 表示三張票券已經成功退費了。因此答案應選(C)。

---

193 What most likely is Oxford-booking?

(A) a department store

(B) a travel agency

(C) a metro company

(D) a hotel

【解析】根據三篇文章內容，我們能得知牛津訂票提供的服務包含火車票預訂和旅遊票券預訂等。因此我們能推斷該公司是一間旅行社。因此答案應選(B)。

194 What is indicated about the tickets?

(A) They were bought at a railway station.

(B) They all became invalid.

(C) They were bought with a student discount.

(D) They were all train tickets.

關於票券的敘述何者正確？
(A) 票券都是從火車站買的。
(B) 票券全都失效了。
(C) 票券是以學生優惠買的。
(D) 票券全都是火車票。

【類型】是非題型

【詞彙】
invalid失效

【正解】(C)

【解析】根據三篇文章內容I purchased on your website five tickets for 表示所有票券都是在網站上買的，而非火車站，因此選項(A)為非。Only two of these tickets will now be valid...表示只有三張票券失效，因此選項(B)為非。5 x Student / Return Rate表示票券為學生票。因此選項(C)正確。而票券不僅有火車票，還有旅遊一日券。因此選項(D)為非。

195 Which of the following is INCORRECT?

(A) The train bound for Cambridge leaves in the morning.

(B) The tickets were purchased on the same day.

(C) The total cost of the tickets is £172.6

(D) One of the tickets is for London tour.

下列敘述何者不正確？
(A) 前往劍橋的火車於早晨出發。
(B) 這些票券都是在同一天買的。
(C) 這些票券總價172.6鎊。
(D) 其中一張是倫敦一日遊券。

【類型】是非題型

【詞彙】
bound for前往／
cost價錢

【正解】(D)

【解析】根據第三篇文章內容Cambridge Day Tour Tour Only 表示其中一張是劍橋一日遊券，而非倫敦一日遊券，因此選項(D)不正確。

關於影印餘額退費的問題
收件人: libraryadmin@york.ac.uk
寄件人: joanna09013@york.ac.uk

給相關人員：

我是就讀於教育學院的碩士生。由於我在九月初就會離開學校了，所以我的圖書館卡很快就會過期。
但是，我的卡裡面還有很多影印餘額，估計在我離校之前都沒有機會用完的。因此，我想要申請退費那些還沒使用的影印餘額。如果可以的話，我想知道退費需要多久時間，還有是不是退到我的銀行戶頭呢？謝謝。

Joanna Chang

Inquiry of print credit refund
To: libraryadmin@york.ac.uk
From: joanna09013@york.ac.uk

To anyone it may concern,

I am a master student in the school of education. Considering the fact that I will be leaving the university in early September, the validity of my library card will soon expire. However, there are still plenty of print credits left in the card, and I doubt there will be a chance for me to use up the remaining credits by the time I leave. Therefore, I would like to request a refund of the unused credits. If this is doable, I would like to know how long it will take for the refund to be processed, and if the money will be wired back to my bank account. Thank you.

Joanna Chang

回覆：關於影印餘額退費的問題
收件人: joanna09013@york.ac.uk
寄件人: libraryadmin@york.ac.uk

Joanna你好
不好意思，我們無法退費影印餘額。就像圖書代幣一樣，影印餘額只能買來影印用，並不能退費轉現金。

如果你同意的話，我們是可以將你的餘額轉給其他用戶，只要你告知我們他的使用者名稱。

Re: Inquiry of print credit refund
To: joanna09013@york.ac.uk
From: libraryadmin@york.ac.uk

Dear Joanna,

Unfortunately, we cannot refund unused print credits. Like book tokens, print credit can only be used for the purpose it was bought for. It is not a refundable deposit.

We will however transfer your credit to another user's account if you reply with their username and confirm this is what you would like.

You might be interested to know how the University uses the income from printing. It is used to keep our student printers and photocopiers working and stocked with sufficient paper and toner; to purchase new or replacement equipment; and to fund new and improved service.

Best wishes,

Amy Peterson
Librarian
University of York

你可能想知道學校是如何運用這些影印儲值的款項的。它們被用來提供每部影印機的紙張，確保影印機能正常使用，並隨時有足夠的紙張和墨水。或者是用來買新的或替代性設備，不然就是用來投資新改善的服務。

祝 學業順利

Amy Peterson
圖書館員
約克大學

University of York
Student Card Information

Card Holder: Ms. Joanna Chang
Student No.: 1607660
Program: International Education (Full-Time)
School of Education
Course Start Date: 20 September 2016
Course End Date: 3 September 2017
Print Credit: £53.05
Recent **Top-up**: £20

約克大學
學生卡資訊

持卡人：Joanna Chang小姐
學生號：1607660
課程：國際教育（全職學生）教育學院
課程開始日期：2016年9月20日
課程結束日期：2017年9月3日
影印餘額：53.05鎊
最近充值紀錄：20鎊

【詞彙】

inquiry詢問／credit餘額／refund退費／concern有關／master研究生／consider考慮／validity有效性／expire過期／plenty許多／doubt懷疑／remaining剩餘的／unused未使用的／doable可行的／wire匯款／unfortunately不幸地／token代幣／refundable可退費的／deposit儲值／transfer轉換／username使用者名稱／confirm確認／income收入／photocopier複印機／stock存放／sufficient充足的／toner影印機墨水／purchase購買／replacement代替品／equipment設備／improve改善／librarian圖書館員／holder持有者／program課程／course課程／top-up充值

這兩封電郵是有關什麼？
(A) 畢業流程
(B) 影印餘額退費
(C) 學費付款
(D) 作業截止日期

【類型】尋找主旨題型

【詞彙】
graduation畢業／
procedure流程／tuition學費／
payment付費／assignment作業

【正解】(B)

Joanna要求多少金額的退費？
(A) 20鎊　　　　(B) 33.05鎊
(C) 43.05鎊　　(D) 53.05鎊

【類型】尋找細節題型

【詞彙】
request要求／refund退費

【正解】(D)

在第二封電郵中提到了什麼？
(A) 錢匯回去需要花超過一週的
　　時間。
(B) 經同意，未使用的餘額可以
　　轉給其他學生。
(C) 學生會被額外收費以支付影
　　印機的升級。
(D) 大學裡所有的印表機和影印
　　機都是全新的。

【類型】尋找細節題型

【詞彙】
transfer匯款／permission允許／
charge收費／upgrade升級／
brand new全新的

【正解】(B)

---

196 What were the emails about?

(A) graduation procedures

(B) print credit refund

(C) tuition payment

(D) assignment deadline

【解析】根據兩封電子郵件的標題Inquiry of print credit refund 及內容，我們能得知本文是有關影印餘額的退費事宜。因此答案應選(B)。

---

197 How much are Joanna requesting for refund?

(A) £20　　　　　　(B) £33.05

(C) £43.05　　　　(D) £53.05

【解析】根據第一封電郵，Joanna要求影印餘額的退費，而在第三篇文章的學生卡資訊中顯示Print Credit: £53.05，因此答案應選(D)。

---

198 What is indicated in the second email?

(A) It will take over a week for the money to be transferred back.

(B) The unused credits can be transferred to another student with permission.

(C) Students would be charged extra for the printers to be upgraded.

(D) The printers and photocopiers in the university are all brand new.

【解析】根據第二篇電子郵件Unfortunately, we cannot refund unused print credits. 我們能得知影印餘額是無法退費的。因此選項(A)為非。We will however transfer your credit to another user's account if you reply with their username and confirm this is what you would like. 表示經同意，餘額是可以轉讓給其他學生的。因此選項(B)正確。It is used to keep our student printers and photocopiers working and stocked with sufficient paper and toner; to purchase new or replacement equipment; and to fund new and improved service. 則表示影印機的升級是由學生所繳交的影印費中支付的，而不用學生額外繳費。因此選項(C)為非。同一句中也提到了某些設備是替代性的設備，而非全部都是全新的。因此選項(D)為非。

---

199 How long is the course Joanna is enrolled in?

    (A) about six months

    (B) about a year

    (C) about two years

    (D) about three years

【解析】根據最後一篇文中資訊Course Start Date: 20 September 2016/ Course End Date: 3 September 2017課程為期大約一年。因此答案應選(B)。

Joanna註冊的課程為期多久？
(A) 大約六個月
(B) 大約一年
(C) 大約兩年
(D) 大約三年

【類型】尋找細節題型

【詞彙】
course課程／
enroll使進入

【正解】(B)

---

200 The phrase "top-up" in the last line in the card information, is closest in meaning to

    (A) fine

    (B) withdrawal

    (C) deposit

    (D) transfer

【解析】top-up表示「充值」，因此與deposit「儲值」意思最接近。因此答案應選(C)。

在卡片資訊中最後一行的片語top-up意思最接近下列何者？
(A) 罰鍰
(B) 退出
(C) 儲值
(D) 轉帳

【類型】同義字題型

【詞彙】
top-up儲值／
fine罰鍰／
withdrawal退出／
deposit儲值／
transfer轉帳

【正解】(C)

New TOEIC Reading Analysis 5
新多益閱讀全真模擬試題解析第5回

沒有簽好的合約我們無法將您的訂單投入生產。

【類型】形容詞詞彙題型

【詞彙】
put sth. into production將……投入生產

【正解】(C)

101 We cannot put your order into production without a _____ contract.

(A) sign   (B) signs

(C) signed   (D) signing

【解析】本句without後面的名詞是要表示「經過簽名的合約」，也就是「被簽上名字的合約」，動作為被動完成，因此需以過去分詞做形容詞用，故正解為(C)。

在協商之後，兩方都已經同意所有的條件與條款。

【類型】介系詞詞彙題型

【詞彙】
party（契約等的）當事人；一方／negotiation協商

【正解】(B)

102 Both parties have agreed _____ all the terms and conditions after negotiation.

(A) at   (B) with

(C) by   (D) in

【解析】本題要考動詞agree搭配介系詞的用法。agree指「同意、意見一致」，用來表示「對……取得一致意見」時，後面的介系詞可以是with、on或about，選項中只有(B)的with符合片語用法，故正解為(B)。

謝謝您給我昨天跟您面試的機會。

【類型】名詞詞彙題型

【詞彙】
interpretation 解釋／induction就職

【正解】(A)

103 Thank you for giving me the privilege of having an _____ with you yesterday.

(A) interview   (B) interpretation

(C) induction   (D) instruction

【解析】根據本句語意，空格中的名詞應為interview（面談、面試），have an interview with sb. 表示「與某人面談」，正解為(A)。其他選項的名詞並沒有這種用法。

104 Gillian has replaced Mr. Garcia, who is no longer in our _____ .

(A) regulation
(B) consideration
(C) employment
(D) reinforcement

【解析】本句逗號後為一形容詞子句，目的是要對先行詞Garcia先生補充描述。根據句意可知Garcia先生已經被其他人給取代，因此空格內填入選項(C)，表示這個人已經不受雇用，是最適合本題句意的答案，故(C)為正解。

Gillian已經取代已經不在我們這裡工作的Garcia先生。

【類型】名詞詞彙題型

【詞彙】
regulation規定／
consideration考慮／
employment 僱用／
reinforcement強化

【正解】(C)

---

105 Raymond is not a good boss to work with as he changes his mind _____ and asks you your opinion more than once.

(A) constantly
(B) generously
(C) perceivably
(D) preferably

【解析】根據語意，選項中的副詞以constantly（不斷地）最適合放在本句空格中，以表示Raymond因為會「不斷地改變主意」，而不是個好共事的主管。其他副詞皆不適合用來形容change one's mind（改變主意）這個動詞片語，因此(A)為最適當的答案。

因為Raymond會不斷改變主意，而且會不止一次地問你的意見，所以不是個很好共事的主管。

【類型】副詞詞彙題型

【詞彙】
constantly不斷地／
generously慷慨地／
perceivably 可察覺地／
preferably 更好地

【正解】(A)

---

106 I would like to set up a meeting to discuss the details of _____ of the proposal.

(A) compensation
(B) recreation
(C) aggregation
(D) implementation

【解析】本句意在表示想安排會議討論執行提案的細節，空格中的名詞應填入選項(D)的implementation，其他選項的名詞放入句子中都會讓語意變得難以理解，因此選項(D)為最適當的答案。

我想安排一個會議討論執行提案的細節。

【類型】名詞詞彙題型

【詞彙】
compensation 賠償／
recreation消遣／
aggregation聚集／
implementation執行

【正解】(D)

會議的日期和時間已經改了，但是地點保持不變。

【類型】動詞詞彙題型

【詞彙】
contain包含／
expect期待／
remain維持／
maintain維護、保持

【正解】(C)

107 The date and time of the meeting has been changed but the location _____ the same.

(A) contains   (B) expects

(C) remains   (D) maintains

【解析】本句but之後的語意是在表示「會議地點維持不變」。選項(C)的remain與(D)的maintain都有「維持」的含義，但是兩個動詞的用法截然不同。remain後面接形容詞，表示「維持某個狀態」；maintain則指「維護；保持」，後面接名詞當受格，如maintain world peace意指「維護世界和平」。因此根據語意，本句空格處應填入remains，正解為(C)。

員工餐廳的菜單會根據食材的可利用性而變動。

【類型】片語詞彙題型

【詞彙】
be eligible for 適合／
be subject to 容易遭受／
be aware of 意識到／
be used to 習慣於

【正解】(B)

108 The menu of the staff canteen _____ change according to the availability of ingredients.

(A) is eligible for   (B) is subject to

(C) is aware of   (D) is used to

【解析】根據空格前後文意，可知本句是要表示「菜單內容會因為食材取得是否而改變」，空格前後的語意即「菜單內容容易因……而變」，be subject to即表示「容易受……」之意，符合本句語意，故為最適當的答案，正解為(B)。使用選項(C)(D)的兩個片語之主詞必須為「人」，而選項(A)放在空格中與句意不符，故均不是適當的選擇。

Bellavita咖啡為慶祝盛大開幕，這個月所有飲品都提供八折優惠。

【類型】片語詞彙題型

【詞彙】
in celebration of 慶祝／
in accordance with根據／
with respect to關於／
for the sake of為了

【正解】(A)

109 Bellavita Coffee is offering a 20% discount on all its beverages this month _____ their grand opening.

(A) in celebration of

(B) in accordance with

(C) with respect to

(D) for the sake of

【解析】本句空格前的句意在陳述「咖啡店本月所有飲品都提供八折優惠」，空格後提到「他們的盛大開幕」，分析空格前後的句意，可知咖啡店提供八折優惠應該是為了慶祝開幕，選項(A)的in celebration of即「為了慶祝……」的片語，是最適合的答案，故為正解。

110 In _____ to expanding its presence in the Europe market, Max Auto is also planning to explore opportunities in Asia.

(A) order   (B) relation

(C) addition   (D) regard

除了拓展在歐洲的市場之外，Max汽車公司也計劃探索亞洲的機會。

【類型】片語詞彙題型

【詞彙】
relation關係／
addition附加／
regard關係

【正解】(C)

【解析】由後半句的關鍵副詞also（也）有「還有」的含義，可知後半句提到的explore opportunities in Asia（探索亞洲的機會）是「除了」前半句的expand its presence in Europe market（拓展在歐洲的市場）」之外，追加跟進的行動，故引導前半句的連接詞以in addition to（除……之外）最符合句意，正解為(C)。in order to表「為了……」；in relation to表「有關、至於」；in regard to 表「關於」，這三個連接詞片語均與本句語意不合，故不選。

---

111 _____ employees who want to participate in the company trip must sign up by the end of this week.

(A) Both   (B) All

(C) Each   (D) None

所有想要參加公司旅遊的員工一定要在這星期結束前登記。

【類型】形容詞詞彙題型

【正解】(B)

【解析】空格後的名詞employees為複數名詞，因此選項(C)的each（每一個）可以先刪除。先行詞employees之後的who引導的形容詞子句是用來表示特定對象為「想要參加公司旅遊的員工」，選項(A)的both用在對象只有「兩個人」的情況，而選項(D)的none用來表示「沒有一人」的狀況，都與本句語意不合，只有選項(B)的all（全部的），表示「所有想參加的員工」，故(B)為正解。

---

112 The processing time for the Taiwan compatriot permit is _____ a week.

(A) normally   (B) considerably

(C) permanently   (D) surprisingly

台胞證的辦理時間通常是一星期。

【類型】副詞詞彙題型

【詞彙】
Taiwan compatriot permit 台胞證／considerably 相當地／permanently長期地

【正解】(A)

【解析】這句是在描述辦理台胞證的時間是一星期。選項(A)的normally是最適合放在空格中的副詞，表示辦理的時間「通常是一星期」。其他選項的副詞均與本句語意不合。

因為衛生因素，泳衣及內衣是不能退換貨的。

【類型】形容詞詞彙題型

【詞彙】
operational操作上的／
confidential 機密的／
hygienic衛生的

【正解】(D)

113 For _____ reasons, swimwear and underwear may not be returned or exchanged.
(A) personal   (B) operational
(C) confidential   (D) hygienic

【解析】泳衣及內衣均屬貼身衣物，會接觸人體私密部位。按常理，一般商店基於衛生理由不接受以上衣物的退換貨，因此空格中的形容詞應選(D)。

Curtis沒有在職場上得到太多成就，因為他屢次因為沒有工作成效而被革職。

【類型】連接詞詞彙題型

【詞彙】
workplace 職場／
productive具生產力的；有成效的

【正解】(D)

114 Curtis didn't have much success in the workplace _____ he was fired repeatedly from his jobs for not being productive.
(A) while
(B) although
(C) even
(D) as

【解析】本題前半句意在表示「Curtis在職場上並沒有得到成就」，後半句說明「他因為工作沒成效屢被革職」，前後兩句在語意上有因果的關係，因此空格中的連接詞必須能表達前後句的關係。選項(D)的as有「因為」的含義，故為正解。

這家餐廳的所有餐點都是現做現吃的。

【類型】名詞詞彙題型

【詞彙】
activation活化／
consumption消費／
assumption假設／
constituent構成成份

【正解】(B)

115 All dishes in this restaurant are cooked for immediate _____ .
(A) activation
(B) consumption
(C) assumption
(D) constituent

【解析】這句的主詞為dishes（餐點），句子中的be cooked for... 是要描述餐點為何而做。immediate consumption 表「立即食用」，可說明這家餐廳的餐點的料理目的是要供消費者「直接立即吃」的，合情合理。immediate constituent指「直接構成要素」，與本句句意不合。其他兩個選項的名詞放入空格內亦無法使句子有意義。故最適當的答案為(B)。

116 Audio guides are free with your _____ entry tickets at the main entrance.

(A) ultimate   (B) intentional

(C) individual   (D) successful

【解析】本句主要在表示「語音導覽隨門票免費提供」。語音導覽是每個人自己利用耳機收聽導覽內容，因此按常理是每張入場門票提供一個語音導覽，因此空格中以選項(C)的individual表示「個人的」為最適當的形容詞，表示「個人的入場門票」，正解為(C)。

語音導覽隨個人門票在主要入口處免費提供。

【類型】形容詞詞彙題型

【詞彙】
audio guide語音導覽／
ultimate 最終的／
intentional故意的／
individual個人的

【正解】(C)

---

117 If you don't go to the restroom right now, you'll have to wait _____ intermission.

(A) since   (B) until

(C) when   (D) after

【解析】本題為if條件句，表示「如果你現在不去廁所，那就得等到中場休息」。wait until...用在句子中是表示「等到……再」，符合本句句意，故(B)為正解。其他選項的連接詞放在句中都沒有until來得合適，故正解為(B)。

如果你現在不去洗手間，就得等到中場休息才能去。

【類型】連接詞詞彙題型

【詞彙】
intermission中場休息

【正解】(B)

---

118 It's not _____ to tip the drivers, but $1-$5 would be appropriate if you want to.

(A) obligatory

(B) complimentary

(C) comprehensive

(D) expensive

【解析】由後半句的if you want to （如果你想給的話），可判斷要不要「給司機小費」是由你自己來決定，而不是經他人強制行使的行為，故空格中的形容詞以選項(A)的obligatory，表示「不一定要給司機小費」，正解為(A)。

給司機小費並非必須的，但是如果你想給的話，一到五美金是比較恰當的金額。

【類型】形容詞詞彙題型

【詞彙】
obligatory必須的／
complimentary贈送的／
comprehensive可理解的

【正解】(A)

一個車內定位系統的花費為一天15美元或一星期70美元。

【類型】動詞詞彙題型

【詞彙】
in-car 車內的／
navigation system 導航系統

【正解】(B)

119 An in-car navigation system _____ $15 per day or $70 per week.

(A) spends   (B) costs

(C) takes   (D) consumes

【解析】本題四個選項的動詞都可做「花費」解，因此必須確實理解每個動詞的用法才能正確做出選擇。本句主詞為navigation system（導航系統），受詞為「錢」，因此本句主要是要表達「某物要花多少錢」。spend主詞應為「人」，故(A)可先刪除不選；take後面通常接「時間」，表示「花費」多少時間，故(C)亦可刪除不選；consume有「耗盡、用光」的含義，因此也不適合作為本句的動詞；cost主詞通常為「物」或虛主詞it，後面可接「金錢」或「時間、勞力」等做受詞，是最適合本句的動詞，故(B)為正解。

這張優惠券只有平日有效，而且不能與其他優惠合併使用。

【類型】形容詞詞彙題型

【正解】(D)

120 This coupon is only valid on weekdays and cannot be combined with _____ offer.

(A) else   (B) one another

(C) each other   (D) any other

【解析】空格後為名詞offer，故空格中應填入形容詞。else為副詞，表「另外、其他」，一般用在疑問詞或不定代名詞後，如what else或something else；one another表「互相」而each other表「彼此」，是名詞，不能做形容詞用，故選項(A)(B)(C)皆不適合本句空格。any other表「任何其他的⋯⋯」，可以接offer表示「任何其他優惠」，是選項中唯一適當選擇，故(D)為正解。

本店所有商品都附有限期一年的保固。

【類型】片語動詞詞彙題型

【詞彙】
warranty 保固／
render up 放棄／
stand for 代表／
come with 伴隨／
set up 設立

【正解】(C)

121 All items in our store _____ a one-year limited warranty.

(A) render up   (B) stand for

(C) come with   (D) set up

【解析】本句意在說明「所有商品皆有一年保固」，選項中的片語動詞，只有選項(C)的come with（伴隨著）能表示「附有⋯⋯」，其他片語動詞放在空格中皆與句意不合，故(C)為正解。

122 The term paper needs _____ to Prof. Adams by September 8th.

(A) to submit

(B) submitting

(C) to be submitted

(D) being submitted

學期報告必須在九月八日之前交給Adams教授。

【類型】動詞詞彙題型

【詞彙】
term 學期／
paper報告／
submit提交

【正解】(C)

【解析】本句主詞為the term paper（學期報告），因此無法主動行使submit（提交）這個動作，故空格中的動詞必須以被動形式呈現，正解為(C)。

＊動詞need表「需要」，只有「人」會「需要」做某事，「物件」不會主動需要，因此當need前面的主詞為「物件」時，通常是要表示「某物需要……」。

| need主詞為「物」的句型用法 |

① sth.＋need＋to be V-p.p.
   need後接不定詞＋被動語態，表某物「有必要做某種處置」。

② sth.＋need＋V-ing
   need後接現在分詞，現在分詞在此可視做名詞，表某物「有……的必要」，但不能與授與動詞如give或submit等字合用。

---

123 The mayor was arrested for taking bribes _____ the use of his official position.

(A) in support of

(B) in memory of

(C) in charge of

(D) in exchange for

市長因為收取賄賂作為行使公職的交換而被逮捕。

【類型】片語詞彙題型

【詞彙】
in support of為了支持／
in memory of為了紀念／
in charge of負責／
in exchange for 作為交換

【正解】(D)

【解析】本題前半句在陳述「市長因收賄而被捕」，通常賄賂的目的是對對方有所求，後半句提到the use of his official position（利用他的公職）可知賄賂市長的目的是要他利用公職之便做某些事情，因此空格中的片語以in exchange for（作為交換）最符合本句語意，故(D)為正解。

驗屍官斷定女子的死是意外而非謀殺。

【類型】動詞詞彙題型

【詞彙】
coroner驗屍官／
conclude推斷出／
integrate使合併／
append 添加

【正解】(B)

---

124 The coroner _____ that the woman's death was an accident and not murder.

(A) promised   (B) concluded

(C) integrated   (D) appended

【解析】本題that子句意在陳述「女子的死因」，主詞coroner指「驗屍官」，由coroner的工作性質判斷，可知驗屍官是在經過觀察及檢驗屍體狀態後作出死因判斷，因此空格應以(B)的conclude為最適當的動詞，正解為(B)。選項(A)的promise指「保證」，通常只是口頭上的允諾，不一定有明確證據，故不是最適當的選擇。其他兩個動詞與本句語意不合，可不考慮。

在開始播放電影之前，首映會將由一場讓賓客可以交流放鬆的茶會展開序幕。

【類型】關係代名詞詞彙題型

【詞彙】
premiere 首映會／
mingle交流；往來

【正解】(C)

---

125 The premiere will begin with a tea party _____ guests can mingle and relax before the start of the film.

(A) which   (B) what

(C) where   (D) those

【解析】本句空格應為一可引導形容詞子句的關係代名詞。先行詞a tea party後的關係代名詞可為which或that，由空格後的句子意在表示「賓客可以在電影開始前，在這場茶會中交談放鬆」，因此which前面需要加上介系詞at，以表示「在茶會上」，而「介系詞＋which」在英語語法中通常會以關係副詞where取代，因此本句空格應填入where，正解為(C)。

因為上個月的火災，分公司的開幕被往後延了。

【類型】連接詞詞彙題型

【詞彙】
postpone 延後

【正解】(A)

---

126 _____ the fire last month, the opening of the branch office was postponed.

(A) Due to   (B) Because

(C) Owing   (D) Resulted in

【解析】本題後半句說明「分公司開幕被延後」，前半句提到「上個月發生火災」，可知「火災」應為「分公司延後開幕」的原因。選項(D)的result in是用來表示「結果」，與本句語意不符，故可先刪除。連接詞because後面要接句子，如果要接名詞要用because of；owing指「未付的」，要與to連用，才能表示「因為」，故選項(B)(C)亦不適用。due to指「由於、因為」，後面接名詞當受詞，故(A)為正解。

127 The gym offers a free session to help their new members _____ the machines.

(A) get acquainted with

(B) be informed of

(C) stay clear of

(D) get familiar with

健身房提供一個免費課程幫助新會員熟悉器材。

【類型】動詞片語詞彙題型

【詞彙】
session（授課活動等的）時間

【正解】(D)

【解析】machine在本句中指的是gym（健身房）裡的exercise machine（健身器材）。get acquainted with sb.表「熟識」，受詞通常為「人」，本句受詞為「機器」，故選項(A)不適用；選項(B)的be informed of sth. 表「得知某項情報」，以及選項(C)的stay clear of sb./sth.表「避免接近某人或某物」，皆與本句語意不合，故都不適用。選項(D)的get familiar with sb./ sth. 表「熟悉某人或某物」，是唯一符合本句用法的動詞片語，故為正解。

---

128 The price does not include breakfast _____ you can add it for £7.50 per person.

(A) but   (B) although

(C) or   (D) nor

這價格並不包含早餐，但你可以用每人7.5鎊的價格加早餐。

【類型】連接詞詞彙題型

【正解】(A)

【解析】本題前半句表示「價格不含早餐」，後半句表示「你可以加價享用早餐」，連接詞應用but最符合句意。although表「雖然」、or表「或者」、nor表「也不」，以上三個連接詞皆與本句語意不合，故(B)(C)(D)均非適當答案。

---

129 If you feel airsick, _____ is a bag in the seat pocket in front of you.

(A) which   (B) there

(C) that   (D) what

如果你感到暈機，你前方的座位口袋裡有個袋子。

【類型】主詞選擇題型

【詞彙】
airsick暈機

【正解】(B)

【解析】這一句是要表示「你面前的座位口袋中有個袋子」，表示「某處有某物」時，通常會用there 做虛主詞，故本句空格中應為there，正解為(B)。

這棟大樓內的所有電梯都正在進行預防性保養。

【類型】動詞詞彙選擇題型

【詞彙】
preventative預防性的／
undergo接受／
experiment做實驗

【正解】(B)

---

130 All elevators within the building are _____ a preventative maintenance.

    (A) taking
    (B) undergoing
    (C) experimenting
    (D) practicing

【解析】本句主詞為elevator（電梯），動詞take、experiment及practice都是主詞需為「人」才能行使的動作，故選項(A)(C)(D)皆不適用在本句空格中。undergo指「接受；經歷」，undergo maintenance意指「進行維護；接受保養」，為最適合本句空格的動詞，故(B)為正解。

▶ **PART 6**

Directions: Read the texts on the following pages. A word or phrase is missing in some of the sentences. Answer choices are given below each of these articles. Select the best answer to complete the text. Then mark the letter (A), (B), (C) or (D) on your answer sheet.

Questions 131-134 refer to the following letter.

親愛的Tucker小姐，
這封信是為了回應有關您在本飯店遇到的問題。
如您信上所述，您的問題是從您聽到隔牆持續不斷的噪音開始。我們很抱歉。這間飯店是一棟七十年的老建築，因此牆壁都很薄，所以其他房客製造的聲音很容易被聽到。我們目前正在進行大樓隔音的工程，以解決這個問題。

Dear Ms. Tucker,

This is in response to your letter concerning the issues you experienced while staying at our hotel.

As you wrote, your troubles began when you heard ___131___ noise from the walls. Our apologies. This hotel is a 70-year-old structure, and the walls are thin, so the noises made by other guests can be heard easily. We're currently in the process of soundproofing the building to solve this problem.

Then, you found that the air conditioner in your room didn't work. You mentioned that you wanted to change a room but your request was ___132___ by our front desk representative, Samantha. I would like to beg for your understanding that we were unable to move you to another room, as our hotel was fully booked on that day.

In this letter you will find an enclosed voucher for a free night's stay and a complimentary breakfast at the hotel. We hope the voucher can ___133___ the unpleasant experience you had at our hotel this time, and ___134___ .

All best,
Daniel Knight
General Manager, Truncheon Hotel

然後，您發現您房內的冷氣不能運作。您提到您希望換房間，但您的要求被我們櫃檯代表人員Samantha回絕了。我想請求您的諒解，我們無法為您換到另一間房，是因為我們的飯店當天客滿了。

在這封信中您會發現附上本飯店免費住宿一晚及一客免費早餐的優惠券。我們希望這張優惠券能彌補您在本飯店這次不愉快的經驗，希望能很快再為您服務。

祝您一切順心
Daniel Knight
Truncheon飯店總經

【詞彙】
soundproofing 隔音

---

131 (A) incessant
(B) attractive
(C) prestigious
(D) imperative

【解析】空格中的形容詞是要形容名詞noise（噪音），選項(C)(D)的形容詞通常不用來形容noise，故可先刪除不考慮。由信件內容可知這封信是要提出抱怨，按常理推測，會讓人提出抱怨的聲音不可能會是attractive（吸引人的），選項(B)亦非適當形容詞。incessant意指「持續不斷的」，當噪音持續不斷的出現時，會讓人感到困擾，故(A)為正解。

【類型】形容詞選擇題型

【詞彙】
incessant持續的／
prestigious 有名望的／
imperative緊急的

【正解】(A)

【類型】分詞選擇題型

【詞彙】
process處理

【正解】(B)

132 (A) welcomed
   (B) declined
   (C) invented
   (D) processed

【解析】由本句前文表示「想要換房間」，以及後文請對方理解「飯店當天被訂滿」，可知想要換房間的request遭到拒絕，因此空格處的過去分詞應為declined（被拒絕的），正解為(B)。

【類型】片語選擇題型

【詞彙】
  put up with忍受／
stay away from遠離／
drop in on順道拜訪／
make up for彌補

【正解】(D)

133 (A) put up with
   (B) stay away from
   (C) drop in on
   (D) make up for

【解析】這一題提到隨信附上了一張優惠券。由本信前文內容，可知收信者對住宿飯店經驗有所抱怨。空格中的片語動詞的受詞為unpleasant experience（不愉快的經驗），而這句是要表示「優惠券的目的」，根據句意，優惠券的目的應為「彌補」這個不愉快的經驗，正解為(D)。

【類型】句子插入題型

【詞彙】
cooperation合作／
without delay立刻

【正解】(C)

★ **134** (A) we thank you for your cooperation
   (B) we hope to receive your order soon
   (C) we look forward to serving you again soon
   (D) we hope you make the payment without delay

【解析】由信件附上飯店住宿及早餐免費優惠券，可知飯店希望對方能使用這個優惠券再次到飯店住宿，因此這裡的句子以選項(C)所表示的「期待能再次為您服務」最為適當，正解為(C)。

Questions 135-138 refer to the following advertisement.

Are you ready for the ultimate Chinese New Year at the Tutu Malaysia Resort?
Join us this February and discover a CNY land with over 30 rides, shows and attractions to create most ___135___ family memories! If you are lucky enough, you will spot Tutu Rabbit, our mascot, ___136___ red envelopes in Dream Park!

You and your family can even extend the celebratory fun by staying in our amazing Tutu Malaysia Resort Hotel for a whole night of Chinese New Year's entertainment and jolly fun that ___137___ kids and adults will enjoy.

Please note that ___138___ for entry into the park.

你準備好要在Tutu馬來西亞度假村享受最棒的中國新年嗎？今年二月跟我們一起探索一個有超過三十種遊樂設施、表演及好玩項目的中國新年城，以創造最歡樂的家庭回憶！如果你夠幸運的話，你還會碰到我們的吉祥物Tutu兔，在夢公園發放紅包喔！

你跟家人可以住宿我們令人驚喜的Tutu馬來西亞度假飯店，享受一整晚小孩大人都能盡情享樂的中國新年娛樂節目，開懷玩樂，讓歡樂加倍延伸！

請注意樂園的入場門票只能事先在網路上購買。

---

135 (A) festive
(B) cautious
(C) persuasive
(D) holistic

【解析】這句要表示在這個樂園要創造「什麼樣的」家庭回憶。由於這篇文章主要是要宣傳度假村的中國新年慶祝活動，因此空格中的形容詞以(A)的festive表示「節慶的；歡樂的」最適合本文語意，正解為(A)。

【類型】形容詞選擇題型

【詞彙】
festive節慶的／
cautious謹慎的／
persuasive 有說服力的／
holistic全部的

【正解】(A)

【類型】動詞變化題型

【正解】(B)

136 (A) deliver
(B) delivering
(C) delivered
(D) being delivering

【解析】這句的關鍵字為動詞spot（發現），spot sb. V-ing 表示「發現某人做……」，這句是要表示「發現吉祥物在發紅包」，故此處的動詞deliver應以分詞delivering呈現，正解為(B)。

【類型】形容詞詞彙題型

【正解】(C)

137 (A) only
(B) none
(C) both
(D) every

【解析】空格後的名詞為kids及adults，因此空格中的指示形容詞應為可以表示「兩者都……」的both，正解為(C)。

【類型】句子插入題型

【正解】(A)

★ 138 (A) tickets can only be purchased online in advance
(B) you may be asked to overwork on the weekend
(C) we will not open for business for the next week
(D) you must bring your original purchase receipt

【解析】本文為度假村的中國新年活動做宣傳，希望吸引讀者來度假村歡度中國新年，因此這裡的句子應與度假村活動有關。選項(A)表示度假村的入場門票需事先在線上購買，合情合理。其他選項的句子都跟度假村無關，因此(A)為最適當的句子選擇。

Questions 139-142 refer to the following email.

From: Joseph Thomas
To: crownhouse-residents@clifton.ac.uk
Date: Tue, Mar 20, 2018 at 5:13 PM
Subject: Notice of Routine Boiler Inspection

Hi,
This is to give notice to residents in Crown House that personnel from the University's Estates staff are due to carry out routine inspection and maintenance of the boilers (providing hot water and central heating) in the flats ___139___ today, Tuesday 20th March. It is ___140___ that this work will take 2 to 3 days.

Work will take place from 9am to not later than 5pm daily.

They will require ___141___ the kitchens and various boiler rooms in the flats but will not require access to bedrooms. The hall will give them access if you are not in your flat when they call. All Estates personnel carry University identification.
___142___
Thank you.

Joseph

寄件人：Joseph Thomas
收件人：crownhouse-residents@clifton.ac.uk
日期：星期二，2018年三月20日下午5:13
主旨：鍋爐例行檢查通知

嗨，
這封信是要通知皇冠樓的住戶，大學住宿組的人將從今天—三月二十日星期二—開始進行大樓鍋爐（提供熱水及中央暖氣）的例行檢查及維護。這項工作預計將會花二至三天的時間。

工作將會在每天上午九時到下午五點進行。

他們會需要進入廚房以及大樓中的各個鍋爐室，但不會需要進入臥室。如果他們到訪時你們不在宿舍內，辦公室會提供他們進入這些地方的權限。所有的人員都會配戴學校證件。
抱歉臨時才通知。

謝謝。
Joseph

【類型】動詞時態選擇題型

【詞彙】
commence開始

【正解】(C)

139 (A) commence
(B) commenced
(C) commencing
(D) will commence

【解析】本句意在表示他們將自三月二十日開始進行……，這個句子已經有動詞carry out（進行），因此後面的動詞commence以現在分詞的方式呈現，表示「自……開始」，正解為(C)。

【類型】動詞時態選擇題型

【正解】(B)

140 (A) estimate
(B) estimated
(C) estimating
(D) estimation

【解析】It is estimated that... 為表示「據估計，……」的句型，故空格處應填入estimated，正解為(B)。

【類型】名詞選擇題型

【詞彙】
access to 進入／
charge費用／
recess 休息／
appeal to 呼籲；請求

【正解】(A)

141 (A) access to
(B) charge for
(C) recess of
(D) appeal to

【解析】本句意在表示進行檢查及維修的人員需要「進入」廚房及其他有鍋爐的地方，access意指「進入的權利」，常與to連用，故正解為(A)。

【類型】句子插入題型

【詞彙】
ASAP (=as soon as possible)
儘速／short notice臨時通知

【正解】(D)

★ **142** (A) Please respond ASAP.
(B) Looking forward to seeing you.
(C) Please fill out the form below.
(D) Apologies for the short notice.

【解析】根據本信件的內容，是在通知佈達即將進行的事，信中並沒有提及需要回覆的事項、需要填寫表格，或是預訂見面時間等事，故選項(A)(B)(C)的句子出現在信件中都顯得很突兀。由於發信日期就是檢查工作將開始進行之日，因此選項(D)表示對於「臨時通知這件事感到抱歉」，是最適合放在此處的句子，故(D)為正解。

Questions 143-146 refer to the following email.

Dear Mr. Cheng,
Maxton Law Office is hiring for the position of law administrator and I am ___143___ information about this opportunity.

The law office administrator will be ___144___ for providing administrative support in our law office. The duties ___145___ overseeing budgeting and payroll operations, managing office space arrangements and gathering supplies.

___146___ in Business, legal administration or a related field. Please contact me if there are any adequate candidates that meet our qualifications for this position.

Sincerely,
Selena

【詞彙】
law administrator 法律行政人員／oversee監督；審查／
payroll薪資

親愛的程先生，

Maxton法律事務所的法律行政人員一職正在徵人，而我正在散播這則訊工作機會的訊息。

法律行政人員將會負責提供本法律事務所的行政事務。職責包括預算審查、薪資計算、辦公室空間規劃管理以及收拾用品。

應徵者必須具備商業、法務行政或相關領域的大學學歷。如果有任何符合我們對此職務要求的適合人選，請與我聯絡。

Selena謹上

---

143 (A) disseminating
　　(B) recommending
　　(C) expressing
　　(D) acknowledging

【解析】這句是要表達「我正在發佈這則職缺訊息」，因此適合的動詞為選項(A)的disseminating（散播），正解為(A)。

【類型】動詞選擇題型

【詞彙】
disseminate散播／
recommend推薦／
expressing表達／
acknowledge承認

【正解】(A)

【類型】形容詞選擇題型

【正解】(C)

144 (A) irrational
　　　 (B) informative
　　　 (C) responsible
　　　 (D) chargeable

【解析】be responsible for sth. 為表示「負責某事」的片語用法，本句意在說明法律行政人員的負責工作內容，故這裡的空格要填responsible，正解為(C)。

【類型】動詞變化題型

【詞彙】
inclusive包含的／
include包含

【正解】(C)

145 (A) inclusive
　　　 (B) including
　　　 (C) include
　　　 (D) included

【解析】這個句子沒有動詞，因此空格處應放入適合本句的動詞。選項(A)為形容詞，可刪除不考慮。主詞為複數名詞The duties（職責），且敘述的是現在存在的事實，故時態用現在式，正解為(C)。

【類型】句子插入題型

【詞彙】
investigation調查

【正解】(D)

★ **146** (A) All candidates show great interests
　　　 (B) That's the reason why I chose this major
　　　 (C) The focus was put on the thorough investigation
　　　 (D) A candidate should have a Bachelor's degree

【正解】由後文的句意表示「若有符合條件的人選請與我聯絡」，因此推斷空格處的句子應是在陳述此職務的具體要求條件。選項(A)(B)(C)陳述內容均與職務條件無關，只有選項(D)表示「應徵者應具備……的大學學歷」，後面以in... 補述哪一領域的學歷，為最適合放在此處的句子，故(D)為正解。

> **PART 7**

Directions: In this part, you will read a selection of texts, such as magazine and newspaper articles, letters, and advertisements. Each text is followed by several questions. Select the best answer for each question and mark the letter (A), (B), (C), or (D) on your answer sheet.

Questions 147-149 refer to the following post.

Event: Alumni Dinner Gathering Set For December 30th

Come join us on Dec 30th at 5:30pm (sharp!) til 7:30 pm for our annual Alumni dinner for UCS at Tapatili downtown!

The evening promises to be a fun time full of fellowship and catching up with friends. In addition, if you haven't received your UCS alumni pin we will be handing them out at the dinner! Bring $30 for dinner and drinks!

DEC 30 UCS Alumni Dinner
Public · Hosted by UCS Alumni Association

🕐 Saturday, December 30 at 5:30 PM - 7:30 PM CST
Next Week

活動：校友晚餐聚會 定於十二月三十日

十二月三十日下午五點半（整！）至七點半，到Tapatili市中心來跟我們一起參加長興大學一年一度的校友晚餐聚會！

這晚必定會是校友們相聚與互相報告近況的愉快時刻。而且，如果你還沒收到長興大學校友胸針，我們會在晚餐時發出去！自備三十元付晚餐及飲料！

12月30日長興大學校友晚餐
公開活動·由長興大學校友會主辦

🕐星期六，十二月三十日中央標準時間下午5:30至下午7:30
下週

Tapatili邊境咖啡 奧克拉荷馬市74103Tapatili 皇后北路89號	Border Cafe Tapatili 89 N Queens Rd, Tapatili, Oklahoma 74103
27 參加 – 15 有興趣	27 Going • 15 Interested

【詞彙】
fellowship聯誼會／
catch up with sb. 與某人更新近況／
CST (=Central Standard Time)中央標準時間

這則貼文的目的為何？
(A) 召開緊急會議
(B) 宣傳一個活動
(C) 邀集活動贊助者
(D) 為一家餐廳打廣告

【類型】內容主題題型

【正解】(B)

147 What's the purpose of this post?

    (A) To call an emergency meeting

    (B) To promote an event

    (C) To invite sponsors to an event

    (D) To advertise for a restaurant

【解析】由貼文內容為大學校友會將在一間咖啡店舉行校友晚餐聯歡會，可知這是一則目的為宣傳活動的貼文，故正解為(B)。

出席者將會在晚餐時拿到什麼？
(A) UCS校友胸針
(B) 校友手冊
(C) 入會申請表
(D) 學位證書

【類型】提問細節題型

【詞彙】
brochure手冊

【正解】(A)

148 What will the attendees receive at the dinner?

    (A) The UCS alumni pin

    (B) The Alumni brochure

    (C) The Membership application form

    (D) The degree certificate

【解析】由活動說明中提到還沒有收到alumni pin（校友胸針）的人，會在晚餐時發放，可知出席校友聯歡會的活動的人將可以拿到校友胸針，故正解為(A)。

149 Who's going to pay for the dinner?

(A) The event organizer

(B) The attendees

(C) The Alumni Association

(D) The event sponsors

誰將支付晚餐費用？

(A) 活動籌辦人

(B) 出席者

(C) 校友會

(D) 活動贊助者

【類型】提問細節題型

【詞彙】
organizer籌辦人／
attendee出席者

【正解】(B)

【解析】活動說明最後提到Bring $30 for dinner and drinks!（帶三十元來付晚餐及飲料），可知出席者必須自付晚餐費用，正解為(B)。

Questions 150-152 refer to the following notice.

Closure of Car Park 1

To facilitate the construction of developing the airport into a Three-runway System, Car Park 1 is closed from 14 January 2018. Hourly parking spaces are available at Car Park 2, 3 and Takashima Outlet Car Park while daily and long-term parking spaces are also available at Car Park 3 and Takashima Outlet Car Park. These car parks provide a total of over 3,000 parking spaces. For any further enquiries, please contact airport car park customer service hotline at 3300-3300.

第一停車場關閉公告

為便利將機場發展為三線跑道系統的施工工程，第一停車場將自2018年一月十四日關閉。第二、三停車場以及高島暢貨中心停車場都提供計時停車位，而第三停車場及高島暢貨中心則有提供計日與長期停車位。這些停車場提供總共超過三千個停車位。需要更進一步的詢問，請撥打3300-3300聯絡機場停車場客服熱線。

這張公告是有關什麼？
(A)一家汽車公司暫時停業
(B) 一個停車場永久關閉
(C) 營業時間變更
(D) 感恩節暫停營業

【類型】內容主題題型

【正解】(B)

150 What is this notice about?

(A) Temporary closing of an auto company

(B) Permanent closing of a parking area

(C) Change of business hours

(D) Business closing for Thanksgiving

【解析】由告示內容表示Car Park 1 is closed from 14 January 2018（第一停車場自2018年一月十四日關閉），可知這個停車場將自該日起關閉，不再對外開放，正解為(B)。

關閉第一停車場的目的為何？
(A) 為了翻修機場
(B) 為了擴增跑道
(C) 為了減少人事支出
(D) 為了興建美食廣場

【類型】提問細節題型

【詞彙】
renovation翻新／
expansion擴增／
gourmet美食

【正解】(B)

151 What is the purpose of closing Car Park 1?

(A) For airport renovation

(B) For runway expansion

(C) To reduce personnel expenses

(D) To build a gourmet court

【解析】告示內容表示停車場關閉的目的是To facilitate the construction of developing the airport into a Three-runway System（為了便利將機場發展為三跑道系統的施工），可知機場關閉是為了讓機場跑道增為三線道，故正解為(B)。

哪一個停車場只提供計時停車位？
(A) 第一停車場
(B) 第二停車場
(C) 第三停車場
(D) 高島暢貨中心停車場

【類型】提問細節題型

【正解】(B)

152 Which car park only provides hourly parking spaces?

(A) Car Park 1

(B) Car Park 2

(C) Car Park 3

(D) Takashima Outlet Car Park

【解析】告示內容表示第二、三停車場及高島暢貨中心停車場都提供計時停車位，而只有第三停車場及高島暢貨中心停車場提供計日及長期停車位，因此第二停車場是唯一只提供計時車位的停車場。第一停車場提供何種停車位在告示中並未提及，故不需考慮，正解為(B)。

Questions 153-155 refer to the following information.

Transport for Special Needs

In addition to public transport, we have a variety of options available for passengers with mobility difficulties, offering more flexible and personalized transport services through advance booking.

★Coach

① Rehabus   Telephone +852 2827 0023

② Easy-Access Bus   Telephone +852 2770 0023

★ Limousine   Telephone +852 8103 0023

★ Taxi   Telephone +852 2766 0023

**Please request a quote before booking.
Thanks!**

特殊需求者的交通

除了公共交通工具之外，我們還有各種可讓行動不便之乘客使用的選擇，提供透過是先預定的彈性及個人化的交通服務。

★巴士
① 復康巴士
　　　電話 +852 2827 0023
② 輕鬆到巴士
　　　電話 +852 2770 0023
★小型巴士
　　　電話 +852 8103 0023
★計程車
　　　電話 +852 2766 0023

請在訂位前先詢問價格。
謝謝！

【詞彙】
mobility行動性／rehabus復康巴士／
limousine 豪華轎車；小型巴士

---

153 Who is the information for?

(A) People carrying large luggage

(B) People with limited mobility

(C) People who are short of cash

(D) Women who travel alone

【解析】由這則訊息內容表示為passengers with mobility difficulties（行動不便的旅客）提供特殊交通服務，可知這則訊息的對象為行動上有所限制的人，正解為(B)。

這則訊息的對象是誰？
(A) 攜帶大件行李的人
(B) 行動受限的人
(C) 缺乏現金的人
(D) 獨自旅行的女子

【類型】提問細節題型

【詞彙】
mobility行動性

【正解】(B)

哪一項有關此交通服務的敘述正確？

(A) 它需要事先預訂。

(B) 它是受歡迎的公共交通工具。

(C) 它是一種機場接機服務。

(D) 他對大部份人來說都是負擔不起的。

【類型】提問細節題型

【詞彙】

pickup service接機服務

【正解】(A)

一個人要預約此交通服務之前，最好要做什麼？

(A) 參觀遊客中心

(B) 詢問價格

(C) 租用語音導覽

(D) 抽號碼牌

【類型】細節提問題型

【詞彙】

tourist counter遊客中心

【正解】(B)

---

154 Which statement is correct about the transport services?

(A) It needs booking in advance.

(B) It's a popular public transport.

(C) It's an airport pickup service.

(D) It's unaffordable for most people.

【解析】訊息中提到we..., offering... transport services through advance booking（我們透過事先預約……提供……交通服務），可知這個交通服務需要事先預約，正解為(A)。選項(B)(C)(D)所述在訊息中均未提及，故不選。

---

155 What is one encouraged to do before reserving the transport service?

(A) Visit the tourist center

(B) Inquire about prices

(C) Rent an audio guide

(D) Take a number

【解析】由訊息最後表示Please request a quote before booking（預約前請先詢價），可知在預約此交通服務之前，要先詢問價格，正解為(B)。

Questions 156-158 refer to the following letter.

December 2017

Dear Michelle,

We received the deposit Rotary Club of Youth made.

We would like to thank you and all your Rotarians for this huge effort. We are definitely sure that this will be of great help for those in need of housing.

We plan to build, at least, twenty houses in March, and there will probably be a second construction in May. We will be sending pictures and whatever news we have concerning the project.

Thank you for becoming a blessing for Mexico.

You set an example of the real essence of Christmas.

We wish you all a very merry Christmas.

Norma Robles,
Rural Reconstruction, Mexico

2017年十二月

親愛的Michelle，

我們收到青年扶輪社匯的存款了。

我們想感謝您以及所有的扶輪社員所做的這個大奉獻。我們相信這絕對對那些需要住所的人來說會是一大幫助。

我們計劃在三月興建至少二十幢房屋，五月很可能會有第二批興建工程。我們會將照片以及任何有關此建屋專案的消息寄給您。

感謝您賜福給墨西哥。

您為聖誕真諦立下了模範。

祝您有個愉快的聖誕節。

Norma Robles，
墨西哥農村重建

【詞彙】
deposit存款／Rotary Club扶輪社／Rotarian扶輪社員／essence真諦

寫這封信的目的為何？
(A) 詢問房價
(B) 討論房屋翻修事宜
(C) 表達感謝
(D) 續約

【類型】內容主題題型

【正解】(C)

156 Why is this letter written?

(A) To inquire about a house

(B) To discuss a house renovation

(C) To express thankfulness

(D) To renew the contract

【解析】由信件內容表示感謝對方的善款，可知這封信的目的是要表達感謝，正解為(C)。

根據信件內容，青年扶輪社做了什麼事？
(A) 他們提供了醫療支援。
(B) 他們創辦了一間學校。
(C) 他們自願做社區服務。
(D) 他們捐了一筆錢。

【類型】細節提問題型

【詞彙】
  community service社區服務

【正解】(D)

157 According to the letter, what did Rotary Club of Youth do?

(A) The provided medical assistance.

(B) They established a school.

(C) They volunteered for community service.

(D) They made a donation.

【解析】由信件一開始表示We received the deposit Rotary Club of Youth made.（我們已收到青年扶輪社所匯的存款），可知青年扶輪社捐了一筆錢。deposit指存到某銀行帳號的存款。正解為(D)。

這筆捐款將可能被用來做什麼？
(A) 蓋暫時住處
(B) 購買聖誕裝飾品
(C) 翻新一間辦公室
(D) 興建一間綜合醫院

【類型】提問細節題型

【正解】(A)

158 What will the donated money probably be used for?

(A) Building temporary accommodation

(B) Buying Christmas decorations

(C) Renovating an office

(D) Establishing a general hospital

【解析】 由信件中表示We are definitely sure that this will be of great help for those in need of housing（我們絕對相信這對那些需要住所的人來說會是一大幫助），可知這筆錢將會被用來提供需要的人住所，選項中以(A)所述為最有可能的答案，正解為(A)。其他選項所述均與住所無關，故不選。

Questions 159-161 refer to the following email.

Dear Mr. Adams,

With regard to your application and the subsequent interview you had with us, we are pleased to offer you the position of Purchasing Assistant in WALTS Company.

As we discussed, this is a full-time position of 40 working hours a week, and your initial salary will be £14,000 per year. Your first day in this position will be March 19th, 2018.

Please confirm your acceptance of this offer by replying to this letter no later than Feb. 28, 2018.

We are looking forward to your joining our staff.

Best wishes,
Diana Watkins, HR Manager

親愛的Adams先生，
有關您的應徵信以及隨後跟我們的面試，我們很高興提供您WALTS公司的採購助理一職。

如我們所談到的，這是一個一星期40個工時的全職職務，而你的起薪將會是一年一萬四千英鎊。你在這個職務的到職日是2018年3月19日。

請在2018年2月28日之前回覆這封信，確認你是否要接受這個職務。

我們很期待你成為我們的一員。

最佳的祝福
Diana Watkins
人事部經理

【詞彙】
subsequent 接下來的

159 What is the purpose of this e-mail?
(A) To confirm the time of a meeting
(B) To invite an applicant to an interview
(C) To negotiate salary
(D) To offer a position

【解析】由信件第一句後半部提到we are pleased to offer you the position（我們很樂意提供您這個職務），可知這封信的目的是要提供職務，正解為(D)。

這封郵件的目的為何？
(A) 確認會議時間
(B) 邀請應徵者面試
(C) 協商薪資
(D) 提供職務

【類型】內容主題題型

【正解】(D)

哪一項有關提供給Adams先生的職務之敘述是正確的？
(A) 這是個約聘職務。
(B) 這是個管理職務。
(C) 這是個全職職務。
(D) 它需要經常出差。

【類型】提問細節題型

【正解】(C)

160 Which statement about the position offered to Mr. Adams is true?
(A) It's a contract position.
(B) It's an executive position.
(C) It's a full-time position.
(D) It involves a lot of business travel.

【解析】根據信件內容，提供給Adams先生的職務是Purchasing Assistant（採購助理），並非管理職務，而且是full-time position（全職工作），選項(A)(B)可刪除不考慮，選項(C)所述正確，故為正解。信件內容中並未提到這份職務是否需要出差，因此選項(D)並非適當選項。

Adams先生接下來應該要做什麼？
(A) 準備第二輪面試
(B) 回對方信告知決定
(C) 打電話給Diana重新安排會面時間
(D) 寄出他的履歷和應徵信

【類型】提問細節題型

【正解】(B)

161 What is Mr. Adams supposed to do next?
(A) Prepare for the second-round interview
(B) Reply to this e-mail with his decision
(C) Call Diana to reschedule the appointment
(D) Send his resume and application letter

【解析】由信件結尾提醒Please confirm your acceptance of this offer by replying to this letter （請回覆此信確定您是否接受這份職務），可知Adams先生接下來應該要回信，告知他是否決定接受這份工作，故正解為(B)。

★**Questions 162-164 refer to the following text message chain.**

------------------ November 25, 2017 ------------------

Mindy0122
22:00

> Dear all, tomorrow we're having the department meeting at 11 AM in Rm 201.

------------------ November 26, 2017 ------------------

Mindy0122
8:45

> Dear all, for those who haven't arrived at the office, the office is closed today due to heating failure. With office closing today, our meeting today will now be on Monday 28th November, at 2:30 PM.

8:46   Carol Chang

> Tks, Mindy.

8:46   Carol Chang

> Are we still meeting in Rm. 201 on Monday?

Mindy0122   8:50

> Yes, we are. See you Monday.

----2017年11月25日----

Mindy0122
22:00

> 各位，明天我們將在上午十一點於201室開部門會議。別遲到了。

----2017年11月26日----

Mindy0122
8:45

> 各位，還沒到公司的人，因為暖氣壞掉，公司今天沒開。因為公司今天沒開，所以我們今天的會議現在改到十一月二十八日下週一下午兩點半。

8:46   Carol Chang

> 謝啦，Mindy。

8:46   Carol Chang

> 我們星期一一樣在201室開會嗎？

Mindy0122   8:50

> 對，沒錯。星期一見。

第一則簡訊的目的是什麼？
(A) 它是個提醒。
(B) 它是個預約。
(C) 它是個提議。
(D) 它是個採購訂單。

【類型】內容主題題型

【正解】(A)

162 What is the purpose of the first text message?

(A) It's a reminder.

(B) It's a reservation.

(C) It's an offer.

(D) It's a purchase order.

【解析】由簡訊告知大家明天開會的時間地點，可知這應該是個提醒，正解為(A)。

公司今天為何沒開？
(A) 暖氣壞了。
(B) 今天有颱風。
(C) 沒有電。
(D) 今天是國定假日。

【類型】提問原因題型

【正解】(A)

163 Why is the office closed today?

(A) The heating is not working.

(B) There is a typhoon.

(C) There is a power failure.

(D) It's a national holiday.

【解析】由第二則簡訊中表示the office is closed today due to heating failure（因為暖氣壞掉，公司今天沒開），可知公司今天沒開的原因是暖氣壞掉，正解為(A)。

由於公司沒開，何者有所變動？
(A) 會議記錄者
(B) 會議地點
(C) 會議時間
(D) 會議主席

【類型】提問細節題型

【正解】(C)

164 What has been changed due to office closing?

(A) The minute taker

(B) The meeting location

(C) The meeting time

(D) The meeting moderator

【解析】由our meeting today will now be on Monday...（我們會議現在改到星期一……）可知會議時間有所更動，但後面的簡訊內容表示會議地點依然在201室，可知更改的只有會議時間，故正解為(C)。會議記錄者及會議主席在簡訊中並未被提及，不需考慮。

Questions 165-167 refer to the following information.

👍*A Tour of Central Library*

ℹ️ Thu, Feb 8 2018 　🕐 2:30 pm – 4:00 pm
🚌 Central Library

This tour will explore the architectural significance and history of Kingsland Public Library's (KPL) landmark Central Library at Grand Crown Plaza. The tour will introduce attendees to the history of the library's spaces and its services. The tour will also give attendees a behind-the-scenes glimpse at the library's underground storage "Cellars" and the Kingsland Collection's "Morgue" of archival materials.

This tour can accommodate up to 20 people on a first-come, first-served basis.

The tour involves climbing and descending stairs. Tours meet in the Grand Lobby next to the Reception Desk and depart 5 minutes after the start time.

👍中央圖書館遊覽團

ℹ️ 星期四，2018年二月八日
🕐 下午兩點三十分至四點
🚌 中央圖書館

這個遊覽團將會探索大皇冠廣場上京士蘭公立圖書館的建築重要性及歷史。遊覽團將會向參加者介紹圖書館空間的歷史以及其服務內容。同時也會讓參加者一窺一般不對外開放的圖書館地下儲藏室「地窖」以及收集京士蘭檔案資料的「資料室」。

這個遊覽團以先到先得的原則，招收最多二十名團員。本團行程需要上下樓梯。集合地點在接待櫃檯旁的大廳，並且在開始時間五分鐘後出發。

【詞彙】
architectural 建築的／significance重要性／
behind-the-scenes私下／morgue 資料室／
archival material檔案資料／accommodate容納／
first-come, first-served先到先得／descend下降

這個圖書館遊覽時間多長？
(A) 一個半小時
(B) 兩小時
(C) 兩個半小時
(D) 三小時

【類型】提問細節題型

【正解】(A)

165 How long will this library tour take?

(A) One and a half hours

(B) Two hours

(C) Two and a half hours

(D) Three hours

【解析】由海報上標示遊覽時間為下午兩點半至四點，可知這個圖書館遊覽行程需時一個半小時，正解為(A)。

遊覽團的集合地點為何？
(A) 在入口
(B) 在大廳
(C) 在噴水池旁
(D) 在電扶梯旁

【類型】提問細節題型

【詞彙】
assembly point集合點

【正解】(B)

166 Where is the assembly point for the tour?

(A) At the entrance

(B) In the lobby

(C) By the fountain

(D) At the escalator

【解析】海報內容表示Tours meet in the Grand Lobby next to the Reception Desk（遊覽團在接待櫃檯旁的大廳集合），可知遊覽團集合點為大廳，正解為(B)。

關於這個遊覽何項敘述不正確？
(A) 要參加必須事先預約。
(B) 它最多能讓廿人參加。
(C) 遊覽過程包含爬樓梯。
(D) 參加者能參觀未開放給民眾的地方。

【類型】提問細節題型

【正解】(A)

167 Which of the following is incorrect about the tour?

(A) To join you need to book in advance.

(B) It can accommodate up to 20 people.

(C) The tour involves stair climbing.

(D) The attendees will visit places not open to the public.

【解析】選項(B)(C)(D)所述內容均在文中有提及，因此都是正確敘述。由海報內容表示This tour... on a first-come, first-served basis.（本團……採先到先得方式），可知參加此團是現場參加，不需事先預約，因此選項(A)所述並不正確，正解為(A)。

Questions 168-171 refer to the following post.

Charlotte Cunningham ▶ Air Rosa
21 hours • Le Mesnil-Amelot, France • 🌐

Yesterday we had a flight with Air Rosa from Maldives to Amsterdam Netherland with a connection at CDG, Paris. The flight from Maldives was delayed and we missed our connecting flight, which we fully understand can happen. However, instead of helping us, your "customer service" would rather treat us as if we were a problem to your company. Your staff sent us in different directions and no one took responsibility or was even nice to us. On top of this you lost our baggage.

We understand mistakes happen and flights get delayed. But our advice is that you shape up your customer experience and start taking care of the people that pays for traveling with you. We are disappointed and will actively advise our friends and family not to travel with you if your don't start showing consideration for your customers.

⌂Like　💬 comment　➡share

Charlotte Cunningham ▶ 留言給 Air Rosa

21小時– 美斯阿美洛，法國 – 🌐

昨天我們從馬爾地夫搭羅莎航空到荷蘭阿姆斯特丹，途中在巴黎戴高樂機場轉機。從馬爾地夫起飛的班機延誤了，因此我們錯過了轉接班機，我們完全了解這是有可能發生的事。然而，你們的「客服人員」寧願視我們如貴公司的麻煩人物，也不願幫我們處理問題。你們的員工要我們到不同的地方詢問，卻沒有人願意負起責任或甚至和顏以對。更糟糕的是你們還把我們的行李給弄丟了。

我們明白錯誤有時候會發生，班機也會延誤，但是建議你們在貴公司顧客經驗上好好表現，並開始照顧那些付錢搭你們航班的人。我們很失望，而且如果你們不開始關心你們的顧客的話，我們會主動建議家人朋友不要搭你們的飛機。

⌂讚　💬留言　➡分享

羅莎航空 早安Charlotte，謝謝您在這裡與我們聯繫。我們非常遺憾聽到您在我們巴黎機場所得到的令人不滿的服務。這深深影響我們，而且不符合我們既有的高客服標準。您的回饋訊息對我們來說非常寶貴，而且會傳達到相關部門。我們想要對此有進一步的後續行動，因此請您將您的訂位證明及／或機票號碼以私人訊息傳給我們。我們更遺憾聽到您行李延誤的事。如果您可以提供行李證明、行李條號碼或是訂位全名，我們將很願意幫您調查。我們樂意以任何我們能夠做到的方式提供幫助，並再次向您遭遇的麻煩向您致歉。

Air Rosa Good morning Charlotte,
Thank you for contacting us here. We are very sorry to hear about the unsatisfying service you have received at our airport in Paris. This concerns us deeply and does not conform with our usual high standard of customer care. Feedback like yours is invaluable to us and will always be forwarded to the departments concerned. We would like to follow up on it further and therefore kindly ask you to send us your booking reference and/or ticket number in a private message.
We're further sorry to hear about your baggage delay. We will gladly look into it for you, if you could provide your baggage reference, tag number or the full name as it appears on the booking. We are happy to help in any way we can and once again apologize for the troubles you've endured.

這則貼文主要是關於什麼？
(A) 顧客投訴
(B) 促銷活動
(C) 飯店翻修通知
(D) 美好的旅遊經驗

【類型】內容主題題型

【正解】(A)

168 What is the post mainly about?
　　(A) A customer complaint
　　(B) A promotional campaign
　　(C) A hotel renovation
　　(D) A wonderful travel experience

【解析】由貼文內容提到「飛機延誤」、「服務人員沒有提供幫助」、「態度不佳」甚至「遺失行李」等關鍵字，可知這則貼文與選項(B)(C)(D)所述無關，選項(A)的「顧客抱怨」是最符合貼文內容的答案，故為正解。

169 How did Charlotte Cunningham feel when she wrote the post?

(A) Excited　　　　　(B) Miserable

(C) Furious　　　　　(D) Calm

【解析】貼文最後表示的disappointed（失望的）並未出現在選項中，因此必須根據內容所呈現的語氣，判斷貼文者貼文時的情緒。由貼文表示will actively advise our friends and family not to travel with you（我們會主動建議家人朋友不要搭你們的班機），推測貼文者的情緒反應較接近「生氣」、「憤怒」，因此選項(C)會是最適當的答案。

Charlotte Cunningham寫這則貼文時，感覺如何？

(A) 興奮的

(B) 悲慘的

(C) 憤怒的

(D) 冷靜的

【類型】提問細節題型

【詞彙】

miserable悲慘的／

furious憤怒的

【正解】(C)

---

170 According to the post, which of the following didn't happened to Charlotte?

(A) Her flight was delayed.

(B) Her baggage was lost.

(C) She missed her connecting flight.

(D) She was forced to give up her seat.

【解析】由貼文內容提到一開始The flight... was delayed（飛機誤點）、we missed our connecting flight（我們錯過轉接班機）以及最後的you lost our baggage（你們弄丟我們的行李），可知選項(A)(B)(C)皆是確實發生的事，只有選項(D)所述之「被迫放棄座位」沒有出現在貼文內容中，故正解為(D)。

根據貼文內容，下列哪件事沒有發生在Charlotte Cunningham身上？

(A) 她的班機延誤了。

(B) 她的行李被弄丟了。

(C) 她錯過她的轉接班機。

(D) 她被迫放棄座位。

【類型】提問細節題型

【正解】(D)

---

171 According to the reply from Air Rosa, what did they offer to do for Charlotte?

(A) To compensate for her loss

(B) To inquire into her missing baggage

(C) To help her book another flight

(D) To provide free pickup service

【解析】由航空公司在貼文回覆中先提到We're further sorry to hear about your baggage delay（聽到您行李延誤我們更加遺憾），並進一步表示We will gladly look into it for you（我們樂意為您調查），可知航空公司提出要為貼文者調查行李下落，正解為(B)。

根據羅莎航空的回覆，他們提出要為Charlotte做什麼？

(A) 賠償她的損失

(B) 調查她遺失的行李

(C) 幫她訂另一班飛機

(D) 提供免費接機服務

【類型】細節提問題型

【詞彙】

compensate賠償

【正解】(B)

在飛毛，我們提供各種題型與大小的狗狗美容以及膳宿服務。我們自2003年起就為社區服務。我們經驗豐富的寵物美容師每年都會參加寵物美容研習會，學習最新的技巧以及有關寵物美容的重要資訊。我們從2011至2017年都被票選為貝爾非斯特最佳寵物美容院，並且自2015至2017年連續三年贏得英國狗狗美容冠軍。

我們待您的狗狗一如自己的。我們的合格美容師及造型師在飛毛為您的狗狗提供他們應有的特別照顧。

我們只接受預約服務，所以請撥打0113-4408-9935聯絡我們有關您狗狗的美容及膳宿需求。

Questions 172-173 refer to the following advertisement.

Here at Flying Fur, we groom and board dogs of all shapes and sizes. We have been serving the community since 2003. Our experienced pet groomers attend grooming seminars annually to learn the latest techniques as well as important information regarding pet grooming. We were voted Belfast's Best Pet Groomers 2011-2017, and won three successive British Dog Grooming Championships from 2015-2017.

We treat your pets as our own. Our certified groomers and stylists are here at Flying Fur to give your dogs the special attention they deserve.

We are by appointment only, so please call us at 0113-4408-9935 for all your grooming and boarding needs.

【詞彙】
groom打扮／board提供膳宿／pet groomer寵物美容師／successive連續的／certified合格的

172 What kind of service does Flying Fur provide?

(A) Elderly care service

(B) Dog grooming service

(C) Child care service

(D) Hairdressing services

【解析】由廣告一開始便表示：we groom and board dogs（我們幫狗狗美容，並提供狗狗膳宿），可知Flying Fur這家店提供「狗狗美容服務」，正解為(B)。

Flying Fur提供什麼樣的服務？

(A) 老人照護服務

(B) 狗狗美容服務

(C) 孩童照護服務

(D) 美髮服務

【類型】提問細節題型

【正解】(B)

---

173 How does Flying Fur do business?

(A) By appointment only

(B) On a first-come, first served basis

(C) By online reservations

(D) By affiliate programs

【解析】由廣告最後表示We are by appointment only（我們只接受預約），可知Flying Fur是採預約制的方式做生意，正解為(A)。

Flying Fur如何做生意？

(A) 僅採預約制

(B) 以先到先服務為原則

(C) 採線上預訂

(D) 採會員制

【類型】提問細節題型

【詞彙】

affiliate成員；成員組織

【正解】(A)

留言給：Louisa Greene

日期／時間：六月十八日下午兩點三十分

來電者：Julia Elliot

留言內容：Elliot小姐希望明天能跟我們早一小時在總公司會面。請在九點半而非十點半到那裡。她要求更改會議時間 是因為其他部門主管也想參加會議。她想確保在他們到達之前有足夠時間可以將一切準備好。請查一下你的日程表，並確認這個時間你可不可以，並打手機給Elliot小姐。

留言記錄者：Angela Bradley

Message for: Louisa Greene

Date/Time: June 18/2:30 p.m.

Caller: Julia Elliot

Message: Ms. Elliot would like to meet one hour earlier tomorrow morning at the headquarters. Please be there by 9:30 instead of 10:30. She requests the change of meeting time because heads of other departments want to join the meeting as well. She wants to make sure there's enough time to get everything ready before they arrive. Please check your schedule to make sure the time works for you and call Ms. Elliot on her cellphone.

Message taken: Angela Bradley

174 What time was tomorrow's meeting originally scheduled?

(A) 10:30 a.m.

(B) 11:30 a.m.

(C) 9:30 a.m.

(D) 8:30 a.m.

明天的會議本來是安排在幾點？

(A) 上午十點半

(B) 上午十一點半

(C) 上午九點半

(D) 上午八點半

【類型】提問細節題型

【正解】(A)

【解析】留言內容表示「會議時間提前一小時」，接著要求「九點半而不是十點半到」，可知原本的會議時間是十點半。正解為(A)。

---

175 What is Louisa Greene supposed to do when receiving the message?

(A) Send an e-mail message to Angela

(B) Take a cab to the headquarters

(C) Look at her schedule for June 19

(D) Meet Ms. Elliot at her office

Louisa收到訊息之後應該做什麼？

(A) 寄一封電子郵件給Angela

(B) 搭計程車到總公司

(C) 看他六月19日的行程安排

(D) 到Elliot小姐的辦公室見她

【類型】提問細節題型

【正解】(C)

【解析】留言最後表示Please check your schedule to make sure the time works for you and call Ms. Elliot at her cellphone（請查你的日程表確認時間沒問題，並打手機給Elliot小姐），可知Louisa收到六月十八日的留言之後，要查隔天，也就是六月十九日的日程，接著要致電Elliot小姐。選項(C)所述符合留言，故為正解。

寄件人：Jerry Moore
收寄人：Steven Harris
主旨：派對邀請

附件：門票訂購單.doc ,📄

親愛的Harris先生，

坎貝爾基金會邀請您出席由巴塞隆納最著名且最受歡迎的劇團——紫瓢蟲——演出的義演。所有收益都將捐給巴塞隆納動物保護協會。

您也許已經知道坎貝爾基金會自2009年起已經在Summerfield地區從街頭拯救了超過一千隻狗狗。但是也許你並不知道我們創立了以絕育及預防針接種為主的計劃，並且每年捐出幾千元給公私立狗狗收容所，以協助地方組織在西班牙各地實施結紮計劃，以人道方式應付流浪狗過剩問題。

您可以透過購買三月十五日晚上七點，在Summerfield大學禮堂演出的義演門票來為這些努力做出一點貢獻。門票費用一個人只要20歐元。

請按此訂購您的門票。如果您無法出席但仍希望能捐款，我們也會感激接受。

我們充滿期盼的等候您的回覆。

最佳祝福
Jerry Moore

From: Jerry Moore
To: Steven Harris
Subject: Party Invitation

Attached: Ticket Order Form.doc ,📄

Dear Mr. Harris,
The Campbell Foundation invites you to attend a special benefit performance featuring Purple Ladybug, one of the most famous and popular theatre troupes in Barcelona. All proceeds will go towards the Animal Protection Association Barcelona.

You may already know that the Campbell Foundation has saved over 1,000 dogs from the streets in the Summerfield area since 2009. But perhaps you didn't know that we created programs that focus on sterilization and vaccination, and donate thousands of euros every year to public and private dog shelters to help local organizations implement spay and neuter programs all throughout Spain to humanely address the overpopulation of street dogs.

You can also make a contribution to these efforts by purchasing a ticket to the benefit performance, which will be held on March 15 at 7:00 p.m. in the Summerfield University auditorium. The cost of the ticket is only €20.00 per person.

Please click here to order your tickets. If you cannot attend but would still like to make a donation, we will receive it appreciatively.

We await your response with anticipation.

Best wishes,
Jerry Moore

Ticket Order Form

To reserve tickets please complete and submit the booking form

Full name: | Steven Harris |

E-mail: S_Harris0918@fmail.com

Phone number: | 077-8475-6884 |

Number of tickets: ⊙ | 5 |

Total amount of payment: | €100 |

Donation options:

⊙ Custom; Enter your own amount: | €300 |

○ Predefined: ☐ €10 ☐ €20 ☐ €50 ☐ €100

Credit card information:

⊙ Visa   ○ Master   ○ JCB   ○ American Express

Credit card number: 5433-XXXX-XXXX-0059

Please mail the tickets to:

| Avenida Diagonal 731, **Barcelona**, 08014 |

| Submit |

門票訂購單

預定門票請提妥並提交此預約單

全名：| Steven Harris |

電子郵件：
S_Harris0918@fmail.com

電話號碼：| 077-8475-6884 |

門票數量：⊙ | 5 |

總費用：| €100 |

捐款選擇：

⊙自訂；輸入您自己的金額

| €300 |

○固定金額：

☐€10 ☐€20 ☐€50 ☐€100

信用卡資料：

⊙Visa   ○Master   ○JCB

○American Express

信用卡號碼：
5433-XXXX-XXXX-0059

請將門票寄至：

| 巴塞隆納市08014，
Avenida Diagonal 731號 |

| 提交 |

寄件人：Steven Harris
收件人：Jerry Moore
主旨：回覆：派對邀請

親愛的Jerry，
謝謝你的邀請。你知道我一直以來都很關心流浪狗的福利問題。下毒、電刑以及射殺等殘忍的方式從來不是適合解決流浪狗過剩的方法。我深深感謝你們為了讓流浪狗更美好的未來所做的努力。

這是一個非常有意義的活動，我非常樂意幫助支持你們的努力。我剛剛提交了線上門票訂購單。我的妻兒都會跟我一起去。希望透過每個人的努力我們能盡可能從各種不同的惡劣環境中拯救更多的狗兒。

三月十五日見。

最佳祝福，
Steven

From: Steven Harris
To: Jerry Moore
Subject: RE: Party Invitation

Dear Jerry,
Thank you for your invitation. You know that I have always concerned myself with the welfare of the street dogs. Cruel means such as poisoning, electrocution and shooting are never appropriate solutions to stray dog overpopulation. I deeply appreciate your efforts in leading the way to a better future for stray dogs.

This is a very meaningful event and I am very glad to help support your efforts. I just submitted the online ticket order form. My wife and children are all going with me. Hopefully together with everyone's efforts we can rescue as many dogs as possible from a variety of bad situations.

See you on March 15.

Best wishes,
Steven

【詞彙】
benefit performance義演／feature由……主演／
theatre troupe劇團／proceeds收益／sterilization絕育／
vaccination預防接種／spay割除卵巢／neuter閹割／
humanely 人道地／predefined 固定的／poisoning毒死／
electrocution電刑處死

176 Why is the first email written?

(A) To evaluate a new employee's performance

(B) To request financial support

(C) To introduce a company

(D) To sell tickets to a benefit performance

第一封信的撰寫目的為何？

(A) 評估一名新員工的表現

(B) 請求財務支援

(C) 介紹一家公司

(D) 賣一場義演的票

【類型】內容主題題性

【詞彙】

　evaluate 評估

【正解】(D)

【解析】由第一封信件內容主要在介紹Campbell基金會，以及舉行義演以募集捐款，並附上義演入場票訂購單以供訂購，可知這封信的目的是要賣義演門票，正解為(D)。

---

177 Which of the following is most similar to a "benefit performance"?

(A) Charitable entertainment

(B) Earning power

(C) Profit-making program

(D) sales volume

下列何者跟「義演」最相似？

(A) 慈善表演

(B) 盈利能力

(C) 牟利計劃

(D) 銷售量

【類型】相似字彙題型

【詞彙】

　charitable 慈善的

【正解】(A)

【解析】benefit performance指「公益表演」，演出門票收入會拿來做公益，與選項(A)的charitable表「慈善的」，charitable entertainment指「慈善表演」，演出收入一樣用在慈善用途，性質與benefit performance相近，故(A)為正解。

---

178 What does the word "proceeds" in the invitation letter refer to?

(A) Original receipts

(B) Annual income

(C) Discount provided

(D) Money donated

邀請函中的「proceeds」指的是什麼？

(A) 原來的收據

(B) 年收入

(C) 提供的折扣

(D) 捐贈的金錢

【類型】詞彙意義題型

【正解】(D)

【解析】邀請信上表示All proceeds will go towards...（所有收益將會捐至……），proceeds做名詞解時表「收益、收入」，根據邀請信前後文，可推測這個字指得應該是義演的收入，由於義演目的不在盈利，因此買票看表演的人也是以「捐款」為出發點購票，因此選項中以(D)的money donated（慨捐的金錢）為最適當的答案，正解為(D)。

根據門票訂購單，Steven除了買票之外還做了什麼？
(A) 他登記成為基金會義工。
(B) 他捐了300歐元。
(C) 他介紹一些潛在客戶。
(D) 他推薦幾個動物福利團體。

【類型】閱讀圖表題型

【詞彙】
sign up登記／
welfare group福利團體

【正解】(B)

179 According to the ticket order form, what else did Steven do in addition to purchasing tickets?

(A) He signed up to be a volunteer at the foundation.

(B) He made a donation of €300.

(C) He introduced some potential clients.

(D) He recommended a few animal welfare groups.

【解析】由門票訂購單的捐款選擇處，可看到Steven填入捐款金額300歐元，可知選項(B)所述正確，故為正解。

第二封信的目的為何？
(A) 婉拒邀請
(B) 接受邀請
(C) 提案邀請
(D) 確認協議

【類型】內容主題題型

【正解】(B)

180 What is the purpose of the second letter?

(A) To decline the invitation

(B) To accept the invitation

(C) To invite proposals

(D) To confirm an agreement

【解析】第二封信件內容提到已經完成購票，並表示「三月十五日見」，可知這封信目的是在「接受參觀義演的邀請」，正解為(B)。

★**Questions 181-185 refer to the following advertisement, information and letter.**

MD Towel Industrial Tourism & Explore Factory

Situated by Sunny Lake in Somerset County, MD Towel Industrial Tourism & Explore Factory is one of the biggest domestic and international towel producers in the U.S. Established in the 1970s, MD Towel Manufacturer remodeled its business, setting up its first tourism factory by Sunny Lake in 2012 and became a popular tourist attraction in the southwest Oklahoma. MD Towel Manufacturer's award-winning tourist factory opens its plants to tourists, introducing visitors how towels that we use on a daily basis are made.

The factory offers a variety of DIY sessions for both adults and children to learn to fold towels into different shapes such as cupcakes, lollipops, ice cream, animals, flowers and other designs and have fun. In addition, group tours of the factory are available to students of primary school, middle school and community-based organizations.

To book a group tour please click ***here*** for more details.

MD 毛巾工業觀光探索工廠

座落在Somerset晴光湖旁的MD毛巾工業觀光探索工廠是美國國內外最大的毛巾製造商之一。創立於1970年代的MD毛巾製造廠在2012年進行改組,在晴光湖旁設立其第一間觀光工廠,並成為奧克拉荷馬西南邊一處受歡迎的觀光勝地。MD 毛巾製造廠的得獎觀光工廠將其工廠對開放給觀光遊客參觀,將我們每日要用的毛巾的製造過程介紹給遊客。

工廠提供適合大人及小孩各種不同的自己動手做課程,可以學習將毛巾折成不同形狀,如杯子蛋糕、棒棒糖、冰淇淋、動物、花朵及其他設計,盡情玩樂。除此之外,工廠的觀光團可以讓小學、中學的學生及社會團體參加。

要預約團體遊覽請*按此*看詳細資訊。

選擇一個團體遊覽省大錢！參觀
MD毛巾工業觀光探索工廠！

➤團體遊覽時間／星期一至星
期五上午九點三十分及下午兩點
三十分

➤團體遊覽選擇
（不超過二十人的團體）

	遊覽時間	費用 （一人）
A 團	兩小時—— 一小時工廠參 觀+一小時自己 動手做課程： 杯子蛋糕毛巾 +棒棒糖毛巾	$10
B 團	一個半小時—— 一小時工廠參觀 +半小時自己動 手做課程：杯子 蛋糕毛巾或棒棒 糖毛巾	$8
C 團	一小時—— 半小時工廠參觀 +半小時自己動 手做課程：杯子 蛋糕毛巾或棒棒 糖毛巾	$5
D 團	一小時—— 工廠參觀	$4
E 團	一小時—— 自己動手做課 程：杯子蛋糕毛 巾+棒棒糖毛巾	$6

請電聯 +1 405-525-7788
或寄電子郵件至
jasonbradman@mdtowel.com
預約團體遊覽。遊覽只提供事前
預約。

Choose a group tour and save big with MD Towel Industrial Tourism & Explore Factory!

➤ **Group Tour Times/** Monday through Friday at 9:30 a.m. and 2:30 p.m.

➤ **Group Tour options**
  (for groups of less than 20 people)

	Length of time	Rates (per person)
Tour A	2 hours— 1 hour for the factory tour and 1 hour for DIY session: cupcake towel + lollipop towel	$10
Tour B	1 1/2 hours – 1 hour for the factory tour and 1/2 hour for DIY session: cupcake towel or lollipop towel	$8
Tour C	1 hour – 1/2 hour for the factory tour and 1/2 hour for DIY session: cupcake towel or lollipop towel	$5
Tour D	1 hour— factory tour	$4
Tour E	1 hour – DIY session: cupcake towel + lollipop towel	$6

Please contact +1 405-525-7788 or e-mail to jasonbradman@mdtowel.com to make an appointment for a tour. Tours are available by appointment only.

From: Katrina Blacks

To: jasonbradman@mdtowel.com

Subject: Factory Tour Reservation

Hi,

My name is Katrina Blacks and I'm a teacher at St. George Primary School. After reading the article about your Towel Industrial Tourism & Explore Factory on your website, I believe taking a tour of your factory would be a nice field trip for my Year 6 class. I'd like to reserve a 2-hour tour on October 25th at 2:30 p.m. for my 20 students.

Please let me know if the factory can take my reservation on the above-mentioned date and time.

Regards,
Katrina Blacks

寄件人：Katrina Blacks
收件人：
jasonbradman@mdtowel.com
主旨：工廠參觀預約

嗨，
我的名字是**Katrina Blacks**，是聖喬治國小的老師。在你們網站上讀到一篇關於你們毛巾工業觀光探索工廠的文章後，我認為到你們工廠參觀對我的六年級班級會是個很不錯的校外教學。我想幫我的二十位學生預約十月二十五日下午兩點半的兩小時遊覽。

請讓我知道上述日期及時間工廠是否能接受我的預約。

Katrina Blacks

【詞彙】
domestic 國內的／remodel 改組

181 Which statement is true about the towel factory?

(A) It is a newly built modern factory.

(B) It specializes in manufacturing towels.

(C) It is not open to the public.

(D) Their DIY sessions are designed for children.

【解析】由第一篇關於毛巾工廠的介紹宣傳文的內容，可知這間毛巾工廠創立于1970年代，並非新建的現代工廠；工廠有開放團體遊覽給遊客參觀，而且是和大人與小孩。因此選項中只有選項(B)所述正確，正解為(B)。

有關毛巾工廠的敘述何者正確？
(A) 它是一間新建的現代工廠。
(B) 它專門生產毛巾。
(C) 它不對外開放。
(D) 它們的自己動手做課程是專為兒童設計的。

【類型】提問細節題型

【正解】(B)

該工廠一天提供幾個場次的團體遊覽？
(A) 五個　　　(B) 四個
(C) 三個　　　(D) 兩個

【類型】提問細節題型

【正解】(D)

Katrina最有可能是在哪裡得到毛巾工廠提供團體遊覽的消息？
(A) 在該工廠的網站上
(B) 在一本月刊上
(C) 在報紙分類廣告上
(D) 在一場電視訪談上

【類型】提問細節題型

【詞彙】
classified ad 分類廣告

【正解】(A)

該工廠將會向Katrina的班級在十月廿五日的參訪收取多少費用？
(A) 80元　　　(B) 100元
(C) 160元　　　(D) $200元

【類型】提問細節題型

【正解】(D)

Katrina為什麼要帶她的班去工廠？
(A) 去野餐
(B) 去聽演講
(C) 去校外教學
(D) 去做歌唱表演

【類型】提問細節題型

【正解】(C)

---

182 How many sessions of group tours does the factory provide a day?

(A) Five　　　(B) Four

(C) Three　　　(D) Two

【解析】由團體遊覽團只有上午九點半以及下午兩點半，可知一天只開放兩個場次。正解為(D)。

---

183 Where did Katrina learn obtain the information about the Towel Factory?

(A) From the factory's website

(B) From a monthly magazine

(C) From classified ads in newspaper

(D) From a TV interview

【解析】由Katrina的信件上這句After reading the article about your Towel Industrial Tourism & Explore Factory on your website... 的關鍵字your website（你們的網站），可知Katrina是在工廠網站上看到毛巾工廠團體遊覽的消息。正解為(A)。

---

184 How much will the factory charge Katrina's class for their visit on October 25th?

(A) $80　　　(B) $100

(C) $160　　　(D) $200

【解析】由Katrina信件內容，可知她班上學生有二十人。她想預約兩小時的團遊，而由團遊價格表上顯示兩小時團費用一人是10元，因此可知全班的參觀費用為200元，正解為(D)。

---

185 Why is Katrina taking her class to the factory?

(A) To go on a picnic

(B) To listen to a speech

(C) For a field trip

(D) To give a singing performance

【解析】由Katrina在信上表示taking a tour of your factory would be a nice field trip for my Year 6 class（到貴工廠參觀，對我六年級的班級會是個很不錯的校外教學），field trip指「校外教學」，可知她是要帶班級去校外教學，正解為(C)。

★Questions 186-190 refer to the following information.

Welcome to the California Country House in Palm Springs!

Situated in the Southern California desert of Palm Springs, the California Country House is all about relaxing, putting your feet up and enjoying a vacation escape. Our classic Italian farm hotel provides just the right amount of rustic charm and fascination. Eighteen comfortable guest rooms surround a swimming pool amid a lush courtyard where palm trees and birds of paradise sway in the breeze complimenting spectacular mountains views!

Vacation Advisor Travelers' Choice Awards
California Country House is voted Number One in service on Vacation Advisor in Palm Springs among 180 properties competing for the spot. We look forward to having you stay with us, by the pool, at California Country House in Palm Springs. Book the room for your stay right now and see why our guests rate us so well time and time again, and year after year. Believe it or not, you'll never want to check out!

歡迎來到棕櫚泉的
加州鄉村屋！

位於棕櫚泉南邊的加州沙漠，加州鄉村屋就是個可以放鬆、翹腳享受假期的地方。我們古典的義式農場飯店提供的正是質樸的魅力。十八間舒適的客房圍繞著蒼翠庭院中的游泳池，享受微風中搖曳的棕櫚樹及天堂鳥所帶來的壯麗山景！

假期顧問旅行者選擇獎
加州鄉村屋在一百八十個競爭者中，在假期顧問被票選為棕櫚泉服務第一名。我們期待您能來棕櫚泉的加州鄉村屋住宿，在泳池邊與我們共度美好時光。現在就預訂您的住宿房間，親自體驗為何我們的房客會一再地年年給我們好評！信不信由你，你不會想要退房的！

Vacation. com

親愛的Miranda H, 你的預約已經獲得保證並且已經付清房價。您不需要致電給我們── 一切都已預訂妥當。

加州鄉村屋	$89 每房每晚價格

棕櫚東路335號棕櫚泉加州 92264-5523
+1 831-228-1234
☑ 免費早餐　☑ 免費網路連線
☑ 免費停車

Vacation.com 確認號碼	10934694756
入住日期	2017年五月三十日，星期二（下午兩點）
退房日期	2017年六月二日，星期五（中午）
您將停留	三晚，一房
支付金額	$267.00
取消政策	2017年五月二十七日前免費取消（凌晨零點）
入住時需要	• 信用卡或現金押金 • 政府核發的有照身分證件 • 最小入住年齡為十八歲

Vacation. com

Dear Miranda H, your booking is guaranteed and all paid for. There's no need to call us – it's all booked!

California Country House	$89 nightly price per room

335 E Palm Canyon, Palm Springs, CA 92264-5523
+1 831-228-1234
☑ Free breakfast　　☑ Free WiFi
☑ Free parking

Vacation.com confirmation no	10934694756
Check in date	Tuesday, May 30, 2017 (2PM)
Check out date	Friday, June 2, 2017 (noon)
Your stay	3 nights, 1 room
Amount paid	$267.00
Cancellation policy	Free cancellation before May 27, 2017 (0AM)
Required at check in	• Credit card or cash deposit required • Government-issued photo ID required • Minimum check-in age is 18

Great stay at California Country House-highly recommended

Miranda H from Chatham, Canada ★★★★☆

California Country House was a great home away from home. A very clean, friendly atmosphere provided a great vacation. We were picked up at the airport and dropped off too at the end of our stay. The limo service is a great addition to the many offerings here. It is available to arrive in style at the down town restaurant of your choosing. Bicycles on the property are also another convenient way of getting around.

The House is located in a great spot with easy walking distance to downtown as well as grocery stores and pharmacies. Ralphs, a supermarket just a few blocks east, has all the fixings for self-catering travellers. We really liked having the kitchen to use to cook meals so we didn't have to go out and eat.

The service and the hotel facility is OUTSTANDING. The staff at California Country House cannot do enough for you during your stay, from offering fresh fruit, a glass of wine, a towel for the pool to a suggestion for an outing such as a hike. Nina and Jake, and the rest of the crew there, made me feel so welcome.

I highly recommend staying here—— with the great amenities, service, friendly faces and reasonable rates, you can't go wrong! I will definitely go back and stay here again and look forward to going back! This family-owned business offers it all!

【詞彙】
fascination魅力／lush蒼翠茂盛的／compliment贈送／
pharmacy 藥房／fixings 配料／self-catering自炊

超棒住宿在加州農村屋──強力推薦

Miranda H來自加拿大查塔姆 ★★★★☆

加州鄉村屋是個讓人賓至如歸的地方。乾淨友善氛圍造就完美假期。來機場接機而且住宿結束也送我們到機場。接駁車是這裡許多服務之外很棒的額外服務。它可以讓你很有格調地到你選擇的市區餐廳。飯店的腳踏車也是另一個四處跑的便利方式。

村屋地點很棒，步行就能到市區以及雜貨店及藥房。Ralphs，一間東邊幾條街遠的超市有各種配料提供給自炊的旅客。我們真的很喜歡有個廚房可以使用來煮餐點，所以我們就不用出去吃。

飯店的服務及設施真的是太棒了！加州鄉村屋在你住宿期間提供各式各樣的服務，從提供水果、一杯酒、讓你在池邊使用的毛巾到要去哪兒出遊散步的建議。Nina和Jake以及其他的員工都讓我們覺得備受歡迎。

我非常推薦住在這裡──很棒的便利設施、服務、友善的面容以及合理的房價，你絕對不會選錯！我絕對會再回到這裡來住在這裡，而且很期待能回來！這個家庭式經營的飯店什麼都有！

根據第一份資料，加州鄉村屋是什麼？

(A) 一座休閒農場

(B) 一座滑雪度假村

(C) 一個度假飯店

(D) 一間地方醫院

【類型】提問細節題型

【詞彙】

leisure farm 休閒農場／
resort 度假村

【正解】(C)

---

186 According to the first piece of information, what is California Country House?

(A) A leisure farm

(B) A ski resort

(C) A resort hotel

(D) A local hospital

【解析】由第一篇介紹文中的這句Our classic Italian farm hotel...（我們的古典義式農莊飯店……），而且提到他們有eighteen guestrooms（十八間客房），適合vacation escape（躲開塵囂的休假地點），可知加州鄉村屋應該是個度假飯店。最有可能的選項為(C)。

根據第二份資料，何者不包含在價格內？

(A) 停車費

(B) 早餐

(C) 網路連線

(D) 加床

【類型】提問細節題型

【正解】(D)

---

187 According to the second piece of information, what is not included in the price?

(A) Parking fee

(B) Breakfast

(C) Internet connection

(D) Extra beds

【解析】由訂房確認信上，顯示房價包含free breakfast（免費早餐）、free WiFi（免費網路）及free parking（免費停車），卻沒有提到加床免費，可知「加床」服務沒有包含在房價內，正解為(D)。

根據訂房確認信，辦理入住時需要什麼？

(A) 確認信函

(B) 身分證明

(C) 機票影本

(D) 原購物發票

【類型】提問細節題型

【正解】(B)

---

188 According to the booking confirmation, what is required at check in?

(A) The confirmation letter

(B) Proof of identity

(C) Copy of flight ticket

(D) Original purchase receipt

【解析】由訂房確認信上，可看到入住時需要提供credit card or cash deposit（信用卡或現金押金）以及government-issued photo ID（政府核發的有照身分證件），可知正確答案為(B)。

189 What does "Ralphs" in Miranda's comment refer to?

(A) A Mexican restaurant

(B) A fitness center

(C) A supermarket

(D) A beauty salon

【解析】由Ralphs, a supermarket... 這句，逗號後為針對逗號前名詞做補充說明的同位語，可知這裡是在補充說明Ralph就是一家超級市場，正解為(C)。

Miranda的評論中的Ralphs是指什麼？

(A) 一間墨西哥餐廳

(B) 一個健身中心

(C) 一家超級市場

(D) 一個美容沙龍

【類型】提問細節題型

【正解】(C)

---

190 According to Miranda's comment, who most likely can Nina and Jake be?

(A) The owners of California Country House

(B) Regular customers of Ralphs

(C) Guests at California Country House.

(D) Companions of Miranda.

【解析】Miranda的評語是針對她在這間飯店得到的各種服務做評論，由Nina and Jake, and the rest of the crew there（Nina和Jake以及那裡的其他員工）這句話，可推斷Nina和Jake也是飯店內的工作人員，選項中只有(A)所指的「飯店老闆」也是飯店內的工作人員，故(A)為最有可能的答案。

根據Miranda的評語，Nina和Jake最有可能是誰？

(A) California Country House的老闆

(B) Ralphs的老顧客

(C) California Country House的客人

(D) Miranda的同伴

【類型】資訊判斷題型

【詞彙】
regular customer老顧客／companion同伴

【正解】(A)

Floyds書店訂單確認信

訂單編號：GB035346
日期：八月二十九日

這個通知信是要通知您，我們已經收到您訂購下列物品的訂單，並且目前已進行處理。請檢查以下資訊確認正確無誤：

顧客姓名：Stacy Perry
聯絡電話：012-2485-8888
寄件地址：曼徹斯特M12湖畔谷Smith宅45號

訂購項目	數量	單價
#59247346 珍珠竊賊 （作者 Elizabeth Wein - 2017出版）	1	$7.99
#23042309 月石： 從不存在的男孩 （作者 Sjon - 2013出版）	1	$8.59
#12083466 普羅旺斯的一年 （作者 Peter Mayle - 1989出版）	1	$7.99
小計		$24.57
新會員優惠		-2.45
運費		$3.00
Total		$25.12

Floyds Books Order Confirmation

Order Number: GB035346

Date: August 29

This notice is to inform you that your order for the following items has been received and is currently being processed. Please check the following details to confirm that they are accurate:

Customer Name: Stacy Perry
Contact Phone: 012-2485-8888
Shipping Address: 45 Smith House, Lakeside Valley, Manchester M12

Requested items:	Qty	Unit price
#59247346 *The Pearl Thief* (by Elizabeth Wein -published 2017)	1	$7.99
#23042309 *Moonstone: The Boy Who Never Was* (by Sjon -published 2013)	1	$8.59
#12083466 *One Year in Provence* (by Peter Mayle -published 1989)	1	$7.99
Subtotal		$24.57
New Member Discount		-2.45
Shipping		$3.00
Total		$25.12

Payment Details:
Debit/Credit Card Number: 22XX-XXXX-XXXX-6609
Card Owner: Stacy Perry
Billing Address: 45 Smith House, Lakeside Valley, Manchester M12

★All orders from Floyds Books ship within 12 hours of this confirmation notice and should be received within 3 business days.

Thank you for purchasing with Floyds.

From: Stacy Perry
To: Floyds Books <customerservice@floydsbooks.com.uk>
Date: Sep 5, 2018
Subject: My Book Order

Dear Floyds Customer Service,
I am writing this letter to inquire about my book order, GB035346, with you for three books on August 29. I received a confirmation letter, which informed me that my order would be delivered within three business days. In other words, I should have received my order no later than September 1st; however, it's already been a week and I'm still waiting for my books.

The delay of the delivery has caused considerable inconvenience as the books are supposed to be a birthday present for my daughter. I must receive them by tomorrow, otherwise I won't be needing them anymore, and I'll definitely cancel my order and ask for a full refund.

付費資訊：
現金卡/信用卡號碼：22XX-XXXX-XXXX-6609
信用卡持有人：Stacy Perry
帳單地址：曼徹斯特M12湖畔谷Smith宅45號

★所有Floyds書店的訂單都會在確認通知信函發出後十二小時內寄出，並應於三個工作日內送達。

感謝您向Floyds購書。

寄件人：Stacy Perry
收件人：Floyds Books <customerservice@floydsbooks.com.uk>
日期：2018年九月五日
主旨：我的書籍訂單

親愛的Floyds客服部，
我寫這封信是要詢問我的訂單，GB035346，在八月二十九日跟你們訂購的三本書。我收到一封確認信，告訴我三個工作天內就會收到訂單，也就是說，我應該最晚就要在九月一日前收到了。但是，已經過了一星期了，我到現在還在等我的書。

寄貨延誤已經對我造成很大的不便，因為這些書應該是我女兒的生日禮物。我明天一定就要收到，否則我將不再需要它們，而且我絕對會取消訂單並要求全額退款。

請你們立刻幫我查詢訂單狀態，並讓我知道發生了什麼事。
請盡快回覆。

Stacy Perry 謹上

寄件人：Floyds Books
收件人：Stacy Perry <stacy0318_sperry@netmail.com.uk>
日期：2018年九月五日
主旨：回覆：我的書籍訂單

親愛的Perry小姐，

在此回覆有關您書籍訂單GB035346一信，我代表Floyds書店為您因寄貨延遲所遭遇的不便向您誠摯地道歉。我們一收到您的信就立刻查詢您的訂單狀態。您的訂單在確認信寄給您當天就已經派送，但是很遺憾地，它被送到錯誤的地址。書已經被收回來，我們的快遞人員會在今天以前將它們送到您指定地址。

為了彌補我們所造成的不便，隨同您的書我們將送上一張下次購物七折的優惠券。

再次致上歉意。

最佳的祝福
Fiona Schmidt
Floyds書店客服部經理

Please could you check the status of my order immediately and let me know what is going on. Please respond as soon as possible.

Regards,
Stacy Perry

From: Floyds Books
To: Stacy Perry <stacy0318_sperry@netmail.com.uk>
Date: Sep 5, 2018
Subject: RE: My Book Order

Dear Ms. Perry

In reply to your letter concerning your book order, GB035346, I on behalf of Floyds Books sincerely apologize for the inconvenience that you faced because of the delivery delay. We checked the status of your order as soon as we received your letter. Your order was dispatched on the day the confirmation letter was sent to you, but unfortunately, it was delivered to the wrong address. The books have been retrieved and will be delivered to your designated address by our express courier by today.

To make up for the inconvenience we have caused, with your books we are sending a coupon for a discount of 30% on your next purchase.

Again, our apologies.

Best wishes,
Fiona Schmidt
Manager of Floyds Books Customer Service

191 According to the first e-mail, how did Stacy Perry make the payment?

(A) By credit card

(B) By cash

(C) By installments

(D) By phone

【解析】由訂單確認信上的付費資訊顯示「現金卡/信用卡號碼」，可知Stacy是用刷卡方式付款。正解為(A)。

根據訂單確認信，Stacy Perry用什麼方式付款？

(A) 刷卡

(B) 現金

(C) 分期付款

(D) 手機

【類型】提問細節題型

【詞彙】installment分期

【正解】(A)

---

192 Which statement about Tracy's order is true?

(A) She was provided a free delivery.

(B) She was offered a discount of 10%.

(C) She will collect her order at the store.

(D) She is a regular customer of Floyds Books.

【解析】由訂單確認信上的金額欄位，有顯示new member discount（新會員優惠），可知Stacy是新會員而非老客戶；優惠金額為小計金額的百分之十，可知新會員優惠為九折，正解為(B)。

有關Tracy的訂單，哪項敘述正確？

(A) 她得到免運費優惠。

(B) 她得到九折優惠。

(C) 她會到店內取貨。

(D) 她是Floyds書店的老客戶。

【類型】提問細節題型

【詞彙】
collect取貨

【正解】(B)

---

193 Why did Stacy write the e-mail?

(A) She received a damaged book.

(B) She wanted to change the delivery address.

(C) Her order didn't arrive on schedule.

(D) She received incorrect items.

【解析】由Stacy信件上表示it's already been a week and I'm still waiting for my books（已經過了一星期，我仍然在等我的書），可知Stacy的訂單還沒有寄達，正解為(C)。

Stacy為什麼要寫這封信？

(A) 她收到一本破損的書。

(B) 她想要更改送貨地址。

(C) 她的貨沒有準時送達。

(D) 她收到錯誤的物品。

【類型】內容主題題型

【正解】(C)

第三封信的目的為何？
(A) 確認購買訂單
(B) 核對會員資料
(C) 處理抱怨
(D) 為缺席致歉

【類型】內容主題題型

【詞彙】
verify 核對

【正解】(C)

194 What is the purpose of the third e-mail?

    (A) To confirm a purchase order

    (B) To verify membership information

    (C) To deal with a complaint

    (D) To apologize for being absent

【解析】Stacy的信件是「寄貨延遲」的客訴，而這封信則是針對Stacy的信件做回覆，因此這封信的目的是在「處理客訴」，正解為(C)。

根據第三封郵件內容，Stacy會連同她的書一起收到什麼？
(A) 一張折扣禮券
(B) 一本免費的書
(C) 一個折扣碼
(D) 一張購物收據

【類型】提問細節題型

【正解】(A)

195 According to the third e-mail, what will Stacy get along with her books?

    (A) A discount coupon

    (B) A free book

    (C) A discount code

    (D) A purchase receipt

【解析】由信件最後表示with your books we are sending a coupon for a discount of 30%（隨同您的書我們寄上一張七折優惠券），可知Stacy在收到書時，也會同時收到優惠券，正解為(A)。

★Questions 196-200 refer to the following information, advertisement and e-mail.

◇Working Holiday Visa Information◇ | ◇打工度假簽證資訊◇

If you're between 18 and 30 (or 35 for certain countries), you could be eligible for a Working Holiday Scheme visa, which enables you to earn a bit of cash as well as acquire some overseas work experience while traveling in New Zealand.

At present, New Zealand has a Working Holiday Scheme agreement with 42 countries around the world. Please note that some countries have quotas, so make sure you get your application in quickly once the quota opens.

The agreements we have with the 42 countries vary, but there are a few rules that apply for everyone. All applicants from all countries must—

➤ Have a passport valid for at least three months after your planned departure from New Zealand.

➤ Be at least 18 years old and not older than 30 (or 35 depending on your nationality).

➤ Meet our health and character requirements.

➤ Not bring dependents with you.

➤ Hold a return air ticket, or sufficient funds to purchase such a ticket.

➤ Have not previously visited New Zealand using the Working Holiday Scheme visa (or been approved for one).

➤ Be coming to New Zealand for a holiday, with working being the secondary reason for your visit.

如果你年齡在十八及三十歲之間（或在某些國家是三十五歲），你可能適合一個打工度假方案簽證，讓你可以一邊在紐西蘭旅遊，一邊賺錢同時在得到海外工作經驗。

現在，紐西蘭與世界上四十二個國家有打工度假方案協議。請注意有些國家有名額限制，所以當名額一開放，你就得立刻申請。

我們與四十二個國家的協議都不同，但是有些關定是適用於每一個人。所有各國的申請者都必須一

➤持有離計劃離開紐西蘭前至少三個月的有效護照。

➤至少十八歲以上，並不得超過三十歲（或依你的國籍為三十五歲）。

➤符合本國健康及資格要求

➤沒有依親者同行

➤持有回程機票，或是足以夠買回程機票的金錢

➤過去未曾持打工度假方案簽證至紐西蘭，或未曾被核發打工度假方案簽證

➤主要是來紐西蘭度假，打工是第二個原因

關於我們

W&T成立於2010年，是一家專門提供背包客來到紐西蘭個人協助的公司。我們為低於五人的團體提供在紐西蘭打工度假整個過程中專業以及個人化的協助與支援。在過去七年來我們在高工作配發率以及高推薦率上都得到極佳的聲譽。本公司所推出的以合理價600紐幣即涵蓋所有所需服務的「新手工具箱」將能幫助你充分利用你的打工假期。

與我們聯絡取得更多資訊。
www.workntravel.com
information@workntravel.com
+64 9 363 1833
或到我們的公司來：
皇后鎮9300峽谷路25號

About Us

Founded in 2010, W&T is a company specializes in providing personal assistance to backpackers arriving in New Zealand. We offer groups no bigger than 5 people professional assistance and personalized support throughout the whole process of a working holiday in New Zealand. Over the seven years we have obtained an excellent reputation for high job placement rate and high referral rate. Our Beginner Kit that covers all the services you need at a reasonable price of NZ$600 will help you make the most of your working holiday.

Contact us for more information.
www.workntravel.com
information@workntravel.com
+64 9 363 1833
or visit us at our office: 25 Gorge Road Queenstown 9300

收件人：
information@workntravel.com
寄件人：DAISUKE MATSUSHIMA
主旨：有關打工度假簽證的問題

嗨，
我是來自日本的Daisuke Matsushima。我目前在紐西蘭旅遊，並計劃在這裡停留久一點。根據規定，我只能在你們國家停留最多三個月，因此我想也許申請打工度假簽證對我來說是個選擇。你們的新手工具箱幫我一個朋友很快地找

To: information@workntravel.com
From: DAISUKE MATSUSHIMA
Subject: Questions Regarding Working Holiday Visa

Hi,
I am Daisuke Matsushima from Japan. I am currently traveling in New Zealand and planning to stay here longer. According to the regulations, I'm only allowed to stay in your country up to three months. Therefore I'm thinking maybe applying for a working holiday visa is an option for me. Your Beginner Kit helped a friend of mine

get hired in NZ fast and thus she recommended me to seek your advice and assistance. I'm wondering if your Beginner Kit also includes working holiday visa application. As I'm already in New Zealand, is it possible for me to apply for such a visa, and how long does it take to get the visa? It is very important that I get my working holiday visa before the expected departure date and get employed as soon as possible; otherwise I'll have to leave on November 19, 2018, and then come back.

I would like to stop by your Queenstown office to inquire about further membership details tomorrow morning. If you wish to contact me, I am only reachable via e-mail as I do not have a phone and contact number in NZ.
See you soon.

Warm wishes
Daisuke Matsushima

到紐西蘭的工作,因此她對見我尋求你們的建議與協助。不知道你們的新手工具箱是不是也包含打工度假簽證的申請。因為我人已經在紐西蘭,我有可能申請這樣的簽證嗎?還有拿到簽證需要多久時間呢?這很重要,因為我必須預定離境日前拿到打工度假簽證並且盡快找到工作,否則我就得在2018年十一月十九日離開,然後再回來。

我想在明天早上到你們皇后鎮的辦公室,諮詢有關進一步的會員細節。如果你想要跟我聯絡的話,只能透過電子信箱與我取得聯繫,因為我在紐西蘭沒有電話和聯絡號碼。很快見。

溫暖的祝福
Daisuke Matsushima

【詞彙】
be eligible for適合／working holiday 打工度假／
quota名額／dependent撫養者／
job replacement 工作更換／referral 推薦

第一則資訊是關於什麼？
(A) 如何申請移民簽證
(B) 如何延長旅遊簽證
(C) 打工度假簽證方案
(D) 如何將學生簽證轉為工作簽證

【類型】內容主題題型

【詞彙】
immigrant visa移民簽證／
visitor visa旅遊簽證／
student visa學生簽證／
work visa工作簽證

【正解】(C)

196 What is the first piece of information about?

(A) How to apply for an immigrant visa

(B) How to extend the visitor visa

(C) The working holiday visa scheme

(D) How to transfer from student visa to work visa

【解析】由第一則資訊標題為Working Holiday Visa Information（打工度假簽證資訊），可知這是提供有關「打工度假簽證方案」之訊息，正解為(C)。

W&T是什麼樣的一家公司？
(A) 打工度假服務公司
(B) 旅行社
(C) 國際人力仲介公司
(D) 移民代辦公司

【類型】提問細節題型

【詞彙】
immigration agency 移民代辦公司

【正解】(A)

197 What kind of company is W&T?

(A) A working holiday service provider

(B) A travel agency

(C) An international human resources agency

(D) An immigration agency

【解析】由W&T的廣告宣傳內容提到We offer... professional assistance and personalized support throughout the whole process of a working holiday...（我們提供……整個打工度假過程專業及個人化的協助與支援……），可知這家公司的工作業務以提供打工度假服務為主，正解為(A)。

198 Where did Daisuke hear about W&T?

(A) From a TV commercial

(B) From the radio

(C) From the Internet

(D) From a friend

Daisuke在哪裡得知W&T這家公司？

(A) 電視廣告

(B) 廣播

(C) 網路

(D) 朋友介紹

【解析】由Daisuke在信件上表示a friend of mine... recommended me to seek your advice and assistance（我的一位朋友……推薦我尋求你們的建議與協助），可知Daisuke應該是透過朋友介紹，才知道W&T這家公司，正解為(D)。

【正解】(D)

---

199 Which word has the closest meaning to the word "quota" in the first piece of information?

(A) situation

(B) allocation

(C) application

(D) segregation

哪個字與第一則資訊中的quota這個字意義最接近？

(A) 情形

(B) 分配額

(C) 申請

(D) 隔離

【解析】quota意指「名額」。選項(A)的situation表「情形」、選項(B)的allocation表「分配額」、選項(C)的application表「申請」、選項(D)的segregation表「隔離」，因此意義與quota最接近的應為選項(B)的allocation，正解為(B)。

【類型】字義選擇題型

【詞彙】
allocation 分配額／
segregation隔離

【正解】(B)

---

200 What's the best way to reach Daisuke in New Zealand at present?

(A) By cellphone

(B) By fax

(C) By e-mail

(D) By Skype

目前與Daisuke在紐西蘭取得聯繫的最佳方式為何？

(A) 用手機

(B) 用傳真

(C) 用電子郵件

(D) 用Skype

【解析】由Daisuke的信件最後表示因為他在紐西蘭沒有電話及聯絡號碼，因此I am only reachable via e-mail（只能透過電子郵件聯繫到我），可知目前在紐西蘭，要要用電子郵件才能聯絡上Daisuke，正解為(C)。

【類型】提問細節題型

【正解】(C)

訓練課程會從十月十二日進行至二十日，在這期間你將會與其他參加者組隊合作。

【類型】介系詞選擇題型

【詞彙】
attendant參加者

【正解】(B)

101 The training program will run from October 12th to 20th, _____ which you will work in a team with other attendants.

(A) for
(B) during
(C) by
(D) at

【解析】先行詞October 12th至20th（十月十二日至二十日）指的是一段時間，關係子句意指「在這段時間你將與其他參加者組隊合作」，因此介系詞要用during，表示「在……期間內」，正解為(B)。

保護公司顧客免受詐騙及財務犯罪對本公司是至關重要的事。

【類型】介系詞選擇題型

【詞彙】
fraud詐騙／
utmost最大的

【正解】(A)

102 Protecting our customers _____ fraud and financial crime is of utmost importance to our company.

(A) against
(B) upon
(C) with
(D) among

【解析】本題句義在表示「公司將保護顧客免受詐騙及財務犯罪視為最重要的事。」本題空格處的介系詞與動詞protect連用，意在表示「使免受……」，正解為(A)。

房屋持有人在新稅法生效前已經競相預付地產稅。

【類型】片語動詞選擇題型

【詞彙】
homeowner房屋持有人／
property tax房地產稅

【正解】(C)

103 Homeowners have raced to prepay property taxes before the new tax law _____ .

(A) takes place
(B) takes exception
(C) takes effect
(D) takes sides

【解析】本題前半句表示「房屋持有人競相預付地產稅」。後半句的主詞為new tax law（新稅法），主詞不是人，因此無法take exception（反對）某事，也無法有自主意識take sides（選邊站），因此選項(B)(D)可先刪除。take place用在「事件」的發生或進行，亦不適用new tax law，故亦非適當片語動詞。根據句義，房屋持有人是要在新稅法生效前，先以舊法繳納房屋稅，因此這裡的片語動詞應填入takes effect，以表示「新法生效」，正解為(C)。

104 The price of bitcoins has _____ more than 25 percent from an all-time high of nearly $20,000 reached last month.

(A) discriminated　　(B) duplicated
(C) deliberated　　(D) depreciated

比特幣的價格從上週到達近兩萬美元的歷史高點之後，至今已跌了超過二十五個百分點。

【類型】動詞選擇題型

【詞彙】
bitcoin比特幣／
all-time空前的

【正解】(D)

【解析】由本題後半句意可知bitcoin（比特幣）在上個月價格達到歷史新高，句子中的介系詞from（從）透露空格中的動詞應該是有「從高處掉落」的含義，選項中的四個動詞只有depreciate（降價；貶值）最適合本句句義，其他動詞放在空格中皆與句義格格不入，故正解為(D)。

105 The theme park is _____ closed and is expected to reopen on November 1st.

(A) personally　　(B) temporarily
(C) successively　　(D) constantly

該主題樂園暫時關閉，預計在十一月一日重新開幕。

【類型】副詞選擇題型

【正解】(B)

【解析】由本題後半句「會在十一月一日重新開幕」，可知主題樂園只是目前暫時關閉，故適當的副詞為temporarily，表示主題樂園目前「暫時關閉」，正解為(B)。選項(A)的personally指「私下地」；選項(C)的successively表「連續地」；選項(D)的constantly指「持續不斷地」，均與本題句義不合，故不選。

106 Passengers without electronic tickets need to pay the traffic fees _____ .

(A) in cash　　(B) in turn
(C) in addition　　(D) in common

沒有電子票卡的乘客必須以現金支付交通費。

【類型】副詞片語選擇題型

【詞彙】
electronic ticket電子票卡／
traffic fee交通費

【正解】(A)

【解析】沒有電子票卡的乘客，無法以電子票卡支付交通費用，必須以其他方式支付交通費用，選項中只有(A)的in cash（用現金）表示「以使用現金的方式支付」，其他副詞片語與「付款方式」皆無關，因此(A)為最適合本處空格的副詞片語，故為正解。

飲用酒精飲料會損害你的駕車或操作機器的能力。

【類型】動詞選擇題型

【詞彙】
consumption消費／
alcoholic酒精性的／
beverage飲料／
prejudice 不利；損害／
machinery機器

【正解】(A)

---

107 Consumption of alcoholic beverages _____ your ability to drive a car or operate machinery.
(A) prejudices
(B) advances
(C) captures
(D) transpires

【解析】空格前為本句主詞：consumption of alcoholic beverages（飲用酒精性飲料），空格後為本句受詞：your ability to drive a car or operate machinery（開車或操作機器的能力），根據酒精性飲料對人體機能的影響來判斷，空格中的動詞應為(A)的prejudice（損害），以表示「喝酒會影響開車」，正解為(A)。

所有有關人事薪資的問題都請直接撥分機1181找Emily Waltz。

【類型】動詞選擇題型

【詞彙】
personnel salary人事薪資／
extension分機

【正解】(C)

---

108 All questions concerning personnel salary should be _____ to Emily Waltz at extension 1181.
(A) introduced
(B) contributed
(C) directed
(D) attributed

【解析】本句意在表示「有關人事薪資的問題要找Emily Waltz」。introduce... to sb.是表示「將……介紹給某人」；contribute to意指「捐助；促成」某事；direct sth. to sb.意指「將某物指向某人」；attribute to則為「將……歸因於」之意。根據句義，放在be動詞後面空格，表被動的過去分詞應為directed，表示「將這些問題導向負責人事薪資事務的人Emily Waltz」，正解為(C)。

109 I'll have to discuss this matter with my supervisor _____ I can give you an answer.

(A) as long as
(B) before
(C) while
(D) besides

我必須先跟主管討論這件事，才能給你答覆。

【類型】連接詞選擇題型

【詞彙】
supervisor主管

【正解】(B)

【解析】空格前的句子表示「我將必須跟主管討論這件事」，空格後的句子表示「我能夠給你答覆」，分析前後兩句的關係，較合理的情況應該是「答覆你之前必須先跟主管討論」，因此根據語意，空格處的連接詞應該填入before，表示處理事情應有的順序，正解為(B)。其他選項的連接詞放入句子中皆無法使句義完整，故不選。

---

110 Owing to the dense fog, the airport will be closed for at least a _____ 6 hours, until 8 p.m.

(A) more
(B) other
(C) further
(D) past

由於濃霧的關係，機場會再繼續關閉至少六小時，一直到晚上八點。

【類型】形容詞選擇題型

【詞彙】
dense fog濃霧

【正解】(C)

【解析】本句是要表示機場因為濃霧的關係，將會關閉至晚上八點。根據句義，機場在之前已經關閉了，但是濃霧未散，會再繼續關閉一段時間，因此空格中的形容詞應填入further（另外的；進一步的），a further 6 hours即「再至少另外關閉六小時」，正解為(C)。

---

111 Let's look over the numbers to see _____ workable this plan is.

(A) where
(B) how
(C) whether
(D) however

我們來檢查一下數字，看看這個計劃的可行程度如何。

【類型】連接詞選擇題型

【詞彙】
workable 可行的

【正解】(B)

【解析】本句意在表示「看看計劃可行程度如何」，並沒有提到地點，因此空格中的連接詞不會放where，選項(A)可不考慮；選項(C)的whether若放在空格中，則後面句子的結構應變成：whether the plan is workable；選項(D)的however意指「無論如何；不管用什麼方法」，與本句語意不合。選項(B)的how意指「程度如何」，放在本句空格中表示「計劃的可行性如何」，是最適當的連接詞，故(B)為正解。

讓眾人驚訝的是，這家新餐廳逐漸把競爭對手給比了下去。

【類型】片語動詞選擇題型

【詞彙】
competition競爭者；比賽對手

【正解】(A)

112 To everyone's surprise, the new restaurant is _____ the competition.

(A) edging out
(B) digging out
(C) reaching out
(D) letting out

【解析】本題句子意在表示「令眾人意外的是，新餐廳將所有競爭對手都排擠出去了」，也就是「打趴所有競爭者」之意。將選項中的四個片語動詞套入空格，只有選項(A)能使整句意義完整，其他片語動詞放在空格中皆會讓句子語意不通，故正解為(A)。

可惜的是，因為事先安排事情了，我沒辦法加入你們的慶祝活動。

【類型】形容詞選擇題型

【正解】(A)

113 Unfortunately, I won't be able to join you for the celebration because of a _____ arrangement.

(A) prior
(B) inferior
(C) better
(D) former

【解析】本句意在表示「因為一個事先安排好的事情，沒辦法加入你們一起慶祝」，根據句義，because of後面應指「事先就安排好的事」，因此(B)(C)可先刪除不考慮；prior與former都有「在前的」之含義，但是prior意指「時間上在先的」，而former則指「兩者中在前的」，因此這裡應該要用prior才符合句義，正解為(A)。

我們的業務人員都是按抽佣薪資機制聘雇的。

【類型】動詞選擇題型

【詞彙】
salesperson 業務人員／
commission佣金／
pay system薪資系統

【正解】(B)

114 Our salespeople are _____ on a commission-based pay system.

(A) assigned
(B) employed
(C) dispatched
(D) underscored

【解析】動詞assign用來表示「分派工作」，常與to連用；dispatch指「派送、發送」，underscore表「在……劃線」，有「強調」之意，根據動詞所代表的意義及用法，選項(A)(C)(D)均與本題句義不合。be employed 意指「受聘用」，放在空格中表示公司內的業務員是以抽佣金為主的薪資機制聘用，句意符合情理，故(B)為正解。

115 Employees _____ to take their seven-day annual leave at once must submit application two months in advance.

(A) planning   (B) to plan

(C) plans   (D) planned

計劃一次請完七天年假的同仁一定要提前兩個月提出申請。

【類型】動詞時態選擇題型

【詞彙】
annual leave 年假

【正解】(A)

【解析】本題空格處的動詞省略了關係代名詞及be動詞who are，因此動詞plan應為分詞形式。因為動作為主詞employees（員工）主動行為，而非被動行為，故分詞應為現在分詞planning，正解為(A)。

---

116 Instead of _____ their hours on paper, part-time employees are required to do that on the company website, starting from July 1st.

(A) recorded   (B) recording

(C) being recorded   (D) been recorded

從七月一日起，兼職人員必須在公司網站上記錄工作時數，而非記錄在紙上。

【類型】動詞時態選擇題型

【正解】(B)

【解析】instead of表「代替」，後面應接名詞或動名詞，因此後面空格處應將動詞record改為動名詞recording，正解為(B)。

---

117 The exact date of the Company Sports Day has not been _____ , but it will definitely be sometime in April.

(A) integrated   (B) preserved

(C) modified   (D) determined

公司運動會的確切時間尚未決定，但一定會是在四月的某個時間。

【類型】動詞選擇題型

【詞彙】
integrate 合併

【正解】(D)

【解析】本題後半句表示「公司運動會舉行時間一定會在四月某個時間」，但由sometime（某一時間）這個字，可知還沒有決定出確定的日期，因此空格中的動詞以determined最適合本句語意，正解為(D)。

Zinova不會拍電視廣告，而是會以網路廣告活動來將其新智慧型手機推出上市。

【類型】連接詞選擇題型

【詞彙】
TV commercial 電視廣告／
advertising campaign廣告活動

【正解】(C)

118 ＿＿＿＿ creating a TV commercial, Zinova will launch its new smart phone with an Internet advertising campaign.

(A) Even though

(B) So as to

(C) Rather than

(D) With regard to

【解析】本句意在表示「Zinova會以網路廣告活動，而不是拍電視廣告，來推出新智慧手機」，選項中的連接詞中只有rather than適合本句句義，故為正解。even though後面通常要接一個句子，而非名詞；so as to後面要接原形動詞，因此(A)(B)都不適用於本題空格。with regard to表「有關」，根本與本句語意不合。

工廠的生產在主機停止運轉後於昨天下午暫時停止。

【類型】動詞選擇題型

【詞彙】
production生產／
break down 停止運轉

【正解】(B)

119 Production at the factory was temporarily ＿＿＿＿ yesterday afternoon when the main machine broke down.

(A) closed

(B) halted

(C) arrested

(D) ended

【解析】本句意在表示「因為主機故障，生產暫時停止」，選項(B)的halt有「暫停」的含義，最適合本題句義，故為正解。

120 VeMo Auto will soon _____ a new CEO to succeed Allen Freeman who is retiring at the end of the month after 40 years of dedicated service.

(A) nominate

(B) assign

(C) allocate

(D) indicate

VeMo汽車公司很快就會提名新的總裁來繼任即將在月底退休，已盡心服務四十年的Allen Freeman。

【類型】動詞選擇題型

【詞彙】
succeed 繼任／
dedicated 專注的

【正解】(A)

【解析】本句意在表示VeMo Auto這家公司將會任命新的總裁人選，以繼任即將退休的原總裁。assign與allocate都可以表示「分派工作」，但經常與to連用，且要接表「工作內容」或「職務」的名詞，本句受詞後為不定詞＋動詞，因此不適用。indicate表「指示」，後面接名詞或that子句，亦不適用於本句空格。選項(A)的nominate表「任命、指定」，放在本句空格中，意指「指定一位新的總裁繼任……」，是為正解。

---

121 East Asia Plastics, one of the country's largest plastic goods _____ , failed to meet this year's revenue target of $5 billion.

(A) provide

(B) provisions

(C) provider

(D) providers

亞東塑膠，該國最大的塑膠製品供應商之一，沒有達到今年五十億營業額的目標。

【類型】詞彙選擇題型

【正解】(C)

【解析】本句兩個逗號中間的one of the country's largest plastic goods _____，為補充說明逗號前面East Asia Plastics的同位語，East Asia Plastics為一公司行號名稱，亦即一財團法人，Plastics指的是「塑膠公司」，並非複數名詞，因此空格處應為provider（供應商），而非providers，正解為(C)。

這款新多功能事務機所擁有的超越之前款式的主要優勢，就是它的影印功能。

【類型】介系詞選擇題型

【詞彙】
advantage 優勢／
multi-function多功能／
photocopy影印

【正解】(A)

122 The main advantage this new multi-function printer has _____ previous models is its photocopy function.

(A) over   (B) on

(C) from   (D) with

【解析】 be動詞is之前都是這個句子的主詞，即「這款新多功能事務機所擁有的超越之前款式的主要優勢」，空格處的介系詞表示的是「凌越」先前的事務機款式，選項中只有over有「超越」的含義，故正解為(A)。

這對夫妻希望由Angela熟食店或Veronica餐廳來負責他們結婚典禮之後的喜宴酒席。

【類型】連接詞選擇題型

【詞彙】
take charge of 負責／cater承辦酒席／reception宴會

【正解】(C)

123 The couple would like _____ Angela Deli or Veronica's Restaurant to take charge of catering for the reception after their wedding ceremony.

(A) both   (B) neither

(C) either   (D) whether

【解析】本題要考的是either... or... ，表示「兩者中非此即彼；兩者擇一」的句型用法。由於句子中Angela Deli及Veronica's Restaurant之間有連接詞or，可知前面空格處必須填either，正解為(C)。

很重要的一點，任何有關我們商議合約的資訊都不應該被透露給第三者。

【類型】形容詞選擇題型

【詞彙】
disclose透露／
third party第三者

【正解】(B)

124 It is _____ that no information concerning our business contract should be disclosed to third parties.

(A) publishable   (B) imperative

(C) confidential   (D) apparent

【解析】本題意在表示「商業合約內容不得透露給第三者」，根據語意，這類要求關係到商業機密，有一定的重要性，故空格處的形容詞應填入表示「極重要的」imperative，正解為(B)。

125 Under the terms of your warranty for this air conditioner, you can receive free maintenance for twelve months _____ the date of purchase.

(A) undergoing

(B) following

(C) passing

(D) preceding

【解析】本題後半句意在表示「你可以自購買日期後十二個月享有免費維修」，選項(B)的following 意指「在……以後」，放在空格中正好可以表示「購買日之後」，故(B)為正解。

在這台冷氣機的保固期內，你可以享有自購買日起十二個月的免費維修。

【類型】詞彙選擇題型

【詞彙】
warranty保固／
maintenance 維護

【正解】(B)

---

126 During the last year, U.S. exports to China expanded by 18%, _____ U.S. imports from China increased by 12%.

(A) as

(B) while

(C) because

(D) since

【解析】本題前後句在做輸出額與進口額的比較，因此連接詞應用有「儘管、雖然」之含義的while。其他選項的連接詞皆不適用於本題句義，故不選。正解為(B)。

去年，儘管美國對中國的進口額增加了百分之十二，美國對中國的輸出額卻增加了百分之十八。

【類型】連接詞選擇題型

【詞彙】
export輸出額／
import進口額

【正解】(B)

---

127 After recent negotiations with government officials, Manila Spinning & Weaving Corp. has announced the _____ of a brand new textile mill in Quezon City, the Philippines.

(A) open   (B) opens

(C) opening   (D) opened

【解析】動詞announce後應接名詞或that子句作為受詞，因此本題空格處應為動名詞opening，正解為(C)。

在最近一次與政府官員協商之後，馬尼拉紡織公司已經宣布要在菲律賓的奎松市開一間全新的紡織廠。

【類型】詞彙選擇題型

【詞彙】
negotiation協商／
government official政府官員／
textile mill紡織廠

【正解】(C)

北約可夏郡的失業率估計將大大提升至28%，造成許多居民必須到臨近城市求職。

【類型】詞彙選擇題型

【詞彙】
unemployment失業率／
gigantic巨大的／
resident居民／
seek employment求職

【正解】(D)

128 Unemployment is estimated to be at a gigantic 28% in the North Yorkshire, _____ many residents to seek employment in nearby cities.
(A) leave (B) to leave
(C) left (D) leaving

【解析】動詞leave在本句中做「使……處於某種狀態」解，由於逗號前後兩個句子的主詞相同，都是unemployment（失業率），因此後半句可以分詞構句表現，將leave改為分詞leaving即可，正解為(D)。

為了維持其對地方發展主要貢獻者的地位，M&Mars公司會再次盡可能地與當地供應商合作。

【類型】副詞選擇題型

【詞彙】
position地位／
leading領導的／
contributor貢獻者／
regional development地方發展

【正解】(C)

129 To maintain its position as a leading contributor to regional development, M&Mars Inc. will _____ work with local suppliers as far as possible.
(A) seldom (B) never
(C) once again (D) briefly

【解析】根據本句前半段句意，M&Mars與當地供應商合作的目的是為保持其作為地方發展主要貢獻者的地位，因此空格處若填入否定副詞如seldom（很少）或never（從未）都與語意不合；填入once again（再次）會比較符合常理，正解為(C)。

藉由在主要的二十五個超市提供當日配送服務，我們預期在下個季度增加百分之二十的營收。

【類型】動詞選擇題型

【詞彙】
same day delivery當日配送／
revenue營收／quarter季度

【正解】(A)

130 By offering same day delivery services in major 25 markets, we _____ increasing our revenue by 20% over the next quarter.
(A) anticipate (B) believe
(C) consent (D) participate

【解析】本題前半句表示「藉由提供當日配送服務」，後半句表示「下一季可提升百分之二十的營收」；根據前後語意，可推測提供此服務的用意是「預期」會提升營收，表示「預期未來會發生的事」要用anticipate這個動詞，正解為(A)。believe後面通常接that子句，因此不適用此空格中的動詞。其他兩個選項的動詞的用法亦與本句語意不合，故不選。

> **PART 6**

Directions: Read the texts on the following pages. A word or phrase is missing in some of the sentences. Answer choices are given below each of these articles. Select the best answer to complete the text. Then mark the letter (A), (B), (C) or (D) on your answer sheet.

Questions 131-134 refer to the following e-mail.

Dear Ms. Wilson,

I am Julia Robinson, the Purchasing Specialist of A&D Garment Company. We learn that your company is a leading manufacturer that produces high ___131___ fabrics; therefore we are very interested in purchasing products from you.

We would greatly appreciate it ___132___ you could send us your latest product catalogue, ___133___ .

As we wish to discuss what products to purchase in our department meeting held this Friday afternoon, we will need the catalogue by Tuesday ___134___ have enough time to review it before the meeting.

Looking forward to hearing from you as promptly as possible.

Best wishes,

Julia

親愛的Wilson小姐，

我是A&D服飾公司的採購專員 Julia Robinson。我們得知貴公司是生產優質布料的主要製造商，因此我們很希望能向您購買產品。如果您能寄給我們貴公司最新的產品型錄，無論是電子檔或紙本，我們都將不勝感激。

由於我們希望能在這星期五下午舉行的部門會議中討論要購買什麼產品，我們將需要在星期二就拿到型錄，如此一來才會有足夠時間在開會前看過。

期待能盡快得到你們的回覆。

最佳的祝福

Julia

【詞彙】
Purchasing Specialist採購專員／garment服飾

131 (A) quality
(B) qualitative
(C) qualification
(D) qualify

【解析】此空格後面為名詞fabrics，因此空格應為一形容詞，選項(C)的qualification（條件）為名詞，而選項(D)的qualify為動詞，故可先刪除。選項(B)的qualitative表示「質的」，為quantitative（量的）的對應字，不適合用來形容一般名詞。選項(A)的quality 除用作名詞表「品質」之外，也可做形容詞表「高級的；優質的」，故是最適合放在此空格的形容詞，正解為(A)。

132 (A) whether
(B) although
(C) if
(D) because

【解析】if與whether都可做「是否」解，在某些句子中用法一樣，但是本句為條件句，意在表示「如果你能寄給我們型錄，我們會很感激」，條件句的連接詞應用if，正解為(C)。

★ **133** (A) as we've already made our decision
(B) around two hours ahead of the meeting
(C) either a soft copy or a hard copy is fine
(D) while the salary is not as good as expected

【解析】這封郵件的主旨在請求對方寄送型錄，選項(A)(B)(D)所述內容與型錄完全無關，只有選項(C)表示「電子檔或紙本都可以」，either... or... 表示「兩者擇一」，soft copy指型錄的「電子檔」，而hard copy指型錄的「紙本」，正解為(C)。

134 (A) so as to

(B) according to

(C) in relation to

(D) with reference to

【類型】連接詞選擇題型

【正解】(A)

【解析】空格後接的是動詞，故動詞前應該要有一個不定詞 to，四個選項中都有to，但是只有選項(A)的so as to（為了）是後面接動詞的用法，正解為(A)。選項(B)(C)(D)的to都用作介系詞，而非不定詞，後面都要接名詞，故不適用於此空格。

Questions 135-138 refer to the following information.

We believe in investing in the future and ___135___ young talent. That's why, as far back as 1975, Zap Inc. started its undergraduate scholarship scheme to help individuals realize their full potential.

As a Zap scholar, you will not only have the opportunity to work on projects that are ___136___ to your field of studies, but will also be able to experience the Zap work culture through our internship scheme. ___137___ completion of studies, Zap scholars will be deployed on various career tracks.

The application cycle will open following the release of JUPAS results and close two weeks later. Please apply via the ZapScholarship website. We thank all applicants for their interest in Zap Inc. and ___138___ .

【詞彙】
JUPAS = Joint University Programmes Admissions System 大學聯招

我們相信投資未來以及為我們的年輕才子們做好準備。因此，遠從1975年起，Zap集團就開始大學獎學金方案以幫助每個人發揮他們全部的潛能。

身為一個Zap獎學金獲得者，您將不僅擁有可以在研究相關學習領域專案的機會，也能夠透過我們的實習方案體驗Zap的工作文化。當結束學習時，我們也會為Zap獎學金獲得者部署不同的事業軌道。

應徵週期將會在大學聯招結果公佈後開始，並在兩星期後關閉。請透過ZapScholarship網站提出申請。我們感謝所有申請者的關注，並對於只有入圍的申請者會接到通知感到抱歉。

【類型】動詞時態選擇題型

【正解】(D)

135 (A) prepare

　　(B) to prepare

　　(C) preparation

　　(D) preparing

【解析】believe in後面接動名詞，表示「相信做某件事是對的」；連接詞and用來連接兩個詞性相同的詞彙，因此空格中的動詞跟前面的investing 一樣，都必須以動名詞呈現，因此prepare（將……準備好）在此需改為動名詞preparing，正解為(D)。

【類型】詞彙選擇題型

【正解】(A)

136 (A) relevant

　　(B) relate

　　(C) reliable

　　(D) relative

【解析】這裡要表示的「與你的學習領域有關的科研項目」，be relevant to sth. 為表示「與……有關的；與……切題的」之用法，正解為(A)。

【類型】介系詞選擇題型

【正解】(C)

137 (A) For

　　(B) With

　　(C) On

　　(D) At

【解析】這句是要表達「學習結束時，我們會為Zap獎學金獲得者部署不同的事業軌道」，on completion 為固定片語用法，表「結束時」，completion並無與其他選項中的介系詞連用的用法，因此正解為(C)。

★ **138** (A) believe that all applicants deserve a second chance
(B) regret that only shortlisted applicants will be notified
(C) welcome any comments you may wish to make
(D) apologize for all inconvenience we may have caused

【類型】句子插入題型

【詞彙】
regret對……感到遺憾／
shortlisted最後入選的／
comment評論

【正解】(B)

【解析】本段落在説明開放申請及申請結束的時間，還有提出申請的方式。選項(A)表示「相信所有申請者值得第二次機會」，這個句子突然提到「第二次機會」，與前後文有點格格不入，並不適合。選項(C)(D)與本段落主題無關，可不考慮。選項(B)接在We thank all applicants for their interest in Zap Inc.（我們感謝所有申請者對Zap Inc.提供的獎學金有興趣）後面，表示「只會通知最後入選的申請者，對此感到抱歉」，合情合理，為最適合放在此處的句子，故(B)為正解。

Questions 139-142 refer to the following advertisement.

All-inclusive Tour Package

全包式旅遊

We are well aware that handling the small details before a big trip is anything but relaxing. So, we're more than happy to ___139___ it for you.

By train or by plane, we organize the appropriate transportation. You will receive all the necessary information before departure. ___140___ .

Your rooms and suites are waiting for you in the very comfortable Village. Lazy sleep in mornings, ___141___ naps, beauty moments, ... you'll love every minute you spend in the room.

Your meals and refreshments are also ___142___ in your package. From breakfast to the evening meal without forgetting breaks for snacks, each Village offers a generous selection of varied dishes and snacks, at practically all hours.

我們深知應付一次大旅行之前的瑣碎小細節一點也不輕鬆，所以我們很樂意幫您處理這些事情。
無論是火車或飛機，我們會為您安排適合的交通工具。您會在出發前收到所有必要的資訊。您所要做的事情只有打包行李。
您的房間及套房已經在非常舒適的度假村中等著您了。晨間的慵懶睡眠、恢復精神的午盹、美容覺等等，您會喜愛您在房間裡度過的每一分鐘。

您的餐點及點心也包含在您的套裝行程內。從早餐到晚餐，甚至是休息時間的點心，每間度假村隨時都提供豐富的各式菜餚及點心。

【正解】(B)

139 (A) look after
(B) take care of
(C) get on with
(D) put up with

【解析】本句前面提到行前準備一點都不輕鬆，因此我們樂意為您處理。take care of這個片語動詞除了可做「照顧、留意」解之外，也有「處理（事情）」的含義，因此空格中的片語動詞應選(B)。其他選項的片語動詞與本句語意不合，故不選。

【類型】句子插入題型

【詞彙】
room service 客房服務／
7/24 一星期七天一天二十四小時（意指全天候全年無休）

【正解】(A)

★ 140 (A) All you need to do is to pack your bag
(B) Our room services are available 7/24
(C) As long as you make a reservation in advance.
(D) Your taxi will arrive in five minutes.

【解析】這一段在說明「有關交通工具方面的打點，我們都會安排妥當」，因此你什麼都不用做，「只需要打包自己的行李就好」，選項(A)的句子放在這裡最符合這個段落的主題，故為正解。

【類型】形容詞選擇題型

【正解】(B)

141 (A) prospective
(B) restorative
(C) innovative
(D) concentrative

【解析】這裡以逗號連接三個性質類似的名詞，空格後為nap（午睡），依午睡的性質與效果，空格中的形容詞以(B)的restorative（恢復健康的）最適合，其他選項的形容詞拿來形容nap並不合理，故不選。

142 (A) includable　　　　(B) included
　　　(C) including　　　　　(D) inclusive

【類型】詞彙選擇題型
【正解】(B)

【解析】這句是要表達「餐點也都包含在包套行程裡了」，主詞為「餐點」，因此這裡要用被動語態，be included in表「被包含進去」，空格中應填入(B)。如果用including，則主詞應為package，且including要用在逗號後，表「包括……」。選項(D)的inclusive表示「包含的」，通常與of連用，以be inclusive of sth.表示「包含某物」。選項(A)的includable表「可被包含在內的」，這裡的行程包套內容已經定案，因此includable不適用於此。

Questions 143-146 refer to the following notice.

=== Home Investment Loans ===

If you are considering ___143___ an income property, or finally buying that home-away-from-home, a First Bank Home investment loan which allows you to finance the purchase of a second property using the equity in your primary home is definitely ideal for you.

Compared ___144___ a personal loan, the First Bank Home investment loan provides a better interest rate and a longer term. Generally, you'll need a down payment of 25% of the purchase price. First Bank will work with you to arrange a smaller down payment by leveraging your own assets depending on your personal circumstances.

Our mortgage specialists can quickly ___145___ a mortgage amount that is comfortable for you based on your personal income and expenses. In many cases, we can even pre-approve to a specified fair market value. Once we receive your application, your First Bank mortgage specialist will contact you within 48 hours, and following the consultation, ___146___ .

＝房屋投資貸款＝

如果您正考慮購買一間收租用的房子，或終於買了一間度假用的房子，利用您原本的房子為抵押資產，以提供您購買第二間房子的資金的第一銀行住投資住房貸款對您來說絕對非常理想。

跟個人信貸比起來，第一銀行住房投資貸款提供更優惠的利率及更長的還款期。一般而言，您會需要一筆房價百分之二十五的頭期款。第一銀行會根據您的個人環境協助您提升資產以準備一筆較低的頭期款。

我們的貸款專員會根據您個人收支迅速地為您計算出讓您能輕鬆償還的貸款金額。在很多的案例中，我們甚至能提前核准指定的公平市場價值。一旦我們收到您的申請，您的第一銀行貸款專員會在48小時內與您聯繫，在諮詢後，您會在72小時內得知申貸結果。

income property 收益用的房產／finance 籌措資金／equity 抵押資產的淨值／interest rate利率／down payment 頭期款／leverage 使負債經營／mortgage 抵押借款／specialist專員／fair market value公平市場價值／consultation咨詢

【類型】動詞時態選擇題型

【正解】(C)

143 (A) purchase
(B) to purchase
(C) purchasing
(D) purchases

【解析】空格中的動詞時態根據本句動詞consider（考慮）的用法，必須為動名詞；consider V-ing表「考慮做某事」，正解為(C)。

【類型】介系詞選擇題型

【正解】(D)

144 (A) to
(B) against
(C) over
(D) with

【解析】這句是要表達「與個人貸款相比……」，compare with即表示「與……比較」之用法，因此空格中的介系詞應選with，正解為(D)。compare to表示「將……比作」，用在將某人或某事以……來做比喻，片語用法上與本句語意不合。其他介系詞如against或over則無與compare連用的用法，故不選。

【類型】動詞選擇題型

【正解】(C)

145 (A) eliminate
(B) plan
(C) calculate
(D) subtract

【正解】這句是要表示「根據收支計算貸款金額」，空格中的動詞後面所接的受詞為與數字有關的mortgage amount（抵押貸款金額），因此動詞用calculate（計算）最為適當。其他選項的動詞放在空格中都會使得句意顯得不合理。

★ 146 (A)your order will arrive at your designated address
(B) we are looking forward to seeing you again
(C) you will receive a decision within another 72 hours
(D) the exact meeting date and time will be announced

【解析】本段落最後主要是有關貸款核貸流程說明，前面已經提到申請貸款與專人諮詢的部分，依常理推斷，接下來應該就是核貸結果，因此最適合放在此空格處的句子應為告知核貸結果的時間，正解為(C)。

【類型】句子插入題型

【詞彙】
designated指定的

【正解】(C)

Directions: In this part, you will read a selection of texts, such as magazine and newspaper articles, letters, and advertisements. Each text is followed by several questions. Select the best answer for each question and mark the letter (A), (B), (C), or (D) on your answer sheet.

Questions 147-149 refer to the following poster.

聖誕市集

2017年十二月十四日至二十四日
每日上午十時至下午九時
單日通行票£5
季票£20
十二歲以下孩童免費

孩童活動

食物・飲料・攤商及手工藝品
抽獎・寫價競標・手工烘焙食品

矮丘公園

克里夫頓BS2矮丘路1200號
www.lowerhillchristmasbazaar.com

矮丘公園停車長提供
停車位 一天£4。

Christmas Bazaar

December 14-24, 2017
11 AM – 9 PM DAILY
£5 for a single day pass
£20 for a season pass
Kids 12 and under free

Kids Activities

Food • Beverages • Vendors & Crafters

Raffles • Silent Auction • Home Baked Goods

Lower Hill Park

1200 Lower Hill Road, Clifton, BS2
www.lowerhillchristmasbazaar.com

Parking is available in the Lower Hill Public Car Park £4/per day.

【詞彙】
bazaar市集／silent auction 寫價競標（參與競標者將出價寫在紙上，價高者得標。非傳統的喊價競標）

147 What is this poster for?

    (A) To invite vendors

    (B) To advertise for a car park

    (C) To promote an event

    (D) To recruit event planners

【解析】由海報內容標示聖誕市集的舉辦時間、地點及市集內容，可知這是一張「宣傳聖誕市集活動」的海報，正解為(C)。

這張海報是做什麼用的？
(A) 招攬攤商
(B) 為停車場做廣告
(C) 活動宣傳
(D) 招募活動企劃人

【類型】內容主題題型

【正解】(C)

148 What do we know about the bazaar according to the poster?

    (A) It's an 11-day event.

    (B) It's an annual event.

    (C) It's a campus event.

    (D) It's a company event.

【解析】由海報上所提供的資訊中，並未提及任何有關「學校」或「公司或部門」等內容，且並未說明這場市集是否為固定每年舉行的活動，因此選項(B)(C)(D)皆非適當敘述。由市集舉行時間為12月14日至12月24日，共十一天，可知這次活動為期十一天，選項(A)所述正確，故為正解。

根據海報內容，我們對這場市集活動知道什麼？
(A) 這是個為期十一天的活動。
(B) 這是個一年一度的活動。
(C) 這是個校園活動。
(D) 這是個公司活動。

【類型】提問細節題型

【正解】(A)

149 What can't people do at the bazaar?

    (A) Bid for the items they like

    (B) Draw lots

    (C) Watch animals doing tricks

    (D) Enjoy handmade cookies

【解析】由海報上的活動內容顯示有silent auction（寫價競標）、raffles（抽獎）、home baked goods（手工烘焙食品），可知選項(A)(B)(D)等活動都可以在市集中進行，只有選項(C)的動物特技並未出現在海報內容中，故這題應選(C)。

人們不能在市集內做什麼？
(A) 競標他們喜歡的物品
(B) 抽獎
(C) 看動物表演特技
(D) 享用手工餅乾

【類型】提問細節題型

【正解】(C)

不像許多新聞組織，為了讓我們的新聞盡可能地開放，我們並沒有設立付費牆。製作調查性新聞需要投入很多的時間、金錢及努力。由於我們自廣告得到的收益減少，我們越來越需要讀者資助我們。如果你讀了我們的報導，喜歡我們的報導，並願意幫助資助我們的報導，我們的未來將會更加有保障。請花一個月£4.99支持我們。

按此成為支持者

Unlike many news organizations, we haven't put up a pay wall so as to keep our journalism as open as we can. Investigative journalism takes a lot of time, money and hard work to produce. With the proceeds we get from advertising coming down, we increasingly need our readers to fund us. If you read our reporting and you like it and you're willing to help fund it, our future would be much more secure. Support us for £4.99 a month.

Click here to become a supporter

【詞彙】
pay wall付費牆（網站為保護其收費內容而設置的關卡）／investigative調查研究的

我們最有可能在何處看到這則廣告？
(A) 在一個新聞網站上
(B) 在一本故事書裡
(C) 在一本汽車雜誌裡
(D) 在班級佈告欄上

【類型】背景推測題型

【詞彙】
journal期刊

【正解】(A)

150 Where most likely can we see this advertisement?
(A) On a news website
(B) In a storybook
(C) In a medical journal
(D) On a class bulletin board

【解析】由we haven't put up a pay wall ...這句的關鍵字pay wall（付費牆），即網站上為某些內容所設置的付費關卡，可推測這篇文章應該是出現在網站上，選項中以(A)為最有可能的答案，故為正解。

151 What's the purpose of this advertisement?

(A) To give a warning

(B) To announce an event

(C) To raise money

(D) To recruit volunteers

這則廣告的目的為何？

(A) 提出警告

(B) 公佈活動

(C) 募集資金

(D) 招募義工

【類型】內容主題題型

【正解】(C)

【解析】由廣告中提到we increasingly need our readers to fund us（我們越來越需要讀者資助我們），並表示If... you're willing to help fund it, our future would be much more secure.（如果你願意幫助提供資金，我們的未來會更加有保障），最後更提出直接請求：Support us for £4.99 a month.（請每月£4.99支持我們），可知這篇廣告目的是在募集資金，正解為(C)。

---

152 Who is most likely to become a supporter?

(A) A party goer

(B) A workaholic

(C) A loyal reader

(D) A shopping queen

誰最可能成為支助者？

(A) 派對常客

(B) 工作狂

(C) 忠實讀者

(D) 血拼女王

【類型】邏輯推理題型

【詞彙】

party goer派對常客（常參加派對的人）／workaholic工作狂

【正解】(C)

【解析】由廣告中這句If you read our reporting and you like it...（如果你閱讀我們的報導並喜歡……）可知這則廣告所針對的對象是喜歡閱讀他們的報導的人，因此選項中以(C)的loyal reader（忠實讀者）為最有可能的支助者，正解為(C)。

進修資金介紹

2018年一月十九日星期四
下午3:15至下午4:00
就業服務處 Christopher大道
六號 – 第二訓練室

這場45分鐘的簡短談話會幫助你們了解有關碩博士資金來源—包含獎學金、助學金、政府貸款及其他資金機會。
這堂課包含：
• 申請資金時可運用的實用資源
• 資助者包含研究理事會及慈善機構的例子
• 去哪裡尋找研究生研究案
• 經驗分享：兩位已經得到資金的學生實例

這場座談會是免費參加，但名額有限，所以需要報名。欲報名請電郵Catherine Rubens。
(C.Rubens630@clifton.ac.uk)。

Introduction to funding further study

Thu 19 Jan 2018, 3:15 PM to 4:00 PM
Careers Service, 6 Christopher Avenue - Training Room 2

This 45-minute short talk will help you come to grips with funding Masters and PhDs, including scholarships, grants, government loans and other funding opportunities.
This session covers:

• Useful resources you can use when applying for funding
• Some examples of funders, including research councils and charities
• Where to find PG student case studies
• Experience sharing: Two examples of students who have been granted funding

The seminar is free but places are limited, so registration is required. To register, please email Catherine Rubens.
(C.Rubens630@clifton.ac.uk).

【詞彙】
come to grips with勉力應付／grant助學金

153 What is the purpose of this seminar?

    (A) To provide funding information

    (B) To recruit higher education students

    (C) To train a group of new employees

    (D) To present a business proposal

這個座談會的目的為何？
(A) 提供資金訊息
(B) 招收高等教育學生
(C) 訓練一批新員工
(D) 做一場商業提案簡報

【類型】內容主題題型

【正解】(A)

【解析】由標題Introduction to funding further study（進修資金介紹），可知這應該是提供如何得到進修資金之訊息的座談會，正解為(A)。

---

154 Who is this seminar for?

    (A) Those who needs funding for business

    (B) Those who needs support for higher education

    (C) Those who are seeking employment

    (D) Those who are getting married

這場座談會的對象是誰？
(A) 需要生意資金的人
(B) 需要高等教育支援的人
(C) 想要求職的人
(D) 即將結婚的人

【類型】邏輯思考題型

【詞彙】
seek employment求職

【正解】(B)

【解析】由座談會提供的訊息內容以「尋求就讀研究所及博士的資金機會」為主，可知需要進修高等教育，且缺乏資金的人最可能對這場座談會有興趣，正解為(B)。

---

155 What should one do before attending the seminar?

    (A) Fill out the request form

    (B) Pay a registration fee

    (C) Contact Catherine Rubens

    (D) Purchase a ticket

參加研討會前應該做什麼？
(A) 填寫申請單
(B) 付報名費
(C) 聯絡Catherine Rubens
(D) 買票

【類型】提問細節題型

【詞彙】
registration fee報名費

【正解】(C)

【解析】公告上表示The seminar is free（座談會免費參加），但是名額有限，若要報名卡位，則必須email Catherine Rubens（電子郵件聯絡Catherine Rubens），因此要參加研討會必須聯絡Catherine Rubens，正解為(C)。

倫敦日報

Charlie Harvey在dailylondon.co.uk
報導2017年一月23日 下午5:25
2017年 下午5:25

倫敦市長首次在今天發出最高空污警告，表示首都的空氣是「健康危機」。今天下午三點的數字顯示首都的空氣比霧濛濛的北京還要更差。英格蘭公共衛生署建議住在首都或其他得到警告的地區的人，依該減少戶外運動。

國王學院的專家認為倫敦最近這一波的空污是2011年以來最糟糕的一次，並且是交通污染合併為了讓住家在冬季保暖而燃燒木柴所帶來的空氣污染所造成。

癌症研究證實空污對人體會致癌並導致肺癌。根據統計，戶外的空污每年都在倫敦造成9,500個早死案例。空污不僅使本來的肺部狀況惡化，也會增加得到肺癌的風險。

有些學校過去幾天已經禁止孩童到戶外玩耍，因為空污已經超過可忍受程度。Khan先生表示：「這是個讓人遺憾的事實，但超過三百六十所小學位在違反法定污染限制的地區。」

Daily London

Charlie Harvey for dailylondon.co.uk   Monday 23 Jan 2017 5:25 pm

For the first time, London Mayor Sadiq Khan issued the highest air pollution alert today, indicating that the capital's air is a 'health crisis'. Figures showed that at 3pm today, the air in the capital city was even worse than that in smoggy Beijing. Public Health England suggests that people who live in the capital, or anywhere else subject to an alert, should reduce exercise outside.

Experts from King's College believe the recent spell of air pollution in London was the worst since 2011, and was resulted from the combination of traffic pollution and air pollution from wood burning, which was to keep households warm during the winter.

Cancer research proved that air pollution is carcinogenic to humans and can lead to lung cancer. According to the statistics, outdoor air pollution contributes to 9,500 premature deaths in London every year. It not only worsens existing lung conditions but also increases the risk of getting lung cancer.

Some schools have banned children from playing outdoors over the past few days, as the air pollution is excess of tolerable levels. "It is a shameful fact that more than 360 of our primary schools are in areas breaching legal pollution limits," said Mr. Khan.

【詞彙】
combination合併物／carcinogenic致癌的／
statistics 統計資料／contribute to促成／premature過早的

---

156 Which is the best title for the news?

(A) Air Pollution Crisis in London

(B) Top Attractions in London

(C) The Worst Victims of Air Pollution

(D) How Air Pollution Measured

【解析】由新聞內容以倫敦的空污情況為主軸，可知選項(A)最適合作為本篇新聞標題。新聞中並未特別提到空污的受害者，雖然有提到figures（指空污指數），但並未提及空污指數的測量方法，選項(B)更是隻字未提，因此(A)為最適當的答案。

何者最適合作為本篇新聞的標題？

(A) 倫敦的空污危機

(B) 倫敦的最佳景點

(C) 空污的最慘受害者

(D) 如何測量空污

【類型】內容主題題型

【正解】(A)

---

157 What do authorities discourage Londoners from doing?

(A) Smoking in public places

(B) Using a wood-burning stove

(C) Doing outdoor physical exercise

(D) Taking children to the parks

【解析】由新聞中提到Public Health England suggests that people who live in the capital... should reduce exercise outside（英格蘭公共衛生署建議住在首都的民眾……應該減少戶外運動），可知有關單位建議倫敦人應減少戶外運動，正解為(C)。

有關單位希望倫敦人不要做什麼事？

(A) 在公共場所吸菸

(B) 使用燃木火爐

(C) 做戶外體能活動

(D) 帶孩童到公園

【類型】提問細節題型

【正解】(C)

下列何者並非造成倫敦空污的原因？
(A) 車輛廢氣
(B) 燃木排放物
(C) 廚房廢棄物
(D) 家庭二氧化碳排放

【類型】提問細節題型

【詞彙】
exhaust 排出的氣／
emission 排放物／
waste 廢棄物／
CO2 (=Carbon Dioxide) 二氧化碳

【正解】(C)

---

158 Which of the following does not contribute to London's air pollution?

(A) Vehicle exhaust

(B) Wood-burning emissions

(C) Kitchen waste

(D) Household CO2 emissions

【解析】新聞中指出這次倫敦空污 was resulted from the combination of traffic pollution and air pollution from wood burning（由交通污染及燃木的空氣污染的合併物造成），選項(A)的vehicle exhaust（車輛廢氣）即traffic pollution（交通污染）；選項(B)與(C)的wood-burning emissions（燃木排放物）與household CO2 emissions（家庭二氧化碳排放）即air pollution from wood burning（來自燃木的空氣污染）。選項(C)的kitchen waste指「廚房廢棄物」，也就是「廚餘」，並非造成空污的原因，故正解為(C)。

Sadiq Khan的身份為何？
(A) 英格蘭公共衛生署的代言人
(B) 倫敦市長
(C) 國王學院的專家
(D) 癌症研究員

【類型】提問細節題型

【詞彙】
PHE=Public Health England 英格蘭公共衛生署

【正解】(B)

---

159 Who is Sadiq Khan?

(A) The spokesman of PHE

(B) The Mayor of London

(C) An expert from King's College

(D) A cancer researcher

【解析】由新聞開頭第一句London Mayor Sadiq Khan issued the...（倫敦市長Sadiq Khan發出……）可知Sadiq Khan身份即倫敦市長，正解為(B)。

Questions 160-162 refer to the following post.

used_auto_supervisor Want to own a Mercedes-Benz E Class E350? We have a beautiful used 2015 Mercedes-Benz E Class E350 for sale and you can have it for only $18,999 now! BlueTEC AMG Night Edition 4dr 9G-Tronic available. Heated leather seats —— 18" alloy wheels —— Cruise Control. Bluetooth-Electric Folding Mirrors —— Paddle Shift.

We are here Mon-Fri 9AM-6PM and Sat 9AM-4PM and ready to get you approved. Give us a call at (313) 635-7600, stop in, or visit our website www.usedautosupervisor.com for more info.

#usedcarforsale #benz_e350

♥ 252 💬 3

---

diva_magicgirl Nice. Wish I could afford it.

....

jonathan_1227 @samwang check this out

....

serena2001 @jackwu88 this might be the one you're looking for!

---

used_auto_supervisor
想擁有一輛Mercedes-Benz E Class E350嗎？我們有一輛美麗的2015年二手Mercedes-Benz E Class E350 要賣，你現在只要花$18,999就能擁有它！有AMG藍色科技夜行版 4dr 9速手自排變速系統。加熱真皮坐椅—十八吋合金車輪—巡航控制。藍芽充電式可折鏡面一方向盤換檔撥片。
我們週一到週五上午九點到下午六點以及週六上午九點至下午四點都在這裡，準備幫您取得貸款批准。打 (313) 635-760來電，親自過來或是參觀我們的網站 www.usedautosupervisor.com 取得更多資訊。

#usedcarforsale
#benz_e350
♥ 252 💬 3

diva_magicgirl
好棒。要是我買得起就好了。

....

jonathan_1227
@samwang 看一下

....

serena2001
@jackwu88 這輛車可能就是你正在找的！

【詞彙】
Mercedes-Benz 賓士（德國豪華名車）／BlueTec 藍色科技（賓士純淨柴油發動機）／9G-Tronic 9速手自排變速系統／alloy wheel合金車輪／cruise control巡航控制／Paddle Shift方向盤換檔撥片

這則貼文的目的為何？
(A) 宣傳一個旅遊套裝行程
(B) 出售一輛中古車
(C) 租一間公寓
(D) 找一名室友

【類型】內容主題題型

【詞彙】
tour package 旅遊套裝

【正解】(B)

160 What is the purpose of this post?

(A) To promote a tour package

(B) To sell a used car

(C) To rent an apartment

(D) To find a roommate

【解析】由貼文表示We have a beautiful used 2015 Mercedes-Benz E Class E350 for sale（我們有一輛美麗的二手2015 Mercedes-Benz E Class E350要賣），可知這則貼文是要出售一輛中古車，正解為(B)。

下列何者最有可能寫這篇貼文？
(A) 一位中古車商
(B) 一個書店老闆
(C) 一個消防員
(D) 一個中學生

【類型】邏輯判斷題型

【詞彙】
dealer經銷商／
fire fighter消防員

【正解】(A)

161 Who of the following was most likely to write this post?

(A) A used car dealer

(B) A bookstore owner

(C) A fire fighter

(D) A middle school student

【解析】由貼文者表示他們要賣一輛中古車，並且在貼文最後貼出聯絡時間及網站，推測貼文者可能是專營中古車買賣的經銷商，選項(B)(C)(D)都不太可能在平日每天做中古車買賣的生意，只有選項(A)為最有可能的人選，故正解為(A)。

何者不是獲取有關這輛中古車的進一步細節的方式？
(A) 參觀網站
(B) 以電子郵件詢問
(C) 打電話詢問
(D) 造訪經銷店

【類型】提問細節題型

【詞彙】
dealership經銷店

【正解】(B)

162 Which is NOT a means to get further details about the used car?

(A) Visit the website

(B) Inquire via e-mail

(C) Inquire via phone

(D) Visit the dealership

【解析】由貼文最後提供的聯絡方式有give us a call「電話聯絡」、stop in「順道進來」、visit our website「參觀網站」，可知選項(A)(C)(D)都是可以取得有關貼文中二手車資訊的方式。貼文中並未提供電子郵件地址，判斷「以電子郵件詢問」不是貼文中建議的聯絡方式，正解為(B)。

Questions 163-164 refer to the following advertisement.

2018 Rosa Airlines
Rock 'n' Roll Buckingham
Marathon & 1/2 Marathon

Saturday, March 10, 2018
Rock 'n' Roll Buckingham Square
3218 West Regent Street,Buckingham, BC10903

The Rosa Airlines Rock 'n' Roll Buckingham Marathon & 1/2 Marathon returns March 10, 2018 and you're invited to ROCK the biggest running festival to hit the city!
More than just a financial city, Buckingham is a cultural city with an endless list of things to do and experience during race weekend. Meet us at the Starting Line and experience it for yourself!

Register Now for $109.99 $99	**Price Increase In:** 5 days 13 hours 21 min

2018 羅莎航空
搖滾白金漢
馬拉松及半馬拉松

2018年三月十日星期六
搖滾白金漢廣場
白金漢市BC10903 西攝政街
3218號

羅莎航空搖滾白金漢馬拉松即半馬拉松在2018年三月十日回歸，您已受邀來這個城市參加這最大的跑步盛會！白金漢市不只是個金融城市，更是個在賽跑週末有一堆活動可以做的文化城市。請到起跑線來跟我們會合，自己親身體驗吧

立刻報名 只要 $109.99 $99	報名費在： 5 days 13 hours 21 min 後調漲

【詞彙】
marathon 馬拉松（24公里長距離賽跑）／Starting Line起跑線

誰是活動的主辦人？
(A) 白金漢市政府
(B) 羅莎航空
(C) 國際馬拉松協會
(D) 以上皆非

【類型】提問細節題型

【詞彙】
city government 市政府／
marathon association 馬拉松協會

【正解】(B)

163 Who is the event organizer?

(A) The Buckingham city government

(B) The Rosa Airlines

(C) The International Marathon Association

(D) None of the above

【解析】由活動公告上標示此馬拉松賽事為The Rosa Airlines（羅莎航空）的活動，可推測這場活動的主辦人應該就是The Rosa Airlines，最有可能的答案為(B)。

根據這則廣告內容，哪一項敘述正確？
(A) 目前報名費有減價。
(B) 參加者必須年滿十八歲。
(C) 此活動僅供羅莎航空員工參加。
(D) 白金漢是個政治都市而非文化都市。

【類型】提問細節題型

【詞彙】
for the time being 目前；暫時／
participant參加者

【正解】(A)

164 According to this advertisement, which statement is true?

(A) Reduced registration fee is available for the time being.

(B) Participants must be at least 18 years old.

(C) The event is for the staff of Rosa Airlines only.

(D) Buckingham is a political city rather than a cultural city.

【解析】廣告內容顯示現在報名費用由原來的$109.99降為$99，且再五天後就會調漲，可知目前報名費正在減價，而選項(B)(C)(D)所述皆與廣告內容所述不符，故正確答案為(A)。

★Questions 165-166 refer to the following text message.

< FE Telecom   [Delete]
------------------- February 24, 2018 -------------------

Dear Ms. Thomason, you have missed your last month's mobile phone payment of $139.59.

Please settle the overdue amount immediately to avoid extra charges. If the payment has already been settled, please accept our apologies and disregard this message.

Thank you very much.

11:02

< FE Telecom   [Delete]
----- February 24, 2018-----

親愛的Thomason小姐，您漏繳上個月的行動電話費$139.59元。

請立即繳清逾期款項，以免被徵收額外費用。如果款項已經繳清，請接受我們的道歉並忽略此簡訊。

非常感謝您。

11:02

【詞彙】
overdue過期的／disregard 忽略

---

165 What is the purpose of this text message?

(A) It's a payment reminder.

(B) It's a reservation confirmation.

(C) It's an apology for a late payment.

(D) It's an appointment reminder.

【解析】由訊息內容是在告知對方「漏繳費用」，並要對方「立即繳款」，可知這是一則帳款催繳訊息，正解為(A)。

這封文字訊息的目的為何？
(A) 這是帳款催繳訊息。
(B) 這是預約確認訊息。
(C) 這是帳款遲繳道歉訊息。
(D) 這是約會提醒訊息。

【類型】內容主題題型

【詞彙】
reminder提醒物

【正解】(A)

下列何者可以取代訊息中disregard
這個字？
(A) 解散
(B) 排除
(C) 忽略
(D) 輕視

【類型】字彙意義題型

【詞彙】
dismiss解散／eliminate排除／
ignore忽略／disvalue輕視

【正解】(C)

166 Which of the following can replace the word
"disregard" in this message?
(A) dismiss
(B) eliminate
(C) ignore
(D) disvalue

【解析】regard表「注意；關心」，前面加了表示「相反、否定」的前綴字dis，則為「不理會；忽視」之意，與選項(C)的ignore同義，可取代disregard，故正解為(C)。

Questions 167-169 refer to the following e-mail.

親愛的Jackson先生，
我謹代表G&P公司感謝您付出時間及心力提供我們這份提案。我們已經仔細看過您的提案。除了您的提案費用太高之外，整體上我們對此提案很滿意。我們希望您能理解我們團隊在這個案子上有拿到具體的預算，因此我們必須在預算內拿到這份合約。
您的價格需要比您在最初提案中的報價再低一點，否則我們必須尋找其他供應商。請考慮我們的提議，並期待能得到您肯定回覆。

最佳祝福，
Jennifer Booth

Dear Mr. Jackson,

I on behalf of G&P Inc. would like to thank you for your time and effort that you have put into offering us this proposal. We have reviewed your proposal in detail. Overall we're quite happy with it, except your proposed price was too high. We hope you understand that our team has been given a specific budget for this project and therefore we must get this contract within the budget.
Your price needs to be lower than what you have quoted in your initial proposal; otherwise we'll have to look for other suppliers. Please consider our offer and look forward to your positive reply.

Best regards,
Jennifer Booth

167 What is the purpose of this e-mail?

(A) To request for compensation

(B) To negotiate for a lower price

(C) To request a deadline extension

(D) To propose a business plan

這篇電郵的目的為何？
(A) 要求賠償金
(B) 協商一個較低的價格
(C) 要求延期截止期限
(D) 提出一個商業計畫

【類型】內容主題題型

【詞彙】
extension延長

【解析】由信件中提到最初提案中的報價太高，希望對方能降價，可知這封郵件目的是在協商一個較低價格，正解為(B)。

【正解】(B)

---

168 Who most likely is Mr. Jackson?

(A) Jennifer Booth's supervisor

(B) Marketing Manager of G&P Inc.

(C) A major shareholder of G&P Inc.

(D) A contracted supplier of G&P Inc.

Jackson先生最有可能是何身份？
(A) Jennifer Booth的主管
(B) G&P公司的行銷經理
(C) G&P公司的大股東
(D) G&P公司的合約供應商

【類型】邏輯判斷題型

【詞彙】
shareholder 股東

【解析】由信件中提到「我們需要在預算內拿到合約」，否則「要另尋供應商」，可知收件者Jackson先生應該是G&P公司簽約合作的供應商，正解為(D)。

【正解】(D)

---

169 What will G&P Inc. do if Mr. Jackson won't change his quote?

(A) Increase their budget

(B) Seek other suppliers

(C) Accelerate their production

(D) Reduce their office expenses

如果Jackson先生不願意更改報價，G&P公司將會怎麼做？
(A) 增加他們的預算
(B) 尋找其他供應商
(C) 加速他們的生產
(D) 減少辦公室支出

【類型】提問細節題型

【詞彙】
accelerate 加速／
office expense辦公室支出

【解析】信件中提出「希望提供比最初報價更低的價格」，否則we'll have to look for other suppliers（我們必須尋找其他供應商），可知如果Jackson不降低報價，G&P公司將另尋供應商，正解為(B)。

【正解】(B)

回收你的衣服——

給舊衣新生命
將它帶來CAP商店！

如果你有任何衣服或布料已經不再想要或需要，無論是什麼品牌或什麼狀態，儘管把它們帶到CAP來，透過我們的服裝回收方案給它們新的存在目的，換一張下次購物可使用的五元優惠券！

現在要給你不想要的衣服一個新生命再容易不過了！舊衣一旦被拿到店裡，我們的合作夥伴W-Pigeon就會來領取並將它們分類為三類：

● 可再穿——能穿的衣服會被以二手服飾出售
● 可再利用——不能再穿的舊衣及布料將被改製為其他產品，如清潔布。
● 被回收——其他的會被轉變為布料織品。

CAP每回收一公斤織品就會捐出0.05美元給地方慈善機構。請至www.cap.charity.com閱讀更多訊息。

RECYCLE YOUR CLOTHES—

New Life to Old Clothes
Bring It to CAP Stores!

If you have any clothes or textiles that are no longer wanted or needed, no matter what brand or what condition, bring them to CAP to give them a new purpose through our garment collecting scheme and receive a $5 voucher for your next purchase in return!

It is now as easy as possible for you to give your unwanted garments a new life.
Once the old garments have been dropped off in a store, our partner W-Pigeon collects and sort them into three categories of

● To be reworn – wearable clothing will be sold as second-hand clothes.
● To be reused – old clothes and textiles that are no longer wearable will be turned into other products, such as cleaning cloths.
● To be recycled – everything else is turned into textile fibres.

For each kilogram of textiles that CAP collects, 0.05 US Dollars will be donated to a local charity organization. Please read more at www.cap.charity.com.

【詞彙】
textile織品／garment服裝／fibre (=fiber) 纖維

170 What is the purpose of the garment-collecting scheme?

(A) To give unwanted clothes a new purpose

(B) To recruit talented fashion designers

(C) To increase the sales volume

(D) To improve the store's reputation

【解析】由公告內容對衣服回收方案的說明，會將衣服依分類give them a new purpose（給予新目的），分別為「可再穿」、「可再利用」、「可回收」，可知回收衣服是為了給予舊衣新的用途，正解為(A)。

衣服回收方案的目的為何？
(A) 給不要的衣服一個新的用途
(B) 招募有天份的服裝設計師
(C) 增加銷售量
(D) 改善店家的名聲

【類型】內容主題題型

【正解】(A)

---

171 What most likely is "W-Pigeon"?

(A) A clothes recycling provider

(B) A fabric supplier

(C) A cleaner

(D) A hypermarket

【解析】W-Pigeon在公告中是負責將collects and sort them into three categories（回收衣服並分類為三類），依其性質判斷，選項(A)是所有選項中最有可能的答案，故選(A)。

W-Pigeon最有可能是什麼？
(A) 一間衣物回收供應商
(B) 一間布料供應商
(C) 一間洗衣店
(D) 一間大賣場

【類型】提問細節題型

【詞彙】
hypermarket 大賣場

【正解】(A)

---

172 What will the store offer in exchange for the unwanted garments?

(A) A free membership

(B) A $5 voucher for the next purchase

(C) A thank you card

(D) A donation certificate

【解析】由公告中提到give them... and receive a $5 voucher for your next purchase in return（將它們交給店家，並換取一張下次購物使用的五元優惠券），in return表「作為交換」。可知店家提供下次購物五元優惠券交換顧客的舊衣服，正解為(B)。

店家將提供什麼作為不要的衣服的交換？
(A) 免費成為會員
(B) 一張下次購物五元優惠券
(C) 一張感謝卡
(D) 一張捐款證明

【類型】提問細節題型

【正解】(B)

參觀Ada Müller的老家

一個探索Ada Müller的世界
絕無僅有的機會

在萊茵河上的科隆穿越五個特別的房舍，一探Ada Müller的生活與時代，任由你的想像力恣意馳騁。看看這個永遠的偉大作家出生及她與家人生活的地方，還有她所探訪過的地方，並用新的觀點看待十六及十七世紀的生活方式。你會驚訝Ada Müller 的世界是如何地被保留下來。

除了下列具體時間之外，所有的房舍都是全年每日開放—

- Ada Müller的出生地，每日上午十點至下午四點開放，除了：
十二月二十四日：上午十點至下午兩點（最後入場下午一點）
十二月二十五日：關閉
十二月二十六日：上午十一點至下午四點（最後入場下午三點）
一月一日：上午十一點至下午四點

- Ada Müller的工作室，每日上午十點至下午四點開放，除了：
十二月二十四日：上午十點至下午一點半（最後入場下午一點）
十二月二十五日：關閉
十二月二十六日：上午十一點至下午四點（最後入場下午三點）
一月一日：上午十一點至下午四點

Visit Ada Müller's Family Homes

A unique opportunity to explore Ada Müller's world

Discover the life and times of Ada Müller across five unique properties in and around Cologne-upon-Rhine and let your imagination run wild. Find out where this great writer of all time was born and where she and her family lived, the places she visited, and gained a new perspective on life in the sixteenth and seventeenth centuries. You'll be amazed just how much of Ada Müller's world remains.

All properties are open daily throughout the year unless otherwise specified below –

– Ada Müller's Birthplace opens daily from 10am- 4pm except:
24 Dec: 10am - 2pm (Last entry 1pm)
25 Dec: Closed
26 Dec: 11am - 4pm (Last entry 3pm)
1 Jan: 11am- 4pm
– Ada Müller's Studio opens daily from 10am- 4pm except:
24 Dec: 10am - 1.30pm (Last entry 1pm)
25 Dec: Closed
26 Dec: 11am - 4pm (Last entry 3pm)
1 Jan: 11am- 4pm

– Ada Müller's House opens daily from 10am- 4pm except:

24 Dec: 10am - 1.30pm (Last entry 1pm)

25 & 26 Dec: Closed

1 Jan: 11am- 4pm

– Eva Müller's Cottage opens daily from 10am- 4pm except:

24 Dec: 10am - 2pm (Last entry 1pm)

25 & 26 Dec: Closed

1 Jan: 11am- 4pm

– Evans Müller's Farm is now closed for the winter.

It will be open 10 March - 4 November 2018

Click here to book now and save 10%!

- Ada Müller的家，每日上午十點至下午四點開放，除了：

十二月二十四日：上午十點至下午一點半（最後入場下午一點）

十二月二十五日及二十六日：關閉

一月一日：上午十一點至下午四點

- Eva Müller的農舍，每日上午十點至下午四點開放，除了：

十二月二十四日：上午十點至下午兩點（最後入場下午一點）

十二月二十五日及二十六日：關閉

一月一日：上午十一點至下午四點

- Evans Müller的農場冬季關閉

三月十日至2018年十一月四日開放

按此訂票並省下 10%！

【詞彙】
perspective觀點／specified 具體指定的

關於Ada Müller的敘述何者正確？
(A) 她是十六世紀的名女演員。
(B) 她是一個名作家的妻子。
(C) 她的家已經成為觀光景點。
(D) 她獨自住在一間農舍裡。

【類型】提問細節題型

【正解】(C)

173 About Ada Müller, which statement is correct?

(A) She was a famous actress in sixteenth century.

(B) She was the wife of a great writer.

(C) Her homes have become tourist attractions.

(D) She lived alone by herself in a cottage.

【正解】由此網頁對於Ada Müller的描述，可知Ada Müller為一個writer（作家），既非女演員亦非作家之妻，選項(A)(B)皆可先刪除；網頁上並未提到Ada Müller生前是否獨居，選項(D)亦非適當選擇；由Ada Müller生前的故居，從出生地、工作室到其家人的農舍住所等開放民眾購票參觀，可知選項(C)所述「Ada Müller的家已經成為觀光景點」符合實際狀況，故(C)為正解。

哪一天所有Ada Muller的房屋都不開放？
(A) 一年的第一天
(B) 一年的最後一天
(C) 聖誕節
(D) Ada Muller的生日

【類型】提問細節題型

【正解】(C)

174 On which day are all Ada Müller's properties closed?

(A) The first day of the year

(B) The last day of the year

(C) Christmas

(D) Ada Müller's birthday

【解析】由網頁上所明列出的休館時間，所有房屋在12月25日都是全天關閉的，選項(C)之「聖誕節」即12月25日休館，正確無誤，故(C)為正解。

哪個房屋除了冬天全年開放？
(A) Evans Müller的農場
(B) Ada Müller的出生地
(C) Ada Müller的工作室
(D) Eva Müller的農舍

【類型】提問細節題型

【正解】(A)

175 Which property is open throughout the year except the winter?

(A) Evans Müller's Farm

(B) Ada Müller's Birthplace

(C) Ada Müller's Studio

(D) Eva Müller's Cottage

【解析】由網頁上表示Evans Müller's Farm is now closed for the winter.（Evans Müller的農場冬天關閉），並在三月份至十一月份之間開放，可知此處冬天是不開放的。正解為(A)。

★**Questions 176-180 refer to the following information and e-mails.**

Isabella Clothing Inc. Order Confirmation

Order Number: AH23986BL235
Order Date: February 12, 2018
Customer Name: Joanna Press
Contact Phone: 033-1288-8821

Dear Ms. Press,

Thank you for ordering products from our company. Your order for the following items has been received and has been processed:

Requested items:	Size	Qty	Price
#35346093 *Ribbed jumper --grey*	L	1	£11.99
#73012948 *Denim super-stretch trousers*	28"	1	£25.99
#88239424 *Hooded fleece top --pink*	14	1	£14.99
	Subtotal		£52.97
First online purchase discount -20%			-£10.59
	Delivery		£0.00
	Total		£42.38

Isabella 服飾公司 訂購確認單

訂單編號：AH23986BL235
訂購日期：2018年二月十二日
顧客姓名：Joanna Press
聯絡電話：033-1288-8821

親愛的Press小姐，

謝謝您向本公司訂購商品。我們已經收到並受理您下列商品的訂單：

訂購項目	尺寸	數量	價格
#35346093 開口針織衫—灰	L	1	£11.99
#73012948 丹寧超延伸緊身褲	28	1	£25.99
#88239424 有帽毛料上衣一粉	14	1	£14.99
		小計	£52.97
首次線上購物優惠-20%			-£10.59
		運費	£0.00
		總計	£42.38

您的訂單已經被送至以下指定超商：

LORRY's 鹿崖店：

萊徹斯特LC2鹿崖路128號

★我們會在商品送達至您指定超商供您提領當日發送簡訊給您。

感謝您在Isabella服飾公司購物。

Your order has been shipped to the designated convenience store as below:

***LORRY's* Hartcliff Store:** 128 Hartcliff Road, Leicester LC2

★We will send you a text message on the day your item has arrived at your designated convenience store for you to collect.

Thank you for shopping with Isabella Clothing Inc.

< QB物流 | 刪除

---------- 二月14, 2018 ----------

親愛的Joanna Press 小姐，您的訂單 #AH23986BL235已經成功送達LORRY'S鹿崖店供您領取了。請在2018年2月21日下午五點之前取貨，否則商品將會退還給寄件人。您的訂單金額為£42.38。非常感謝您。

09:12

< **QB Logistics** | Delete

--------------- February 14, 2018 ---------------

Dear Ms. Joanna Press, your order # AH23986BL235 has been successfully delivered and is available for pickup at LORRY's Hartcliff Store. Please collect your item before 5:00 PM, February 21, 2018; otherwise your order will be returned to sender. The total amount of your order is £42.38. Thank you very much.

09:12

From: Joanna Press
To: Isabella Clothing <u>customerservice@isabellaclothing.co.uk</u>
Date: Feb 14, 2018
Subject: Item Arrived Defective

Hi,
I am writing this letter regarding my order, AH23986BL235, with you for three items on Feb 12. I hate to cause trouble but an item I purchased arrived defective. The zipper of the denim trousers is broken. The zipper cannot work at all because the teeth don't line up. I have taken some pictures of the defect and would like to return this item for a full refund. Please contact me as soon as possible.

Looking forward to your prompt reply.

Regards,
Joanna Press

【詞彙】
designated指定的／defective有瑕疵的／zipper拉鏈／
teeth齒輪／refund退款

寄件人：Joanna Press
收件人：Isabella服飾公司
<u>customerservice@isabellaclothing.co.uk</u>
日期：2018年二月十四日
主旨：商品到貨瑕疵

嗨，
我是為了我在二月十二日跟你們訂購的三件商品，訂單編號AH23986BL235，而寫這封信的。我很不願意造成麻煩，但是我購買的其中一件商品到貨後發現有瑕疵。丹寧長褲的拉鏈壞掉了。拉鏈因為齒輪沒有對齊，完全沒辦法用。我已經照了幾張瑕疵處的照片，並希望能全額退還這件商品。請立刻與我聯絡。

期待你們盡速回覆。

Joanna Press 謹上

關於此訂單，下列何者正確？
(A) 買家是用分期付款的方式支付訂單金額。
(B) 訂購商品將會被送到買家住處。
(C) 買家被索取三鎊運費。
(D) 買家將會在超商取貨。

【類型】提問細節題型

【詞彙】
by installment 分期付款

【正解】(D)

176 About the order, which of the following is true?
(A) The payment was settled by installments.
(B) The order will be delivered to the buyer's place.
(C) The buyer was charged a delivery fee of £3.00.
(D) The order will be collected at a convenience store.

【解析】由訂購確認單顯示內容，可看出此訂單的運費為£0.00，也就是免運費。訂單派送地點為買家指定超商，因此買家將會至超商取貨。由簡訊內容，可知買家取貨時必須支付整筆訂單費用，故除了選項(D)之外，選項(A)(B)(C)所述皆與訂購確認單及簡訊不符，正解為(D)。

簡訊的目的為何？
(A) 取貨通知
(B) 會議通知
(C) 活動邀請
(D) 取消訂單

【類型】內容主題題型

【正解】(A)

177 What is the purpose of the text message?
(A) It's a pickup notice.
(B) It's a meeting notice.
(C) It's an invitation.
(D) It's an order cancellation.

【解析】由簡訊中表示your order... is available for pickup（你訂購的商品已經可以取貨），可知這是一則「取貨通知」，正解為(A)。

根據簡訊內容，便利商店會幫買家保留商品多久？
(A) 兩天
(B) 五天
(C) 七天
(D) 兩週

【類型】提問細節題型

【正解】(C)

178 According to the text message, how long will the convenience store keep the item for the buyer?
(A) Two days
(B) Five days
(C) Seven days
(D) Two weeks

【解析】此簡訊發送日期為二月14日，簡訊內容表示須在二月21日前取貨，否則將退回給寄件人，可知便利商店會保留此商品七日，正解為(C)。

179 Why is Joanna writing this e-mail?

(A) She is pleased with the items.

(B) One of her items arrived defective.

(C) She wants to change the order.

(D) Her order has not arrived yet.

【解析】由Joanna的信件中提到an item I purchased arrived defective（我購買的一件商品到貨後發現有瑕疵），可知Joanna寫這封信是因為他的商品有瑕疵，正解為(B)。

Joanna為何要寫這封郵件？

(A) 她對商品很滿意。

(B) 她的其中一件商品到貨時有瑕疵。

(C) 她想要變更訂單。

(D) 她的訂單還沒有送達。

【類型】內容主題題型

【正解】(B)

---

180 What will Joanna do with the trousers?

(A) Return it for a refund

(B) Exchange it at the store

(C) Give it to her sister

(D) Take it to the store for alteration

【解析】Joanna在信件中表示... would like to return this item for a full refund（……希望能全額退回此商品），可知Joanna希望能將這件褲子退貨，並全額退費，正解為(A)。

Joanna將怎麼處理這件褲子？

(A) 全額退貨

(B) 到店內換貨

(C) 送給她妹妹

(D) 拿到店裡修改

【類型】提問細節題型

【詞彙】

alteration修改

【正解】(A)

電話留言

留言給：Wellington教授
留言者：Davenport小姐
日期：十二月十二日
時間：16:02

留言內容：

布萊頓市科技大學希望能邀請您在他們2018年六月十六日的畢業典禮上擔任主賓及致辭。校方在十二月一日已經記正式邀請函給您，但還沒有得到您的回覆。請盡快以電子郵件確認您是否出席。管理部及畢業典禮籌備小組希望能得到您肯定答覆。謝謝您。

行動要求：

☐ 請回電 電話號碼 _____
☐ 來電者會再打來
☐ 不需要行動
☑ 其他：請以電子郵件確認

留言記錄者： Brenda

Telephone Message

For: Prof. Wellington   From: Ms. Davenport
Date: December 12   Time: 16:02

Message:

Brighten City University of Science & Technology wants to invite you to be the Chief Guest as well as deliver a speech on their commencement on June 16, 2018. The school sent you a formal invitation on December 1st, but hasn't received a reply from you. Please could you confirm your attendance by sending an e-mail at your earliest convenience. The management and the Graduation Preparation Team are expecting your positive response. Thank you.

Action required:

☐ Please call back Tel No. _____
☐ Caller will call back later
☐ No action required
☑ Other: Please confirm by e-mail

Message taken by:___Brenda____

From: David Wellington
December 13, 8:25AM
To: Linda Davenport
Subject: Invitation Acceptance

Dear Ms. Davenport,

I got a message from you yesterday regarding the commencement speech invitation. Please accept my sincere apology for not replying earlier. I was attending an academic conference in Beijing when I received your invitation and just returned to UK two days ago. I had been considering whether to accept the invitation before my assistant handed me the message note yesterday.

It's an honor for me to be invited to give a speech as the Chief Guest. I am pleased to accept your invitation to address the graduates at the Commencement on June 16th, 2018. As you requested, I am sending you this letter to confirm my attendance.

Best wishes,
David Wellington

寄件人：David Wellington
十二月十三日上午8:25
收件人：Linda Davenport
主旨：接受邀請

親愛的Davenport小姐，

我昨天收到您有關畢業典禮演説邀請的留言。沒有早一點回覆您，在此誠摯地向您道歉。我收到邀請函時正在北京出席一場學術會議，兩天前才回到英國。在我的助理昨天將留言條遞給我之前，我一直都在考慮是否該接受邀請。

受邀擔任主賓對我來説是無上的光榮。我很樂意接受您要我在六月十六日的畢業典禮上對畢業生致辭的邀請。如您所要求的，我現在就寫這封信給您，確認我會到場。

最佳的祝福
David Wellington

寄件人：Linda Davenport
十二月十三日上午10:11
收件人：David Wellington
主旨：回覆：接受邀請

親愛的Wellington教授，

我們想要向您接受擔任我們在2018年六月十六日的畢業典禮上的主賓及向畢業生致辭的邀請至上誠摯的感激之情。您的出現將使這個紀念性的場合蓬蓽生輝。典禮將會在布萊頓大禮堂於上午九點四十五分舉行，並預計於上午十一時結束。

籌備小組正計劃在典禮之後舉行午餐派對，我們希望能邀請您加入我們。

我會在六月第一個星期與您聯絡，告知您最後的安排。

再次感謝您參加我們的畢業典禮。

溫暖的祝福
Linda Davenport
畢業典禮籌備組組長

From: Linda Davenport
December 13 at 10:11AM
To: David Wellington
Subject: Re: Invitation Acceptance

Dear Prof. Wellington,

We would like to extend our sincere gratitude and appreciation to you for kindly accepting our invitation to be our Chief Guest and speak to our graduates at their commencement on June 16th 2018. Your presence will grace this memorable occasion. The ceremony begins at 9:45 AM at Brighten Hall and is estimated to end by 11:00 AM. The preparation team is planning on giving a lunch party following the commencement, and we would like to invite you to join us.

I will contact you the first week in June to finalize the arrangements.

Once again, thank you for taking part in our commencement.

Warm wishes,
Linda Davenport
Director of Graduation Preparation Team

【詞彙】
commencement畢業典禮／attendance 到場

181 What is the purpose of the telephone message?

(A) To request an interview

(B) To request a meeting

(C) To ask for a reply to an invitation

(D) To ask for payment

【解析】由留言內容可知校方在十二月初寄出邀請函，但一直沒有收到回覆，因此這則留言的目的是要請對方：Please could you confirm your attendance by sending an e-mail（以電子郵件確認你的出席），即「回覆邀請」，正解為(C)。

該則電話留言的目的為何？

(A) 要求面試

(B) 要求會面

(C) 要求回覆邀請

(D) 請求付款

【類型】內容主題題型

【正解】(C)

---

182 What is Prof. Wellington invited to do at the commencement?

(A) To award prizes

(B) To address the graduates

(C) To give a presentation

(D) To interview the job candidates

【解析】留言內容提到這間大學除了邀請Wellington教授擔任典禮主賓之外，還邀請他deliver a speech on their commencement（在他們的畢業典禮上發表演說），可知正解為(B)。

Wellington教授受邀在畢業典禮上做什麼？

(A) 頒獎

(B) 向畢業生發表演說

(C) 做簡報

(D) 面試工作應徵者

【類型】提問細節題型

【詞彙】

award 頒獎／

address對……演說

【正解】(B)

---

183 How long is the commencement estimated to last?

(A) One hour

(B) One and a half hours

(C) One hour and a quarter

(D) Two hours

【解析】第二封信件中提到典禮將會在9:45開始，並預計在11:00結束，可知典禮預計會持續一個小時又十五分，正解為(C)。

畢業典禮預計持續多久？

(A) 一小時

(B) 一個半小時

(C) 一小時十五分

(D) 兩小時

【類型】提問細節題型

【正解】(C)

根據第二封郵件，典禮後會舉行什麼？
(A) 午餐派對
(B) 茶會
(C) 學術會議
(D) 臨時會議

【類型】提問細節題型

【詞彙】
impromptu meeting臨時會議

【正解】(A)

184 According to the second e-mail, what will be held following the ceremony?

(A) A lunch party

(B) A tea party

(C) An academic conference

(D) A impromptu meeting

【解析】由第二封信件中提到「我們正計劃在典禮後舉行午餐派對」，可知典禮後會有「午餐派對」，正解為(A)。

Wellington教授何時將獲知最後的安排？
(A) 聖誕節前
(B) 畢業典禮前一週
(C) 六月初
(D) 六月底

【類型】提問細節題型

【正解】(C)

185 When will Prof. Wellington be informed of the final arrangement?

(A) Before Christmas

(B) A week before the graduation

(C) At the beginning of June

(D) By the end of June

【解析】由第二封信最後表示I will contact you the first week in June to finalize the arrangements.（我會在六月第一週與您聯絡最後的安排），故Wellington教授會在六月第一週獲知最後的安排，正解為(C)。

★**Questions 186-190 refer to the following advertisement, reservation and e-mail.**

Sky Tower Restaurant

Champ de Mars, 101 Avenue Anatole France, 75007
Paris, France
dineandwine@skytower.paris
+33-1-4573-8666

Sky Tower Restaurant is a food experience not to be missed - the menu is best described as French contemporary with a delicious selection of exceptional dishes beautifully presented. Sky Tower offers splendid views of city Paris and sumptuous interiors, including the deluxe private dining room, Adèle, which is suitable for up to 16 guests. To reserve this space please contact our events team groups@skytower.paris.

Dining at our rooftop bar is also a delightfully classy experience where guests can enjoy an impressive list of wine and cocktails as well as the full a la carte menu. Bookings for tables at the bar can also be made through our reservations system.

We welcome and encourage style, but please note that we do not permit shorts, sportswear, sports trainers or flip flops. Our management reserves the right to refuse admission to anyone we feel is inappropriately dressed. Guests aged 16-17 are welcome in our bar and lounge areas accompanied by an adult (aged 21+).

Lunch: Mon-Sun: 11:45am-2:45pm /
Dinner: Mon-Sun: 5:45pm-10:15pm

We accept bookings 60 days in advance.

天空塔樓餐廳

法國巴黎市75007阿納托爾大道
101號戰神廣場
dineandwine@skytower.paris
+33-1-4573-8666

天空塔樓餐廳是個不容錯過的美食體驗—這裡的菜單被形容為法國當代美食——美麗的擺盤完美呈現道道精選的美味佳餚。天空塔樓提供精彩絕倫的巴黎景觀以及奢華的餐廳內景，包括適合最多十六位賓客的豪華私人用餐室Adèle。欲預訂此空間請與我們的活動組groups@skytower.paris聯絡。

在我們的屋頂吧台用餐也是非常時髦的用餐經驗，賓客可以在此享受各種令人印象深刻的酒飲及雞尾酒飲料，還有完整的單點式菜單。吧台的桌位亦可透過我們的訂位系統預訂。

我們歡迎並鼓勵各種時尚造性，但請注意我們不接受短褲、運動服、運動鞋及夾腳拖。我們的管理部有權拒絕任何我們認為服裝不合宜的賓客入場。我們的吧台及休息區歡迎有成人（21歲以上）陪同的16至17歲賓客。

午餐：週一至週日上午
11:45至下午2:45
晚餐：週一至週日下午
5:45至下午10:15
我們接受六十天前的定位

寄件人：Josephine Cochran
收件人：
<groups@skytower.paris>
主旨：Adèle 訂位

嗨，

我在頂尖巴黎雜誌2018年三月號上讀到一篇關於你們餐廳的文章，發現這是個很適合我們家庭聚會的地方。因此我寫這封信想預約四月二十四日星期二的私人包廂。我們有十五個人，而且我們六點至九點需要這個地方吃家庭晚餐以慶祝我祖父母的六十週年紀年日。請告訴我Adèle是否能接受我在上述時間的預訂。

還有，我想知道我們是不是能帶自己的酒到餐廳去。我知道你們的屋頂吧台提供賓客許多酒類及雞尾酒飲料，但是我們想要帶我爺爺的葡萄園釀製，對我們來說很特別的酒去。

期待你們快速回覆。

Josephine
謹上

From: Josephine Cochran
To: <groups@skytower.paris>
Subject: Adèle Reservation

Hi,

I read an article about your restaurant in Top Paris magazine Issue March 2018 and found it a nice place for my family gathering. Therefore I am writing this letter to reserve the private dining room on April 24, Tuesday. There are 15 of us, and we'll be needing the room from 6 pm to 9 pm for a family dinner in celebration of my grandparents' 60th anniversary. Please let me know whether Adèle is available at the time mentioned above.

Also, I'd like to know if we could bring our own wine to the restaurant. I understand that your rooftop bar provides the guests with a wide range of wines and cocktails, but we'd like to bring our own special wine from my grandpa's vineyard.

Looking forward to your prompt response.

Regards,
Josephine

From: Adèle Room

To: Josephine Cochran

Subject: Re: Adèle Reservation

寄件人：Adèle廳

收件人：Josephine Cochran

主旨：回覆：Adèle Reservation

Dear Ms. Cochran,

Thanks for your making a reservation with us. Adèle Room is reserved for you for your designated date and time. We will be very glad to receive you in our establishment. We warmly welcome you and your family to spend the meaningful and memorable night of celebration with us.

In regard to your request to bring your own wine, please note that according to the restaurant's policy, we will charge a €30 corkage fee for wine (€60 for a magnum) and €75 for Champagne (€150 for a magnum). Thanks for your understanding.

We look forward to receiving you on April 24.

Best wishes

親愛的Cochran小姐，

謝謝您向我們訂位。Adèle廳已經在指定日期與時間保留給您了。我們將很樂意在我們的餐廳接待您。我們誠摯地歡迎您與您的家人在我們這裡慶祝這個有意義及具紀念性的夜晚。

有關您想帶自己的酒的要求，請注意根據我們餐廳的規定，我們會酌收開瓶費，一瓶酒€30（大酒瓶€60）及一瓶香檳€75（大酒瓶€150）。感謝您的諒解。

我們期待在四月二十四日接待您。

最佳的祝福

【詞彙】

contemporary當代的東西；最現代的東西／sumptuous奢華的／classy時髦的／a la carte單點菜單／flip flop 人字拖鞋／vineyard葡萄園／establishment 機構；企業／corkage fee開瓶費

廣告中的Adèle指的是什麼？

(A) 餐廳經理

(B) 用餐包廂

(C) 屋頂酒吧

(D) 主廚招牌菜

【類型】提問細節題型

【詞彙】

signature dish招牌菜

【正解】(B)

---

186 What does "Adèle" refer to in the advertisement?

(A) The restaurant manager

(B) The private dining rooms

(C) The rooftop bar

(D) The chef's signature dish

【解析】由廣告中這句the deluxe private dining room, Adèle, which is suitable for up to 16 guests（豪華私人包廂Adèle適合最多十六人），可知Adèle指的是一個用餐的包廂，正解為(B)。

下列何者最有可能是該餐廳的服裝規定？

(A) 正式服裝

(B) 上班服裝

(C) 海灘服裝

(D) 時尚便服

【類型】提問細節題型

【詞彙】

attire服裝／

cocktail attire雞尾酒會小禮服（男士著西裝加領帶，女士著半正式禮服）／

business attire上班穿的服裝／

smart casual時尚便服（休閒不失時尚的服裝）

【正解】(D)

---

187 Which of the following is most likely the restaurant's dress code?

(A) Cocktail attire

(B) Business attire

(C) Beach attire

(D) Smart casual

【解析】由廣告中表示we welcome style，style意指衣服等的流行款式，可知這間餐廳並沒有規定賓客必須穿特別正式的衣服，但是他們也不歡迎shorts（短褲）、sportswear（運動服）、sports trainers（運動鞋）或flip flops（夾腳拖）。可知smart casual（時尚便服）最有可能是該餐廳的服裝規定，正解為(D)。

188 Where does Josephine hear about the restaurant?

(A) From a journal

(B) From the social media

(C) From TV

(D) From a friend

Josephine在哪兒得知這間餐廳？

(A) 一本雜誌

(B) 社群媒體

(C) 電視

(D) 朋友

【類型】提問細節題型

【正解】(A)

【解析】由信件一開始表示I read an article about your restaurant in Top Paris magazine Issue March 2018（我在頂尖巴黎雜誌的2018年三月號讀到有關你們餐廳的文章），可知Josephine是在雜誌上得知這間餐廳，正解為(A)。

---

189 According to the first e-mail, what is the purpose of the dinner gathering?

(A) To celebrate a colleague's promotion

(B) To celebrate a couple's anniversary

(C) To celebrate a friend's birthday

(D) To welcome new employees

根據第一封郵件，這場晚餐聚會的目的為何？

(A) 慶祝一位同事陞遷

(B) 慶祝一對夫妻週年紀念

(C) 慶祝一位朋友生日

(D) 歡迎新進員工

【類型】提問細節題型

【正解】(B)

【解析】由信件中提到we'll be needing the room... in celebration of my grandparents' 60th anniversary（我們將會需要這個房間……慶祝我爺爺奶奶的六十週年紀念），可知他們晚餐聚會的目的是為了慶祝爺爺奶奶的週年紀念，正解為(B)。

---

190 According to the second e-mail, when will the restaurant charge a "corkage fee"?

(A) When the guests bring their own food

(B) When the guests don't reserve in advance

(C) When the guests don't show up on time

(D) When the guests bring their own wine

根據第二封郵件，餐廳何時會收取「開瓶費」？

(A) 當客人自帶食物

(B) 當客人沒有事先訂位

(C) 當客人沒有準時出現

(D) 當客人自帶酒

【類型】提問細節題型

【正解】(D)

【解析】corkage fee意指「開瓶費」。第二封郵件在回應Josephine信上有關自己帶酒的詢問，說明餐廳規定要收corkage fee，可知這筆費用是在客人要自己帶酒進餐廳時會收的費用，正解為(D)。

寄件人：Abby Gilmore
收件人：研發部門
主旨：月會通知
附件：📄2018三月會議議程. doc

親愛的各位，
我們已經將研發部月會定在三月十六日星期五上午十點於會議室舉行。

在Brian和Lillian做完他們跟日方對應人員開會內容的報告後，我們每個人都應該要準備好報告我們目前工作項目的最新進度。我們還會在會議中討論未來六個月即將進行的工作項目。請看附在本信中的會議議程。

如果有任何有關此會議通知的任何問題，或是安排的會議日期、時間或地點對你們來說不方便，請儘管打分機331與我聯絡。

我們期待各位參加這場重要的會議。

誠摯地
Abby Gilmore
研發部助理

From: Abby Gilmore
To: R&D Department
Subject: Monthly Meeting Notice
Attachment: 📄 Meeting Agenda for March 2018. doc

Dear all,
We have scheduled our monthly Research & Development meeting in the conference room at 10:00 a.m. on Friday, March 16.

Each of us should be prepared to give an update on our current projects, following Brian and Lillian's report on the meeting with their Japanese counterparts. We will also discuss the upcoming projects for the next six months in the meeting. Attached please find a draft agenda for our meeting.

Should there be any questions with regard to information contained in this meeting notice, or if the scheduled date, time or location of the meeting is not convenient for you, please do not hesitate to contact me on extension #331.

We look forward to your participation in this important meeting.

Sincerely,
Abby Gilmore
R&D Department Assistant

6

Agenda for March Meeting, 2018	
10:00	-Meeting begins-
10:00 – 10:15	-Brian and Lillian's report-
10:15 – 10:45	-Updates on current projects-
10:45 – 12:20	-New product development- 1. New product ideas 2. Possible applications of new product 3. Cost of product development 4. Workable development plan 5. Realistic schedule
12:30	-Meeting adjourns-

From: Helena Sunders
To: R&D Department
Subject: Monthly Meeting Minutes

Dear all,

Thank you all for another worthwhile meeting yesterday. I am excited about all the accomplishments we have made in the meeting.

The meeting minutes have been compiled, transcribed and proofread and are now attached to this mail for your review. Please take a few minutes to review the meeting minutes and feel free to contact me if you notice any discrepancies between the minutes and the actual meeting content.

2018年三月會議議程	
10:00	-會議開始-
10:00	-Brian與Lillian的報告-
10:15	
10:15	-目前各項工作進度報告-
10:45	
10:45	-開發新產品- 1.新產品點子 2.新產品可能的應用 3.產品開發的成本 4.可行的開發計劃 5.可行的進度表
12:20	
12:30	-會議結束-

寄件人：Helena Sunders
收件人：研發部
主旨：月會會議紀錄

親愛的各位，
感謝昨天各位又開了一場有意義的會議。我對於我們在會議中完成的事感到非常興奮。

會議紀錄已經經過匯整、謄寫及校對，現在附件在這封郵件中供各位審閱。請花幾分鐘的時間看一下會議紀錄，如果有發現任何與實際會議內容不符的地方請儘管與我聯繫。

研發月會將會在四月十三日上午十點在大會議室再次召開。期望能再次看到各位並與大家一起腦力激盪。

最佳的祝福
Helena Sunders

The R&D Monthly Meeting will reconvene in the main conference room at 10:00am on April 13th. Look forward to seeing you again and brainstorming with you all.

Best wishes,
Helena Sunders

【詞彙】
counterpart （地位相同的）對應者／compile匯整／transcribe謄寫／proofread校對／discrepancy 不一致／reconvene 再開會／brainstorm 腦力激盪

所有與會者被要求要做什麼？
(A) 跟會議主席簡短談話
(B) 登記參加會議
(C) 報告目前工作進度
(D) 加入一項會議議程

【類型】提問細節題型

【正解】(C)

191 What are all attendants of the meeting asked to do?
(A) Have a short talk with the moderator
(B) Register for the meeting
(C) Give an update on the current projects
(D) Add an agenda item

【解析】第一封信件中提到：Each of us should be prepared to give an update on our current projects（我們每個人都要報告自己目前負責工作的工作進度），update指「為……提供最新訊息」，可知正解為(C)。

Brian和Lillian將要針對什麼作報告？
(A) 他們跟日方對應人員的會議內容
(B) 新產品開發進度
(C) 新產品上市計劃
(D) 在職訓練課程

【類型】提問細節題型

【詞彙】
on-the-job training在職訓練

【正解】(A)

192 What will Brian and Lillian report on?
(A) The meeting with their Japanese counterparts
(B) New product development schedule
(C) New production launch plan
(D) The on-the-job training program

【解析】由這句Brian and Lillian's report on the meeting with their Japanese counterparts（Brian與Lillian對他們跟日方對應人員會議所做的報告），可知這兩人是要報告他們跟日方對應人員的會議內容，正解為(A)。

193 According to the agenda, what will the meeting focus on?

(A) New product development

(B) New marketing strategies

(C) Staff requirement

(D) Budget revision

根據議程內容，會議的重點將會是什麼？
(A) 新產品開發
(B) 新行銷策略
(C) 員工規定
(D) 預算修訂

【類型】提問細節題型

【正解】(A)

【解析】由會議議程在Brian與Lillian做完他們的報告，以及所有人做完各項工作進度報告後，整個會議會有三分之二的時間用來做new product development的討論，可知這個月會會將重點放在「新品開發」上，正解為(A)。

---

194 Who is most likely in charge of the minutes in the meeting?

(A) Brian

(B) Helena Sunders

(C) Abby Gilmore

(D) Lillian

誰最有可能在會議中負責記錄？
(A) Brian
(B) Helena Sunders
(C) Abby Gilmore
(D) Lillian

【類型】提問細節題型

【正解】(B)

【解析】由主旨為「月會會議記錄」的發信人為Helena Sunders，而且信中表示若紀錄內容與實際會議內容有任何不符之處，要聯絡寄件人，可推測Helena Sunders最有可能是負責做會議記錄的人，正解為(B)。

---

195 Which of the following is closest to the word "reconvene" in meaning?

(A) Reunite

(B) Redeem

(C) Rewind

(D) Revert

下列何者與「再集會」這個字意義上最接近？
(A) 重聚
(B) 償還
(C) 倒轉
(D) 重提

【類型】詞彙選擇題行

【詞彙】
reconvene再開會

【正解】(A)

【解析】這次的會議是三月月會，信件最後告知四月份會議時間，即使不認識reconvene這個字，也可依文意推測此字意指「再開會」。選項(A)的reunite表「重聚」，選項(B)的redeem指「償還」，選項(C)的rewind表「倒轉」，而選項(D)的revert指「重提」，故意義上最接近reconvene的應該是reunite，正解為(A)。

職位：資深公司經理

公司：Halvard 財務規劃 愛丁堡分公司

Halvard 財務規劃公司預備在2018年五月於**愛丁堡**開一間分公司。該地點的翻修工程將會在四月底結束。因此Halvard財務規劃公司有意為新辦公室招聘一位資深公司經理。

應徵者必須有至少五年以上在相關領域擔任公司經理的經驗。必須有大學以上學歷。擁有商業管理及金融系學位的將優先考慮。有財務規劃經驗會是很重要的資歷條件。

此職務的主要職責包含招聘新員工、薪資觀禮、帳務管理、及時回應客服問題以及所有其他有關公司環境順暢作業的職責。

我們歡迎任何能在這個高需求的工作環境中有創意表現的人來應徵這個職位。請將三月二十日前將包含履歷表的應徵信寄至 hr_hiring@hvfinancialplanning.com。

Position: Senior Office Manager
Employer: Halvard Financial Edinburg

Halvard Financial Planning Inc. is opening a branch office in **Edinburg** in May 2018. Renovation on the location is expected to be concluded by the end of April. Thus, Halvard Financial Planning is interested in hiring a Senior Office Manager for our new location.

Candidates must have at least five years experience as an Office Manger in a related field. A Bachelor's Degree or higher is required. Preference will be given to those who hold degrees in business administration and finance. Experience in financial planning is a considerable asset.

Key responsibilities of this position include hiring new staff members, payroll managements, accounts management, responding to customer service issues in a timely manner and all other duties related to the smooth operation of an office environment.

We welcome anyone that can creatively perform in this demanding environment to apply for this position. Please send an application letter including your resume to hr_hiring@hvfinancialplanning.com no later than Mach 20th.

親愛的女士/先生，

我極富興趣地在您的網站上看到您徵求資深公司經理的廣告，想要自我推薦爭取Halvard財務規劃公司的這個職務。

Dear Sir/Ma'am,

I saw, with interest, your advertisement looking for a Senior Office Manager on your website and would like to recommend myself for this position at Halvard Financial Planning Inc.

I am currently employed as the Financial Controller for NHP Corp, where I have been working for 6 years since I earned my Master's degree in Business Administration from the University of Washington. I believe the skills and experiences I have obtained make me an ideal candidate for the position.

My experience in NHP Corp as a financial controller has afforded me the opportunity to develop considerable skills in payroll management and accounts management. In addition, through my work with NHP Corp., I have become heavily involved in handling customer complaints and related issues. I am confident that my experience in NHP and my academic background in business administration qualify me for consideration.

I am enclosing my latest resume for your review in hopes of meeting with you to discuss my qualifications in more detail.

Sincerely,
Danny Peterson

我目前是NHP公司的財務主任，自我拿到華盛頓大學的商業管理碩士學位之後就在此工作，至今已有六年的時間。我相信我已經獲得的技能與經驗讓我成為此職務的理想候選人。

我在NHP公司擔任財務主任的經驗培養我在財務管理及帳務管理方面的重要技能。除此之外，我在NHP公司的工作非常需要處理顧客投訴及相關問題。我有信心我在NHP的經驗以及我在商業管理的教育背景使我具備被考慮的條件。

隨信附上我最新的履歷表讓您參考，希望能與您見面，詳細討論我的資格條件。

誠摯地
Danny Peterson

Dear Mr. Peterson,

Thank you for submitting an application for the position of Senior Office Manager with Halvard Financial Planning Inc. in Edinburg.

We have looked over your resume and would like to invite you to have an interview with us. Your interview has been scheduled for April 2, 2018, 10 am in our head office, located at 212 N Business Highway 181, Edinburg TX15845-6264

Please bring along the following documentation with you to the interview: two passport-size photos, proof of ID, and your highest degree diploma.

親愛的Peterson先生，
感謝您提交Halvard財務規劃公司在愛丁堡分公司的資深公司經理一職的應徵信。

我們已經看過您的履歷，並想邀請您來與我們面試。您的面試被安排在2018年四月二日，上午十點，地點是我們位於愛丁堡TX15845-6264商業大道北區212號的總公司。

請帶著以下文件前來面試：兩張護照尺寸照片、身分證件以及您最高學歷證書。

請在三月三十日下午五點之前撥打877-222-3333聯絡Becky，確認您的出席，或是如果你有任何問題或需要另外安排時間的話，請以電子郵件與我聯絡。

Patty Johnson
Halvard財務規劃公司人資部經理

Please call Becky at 877-222-3333 to confirm your attendance by 5pm on March 30th or email me if you have any questions or need to reschedule.

Regards,
Patty Johnson
HR Manager
Halvard Financial Planning Inc.

【詞彙】
bachelor's degree 大學學位payroll薪資／demanding高要求的／financial controller財務主任／qualify使具資格／documentation文件

這則啟示的目的為何？
(A) 公佈就業博覽會活動
(B) 公佈翻修訊息
(C) 公佈假期休業訊息
(D) 公佈職缺訊息

【類型】內容主題題型

【詞彙】
job fair就業博覽會／
vacancy 職缺

【正解】(D)

196 What's the purpose of the notice?

(A) To announce a job fair

(B) To announce a renovation

(C) To announce a holiday closing

(D) To announce a vacancy

【解析】由公告內容表示要招聘一位senior office manager（資深公司經理），可知目前該公司這個職位是有空缺的，而這則公告則是要對外宣布這個職缺，以招募有意應徵的人，vacancy意指「職缺」，正解為(D)。

何者不是資深公司經理的要求條件？
(A) 大學學歷
(B) 管理經驗
(C) 優異英語能力
(D) 相關領域公經驗

【類型】提問細節題型

【詞彙】
proficiency 精通

【正解】(C)

197 Which is excluded from the qualifications for the Senior Office Manager?

(A) A Bachelor's degree

(B) Management experience

(C) Excellent English proficiency

(D) Work experience in related field

【解析】由公告中關於應徵者要求條件的第一點就是應徵者必須具備at least five years experience as an Office Manger in a related field（至少五年擔任相關領域的公司經理之經驗），這一句便包含了選項(B)及(D)所述的條件；此外提到A Bachelor's Degree or higher（大學以上學歷）也是必要的，這一句則為選項(A)所述條件。除了以上三點之外，對於應徵者的語言能力要求，在此公告中並未提及，故選項(C)所述並不包含在其中，正解為(C)。

198 What's the purpose of the first e-mail?

(A) To request for a meeting

(B) To inquire about the status of application

(C) To apply for a job vacancy

(D) To reply to a request

【解析】由第一封信件表示自己看到徵才廣告之後有意應徵，除了簡單介紹自己的學經歷之外，也附上最信履歷表，可知這封信的目的是要應徵工作職缺，正解為(C)。

第一封郵件的目的為何？
(A) 請求會面
(B) 詢問申請進度
(C) 應徵工作職缺
(D) 回覆請求

【類型】內容主題題型

【詞彙】
status狀態

【正解】(C)

---

199 According to the Danny's e-mail, which statement is correct?

(A) Danny doesn't meet the academic qualifications.

(B) Danny is planning to change jobs.

(C) Danny lacks experience in management.

(D) Danny is now between jobs.

【解析】由Danny的信件表示I am currently employed as the Financial Controller（我目前是NHP公司的財務主任），這句話說明Danny目前並非失業狀態，而且依「財務主任」的職務稱謂可知此為管理職位，因此選項(C)(D)皆非正確敘述。由接下來的句子... since I earned my Master's degree in Business Administration（自我拿到商業管理碩士學位起），可知Danny是符合大學以上畢業學歷的要求的，故選項(A)所述亦不正確。Danny既然目前仍在職，卻對另一個職務空缺有興趣，可推測Danny應該是計劃換工作，正解為(B)。

根據Danny的信件內容，哪一項敘述正確？
(A) Danny不符合學歷要求。
(B) Danny正計劃換工作。
(C) Danny 缺乏管理經驗。
(D) Danny 目前待業中。

【類型】提問細節題型

【正解】(B)

---

200 What is Danny supposed to do by March 30th?

(A) Pay Patty Johnson a visit

(B) Register for a place online

(C) Resign his position at NHP

(D) Confirm his attendance

【解析】由第二封信邀請Danny前去面試，並告知Please call Becky... to confirm your attendance（請打電話給Becky確認你會出席），可知他必須在三月三十日前打電話去確認自已會參加面試，正解為(D)。

Danny在三月三十日前應該要做什麼？
(A) 拜訪Patty Johnson
(B) 在線上報名
(C) 辭去他在NHP 的職務
(D) 確認他會到場

【類型】提問細節題型

【詞彙】
pay sb. a visit拜訪某人／
resign辭去

【正解】(D)

原來如此 系列 *E244*

TOEIC新多益考試金色證書一擊必殺 —— 閱讀全真模擬試題(高手影音解說版)

高手陪你迎戰,多益金色證書不是夢!

作 者	李宇凡、蔡文宜、徐培恩◎合著	
顧 問	曾文旭	
社 長	王毓芳	
編輯統籌	耿文國、黃璽宇	
主 編	吳靜宜	
執行主編	潘妍潔	
執行編輯	吳欣蓉	
美術編輯	王桂芳、張嘉容	
法律顧問	北辰著作權事務所 蕭雄淋律師、幸秋妙律師	

初 版	2021年02月初版1刷 2023年初版5刷
出 版	捷徑文化出版事業有限公司
電 話	(02)2752-5618
傳 真	(02)2752-5619

定 價	新台幣699元/港幣233元
產品內容	1書

總 經 銷	采舍國際有限公司
地 址	235 新北市中和區中山路二段366巷10號3樓
電 話	(02)8245-8786
傳 真	(02)8245-8718

港澳地區總經銷	和平圖書有限公司
地 址	香港柴灣嘉業街12號百樂門大廈17樓
電 話	(852)2804-6687
傳 真	(852)2804-6409

本書圖片由Shutterstock 提供

捷徑 Book站

國家圖書館出版品預行編目資料

TOEIC新多益考試金色證書一擊必殺閱讀全真
模擬試題(高手影音解說版)/李宇凡,蔡文
宜,徐培恩合著. -- 初版. -- 臺北市:捷徑文化,
2021.02
面; 公分(原來如此:E244)
ISBN 978-986-5507-58-9(平裝)

1. 多益測驗

805.1895 110000365